Praise for Ann-Marie MacDonald

"MacDonald can capture, deftly, the fleeting moment, the fragmented feelings that make up so much of what we term 'understanding'. Thus, complex experiences become single, vivid images. It is a rare talent that can produce it for others to see."

The Times (London)

"MacDonald is a master of exciting story-telling, of suspense and surprise."

The Gazette (Montreal)

"MacDonald is a stunningly good writer."

The Calgary Herald

Fayne

a novel by

Ann-Marie MacDonald

Alfred A. Knopf Canada

PUBLISHED BY ALFRED A. KNOPF CANADA

Copyright © 2022 A.M. MacDonald Holdings Inc.

www.penguinrandomhouse.ca

Knopf Canada and colophon are registered trademarks.

Library and Archives Canada Cataloguing in Publication

Title: Fayne : a novel / Ann-Marie MacDonald.
Names: MacDonald, Ann-Marie, 1958- author.
Identifiers: Canadiana (print) 20220146888 | Canadiana (ebook) 20220146889 | ISBN 9780735276635 (hardcover) | ISBN 9780735276642 (EPUB)
Classification: LCC PS8575.D38 F39 2022 | DDC C813/.54—dc23

Book design: Kelly Hill
Image credits: (jacket) Simon Antony Wilson; (interior) Fire Salamander (Salamandra salamandra) / vintage illustration from Meyers Konversations-Lexikon 1897, by Hein Nouwens / Adobe Stock; (beetles and butterfly) *3,800 Early Advertising Cuts*, Dover Publications Inc., 1991; (wooden box) Iryna Melnyk, Adobe Stock

Printed in Canada

10 9 8 7 6 5 4 3 2 1

Penguin
Random House
KNOPF CANADA

I am different. Let this not upset you.

PHILIPPUS AUREOLUS THEOPHRASTUS
BOMBASTUS VON HOHENHEIM, A.K.A. PARACELSUS

AS A COURTESY to those whose sole aim in opening this book be to obtain an answer to the question most often posed me, to wit, "What is the secret of long life coupled with mental vigour?"; and to spare them fruitless perusal of these pages, herewith my answer: I am immortal.

The latter assertion may cause the reader to question my claim to "mental vigour"; but where is the proof that I am mortal? I have not yet died. And if you are reading this, neither have you.

omprising upwards of twelve-thousand acres of swelling moorland, the estate of Fayne is situated on the southern border of Scotland—or the northern border of England, as the case may be. Here it is that a trick of geology cut off an ancient lake, such that over the course of millennia the lake became an expanse of moorland, to the which, some nearly six hundred years ago, the present peer's ancestors, having left off cattle reiving, laid claim together with a vast surround of arable land. The family prospered for a century or so in rents until it found itself, like many others, in reduced circumstances owing to a general economic malaise; unlike others, however, the Bells did not rally with the general recovery, owing to the county having been bypassed by the railway. Moreover, the Fifteenth Baron Bell had, in the meantime, sold all but the valueless moor.

Originally constructed as a castle with a view to defence, the house is engirdled by the remnants of a moat (to the existence of which the visitor is kindly alerted, the tall grasses sprouting therein lending an impression of continuity with the surrounding level ground). Between the vestigial moat and the house, an influx of bluebell and stitchwort hints at a formerly terraced lawn in its upward slope to a cindered forecourt, itself testament to the triumph of utility over taste in the face of variable weather.

Fayne House is an imposing four-storeyed manor principally of Scottish granite, with the notable exception of the limestone scutcheon which bears the coat of arms: a much-weathered *Salamander Rampant*, whose origins are involved in obscurity (no less than its scarcely legible but clearly apocryphal motto: *NEMO VENIT AD MATREM, NISI PER ME*).

It is impossible to designate the architecture of Fayne House by any given or familiar term, for the variety and eccentricity of its parts are not to be defined by any words of common acceptation. A structure perhaps more ponderous than elegant, its high roof attests the strong influence of the Scottish baronial style. The great oak doors, however, are ornamented by a portico and four Doric columns, and the Romanesque arch of the frontispiece is flanked by rows of high, rounded Norman-topped windows in the Anglo-Flemish style, the which retain the glazing that conferred boasting rights on the forward-thinking lord of the manor who installed them as a lure to Good Queen Bess, who nonetheless failed to visit. Had she known of the trout stream,* Her Majesty might perhaps have altered her progress up the North Sea coast in favour of making a left turn at Berwick-on-Tweed.

The present structure stands on the spot formerly occupied by the Abbey of Saint Brigid. Close inspection of the foundational stones reveals, as well, traces of Roman brickwork, such that the site is thought to have been at one time a fort. Located between Hadrian's Wall to the south and its unfinished Antonine counterpart to the north, it is difficult to determine what precisely the fort was protecting. If, bending down, we pull away the moss and couch grass concealing the ruined imperial masonry, we find here and there evidence of drystone construction of the type used in the building of a broch, likewise a type of fortified dwelling dating to Iron Age Celts, prior to which the historical record is mute. Taken together, these traces might be seen to support the suggestion that Fayne has long been contested ground, although what its value may have been, whether strategic or economic, is lost to time.

Guests are invited freely to roam the principal rooms of the House upon the filling-in of a brief indemnification form. Among divers curios to be found within, of particular interest are extensive lepidoptera and beetle collections.

The surrounding moorland encompasses bog, stream and fen; wooded glen and windy fell; lochan and secluded dell, all sure to divert the seasoned naturalist and amateur alike, as well as to reward the weekend rambler. (Walkers are encouraged to keep to the paths lest the greenest ground prove the least solid. In the event of a sudden mist, the walker is advised to remain still until such time as it should lift.)

Thank you for visiting Fayne House, Stateless Home. For the benefit of future visitors, kindly deposit this guide on the console table in the great entry hall as you leave.

* *Regrettably off-limits to visitors.*

Part One

Scientia potentia est.
FRANCIS BACON

I

"FATHER, I HAVE an idea."

"Mmm?"

I was peering through his magnifying glass at the feather of a *Vermiphagiora rubifortan.* I had plucked it from amid a frowzy heap, the which a housemaid might mistakenly sweep from the desktop into the dustbin and expect to be forgiven. (But she would not be forgiven.) "Let us travel to the nesting ground of this bird."

"And where might that be?"

"'A sheer rock face jutting from the sea, it forms the extremity of an unnamed archipelago in the southern antipode, and is visible at night owing to the phosphorescence of the guano with which it is liberally daubed.'"

"Heh-heh." He squinted, took the red feather between the points of his tweezers, and applied to its quill a drop of glue no bigger than a grain of sand.

"Father, why is that amusing?"

"It is . . . not amusing per se, rather, in point of fact . . . Tell me, have you been memorizing again?"

"Father, that which you term memorization is to me involuntary. I read, I retain. 'Tis no strain to me."

"I say, how are the L's coming along?"

"Oh I've long since tackled the M's."

"Have you, indeed? Dear old Menander."

"Shall I fetch him now and you may quiz me?"

He smiled. "I fear I'm apt to be woolly-headed at this hour."

"Very well then, Father, tomorrow, depend upon it."

"I shall of course be delighted. Do bear in mind, however, there is no great hurry. The Ancients have been with us for over two thousand years, I daresay Meno will keep 'til Monday."

We were in his study, he in his oaken armchair, I perched on a stool at his side. About us on the desktop, a tableau of partially re-membered birds was taking shape from the frizz of bits and beaks and bones—here a headless robin, there a legless lapwing. He inserted the red feather into the wing of our latest specimen, and I watched as the lamplight played at the edges of his spectacles.

"Father, what is light?"

"Why, 'tis . . . a property of the sun. And of fire, of course."

"But what *is* it?"

"It . . . Why I shouldn't think it qualifies as a 'thing' *per se*."

"Then how do we come to perceive it?"

He paused but did not reply.

I asked, "What is colour?"

"Ah. Colour is a property of light."

He replaced the cork on the glue bottle.

"Aristotle believed light to be a disturbance of the air, but Democritus said it is made of bits called atoms and Lucretius said atoms rain down from the sun, in which case the sun must be running out of atoms, what do you think, Father?"

"Mm? Oh, I should think the sun has plenty of atoms in reserve."

"But if not an infinite number, the sun must one day extinguish like a lamp."

"Pass me the . . ." I handed him the sandpaper thimble. "Thank you."

"And when the sun dies, so must life on Earth—save perhaps whatever giant worms ply its bowels and serpents swim the uncharted depths of its oceans. Does not this give one pause, Father?"

"I shouldn't worry. I expect the sun's atoms are replenished by a . . . celestial process."

"Of course! Thank you, Father, I am relieved. To what process do you refer?"

He let out a breath that was half a chuckle and shook his head. "I see I shall soon have exhausted my store of knowledge."

"Certainly not, Father. No one can touch you for birds."

He smiled.

In addition to being my principal companion, Father was my teacher. He gave me the benefit of the education he had himself received as a boy, first from his tutor (an elderly scholar whose nose dripped perpetually) and then at Straifmore School. I entertained reveries wherein I was myself his boyhood friend: the two of us stoical in the face of canings by masters and bullying by older boys. Father taught me to debate, and many were the evenings we spent working away at our ornithological specimens whilst refuting and affirming by turns: Ought Caesar to cross the Rubicon? Ought Alexander to turn back at the Indus? Why? Why not? What Father lacked in Euclid he made up for in philosophy. Thus he instilled in me the Virtues: Courage, Justice, Piety, Temperance, Wisdom. And containing all of these: Truth. He was at pains that I should attain, as had he, a Good Life. The trick of achieving such a life was to accept whatever was beyond the influence of one's will; what the Stoics called "nature." Father taught me that it is helpful to envisage a dog tied to a cart. The cart is nature. The dog is oneself. When the cart begins to move, the dog may either trot cheerfully alongside it, or be dragged behind. The dog's choice alters its experience of the journey, but not a jot its course. And how might one discover what nature required? By dint of unflinching self-examination. Thus, I knew Latin, Logic, Rhetoric, and Father had managed even to insert into my head a tolerable grasp of Greek, *id est* Τί δύσκολον; Τὸ ἑαυτὸν γνῶναι. Or, as Thales of Miletus might put it in our own day: "What is the most difficult thing in life?" Answer: "To know oneself." I, however, knew myself fine well: I was the Honourable Charlotte Bell of the DC de Fayne. I possessed several intervening names waiting to be brought out of storage and packed in trunks for the trip to Court when I should be of age, health permitting; for my father was Lord Henry Bell, Seventeenth Baron of the DC de Fayne, Peer of Her Majesty's Realm of the United Kingdom of Great Britain and Ireland. For now, however, my Condition kept me apart.

"Father, I've come up against a Latin conundrum."

"Ah, now you are speaking my language," and he smiled, eyes trained on the ever-more colourful bird taking plumage before us, as I recited:

"Memmi, bene me ac diu supinum
tota ista trabe lentus irrumasti.
sed, quantum video, pari fuistis
cāsū: nam nihilō minore verpa
farti estis."

Father's hand had stilled in the act of reaching for a magpie feather (green), and I hastened to provide my translation:

"O Memmius, while I lay on my back for a long time,
you fed me well and slowly with that entire beam of yours.
But so far as I can see, you fellows have met with the same fate:
for you have been stuffed with a verpa no less large!"

"Now, Father, one might take 'beam' to mean a 'board' upon which foodstuffs are arrayed. But what is 'verpa'?"

He folded his hands, knit his brows and addressed the desktop. "Where did you . . . ?" He cleared his throat. "Where did you come across this . . . obscure verse?"

"It is by Catullus."

"Quite."

"Funnily enough, the volume had somehow fallen down the back of the bookcase."

"Charlotte. My dear. I forbid you nothing you may find on the library shelves, but now that you are approaching maturity, you must understand that knowledge is . . ."

"*Scientia potentia est.*"

"Quite, and power, without a scaffolding of, of . . ."

"Learning."

"Just so. Raw power is like fire. Left to its devices it consumes everything, including itself."

"Then send me to school!" The words were out before I gave them leave, I saw him flinch, and I felt my face grow hot.

Father never spoke of my Condition, for it pained him, and I had rather drive a pin through my thumb than inflict upon him a moment's suffering by raising the subject . . . which I had done just now, however inadvertently. "Forgive me, Father, I was carried away. Have I always been like this?"

He smiled sadly, removed his spectacles, rubbed the bridge of his nose and turned his mild blue eyes upon me. "You are apt to be carried farther now, the which is to be expected, approaching as you are, the age of—" He swallowed. "An age when, no longer a child, you are not yet a woman."

"I do not wish to be a woman."

"My dear. I'm afraid we none of us has the choice."

"I do not wish to be a lady, then."

"I cannot blame you. I myself should fail miserably at it."

We resumed in companionable silence, heads mutually inclined over our specimen. "What shall we call it, Father?"

"Why, let us first see what it looks like once we have finished assembling it."

I passed him the left fibula of a ptarmigan and watched as he speared the tiny bone home to its tiny kneecap.

"Well done, Lord Henry."

"Thank you, Miss Bell."

Here it must be stated: Father's specimens were long dead before he acquired them. Not for him the killing jar, the bird-shot prize, for he could not bear to inflict suffering.

Presently he handed me the tweezers. "Would you care to do the honours?"

I selected the wing feather of an amethyst starling—*Cinnyricinclus leucogaster*. I applied a drop of glue, and tucked the purple feather next to the red. "Father, when once we have completed our creature, how if we send it to the Royal Society of Edinburgh as a newly discovered species?"

He fairly chortled. "What might the learned members make of our 'rare bird'?" He laughed outright, and I joined in.

My jest turned as much on the absurdity of our "specimen" as on the notion that either of us would stoop to falsehood; for Father was the embodiment of Virtue. And I was my father's daughter.

I rose and kissed his forehead. "Don't stay up too late, Father." He patted my hand and murmured, "My treasure."

I slipped from the glow of his study into the gloom of the great entry hall, as chill and tall as a sunken ship. High overhead, all but lost in shadow, mounted antlers, crossed swords and battle axes, along with shields, flying colours and other such "gabions" were testament to a turbulent past when Bells hunted for sport and fought for honour. I crossed the wide paving stones on silent kid soles to the great oak doors and, grasping the iron rings, I pulled them wide. Daylight rushed in, dazzling my eyes, for though the morning was overcast, the veiled sun easily outshone the lamp in Father's study.

My eyes adjusted and I beheld, clear to the grey horizon, the moor; laid out in mighty swells of emerald and dun, creased in dark brown, spumed in yellow. Come August, whole tracts would blaze with heather stained purple by the blood of the Picts. But this was the moor in April, and I loved it not the less for its subdued mantle.

I stepped out onto the portico and, pulling closed the doors behind me, tarried long enough to thrust my feet into a pair of greased Wellingtons. To either side of me, marble urns brimmed black, their pedestals grimed with the dreich of centuries. I sprang from the stone steps into a puddle, pelted across the cindered forecourt and over the margin of scrub and creepers; I slid on my heels down the brackeny moat, scrambled up the other side and ran onto the moor in a bid to discharge a buildup of energy that threatened fairly to explode.

It is not possible to run across a moor. Moorland looks smooth from a distance but with its tufts and tussocks and heathery hummocks, it is convolute as brain; such that, as in accounts of travellers who have been carried off by Faery only to return and find fifty years have passed in our world in the space of five days in Faery Wyrld, so it is with distance, whereby a quarter mile across moorland is like a league over ordinary ground. Soon enough I was no longer running but plodding, then staggering, joyful to my marrow, for the moor never failed to meet me and best me and buoy me.

"Keep off the bog!" came Knox's cry behind me.

I raised a hand in acknowledgement but neither slowed nor turned, for my old nurse squawked the same warning every day.

In fact, there was no single "bog" but a shifting array of boggy expanses which were part and parcel of the moor. As I tramped along, I drew a line of sight all the way to the horizon where the great standing stone jutted from the brow of the North Fell. Off to my right was a track that followed an old Roman road and ran like a spine from Fayne House, all the way up to the North Fell. It had been laid down generations before with crushed limestone and crockery that glimmed on a moonlit night to guide the wayfarer.

I walked through heather, even now budding mauve; I waded through sedge and wove through thistles, sweeping my free-flying locks out of range of burs. I breasted crowberry bushes—and was scolded by a red grouse for coming near its nest. I picked up a sheep path but presently grew tired of avoiding their droppings not to mention the sheep themselves who were wont to stand singly or in pairs in the middle of the path, staring impassively up at me. They were not all our sheep; any within herding distance had free right to batten by day, and batten they did along with the deer whose dung was nearly as plentiful.

I pressed on. Bees danced across my line of sight, I caught a coconutty whiff of gorse; high above, I glimpsed a kestrel hovering and I squinted, for the sun had burnt through its veil. All the while, the standing stone winked in and out of sight with the rise and fall of the ground beneath my feet and I took care to keep not only to the high ground, but to the drab, for I knew the greenest grass might prove the merest mantle over a depthless pool.

I had it from Byrn that the Old Folk used to toss treasure into just such pools as gifts to the Mother. The Romans knew this and set about draining the lochans and looting the treasure. (Rome fell.) Byrn it was who had taught me to walk safely across "Fenn" without restricting myself to a sheep path. Our old man-of-all-work taught me songs and tried to teach me to "borrow" the eyes of the plover. He alone braved the moor by night, filling his buckets according to his own system of Moon phases. Byrn could find his way by smell, for moorland is an olfactory buffet of stinky peat and fermenty loam, of earthworms, rain and musk—peril lies in that which one cannot smell, namely bog fumes. Byrn did not believe in bog fumes, he believed in marsh sprites. Byrn's mouth, when agape with misdoubt, was black like ink, a pool of never-to-be-written words. I do not know how many teeth he had, he must have had some for he ate and was obstinate with life, as though his doubt extended to the idea of mortality itself. Indeed, it was not because Byrn was credulous that he believed in marsh sprites, but because he was skeptical; and of nothing so much as the scientific presumption to parse what he understood fine well, to wit: on nights when marsh sprites are about, keep off the moor.

He was right, for bog fumes, being noxious, are liable to befuddle the wits and prove fatal owing, not to the fumes *per se*, but to the treacherous terrain of the moor; now solid, now liquid, now something in between consisting of a stew of sucking force. A sudden mist is hazard enough (if caught in one, stand still 'til it lifts) but clear days pose their own danger, lulling one into a false sense of solidity for, after all, there appears to be land clear to the horizon. Cattle have disappeared, swallowed whole. As have people; gone out for a walk, never to be seen again—I had the latter from Knox, she never being one to pass up a chance to deter me from danger by instilling fear, whether reasonable or not *id est*, "Dinnae lock eyes with a wild hare lest he carry the sight of you to Faery." "Knoxy, how does Faery square with your Christian faith?" "Go to sleep now, pet."

It was true, however, that nothing about Fenn—the moor, that is—was certain. Not even its name.

The ground grew spongy underfoot and I took care to keep a tussock within reach, for swallets were known to surface suddenly. It is possible to hear them rippling along underground, and tempting to follow their song in hopes of seeing them rise up as though to bask and blink. Do not follow them, lest their waters rise about your feet and take you with them when they disappear just as suddenly back into the earth. Swallets are oft heralded by a singular myst with which the Wee Folk conceal the entrance to their Wyrld (*ibid*. Byrn). Off to the east now, beyond the cart track, I spied just such a rogue patch of mist; and though my faith in Faery was fast evaporating, I longed to go to it, to hear the swallet's song, to glimpse it rise . . .

I did not go to it. Not for fear of drowning, still less of "Wee Folk." No, Reader, it was the thought of Father—bewildered, betrayed and beset by worry at the spectre of my scarlet tunic disappearing into a shroud of mist—that clutched at my heart and stayed my steps.

Never to be seen again? Not quite. It is well known that perfectly preserved bodies have been pulled from bogs, and I cherished a particular hope I might one day stumble upon the leathered corpse of a Roman centurion, complete with cape and sword. Indeed, in the unlikely event I should disobey Father and come to grief in a mantle of mist, I might one day be dug out of the peat and be mistaken for a Crusader—it was not directly owing to my Condition that I wore tunic and leggings, but it was a benefit thereof. Do not say "invalid," for where was weakness in my body which carried me from fell to dell? Where feebleness in my mind which had battened on the books in Father's library? *Mens sana, in corpore sano!*

Owing to Father's silence on the subject, my knowledge of my Condition was supplied by my old nurse: "There be contagions, miasmas and the like, as may be brought in on drafts and by folk from outside, causing you to fall ill and be carried off. And not for the world would I lose my darling pet." Practised as I was at translating Knoxy's mode of speech, I understood my Condition thus: I was morbidly susceptible to germs.

Though it deprived me of playmates and a place at one of the several schools for gentlemen's daughters which had sprung up even here in the north of England—or the south of Scotland, as may be—my Condition conferred upon me a liberty of body and mind which I cherished, for in being kept from society I was likewise kept from its strictures, including those appertaining to the female sex, *vis-à-vis* frocks and sitting still. Thus, insofar as my Condition was an impediment, it was also a portal, bearing out the wisdom of Emperor Marcus Aurelius who wrote: "That which obstructs the way, becomes the way." For when I should one day outgrow my Condition, I would be well prepared to become what I so fervently desired: the Hon. Charlotte Bell, intrepid female traveller.

I was now out of sight of the House, lone human on the windswept vasts. Rolling hills became Arabian dunes; browsing deer, a herd of camels; the standing stone, a palm tree in a desert oasis . . . I traversed Egypt to the Mediterranean Sea, where I boarded an Athenian barque laden with indigo silks, bound for the wild shores of Caledonia. Making landfall, I paused to kill a wild boar, thence onward and upward to the Highlands, where I rallied a horde of painted Picts in a rout of Hadrian's sandalled forces. Then, in a bold historical leap, I vanquished the Duke of Cumberland's army on the field of Culloden. I slew a lion (in fact I saw a Scottish wildcat—truly I did, it disappeared in a ripple of furze). Meanwhile, beneath my feet the ground had grown firmer, the vegetation thinner as I ascended to the crest of the North Fell and met the ceaseless wind which seemed fair to blow the hair from one's head and a grin onto one's face. (Unlike treacherous indoor "drafts," outdoor motions of air were counted of no consequence *vis-à-vis* my Condition.)

Here a drystone wall prevented sheepfall onto the riverbank below, for on this side of the fell was a sheer drop. I turned to the standing stone that towered upwards of twelve feet and scaled it by means of notches worn by weather or ancient hands. At the summit I stood, feet planted firmly apart, fists on hips, and surveyed the scene laid out before me, pronouncing as usual: "There be dragons."

And today, for the first time, the phrase rang hollow in my ears. Childish.

I knew of course there were no dragons in the village of Aberfoyle-on-Feyn, at least not in our day, and while the North Fell might be the antipode of my world, it was merely a stony bank and the highest point on our moor. Below me flowed gently the Water of Feyn, itself a tributary of the River Tweed, and I fancied I beheld the same water upon which Sir Walter Scott gazed from the windows of his beloved Abbotsford. Spanning the river was a stone bridge, on the far side of which clustered the village. A steeple anchored each end of its curving high street lined with shops and dwellings. Smoke drifted up from chimneys, for it was a raw day. Beyond the village, plump fields were hemmed with greening hedgerows; pastures were tufted with sheep and nestled here and there amid stands of elms could be seen the thatched roofs of farmhouses and stone byres; the whole couched about with lush woodland. The contrast with our estate could not have been more pronounced—indeed, from a geological viewpoint it seemed the Water of Feyn divided two continents rather than one county.

We had, at one time, owned the lot. We now retained a single holding in the village: St. Foy Church of England and Scotland along with its churchyard and vicarage. Notwithstanding neither Father nor I attended services, it was a matter of *noblesse oblige* that we Bells maintained the living for the benefit of the inhabitants of Aberfoyle-on-Feyn, all of whom—including those congregants, higher in number but lower in steeple, of the kirk—had once been our chattel.

I clambered down from the stone. Beyond it, was I forbidden to venture. I turned back to face the moor, and it began to rain.

I kept the house dead ahead as I plodded through a landscape now oddly bereft of enchantment . . . composed of drab vegetation and the familiar rustlings of familiar creatures (wildcat notwithstanding—in truth probably a badger); the pastel pinks shimmering in the rain, merely moss, the shred of myst off to the east, merely mist. Merely springtime. Merely the moor.

"Hai, Miss Charlotte!"

The small-faced boy marching toward me now, whipping the hummocks with a riding crop, was Murdoch Mungo. I'd grown up with him about the place. He fancied himself a "lad o' parts" but I could best him at tug-of-war, and he knew to fear me in a fight with pointed sticks. I was, of course, unfailingly civil for his father was our estate manager, thus, "Go away, Mungo, I'm busy."

"I am not a servant, Miss Charlotte."

"Quite. Well, Murdoch then. And 'tis Miss Bell to you, we're no longer bairns."

"There's a mist gathering, you must hie home for your own safety." Chin held impudently high, he raised the crop, pointing the way.

"Murdoch, the house is plainly visible."

He dogged my steps. "You'll not be seeing me about the place so much in future, Miss Bell."

This I judged as not meriting a response.

"I'm to attend the grammar school in the village," he added.

I kept walking.

"I shall learn mathematics."

I stopped and looked at him. I was accustomed to scrambling through mud and briars and I was no stranger to the byre where Byrn sang to the pregnant ewes; I ate bread and cheese in the scullery and, when I could get away with it, slept on the hearth rug in the great hall—indeed, I disdained all manner of hardship (insofar as I was permitted, given my Condition). But I was a Bell; of one blood with the barons framed and glowering in the upper gallery of the house, and I would not be trifled with. I feinted a lunge. He jumped back. I turned my steps toward the house, nettled that in so doing I but obeyed Murdoch Mungo.

Luncheon was a solitary affair as usual which I took in the dining room. Scotch collops in suet with mash. Wholly satisfactory. Dollop of crowdie on toast by way of pudding.

Afterwards, I slipped through the service door and along the passage into the steamy scullery where Cook was boiling bones, then outside past the ash heap and the henhouse to squelch across the barnyard. The rain-washed air imparted a crispness to the tinkle of a goat bell, a sharpness to the scent of peats stacked and drying in the lee of the byre.

Within, the air was pungent with hide and hay. Ancient timbers exhaled overhead, and the walls streamed with the sweat of stones.

I sought solace in my wonted employments. Solace, for that I felt more and more out of sorts. I leaned my cheek against Gossamer's great white head whilst Byrn sang her milking song, and allowed the music of her milk against the pail to soothe me. The old man had a song for everything—nonsense words that, as a wee one, I used to warble along with him—and never the same tune twice. Gossamer always gave at the first notes.

He was crouched on the stool with his head against her flank. Bald as a stone he was. A pair of bumps on his crown bespoke, according to Knox, his having either fallen on his head or been beaten, either way winding up "addled in his wits." Byrn himself put the bumps down to his "braw brains." Or words to that effect.

Byrn was as familiar to me as my own hand before my face, and my earliest memory was of seeing the ground rise and fall from my vantage point under his arm as he loped along with me tucked like a runaway piglet after I had strayed onto Fenn—the moor, rather.

Now he rose from his stool—for all he was stooped, the old length of bones was taller than Father—and held out the pail for me to drink. The milk of the white cow, warm from her body, never failed nearly to fell me with richness.

Byrn set about his work and I shadowed him as he physicked the goats, and pitched in when he mucked out the pen. I rubbed a gob of Byrn's balm onto a bare patch in Nolan's black-and-white coat where he had worried a hornet's sting (Nolan it was had pulled my wee cart years ago, submitting to the harness and my cries of "gee-up!" with surpassing canine patience). I pumped water into the stone trough, I picked bur-docks from the lambs' fleece, and forked fresh straw into Achilles's stall. I sought out Cato where she was curled in the loft with her litter, and left her a saucer of milk. I roused Maisie roughly and rode her across the yard, despite the mud and the risk to my tunic. She tried to buck me off and would cheerfully have trampled me too but I had hold of her ears and could feel her grinning. I could feel as well her bristles embedding in my flesh right through my leggings and this along with all of the above went some way toward restoring my good humour.

On my way back to the house, I lingered in the scullery yard to watch Cook catch one of the roasters. I held the bird on the block as she chopped off its head. I thought of Mary Queen of Scots, and wondered: Would I be that brave? Answer: yes. My reading had taught me that peoples of the East believe we return to life as other folk and even other creatures, depending upon the merit of the lives we have led. Perhaps that roaster had been the Duke of Cumberland. And perhaps Maisie was working her way up to a war-horse in her next life.

Solitary dinner. Chops and boiled tatties. Cabinet Pudding consumed entire. (Can any civilization which knows naught of its sweet sodden sponginess, its custard and scolded almonds, be said to be truly civilized?)

After dinner I repaired with a lamp to the library and resumed the M's. When I got to Meno I surprised myself by snapping shut the book, suddenly loath to cross the alphabetical meridian now that Z loomed on the horizon. The monsters that lurked for the Ancients beyond the edge of their flat Earth were as nothing compared to what I dreaded when once I should arrive on the shores of Z: namely, a return to A. The tall windows were filling up with gloom. I abandoned the book, doused the lamp and quitted the room, spinning the globe as I passed.

Out in the great hall, a draft set to dancing the flames of the candelabra at the foot of the marble staircase such that high overhead, the antlers seemed to leap in fear from the huntsman; swords and axes clashed anew, captured colours seemed once more to fly. On the far side of the staircase, a triangle of light from Father's study door signalled he had begun his day's work. My father's nocturnal habits were owing to the weakness of his eyes which rendered him prey to headache with exposure to sunlight—even in its oft-dimmed form at Fayne. Thus his day began when mine ended.

I crossed the hall and put my head round the door. He looked up with a smile. "Charlotte, my own." He shifted his chair, making space for me at his side. I, however, did not take my place on the stool. "How was your day, my dear?"

"Capital, Father. I saw a badger."

"Did you, now." He returned his attention to his desktop where he was restoring the head of a great tit.

It was our habit to while away an evening's hour in sorting and restoring specimens or reading aloud; tonight, however, I was at a loss to dispel the dullness that had descended unaccountably upon me, and so pleaded sleepiness brought on by wholesome exertion. "Goodnight, Father." I bent and kissed his temple. He reached round and patted my head.

"Goodnight, my treasure."

I plucked a candle and ascended the marble stairs, careful as usual to lower my eyes lest they meet those in the portrait that towered above the landing. Nor, as I passed by the heavy gilt frame and commenced to mount the leftward branch, did I draw breath until the turning at the top of the stairs dispelled the sense of a painted gaze upon my back.

My bedtime ablutions were attended by the usual fuss and prayerful palaver of Mrs. Knox, with the addition this evening of a poultice of moor moss applied to the angry abrasions on my inner thighs, thanks to Maisie. "You're wanting a saddle, lassie."

"Really, Knoxy, who ever heard of saddling a sow?"

My day had been perfectly ordinary. And for the first time, I deemed this unsatisfactory.

2

ON THE EVE of May 1, I helped Byrn to lay the bonfire as usual—first shaking loose the kindling lest any critters had nested therein—piling on larger sticks, then whole limbs of seasoned alder gathered from deadfall over the previous year (it is inadvisable to cut a living alder lest you carry its blood on your conscience). We lit it at sunset and though I sang along, I did so half-heartedly, suddenly embarrassed to be disporting myself with the old pagan at the fire's edge, despite there being none to see us but the denizens of Fayne House; including Father who looked on with indulgent amusement as Byrn seemed to snatch something from the fire, then dropped it, wriggling, into my hand: a wee dun-coloured salamander— not nearly so fierce as its stone counterpart on the scutcheon over the door of the house. I was careful to release it without keeping hold of its tail or any of its limbs lest it come away in my hand—as had been wont to happen, to my chagrin, when I was a wee bairn. Now as it skittered away, I saw—doubtless by a tryck of the firelight—it flash blue.

Father poured mead all round and small beer for me, and Cook did a step dance while Knox played the spoons 'til she declared an end on the highjinks and sent me to bed "afore you catch your death."

Next morning, I dutifully snipped twigs from the witchwood that scraggled next to Byrn's stone bothy and tied them to the milking pail, making fast 'gainst Faery Folk who had their own ways of celebrating Beltane. Byrn believed in Faery, as did Cruikshank; Cook was avowedly superstitious which in no wise contradicted her faith in the Scots Confession, while Knox was content to hedge her bets as "better safe than sorry." Father was, of course, above folkloric fust but, as became a true aristocrat, he honoured those traditions more ancient than his family name, thereby bolstering the bond 'twixt master and servant that went deeper than the peat beneath the moors. Thus, I took a basket of fresh bannocks out to the byre and shared it among the goats, the sheep, Achilles, Hector and Maisie—the latter devoured it with a nip at my knuckles. And yet these festive pursuits were somehow stale; the fire had failed to thrill, the salamander was but a common palmate newt, the bannock dry in my throat—even the crowning of Gossamer with cornflowers was tinged by rote.

May advanced along with the snowy stitchwort that ran riot from forecourt to moat and amid whose blooms floated butterflies, themselves like errant blossoms. The whole of the moorland rustled with renewed industry, but my daily expeditions were become desultory walks. Each morning I joined Father before he retired to bed, and each night I assisted him with his silent beloved birds before making my way up the great staircase.

And then, at the beginning of June, life took an extraordinary turn.

On the day in question I breakfasted with Father—itself a dispensation, for he seldom took that meal in company. We sat, he at the head, I to his right, at the long dining table; its green cloth drank up what light was admitted by a high row of leaded panes over the French doors to the terrace—the doors had been my mother's innovation; the heavy velvet curtains now covering them, my father's.

I made short work of the finnan haddie followed by oatmeal porridge and blood sausage. Father was a vegetableist but believed it folly in the young or female (the which suited me, for much as I would rather have died of inanition than put Gossamer to the axe, or even Maisie, I had no scruples eating creatures outside my personal ken).

Father blinked behind his spectacles and addressed me: "The light of my life is today twelve years old. I wish you, my child, many happy returns of the day." He scraped butter onto his toast and ate in silence, his pale blue gaze resting on the empty chair at the opposite end of the table.

Lest you think him cold, allow me to disabuse you. *Cold?* Never. Subdued, rather, and never more so than upon the second day of June when, along with my birthday, our household observed another, sombre anniversary: that of my mother's death.

"Thank you, Father." Something in my own voice surprised me. I heard—and felt—something new: a power. Surging in my veins, almost painful. To what does the honey bee owe its knowledge of pollen and hive? What tells the seed pod to burst, the sap to rise? Reader, I was suddenly glad. Glad to an unseemly—a heathen—extent, to be alive. Fearful lest I let fly a fresh volley of *Send me to school!* I willed myself motionless and sealed my lips amid the familiar scene: Father crunching. Crimson curtains fading. Empty chairs ranged like mute witnesses—the emptiest of all stationed at the far end of the table, about it a penumbra of motion as though it had only recently been quitted. And I knew that my life had begun.

"Father, who is that with Byrn?"

Following breakfast, Father had invited me to join him outside; rarely did he venture out of doors on even a dull day, but he stood next me now on the forecourt, squinting into the blue. Sunlight rendered crisp the horizon where a black dot had crested the fell and grown larger along the track 'til it took on now the outline of our dog cart, in which, beside the familiar bend of Byrn, was seated a second figure, upright and top-hatted.

Visitors to Fayne were few.

Father's answering smile, with its trace of sadness, touched the old bruise on my heart, and I smiled the harder back up at him. *Up?* Fairly across, rather, for I had of late grown taller. I marshalled meekness in my tone the better to reassure him: "I'll withdraw into the house now, shall I, Father?" Such visitors as we had were barred from my presence lest they carry disease. I had, over the course of my twelve journeys round the sun, spied from behind the service door to the dining room but one guest: the Curator of Birds from the Edinburgh Museum of Science and Art, now dead (he was all but dead at dinner). I was turning already toward the house when Father said, "Stay, child. It is your birthday gift. That is to say, '*he*.'"

"'He'? Who? Father, whatever can you mean?" And I jumped up in place, as though better to descry the figure on the cart.

Father chuckled. But the next instant, "You tremble, my darling, shall I call for a cloak?"

I forbade my eyes to blink, I clamped my teeth against their chattering and by dint of a self-command which certain Oriental fakirs are said to employ when in a trance, willed myself immobile against an inner onslaught of excitement. At last Achilles's hooves rang out on the forecourt.

Byrn slid from the bench and busied himself with cargo lashed to the rear of the cart. A young gentleman alighted, clutching a leather carry-all. He approached and halted a deferential five feet short of us, removed his dusty silk hat and bowed.

Father said, "Mr. Margalo, you are welcome."

"I thank Your Lordship."

He was tall. His voice was deep—like the scent of split pine. His eyes were brown like roasted chestnuts. (Fanciful, but I am bound to report faithfully my contemporaneous impressions.) His name was curious for I knew it to be Greek, and yet nothing in his speech or manner betrayed foreignness—although his high forehead did recall the statues in our marbles room. His overall angular physiognomy, together with a slight perturbation of brow, lent his countenance a solemnity verging on severity, chestnut eyes notwithstanding. I liked him fiercely.

"Allow me to present my daughter, the Honourable Charlotte Bell."

The young gentleman bowed in my direction and, upon straightening, swept a refractory lock of thick dark hair from his eyes as he returned their gaze to my father such that I knew he could not possibly have seen me.

"Well," said Father. "You may as well get started." Whereupon he made toward the house.

I was mystified. What were we to "start"?

"Your Lordship!" he croaked—doubtless dry with the journey—"If you please, Lord Bell—" Father turned. "Might I inquire . . . ?" There was a burr to the young gentleman's speech, his words rather more cinched than Knox's or even Father's.

"Of course, Mr. Margalo, how might I be of assistance?"

"Your Lordship, as to—insofar as 'getting started,' where might I—when, that is, might I expect to have the honour of making the acquaintance of my pupil?"

"Why sir, she stands before you," Father said affably. "Charlotte, my dear, you may wish to show your tutor about the library." With that, he cast me a wistful smile, turned once more and disappeared into the house.

I looked up—aye, up—at *my tutor*. He stood before me like a cabinet of wonders, packed with planets, stars, insects, oceans . . . I waited for him to turn to me with a smile to mirror my own, and noted the flush patching his lean cheeks.

Byrn addressed a guttural syllable to Mr. Margalo and I could not fault the young gentleman for flummoxing at the sound—even at Fayne, Byrn's style of speech was an acknowledged singularity. The old man was holding a great brass-bound trunk by its leather grips, and I answered, "Take it to the library, Byrn."

"No!" cried Mr. Margalo, hastening to add, "Begging your pardon . . ."

From this I surmised the trunk must be more *portmanteau* than *port-école*. "In that case, Byrn, take it to Knox and she'll tell you where my tutor is to be quartered."

"Stop. If you please, sir, return the trunk to the cart." With that Mr. Margalo donned his hat then doffed it immediately and addressed the ground at my feet. "Your Ladyship—"

"Ha-ha, I am no such, you must address me as Miss Bell."

"I . . . see. Forgive me, I must return, sooner than expected, to Edinburgh. Miss Bell." And he bowed from the neck and made for the cart.

"Why? Did you forget something? Byrn can fetch it. We have a house in Edinburgh, I've never seen it, my aunt lives in it, I've never seen her either, what did you forget? Byrn has never been in a train, nor have I, certain heathen peoples believe the soul can travel only as swiftly as a person can walk, by which I calculate your soul to be somewhere near the Lammermuir Hills, whereas Byrn's is right there, slipping back into his side, I jest." I was prattling. And nigh on shouting in my enthusiasm. Byrn had hoisted the trunk back onto the cart and now mounted to the reins once more whilst Achilles lowered his head balefully for he knew fine well it was time for oats—

"Mr. Margalo," came the voice behind me, "I bid you welcome to Fayne House, sir." It was Knox, bustling down the broad stone steps and crossing the forecourt. "I am the housekeeper, Mrs. Knox, allow me to show you to your chamber, and Byrn . . . Byrn!" The old man blinked but did not stir. "Dinnae be dawdling, fetch down the young gentleman's trunk."

"It's been down, he'd have it up again," said Byrn. (I endeavour throughout to translate Byrn's words, but a degree of uncertainty is unavoidable, *ergo, caveat lector*.) But the old man dropped the reins in obedience and stepped down once more.

"Mr. Margalo forgot something in Edinburgh, Knoxy. Still," I turned to my tutor, "no reason to tote the trunk all the way back there, unless— did you bring the wrong one?"

"Sir," Knox's tone turned solicitous, "are you poorly?"

Indeed, my tutor was as pale now as, moments before, he'd been flushed.

"Och, you'll be forfochen with the journey, and faimished too I'll warrant." She dispossessed him of his leather carry-all and, plunking it atop the trunk, ordered him, "Follow Byrn into the house, young sir, I'll no be a minute."

Mr. Margalo obeyed her (people did).

She put a broad arm about my shoulders, squeezed me close and smiled. "Are you pleased with your gift, child?" I could not refrain from hugging her, noting as I did that the last time I had flung my arms round my old nurse, my fingertips had not quite met at the back—and it was not she who had diminished in girth, but I who had increased in length.

"Knoxy. Am I to surmise by the arrival of a stranger that I have outgrown my Condition?"

"Och, pet, that's for your father to say. But he'd ne'er bring a guest under his roof if he didnae think you hale eneuch."

I bounded about in a mad circle before pelting toward the house, but Knoxy admonished me to "Let the young gentleman catch his breath afore you pounce."

"I'll give him twenty minutes, shall I?"

"You'll give him 'til luncheon!"

There was nothing for it but to wait.

Lord Henry Bell has ceded his desk to a great migration of Pacific terns, some whole, most in parts, all dun-coloured in death, frowzy with their journey from sea cliff to net to glass-top case to dust-bin—yes. Hardly to be credited, this latter. Lord Henry retains the after-shock he sustained more than a decade ago upon spying the batch of remains in the wheeled bucket of a caretaker in the Bird Gallery of the Edinburgh Museum. "Hold!" cried Henry, the word escaping him—an old reflex from his fencing days—and the caretaker had stopped and explained. "A mishap involving a display case, Your Lordship. Take care now, there be splinters of glass in amidst the debris." *Debris!*

At the moment, however, his tweezers sit idle, for his head is in his hands. Splitting. A tap at the study door causes him to look up. The door opens to admit Mrs. Knox with a tray.

"Bless you, Knoxy."

"You're sun-smote, My Lord."

"It was worth it, I'll wager." And he manages a smile.

The old housekeeper is about to set the tray down on a low table before the fire but Lord Henry carefully makes space on his desk. "I'll have it here."

"So long as you have it, My Lord."

"I promise."

Knox purses her lips but obliges her master, setting the tray between two piles of bird bits. "Lord Henry, 'tis time you were abed, you'll wear out your lights." She pours the brew into his mug. The aroma of anise and willow bark appears to revive him for he removes his spectacles and rubs his eyes. "Is she happy, do you reckon? With her gift?"

"She is over the moon, My Lord."

He reaches for the cup. "Twelve years, Tabby."

"And all for the best, My Lord."

"Has she . . . ? Is there any change?"

"I would tell you, sir."

"I hardly know whether to be relieved or dismayed."

"Your Lordship . . . surely the latter."

"Of course. Still . . ." He sighs. "At times, when I see how mentally keen Charlotte is, I wish . . . well, I wish I could have shared Marie's delusion."

"Och, Lord Henry, you're not one to dwell in a fool's paradise."

"I did dwell there, Tabby. And I was happy while it lasted."

Tabitha Knox waits, hands folded at her apron.

"Here's to fools," he says, and sips.

3

THE REST OF THE MORNING was an eternity.

I confined myself to the library, loath to leave it lest Mr. Margalo enter it. My heart thrummed in my ears like a war drum. My Condition was in retreat. I would soon see the world! Just as soon as I had learned about everything in it.

I sat cross-legged in the middle of the Turkey carpet, staring at the padlocked trunk as though I might by sheer mental force cause it to pop open.

I waited.

I could hear the very dust motes colliding.

At the sound of the luncheon bell I leapt to my feet, flew from the room, skidded across the great hall and took a shortcut through the drawing room—the drawing room had been redecorated by my late mother such that, while it was the newest chamber, it seemed, by virtue of its being permanently sheeted and shuttered, the oldest.

Before the doorway to the dining room I paused to muster dignity, then slow-marched over the threshold to see . . . the table set for one. As usual.

Luncheon was a trial—pudding notwithstanding, an aptly sticky and gingery parkin—for to the torment of waiting was now added anxiety lest Mr. Margalo be gravely indisposed. When I rang for Knox, however, she told me my tutor was well and taking the meal in his room.

On my way back to the library, Cruikshank slipped, waif-like, from the service door in the great hall, and thrust at me a letter, somewhat begrimed, in her fingerless-gloved and perpetually trembling grip. I knew full well what it was without looking and, opening it on the spot with a sigh, I perused the usual birthday greetings from a friend of my late mother's, a Mrs. Blanchard, along with her daughter who persisted in referring to me as her "cousin" and never tired of wishing I might "get well soon." I thrust it back at Cruikshank. "Take it away, Shanky." She bobbed and scurried off to feed the nearest fire.

I resumed my post on the library floor.

The trunk had not moved. Its keyhole eye returned my stare, implacable as Cyclops.

I waited. As do you now, gentle Reader. In mitigation whereof, I condescend to offer the following:

Situated in the east wing, this august apartment had served as the scene of my father's early tutelage, and his father's before him, and his before him, and his before—see Deuteronomy. I jest. In fact we Bells went back a mere four and one half centuries on this spot. Along the library's north wall, a rank of round-topped Norman windows overlooked the moor; two interior walls were lined with bookcases where a wheeled ladder provided access to the higher volumes, while a set of winding iron stairs led to more shelves in the balustraded gallery above. The Bell Collection was modelled on the Great Library of Alexandria, and housed works from Achilles (not our horse) to Zephyrus. At one end of the room was the fireplace; at the other, to one side of the door, a range of glass-fronted specimen cabinets was home to ranks of mounted moths, divers shells, a swan (gift of Charles I), an inexplicable mongoose and pup, and a petrified oatcake said to have been baked by Flora MacDonald. In the corner where the bookcases met, two leather armchairs flanked the globe of Earth, its surface corrugated where mountainous, sapphire where liquid, pink where Imperial. Commanding the centre of the room, a mahogany table bore the scars of scholars past. (See above *re* Deuteronomy.)

Between the soaring windows hung divers oils of dead grouse and live dogs, as well as of horses, variously mounted and riderless, in attitudes ranging from the bucolic to the bellicose. Above the fireplace hung numerous maps, chief among them, a fourteenth-century reproduction of Ptolemy's *Cosmographia* featuring a Scotland which protruded like a goitre into the North Sea. Next to it hung a more recent map of our own portion of the Empire, but whereas the village of Aberfoyle-on-Feyn duly appeared as a black dot some fifty miles south of Edinburgh, our estate, in accordance with protocols dating back to the final [*sic*] War of the Roses, did not.

Thus, the library.

And still we wait.

And still I stared at the trunk.

And still it failed to open.

The door, however, did at last open to admit Mr. Margalo, who bowed. I shot to my feet and declaimed, *"Te salvere iubeo in domo Faenis, magister! Me discipulam diligentem futuram esse promitto!"*

He regarded me uncertainly. Worried lest I had put a foot wrong in bidding him welcome to Fayne and pledging diligence in the language of Cicero, I hastened to assure him of both in the language of Plato, "χαῖρε, ὦ εἰς Φαίνης ἀφικόμενος. ὑπισχνοῦμαι, ὦ διδάσκαλε, λιπαρῆς περὶ παιδείας ἔσεσθαι."

He cleared his throat. "Miss Bell, I . . . confess to some doubt as to how to . . . commence."

"Why not commence by opening that trunk?"

He looked at it as though seeing it for the first time. "That will not be necessary, in light of . . . circumstances."

"What circumstances might they be, Mr. Margalo?" His name felt like boiled sweets in the mouth, *Margalo, Margalo, Margalo*. It meant "pearl" in Greek, the which augured well for a tutor *re* wisdom.

He cleared his throat again and said, with compressed Edinburgh vowels, "To begin with is the fact of your being, Miss Bell, in fact, a young lady."

"I see you mean to commence with the basics, but at this rate I fear my education will proceed at a *Cochleaa sarmatia*'s pace."

"A . . . what?"

"Species of giant snail, native to the East Germanic Sea, size of a wine cask, and slow-moving."

He cleared his throat. "The fact is, Miss Bell, I have come supplied with such tools and appurtenances as may be counted . . . infelicitous in light of . . ."

"'Circumstances.'"

He nodded. And suddenly I understood. "Sir, be assured my Condition is no impediment. Though I have been sheltered, I have not been idle." I made to reassure him on this point with a recitation of Caesar's *Commentaries on the Gallic War* but he interrupted me before I could say "*Gallia est omnis divisa in partes tres—*"

"'Condition,' Miss Bell?"

"Do you mean to say you are not apprised of it?"

"No. That is, yes, I am not. Apprised."

"Oh. Then what circumstances could possibly prevent you opening this trunk?" He did not immediately answer, and into this vacuum rushed visions of pythons and potions, explosion machines and a spyglass capable of annihilating the viewer with a vision of the monstrous ants which must inhabit our Moon. My palms grew moist with dread and longing.

At length, he spoke. "The fact is . . ."

"You said that already."

"Miss Bell, it is customary for the education of a young lady to be undertaken by a governess."

"Rum custom, I agree."

"I am a tutor."

"I know!" I clapped my hands delightedly then forced them to my sides to forestall further childish display.

"Miss Bell. Tutors are customarily the preserve of young gentlemen."

"I am keenly sensible, Mr. Margalo, as to the rarity of my birthday gift."

". . . And I am by way of being said . . . 'gift'?"

"Of course."

"Not unlike a pony, as 'twere."

"I am too old for a pony, I am today twelve years of age."

"Miss Bell, I fear there has been a grave misapprehension."

"No, truly I am twelve, my height is precocious but not without precedent as you may see in the upstairs picture gallery where each of my forebears is immortalized—with of course the exception of the Blighted Heir. See above *re* my Condition being no impediment, and add to that my age."

"'See above' . . . what?"

"Figure of speech. I am favoured with an audiographic memory such that I am able to read, as though laid out in print before my eyes, our conversation." Here I lowered my pitch and borrowed his compressed Edinburgh brogue: "'Your Lordship, as to—insofar as 'getting started,' where might I—when, that is, might I expect to have the honour of making the acquaintance of my pupil?'"

"My word."

"Ha-ha." I saw by his continued gravity, however, that he had failed to appreciate his own witticism.

"I refer, Miss Bell, to a misapprehension as to the post for which I was engaged."

"Father engaged you to undertake my education."

"Lord Bell engaged me to undertake the education of his . . . 'child.'"

"The which I am."

He cleared his throat once more. I noticed the protuberance at his throat was more pronounced than that of either Father or Byrn and bobbed animatedly above his stiff collar when he spoke or cleared his throat.

"Miss Bell, the fault is mine. I assumed I had been engaged to undertake the education of His Lordship's son."

". . . Oh. You thought I was a boy."

He lowered his head in assent.

I laughed. "And in consequence, you brought the wrong trunk. That explains everything, and easily remedied too. Meantime, we'll make do with this one." And I dealt the lid a friendly blow.

"Miss Bell, please be so kind as to excuse me while I seek out Lord Bell for clarification."

"You won't see him 'til dinner. Shall I show you round? You'll want to see the gallery, and meet Gossamer."

"With your permission." With that, he bowed and quitted the room.

I called after him, "And there are pathways across the moor which are perfectly safe." But he had fled, and I concluded he had been taken short, bearing out Mrs. Knox's dim view of train victuals. I resigned myself to the prospect of dinner alone as usual.

Dinner.

Candlelight danced on Father's glasses as he applied himself to his soup (white soup, my favourite). Across from me, Mr. Margalo ate his with downcast eyes.

I had been at pains to suppress an undignified degree of joy when I entered the dining room to find Father already seated and, at his left hand, Mr. Margalo! Having risen at my entrance, he was constrained upon sitting to fish beneath the table for the dinner napkin which had slid from his lap.

Since then, not a word had passed his lips, and it was with a sinking sensation that I wondered whether all gentlemen shared Father's customary silence at meals.

At length, Father spoke. "Might I inquire, Mr. Margalo, what lessons you undertook today with your pupil?"

Mr. Margalo coughed. "Your Lordship. I confess a degree of doubt as to whether I am best qualified to fill the present post." He reddened.

Father tilted his head, rather in the manner of his beloved bobolink. "How's that? Your qualifications are impeccable, your degree first-class, your references sterling."

"I refer, Your Lordship, to . . . circumstances regarding your . . . my pupil."

"What circumstances are they, Mr. Margalo?"

Mr. Margalo's lips parted but no sound issued thence. I came to his aid. "He thought I was a boy."

"What?" Father turned to me as though surprised to find me seated next to him.

He then addressed Mr. Margalo, "I fail to see, sir, how anyone could mistake my daughter for a young man."

"Your Lordship, my misapprehension preceded my-my-my meeting Miss Bell. I refer to the expectation I formulated, in error—my error—when I accepted the post of tutor to your . . . ."

"'Child,'" I supplied.

Father finished his soup. Cruikshank wavered from the shadows and removed his empty bowl then withdrew through the service door behind Father's chair. (Reader, I anticipate your objection: while it is true that women did not generally wait at table in the great houses, this was Fayne and Father was the old style of aristocrat for whom such protocols were no more than middle-class trumpery.)

My tutor sat as still as a parsnip. I reassured him. "Mr. Margalo, if Father says you are the best tutor, then there's an end on it, no need to fret. And no need to finish your soup if white is not to your taste, plenty of food to come." And I fell to finishing my own.

Father fixed Mr. Margalo with a look over his spectacles and said, "Do you mean to imply I deliberately misled you?"

My spoon fell with a clatter from my grasp. Mr. Margalo appeared likewise stricken, his brown eyes wide with alarm. Father placed both hands calmly on the table. He had once fought a duel in his youth—shot deliberately wide and was grazed in return. Mr. Margalo was hardly an equal, thus incapable of providing satisfaction in the event of offence. But how soon might he be turned from the house? And might we confiscate his trunk in recompense?

He answered, barely above a whisper, "Certainly not, Your Lordship."

My relief was short-lived, for Father patted his lips with his dinner napkin and stated coolly, "I did."

Cruikshank re-entered with the fish and a head of boiled cauliflower for Father. I was speechless. So was Mr. Margalo—the two of us united in bafflement.

Father addressed his cauliflower mildly. "I was quite aware, Mr. Margalo, that the services of a reputable tutor might be otherwise unattainable." He picked up his knife and fork and commenced to eat, lobe by lobe.

I was not more amazed by Father's admission of deceit than by the notion of its necessity in securing the services of a tutor for me. And it hit me with the force of Gossamer's hind hoof that if girls did not customarily have tutors, it was not because girls did not wish to have tutors but because tutors did not wish to have girls!

"Claret, I think, Cruikshank," said Father.

She trembled forth with the decanter. Father indicated with a raised finger Mr. Margalo's glass, and Cruikshank filled it to the shaky brim. Mr. Margalo regarded it—longingly or charily, I could not tell.

"You fear irreparable harm to your reputation and therefore your prospects should it get about that you have tutored a female; your hopes of a professorship at the university supplanted by a teaching post at a lesser public school; or even . . . emigration."

I looked at Mr. Margalo. He did not contradict my father. I understood now why my strong sense that he and I were to be friends—a sense unfounded, considering I had never yet had a friend—had gone unrequited by look or word. I understood as well that what I had taken for illness on his part was revulsion. At me. Hard on comprehension followed the sting of I knew not what, and I felt my face grow hot.

Father continued. "Not to mention the unfortunate sequel attendant upon it becoming known that, having accepted such a post, you were swiftly dismissed sans letter of reference by a peer of the realm."

Mr. Margalo, pale now, spoke. "Your Lordship, I know neither what nor how to teach a young lady."

Father rested his gaze upon the empty chair at the far end of the table just beyond range of the candlelight, and spoke softly. "Hath not a woman eyes? Hath she not brain? If you teach her, does she not learn?"

Mr. Margalo seemed about to reply but, perhaps thinking better of it, looked down.

"Mr. Margalo." Father was suddenly businesslike. "I give you my word, the sex of your pupil shall not be broadcast. As to the pecuniary terms of your employment, do you find them sufficient?"

"I find them generous, Your Lordship."

"They are hereby doubled."

"Your Lordship—"

"Teach my daughter as you would my son. Had I one." With that, Father rose and left through the service door, passing Cruikshank who was entering with a covered dish.

Mr. Margalo half rose as though to follow, but Cruiky forestalled him with a serving of roast chicken. Rounding the table, she dropped a leg and thigh onto my plate but I felt my stomach seal over at the prospect of eating a single morsel. Mr. Margalo continued to stare at the swing door as though Father might return any moment bearing the pudding. Presently, he transferred his gaze to his glass which he carefully raised with two hands and drained, throat madly bobbing. The sight seemed to break a spell, and I rose. He rose.

"Sir. I trust Mrs. Knox has put you in the blue room overlooking the garden."

"In fact, Miss Bell, I have been quartered in a somewhat dun-coloured chamber overlooking the moor."

"In that case, make fast your window. Cries are known to issue from the bog. A skraik there is, walks by night, hungry for human blood. Male blood. With the exception of Father's, of course." Whereupon I turned and swept from the room—we dressed for dinner at Fayne, thus I made the most of my cape.

Plunging into the deeper gloom of the drawing room, my cheeks burning with outrage, I walked the gauntlet of dust-sheeted chairs and tables forever arranged in ghostly tête-à-têtes and games of whist.

It was my intent upon gaining the entry hall to ascend immediately to my bedchamber, for I wished to be alone with my thoughts which were cloudy and low to the ground like fog. But I reluctantly crossed the hall in obedience to the triangle of light from Father's study door.

"Hello, Father."

"Hello, my treasure."

I experienced a stab of remorse for having taunted Mr. Margalo who was, after all, Father's birthday gift to me. "That's coming along," I said of a bedraggled swift taking shape between tweezers and dropper.

"There's hope for it yet."

I beheld his pale brow, his face framed by side-whiskers as subdued as the wings of his dear specimens, and felt a dangerous lump forming in my throat.

"Hold this, if you please . . ." he bid me. It was a beak, the point of which I held 'twixt thumb and forefinger whilst he pearled its inner edge with glue. He took it and carefully pressed and held it to the bird's vacant face with the tip of his forefinger. Contemplation is the companion of calm and, as oft occurred when in company with Father in his study, the mist cleared from my thoughts.

"What is it, my own?"

"Father, is the world—the world out there—really so unfit for female habitation? Leastways, female education?"

"I am afraid Fayne is something of an oasis in that regard." He favoured me with a twinkle of amusement and I was near to climbing aboard his lap as of old. Alas for the days spent snuggled, nay swaddled in that tweed embrace, our two heads bent over books and birds and shells, a world of tiny wonders. "Father, I would rather you sent Mr. Margalo away than retain him for my sake."

"Is that so? And to what do we owe this misgiving?"

"Only, I would not for the world be the occasion of—of anything . . . dissembling." The last word bumped against the lump in my throat.

Mercifully, he kept his eyes on the bird as, with his free hand, he dug a handkerchief from the pocket of his waistcoat. I held the silk to my eyes and nose. Tears were a type of personal precipitation all but foreign to me.

"You wonder at my deception," he said, his voice as kind as ever.

I looked away.

He continued, "In that I deliberately obfuscated the fact of your sex."

"Yes."

"I lied."

"No! Mr. Margalo made an assumption for which he is alone responsible."

"My Portia," he smiled.

"Nevertheless, Father, you did promise to keep secret the nature of . . . me."

"I did so."

"Secrets are ignoble."

"And sometimes discretion is the better part of valour."

". . . How is one to know the difference?"

He took his finger from the beak ever so slowly and it held. "My dearest child, it has for these many months been plain to me that, in accordance with my most cherished hope, you evince robust good health, and that the strictures which characterized your infancy admit of some relaxation."

I hugged him. He continued. "And that, what's more, I have reached the limit of what I am able to teach you."

"Of course you haven't! Oh, send him away, Father, let us be as we were." He gently extricated himself and sought my gaze. "If at the end of one week—hush now and perpend: if at week's end your present animus persists, I shall dismiss your tutor. And engage a governess."

"Will a governess teach me mathematics?"

"No."

I blinked, and my glance fell upon our "creature." Propped atop the bank of pigeon holes, it stood long and lanky with feathers of every hue and texture. As yet headless.

I kissed his cheek. "Thank you, Father."

"Goodnight, my own. Many happy returns."

———

Candle in hand, I mounted the staircase, averting my eyes as usual from the portrait that presided over the landing. As on previous nights, I felt the gaze upon my back as I made to mount the leftward branch. Tonight, however, I stopped. Tonight, I turned. Tonight, I looked up at the portrait. Tall as a huntress, barefoot like one too, raven-haired and statuesque beneath the shimmer of a silken shawl that slipped from milky shoulders, my mother. Framed in gilt. But far from following me with her emerald gaze, she had eyes only for the babe in her embrace. He smiled out at the world, wee fingers entangled in the fringe of her shawl. Thus, as with the chill baptism of new maturity, I affirmed that paintings are inert, mothers die, and mine had never gazed on me at all, whether in paint or in flesh. She died, Charlotte. Exactly twelve years ago. Because you killed her.

~๑๏

Rome, Italy
April 30, 1871

Dear Taffy,
Don't be cross. I'm to be married. I know, I know dearest, we promised, I promised, etcetera etcetera, and now you will never clutch a trailing nosegay in my wedding procession, much less put my hair in curling papers the night before (which old Annie would re-do in any case) nor gaze upon my intended, and giggle with me into the wee hours before the day of <u>the wedding night.</u> And by the time you receive this, I will have been married for weeks and will no longer be a . . . EEK! ("maiden," to put it politely). I promise to tell you all about it, or nothing about it, just as you please, or . . . Oh heavens to Betsy, Taffy, it's all happened so fast, and this time tomorrow I shall be Lady Marie Bell of the DC de Fayne. I am to marry a baron! That sounds so formal—his name is Henry and he is a dear. We met at Fanny Bunker's palace in Rome (everyone here has a palace). Fanny is of course La Principessa della Montesilvio von Badenkreuzer. The Principe is dead. All *comme il faut*, as he was ancient, but lest you think Pappy has sold me to the oldest bidder, I give you Henry (five middle names) Bell: all of thirty-two years old, tallish, trim, pretty much wheat-coloured all over, with smallish light blue eyes (for me only). I don't know if I'm in love with him (that's his department *vis-à-vis* yours truly) but I can definitely say I'm head over heels in like.

Now, Miss Timothea Weaver, I order you to forgive me. I know we were to be one another's bridesmaids, and even though I have deprived us both of your attending me in that role, I promise I'll come home at the drop of a veil to be your Matron of Honor when you and a certain Harvard man set a date . . . And after my honeymoon, and having tasted "the Season" in London where Henry has a house, and once I've visited his country seat (sounds indecent somehow, let's call it his country house), we'll sail home to Boston. I don't know if you've been counting, but that brings us up to Christmas which will be perfect. Katie Buxton will be giving her annual oyster party and I'll sashay in with a real live British lord. I can't wait to see her face! And, without going into unladylike detail, I just may, in the natural course of things (see above, "EEK!") either have, or be expecting, not just any old baby, but an heir. Oh, Tiff-Taff, hurry up and get married so our children can grow up together—Atlantic Ocean notwithstanding-or-swimming.

I love you love you love you, think of me tomorrow (oh all right, three weeks ago, by the time you're reading this) when I shall be wearing the most scrumptious veil of Venetian lace in a dreamy cream colour called "dust of ruins"—I swoon as I write these words!

Yours forever,
Mae

❧

Beneath a gibbous moon, the moor lies in breasting swells like a sea stilled by a sorcerer. Creased in charcoal, bruised in violet. Not so light as to lure a hare from its burrow. Light enough to make out the standing stone away off on the North Fell. Light enough to ask, What is that? Something slipping through the gloom. A huddle of darker darkness. On the move . . . coming closer. A human shape. Closer . . . Staggering . . . Closer . . .

I sat straight up. I flung aside my bed curtains. The sound of the door latch was like the report of a gun. "You heard it too!"

Knox was rustling toward me. "Indeed I did, pet."

I sprang from bed. "I'll tell Father, you get Byrn"—doubtless the old man had heard the cry from his bothy and was already up and out with a lantern.

"Snuggle back into bed now."

I made for the window—"There's someone on the moor, we've got to help." I tore open the drapes, leaned both hands on the ledge and peered out—the moor was drenched in light from the full moon, Byrn would need no lantern.

"There is no one on the moor, child, gracious me."

"There is, they cried out!" I turned and snatched up my boots.

"'Twas you cried out."

"What? No, no, it came from out there."

"It didnae."

"I heard it. You heard it."

"I heard you." She stroked my cheek. "Och, lass, not for nowt have I watched o'er your slumber since you were born. I know every whumper, giggle and cry."

"Do you mean to say . . . ?"

"We all ride the nightmare from time to time, pet. Tonight it seems she bucked you off."

The sight of old Knoxy standing there plain as porridge in bedsocks, nightgown and cap dispelled any lingering fancy on my part, but I was seized the next instant by a fresh misgiving: had Mr. Margalo heard my cry? And did he think me a great babby on top of being a useless girl? I flung myself back onto my bed and yanked the quilt to my chin, thrashing once or twice to subdue the linens. Knox closed the window drapes against the moonlight and I heard her settle into the upholstered chair that had acquired, through years of bedside watching, the impression of her broad back and generous beam. "There, there, pet," she crooned.

"I am no pet and I'll prove it if you don't leave off stroking my head."

"Just so, pet."

I sighed, soothed in spite of myself by her firm, dry palm on my brow. The following question took me by surprise, notwithstanding it issued from my lips: "Knox. Did my mother love me?"

"Och, dearie, she'd've treasured you."

"Would she have loved me as much as she loved him?"

"Who?"

"My brother."

"Of course she would have. She never had the chance."

I curled on my side, suddenly drowsy. "You needn't stay 'til I'm asleep."

"Whyever not?"

"Knox, I'm twelve. I have a tutor. It's time I went to sleep without my nurse."

She sighed, rose and made to close my bed curtains.

"Leave them open."

"'Tis one thing leaving you to drift off on your own, I'll not have you beset by drafts."

"I like the air."

She looked as if I'd voiced a morbid craving, but did my bidding.

"Knoxy?"

"Yes, child?"

"Are you sorry I was born?"

"Och, lamby, I love you to the ends of the Earth and back, nor would I trade you for another soul." This with a firm kiss to my forehead.

"Not even for him?"

"For . . . ?"

"For Charles?"

". . . Not even for him."

I closed my eyes. Presently I heard her stolid footfalls retreating, followed by the click of the door latch.

I opened my eyes. The cry had been so real—*manifesto*, for it had come from me. Still . . . I rose and crept to the window.

The moor lay perfectly still. Now that I was fully awake, I fully appreciated the impossibility of what I had heard, for the piteous cry that had shocked me awake had been the cry of a child. And as unlikely as it was that anyone at all might be out there (save Byrn, with his buckets), it was absurd to believe a real live child could be lost and wandering alone on the moor in the dead of night. I returned to bed and sank among my pillows, relieved yet oddly bereft.

～ତ

Paris, France
July 15, 1871

Dearest Taffy,
Having only this morning dispatched by ocean liner, all of the missives which I penned to you over the course of our Grand Tour of the

Quatro Cento and the South of France, you will now be in possession of an epistolary bundle, for the superabundance of which I crave your pardon. Taffy, this is how they speak! (Henry and his well-bred compatriots with whom Paris is packed.) Remember Miss Jolly with her wooden tongue depressors? "Young ladies, if you can recite 'The Wreck of the Hesperus' with this depressor lodged between tongue and teeth, you may with confidence converse with the queen." Tongue depressor was one thing, tongue <u>twister</u> is another. I fear I may go mad with their "parlance" if I don't die laughing first.

And now to the question that is burning in your brain: What is married life like? You are dying to know about the conjugal act (sounds like "jungle act"!). Well (and burn this after reading or our friendship is cancelled and I will tell your mother who it really was that laced last year's Thanksgiving cider with licorice water), <u>it</u> is not terrible, my dear. <u>It</u> contains a flicker of . . . something short of but perhaps on its way to . . . nice. Which is about three whistle stops short of the Terminus called Wonderful. I think we may be on our way to Wonderful. Stop it, stop it you silly girl, you are doubled over, pinching your giggles in by the nose. On the other hand, enjoy your hysterical laughter, chickadee, it is due to your still being a Maiden, while I am a Married Lady. Ha-ha! Henry is the sweetest, the nicest, the abashed-est, and I think I'll be able to make him do anything I want. My prediction: marital bliss.

Henry has promised to whisk me directly from Dover to his house in town, thence to his noble pile. (Pile as in country house, not $$$, for as you know they haven't any. Rather, they hadn't until yours truly, tra-la!)

Love, licorice, laughter and more "missives" to come from your if-not-older-then-certainly-wiser (here a saucy wink) cousin,

Mae, a.k.a. Marie, Lady Bell, Seventeenth Baroness DC de Fayne
(No one here has ever heard me called "Mary" and they never shall!)

PS You *will* burn this. Send me the ashes with a few legible fragments as proof.

4

MR. MARGALO WAS STANDING next to his precious trunk when I entered the library after breakfast. If he had heard my nocturnal cry, he gave no sign. Still, I was vexed to feel my face flush, and so cast him a severe look. "I deem it fair to inform you, Mr. Margalo, I am a physical Epicurean and a moral Stoic, but remain agnostic as to the nature of free will."

"Miss Bell, of what, may I ask, has your education consisted thus far?"

I gestured to the shelves. "Achilles through Pythagoras." He glanced at the book-lined walls, then returned me a quizzical look. I added, "Had I known you were coming, I'd have put on a push to Zeno."

"Do you claim to have—That is, do you mean to say, Miss Bell, you have read . . . these volumes?"

"'Achilles was son of Peleus, king of Pythia in Thessaly, descended of Zeus, son of Thetis, daughter of Oceanus. Divers accounts of the hero's infancy are extant, chief among them that of his consignment to the care of Chiron, the Centaur—'"

"Miss Bell . . . I am familiar with Achilles."

"Of course you are, it is *my* familiarity with which we have to do here, but very well. 'Aeschylus: born five hundred and twenty-five BC, died four hundred and fifty-six BC. Aeschylus, acknowledged father of Tragedy—'"

"Miss Bell—"

"Shall I jump to Pythagoras? Pythagoras was—and here I do not quote, but comment—a vegetableist like Father, for he believed that in consuming animals one risks consuming one's own grandfather *vis-à-vis* the doctrine of reincarnation. Beans, likewise, he forbade his disciples, but I cannot find out why. Why?"

"Why did Pythagoras refuse to eat . . . beans?"

"Yes."

"I do not know."

"Really. What else do you not know?"

". . . I hardly know where to begin."

"Begin at the beginning."

"And where, I wonder, might that be?"

"Not 'where,' 'when.'"

"All right, when?"

"October twenty-third, four thousand and four BC at approximately two o'clock in the afternoon. Likely a Tuesday." I smiled, for I knew he had thought to trip me up.

"And what is supposed to have occurred at that precise moment?"

"God formed the Earth and set the heavens in motion. Don't tell me we have stumbled onto another lacuna in your store of knowledge, Mr. Margalo?"

"Miss Bell . . . Have you heard of James Hutton?"

"Homer, Horace, Ithaca . . . no."

". . . Charles Lyell, perhaps?"

"Lucretius, Lyceum, Lysias."

"Charles Darwin?"

"Corinth, Democritus, Diogenes."

He sighed.

He reached into his trouser pocket—a gentleman keeps nothing in the pockets of his trousers—and drew forth a stone. "Do you know what a fossil is?"

"Fossil. *Fossor.* Something one digs up?"

He held it out and I approached. He placed the stone in my hand, warm from his pocket. Oblong and grey, it was bisected lengthwise with a dark stripe, from either side of which there fanned numerous thinner stripes.

"Does it remind of you of anything?" he asked.

"It . . . Well, it looks like a plant of some kind, a bit of a fern, perhaps. Did you carve it? It's not very good, is it. Byrn whittles and carves, very skilled he is, he could help you."

"I did not carve it."

"Who did then?"

"Time did. This stone bears the impression of a fern which lived, then died, some three hundred and fifty million years ago." I looked up at him. The gaze which met mine, far from trifling, was grave. "I found it on a cliff-face in the Northwest Highlands near Cape Wrath. It was embedded in a stratum of red sandstone, above a stratum of limestone itself encrusted with the fossils of creatures born some five hundred million years ago, now long extinct."

"Then . . . how old is our Earth?"

"'We find no vestige of a beginning, no prospect of an end.'"

". . . Do you mean to say Aristotle was right?"

"I quoted our own Mr. James Hutton just now."

"Then Mr. Hutton must be a heathen like Aristotle, for he too said the world has always been."

"Sir Isaac Newton was an alchemist, but that did not prevent him discovering the law of gravity."

"Sir who?"

"Miss Bell. The whole of Earth is a vast record. All that has lived has left its trace. Every event great or small is written. And the living world we see around us today is but a fleeting manifestation, a mere . . . blossom, as it were, of Time."

I looked down at the humble stone in my palm. "This . . . happened."

"Yes. It did."

I felt I was privy to a secret. A life. A fall. A death. What eyes had seen this frond green with life? Tears arose in mine. I dared not look at Mr. Margalo.

He continued, "If we could hear the life that is unfolding within a single spore of fungus out on your moor, we would be deafened and run mad."

"Perhaps we do hear it. And call it silence."

He regarded me. Then he reached into his other trouser pocket—truly, he had no breeding—and came out with a key. He bent to the trunk and opened it. Had it been sunny up to then? Does memory embellish what came next? Or is it meteorological fact that high above Fayne the sun pierced the clouds and shot a beam through the library windows that transformed a heap of packing straw into gold?

Mr. Margalo removed his morning coat and cuffs, rolled back his sleeves and, plunging in both hands, lifted out an object of gleaming brass. Like a miniature cannon or a captain's spyglass it was, mounted on a sturdy tripod base. He placed it on the table. "Do you know what this is?" he asked.

"It is either a weapon or an ocular device."

He smiled. "It is in a sense both, for it renders visible the invisible."

"Do you mean to say that with the help of this instrument one may see ghosts?"

"Ha-ha!"

I reddened.

"Forgive me, Miss Bell. Are you familiar with an implement called a magnifying glass?"

"Of course," I sniffed. "Father keeps one for his specimens. And I possess field glasses with which I survey the moor on clear days."

"This is called a microscope. It is an extremely powerful magnifying glass. Allow me."

He reached back into the trunk, withdrew a morocco-bound chest and set it on the table—by its look, one might have expected it to open upon a heap of gold coins. He lifted the lid to reveal, instead, several dozen velvet-lined slots, each of which housed a small rectangle of glass. He selected one and held it up to the light. The glass appeared clear but for a speck at its centre. He slid the glass into a small platform between the lens of the microscope and a tiny tilted mirror below it. He bent to the eyepiece and began slowly to turn a dial affixed to the brass cylinder. He straightened and stood aside. I took his place, pressing my eye to the warmed rubber. At first a blur, then I felt for the dial and turned it. Into focus came the most hideous creature I had ever beheld. And the fiercest. Bulbous body of segmented armour bristling with spines. Fixed blank eye. Hooked probosces where there ought to be a mouth such that the monster appeared to be devouring the hind-quarters of another creature. From its underbelly protruded multiple legs like those of a lobster. "And how old is this specimen?" I asked, reassured by my assumption it was as long extinct as everything else in Mr. Margalo's cliff-face.

"Why, some months," he said.

I sprang back. "You don't mean to say that such creatures walk the Earth today?"

"They hop more than walk. You are looking at a flea."

He went to the window and ran a corner of his handkerchief along the ledge. Returning, he shook dust onto a fresh rectangle of glass—"it is called a 'slide'"—I adjusted the dial and . . . the mess was alive! Writhing, foul, foreign. I shrank inwardly but forced myself to stand firm. After a decent interval I straightened. "You laughed when I asked about ghosts, you scoffed at my *Cochlea sarmatia*, but nothing could be more fantastical than what I have just seen."

"Precisely, Miss Bell."

He handed me a splinter of wood, one end swabbed in cotton. "Swipe that along your gums." I did so. He smeared it on a fresh slide, and I looked. Swirling denizens of slime. I drew back, fairly faint. "Do not you fear contagion, Mr. Margalo?"

"Not in the least. The presence of these creatures is perfectly normal."

"You are accustomed perhaps to a grubbier class of student."

"Miss Bell, be assured, the same creatures dwell in—and on—all of us. Our skin, our hair, the whole of the oral, digestive, urogenital—that is . . ." He cleared his throat. "We teem with microscopic life." Clearly he had warmed to his subject for he was flushed.

"Do please continue, Mr. Margalo."

"Yes, well, it was the Dutch lens-maker, Van Leeuwenhoek, who first saw them in a drop of rainwater. He called them animalcules. We know them as micro-organisms, among which are numberless bacteria, and we can but surmise that of these creatures, some—perhaps many—must be our allies in health, or at least not our enemies. You may wish to take notes."

"So . . . they are not peculiar to my Condition?"

"Your . . . Miss Bell, what is the nature of your condition?"

"I am morbidly susceptible to germs."

His brow stirred but he remained mum.

I continued, "It is why I may not venture from the estate until such time as I may have outgrown it. It is why we have so few visitors, lest I fall ill."

"Are you often ill?"

"I am never ill."

"Ah."

"Unlike my brother."

". . . You have a brother?"

"He died."

"I am sorry."

"I am not."

He flinched.

"Allow me to adumbrate, lest you think me unfeeling. You see, had he lived he could hardly forget that my life was in forfeit of his mother's."

"I see."

"One could not blame him for hating me."

"He might not hate you."

Something in Mr. Margalo's look prompted me almost to ask whether he had heard a cry in the night. I pushed aside the impulse, for what had it to do with microscopic monsters, ancient ferns and intimations of infinity? For if our world was without beginning or end, then our world itself was God, and we specks of that divine spark . . . "Electricity," I said. It was a word I had heard from the lips of Father's estate manager, Mr. Mungo.

"What about electricity?"

"Everything. Go ahead, I'm listening."

Dinner that evening could not have been in starker contrast to that of the previous. Father posed the same question: "Might I inquire, Mr. Margalo, what lessons you undertook today with your pupil?"

Tonight, however, Mr. Margalo replied, "Your Lordship, it was my privilege today to introduce Miss Bell to current concepts of geology, microbiology—"

"Father, the world is hundreds of millions of years old, perhaps even older." I stated this with barely contained urgency.

Father blinked over his spectacles and rejoined mildly, "Is it, indeed?"

"And there are creatures, invisible to the naked eye, creeping and crawling over each one of us, even now as we eat our soup, nay our soup itself seethes with unseen life!"

Father drew back slightly. "Well, well," he chuckled. "''Twas a brave man that first et an oyster.' I suppose one must now say the same of a bowl of soup."

"They are harmless, Father, they are—why, they may even be useful, is that not so, Mr. Margalo?"

"It is a subject of debate at the highest levels of scientific research."

"Father, did you know that a pine cone grows in spirals of eight in one direction and thirteen in the opposite direction in accordance with a sequence known as Fibonacci numbers, each of which is the sum of the two preceding numbers, that is unless the pine cone grows in spirals of seven in one direction and eleven in the other, in which case they accord with the less common but equally serviceable Lucas numbers which, despite their difference from Fibonacci numbers, tend toward the same destination, namely dear old Euclid's golden mean!—the which ratio we may express as the irrational number one point six one eight zero three three nine eight eight seven four nine eight nine four ad infinitum, for the ease of which decimal notation we are indebted to our own John Napier no less than for the wonderfully congenial logarithms that account for the horns of sheep and myriad other living and non-living structures?"

"I confess I did not know that."

Mr. Margalo said, "At Miss Bell's request, we touched upon mathematics in addition to natural history and electricity."

"You sound surprised, Mr. Margalo."

"The pace is . . . notable."

"For a female scholar, you mean?"

"For any scholar."

Father turned to me and for a moment I feared lest he renew his misgivings *vis-à-vis* over-exertion of my mental faculties, but he said, "I am, of course, unsurprised." He bestowed upon me a smile of paternal pride such that I fairly glowed. And behind his lenses, I saw his eyes had misted over.

Cruikshank carried in a platter of mutton with caper sauce, and a basin of neeps and tatties. Far from the silence of dinners past, there was much of mirth and lively intercourse. "Claret, I think, Cruikshank," said Father, midway through the meal. Mr. Margalo posed apt questions and Father held forth obligingly on the history of Fayne and waxed eloquent as to the variety of our moorland birds, the which he only rarely now viewed in their habitat owing to the sensitivity of his eyes, eliciting from Mr. Margalo the shy admission, "I am myself a devoted botanist." At one point, Mr. Margalo even queried Father as to, of all things, Byrn. I soon gathered, via my tutor's questions and my father's amusement in answering, that Byrn's singularity extended beyond his manner of speech. Father went so far as to summon the old man-of-all-work before us in the dining room. Thus I beheld Byrn through the eyes of a newcomer, and it seemed a familiar fixture of Fayne had been turned on its axis, affording me a fresh perspective: Byrn resembled a fossil. In clogs and begrimed linen smock. I was prompted to wonder whether there were other inhabitants of Fayne who had struck Mr. Margalo as out of the ordinary. Cruikshank entered just then with the pudding. Jaune mange. Two helpings.

I. MARGALO. FIELD NOTES. JUNE 5, 1887

Pupil, twelve-year-old female.

Prodigious memory for facts, appetite for knowledge. She may learn to think.

Pupil's dress quasi-medieval, *id est* scarlet tunic embroidered with Bell coat of arms (blue *Salamander Rampant* on field of vines), deerskin leggings, boots. Unconventional if not eccentric, but practical, given remote situation, rugged terrain (therefore retract "eccentric").

Arrived yesterday morning by post-chaise at the Inn at the Kenspeckle Hen in Aberfoyle-on-Feyn. Met by elderly man, relieved me of trunk, swung it onto back of dog cart. I could make out neither his name nor his answers to questions pertaining to county, but was struck by physical strength in one so aged. Queried Lord Henry over dinner. He replied that old man had been born "on the bog" of local stock that went back to "before the Conquest" and had "come with the house, as it were." Lord Henry evinced pleasure at my interest, told dining-room servant (female, mute, Cruikshank) to fetch old man to us.

He entered dining room, accompanied by gamey odour which I had not remarked whilst near him out of doors. He was dressed, as before, in rustic smock and leggings. Bald, bowed but tall and sinewy. Lacking several teeth, mouth has black look, but a few yellowed molars in evidence must furnish sufficient chewing power, for no man may long outlive his teeth.

Lord Henry instructed "Burn" to tell me "the secret" of his vitality to which the old man muttered a reply. L. H. thanked him, sent him away, then turned to me, saying, "Well, Mr. Margalo, does that answer your question?"

"Your Lordship, I heard your servant say that he takes oats, mush and muck."

L.H. laughed. Miss Bell translated old man's words: "'Goat's milk and mud.'"

Curiosity piqued as to whether these moorlands be among those purported to contain chemical properties which, if we were able to isolate and identify, might yield benefit to mankind. Paracelsus mentions drinking of moor mud by Romans and ancient Celtic peoples who also encouraged livestock to partake, attributing medicinal properties. While Paracelsus is not to be taken at face value (if at all), folk wisdom has been seen on occasion to point toward scientific discovery.

Housekeeper, Mrs. Knox, is of peasant stock. Her head is shape and hue of a turnip, prompting me to wonder whether, in this case, Lamarck's theory of acquired characteristics is not borne out, for that stolid tuber is abundantly grown as feed hereabouts. (The latter, fanciful. L. H. is liberal with his claret.)

With newfound boldness did I climb the stairs that night, and once again raise my candle and my eyes to the portrait on the landing. This time I looked straight at my brother. The grey-eyed cherub nestled in his mother's arms gazed merrily outward. I hated him a little less tonight. After all, I had a tutor, and he was dead.

∿☉

Calais, France
August 10, 1871

Dearest Taffy,

I didn't mention this before because who needs gloomy news, so I have waited until it no longer bothers me a whit. It's this: I was expecting, but I'm not anymore. And really, it was ages ago, last month in Paris where it began and ended before it could really get started. I didn't tell Henry, and I tried my best to launder the offending petticoat myself—I couldn't leave it for the help at the Grand Hôtel du Louvre, and in this I guess I am incorrigibly Yankee: I care what the lower classes think— at least I cared what the Parisian chambermaid, who was likely a guttersnipe but made me feel like an imposter, would have thought (I'm still convinced she saw right through my "Marie" to "Mary" underneath). I pictured her scorn upon finding the evidence of my *petite* disaster: "moi," the jumped-up Yank putting on airs, meanwhile, splat. It was no more than a "monthly" gone queer though, really, so I'm not worried and neither should you be 'cause at the rate my marriage is going, I ought to have happier news quite soon (herewith you may imagine a saucy wink on my part, as I imagine a blush on yours).

When next I write you, it will be from our establishment <u>in town</u>.

Love,
Mae

5

I HAD EXPECTED that a tutor was a sort of vessel which would tip and empty its contents into my brain and I would be full of education. Instead, my tutor opened for me daily the Book of Life and bid me peruse where I would in pursuit, not so much of answers—for answers are abundant as drones in a hive—but Questions. A good Question is the queen bee.

Each day was packed as full with wonders as Mr. Margalo's trunk. The first day was characterized by "A general introduction to chemistry. Let us begin with the known elements."

"That's easy: earth, air, fire and water."

By way of answer, he laid before me a sheet of vellum whereon was depicted an asymmetrical chart divided into squares, in each of which appeared words—many unfamiliar—accompanied by initials and numbers. The whole effect was nothing if not runic and for a mad moment I wondered whether my tutor had transcribed Byrn's dialect. "This, Miss Bell, is the Periodic Table. Your first task shall be to commit it to memory, one line per day, such that in due course—"

"I have it, Mr. Margalo."

"You have . . . ?"

Taking up a pencil, I turned the sheet of paper over and rendered a reproduction of the "table." He looked perturbed. "Have I left something out?" I asked.

"No . . ."

"What do these letters and numbers mean?"

"They are abbreviations denoting the known elements."

"Do you mean to say there are in excess of four elements?"

"There are sixty-three. And counting."

"Huzzah!"

On the second day, the library table became a laboratory bench. I began by combining several drops of a pale blue liquid known as hydrogen peroxide with a measure of pig's blood (not Maisie's) to produce a foaming pink mixture which overflowed its "test tube"! This I followed with a chemical sleight of hand involving a granular purplish substance called potassium permanganate ($KMnO_4$ to the initiated), ordinary H_2O (water, to the layman), sugar and sodium hydroxide (lye), the which I stirred

together in a "beaker" whereupon the clear liquid turned violet, then
green, then yellow, then red!! After luncheon—I scarcely noticed what I
ate (stovies)—the sorcery of combining crystals of iodine with dust of
zinc and a drop of water produced an audible "poof" simultaneous with a
puff of bright purple smoke, such that I fancied myself a budding Merlin!!!

On the third day, Mr. Margalo introduced "some principles of mechanical engineering." Reader, I built a steam engine; diminutive, to be sure,
nonetheless capable of setting a cork disk to spinning in a basin of water
by means of a loop of copper tubing and a candle. Thus did I wield with
my own hands the power that had ignited the Industrial Revolution
and drove it still, for what was my spinning cork but a flywheel writ
small? A thundering locomotive, a chugging ocean liner, a piston-pump
in a mine where coal was dug to make the heat to turn the water into
steam to drive the pump to keep the mine from flooding?!!!!

As Mr. Margalo observed, "Some of the simplest feats of applied
physics are among the most profound. Archimedes said—"

"'Give me a long enough lever and a fulcrum and I shall move the
Earth.'"

"Quite right."

"I say, Mr. Margalo, how long a lever might be required to lift
Mrs. Knox and Cruikshank with the touch of a finger?"

"We merely must calculate their combined weight in relation to the
amount of force exerted by your finger . . ." I applied the formula and
found said lever would need to be impracticably long in relation to a
fulcrum impracticably high in order to send the two of them sailing, at
the touch of my finger, over the house. (Safely into a bed of hay.) But it
was possible. "Theoretically."

Following luncheon—it signifies not what we ate, but that we ate
together (sausage and mash)—my tutor sketched a diagram with
mathematical notations, of a magnificent structure even then under
construction in Edinburgh: a cantilever railway bridge. !!!!! It was dizzying to envision arm after steel arm thrown out over the void whilst the
whole remained stable and sound. "Unlike the Tay Bridge." Whereupon
he told me a tale of manmade disaster that haunts me still—the darkness,
the freezing water, the plunge of a passenger locomotive . . . the drowned

hopes of Yuletide. And yet, the ponderous grid of the Tay Bridge had appeared sounder to the untrained eye than the elegant geometry of the Forth Bridge. So much for appearances.

We spent the remainder of the afternoon in fashioning a suspension bridge out of matchsticks with needle and thread—

"And here's me thinking pixies had took it, what're you after with me sewing basket?!"

"Science, Knoxy."

On the fourth day, Mr. Margalo schooled me in the law of gravity.

"Mr. Margalo, I have seen the drawing of Leonardo's flying machine, and Father says we shall, within my lifetime perhaps, take to the skies on manmade wings. Do you believe we shall defy gravity?"

"That which we do every day would have been counted magic less than a century ago—capturing lightning in a bottle, taming it to run along copper wire, sending messages through cables that span the ocean floor."

He illustrated the physics of bodies in motion by way of an experiment: we ascended to the upper gallery of the schoolroom (as I now called the library) whence he dropped a piece of chalk.

"Why does the chalk not fall upward, Miss Bell?"

"Silly question."

"Is it?"

"Because that would be . . . impossible."

"Why?"

"Um."

"We take it for granted. And yet it is the force of gravity. Newton showed that every object attracts every other object, which is why all things—including these books, this house, ourselves—do not simply fly asunder. And float away."

He paused. I gaped. He continued. "When I dropped the chalk, Earth exerted a force upon it, drawing it to Herself. But the chalk, likewise, exerted a force on Earth. These forces, we can measure." His brown eyes were gleaming now and I was rapt. "Which of these two objects, if we drop them simultaneously, do you predict will land first, Miss Bell?"

"Why the heavier, of course. Aristotle is clear on that point and common sense bears him out."

We extended each an arm over the railing; he dropped an egg (boiled) and I, simultaneously, a cabbage. They landed at the same time. I could hardly credit it. We reproduced the results with a turnip. A yelp from below alerted us to Cruikshank and thus us to luncheon.

On the fifth day we constructed a ball-and-stick model of CH_4 (methane) molecules. *Molecules.* They sounded like the sort of critter Byrn would drive off the moor. "They are not alive," said Mr. Margalo. "In fact, no one has yet proven their existence."

"Then how do we know they exist?"

"By mathematical inference. Our very own James Clerk Maxwell points out that 'molecule' is so modern a notion that the word is not to be found in Johnson's *Dictionary*."

"Who is this Mr. Maxwell?"

"The world's pre-eminent physicist, and a Scotsman."

"Let us summon him to Fayne."

"He is deceased."

"Bother."

"I do, however, have in my possession his article as it appeared in *Nature*, if you—"

"Yes please."

"As well as a treatise in which he advanced the late Mr. Faraday's work—"

"Faraday?"

"British scientist concerned with electro-magnetism—"

"Electro . . ."

"The theory that light consists of a propagating wave of electric and magnetic fields. Another time, perhaps."

"Now, if you please."

Reader. From the Ancients right up to Sir Isaac Newton, light was held to be corpuscular—that is, made up of matter—but Newton's rival, Sir Robert Hooke, along with a Dutchman, held it was a wave; a century or so later, Sir Thomas Young showed as much with a slip of card and a mirror one sunny day to the amazement of the grizzled worthies of the Royal Society in London. More recently, Mr. Maxwell backed this up with exquisite equations, thus it seemed the waves had it. Maxwell was, however, intrigued by his electro-magnetic wave being wont to betray signs of matter-like behaviour. The mathematics required to prove a dual state of wave and matter, however, required the positing of a pervasive *something* called "luminiferous ether."

"An acknowledged infelicity," said Mr. Margalo. "And an embarrassment in his final years."

I quoted Pliny: "'The more I observe Nature, the more I am compelled to deem nothing about Her impossible.'"

He smiled.

"Mr. Margalo, in this world of scientific wonders, might we not one day discover that two opposite states might indeed coexist?"

"... Theoretically. For now, however, it remains a matter of dispute."

"Or a wave of dispute."

"... Oh, I see. Ha-ha."

On the sixth day, Mr. Margalo hauled up from his trunk what appeared to be a heftier sort of microscope on a squat wheeled carriage. He plunked it onto the table—bench, rather.

"Where is the eyepiece?"

"There isn't one."

Nor was there a lens. At his instruction I packed the open end of the brass cylinder with a pouch of powder into which he planted a wick. "Remove your boots, Miss Bell. If you please." I obeyed. "Now, rub the soles of your stockinged feet vigorously along the carpet." I did so, whereupon he bid me touch the end of the wick. A spark leapt from my fingertip to the wick at the same time as he clapped his hands over my ears and the air exploded! I cried out in terror and joy, "Again!"

Cruikshank came running, followed by Knox. "Mercy!" cried she, once having registered I was all of a piece and the library intact. "What's all the rumpus?"

"I beg your pardon, Mrs. Knox. We have reproduced here Lord Kelvin's firing of Volta's cannon."

"Lord Kelvin's no business firing upon Fayne, never mind whose cannon, what am I to tell His Lordship?"

"Please tell Lord Henry that I am teaching his daughter as I would his son."

No one intruded when, luncheon out of the way, we reproduced Helmholtz's polyphonic siren.

———

"Well?" said Father at the conclusion of that first week.

"'Well' what, Father?"

"Am I to dismiss your tutor?"

"No!"

His smile as he bent over his desk and affixed a head to our creature jogged my memory (since when had it required "jogging"?!) as to the bargain we had made at the beginning of the week, and I laughed and threw my arms about him. He patted my wrist and righted his spectacles. Summoning temperance, I turned my attention to our "rare bird." Its long, extravagantly plumed body now bore the head of a green parrot and wanted but one feature, the selection of which fell to me. I hovered over a nacreous heap and selected the beak of a herring gull.

"Are you certain?" asked Father.

"Never certainer."

When the glue had dried, we surveyed our creature. I observed solemnly, "It's laughing."

"It is that."

And in a moment, so were we.

"Imagine if our bird were to come to life, Father. I wonder where it would fly?"

"Oh, we oughtn't to wish life upon it."

"Why not?"

"It is a chimera. It would have no fellows. What is more, other birds would peck it to death."

I sobered. And found I could not now look upon its laughing face without a pang of pathos at how the creature was innocent of its own monstrosity.

Father, however, was still smiling, so I composed my features to mirror his own. "Goodnight, Father."

"Goodnight, my own."

I dashed up the stairs without a candle—"Boo!" I shot at the portrait—after all, no more than an arrangement of chemicals—eager to get the night over, for tomorrow was Sunday and I had in mind to share with Mr. Margalo that most solitary of pursuits: trout fishing.

꩜

No. One Bell Gardens
August 2, 1871

Darling Tiff,
"Town" as in Edinburgh, alas, not London. Apparently the Scottish
capital is at the forefront of science, technology and medicine.
Unfortunately, it is at the backend of fashion. Thus the house:
mercifully gas-lit, serviceably carpeted throughout, well-plumbed,
but utterly lacking in charm. It is a tall four-story Georgian cracker box
in the New Town, stuffed with Empire furniture, and I would be quite
content to set about making it over but that—brace yourself—we are
not its sole inhabitants. I refer here not to the servants, but to the
tenant of No. One Bell Gardens: Henry's sister. Who knew he had
one? The Honourable Clarissa Bell. Spinster. All watered silk and jet
jewelry. (And ringlets, oh dear.) She says little and manages to be
everywhere, all while seeming never to leave her armless rocking chair
in the parlor. Henry has asked me to be patient regarding my decorat-
ing plans. I said, "Henry, just so I'm clear. This is your house, yes?"
"Of course it is, dearest. But it is Clarissa's home." He said it with
a sort of wistful finality—a kind of reverent resignation which I am
coming to recognize as the tone he takes whenever he is saying to me
what amounts to "No." It makes me feel a brute, as though I might just
as soon mention flocked wallpaper to Clarissa as drive a dagger through
her heart. And yet, Taffy, Henry's elder sister is far from fragile. She is
merely plain as hard tack. She is suspicious of vegetables. And frowns
on fruit. "Henry, it's an orange!" "Keep your voice down, please, Mae."
Our first tiff. I feel like a hussy just knowing I'm pregnant (yes!)
    When are you coming?

Love,
Mae

PS I am picking up on the local argot. They don't eat dessert here,
instead it's "pudding." Or, more accurately, "pooding." More anon . . .

6

SUNDAY: INTERMINABLE. I was forbidden by Knox—"How dare you forbid me aught, I can have you put to death!"—to "molest the young gentleman's quiet." I stood in the gun room doorway (no guns, fishing tackle only) perspiring in my waders and waxed jacket, with my tweed bunnet pulled low on my brow, basket over my arm, landing net and canny eight-ounce rod of split cane over my shoulder, and watched as my tutor set off on foot up the cart track. I sighed. He veered onto the moor. "He'll drown in a sinkhole!"

"He knows to keep to dry ground, pet."

I was torn. The drizzly day was perfect for angling—even now the speckled beauties would be flashing in our stream. But I chose to forgo fishing in favour of keeping vigil lest my tutor tire of his solitude and crave fellowship.

Two and one half turns of the glass later, I observed, from my bedchamber window, Mr. Margalo tramping back from the moor toward the house. Without breaking stride, he disappeared into the moat. I counted thirty-seven seconds before he emerged on the near bank (had he exceeded forty seconds, I would have undertaken rescue). At the sight of him limping, however, I quitted my post and hastened down the service stairs, through the kitchen and out in time to see him hobbling off with Byrn past the byre and up beyond the well, toward the old man's bothy— ah well, he was in good hands. I watched him duck through the bothy's low door that was overhung with wisps of thatch. Just then a nickering from the direction of the stables alerted me to the arrival of Reginald, and I ran back to the kitchen where I raided a basket of winter apples before Cook could stop me.

Mr. Mungo's great black shire horse was hitched outside the stables beyond nipping-range of Hector and Achilles in their stalls—the estate manager called once a month and Father stayed up "late" to receive his report touching on our few tenants as well as the upkeep of the vicarage and other quotidian matters into which it had never crossed my mind to inquire. Reggie whinnied and nodded at my approach. His lips nuzzled the flat of my hand as he crunched the apple, making it seem the most delicious food imaginable.

"There's a good Reggie," I murmured, stroking his nose, leaning my temple against his cheek.

"Hai, Miss Charlotte, you'll spoil him for work."

Murdoch Mungo sauntered up, smacking his riding crop against his boot.

I produced a second apple for Reggie.

"I will take over management of this estate from my father in due course, Miss Bell." His tone implied the resumption of a grievance. I condescended to bestow upon him a glance.

He lingered.

"You may go, Murdoch. Shoo."

Into his gaze there crept a look both sullen and sly, he lowered his voice and, in a confiding tone, said, "Will you show it me?"

"Show you what, Murdoch?" I sighed. Of all our underlings Murdoch Mungo was the most tedious.

"Your tail," he whispered.

We stared at one another, oddly united in being rooted to the spot by what he had said. Speechless, I watched as he backed away, then turned and fled round the back of the house.

I was suddenly furious. I would run him to ground and thrash him! No. I must not vent my spleen on an inferior—as Socrates said to his slave, "I would beat you if I were not enraged." I would tell Father. And Father would tell Mr. Mungo. And Mr. Mungo would thrash him! My heart pounding, I strode back to the house.

Muffled voices reached me through the study door. I waited. Presently it opened to emit Mr. Mungo, ledger under his arm, customary scowl upon his face. He bowed to me in passing and exited by the principal doors as was meet, for he was no tradesman.

Father smiled up at me, but I had caught the look of weariness in the wake of Mr. Mungo's departure. "How was your catch?" he asked.

"What? Oh, I didn't go." I felt a twinge of self-reproach, for by rights I ought to have been off angling rather than moping and placing myself in the way of insult by the likes of Murdoch Mungo.

"What is it, dear one?" Father removed his pince-nez and regarded me tenderly.

My zeal to heap pain upon Murdoch melted away at the prospect of inflicting any at all upon Father. For how could he mete out punishment without knowing the cause? As grievous an affront as it was to me, Murdoch's query would give graver offence to Father—I knew of a sudden that I could no more allow the report of it to pass my lips than I could bring myself to utter a falsehood. And it occurred to me that Murdoch's absurd question must refer, however obliquely, to my Condition—for he knew full well I was confined to the estate. That he had hit upon an outrageous explanation for a perfectly ordinary precaution was a reflection of his own credulity—or cruelty. All the more reason to spare Father. And to leave lie a subject that I had reason to hope was all but in the past.

"What did Mr. Mungo have to tell you, Father?"

He sighed. "Much the same as he tells me every month."

"And what is that?"

"'The estate turns no profit.'"

This gave me pause, being a concept wholly foreign to me. "Need it do so?"

"Certainly not."

"Then of what concern to him, if none to you?"

"The man is ambitious. And bored. Frightful combination. He . . ." Father chuckled mirthlessly, "He proposes to 'cure the bog.'"

"But there's nothing wrong with the bog. Is there?"

"Not a thing."

"What need has it then to be cured?"

"None at all, but that 'tis a bog and bogs are worthless."

"How does he propose to effect this needless 'cure'?"

"Why with digging and draining and lashings on of lime and putting the lot under plough. He proposes, moreover, to harvest the peat out from under the heather to sell in the city and to undertake a geological survey."

"Whatever for?"

"Coal."

"Ridiculous."

"Not a bit of it, the Romans mined for coal hereabouts."

"Did they. I say, Father, perhaps Mr. Mungo has a point. Think of the feats of agriculture and engineering we might undertake. Why, our farm might rival any in the county. We could acquire a fleet of *machines*," I breathed, savouring the word.

He grew grave. "Charlotte. We must never lay a hand on these moorlands. They are home to many more creatures than we few human residents. Wither the birds, and the . . ." His words caught in his throat. He looked away, and spoke, "The merest midge must have her day . . ."

"Forgive me, Father." I thrust from my mind's eye the picture of rail tracks laid at last along the Water of Feyn; of a mighty goods train thundering through the village, its iron sides painted with *Bell Mine Works and Agricultural Estate*.

He turned to me once more, and with a show of heartiness that only cast into relief his weariness, said, "There is nothing to forgive, my dear."

"Shall I teach you the rudiments of Morse code, Father?"

"Nothing could please me better."

We dotted and dashed our way through the first few pages of Thomas Bewick's *A History of British Birds* until the bell summoned me to luncheon and Father to his long-deferred bed.

I lunched alone.

In the afternoon I consoled myself with graphing trigonometric functions.

Dinner likewise solitary. I came near to refusing pudding. (Baked spiced apple.)

I. MARGALO. FIELD NOTES. JUNE 12, 1887

Two hours' ramble over moorland. Numerous species.

Turned ankle.

Burn applied poultice: sphagnum moss soaked in dark organic matter drawn from bucket: "Burn's balm," so-called by Mrs. Knox. Stench of methane and hydrogen sulphide. (Presume presence carbon dioxide.) Judged polite to accept Burn's ministrations. Observed him mix same matter into animal feed. Question: could this be "muck" he claims to eat? I asked him whence it came. Garbled reply sounded like "Shooharuthy."

Burn accompanies work by humming and muttering. No discernible words. Continues to show remarkable vigour.

———

Cruikshank had filled the great copper tub. I sat hugging my knees, and as Knox poured a pitcher of warm water down my back I pondered Murdoch Mungo's question.

"Knoxy. What was wrong with Charles?"

"Och, your brother was aye a sickly bairn."

"I know, but what killed him?"

"Carried off he was, in his second year, the lamb." She commenced sponging me with a clump of moss.

"Never mind," said I, "I'll ask Father."

"Bowel hive."

After Knox dried me, after she drew the chamber pot from under my bed and exhorted me to "piddle afore you sniggle"; after I had obeyed, and after she left, I rose and crept to my window.

The moor was suffused with the lengthening spring sunset. As far as the eye could see lay swell upon swell of gleaming green and slumbering dun, pools of gorse like spilt sun, the more vivid with the veil of evening. I looked off to my right and waited 'til, from the direction of the bothy, there came a familiar figure in the supple shape of two wands crossed. It was Byrn. Moving swiftly, empty buckets swinging from either end of his yoke, he crossed the forecourt and the margin of scrub, then, blue-bells bobbing in his wake, he leapt over the dry moat and bounded onto the moor. I watched as he loped with ease, growing smaller in the distance until he was lost to the gathering mist.

∼◉

No. One Bell Gardens
October 2, 1871

Dear Taffy,

I am over the moon and fending off fits of vapors! You are coming! You will be here when he (of course it might be a she, which wouldn't be a tragedy) arrives. Dear, I shall soon be big as a house—a country house! Here's the plan: you spend the winter with us in Edinburgh, then Henry and I and the baby go home with you for the summer where we'll show ourselves off all over the length and breadth of the south slope (not neglecting Katie Buxton, Brahmin Bitch of Beacon Hill) with our titled little baby boy—just imagine, Taffy, one day my 'bairn' will be a baron! He's got to get born first of course, and I hope his nobleness doesn't signify a larger than normal head. I wax indelicate. It is part of my charm, as you know, and since I know you burn my letters immediately upon reading, I don't mind telling you, my beloved Taffy, that not only has pregnancy and impending motherhood not muted me, it has AMPLIFIED me!!! I am more MAE than ever!

Demurely,
Lady Marie, 17th B of the DC de F

Merciful Monday.

Mr. Margalo's gait as he entered the schoolroom was near to normal. "Byrn physicked you, did he?"

". . . Why, yes."

"Only, I happened to be at my window when you fell into the moat."

"Ah." He reddened. "It would seem the injury was less acute than it appeared."

"I was not spying, merely watchful lest you come a cropper on the bog."

"Burn appears to navigate it safely."

"'Tis Byrn."

"What?"

"His name. B Y R N. There is no U."

". . . How did you know I had misspelled it?" and he felt for his notebook as though I might have pickpocketed it (I took no umbrage at the reflexive gesture).

"I heard you mispronounce it. Say it again now, properly."

"Byrn."

"There you are."

He looked a titch uncertain but opened his notebook and corrected his spelling. Without glancing up, he asked, "What does this word mean?" And showed me the page. His name appeared at the top preceded by the lone initial, "I." (It had not 'til then crossed my mind to wonder what his given name might be, much less whether he had one, and the name that came to mind now was Ivanhoe.) I sounded it out, "'Shooharuthy' . . . Oh, 'tis Gaelic. Rum spelling."

"No doubt."

"It means 'Eye of Creation.'"

He jotted this down.

"Mr. Margalo, is this notebook by way of being your diary?"

"Not as such, these are field notes."

"Which field? Fayne has several."

"Heh." He cleared his throat. "'Field' as in a subject of inquiry."

"Why make notes? Have you difficulty retaining facts?"

"Notwithstanding my memory is less prodigious than your own, Miss Bell, it is not solely for the purpose of retaining facts that I make notes."

"What other purpose could there be?"

"Facts . . . by themselves, are . . . You see, the act of writing is a means of stimulating the brain whereby facts may be seen to arrange themselves in patterns. Others had to hand the same facts as Mr. Darwin and Mr. Wallace, but those others did not see those facts in relation to one another as the great 'web of affinities' we now call Evolutionary Theory."

"Mr. Margalo, what is bowel hive?"

"'Bowel hive.' A term from a bygone age, denoting an illness whose symptoms are so general and varied as to void the term of diagnostic utility."

"So to say that someone died of bowel hive is to say . . ."

"It is to say, 'We have no idea how they died.'"

We spent the day on a soap bubble. Mr. Margalo said we might spend a lifetime on it, and barely touch the surface of the science of physics.

"Mr. Margalo, if, as modern physics avers, all matter is made up of molecules, themselves aggregates of atoms as *per* Democritus, then there must be a degree, however small, of space between each atom *vis-à-vis* Zeno's Paradox of diminishing yet infinite space between the tortoise and the hare in their eternal race, *ergo* if I calculate the correct angle and speed of entry, I ought to be able to walk through the schoolroom wall and onto the forecourt."

". . . Theoretically," replied Mr. Margalo.

I. MARGALO. FIELD NOTES. JUNE 13, 1887

Observed Byrn from window in wee hours coming from bog with buckets. Mrs. Knox says he follows system of farming according to moon phases. "He has his ways."

"Knox, there be no such thing as 'bowel hive.'"

She did not pause in her brushing of my unruly mane. "Aye, 'tis what carried off your brother."

I slouched and all but groaned. "You may as well say he was 'carried off' by faeries."

"Nay, pet, there's no malice in our Fayne faeries, leastways—"

"Knox." My mouth dried as it struck me—"Was Charles like me?"

"Och aye, you favour him about the brow, and you'd both bonny grey eyes—"

"No. Did he have the Condition?"

"What? Nay. Nay, nay."

I turned to face her, parrying the brush with my wrist. "He did, and it 'carried him off' all right, and it's going to do the same to me—"

"No, pet—"

"That's why I've got a tutor, not because Father thinks me well, but because he knows I'm going to die, you all know it—"

"Not a bit of it!"

"Then—?"

"Your brother was . . ."

"What? What was he?"

She sighed. "He was Brigid's child."

". . . I thought we were all of us Brigid's children."

"Aye, but some of her children . . . she gathers them to herself betimes."

"Why?"

"'Tis kinder."

"Kinder how?"

"Brigid knows—that is, Our Lord knows . . ." She crossed herself here like a papist. "Some children are better off out of this world."

"Why?"

"Because they are different."

The other birds would peck it to death.

"Was he . . ." I whispered, "Misshapen?"

"Nay, pet, you may see for yourself in the portrait, he was bonny."

"Portraits may lie."

"Hush now."

I sat up straight. "Did he have a tail?"

"Of course not, what put that notion—?"

"Then what was wrong with him?"

"Your brother was aye a sickly bairn—"

"Tell me!" I shot to my feet, and the hairbrush clattered to the floor. "Tell me or I'll ask my father!"

Knox closed her eyes and, clasping her hands together on her apron, drew a slow breath. When she opened her eyes, I saw a new sort of sadness in them. "We dinnae always know why a babby dies, pet. There be times a mother or its nurse lays them safe and warm in their crib, only to find them still and cold in the morning. We dinnae know why."

"They just . . . die?"

"Aye. It happens. You may ask your Mr. Margalo."

❧

No. One Bell Gardens
November 14, 1871

Darling Taffy (or shall I say "Miss Weaver," as opportunities to address you as such are now numbered!),

Of course I forgive you. Whether or not Carter Blanchard deserves my forgiveness is another matter, but considering the two of you are made for one another, I may see fit to extend my pardon to him as well. Congratulations! You are going to be almost as happy as I am! I say "almost" because, knowing you to be of a slightly less robust constitution, I would not wish a degree of frame-stressing joy upon you. In fact, I feel an attack of happiness coming on . . . You are getting married, sweetheart! And—be still my heart—our children (for I urge you not to dilly-dally on your way to Wonderful) will be almost of an age and . . . let me see, if you have a girl, and I have a boy—whee!

Know this, in all solemnity, dear sweet Taffeta, if I could safely travel in my condition, I would defy my husband (well, that's hardly a labor of Hercules, but still) and board the next packet home to witness your

Christmas (so romantic!) nuptials and attend you as Matron of Honor. Katie Buxton will serve admirably in that capacity, and as Carter's sister's confidante, you could not hope for a better ally (save, perhaps, a British Noblewoman . . .)

Oh Chère Taffée, I am already looking forward to summer when we shall punt together on the Charles River, I with my bundle of boy (if I have my way!), and you, perhaps, carrying your own special cargo—make sure it's a girl!

All my love and grandest wishes for you and Carter,
Mae, the Lady Blah-blah

7

THE NIGHTS GREW shorter and the evenings brighter, and on the estate, all proceeded as usual. Of a Sunday I helped Byrn to wash the sheep before he sheared them where they lay on the floor of the shed, lulled nearly to sleep by the low hum of his words. Of another Sunday I sat with Knox and Cook and Cruikshank as we combed and carded the wool, some of which Knox would spin and weave into a new tunic for me.

Meanwhile in the schoolroom, there unspooled days of discovery and delight more scintillating than a magic lantern show.

"Mr. Margalo, how distant is the North Star?"

"Mr. Margalo, how do you know the continents are moving?"

"Mr. Margalo, does the butterfly remember being the caterpillar? Is it one creature or two?"

"Mr. Margalo, does $\cos(\arcsin [1/7])$ equal $4\sqrt{3}/7$?"

On an ordinary Tuesday night, with my feet planted on the forecourt, I trained heavenward a telescope of polished brass and came face to face with our pockmarked Moon. With one fine adjustment I all but forgot myself in the clustered stars of the Milky Way. (Except I did not forget myself because Knoxy would not leave off fussing with a muffler about my neck.)

"Miss Bell," said Mr. Margalo at my side, "you now behold what William Herschel himself saw when he discovered the nebulae to consist of stars, and found the planet Uranus along with its moons." I traced the constellation of Gemini and listened to Mr. Margalo's account of the great quantities of light we cannot see but can measure thanks to that great man.

I. MARGALO. FIELD NOTES. JUNE 27, 1887
Byrn speaks mix of localized Gaelic and Doric Scots sprinkled with Saxon precursors. Conversing with him—notwithstanding he is man of few words—tinged with uncanny sense of listening to a language both familiar and strange.

I seemed to see everything differently. In the cart track, pricked with light on nights with a moon, I now saw the embedded phosphorescence of extinction—our forebears caught in the act of growing spines and sprouting fins. Everything, from a grain of sand to the unseen vasts of the cosmos, was part of an inextricable web of which I was an unlikely and inevitable thread.

I learned of carbon, "the gregarious element" and the smallest one to form stable bonds with a host of others. Mr. Margalo spoke of the search for the smallest unit of matter, what the alchemists called *prima materia*, the stuff of which all matter, both living and non-living, is made. That which enables the scientific sorcery of transformation. Something smaller than an atom. Something that is in everything.

"Mr. Margalo, if this so-called *prima materia* is the basis of everything, then everything is alive."

"Not in . . . Not in any . . ."

"Theoretically?"

". . .Theoretically."

"Let us fire the cannon again."

"Very well."

I. MARGALO. FIELD NOTES. JULY 15, 1887
Observed Cruikshank carrying dead weasel from henhouse. Mrs. Knox credits "Byrn's bane" ("bayn"?): dark organic matter drawn from buckets and daubed about the roosts.

I: "How do the hens avoid being similarly poisoned?"

She: "He has his ways."

I: "What ways might they be?"
She: "Old Ways."

On a Thursday afternoon the rain sheeted down the schoolroom windows while I dissected a worm. They are hermaphroditic. They are
stronger than any known creature in proportion to their size. They
regenerate when severed. "God might just as well have stopped when He
created Worm," said I.

"Or Salamander," said he.

I. MARGALO. FIELD NOTES. JULY 29, 1887
Took samples of "Byrn's balm" and "Byrn's bane." Examined both
under microscope. Identical.

I was contentedly factoring quadratics. "Mr. Margalo, I should like to
be a scientist."

He looked up from *Principles of Geology* but did not immediately
answer.

I faltered. "Are there lady scientists?"

"There are . . . a few." I must have appeared disheartened, for he went
on, "But the very term, 'scientist,' was coined for a woman. Scotland's
own Mary Somerville—" And before I could ask, he added, "Born 1780,
deceased 1872. Until she came along, the term was 'Man of Science.' In
light of her contributions, a new term was needed." He jotted something
in his book.

"Are you making a field note, Mr. Margalo?"

"I have made a note to send for her chief published works."

"What of the others? You said there were a few."

"Mary Anning, the great fossil hunter, discovered an intact Ichthy-
osaur."

"Alive? I refer to Miss Anning."

"Regrettably, no."

"Who else?"

"Charles Babbage's Analytical Engine owes a debt of mathematical
calculation to Ada, Countess of Lovelace."

"Dead?"

"Aye."

"Who else?"

"William Herschel owes his fame in large part to the calculations of his sister, Caroline, to say nothing of her having discovered a comet."

"By Jove."

"She and Mary Somerville were the first women to be named honorary Members of the Royal Astronomical Society. Likewise deceased."

"How tiresome."

"You shall yourself, perhaps, increase the ranks of those living."

"I shall have the good grace not to die."

He laughed.

"Let's set off the siren again."

"Aye, let's."

"Father, did you know that Scotland was once in the tropics, and England was fused with France?"

"I confess I did not know that. But it explains a good deal."

"What would you say if I told you that this dining table is hurtling through space at the rate of sixty-seven thousand miles per hour?"

"I would say it is a wonder we are able to take any nourishment at all."

"That is because gravity bolts us to the Earth. The Earth, however, is spinning on its axis, therefore, if I stood upon the table and jumped, I would not land in the exact same place."

"East of the salt cellar as it were."

"Unless of course, we were at one of the poles in which case I might jump as high as I liked and land in the very same spot."

"As indeed you'd be well advised to jump up and down if only to keep warm."

"And did you know the light we see from the stars was produced millions of years ago, which means time is dependant upon distance and therefore not absolute, therefore what is it?"

"Half eight or thereabouts."

Mr. Margalo chuckled. Father smiled.

I said, "The brightest star is no more than a dead sun."

He looked up from his soup. "And you, my dear, are the light of my life."

Cruikshank apportioned a cottage pie and a heap of root vegetables with extra parsnip for Father (parsnip bears an olfactory resemblance to pork, I wondered he could stomach it).

"Father, did you know that fungus is neither plant nor animal, but both? Did you know that lichen is in fact two species, one plant, one animal? Perhaps we are witnessing evolution in action as two members of different kingdoms combine to become an entirely new species—"

"That they may not, Miss Bell," interrupted Mr. Margalo.

"Theoretically."

"Not even theoretically."

I rallied. "Father, did you know there is a germ in the roots of trees that sends messages to neighbouring tree roots?"

"Talking trees, you begin to sound like Byrn."

"Chemical messages, of course, Your Lordship," said Mr. Margalo.

"Well, well, Mr. Margalo," said Father at length, "you have strayed a good distance from Plautus and Plato. The smells and sounds issuing from the schoolroom rival those of the Lawnmarket on a Saturday—to say nothing of the Battle of Waterloo."

"It is true, Miss Bell has made short work of such indoor instruction as I came equipped to provide."

"I doubt the nerves of my household can withstand much more indoor instruction."

"With Your Lordship's permission, I thought to conduct tomorrow's lessons out of doors."

I clapped my hands excitedly—then sat on them.

Father smiled indulgently. "By all means. Mind you don't stray onto boggy ground in chasing butterflies."

"Father, I'm not a child!"

He laughed. "It was to Mr. Margalo I spoke, my dear, whereas you are charged with the safe conduct of your tutor. See you bring him back alive and well to teach another day."

"You have my word."

Mr. Margalo and I exchanged a smile across the table, and Father refilled Mr. Margalo's glass of claret, saying, "I caught sight of a sparrow hawk over the east moor this morning, from my study window."

"Did you, Your Lordship? What a fortunate sighting."

"That was a kestrel, Father, we saw it too, didn't we, Mr. M?"

Father said quietly, "If you saw it, why then you'd have known it a sparrow hawk," and applied himself to quartering a beet, whilst Mr. Margalo undertook the close perusal of his fish fork.

"Come with us, Father."

He looked up in mild surprise.

"We can set out at dawn and return before the sun is high, do come, it won't be half as edifying without you." And to my tutor, "If you'll forgive my saying so, Mr. Margalo."

"I couldn't agree more, Miss Bell, indeed I would be grateful for Your Lordship's guidance as to the many species of flora and fauna with which I am unfamiliar."

Father knit his brows, firmed his chin and appeared to consider. "I would of course spare no effort to oblige you, Mr. Margalo, but that I am at a critical point in penning a long-promised treatise for the *Journal of the Edinburgh Ornithological Society*." Turning the full warmth of his gaze upon me, he added, "You are in good hands with my daughter."

I smiled back, inwardly relieved that Father had declined my invitation— and experienced a prick of conscience. I resolved to keep a lookout tomorrow for some specimen or other that I might carry home to him.

~◦

February, 1872

Dear Taffy,

It was a girl. Dead.

Your,

M

8

"KNOX, WE ARE not seeking the Northwest Passage, merely rambling over the moor." Her basket of provisions weighed more than my specimen case, field glasses and water flask together. She sought now to press upon us a picnic rug—"Don't be absurd, Knoxy. And—what're you doing, stop that!" For she had made to cram a sausage into my specimen case.

"As why not, 'tis empty."

"Aye, for specimens!"

"Stay off the bog."

"Knoxy, there is no one bog, rather a shifting array of—"

"Stay off them all."

"I promise to take the utmost care of my pupil, Mrs. Knox."

"Mind you do, there be specialmans enough on dry ground."

Mr. Margalo gallantly took up the lunch basket and, with a spade slung across his back, a rope coiled over one shoulder and his own field glasses and specimen case over the other, we set out.

The day was sunny and clear.

Off we tramped, wending our way through the blooming heather. All about us the air was etched with birdsong and suffused with the sweet and musky smells of summer.

After three quarters of an hour, the standing stone on the North Fell had grown no larger and, stepping over a stripe of water in a sedgy ditch, we paused while Mr. Margalo trained his field glasses on it.

I said, "A moor mile is equal to three across ordinary ground, therefore time moves more slowly on the moor."

"At a *Cochlea sarmatia*'s pace, as it were."

"Theoretically."

We chuckled.

"What is that sound?" he asked, as a high warble reached us.

"That'll be Byrn."

Sure enough, all about us the bracken commenced to stir, sending up a cloud of butterflies along with a spray of hares that bounced away in all directions. Mr. Margalo froze. "What is happening?"

"Moles."

Where there is one there are a hundred, and now the critters set the heath to rolling like a wave as they fled for the silence of the North Fell.

"Has someone set off a phosphorus bomb?"

"'Tis Byrn. He drives them off with it," I said.

"With what?"

"Why, his song."

The song was louder now and Byrn himself appeared over the next rise, advancing steadily behind the wave. Mr. Margalo appeared transfixed, not only by the sight of the fleeing rodents but the sound of the old man: high and winding.

Mr. Margalo murmured, "It must have to do with frequency and . . . ?"

"Pitch?" I supplied.

"Quite."

"Good evening, Byrn," I called when the heather stilled and he ceased his singing. He nodded in reply.

"Miss Bell," said Mr. Margalo, "it is yet morning."

"Byrn follows the old day. From moonrise to sunrise."

Just then the old man gave a series of short sharp whistles and our flock appeared over the rise and streamed past like spring runoff, with Nolan zig-zagging at their heels. Mr. Margalo said, "That sound, at least, I recognize."

Byrn loped off behind them and was soon gone from sight.

"He's never lost a sheep. Nor a lamb."

I led the way along an old shieling path until we came to a grove of alders—a charm of goldfinches arose chattering from the upper branches to harmonize with the notes of a nearby stream. "Follow me," I said, trembling with excitement. The sound of water grew louder as we passed between grey trunks, their fissured bark furred green, and came to the edge of a brawling brook. Its peat-browned waters rushed over stones before plunging into a deep wooded dingle. We picked our way down, skidding at times, alongside the waterfall. "I say!" cried Mr. Margalo upon spotting one, then three, then five and more speckled beauties. I turned to him with due solemnity. "Mr. Margalo, I hereby grant you lifetime licence to fish my trout stream."

"I thank you, Miss Bell." He bowed from the neck. "I am honoured, and look forward to learning from you the appertaining craft."

"It is an art, Mr. Margalo."

We hopped from stone to slippery stone and scaled the opposite slope with the aid of rocks wedged into the turf by some canny angler of old. Up and onto the moor once more, we pressed on over the next rise, and the next, and the next 'til we had lost sight of house and stone altogether and found ourselves in a wind-whipped sea of scrub and stunted heather. The old temptation to run beyond just one more rise *ad infinitum* took hold of me, but Mr. Margalo crouched, took his spade and sank it into the ground. He uprooted a square of turf, trailing roots like a Medusa head. He tossed it aside and excavated a chunk of peat—inexpertly, I might add, for he had neither Byrn's trusty tairsgeir nor Byrn's way of cutting and easing out the sods.

"We've plenty of peats at home, Mr. Margalo, no need to carry that back."

He ran his long fingers from the lighter fibrous stuff at the top to the dense black at the bottom, where he rubbed a clump between thumb and forefinger. "Do you know what this is, Miss Bell?"

"Aye, 'tis the dark stuff," I said.

"It is the packed energy of the sun."

The moor had been my playground. It now became my classroom. Mr. Margalo explained how moss decays and the peat grows upwards by slow degrees, all of which begins with "the process of photosynthesis."

"Explain."

"Plants and plant-like organisms absorb carbon dioxide from the atmosphere and convert it, using the power of sunlight, to energy. When the plant drops its leaves or dies, that CO_2 is returned to the atmosphere. Not so in a bog. In anaerobic—that is, without oxygen—conditions, plants die without rotting. Their carbon is stored."

Given enough time, the peat would turn to coal, the coal to diamond, and diamond into layers of graphite.

"And when we burn peats, we burn the buried sunshine," said I.

"We burn in an instant what it has taken Nature millions of years to make."

"Good job there's loads of it."

He did not reply but tucked the turf carefully back into the ground, pressing it with his spade. Presently, he said, "Already the peppered moth has adapted such that the markings on its wings mimic the face of a soot-covered sphinx, thanks to the smoke-stacks of the Industrial Revolution."

"How clever of it."

"We must take care not to attribute conscious agency to evolution."

With the next rise we came upon a meadow strewn with bog cotton like snowballs. We ploughed through drifts and the land fell away gently, growing spongier underfoot and rosier to the eye until it seemed we walked on a carpet the colour of dawn, for all about us was moss. "Sphagnum moss," said Mr. Margalo as he bent and turned his magnifying glass on the tiny massed flowers—"bladders"—each in its star-shaped leaf, each holding "in excess of eight times its weight in water."

"Do you mean to say . . ." A quick calculation yielded a dizzying tonnage on Fayne alone. "Why 'tis a deluge held in check."

"It is a vast reservoir."

"Mr. Mungo has great plans for the moor. He proposes to cure the bog and mine for coal and plant crops."

". . . And what is your father's view?"

"Father says there is plenty of food and fuel depending upon whom, or what, one asks."

He nodded. "I suppose we might, in a manner of speaking, inquire of that damselfly."

As I watched, the emerald creature caught a midge on the wing and flew off with its prey. It did not "know" how to build its own large compound eyes any more than I "knew" how to staunch a nick in my skin by forming a scab, but build it did, and staunch did I—to say nothing of photosynthesis. What, therefore, was intelligence?

"That question strays into the philosophical, Miss Bell. Thanks to the fossil record, however, we do know that damselflies are today smaller than they were millennia ago."

"For the which we might be thankful."

"Undoubtedly."

We walked on, 'til a dip in the land brought us to a dell where a tiny lochan sparkled, bedecked with lilies and overlooked by sturdy bog willows, in whose budding branches spiderwebs caught the glitter of high noon. The pond was ringed with the alluring green of liquid land and we knew not to stray beyond a frizzy hem of white five-petalled flowers— "Frilly knickers," said I. "That's what Knoxy calls 'em." Mr. Margalo cleared his throat and corrected me, "*Menyanthes trifoliata*—bogbean."

He paused and stooped to a cluster of small pink-and-green petals. I watched as they curled round his fingertip. "Like to eat me whole, eh?" he chuckled and, withdrawing his finger, rubbed it against his thumb. I then touched the "petals," triggering a sticky embrace as inexorable as the jaws of a reptile. Mr. Margalo explained that this tiny *Drosera*, commonly "sundew," was every bit as carnivorous as its giant cousins in equatorial Africa and the Amazonian jungle. How, I wished to know, did that square with their designation as "flora"? Surely only "fauna" were capable of such a feat.

"Photosynthesis is eating by any other name," replied my tutor.

"Aye," I said, "but 'eating' sunshine and 'drinking' rain are of a different order to consuming a living being." And as I watched, a gnat landed and fluttered its wings in a doomed attempt to free itself as the tentacles closed over it.

"Miss Bell, you have yourself seen the promiscuous multitudes that dwell in a drop of rainwater. Nature's so-called lines are often in fact a blur. That is evolution in action. Nature does not care if something fits a manmade category. She does not care if what arises is beautiful or useful to man. She is a Vesuvius, spewing forth variations, many of which we are pleased to call 'mistakes.' Yet who knows but that one of those mistakes might someday prove the key to our survival.

We picked our way cautiously to a fall of stone where we judged it safe to sit, and broke out the lunch Knox had packed for us. Glad now of her over-provisioning, we feasted on sausage rolls, fowl, scones with sloe-berry preserve and Eccles cakes. Mr. Margalo unstoppered the water flask but I reached down, tore free a clump of moss and, tilting my head back, squeezed a stream of water into my mouth. As it slipped down my throat, I was struck suddenly humble that a substance so pure would consent to pass through me on its way to the sea and back to the air to fall as rain in Heraclitus's river that is never and always the same . . . Mr. M. was regarding me closely. I reassured him, "It is perfectly clean, Mr. Margalo."

"It is not only clean, Miss Bell. It is oligotrophic."

"Explain."

"The absence of decay means a low nutrient level, therefore water of exceptional purity." He likewise plucked a handful of moss and drank.

"We have just committed cannibalism," said I.

He looked doubtful.

"Are we not largely water, Mr. Margalo?"

He smiled. "Nature is a great consumer and recreator of Herself. You, Miss Bell, are grass in another form. I am indebted to the sundew as much as the sun. We are all of us carbon and water."

"Then how is it you and I may converse but a sundew may not?"

"They communicate as surely as do birds with their calls and bees through their dance. Consciousness, however, is another matter. Only Man possesses that."

In that instant I became aware of a muffled burbling.

"What is it?" he asked.

"Water."

"Where? I don't hear anything." He looked about.

"Underground." It grew so loud I feared the waters might rise up about us.

Mr. Margalo stood up. "Make haste, Miss Bell."

But I laid down and pressed my ear to the ground. A sound so familiar, yet out of reach—words shimmering just below the surface of comprehension. The water was singing. I ached suddenly to follow the song but I gripped the earth with my fingers for I knew I must resist or come to grief. Reader, I was in that moment possessed of two knowings: one was seated in an English-speaking region of my brain, the other submerged in an older pool of forgotten language . . .

The sound receded as swiftly as it had arisen. I loosed my grip and looked up as though waking from a dream, to see Mr. Margalo kneeling over me.

"It's gone," said I. "A swallet."

He sat back down. "Not unusual in these parts."

"Quite common in fact," I said airily.

"You have a keen ear, Miss Bell."

"Byrn taught me to listen."

"I hope he taught you to seek higher ground."

"He rescued me once. I strayed onto the bog, oh long ago, when I was a bairn. He brought me home, tucked under his arm." I grinned at the memory of watching the earth rise and fall beneath my eyes as we bounded along. "He taught me not to follow the Wee Folk."

"Who?"

I felt myself blush and, chuckling by way of disclaimer, gave a fair imitation of the toothless old man, "'Lest they pull you to your deeth.'"

"Why would they do that?"

"They're Brigid's guardians."

"Who is Brigid?"

"She's the Mother."

"Whose mother?"

"Why, everyone's."

Oddly light-headed of a sudden, I lay back once more on the ground.

"I would suggest you remain upright, Miss Bell."

I obeyed. I understood. Like will-o'-the-wisp, bog fumes were supposed not to be abroad in the day when sunshine burns them off, but we were in a dell and I had pressed my face to the very ground. I drew a breath and shook the fog from my brain. "I have, before now, come across hares lying limp, felled by fumes."

"Ammonia," he said.

"One nitrogen, three hydrogen."

"Very good, Miss Bell."

We hiked northwest 'til the standing stone pierced the break of slope, and made straight for it. Leaning into the wind atop the fell, I showed my tutor the handholds in the stone but instead of climbing, he looked down. "What's this?" In its lee there lay the remains of a feast of carrots, runner beans and potatoes.

"Lughnasadh," said I.

"An offering for Brigid?"

"For the rascally guardians more like."

I turned and ran pell-mell back down the slope, suddenly wild with happiness. I waited at the bottom for Mr. Margalo who proceeded more prudently, and together we walked in wordless contentment back to the house.

Only when I had pulled off my Wellies on the steps did it strike me. "Mr. Margalo, we collected not a single specimen."

He tapped a finger to his forehead in reply. Indeed, my specimen case was empty but my mind was full.

That evening, the triangle of light shone from Father's study door and it was all I could do to obey the beacon.

"Well, my Lady Scientia, you are most welcome." He had already made room for me by his side and drawn up my stool. He handed me the dropper and took up his tweezers.

"Father, I do not trust myself not to fall asleep in the glue pot so weary am I."

"Is your tutor overworking you?"

"On the contrary, I wish for nothing more than an extra hour in the day."

"Despite the non-existence of time."

The twinkle in his eye forestalled a renewed disquisition on my part as to the relative nature of time and distance. I entered his embrace along with the spirit of his jest. I felt him pat my head. He said, "Sleep well, my own."

I. MARGALO. FIELD NOTES. AUGUST 1, 1887

Queried Byrn *re* both Lughnasadh offering and "mole song." His reply took on chanting quality as *per* oral tradition/pagan culture. Herewith his words, set down as best I can, with liberties of syntax/sense:

It is of a colour with the ground for 'tis ground but in softer form, 'tis what makes the pool easy to miss and easy to find by accident. Do not wander there. Do you know the ways of Fenn? Do you know the plants and can you judge by feel the mud whether silk or soup 'twixt finger and thumb, whether 'twill heal or harm or do aught but muck your boots? Do you know by smell what plants will yield a ewe or sheep, what keep the unborn in the womb and what will loose it? To these add riddles like in length to Domesday Book, and if you answer but a moiety, go ahead and roam the face of Fenn. But have a care. Fenn keeps not still but shifts perpetual. Fenn breathes. Fenn sleeps, betimes opes an eye, Fenn rolls over, belches, eats. Scats. Fenn dies and gives birth. Fenn lives.

Knox palpated both sides of my neck to check for glandular swelling.

"You'll bring on the swelling if you don't leave off palpating," I grumbled.

At length, satisfied that my long day on the moor with Mr. Margalo was unlikely to prove fatal, she watched while I drained a mug of elderberry tea with honey, then suffered me to lie back amid my pillows. "Now go to sleep, lamby." I closed my eyes until I heard her leave, then I sat up, lit my lamp and drew from beneath my covers Mary Somerville's *On the Connexion of the Physical Sciences.* "'The progress of modern science, especially within the last five years, has been remarkable for a tendency to simplify the laws of nature, and to unite detached branches . . .'"

The portrait on the stairs.

I am facing it.

I am on a level with my brother, as though hovering in midair.

I am looking at him.

But he is staring past me.

I turn, and see the moor.

I do not think it strange that the wall of the house has disappeared.

I see the moor . . .

The cry woke me. I sat up, my heart thumping. I waited, but Knox did not appear. I rose and went to the window. I opened it wide. The night was starry and sultry too, but as I looked out upon the still and silent moor, I commenced to shiver. Was this fever? Had I in truth not outgrown my Condition, and would it now rear its fanged head and devour me? I placed my cold hands against my burning cheeks and felt . . . moisture. On my tongue, salt. Inescapable was the conclusion that I had shed tears in my sleep. I returned to bed.

Artemidorus of Ephesus believed dreams were products of the mind rather than messages from the gods. But why either my mind or the gods sought to produce the cry of a child on the moor at night, I could not fathom. I lay wide awake. (Hereupon, I resorted to a practice of private gratification in the interests of quelling a part of my anatomy which had likewise been roused from sleep. This do I report in a spirit of that transparency without which scientific inquiry is in vain.) I slept 'til morning.

❧

May 23, 1872

Dear Taffy,
The doctor, Mr. Moore said the first two were practice runs. Third time the charm? I hope. Especially as things appear to be heading in the right direction, after all, the second one got a whole lot further than the first. Yes dear, I am once more "en ceinte." Don't tell anyone yet! . . . .

9

IT WAS RAINING. We were in the schoolroom, a week or so following our expedition. Mr. Margalo stood facing the fireplace, hands clasped behind his back.

"A word on your progress, Miss Bell."

"Yes, Mr. Margalo?"

"Excellent."

"Thank you."

He turned and regarded me gravely. "You have, in the space of two months, exceeded the course of a year's tutelage for which I was engaged."

"You're not leaving."

"Miss Bell, do you know what a university is?"

"Certainly. Father attended one in his youth, in Oxford it was. He read classics for a year then came down before his liver could give out."

"Ha-ha!"

"Why is that humorous?"

He sobered. "A university is not only a rite of passage for gentlemen. It is far greater in scope, learning and influence."

"Did you attend a university, Mr. Margalo?"

"The University of Edinburgh is an institution of higher learning esteemed throughout the world; it is a beacon of scientific research; engine of the Scottish Renaissance; pride of the Athens of the North. It is also my alma mater. With your father's permission, and your willingness to redouble your efforts—I shall prepare you to sit the entrance examination."

A thrill erupted in my stomach and spread like electricity through my frame. I wanted to leap and laugh because something invisible had been glimpsed, something as impossible as a unicorn. It was my self! In that moment I stood wide awake to a world of pulsating possibility that rivalled the burgeoning, secret life of the moor.

"Mr. Margalo, I give you my word. I shall best the examination. I shall gain admittance."

"I fear 'tis not solely up to you, Miss Bell."

"Father is sure to agree, my Condition permitting."

"Your Condition. I had forgotten."

"What other impediment could there be?"

"'Tis a question of your—That is, while females have been admitted of late, they are but few. Nor has a degree been conferred on any. However deserving."

"Still, it is possible. Theoretically."

He smiled. "Theoretically."

We spent the remainder of the afternoon in fermenting a test tube of beer according to an ancient Sumerian formula.

I donned my green tunic embroidered with a roe deer grazing, for I felt celebratory—even though I knew there could be no question of broaching the subject of my university prospects over dinner. I expected Mr. Margalo would repair alone with Father to his study for that purpose, and I hoped it might be this very night. Eager as I was for it to take place, I was grateful to be barred from an interview which must perforce touch upon the delicate subject of my Condition, for though obsolete in all but name, there hung about the subject an uncomfortable air of . . . intimacy. Doubt nibbled the corner of my mind. I shooed it away. Father would not refuse Mr. Margalo's offer. Hath not a woman brain?

I quitted my chamber and at the head of the stairs squared my shoulders and composed my features. Then, inwardly vibrating as though my veins were made of copper wire, I descended.

"Father, did you know the skeletons of the notorious murderers Burke and Hare are on display in the Anatomy Hall at the University of Edinburgh where the medical students may study them? Suspended in glass cases and flayed of their skin—*post mortem* of course."

"That is reassuring."

Cruikshank plonked a basin of butter onto the table. Father rubbed his hands together and exhorted Mr. Margalo to join him in smearing a pat of it onto a thick slice of bread. "You'll ne'er get butter so rich as this, Mr. Margalo, even from the cattle of the sun."

Mr. Margalo nodded, chewing. "Delicious. From Gossamer, is it?" I could see he enjoyed being able to refer to our cow by name and I took pleasure in his familiarity with things Fayne—even if he was, in this instance, mistaken.

"No," said Father. "Though quite possibly from one of her ancestors."

"Her . . . ?"

"'Tis bog butter," said I, between mouthfuls.

Mr. Margalo lowered his slice of bread. A smile played about Father's lips—he was enjoying himself, not unkindly, at my tutor's expense.

I explained. "Byrn hauls it out from the bog."

Father pointed with his butter knife at an inscription on one side of the wooden basin:

MCDLXXVIII

Mr. Margalo regarded the butter as though fearful it might rise and slither onto the table.

Father explained, "'Twas common practice to bury butter in chests against future scarcity."

"Or as a gift to the Mother. 'Tis perfectly hygienic, owing as you know to the oligotrophic environment."

He smiled wanly.

I added, "Sometimes we'll get a chest with an Anglo-Saxon inscription and one can surmise thereby a butter of some antiquity."

"Six hundred and twenty-five AD," pronounced Father, "was a particularly good year," and he broke into a laugh. "Claret, I think, Cruikshank."

It was doubtless owing to the unprecedented brew of merriment and erudition which followed that I forgot myself in saying, "Father, are you acquainted with the works of a lady named Mary Somerville?"

"Hmm. Don't know that I've had the pleasure."

"A Scotswoman and a scientist."

"Well, well. Let us summon her to dine."

"She is dead."

"Ah well. Another time, perhaps."

"Then there is Miss Caroline Herschel—Father, she had a comet named for her!"

"Did she? Good show."

"She was the first woman to be paid a salary for scientific work."

"Pity. That does rather tarnish her achievement."

Then, for the second time that day, the world changed when Mr. Margalo opened his lips and released words as irretrievable as the arrows of Apollo. "The great Mrs. Somerville was debarred from attending university because of her sex."

My tongue cleaved to the roof of my mouth. I dared not look at Father. Mr. Margalo continued, "In our day there is no formal impediment to a female being admitted to the University of Edinburgh. It is, however, sufficiently uncommon as to merit uncommon effort. To which end, I propose, with Your Lordship's permission—"

Cruikshank banged through the swing door bearing a roast of lamb, and a head of boiled cabbage for Father.

She withdrew and Mr. Margalo resumed. "With Your Lordship's permission, and Miss Bell's health permitting—" There it was: *health*. A fig leaf of a word, concealing another: *Condition*. Immobilized, my palms grown clammy, I watched Father's jaw working rather more vigorously than one might suppose needful to the mastication of cooked cabbage. Mr. Margalo continued, "I propose to prepare your daughter to sit the entrance examination for the University of Edinburgh."

My heart pounded in my ears. Father set down his fork, eyes on his plate. Mr. Margalo concluded, "The examination might be conducted here at Fayne, with myself as invigilator."

Silence.

Presently, Father looked up and, seeming to address the far end of the table where the empty chair sat in shadow, spoke. "Though there be no longer formal impediments to the admission of females, Mr. Margalo, there remain significant *in*formal impediments, witness the late events in the medical school."

"Ah. Your Lordship refers to the objections raised by male students to the presence of females in the Anatomy—"

"'Objections'?" Father's tone was the more withering for being mild. His brow darkened as he turned to Mr. Margalo. "There was a riot, sir. The students hurled a live sheep, not to mention dung, at the petticoated would-be scholars. Nothing could induce me to expose my daughter to such barbarity. I wonder, sir, that you lift her hopes."

I had 'til then never witnessed Father's wrath. I shrank in my chair— even as my mind queried the spectre of a live sheep flying through the air. Mr. Margalo had gone as pale as a statue in the marbles room. He murmured an apology.

Father drew a long breath. He let it out. He placed his hands flat on either side his plate and I witnessed a battle raging, however subtly, in his countenance. Father, I realized to my horror, was on the point of tears, here at the dining table—in company with an inferior. He turned to me once more, and smiled so sadly I feared my heart would seize. And in an infinitely gentle tone, he asked me, "And what, my dear, is your wish?"

"Father, I wish to become a physician."

If he was surprised, he did not show it. I had, however, surprised myself, and as I spoke now of my vocation, it was with the sense that I had known of it long before I knew that I knew. "And if ever you should fall ill, I shall cure you."

Tears now frankly coursed down my own cheeks and I brushed them away, unashamed for they felt in no way personal. Father took another deep breath, and addressed Mr. Margalo. "Insofar as my daughter continues in good health, I accept your kind offer, Mr. Margalo, and give you leave to adapt your pedagogy in accordance with the criteria of the entrance examination of the University of Edinburgh."

Reader, I leave it to you to imagine my inward rejoicing; my outward restraint; as my heart came near to bursting with love for him who had so selflessly set my happiness above his fears.

"Whisky, I think, Cruikshank."

We toasted. I fought choking as the liquid fire scorched my oesophagus. Father and Mr. Margalo talked of Edinburgh, that shining City on a Hill and my soon-to-be abode. It came home to me that Father had led a full life before ever I was born, one caught up in the great industrial and intellectual roar of the metropolis. I felt vicariously his pleasure in hearing that a certain pub still stood in Fleshmarket Close; his regret at the Hope Park factory building fire; his determination to skate once more on Duddingston Loch come winter. And in joyously anticipating my own imminent release into the city, I understood for the first time a little of what Father had sacrificed in keeping so long away from it for my sake. Indeed, he had not set foot in Edinburgh for upwards of twelve years.

Mr. Margalo quizzed Father as to Fayne and its history, remarking, "Nowhere can I find it on any map."

"Nor shall you so long as it exists," said Father.

". . . Why is that?"

"For that it falls neither in Scotland nor in England, therefore must not be depicted as being in either one."

"Ah, yes, being in the Borders and therefore among the 'debatable lands'—"

Father tut-tutted, "Our borders are not and never have been a matter of debate." And refilled both their glasses.

"They are a matter of Dispute," I explained.

"But if Fayne is in neither Scotland nor England, then . . . ?"

"It is in both."

"I'm not certain I understand. Fayne is in neither England nor Scotland, but in both simultaneously."

"You understand perfectly," said Father, and sat back in his chair expansively. Mr. Margalo followed suit. Father called for his pipe and the gentlemen smoked, right there at the table, custom be dashed. I kept quiet as a mouse, for though I knew myself to be the inciting cause of this bacchanal, I was young enough to be sent to bed and old enough to know it. Thus did I refrain from filling a pipe of my own.

In the end it was not my father but my own fatigue that prompted me to retire from the table and the garrulous cloud of smoke. I mounted the stairs with a high heart and, glancing up at the portrait, acknowledged for the first time a kinship with the laughing cherub in his mother's arms.

10

WITHIN TWO WEEKS another trunk arrived from Edinburgh, similar to the first, but crammed full with books. Books on astronomy, physics, law, geology, cosmology, mathematics and more. Mr. Margalo was determined I should not only meet the standard, but exceed it.

My earlier endeavours now seemed mere high-jinks by comparison as I hammered away at higher studies, indifferent to the golden light of August bathing the schoolroom windows, unmoved by the rain that glimmed them with promise of flashing trout. We were deaf to the luncheon bell and Knox herself took to carrying in trays, exhorting me to eat lest I collapse with brain fag, and cautioning Mr. Margalo against a dangerous buildup of "black bile." During these breaks I drew out Mr. Margalo on university life. I listened, rapt, to his accounts of the medical school at Teviot Place with its stone arcade through which those seven women had dared to pass; of the great clock above the quadrangle and the motto inscribed in stone thereunder, ARS LONGA VITA BREVIS. Of lecture halls and distinguished professors; of the cranky landlady who ruled his student "digs" with an iron crochet hook. Of "cramming" in the library, of singing in the student ale house. Mindful that life was indeed brevis, and the acquisition of medical art long, I scarcely lifted my head from the pages. The lengthy northern summer evenings obviated the need for lamps until nigh on ten o'clock at which time Mrs. Knox, by the power vested in her by my father, banished me to bed.

Thus we continued diligently through the final weeks of August.

I. MARGALO. FIELD NOTES. AUGUST 25, 1887

Miss Bell's condition deemed no obstacle to university.

Doubt existence of "condition."

Possible Lord Henry kept daughter confined due to anxiety *re* sole remaining child?

Of note: L. H. does not object to higher female education. Gentleman of advanced views.

September was yet young when Mr. Margalo pronounced me within sight of shore. It wanted but to send for the examination papers. "Which I shall do after dinner this evening." He then declared it too fine a day to spend indoors whilst "our sacred parent" basked without in all her glory.

We waded through a sea of heather—its purple no less vivid now I knew it derived from anthocyanins rather than the blood of the Picts. We were not burdened by so much as a pair of field glasses—nor had we announced our intention to ramble, so no fuss had attended our departure.

On we sauntered and time seemed to suspend. The whole of the moor drowsed with moths and bumblebees, and I became aware of a sort of buzzing well-being. Mr. Margalo removed his coat ("With your permission, Miss Bell") and I pushed up the sleeves of my tunic.

He bent to free a blue butterfly from a web on a bilberry bush. "There," he said. "We have altered the course of Nature." A salamander scuttled across the toe of my boot and I made a grab for its tail but missed. I caught a whiff of something . . . dark and loamy, at once strange and familiar. I crouched on my haunches and perused the progress of a click beetle up a blade of bent-grass. Mr. Margalo hunkered beside me, took his penknife and bored a tiny hole in the ground, extracting a dollop of mud. He reached into his waistcoat pocket for his loupe. With the weight of the mellow September sun upon our heads, we took turns peering into the tangled fibres where tardigrades lumbered and tumbled endearingly, and less comely nematodes probed about like living wands amid the shadows of numberless other beings as yet unnamed, knowing we but glimpsed the surface of a universe many orders of magnitude below the reach of the most powerful microscope known to man. "You could do a doctorate in a teaspoon," said Mr. Margalo. As I listened and looked, it seemed to me the division 'twixt Faery and

biology blurred and I understood something about the power of naming and the claiming of meaning and the taming of time and my thoughts
commenced to rhyme when . . . So intent had we been on our teaspoon
of earth, we were wholly unprepared, upon rising to our feet, to find our
heads in the clouds.

We looked at one another, wreathed in mist, and laughed. I watched
as, the next instant, Mr. Margalo's face disappeared, along with the rest
of him. "My word," he said. His hand groped for mine and closed upon
it. He knew as well as I that we daren't move lest we stray onto bog. Even
my feet were gone. Presently we agreed we might sit—albeit straight-
backed, lest any ammonia be pocketed about.

If time had distended under the sun, within the mist it seemed to
cease altogether. I know not how long we sat in silence, his hand gripping mine, before I said, "Mr. Margalo. I have heard . . . sounds. At
night. Do you think the bog fumes can reach my window?"

His voice seemed closer in the mist. "What do you hear, Miss Bell?"

"A child. Crying out." I sensed him shift. "Mr. Margalo, have you
heard it too? Perhaps on your first night at Fayne?" My face grew warm
and I was grateful for the fog.

"I heard a cry on the night in question. But it issued from within the
house. I thought . . ."

"What did you think?"

"I thought it was you. That you meant to tease me thereby."

"I assure you I did not. But Knox too said it was I. She says I often
cry out."

"And do you always say the same thing?"

"What . . . do I say?"

"Forgive me."

"Tell me."

"'Tis but one word."

"What word?"

He was silent. I proffered my palm. With the tip of his finger he
traced the letters and I read, silently, *Momma.*

Together, we passed the timelessness in that opaque no-place. Was it
one hour or one year? Would the mist lift on a world subtly changed?
Or radically? I wondered suddenly whether my tutor had brothers or
sisters; whether his father was likewise a man of science—and did his

mother yet live? As swiftly as these questions arose, I posed them, and in the intimate muffle of myst, he obliged with the story of his life. It was brief. He had not been brought up in a family at all. He was a foundling. "Found where?"

He had been delivered to Edinburgh's Heriot's Hospital School for boys in a basket. "Like Moses," I said.

"Like bread," he demurred.

"And did your parents, once having misplaced the basket, never seek you out?"

"They did not misplace it . . . as such."

Mr. Margalo had grown up at the school.

"I have neither father nor mother. I have a benefactor."

"The eponymous Mr. Margalo?"

"No. I know only that my name was affixed to the basket, penned by 'an educated hand.'"

"And are you Greek?"

"Not according to my benefactor."

"Well, 'tis a perfectly serviceable name. Nothing wrong with a pearl."

"Except that in addition to being uncommon, Margalo is customarily a woman's given name—in English 'tis Margaret."

"Mr. Margaret, as it were."

"Ha. I don't mind it now. Though I put up with a deal of teasing from the other lads."

"Why did they tease?"

"Well. Boys do not normally take kindly to being associated with females."

"They frequently marry them."

He chuckled. "Yes. But." He sighed. "Miss Bell, before I came to be your tutor, I myself subscribed to certain backward notions *vis-à-vis* the female sex."

"Were you among those apt to hurl livestock?"

"No. But I was wide of the mark in my estimate of female intelligence."

I learned that, courtesy of his benefactor, he had entered the University of Edinburgh at the age of sixteen, and earned a "Bachelor of Science with Honours degree" in a mere three years. "Mr. Margalo, it would seem your intelligence is nearly on a level with my own."

I heard him laugh. I felt him squeeze my hand. I was summoning the cheek to ask what the "I" stood for in his given name when the mist lifted and we let go our hands.

About us, the mellow light had deepened, the afternoon was well advanced, we would be missed at home. I jumped to my feet . . . only to sink several inches. We looked down. Water had risen silently; it limned the soles of Mr. Margalo's boots, and closed about my ankles. As though my sense of smell had likewise been suppressed by mist, my nostrils were now assailed by a swampy stench and as I watched, a toad splashed past my legs and hopped away over what was now effectively an open stretch of quaking bog. Plain as a pikestaff stood the stone to the north for we had not been wayward in our wending, yet here we were set to sink within sight of home. Mr. Margalo rose slowly; and sank three inches. His voice was calm. "You see that hummock not eight yards off, Miss Bell? We shall be on solid ground there. Walk in my footprints. And if I sink, you are by no means to approach me."

He proceeded gingerly, his footprints flooding the moment he lifted his boot. I took a step. A glance behind me showed my own boot-print and . . . Was it a tryck of bog light? For where the imprint of my sole ought to be, there was a face . . . rudimentary. Round. Shocked. Gazing up at me, its eyes large and supplicating like a carved squash. Or a baby.

I was suddenly thigh-deep in mire. Mr. Margalo did not turn, for the earth had given way to the liquid side of its nature silently. I was mute, as though my voice had been snatched, unable to utter a cry. I was saved by a stag.

The appearance of the animal was not downright rare—the moor was home to abundant red and roe deer, and among them must be bucks and stags. But Mr. Margalo was new to the countryside and for him the appearance of a fourteen-point set of antlers was remarkable (I had leisure to count them as I sank)—so it was he turned to me with a rapturous look which changed instantly to horror. Tearing off his coat, he flung himself prone and with his toes hooked in heather and the rest of him half-submerged, threw the garment to me. I caught the sleeve and, hand over steady hand, he hauled me toward safety.

I was all but free when my ankles were seized in a powerful grip. "Something's got me," I whispered, finding my voice even as I was pulled downward. I set to thrashing, thereby aiding the bog in its swallowing of me. Mr. Margalo lunged and grabbed my wrists. He locked eyes with me—his, brown like the wet earth and containing nothing but truth—and I ceased struggling. Prone and sinking himself, Mr. Margalo counted to three then pulled and, by increments, I was delivered of the bog.

I, along with a twisted vine-like mass wound about my legs. "Vegetable matter of some sort," said Mr. Margalo, applying his knife, cutting me free. It looked like a great fibrous shroud. "A mat of peat, perhaps?" We laid it out on a bed of moss, blackening the massy pinks with mud.

"Why, 'tis a cloak," said he.

"By Jupiter and by Jove," I breathed, for here at last was my legionnaire's cape—could the sword be far behind? I looked back at the site of my near-demise where even now the treacherous green carpet was reconstituting itself, in hopes of spying a hilt jutting forth.

"Jenner & Co. Edinburgh," said Mr. Margalo.

He had scraped away the mud to reveal a label embroidered inside the collar. I had never been to Edinburgh, nor had I heard of the shop, but I knew Caesar's legions had not been provisioned by Scottish drapers.

Mr. Margalo said, "One hopes the lady met with no misfortune."

"'Lady'?" I was crestfallen. But cheered the next instant—"You think she drowned in the bog?"

"One sincerely hopes not."

"One sincerely does," said I, summoning gravitas.

"It is certainly a lady's cloak, however, for I have never seen a gentleman's with buttons such as this . . . sort of shaped like scallop shells, and they're ivory, quite costly I shouldn't wonder." He rose, hefting it by the shoulders. It was already stiffening and looked fair to stand up by itself. The thing had rather a sepulchral air, like a headless monument.

We both were caked in mud, drying now to a wrinkled grey on skin and hair as though we had aged an eon in an afternoon.

"In any case, it behooves me to bring this to your father's attention. He will know best how to proceed with inquiries."

"If you please, Mr. Margalo, do not do any behooving without me, I wish to be kept abreast of developments. However grisly."

He grinned and tousled my hair, then immediately apologized. I grinned back.

We lugged the thing homeward and I fancied it was heavy as a dressed doe. Moreover I had lost my left Wellie to the clabber and so limped along (uncomplaining). I harried my tutor about what he might have told my father had he returned home without his pupil, and laughed at his dismay, assuring him, "Mum's the word, Mr. Margalo."

He turned grave. "I cannot countenance deceit, Miss Bell, even by omission."

"Mr. Margalo, I apologize for my unwarranted slight to your honour. We shall tell Father together. The facts reveal nothing untoward insofar as the perils of fog and bog, but they do reflect on your quick-wittedness and skill in having rescued me."

He bowed. I bowed back.

In my mind's eye I saw the two of us amid jungle fronds, collars dark with sweat, heads mutually inclined over a giant slug, jotting notes. I saw us subsequently upon a dais—sunburnt but erect—before the Royal Society. Margalo & Bell.

We dropped the cloak on the forecourt with a thud and stood over it, wiping mud from our hands. "I say, Mr. M, we ought to check the pockets."

"If it has pockets." No sooner did he bend to investigate, than:

"Thank Brigid, Mary and all the saints!" Knoxy was bearing down on us from the bothy. "Here's me after sending Byrn to seek you!" Turning now to bellow over her shoulder, "Stand down, Byrn, they're found!"

"We were not lost, Knoxy."

"I was on the point of waking your father!"

"Look what we found in the bog."

"Never mind what you found, you look to have been in the bog yourself."

"Indeed I was."

"Mr. Margalo, what is the meaning of this?"

"I assure you, Mrs. Knox, Miss Bell is unharmed."

"I'll be the judge of that, she's soaked and covered in Lord knows what—"

"Moor mud," said I. "'Tis anaerobic."

"Anna who?"

"Knoxy, look what we found, a lady's cloak! Oh, and it might prove a very sad object for some in the county as may be missing a female relation."

Her expression changed as she regarded it. "Knoxy, do you know whose it is?"

She looked up sharply. "Into the house with you now, in, in, in" and she made to shoo me as though I were a flock of hens. "Straight up to your chamber, lassie."

"'Tis 'Miss Lassie' to you." But I headed obediently toward the house.

Behind me Mr. Margalo said, "I shall inform Lord Bell of the find."

"You'll do no such thing," barked Knox.

"Really, Knoxy!" I whirled.

"I take no offence, Miss Bell," said Mr. Margalo.

"Well you ought to," I retorted, backing up the steps before the force of Knox's oncoming bustle.

Really, this perfect day was going swiftly south. I grumbled but preceded my old nurse, making as much of a mess as I could with the shaking of dried mud onto the floor and the stairs. O, how I yearned to be gone from this heap of home to the spires of Edinburgh and its university!

June 21, 1872

Dear Timothea,
I am no longer pregnant. Please encourage Daddy and everyone there to take it lightly. I will have another. There is nothing wrong with me, says the doctor.

Your Mae

Lord Henry raises himself on an elbow and blinks at the lamplight. "What is it, Knoxy? Dinner already? Have I o'erslept?"

"Nay, Your Lordship, dinner's a glass or more off yet."

"What then?"

"It concerns Miss Charlotte's excursion onto the moor with her tutor today."

He has sat up, is swinging his legs over the side of the bed—

"All's well, Your Lordship, the lass is muddy but unharmed, it concerns what they found. In the bog."

He sits back. ". . . What?"

"A cloak."

Five seconds pass.

". . . Hers?"

She nods.

His hands find his face. He sighs. Shudders.

"Do you wish to view it, Your Lordship?"

He shakes his head, no. She waits. He draws a deep breath, lifts his face from his hands and exhales.

"Shall I . . . What would Your Lordship have me do with . . . the garment?"

"Why, burn it."

I reclined in my bath, basking in the light that poured pink and golden through my window. I was as blissful now as I had been recently fractious. Cruikshank had laid a fire despite the warmth. Knox stood sentinel as usual, lest I fall asleep and drown—I suspected even she knew this to be something overcautious.

"You may go, Knoxy."

She did not budge. I might as well have been speaking ancient Greek. To the cupboard. I splashed her. She stepped back but failed to retreat. I slid underwater, keeping my eyes open 'til her worried face appeared above, then I surfaced and spouted like a whale.

"Two minutes, missy, then I'm coming back in."

I opened my lips to object and she dosed me with a spoonful of Byrn's balm. (Foul stuff—a point in its favour, according to Knox.) She withdrew.

A rare two minutes of solitude in my bath. I mused that, whereas solitude was commonly employed as a punishment, to me it was a privilege. I folded my hands behind my head and relaxed—that is, ninety-eight percent of my body relaxed; all but that dissenting bit of flesh that waxed every day more intractable. By turns lazy and limp, then alert and headstrong. "No," said I, addressing it. There it stood amid the fine curls between my legs, chipper and devoid of malice. This negligible bit of me—long a minor distraction—had come to exert a disproportionate claim upon my attention. But I was fond of it—protective even, for were it a person, it would be given to ecstatic leapings from the nearest precipice. Fond? I loved it. It was part of me, yet separate too, like an external little beating heart—nay like another self; as if within it lay a little mind and soul and history . . . I wondered if everyone's—that is, every female person's—appendage was so troublesome and so dear. And did everyone call it a prickle? Or was that nomenclature particular to me? I reached into the water with the intention of a friendly pat but soon found myself at one with its cheeky all-consuming drive toward—the click of the latch signalled Knox's return and I arose abruptly, shedding half the bath as I stepped from the tub and made a grab for the linen warming on the fender—

"Here now, you'll catch your death."

I wrapped it swiftly about my waist and drip-toed over to the window so as to afford Prickle the chance to subside on its own. Steam had smeared the sunset and without thinking, I applied my forefinger to the pane and drew a circle, then two eyes, a nose, an "O" for a mouth—it was the rudimentary face that had appeared on the bog that afternoon. I swept my hand across the glass, obliterating the face and liberating what was left of the sunset before yielding to Knox, who dried me brusquely head to toe with practised skill.

I instructed her to lay out my best purple cape and scarlet tunic with the blue *Salamander Rampant* emblazoned across the chest—I craved to be fully kitted out with sword and shield. Thus the interval 'twixt infancy and maturity wherein a girl might fancy herself both medieval knight and budding scientist. I was spoiling to tell Father of the cloak I'd exhumed from the murky maw and I fairly pranced with joy as it struck me, I had indeed brought him back a specimen!

I turned to see my nightgown laid out on my bed. Knox informed me the directive had come from Father himself: I was to take the evening meal in my room and keep to my bed 'til morning. "For the sake of your health."

"There's nowt amiss with my health!"

She spoke quietly. "Aye. And your father means to keep it that way."

She went to see about a tray for me. I paced, I kicked at the carpet, ribboned the air with my 'sword,' I . . . sulked. I felt for swollen glands in my neck. Nothing! Cruikshank entered with my meal—"Take it away!"—and Knox stood guard 'til I'd finished every bite. (In truth I was suddenly famished—and tired.) Still, I feared lest Mr. Margalo think I lacked pluck in failing to appear at table after a bit of a wetting.

"You can set him straight tomorrow, now eat up and snuggle down if you hope to go a-heather-loping ever again."

I lay strangely alert despite my fatigue and only then, in the tranquility of my bed in the fading light of the summer sky, did the full force of my narrow escape visit itself upon me. My nerve strings set to thrumming, my blood grew hectic in my veins; and I heard a sound like heavy footfalls in an empty chamber, forever approaching, never arriving—'twas the beating of my own heart. I lulled myself with the knowledge that tomorrow promised fair; my tutor was in favour with my father; I was in good health and on the path of higher learning. I formulated a plan to have Byrn return with me and Mr. Margalo to the scene of the drowned cloak, this time with rope and grappling hook. If aught remained—however gruesome—we would find it.

I quelled the prickle.

Then I slept.

I. MARGALO FIELD NOTES. SEPTEMBER 8, 1887

Moor foray ended with near loss of pupil to dual nature of bog. Unearthed woman's cloak. Mrs. Knox forestalled my telling Lord Henry. "No need, sir. The cloak belonged to a local woman, known to walk the moor by night." Declined my offer to return cloak to woman. "Dead and gone these many years, sir." I expressed misgivings lest body be yet in bog. "Never worry, sir, she had a Christian burial."

Above exchange took place in Mrs. K's pantry where I sought her out following solitary dinner. I asked after Miss Bell's health, concerned lest "condition" be genuine after all.

"She is in fettle, sir."

Relieved.

Asked after L. H.'s frame of mind in light of daughter's mishap (concerned for my post).

"His Lordship bade me thank you for bringing his child home safe and sound. Had you no been there . . . Well it doesnae bear thinkin' about."

Doubly relieved.

Cloak had pockets in which document found, now air-drying on toiletry case preparatory to unfolding.

This time the cry came not from out on the moor, but from much closer. I woke instantly and knew this was no dream, for the cry yet hung in the air, palpable, wet. I sat up. The darkness felt substantial . . . animate. Again came the cry! It was a cry of terror. Of sorrow. Of pleading. It was the cry of a child—the same one I had heard before. And it was coming from my window . . . where a whitish glow I took to be moonlight suffused the pane. I rose. Chills skittered up my spine yet I walked to the window, for what had anyone to fear from a wee bairn? Reader, even now the hairs stir at the back of my neck and my eyes water at the recollection of the sight of *A FACE AT MY WINDOW*. Large as my own, and yet a baby's. Full in the pane he—yes, *he*, for I recognized him now! With his halo of curly locks, but no longer laughing, he was staring, tear-stained and unblinking; not at me . . . at something—or someone—just behind me. "Go away!" I screamed.

His high baby brow dimpled in distress, he turned to me his pleading eyes—I knew what he wanted. He wanted me to turn round, to look behind me—"No!" I sobbed in terror, "Go away! You're dead!"—and raising my fists, brought them down with all my might against the pane, smashing it, obliterating the face of my brother.

The jags of glass leapt like flames in the sudden candlelight and I spun about to see—"Knox!" I raised my hands like some pagan priestess, "I'm bleeding."

"Aye, pet, 'tis natural, come awa' from the window now."

"Help me!" I cried, shocked to hear in my own tone the echo of the spectral baby, and I thrust forth my gory arms . . . to find they were spotless. I pivoted to the window. It was intact. And blank as the moonless night.

"You were riding the nightmare again, pet. Come now, we'll make you fresh."

In my haste I had thrown back the bedclothes, and the bottom sheet lay exposed like a slab in the candlelight. I gasped—did I yet dream? There, as though evidence of a crime forgot, was a splotch of blood.

"'Tis natural," she repeated, with a familiar gesture that meant I was to lift my arms to be undressed. Instead, I clutched at the back of my nightgown, snapping my head round to see a twist of bloody fabric. My blood. *My Condition*. "Am I dying?"

"You are preparing to carry life."

She was sponging me, helping me into a pair of bloomers wadded at the crotch with clean linen, all the while explaining something in her slow, kind way while my mental faculties revived and flew ahead to the conclusion where they had time to sit and unpack a picnic by the time Knox's words caught up. *Breviter*: Reader, I was a mammal.

I dwelt on a farm. I knew mares, cows, ewes, nannies, dams and bitches experienced oestrus; I was no stranger to divers couplings and tuppings, including the caterwauling coitus of barn cats. I knew that women fell pregnant, for I had seen Mrs. Mungo before she died. None of this was a mystery, so how had I failed to register the same applied to me?

"And so you see, m'luvvy, you need take measures in accordance with the waxing and waning of the moon, for like to the tides of the ocean . . ." I was once more abed, she having changed me and the sheets and shown me "the necessary" for next time; for there would be a next time, and a time after that and another and another until "the joyous day ye might carry a bairn of your—"

"Knoxy, it was so real. I saw him."

"Who?"

"My brother," I whispered. "At the window."

She hugged me.

"Hush, 'twas but a dream."

"What does he want?"

"We'll say a wee prayer for him."

"Why?"

"For the repose of his soul."

"Why isn't his soul reposed?"

"He lost his mother, dearie."

"So did I."

"Aye, but . . . you didnae lose your life."

"He wishes me dead."

"Och no, why would he wish such a thing?"

"I killed his mother."

"'Twas none of your fault, she died in child-bed like many a woman afore her."

"Then why is he haunting me?"

". . . Belike he's watching over you."

"No. He wants me to turn around and . . ."

". . . And what?"

I shivered. I had no words.

"Now lass, 'tis a part of your woman's time to feel . . . feelings."

"I don't want them! I hate feelings! I hate woman's time!" I smote the mattress, dispelling fear with anger.

"Nay, 'tis a time some call fey."

"Phooey!"

I pushed her away. She returned and stroked my head. I bit her wrist. She did not flinch. I buried my face in the pillow and wept with a sorrow I could not fathom, wept with rage that I should weep, the while she softly sang. Finally she made to withdraw. "Don't go," I whimpered. She stayed.

It is shortly after midnight, Lord Henry is bent over a set of tweezers—between its fine points a finer bone—in the act of reconstructing a spine when there comes a knock and Mrs. Knox enters with a candle.

"Lord Henry, sir, a word if you please?"

"At this hour?"

"Forgive me, Your Lordship, yes, I believe now be best."

"What's the matter?"

"All's well, My Lord, but all's not as it was. Miss Charlotte, Your Lordship—"

He clasps the arms of his chair. "Dear God—"

"She is well, Your Lordship, she is, today—tonight . . . My Lord, she is a woman."

He blinks.

"Do you take my meaning, Lord Henry?"

His breath assails him, the air forcing between his lips like a mother with a spoon. He drops his brow to his hand, cradling his forehead.

She goes to him. "There, there, My Lord."

The breath that invaded him now retreats and he shudders.

"Your Lordship. It is good news."

"I know," he says, weeping.

She places both hands on his shoulders. "Poor Henny-Penny."

~◎

Fayne House
October 21, 1872

Dear Taff,

I have barely removed my hat, having been whisked directly up the
grand staircase and into the "family wing" by the housekeeper whom
I judge to be somewhere between forty and one hundred years of age.
Yes, I am at the vaunted Bell family seat. You recall Pappy made much
of the fact that Henry owns a "stately house" and not by way of vulgar
purchase, no, this ancestral keep has been in his family for nigh on
these four hundred and fifty years. Ancestral *heap* more like! Oh Taffy,
burn this after reading! But really. I knew Henry was in Rome on more
than a sightseeing tour, but if I did not have ample evidence that his
interest in me extends well beyond the pecuniary, I could swear he
married me <u>only</u> for my mountain of beans. Apparently the air will
do me good. Taffy, pray for me, darling, I'm expecting again and it
must work out this time. Enough of that! Nice thoughts, only!

We boarded the "snorting iron horse" as Henry calls the train,
and the journey started out promisingly, for the countryside really
is charming and, in places, quite dramatic. On we chugged until we
disembarked at a sleepy one-horse station and boarded a carriage.
We passed in and out of broad valleys, slowing to admire a village
"than which nothing could be more picturesque"—except perhaps the
next village in the next valley (with all due respect to Baedeker). With
each glimpse of manicured grounds or a tree-lined drive, I waited for
Henry to say, "We're here." And on we rolled. (I am smoothing my
frown lines as I write.)

Henry nudged me awake when we came at last to the village
of Aberfoyle-on-Feyn. (Everything in Britain is called Something-
on-Something-Else.) It is pretty enough; there is a mill with a wool
factory; there's a market square, and a "high" street with a dear
little glass curiosity shop. In its window is a sign in Gothic script:
WE SAY NO TRAIN IN FAYNE. "They'd rather not see their
valley stitched up in steel," said Henry, adding, "As who can blame
them?" Well, I can. The village really is sweet, though. Along with

the butcher, baker and honest-to-goodness candlestick maker, there is the Inn at the Kenspeckle Hen where a post coach delivers packages and passengers including, today, my extra trunks. At one end of the village, there's an Anglican Church with a tall spire, while at the other end there hunkers a Scottish kirk. Nowhere is there a Catholic Church.

It's all very romantic as seen on a sunny day from a well-sprung carriage—and here it must be said, Henry shows no Scottish bent for stinginess, at least when it comes to spending my dowry (but then, is Henry English or Scottish?!)—and I was expecting at any moment the stately roofline of Fayne House to appear over treetops. But we turned abruptly, crossed a bridge, and the rolling green landscape fell away behind us as we ascended a steep hill, at the brow of which an entirely different prospect greeted us, such that . . . Baedeker be darned, Taffy, it's bleak. And it's all that's left of the Bell estate: a stony ridge ("fell") overlooking an enormous moor that's good for nothing, with a lot of boggy patches that are good for even less. I thought of what Daddy said when I told him I had accepted Henry's offer of marriage—"Not bad for a bog-hopper from County Leitrim." And now here I am back on the bog! Oh well, at least we own this one.

Henry claimed to distinguish umpteen shades of purple and I'll give him that, the heather is lovely. But as for the rest, maybe my eyes aren't yet accustomed to the thin light here, because I saw mostly dun.

As for my first view of Fayne House, I wish I could say it filled me with a nameless foreboding, that I sensed a menace lurking behind its stone façade and sinister watchers at its many dim windows. But all it is, Taffy, is gray. And gaunt. Flanked by a timbered stone barn, stables, a dumpy outbuilding with fly-away thatch and no tree-lined drive, much less a lawn. (Forget gravel, there's cinders.) The whole place looks to be suffering from a miserable cold. I could feel Henry's eyes on me, desperately wanting me to love it. Finally I said, "Henry, it's really striking." The smile he gave me was . . . pathetic. Sigh. He said, "This is the new house of course. The old house burned down in sixteen twenty." Small mercies, Taff.

There is not a neighbour in sight, never mind "society." After I have finished this letter to you, and before I descend the stairs to take a glass of thousand-year-old mead, I am determined to ascend to the attic in the faint hope there may be a madwoman confined up there.

I am, at present, seated at the dressing table because I can't face the long walk from here to the davenport (which is what they call the desk, not to be confused with the sofa) on the other side of the room. Everything is vast, including the bed which sits like an island in an ocean of drafty space. How many Bells were conceived within those four posts, how many went thence to their maker, and how old is that mattress? I wonder if there's a shop in Aberfoyle-on-What's-It that sells bedding?

More anon.

Love Your own,
Lady Marie Bell-on-Tenterhooks

II

I AWOKE THAT MORNING and parted my bed curtains to find sun invading the chamber. What?! Mr. Margalo would be vexed and rightly so! Up I leapt, only to feel a warm gushing between my legs. "Knox!" I doubled over.

She was there in an instant, dragging the copper tub, followed hard upon by Cruikshank who came and went with steaming ewers of water.

I sat in the bath, head bowed, hugging my knees against the dark ache that girdled me about, watching the blood balloon and disperse whilst Knox poured warm water over me. It soothed my low back. Was it owing to its outlet in the "unmentionable" nether region of the anatomy, that Knox had omitted to warn me the menarche would hurt like the deuce?

"It doesnae hurt every woman every time in the same way."

"I say, that is consoling!"

I rose abruptly, but she was on me with the towel as though smothering flames and I, made docile by pain, suffered her to dab at the crimson trickle on my thighs before stepping into a pair of bloomers padded with moor moss wrapped in linen—like a field dressing for a battle wound.

I straightened stoically despite the sensation of gears in my guts. "Knox, tell Mr. Margalo I shall join him presently."

"That I cannae, lass—"

"Cruikshank, go directly to Mr. Margalo, do you hear?" She bobbed and made for the door but Knox stopped her—"No need, the young gentleman has left."

"Bother, why did you let me lie in?!" I crossed to the window.

"Child, you're in your smalls!"

"And who's to see me, the rooks?"

It was a fine day and Mr. Margalo was nowhere in sight—as no wonder, he'd be halfway to the North Fell by now—I only hoped he would not exhume any more artifacts without me. I'd hasten and overtake him before luncheon. I turned to the bed where my tunic and leggings were laid out but, like a shipwrecked mariner in view of shore, I foundered and sank to the floor. Reader, it hurt.

The pain did not lessen with being abed. I lay curled. Writhing only waked the snake of pain. In stillness it sank its fangs. I could take no nourishment, I could think no thoughts. Knox plied me with peppermint tea. Somewhere in the afternoon, pain abated and I slept.

Awoke in time for dinner. Refreshed. My very thoughts, dewy. I arose, pain-free but bleeding from the crux of me—no matter. I wrested from Knox the fresh arrangement of moss, stuffing it into my drawers as a soldier might staunch his own wound. I donned my finest scarlet tunic— aye, so's none should see me bleed. "What did you tell Mr. Margalo?"

"Why, nowt, pet."

"Good."

I froze. "Does Father know?"

"Know what?"

"Why, that—that is, about my—about . . . the woman's time?" I could hardly get out the words.

"Of course not. Men have no truck with women's troubles."

"So you admit 'tis troublesome."

"All in a good cause."

"Then why not drape the halls in gay bunting?" I snarled.

"Och pet, you'll wear me out, so you will."

I did my best to stride past her despite the bulk between my legs. This spot of bother would soon be over and no one—certainly neither Father nor Mr. Margalo—would be any the wiser. I ran down the stairs and reported for duty in the dining room.

Father rose at my entry, but Mr. Margalo was absent and no place had been set for him.

"Is my tutor not to join us this evening?"

Father's mild expression did not alter as he said, "Mr. Margalo is no longer with us."

"He . . . what?"

"He has gone, I'm afraid."

"'Gone'?"

Father took a sip of water.

"Do you mean to say . . . ? Oh Father, he went out onto the moors by himself this morning—"

"No, no, he is quite safe, my dear—that is, one may reasonably assume so, insofar as he is certainly not lost to the moor."

Faint with relief, scarcely had I formulated my next question when Father answered it: "He has returned to Edinburgh."

"When will he be back?"

"I shouldn't expect him back, my dear."

"I do not understand."

"He packed his personal effects and cleared out before dawn. I am sorry, Charlotte."

"But . . . I do not understand," I repeated.

"I do not presume to know his mind."

Cruikshank spooned white soup into Father's bowl. Then mine.

"What did he say?"

"Nothing at all, to me."

"Did he . . . leave a note?"

"He did not."

Father took a spoonful of soup. Another. Presently he addressed the table. "Charlotte. Young men like Mr. Margalo are ambitious. You saw yourself his reluctance to take you on as a pupil. If the offer of a more suitable position has presented itself, we may blame him for failing to take his leave like a gentleman, but we must not stand in his way."

I felt dazed. As though at a blow. ". . . Father, we cannot know for certain, he may have received an urgent message." Perhaps from his benefactor to whom he owed so much—"We must . . ." But a message required a messenger and none could approach the house without setting Nolan to barking and Byrn to waking, if the old man wasn't already up and on the wander—what's more, Father himself would espy any nocturnal comer from his study window. I felt my spirits sinking as though into the mire.

"He did not fail to collect his wages yesterday. A month's in advance."

"But . . . he was going to conduct my examination."

Father lifted his eyes to me with such a look of regret, it struck me now that he too had been deserted; and added to my bewilderment was a tincture of shame, for if Mr. Margalo had abused Father's trust, was not I the instrument of that abuse? *Send me to school!* Tears pricked my eyes and I dropped my gaze.

I felt Father's hand alight upon my own; heard him say with infinite gentleness, "Be assured, my own, I have not forgotten your hopes. And I shall . . ." Here he broke off and I heard him clear his throat. I looked up and was shocked to see, though he looked quickly away, his own eyes glistening. I dreaded lest the slightest breath cause either Father's or my own tears to breach their banks. He squared his chin. I did likewise. He directed his gaze to the shadows at the far end of the table. His voice was steady. "I shall do all within my power to secure your happiness. I give you my word."

Despite a cratering grief in my chest, I wished more than anything to buoy Father's spirits by assuring him that he had restored my own and so, casting about for an offering, said, "We found a cloak. In the bog."

"Claret, I think, Cruikshank."

We spoke little. I ate less.

Following the meal, I ventured into the schoolroom. I raised my candle. All was as we had left it. Books were piled precariously on the table. Pencil shavings lay curled. My protractor was speared, Excalibur-like, into the tabletop. The Sumerian beer fizzed softly in its test tube. My chair stood askew and a corner of the carpet was flapped where I had tripped in hastening after Mr. Margalo when he suggested a spontaneous foray onto the moor . . . yesterday. Nothing in all I surveyed bore signs of finality. Even the microscope stood at the ready—surely he would wish to retrieve his microscope! In that instant I witnessed another illusion depart like a shred of mist, for of course the microscope along with all the wonders of the trunk, nay the trunk itself, were Father's property. A pang smote my heart and I felt it bleed as surely as I bled from that other place. Poor Father.

I lingered at the foot of the staircase, but no beckoning triangle of light spilled from his study door. It was closed.

I clung limpet-like to the faint hope all might yet be honourably explained.

All the next day I waited in vain.

In the evening I dressed for dinner, and descended only to cross paths with Cruikshank carrying a covered tray into Father's study. Following the solitary meal, I lingered at the foot of the staircase; but the study door remained closed. I plucked a candle from the sconce and ascended the gloom, careful once more to avoid the eyes of the portrait—no longer those of my indifferent mother, but of my mocking, demon brother.

In my bed I was prey to a thousand moving images; scenes of remembered joy and camaraderie with Mr. Margalo. I drove my palms against my lids 'til I saw only blood and black and dying stars. If I could have strangled the sorrow in my throat I would gladly have choked along with it, but I kept on breathing, and there seeped from beneath my lids hot tears from a swallet too cruel to rise up and drown me.

In the morning I awoke, ashamed at my lack of fortitude. I resolved to attain equanimity in the face of a hardship which did not admit of my remedying.

And failed.

On the third evening, I encountered Cruikshank on her way to Father's study with the tray; this time, propped against its pewter lid was a letter. My heart leapt painfully.

I dined alone.

And went up to bed none the wiser.

Mrs. Knox sets a mug of alder-bark tea before His Lordship. An envelope, addressed to him, sits unopened on the desk. She recognizes the hand but says nothing. Lifting the cover from the dinner tray, she sees

His Lordship has eaten no more than would one of his birds, were they alive to do so.

"Your Lordship, you must eat." He does not reply. She moves to leave, but he says in a ragged whisper, "I betrayed her."

". . . Who?"

"My daughter."

"Nonsense—begging Your Lordship's—"

"Tabby, you know, as well as I, that I have been selfish."

"I know no such—"

"My sister was right." He cradles his forehead.

She places a hand on his shoulder. "You're no good to the lass if you 'llow your own health to fail." She slides the tray in front of him. "Eat. Your Lordship." He sighs, steals a look at his old nurse, and takes up the spoon.

⟞◉

Fayne House
October 25, 1872

Dearest Taff,

There is no running water except in the scullery. Need I say more? Probably not, but just try and stop me. There are trophies everywhere; I can't look up without meeting the glassy gaze of some dead brute, nor tread on a rug without having it stare back at me. And there are altogether too many pictures: gummy oils of dead Bells dating back to the Middle Ages. "Saved from the fire, remarkable good fortune," said Henry. Who, I wonder, rushed into the burning mansion to rescue those dour depictions of beetle-browed Barons united in adherence to the eleventh commandment: *Thou shalt not smile*? Where did Henry come from? He has the mildest face, the kindest eyes, he must be a throwback to a weak, sweet, murdered minor Bell—hopefully not the one in the blank portrait (!). All of which is to say, Fayne House is not precisely the *beau idéal* of domestic comfort. A full suit of armor scared me on the way up to the baronial bedchamber just now.

Two chambers, actually, adjoining bedrooms, his and hers, Lord's and Lady's, divided by a great groaning door such that nocturnal trysts are announced to the entire household and threaten to tax a man's vigor before he can part the bed curtains. Taf, I don't know whether to laugh or cry.

The old housekeeper is so proud of this place and I know she must have toiled to beat out the dust of epochs, but to give you a teensy example of barbarism: there is no mirror—sorry, "looking glass"!— rather a beaten bronze oval hangs above my dressing table. How I am to gauge the full effect of my toilette is beyond me; I suppose I am to seek for that in Henry's eyes, but he is so hopelessly biased in my favor (may it be ever thus!) he is hardly a reliable reflection. Oh, for Annie back home, whom I tormented and teased but who kept me presentable and knew how to lay out a dress and confect a chignon. There is here, a hired girl, a timid spindle of a thing, who cannot keep her finger from her nostril. And to crown all, there is no running water except in the scullery (it bears repeating).

Ta-ra for now, Taffy, dear.

Love,
The Lady Mae,
British Isles (walk down Beacon Hill to Charles River, follow to Boston Harbour. Dive in. Swim east straight on to landfall)

PS No "water closet" (because no running water, did I say?). Instead, a vestibule off my room called a "garderobe" wherein . . . a CLOSE STOOL! I stand amazed and know not what to say. But I'll think of something.
PPS The hired girl just came in and informed me, with a series of squeaks, that a lady has been and gone and left a card in hopes of paying a call at my convenience! Just the vicar's wife, but "needs must."

❧

Knox entered my chamber and I pounced. "Has there been word?"

She sighed. "No, pet."

"Father got a letter this evening."

"So he did."

"Is it from . . . ?"

"'Tis no from Mr. Mar—"

"Speak not his name!" I meant it to sound imperious. It came out petulant.

She pulled back my bedclothes and I climbed in, careful not to dislodge the fresh wad between my legs. "Knox?"

"Aye, pet?"

"Why . . . ?" My voice wobbled. She enfolded me in her ample embrace and answered the question I could not utter.

"Well now . . . if he's the sort of young man could do a bunk in the night, then he's no fit to be under your father's roof."

"I cannot credit it, Knoxy. His conduct, his countenance, all bid fair . . ."

"Ah well. *Is minig a bha sùil-chruthaich air blianag bhòidhich.*"

I crumpled. "There, there," she said.

I moaned, "And now Father is cross with me-e-e." I blubbed like a babby. What child was this?

"Fiddle-faddling nonsense." She rocked me as of old. "The sun rises and sets on his darling dear Charlotte and there's nowt as'll e'er change that."

I swiped my soggy cheeks against her starched bib. "Where's the cloak?"

"What cloak?"

"The one I found with Mr.—he who shall remain nameless."

"Why 'tis burnt."

"The deuce! Why?"

"Why not? 'Twas rubbish."

"I wished to turn out the pockets!"

"What for?"

"A clue." I meant it to sound haughty. It came out pouty.

"What sort of 'clue'?"

She looked stern yet indulgent and I saw myself as Mr. Margalo must have: a foolish child—worse, a foolish girl. He had only ever humoured me. For wages. "A clue as to the identity of the owner, donkey! She may have fallen in, she may be there still." I felt suddenly hot. Knox made to feel my neck and I slapped her hands away.

"She's no there, pet."

"How would you know?"

She folded her hands and looked down. "Do ye no reckon, child, if a lady went missing in the county there'd be a hue and cry?"

"Maybe she was a stranger. I'll ask Father—"

"Come your ways!"

I was too taken aback to chastise her. She continued, apparently contrite, for she spoke carefully. "There was a woman. Who walked the moor by night. Long, o long ago afore you were born. And she was seen to wear just such a cloak."

I shivered, delighted into momentary forgetting of my woes. "What happened to her?"

"Well. One night, when she was off on the wander, she strayed from the path and . . . sank into the earth.

I drew a slow breath. "She lies there still."

"She was pulled out and . . . ta'en away."

"Where?"

". . . That I cannae say."

"A madhouse."

"No!"

"Then where?"

"I'm not to know that, am I?"

"She'd have had to be mad to stroll about the bog at night."

"What bodes it, pet? I tell you only so's you'll leave off rooting for fen bodies where there be none."

"Bog bodies."

"You'll wind up one yourself, now promise."

"I'm not likely to stray now I've no companion, am I?" Adding bitterly, "And what care I for the moor, nothing could induce me to step foot on it again."

"I'll have Cook make up a basket, and you and Murdoch Mungo can—"

"Shutup."

"And there was nowt in the pockets, pet. I did look."

I curled up beneath the quilt. She sang to me as of old, and I drifted off.

But her words about my traitorous tutor shadowed me into the land of Nod.

'Tis oft a quagmire's to be found in fairest, greenest level ground.

On the desk before him lies a letter. Lord Henry steeples his fingers. Threads them. Squeezes his hands together. And reads.

No. One Bell Gardens
Edinburgh
September 10, 1887

Dear Brother,
I take up my pen to reply with due haste to your letter of the ninth which I received this morning. I bid you rest assured that I continue in tolerably good health, bouts of indisposition notwithstanding. I thank you for your solicitous inquiry and trust I may remain confident in your own continued good health.

In answer to your query *vis-à-vis* the physician, Dr. Chambers: He is still to be found in Ainsley Place. Chary of overstepping, I shall not here make bold to inquire whether you mean to revisit a subject which was laid to one side these many years ago.

With regard to the other matter: If I have understood aright, my niece has passed the meridian from childhood into womanhood. You honour me in requesting what is yours to command. Look for delivery within the week.

Your devoted sister,
Clarissa Bell

I waited next morning, but Father remained sequestered before retiring to bed.

I undertook to compose a treatise on the inevitability of human suffering and the happiness to be derived from patient resignation to same. Through my chamber door I heard Knox laying into Cruikshank for some petty misdeed to do with the washing—I tore open my door and demanded, "Silence!" I returned to my escritoire but it was no good, I had lost the thread. I abandoned the effort and consigned it to the flames.

I summoned Patience. Dullness came in its stead.

Dim to my eyes was the golden light of September. The sky itself seemed lower. All appeared curiously flattened.

Even the portrait on the stairs was drained of import, and I wondered that a dead brother—older than I, but forever a babe—had ever struck terror in my heart. What need had I now of phantoms when the living dealt such blows?

I was solitary as of old. But for the first time, I felt alone.

Friendship, Reader—that which Aristotle had named as a Good in and of itself. Friendship, without which the philosopher declared life not worth living—Friendship had been torn from me. No. The relation that existed between me and my tutor had never been Friendship, merely its counterfeit. I summoned Wisdom. Anger arose.

In the midst of that vapid afternoon, I spied from my window our cart approaching with Byrn bowed over the reins. The cart was laden with cargo of some kind—a trunk, perhaps? Herald of Mr. Margalo's return?! I flew from my chamber, down the stairs and out onto the forecourt in time to see the old man pull up and slide from the bench. Then, like a mockery of that previous arrival, he unloaded a large crate; this one shaped, for all the world, like a coffin. "What is that, Byrn?"

"'Tis for Missus," he replied (or sounds to that effect).

Before I could withdraw in the face of this fresh defeat, I was waylaid by Murdoch Mungo who, clearly acting on orders and cringing as though in anticipation of a thump, sought to entice me onto the moor with a promise of showing me where moles had turned up lumps of coal in "a stream." I suffered his nattering long enough to ascertain he meant not my trout stream, then dismissed him—though with less scorn than he merited, owing more to my want of vim than self-mastery—and stalked off to the byre. Besides, I was newly inclined to agree that the moor was indeed "useless": twelve thousand acres fit only for foolish children, treacherous tutors and madwomen in unsuitable cloaks. And for Byrn who hauled buckets like a Bronze Age bumpkin—O, how Mr. Margalo must be laughing at us now! I pictured him among his fellow students, standing them a round of ale at my father's expense, the loudest guffaws reserved for the ridiculous girl who dared dream of a place in their midst. I'd show him. I'd show them all! I'd pick up their sheep and hurl it straight back! My father would find a better tutor and one day soon I would stride into that ale house and Mr. M and his jeering cohort would fall silent and . . . Here my imagination petered out. I kicked Maisie. She kicked me back.

12

THE BLEEDING CEASED some five days after it began. On that happy blood-free morn I awoke, sat up, stretched and yelped: a headless woman stood at the foot of my bed. By the time Knox arrived, I understood it to be merely an effigy of some kind. "What on earth is it?"

"'Tis a dressmaker's form, Miss Charlotte."

She—it—stood, decapitated yet elaborately gowned and beribboned. "What's it doing here?"

"'Tis to aid you in your toilette."

"My what? Where'd it come from?"

"Edinburgh."

Before my mind's eye there flashed an image of the thing seated, headless, in a railway carriage.

"It is a gift from your aunt."

"My aunt? Has given me a . . . headless doll? Does she know I've ne'er been wont to play with dolls, be they never so large? Not to mention I am too old for toys of any kind." (Sirens and cannons and miniature bridges did not count as "toys.")

"Pet, 'tis no the dressmaker's form that's the gift, but the dress itself."

". . . Oh. Why then, see it is returned to her with a note indicating her mistake and requesting a more suitable garment."

"Your Aunt Clarissa has selected garments as befit a young lady of your station."

"Well you needn't go blaming her, she's ne'er laid eyes on me." I flipped off the coverlet and arose. "Now fetch my clothes."

"These are your clothes."

I laughed. "I'm not likely to venture onto the moor in a ballgown." For I was up from the slough of self-pity, determined to scavenge grouse

feathers for Father before plunging back into studying for the examination—it was high time I set about meriting Father's efforts on my behalf.

"'Tis a day dress, Miss Charlotte."

"I shan't wear it no matter the o'clock, Mrs. Knox, and . . . what is
that?" Draped across my nurse's arms was a loosely-strung assemblage
of . . . "I say, they're not bones?" Mayhap a primitive Celtic musical
instrument?

"They are stays."

Before I could formulate my next question, Cruikshank entered bearing a cone-shaped arrangement of hoops, such as one might use to cage
a wild cat.

Knox said, "It is your father's particular wish that you wear it today."

I stood amazed and knew not what to say.

Fayne
October 27, 1872

Chère Taffée,

I told Hank I would stay on condition I be given free rein—and
wallet—to spruce up the place. He agreed, the lamb. My lord and
master can deny me nothing, even the freedom to return to town,
so you see I am far from a prisoner, and healthy as a horse. Still, say
a little prayer for me, dearest, a novena if you can manage it. There's
no darn church around here. Not a real one. Not an alabaster Mary
in sight.

How I wish I could lay eyes on you, especially now, sweetheart, that
you are a ship in full sail. I just know pregnancy becomes you. Although
I giggle when I try to picture you with a belly!

The grub here is first-rate, I'll say that much. There is a garden out
back of the house. It's walled against deer, but why a deer would cross the
moor for a nibble of lettuce is beyond me. On the other hand, I crossed
the moor for a cup of tepid tea at the vicarage and was grateful for the
society of a female within hailing distance of my own social station even
if her lips were stained with cordial. (Mrs. Reverend Haas, the vicar's
wife. I'll save her for later. She'll keep. She is well-preserved.) . . .

꩜

It began with an assortment of underlinens and petticoats which I assumed were laid out for my choosing, but all of which, it transpired, I was to wear. Knox held out a pair of drawers and I waved them away, "They're torn, fetch a new pair." Reader, I was then given to understand that the tear from front to back along the crotch was not a flaw but a feature: "They're ladies' open drawers." Stunned by this intelligence, I failed to object when a pair of stockings was unrolled from my toes to the tops of my thighs and fastened there by means of a "garter" that had naught to do with chivalry; obligingly, I raised my arms, lowered them, turned about, held my breath and let it out upon command as I was tied, cinched, hooped, trussed, hooked and buttoned into the "combinations," then the under-cladding, and finally the façade of the cornflower-blue silk "day dress." My feet were then seized and jammed into a pair of painfully pointed boots—more buttons, these requiring a special tool in the fastening thereof. Thus I teetered on elevated heels in full feminine armour. Like a knight of old, I felt myself to be helpless if once knocked to the ground.

Cruikshank crouched at my feet, her lips bristling with pins as she let down the hem, whilst Knox set about subduing my hair—"Why not simply drive the pins into my brain?"

"There now, Miss Charlotte, you may look."

My chamber door had opened and a full-length looking glass was advancing toward me. It plunked onto its filigreed stand and Cook stepped out from behind it. She looked me up and down as though I were a side of mutton and left.

Before me in the glass stood a simulacrum of my former self. My head looked to have been grafted onto the body of the dressmaker's form. My hair was braided to the scalp and wound like a crown of thorns; my shoulders sloped under sartorial pressure; a high-boned lace collar tormented me like a ligature of live ants. My waist was unnaturally narrow (whence the twenty-five feet of human digestive tract?). I was bell-shaped from the waist down. I looked absurd!

Then it dawned on me. Father must have realized, when the "gift" arrived, that it was preposterous; and that he and I might share a

moment's sorely needed mirth (my aunt's good intentions notwithstanding). In the glass behind me, Knox's eyes were brimming and Cruiky
trembled with her hands clasped. Clearly they could scarcely contain
their own mirth. I laughed by way of granting them permission to do
likewise but they did not.

"Shall we?" I said, and led the way—haltingly, for the boots were as
stiff as the "stays." The sleeves did not admit of my extending an arm
beyond a twelve-inch, so Cruikshank opened the door for me with a
bob. The whole getup itched, but "A lady doesnae scratch," said Knox.
Nor *could* a lady scratch, for there was no bending at the elbow. Ordinary
perambulation was out of the question owing to the circumference of
the skirts and their cumbersome undercarriage such that only a timely
grab for the banister prevented my tumbling headlong down the stairs—
"The deuce!"

"Language."

I sighed—rather, I attempted to do so, for as much as I was prevented
from drawing a full breath, no more was it possible to fully exhale, and
it occurred to me that retention of carbon dioxide in the lungs must put
a lady at risk of fainting. I wondered that such garments could be quite
lawful. Ah well, anything could be borne for a morning.

"That's as may be," said Knox.

"You don't mean to say I'm to remain in this rigamarole for the entire
day?"

"Och no. There's a bonny dinner gown's been put to one side."

PS Dear girl, the oddest thing: I had a dream that I could have sworn
was real. Nothing could have convinced me that I hadn't been out
traipsing over the moor and onto the bog—the old scarecrow man-
of-all-work calls it "Fenn" (as if it were a proper name). In fact, now
I come to think of it, he was in my dream—picture me shuddering
here—but luckily so was Momma. Although, what Momma was doing
out on the bog in the middle of the night is . . . well, it's not beyond
me, but you'll have to wait 'til we're together to hear the rest . . .
"Pregnant women are given to vivid dreaming." Nothing fazes
old Knoxy.

I made my way across the hall amid the rustling of the dress to the study door. I swallowed a grin, knocked and entered.

Father looked up and rose from his chair. He removed his spectacles. "Well, well. My dear. You are a Beauty."

I felt my brow furrow. Our many-coloured chimera stood atop the bank of pigeon holes—it alone was laughing.

I said, "Should I ever have occasion to attend a fancy-dress ball, I am furnished with a suitable costume." He looked bemused. I added, "How kind of Aunt." He smiled. Wistfully, I thought. I noticed a heap of feathers on the desk. "Might I be of assistance, Father?"

"Why certainly. If you like."

This fell oddly upon my ear, as when had I ever not liked to assist him? I made to draw up the stool but he took it from me and himself placed it next his chair as though I were incapable of doing so myself—which in truth I may have been, restrained as I was.

He said, "I am in search of the femur of the *Xenicus lyalli*. So tiny as to admit of one requiring this." And to the novel note of deference in his tone, Father added a courtly inclination of his head as he proffered the magnifying loupe.

He remained standing and I realized he was waiting for me to sit first. I did so, and my skirt frontage sprang up alarmingly, sweeping the whole heap of feathers and bits from the desk. "I'm sorry, Father!" I bent immediately to assist him but could not reach the floor because of the corset—moreover I was besieged by light-headedness at which I straightened smartly only to lose my balance and topple backward from the stool. "Charlotte!" cried Father from beyond the horizon of my hoops. I flipped onto my stomach like a trout, got my feet under me but, in rising, trod on the hem of my skirt and fell a second time. Knox hustled in, followed by Cruikshank, who hooked each an elbow under my arms and hauled me upright.

"Dearest," said Father, "are you hurt?"

"Not a bit of it—leave off, Cruiky! Father, I'll go change and rejoin you presently—"

"In fact, my dear, 'tis time I retired for the day."

"Oh, of course, but—oh dear, Father, what about your bone?"

"A trifle," he said with a wave of his hand.

"It is no such thing, oh Father, I shall find it, I promise—mind where you step, Knoxy!"

Father inclined his head with a smile then looked away—for all the world as if he were dismissing me, politely.

"Come along, Miss Charlotte."

It was with a slight sense of unreality that I withdrew—brought on no doubt by lingering hypoxia (a lady does not breathe).

I eschewed breakfast, unable to imagine how food was to fit behind my "stomacher." (Neither does a lady eat.)

The day yawned before me. There was naught to do because, garbed as I was, there was naught I could do. There was no nearing the moor in these thirsty trappings. One foot wrong, and I'd be food for the bog. Unbidden to my mind's eye arose the image of a woman, face shadowed by the hood of her cloak . . . sinking . . .

The remainder of the day passed in a sort of stupor. I picked at luncheon, tantalized by the cabinet pudding of which, owing to the "corset," I was unable to swallow more than a morsel. I wandered aimlessly about the house accompanied by the swishing and hissing of the skirts.

An hour prior to dinner, Cruikshank ran me to ground in the trophy room where I stood amid the blank stares of extinct bears and wolves, as still as though I too were stuffed and mounted. I followed her meekly back to my chamber, the dress whispering with every step—why, I wondered, ought it be necessary at all times to hear a lady's approach? What of stealth? How was one to steal up on a vole or a ground swallow? I stood once more before the glass and submitted to the elaborate exchange of the cornflower-blue day dress for the cream-coloured dinner gown. Anything could be borne for a day.

At my entry to the dining room, Father rose, came round and drew out my chair. I did not wonder at this, for presumably he was at pains to prevent a reprise of the morning's mishap. Thus, I lowered myself gingerly onto the seat as he pushed it gently to until my unpredictable bottom half was safely stowed beneath the table.

Cruikshank came and went. Father ate with the same deliberate working of jaw as though he took care not to injure his food in the chewing be it never so much as a potato. Before me, the lamb sat untouched and bleeding on my plate. "Father?"

"Yes, Charlotte?"

"I . . . Merely, I wondered whether you have . . . Rather, when you might see fit to—Rather, whether you might not already have . . . made inquiries on my behalf."

He looked up mildly, "In what regard 'inquiries,' my dear?"

"In regard to the matter of engaging . . ." I swallowed. "That is . . . a new tutor." My face grew hot. I feared lest I give offence either by seeming to doubt Father's word or by rekindling the insult dealt him by the blackguardly Mr. Not-to-be-Named.

"As to that, my dear. Be assured, I have not forgotten."

I waited.

He did not dilate further.

"Father?"

"Mm?"

"Tomorrow. If the weather's dreich, might you fancy an early walk before you retire for the day?"

He did not immediately reply, occupied as he was with a particularly fibrous morsel of parsnip. I continued, "You recall the black grouse that were in fledge when last we walked out in May? Well there's a scolding wee male has found his voice and staked his claim in the shrubbery on the east moor." This brought a smile to his lips—a reply more satisfying than words, and more nourishing than the food which I scarcely touched.

I went to bed hungry but happy.

In his study, Lord Henry sits, elbows on his desk either side of a sheet of notepaper, his forehead resting on the heels of his hands. He closes his fists and grinds his knuckles into his brow. He raises his head, puts pen to paper and writes.

13

NEXT MORNING I ROSE and rang immediately. "Take that away and fetch my clothes." For the monstrosity was still there, fully dressed once more as though by elves in the night.

Cruikshank had the cheek—thin though it was—to shake her head, *No*, and I really was on the point of striking her when Knox entered. *Breviter*: I was to repeat the sumptuary ordeal.

"But why?!"

"'Tis your father's particular wish, Miss Charlotte."

"What, again?"

She nodded.

"Blast my aunt."

Knox felt or feigned shock. And drawing out the syllables for maximum reproach, "Now, now, for shame, Miss Bell, what with your aunt a poor invalid."

An image arose of a frail and kindly maiden lady of years something in advance of Knox's—the latter being patently illogical, since I knew Knoxy to have been both Father's and Aunt's nurse.

I squared my chin and submitted once more to the manifold procedure of attaching hoop to cage to bustle to camisole to corset like a suspension bridge—and I had rather build a bridge than wear one. Not to mention the layers of underlinens (those split drawers!)—oh, to be a laddy rather than a lady. Thus, the time-devouring construction of my "toilette."

By the time I was dressed, Father had long since retired to bed, raising the question of why I must remain thus banded and plumed like a flightless bird.

Seneca said, "Leisure without learning is death," and indeed I wandered the house like a ghost. Perhaps I was dead and did not know it—Knox had explained thus the restless wanderings of my dead brother. At some point in the course of that vapid afternoon I found myself, like a wakened somnambulist, stranded midway along the portrait gallery with no clear sense of how I'd got there. I "woke" to find myself staring into the blank frame of the would-be Thirteenth Baron Bell. The Blighted Heir.

"Father, I presume you shall not require of me this raiment on a daily basis?"

"Hm?" He had risen at my entry to the dining room. "Yes, quite."

I stumbled—not on my hem, but at the gap between the lightness of his tone and the enormity of his words. "But Father, why?"

He pushed in my chair. "I daresay, my dear, you shall be glad of it."

"When shall I, Father?"

"All in good time, my own."

Cruikshank came and went.

"Father?"

He turned and looked at me. "Hm?"

Against all logic, Reader, was my discomfiting impression that Father was looking at someone else—even as his eyes met mine. And within me arose an uncanny question: *Who is Father looking at?*

Thus it was that, as though by a spell, there at the dining table I was robbed of speech. And so as not to draw attention to my sudden deficit, I smiled.

He smiled back . . . at the someone else.

Day after day I rose to the awareness that this was no dream. The phantom had taken up residence in my chamber. Day after day it was methodically stripped until it stood, headless, limbless, impaled on its post, and I stood swathed in its stead.

And every evening Father's study door stood closed, and I mounted the stairs, past my gloating brother and his adoring mother—*gloating*, aye, for had he lived he would have faced no more irksome prospect than a stiff collar.

"Knoxy," I moaned, "what have I done?"

"Och Miss Charlotte, you've done nowt wrong."

"Why does Father shun me?"

"He does no such thing."

"He does! He treats me as a stranger."

"He treats you like a lady."

". . . So that's it."

"What?"

"My crime."

"What crime?"

"Being born a girl."

"'Twas no crime—"

"I wish I had died instead of Charles. Everyone would be happier."

"Niver say it." And she hugged me hard.

~◔

Fayne House
June 3, 1873

Dear Taffy,
I have a son. The future Eighteenth Baron, Lord Bell of the DC de Fayne.
Little Charles Bell. And when he is big and strong enough, we will come
home to Boston and I will show him his namesake River and we shall feed
the ducks together, I with my Charlie and you with your darling little Tess.
I shall write again soon, but I feel my milk "coming down"! Glory be!

Love and kisses!!!!
Your Mae

~◔

The days ran one into another like a ruined watercolour. Nothing happened. I lie: on a Tuesday (unless it was a Wednesday) Knox presented
me with a square of linen, a wooden frame, a needle and coloured thread.
"'Tis a sampler, Miss Charlotte."

"A sample of what?"

On a Thursday (unless it was Saturday) Knox brought to my chamber
a jar of heather and thistles. "Make out like as if they be roses and such
and arrange them into a bonny . . . arrangement."

"I have never seen anything so pointless, take it away at once and
rubbish it!" I hurled it across the room, winging the dressmaker's form
and setting it to trembling on its post.

And on a Monday (?) Nothing at all.

Powerless to resist, I compensated with kicks and complaints, in short
all the temper I would never dream displaying before my father, I rained
upon his servants.

It was the only physical exercise I took.

I breathed little and ate less. Knox took to bringing me "a wee bitty"
at bedtime—in reality, whole meals the which I devoured in my nightshirt, freed from stays. "Was it to your taste, Miss Charlotte?"

"Speak not to me on pain of death."

"As you wish, Miss."

———

Father, on the dwindling occasions when he dined in company with me, persisted in his unsettling formality; nor could I recall the last time Knox had called me "pet." Even Cook bobbed as I swished through the scullery in search of slops for Maisie.

Byrn alone remained unchanged, handing me the milking pail when, finally, I braved the byre. But I was incapable of raising the pail to my lips, never mind forking straw or chasing down piglets, and I did not repeat the dispiriting visit.

I knew that insofar as my new manner of dress was a tangible obstacle, it did not merit the name of suffering. But insofar as it was an intangible obstacle . . . Reader, I suffered. Nor, try as I might, could I work out how I might convert the Obstacle into the Way.

October dawned and the moor loosed hold of its greens and purples in favour of golds and crimsons so dark as to be almost black. Some birds were preparing to depart for the winter, others were bolstering their moorland nests. The sound of the rams clashing heads reached me in my chamber—I glimpsed Cook shoving one good and proper when it bumped her in the yard. She and Cruikshank took empty baskets into the garden and emerged with them laden.

Then it happened again. The lunar disaster referred to by Knox as my "woman's time."

I repaired to a pew in the crypt chapel with a well-intentioned slate of trigonometric functions, but I soon flagged. Beneath me slumbered the Barons Bell in full armour. I rose and gripped the back of the pew before me. I summoned logic: Father was good. The new regimen of apparel was decreed by Father. Therefore it was good. That I could not perceive its good did not change its nature. If I suffered it was because I assented to the impression of suffering. If I assented to the impression of suffering, it was because I was not in accord with Nature. Rather than trotting cheerfully alongside the cart, I had chosen to be dragged behind—in all my finery.

I determined henceforth to trot, if not cheerfully then with dignified indifference; no more to rail against my Fate, nor its emissary, my Father. To do otherwise was unworthy of the barons beneath the floor.

Newly girded, I tapped on the study door that evening and entered, hoping that by drawing near to reminders of my formerly happy estate, I might inure myself to their power to awaken suffering.

Father rose. The lamplight reflected on the lenses of his eyeglasses, and I faltered . . . 'twas all I could do not to run to him, to nestle at his side, to drink in his scent of tweed and tobacco and soap. I stood firm. I seated myself on a low stool and did not approach his desk.

Father resumed his chair and bent over a bit of a swift.

Certain monks took a vow of silence. I would do as much until or unless Father himself should speak to me. I allowed my eyes to rove about the most familiar of rooms, in which I now knew myself to be a guest. Atop the bank of pigeon holes stood our phantastical bird. Propped against its long legs was a letter. "Who is Dr. Chambers?" I asked, instantly reproving myself for being so soon forsworn.

Father looked up sharply. I shrank. "Only . . . you've a letter there, Father, waiting to be posted."

"Ah. Quite. He is, in point of fact, a physician of my acquaintance."

I felt the blood recede from my head. "Father. Are you ill?" And was the sight of me in woman's weeds a dying wish?

"Certainly not," he chuckled, and for a moment I fancied we were back on our old footing. Fear dispelled and I was able to sequence a series of facts to which I failed to remain indifferent: (i) Father knew that I wished above everything to attend the University of Edinburgh and become a physician. (ii) Father had promised to do all within his power to secure my happiness. (iii) Father had penned a letter to an Edinburgh physician.

I watched as he drew a tiny claw from a pot of cedar-wood oil.

I trembled with gratitude.

I did not seek to know more.

Presently, I rose. He rose. "Goodnight, Father."

"Goodnight, my own."

Having been vouchsafed a sign that my prospects were still aligned with my hopes, it behooved me to redouble my efforts to cultivate patience— certainly I would need it as a wayfaring physician. Thus, the very next morning, when Knox cautiously produced another gift from my aunt—a cloth-bound book this time—I did not immediately demand it be binned.

I accepted it with equanimity and perused the title: *The Young Ladies'
Treasure Book*. I harboured a keen interest in treasure, as the Reader
knows, especially of the buried variety. I sat up in bed and opened it.

Inscribed upon the flyleaf in a spidery hand, *For my niece, the Honourable Charlotte Bell, from her devoted aunt, the Honourable Clarissa Bell*.
The dear blameless invalid.

I read aloud: "'A disused chiffonier may be made over into a vessel
for potted ferns.'" My brow ruffled. Knox stepped back. I turned a page
at random.

"'Reliably fill the gap in a whatnot case with a hand-embroidered
pincushion beribboned with cast-offs from last spring's bonnet.' Hmm."

"Miss . . . ?"

"'A gift of a glass oddments bowl inverted over a scene of faux furze
salvaged from Christmas ornaments is never amiss.' Well, well."

Knox flinched. I regarded her with terrible serenity and said, "I for
one should never think it amiss. How kind is Aunt." I returned to the
book, determined to mortify my intellect.

I glanced up to see Knox exchange a doubtful look with Cruikshank,
who trembled afresh.

When it came time to dress and have my hair mangled into a knot at
my nape, I kept my elbows to myself and stood straight as a soldier; when
Knox held out the split drawers I kept mum and did not step both feet
into one leg. I carried the fatuous book about with me all through the
day like a talisman . . . or scourge.

Later, when Knox brought me my customary meal in bed, I ate slowly.
"Thank you, Knox. That was most satisfactory."

"Are you feeling poorly, pet?"

I smiled beatifically. She felt my forehead. "I don't know but what you
ought stay abed tomorrow."

"Oh but Knoxy, not for anything would I lose out on a single day in
the suitable dress."

She narrowed her eyes. "You needn't try pulling the wool over my
eyes, Miss Charlotte, I know you hate the dress."

"I do not hate it, Knox. It is merely an unpreferred indifferent."
I closed my eyes and murmured, "Draw my curtains before you leave,
if you please, Knoxy. I'd not court a draft."

——

"Your Lordship."

Mrs. Knox has entered his study empty-handed, itself enough to cause His Lordship to have looked up in alarm, for absent tea and victuals there can only be news and news is rarely good. "What is it?"

"'Tis Miss Charlotte—"

He drops his forehead to his fingers. She hastens to add, "She's well, My Lord, but she is . . ."

"What?"

"She is not herself, Your Lordship, the lass is . . ."

"Rebellious is she? One can hardly blame her."

"That's just it, Your Lordship, she's . . . meek. Says she prefers to be different, or some such—"

"'Different'?" he asks warily, "In what way . . . 'different'? You don't mean—"

"No such, Your Lordship, different only in the way of not minding what she eats nor wears nor anything."

"I see. She seeks the consolation of philosophy. Quite right." His brow clears with a sigh as he returns to *The Transactions of the Royal Midlothian Ornithological Society*. But a moment later looks up. The old woman is still there.

"'Tisnae working, Your Lordship. She's no consoled."

His eyes narrow.

"Begging Your Lordship's pardon," she clasps her hands and addresses the carpet, "there be a limit to what I can teach the lass in the way of—in the ways of a lady. She wants example, sir."

"I shall engage a governess, ought to have done so immediately of course, I'll write to my sister." And he reaches for his pen.

"I'm a foolish old woman, Lord Henry, but I don't know as Miss Charlotte might take unkindly to such a personage."

". . . You're right, dash it." His shoulders sag. "What am I to do?"

"Och the lassie needs a friend is all, My Lord."

"She has friends. She has me, there is her aunt in Edinburgh, why if memory serves we've a distant cousin, a colonial governor in the Far East—"

"A friend, My Lord, like—" She swallows and continues, "A friend in the American sense."

His mouth becomes a line. Mrs. Knox adds gamely, "Someone of her own age. And sex."

At length, he nods. "Where are we to obtain such a one? I'll ask Clarissa." He reaches once more for his pen.

"There is someone nearer to hand, Your Lordship."

14

I SUSTAINED MY STOIC demeanour with the result that by week's end I could be found in various reaches of the house in an attitude of insensibility, having attained a trance of indifference.

Knox sought me out and roused me with an unprecedented announcement: we were to receive guests for tea.

I submitted willingly to the frockery, keen to make a favourable impression upon my new tutor—for so the guest must be—and to be a credit to Father, who himself was to rise early for the occasion. The plural, "guests," gave me pause, then a frisson as I reflected it might be Dr. Chambers himself, perhaps in company with his wife, or—better— a nursing sister, fresh from the Crimea.

Knox dashed these hopes whilst scraping my hair into a topknot. "You shall at last meet the daughter of Reverend and Mrs. Haas."

"What? Who? Why?"

She wittered on. Something about the vicarage in Aberfoyle-on-Feyn and "Miss Haas is almost of an age with you and nothing's to stop you becoming bosom friends."

I slouched as far as the dress would permit, and allowed my eyes to roll heavenward. "Based on what shall this bond burgeon in our respective thoracic cavities, pray tell? The near concordance of years spent on Earth? The random selection of sex?"

I said it to confound her but she inquired gently, "Has it started up again then, your woman's time?"

"No!"

I tried to regain my state of indifference but was betrayed by curiosity which, like a ball that's been held under water, sprang up with redoubled force. Thus I pumped my old nurse for intelligence, and she schooled me in the finer points of polite intercourse, summed up as follows: (1) Draw out one's guest on any suitable subject likely to be of interest to them. (2) Do not linger on any single subject. (3) Do not wax overly familiar, whether via statement or question such as, "To what do you owe that scar above your eye?" (Here I inquired, "She has a scar? What's it from?" "She hasn't," replied Knox, "Leastways not so far as I know." "Then why say it?") (4) Do not gorge at tea, "a lady eats like a bird." (As though gorging were possible in a corset!) Thus did my nurse exhaust her store of knowledge touching refined society. This was followed by a hasty tutorial in the kitchen on the proper taking of tea, along with the alarming news that I was to "pour."

Gone were the sheets, down were the carpets and blazing was the hearth in the drawing room which, fairy-tale-like, appeared to have awakened from a twelve-year slumber. It fairly shone like the sun, what with its yellow walls and silk-upholstered furnishings in white and gold.

I arranged myself in a window seat with Bewick's *A History of British Birds* resting open on my knee, determined I should be discovered absorbed and, yes, indifferent. I watched at a gap in the curtains as, through a veil of rain, our heavy black carriage materialized, drawn by Hector and Achilles with Byrn spectrally hooded at the reins. It rolled up to the portico and its door opened, disgorging a gentleman, a lady, then a girl—the latter clutched a drooping nosegay to her chest.

I had no experience of females of my own vintage—up 'til that moment I would have been less surprised to meet a unicorn on the moor than a girl at my door. Her lean frame and downcast gaze, her soggy cloak like the dull plumage of a bog-sparrow, dampened my curiosity. Nonetheless, I slipped from my window seat, rustled to the doorway and, keeping to one side, listened to the voices echoing in the entry hall. Father was speaking in a heightened version of that mode in which he had of late addressed me. "Mrs. Haas, how do you do?" Though I could not make out the lady's words in reply, her tones reached me like the chiming of crystal bells—up to then all I knew of females and their native calls were Knox, Cook and Cruikshank: sturdy, strident and squeaky. The sweet timbre of this lady's voice touched a chord within me like a fragment of forgotten music, and in that instant not only did I crave to hear the song in its entirety, I marvelled I had survived so long in a realm parched of those notes. (I acknowledge the latter is fanciful, but the Reader may thereby rest reassured I report faithfully all memories and impressions, even when they minify my claim to scientific observation.)

"Reverend Haas," I heard Father say in airy tones, "you are welcome, sir, at Fayne, I thank you for venturing out on a dreich day such as this. Ah, and Miss Haas, I am delighted to make your acquaintance. If you will permit me . . ."

Alerted by footsteps, I hastened as best I could back to the window seat where I opened the book at random in time to look up with an absent air from an engraving of the female merlin, as the guests entered the drawing room.

"Charlotte, my dear, may I present Reverend Haas, Mrs. Haas and Miss Haas." I rose. Father continued, "Reverend Haas, Mrs. Haas, Miss Haas, allow me to present my daughter, Miss Bell."

I extended my hand in keeping with Knox's instructions, "How do you do, Mrs. Haas." She was a pretty creature with a crown of pincurls and a nervous smile. She curtsied. "Miss Bell," she trilled—and stifled a cry, touching the back of her hand to her lips. "Forgive me, only you do so resemble your mother."

I was shocked.

Father smiled and remarked with ease, "I am glad you see it too, Mrs. Haas."

Father turned now to Reverend Haas and I offered my hand, over which that gentleman bowed with—mercifully—no ejaculation of either joy or sorrow. A man of unprepossessing appearance, he was framed with a paucity of particulars such that, even with his head on, he might have served as a tailor's form.

As for Miss Haas, she resembled her mother not at all. Her thin face was smattered with freckles and framed by pale ringlets that drooped along with her proffered nosegay. She had light blue eyes (both eyebrows were noticeably free of any scar) and her scalp showed pink and straining where the hair was quilted in sections to feed the ringlets—as I could not help but observe, she being a head my inferior in height.

I extended my hand and spoke the words which I had rehearsed that morning with Knox. "I am pleased to make your acquaintance, Miss Haas."

She curtsied, and in a voice as dry as her expression, replied, "And I yours, Miss Bell."

I decided I'd best hate her first.

"I hope you shall be great friends," warbled Mrs. Haas.

The words hung in the air and even I recognized them as somehow untoward. ("Familiar," Knox would humph later as she poured my bath.)

"Well well," said Reverend Haas approvingly.

"Quite," added Father.

I would soon learn that much of adult conversation consists of this verbal bunting—no, less useful than bunting. Ballast? Again, too useful. Dross.

Knox wheeled in the tea tray. Tinkling upon it was the bone china service adorned with daffodils, upon which I had set eyes for the first time that morning ("'Twas your mother's") when I was pressed into a practice round involving water, about which the less said the better.

I held my breath. I grasped the dainty handle of the shapely china pot—I would need a steadier hand if I aimed to be a surgeon!—and poured a quaking stream of amber liquid into a translucent cup which I then passed, rattling on its saucer, to Mrs. Haas. I repeated the ordeal thrice more and would gladly have eschewed pouring one for myself but that Knox shot me a dark look and I completed the ceremony. I was sweating ("Horses sweat, ladies glow") and longing for an earthenware mug. I dried my palms on my skirt. Miss Haas's hands were folded primly in her lap; they were likewise freckled.

"And how are your studies progressing, Miss Haas?" asked my father.

"Very well, I thank Your Lordship."

"You go to school?" I blurted.

"I do, Miss Bell," she replied.

"You are fortunate."

"Am I?"

Mrs. Haas tittered in reproach. "Gwendolyn plays the pianoforte and reads French."

"At the same time?" I inquired, my interest piqued.

Reverend Haas chuckled, but his daughter did not deign to answer my question. The Reverend turned to my father, solemn once more. "As with so much else, we are indebted to Your Lordship for having recommended Gwendolyn to Miss Gourley."

"I trust then the school meets with your approval?"

"Oh the school is a marvel, Lord Henry," gushed Mrs. Haas, "not to mention Miss Gourley herself is a most admirable lady."

"Most admirable," concurred her husband.

More tinkling of china.

"Charlotte," said Father, "perhaps you might show Miss Haas the library."

"What for?" Then quickly, "Certainly, Father. Miss Haas, if you please."

I strode from the drawing room; that is, I made to stride but, forgetful of the swaddlesome skirts, stumbled before moderating my pace.

Miss Haas followed me out and across the hall. I opened the door to my former schoolroom. "There it is," said I, then promptly closed the door. I returned to the drawing room and she followed. With our re-entry, Father broke off mid-sentence—". . . with the return of the northern ptarmigan of course—" I resumed my seat. Silence. Father said, "Charlotte, perhaps Miss Haas would care to see the trophy room."

I turned to Miss Haas. "Miss Haas, would you care to see the trophy room?"

Her face was inscrutable but she replied, "If it please Miss Bell, I should be much obliged."

She followed me out and up the staircase to the landing where I ascended the rightward branch to the west wing. I proceeded to the far end of the gallery where, intent upon emulating Father's gentlemanly manner, I lifted aside the tapestry and bade her precede me. "Within this commodious chamber, Miss Haas, are trophies dating back to the days when wolf, lynx and bear roamed the British Isles. All you see before you, killed by Bells."

I led the way amid silent snarls and frozen lunges, taking care to draw her attention to the plaque at the base of each trophy whence its proper Latin name. "And here we have rather a fine example of *Ursus arctos*, possibly the last brown bear ever to have been bagged on these shores." I glanced over my shoulder and caught her stifling a yawn. I turned on my heel and quitted the chamber, judging she had forfeited the privilege of viewing the rare spot-bellied Scottish wildcat.

Fain would I have left Miss Haas to make her own way back to the drawing room but, constrained as I was to descend cautiously the stairs, she was once more stuck like a burr to my side before I reached the land-ing, where she hung back and I heard her say, "I don't think you look a bit like her."

I turned to see her looking up at the portrait. "You refer, I presume to the Lady Marie Bell, Seventeenth Baroness of the DC de Fayne." I expected she could hardly mistake the asperity of my tone and would therefore check the familiarity of her own.

But she merely tilted her head to one side. "Well . . . perhaps about the jaw."

"I am not in it." I was instantly vexed at myself for encouraging her in this vein.

"Of course you are." Her familiarity now bordering on insolence.

"That is not I, Miss Haas, that is the Honourable Charles Bell, erst-while heir to the Barony of the DC de Fayne, now deceased."

"Of course it is, I'd know him anywhere."

I was struck dumb.

At last she turned to me and, with a nonchalance out of keeping with the outlandishness of her words, said, "We were nursery mates of a sort."

"You . . . knew my brother?"

"If one can claim to 'know' anyone at the age of two. We rolled about together on the grass in back of the house. All fat cheeks and chuckles."

I gaped.

She said, "I was fat then."

I shook my head.

"Difficult to credit, I know."

"How did you come to make his acquaintance?"

Her tone continued matter-of-fact. "Our mothers were friends . . . of a sort. That is, Lady Marie Bell, Seventeenth Baroness of the DC de Fayne, condescended to receive Mrs. Reverend Haas and her whelp. Not much society hereabout, as you may have noticed."

I stood as mute as the figures in the painting. Reader, I knew my brother had been born, lived and died. I knew he had been loved in life, mourned in death and remained as a sort of hush that permeated Fayne—and a spectre that haunted my dreams. But a live chortling baby, "rolling about" in company with this scrap of a girl before me?

"So you haven't noticed?" she said, cocking her head.

"Noticed . . . ?"

"The dearth of society. On account of which I have been inflicted upon you, Miss Bell."

"Seeing as you are so well acquainted with my family, Miss Haas, I wonder you assert that I am in this portrait."

"Why, you'd be right about there of course." And she pointed boldly at my mother's mid-section.

I made to mount the few steps back up to the landing, but succeeded only in ascending the hem of my dress—hitching it in both fists I stomped up and leaned in to look. Compared with the idea that the girl next to me had frolicked with my brother, the notion that I might myself be present in the portrait seemed downright plausible. Was my face concealed by means of a clever *trompe l'oeil* in a fold of my mother's gown? I was peering intently when, in a distinctly sarcastic tone, she said, "I don't mean to say literally, Miss Bell."

She was trifling with me. My inexperience of the society of persons of my own years and sex had unfitted me for survival in their midst; had marked me out as weak, to be pecked, driven over a cliff . . . Well, I had an evolutionary advantage of my own, quite apart from the power and privilege of rank. I drew myself up to my full height, planted my feet, and weighed the merits of pushing her down the stairs.

Presumably she took my meaning for she looked up at me and said, "I beg your pardon, Miss Bell. When I said you were in the picture, what I meant was that of course your Mother was . . . expecting at the time it was painted. So you are, in a sense, there." She pointed again. And we both stared at Lady Marie Bell, Seventeenth Baroness of the DC de Fayne's belly.

"But the abdomen is quite flat," I said, restored to self-mastery in the presence of an inferior whose offence arose from ignorance.

"Aye, even nowadays 'tis counted improper to depict a lady who is . . . big with child." Her mouth twitched.

"'Improper'?"

She nodded.

I was struck that I had never noticed this conspicuous absence; of course the portrait, depicting as it did my brother round about the age of two and thus near the end of his life, ought indeed to depict my mother big with child—big with me. I turned to her. "Why 'improper'?"

"You really have been kept from the world."

"I take umbrage."

"I'm sorry—" She turned, as though to flee.

"Stay."

She obeyed.

"Pray continue, Miss Haas."

"Well . . . 'tis a matter of female modesty. Our gracious queen herself was never seen in public while she was . . . B with C." She bit back her lips. She continued. "And in fact, all her ladies-in-waiting had to strap on padded stomachers so they'd look B with C too."

I wrestled with the logic. Finally, I said, "Rum word, 'stomacher.'"

She burst out laughing. I waited. I offered her my handkerchief, with which she dried her eyes.

"Do you remember him?"

"Who?"

"My brother."

She thought for a moment. "Yes."

"What was he like?"

"He was merry."

"Merry?"

"Aye. Mother says no matter how I poked and pinched, he laughed."

"So he was . . . much as he appears in the portrait?"

"The spit and image—begging pardon, that is I believe the portrait to be a fair likeness of your brother, the Honourable Charles Bell, Miss Bell." Adding piously, "God rest his soul."

A heavenly smell of baking reached us and I looked down to see Cruikshank crossing the hall with a linen-covered tray.

"Would you care to take refreshment, Miss Haas?"

"Yes, please, I'm starving." Thin though she was, I took this to be an exaggeration.

Miss Haas descended the stairs trippingly without actually tripping. How much, I wondered, did her facility for perambulation owe to the style of her skirt, which fell more or less straight from the waist? And was her want of a hoop crinoline a sign of slender means or a signifier of social inferiority?

Back in the drawing room I endured the sight of my guest enjoying, warm from the oven, a raisin scone with lashings of butter. (Were her stays, too, of a lesser order of tension? Or was she practised in the art of constricted digestion—like a snake swallowing a rabbit?) Amid the clitter-clatter of plates, the adult dross piled up to the point where I felt a sneeze coming on until, all having agreed that rain was wet, trains were rather swifter than horses, and fresh air congenial to the lungs, the Haases took their leave some forty-nine minutes subsequent to their arrival.

That night, Knox ground a wash cloth round my ear whorls. "How was your visit today with Miss Haas?"

"She is common, impudent and frivolous."

"Well you needn't have her back."

"I've invited her for Saturday next."

15

I RE-CONSECRATED MYSELF to the getting of patience (falling short on Thursday evening when I looked in on Father, ostensibly to bring him his slippers, in truth to ascertain whether the letter to Dr. Chambers had been posted—it had not) but was sleepless with anticipation on the eve of Miss Haas's second visit. I watched eagerly as Byrn delivered her, this time in the dog cart. Once shown into the drawing room and seated across from me, however, she was mum.

I rifled about inwardly and laid hold of some dross: "I trust you have passed a satisfactory week at your school, Miss Haas."

"Yes, thank you, Miss Bell."

The earth sped at 67,000 miles per hour, thus we travelled 1,116.66667 miles in silence before: "I trust yours was likewise satisfactory, Miss Bell?"

"It consisted of the usual complement of seven days."

Another 558.333333 miles.

Having formed an impression of Miss Haas as being of a more voluble nature, I surveyed her now as a child might a mechanical toy whose key has been lost. "Miss Haas, would you care to meet Maisie?"

"I should be honoured to meet a friend of yours, Miss Bell. Or is she a relation?"

"She is a sow."

"Ah." She reddened.

"Perhaps a pleasure deferred."

"It is rather wet today."

"It is."

Silence.

I sneezed. I was on the point of turning her out when I recalled, half contrite, my omission of the previous week. "Would you care to see the rare spot-bellied Scottish wildcat?" I rose and, conjuring Father's airy condescension, said, "Do follow me, Miss Haas."

Standing to one side, I indicated the jewel in Fayne's taxidermical crown. "It is estimated there remain but a handful in all of Great Britain."

"How fortunate that your ancestors managed to kill one."

"Quite."

The cat, fangs bared, its spotted belly exposed, black paws poised to pounce upon an unsuspecting stuffed vole—this, my guest gave no more than a glance, her eyes straying back to the fatigued Flemish tapestry, no doubt signalling her desire to be gone through its flap. Surely I was now exempt from showing her my collection of beetles. "I expect you're disappointed."

"Not at all, Miss Bell, the tapestry must have been very fine in its day," and she appeared lost in admiring its faded hounds and horses, its ladies at their harps, "I daresay it could be restored."

"I meant, I expect you would rather my brother were here, showing you about." I was disconcerted to feel myself flush.

"Well, but he wouldn't be showing me about, would he?"

"Why not?"

"Miss Bell, I am already of doubtful . . . utility to you. To him I would be irrelevant."

"But you were playmates."

"The only way our circles might overlap now is if I were to be one day engaged as governess to his children."

"Ugh."

"Much obliged."

"Forgive me, Miss Haas, I simply cannot think of a worse fate."

"Of course you can't," she murmured under her breath.

Curiosity trumped umbrage. "Name one."

"One what?"

"'Worse fate.'"

". . . the Cowgate," she said, unaccountably as an imp in a fairy tale.
"What?"

She did not answer, but continued brusquely, "Your brother would not be here to show me about even if he wished to, Miss Bell, he'd be at school unless . . . He'd be at school."

"Unless what?"

"Unless, well. Unless he were like you."

I fixed her with my gaze. I had refrained from querying her as to the extent to which the landmass of her body was covered in freckles, yet here she was coming near to quizzing me as to my Condition. Familiar indeed. Ruddy cheek! I summoned *sang froid*. "In what respect, 'like' me?"

She flushed to the roots of her freckles. "I'm sure I don't know, begging your pardon, Miss Bell."

"Do you imply I am out of the ordinary?"

"Certainly not, please forget I said anything."

"I'm afraid I cannot."

She glanced about as though in hope of enlisting an ally among the stuffed brutes. "With your permission, Miss Bell, I ought perhaps take my leave—"

"'Miss Bell,'" said I, "'I am already of doubtful utility to you to him I would be irrelevant the only way our circles might overlap is if I were to be one day engaged as governess to his children much obliged of course you can't one what the Cowgate your brother would not be here to show me about in any case even if he wished to Miss Bell he'd be at school unless he'd be at school unless well unless he were like you.'" I drew a breath. "You see, Miss Haas, much as it would please me to oblige a guest, I am quite incapable of forgetting anything." I had thought to flummox her, but succeeded only in frightening her, for she stood before me transfixed as though before a . . . well, something frightful. I formed a smile. This appeared not to assuage her dismay. "Would you care to see the oatcake baked by Flora MacDonald for Bonny Prince Charlie? There's a spot where he nibbled it."

Silence.

"Miss Haas, pray be not discomfited, I possess an overdeveloped mnemonic faculty."

"Crikey." She swallowed. "I suppose we each of us has our . . . quirk."

"What is yours?"

"Mine is an unfortunate tendency to speak in advance of thinking."

"I concur."

"How pleasant to know we see eye to eye on something."

"Are you freckled in your entirety?"

She blushed, compressed her lower lip and I perceived I had wounded her.

"I don't mind your freckles."

"I do."

"What can't be cured must be endured."

"With compliments like that . . ."

"It was not a compliment, it was a fact."

"I feel so much better now."

"Were you unwell?"

She stared. Sighed.

I said, "Do you like oatcakes? Fresh ones, that is."

"I prefer madeleines."

"What are they?"

"French biscuits. I shall live on them when I move to Paris."

"When are you to remove to Paris?" I did not recall Father having mentioned the need for a new vicar at St. Foy.

"As soon as ever I can scrape together the price of passage and a month's rent at the top of a house."

"Why the top?"

"The light, of course."

"Of course." She might as well have been speaking the lost language of Norn, but I bid her, "Please continue, Miss Haas."

She did. And for the first time it occurred to me that intriguing specimens are not to be found exclusively out of doors, behind glass, stuffed and mounted or beneath a lens. Indeed, I suspected Miss Haas was an entire branch of learning.

Onto the scullery table, Cook plunked a griddle of hot, pliant bannocks and Miss Haas scarcely paused for breath as, between bites, she described a life of privation and pleasure in a light-drenched "loft" where she would ply her art on stretched canvases until nightfall saw her gallivanting with her fellow "Bohemians," spouting poetry and quaffing wine along the Champs Élysées. She spoke of a "demi-monde" devoted to elongated loaves of bread and, of course, madeleines. Of "taking a lover."

"Do I shock you?"

"Oh yes." For I had determined to be agreeable, never more to see the look of fear in her eye. Thus she sketched in words the chiaroscuro of the "*rive gauche*"; the bold colours of the "Folies Bergère"; the pastels of "*les jardins*"; all of which she would capture with charcoal and paint.

"You do not laugh at me," she said with her mouth full.

"Am I remiss in failing to apprehend humour?"

She smiled. "*Au contraire*. You are the first person who has listened to my plans and neither ridiculed nor chided."

"Why might I do either?"

"For one thing, I 'possess ambition in advance of my pecuniary means.' For another, I'm a lass."

"The first admits of remedy. The second is an impediment in the mind only."

"In the body, more like." She seized a third oatcake. "Are you not hungry?"

"I am famished."

"Then why not eat?"

"My garments prevent me."

"Oh I can fix that." She demurred. "That is, if you will permit me, Miss Bell."

I rose and she set to work on my bodice in back where the line of hooks-and-eyes overlay my spine. Her nimble—and cold!—fingers found the laces and in a trice I felt a seismic relief as the stays were loosed . . . but not entirely. She retied my corset tightly enough to permit re-closure of the bodice but not so tightly as to prevent my taking nourishment. I resumed my chair, near giddy. "Treacle, I think, Cook."

Knox was in the process of dismantling my toilette as I stood before the glass. A layer of clothing dropped about my feet. She set to work on my stays. "They've come loose, so they have."

"Knoxy, what is the Cowgate?"

She knit her brows. "'Tis a place in Edinburgh."

"What sort of place?"

"Why . . . 'tis a street with a great gate where livestock are driven on market day."

"Unsuitable for ladies then." I pictured a bevy of bonneted females mired in manure as cattle streamed past. I chuckled.

"Most unsuitable," she averred, adding sharply, "Who's been talking of the Cowgate?"

"I read of it. In an atlas." My first lie.

"Into bed now, lamby."

I justified it thusly: According to Aristotle, Friendship was a relation superior to that 'twixt master and servant. I had lied to Knoxy lest she bar Gwendolyn Haas from future visits. Did that mean Gwendolyn was my . . . friendolyn?

"What's funny, pet?"

"Nowt." My second lie . . .

"Goodnight, pet."

16

THE FOLLOWING SATURDAY, mindful of her interest in painting, I offered to show Miss Haas the portrait gallery on the third floor. She trotted up the stairs as if she were in leggings, not skirts. At the top, she turned to wait. "Are you . . . ?"

"Am I what?"

"Only you stumble a good deal, so I wondered if . . . nothing."

"Out with it. I shan't take umbrage."

"Are you lame?"

"How dare you?"

"I'm sorry."

Abashed, I replied, ". . . 'Tis the garments trip me up."

"I see. Um. Why've they got you in a cage?"

I had no rejoinder.

"Forgive me, Miss Bell, only, cages and hoops are hopelessly out of fashion."

"I am indifferent to the vicissitudes of fashion."

"The vissict . . . vivisicti—what?"

"Trifling changes."

"I couldn't agree more, but some changes are to the good, *n'est-ce pas?*"

I looked down at my spherical lower half. I could not see my feet. "My aunt, the Honourable Clarissa Bell, sends me these clothes," I mumbled, adding, "She is an invalid."

"That's no excuse for poor taste," she said tartly, then, "I'm sorry!"

"I shall overlook the offence. For the present."

Hiking my skirts, I pressed on up and led the way to the gallery where I slow-marched with due solemnity between the ranks. "Here, in ascending order, are pictured the Barons Bell . . ." I was careful to give ample time to each portrait. ". . . We come now to Lord Bell, Sixth Baron of the DC de Fayne, beheaded by Lancastrians, and next to him his son, Lord Bell, Seventh Baron of the DC de Fayne, beheaded by Plantagenets—"

"So they're all your relations."

"They are my lineage."

"On your father's side."

"Of course."

"What about your mother's lineage?"

"She hadn't got one. She was American."

"Everyone's got a lineage."

"On the contrary. Everyone has forebears."

"Well then?"

"'Corcoran.' Boston."

"Irish, then."

"American," I corrected her, and carried on until we came to the blank portrait—"And here, commemorated *in absentia*, is the would-be Thirteenth Baron. Known as the 'Blighted Heir,' for reasons long forgotten. Which brings us to the Fourteenth—"

"I thought it was because he had a tail."

I froze. "Why would you say such a thing?"

"Oh. Only, it's a legend. I thought everyone knew it."

"I do not know it."

"I'm sorry, Miss Bell."

"Tell it me."

"Well, that's it really. Blighter was born with a tail and got banished. It's just an old story. I heard it in the village."

"What else have you heard? In the village?"

". . . Nothing."

"Do they say I have a tail?"

"What, no! . . . That is, no one believes it."

It felt like a blow to the stomach. But at least now I knew the origin of Murdoch's idiotic question.

"Pay it no mind," she hastened to add, "folk make up silly stories what with your being a shut-in is all."

"'Shut-in'? I am forever out of doors! Leastways I used to be."

"But Miss Bell, even my parents had ne'er laid eyes on you. I was prepared to meet—well at the very least, an invalid."

"I am no such."

"Then why are you confined to the estate?"

". . . I have a Condition."

"What kind of condition?"

"I am delicate."

"You don't look delicate."

"Neither do horses, but they are brought down by moles."

"Are you a bleeder?"

"You refer to the monthly function."

"Ha—No, I'm talking of a condition that afflicts members of the royal family."

"Germanic upstarts, in no wise equal in pedigree to the Bells of Fayne."

"'Course not."

"Which brings us to the Fourteenth Baron—"

"What's up there?" She pointed to the ceiling.

"The upper floors."

"You don't say."

"I just did."

She laughed. I waited, as one waits to see what a pine marten might do next when spied in the open. She composed herself and said, "Might I see the upper floors, Miss Bell?"

"Little enough to see. Although Bonny Prince Charlie is said to have spent a night secreted in a false-bottom bed, the while the Duke of Cumberland feasted and caroused below with the pursuivants."

"Aye, show me that, please."

"I may not."

"Why?"

"It is in Mrs. Knox's chamber."

"Have you at least got an attic?"

"Of course we have."

"Might I see it?"

"Whatever for?"

"Have you got a madwoman locked up there?"

"Certainly not. What an idea."

"I'm joking."

"Ah."

"Do you not know *Jane Eyre*?"

"I know you and Murdoch Mungo. There be the antipodes of my social acquaintance."

"'Jane Eyre' is the title of a novel. You do read novels."

"I do not." I cleared my throat. "With the exception of Sir Walter Scott's, which are more historical than fanciful and therefore of some utility." I blushed, knowing my keenness resided at least as much in their scenes of fervid attachment and moonlit ruins. "I have them by heart if you care to—"

"What's on the floor below us?"

"The guest wing."

"I thought you hadn't ever any guests."

"We seldom have guests. Unless one counts my tutor."

"You have a tutor?"

"I had a tutor."

Her amazement gratified me, but rather than quiz me as to what I had learned (the which I was ready to impart), she asked, "What did he look like?"

". . . Why, like a man."

She giggled and gazed at me expectantly. I did my best to satisfy my guest's curiosity. "Tall. Lean. Hair, dark. Eyes, likewise."

"Aye, but was he handsome?" She drew out the last word.

"I really couldn't say."

"Features regular? Symmetrical?"

"Quite symmetrical."

"Handsome." She smiled knowingly. "And what was his name?"

"He shall not be named," I replied curtly. Then, softening my tone lest I frighten her, "He departed under a cloud."

"Oh dear. Why?" And lowering her voice, although we were quite alone in the gallery, "Did he try it on with you?"

"Try what on?"

"Rector Grushen tried it on with me but I went taut as catgut and he called me a minx and never tried it on again. Did he show you his hideous member?"

"His . . . Member of Parliament?"

Miss Haas doubled over. "Oh, *je vais me pisser!*"

I waited for her to compose herself. "Would you care to see my collection of beetles? It is rather fine, if I do—"

"Might I see his room?"

"'Tis an ordinary bedchamber."

Noblesse oblige, however, so I conducted her to the guest wing via a shortcut through a service door, down the narrow stairs, out into the corridor and along to the chamber of He Who Must Not Be Named. I pressed the latch, pushed open the door and stood aside, for I had no intention of setting foot on sullied ground. Moreover, there was naught to see, the furniture being dust-sheeted—on second thought: "Of note is the coffered ceiling wherein a scene of the execution of Robert the Bruce."

"Crikey, it's a mausoleum. Remind me to be buried here when I die. I don't suppose it's been redecorated since the snakes were driven from Ireland."

"In fact it was freshened when Oliver Cromwell billeted here."

She tested the bed. "Hmm. It's actually quite soft."

"We are aristocrats, not anchorites. I say, are you sleepy?" For she had lain face-down and now drew a great breath.

"Mmm, I like the smell of man."

"I have no rejoinder."

She rolled onto her back with her hands folded behind her head, legs crossed at the ankles. "Are you joking?"

"I rarely jest."

"No offence, only most people would say 'I have no *reply*'"—why do you choose the least common word?"

"It is the more accurate, therefore the less recondite."

"'Recondite'?"

"It means—"

"I know what it means, I attend school."

"Then have a care for those of us debarred from that *locus eruditionis*." She looked blank.

"I was 'joking' that time."

"Oh. Hah." She ground her cheek against the mattress. "There. Now it smells of woman."

"Would you care to see the crypt chapel?" But she remained, positively lolling. "Come, Galapagos," I urged.

"What did you call me?"

"Blue-footed booby, could you be any slower?" I held the door for her and closed it after us. "Along with its singular morphology, the blue-footed booby displays no fear. Having evolved in the Galapagos without predators, it is incapable of recognizing one. Happily for it, the first human it encountered was the ship's naturalist and not its cook."

The bell tolled for luncheon.

We spread our picnic in the window seat of the drawing room whence I had, only two weeks ago, first spied Miss Haas. She had the physique of a filly and the appetite of a horse. I had prevailed upon Knox to back off my stays and so was able to keep pace as we tucked into large portions of shepherd's pie, followed by scones stuck with currants and slathered with gooseberry preserve and quantities of clabbered cream courtesy of Gossamer.

"Knox says a lady eats like a bird."

"Aye, an eagle!"

"Would you care for the last scone, Miss Haas?"

"Shall we go halves?"

"Certainly, Miss Haas."

"Please. Might you call me Gwendolyn?"

With the solemnity due the consecration of a sword, I said, "Very well . . . Gwendolyn." I hesitated. Then, "And you may call me Miss Charlotte." Something in her smile inspired confidence, and there in the alcove of the window, artfully draped long ago by my mother—perhaps in anticipation of just such confidences, I said, "My mother died abroad, in childbed . . . of me. My father, having buried his wife and son in foreign soil, feared lest he lose me to my Condition. He took care to shield me from harm in hopes I might outgrow it." I dropped my voice. "Your presence here, along with your parents' and Mr.—my former tutor's—suggests Father believes I have outgrown it. But while it may end happily, it is rooted in grief. And is therefore not spoken of."

"I apologize for bringing up a painful subject."

"Oh it is not painful to me, Miss Haas—that is, Gwendolyn. You see I live in the midst of pain, but feel it not myself. Rather, it is a presence in this house, a . . . a sort of . . ."

"A sort of hush."

I regarded her. "Precisely."

"Where abroad?"

"Why, the Alps."

"Which Alp? There are several."

"I don't know." No sooner was I taken aback by the fact that I did not know, than it broke in upon me that I had not known I did not know. Thus did I come face to face with Socrates's Wisdom. What else, I wondered, did I not know I did not know?

She heaped cream on her share of the scone, saying, "I'm always ravenous when I've got the curse."

"What curse?" I immediately thought of Byrn, for if anyone could lift a curse—

"The curse of Eve."

"You refer to the loss of man's ability to converse with animals?"

A spray of tea shot from her nostrils, and she laughed outright. "Forgive me, only 'curse' is schoolgirl slang."

"'Slang'?"

"Oh, um, vulgar speech."

"Vulgar speech with reference to what?"

"Oh dear, well, the monthly function."

". . . Ah."

"Aye."

"What's Eve got to do with the menarche?"

"The what? Sounds like a butterfly."

I laughed, aspirated a crumb and set to coughing. Miss Haas thumped me on the back and immediately apologized. "Not at all," said I, "We can't have Knox bustling in, worried I'm getting chesty."

She said gravely, "Rum word, 'chesty.'"

We succumbed to gales of laughter, in the throes of which I could not have explained why.

"Knox, where was I born?"

I had insisted upon brushing my own hair but she was hovering. "Why, abroad of course, pet."

"Where abroad?"

"In the Alps."

"Which Alp? There are several."

She turned away and shook out my quilt. "Blessed if I remember, what does it matter?"

"I shall ask Father."

"You mustnae—"

"I know." I sighed. But I was nettled.

On the Eve of Samhain I assisted Byrn in making fast the byre 'gainst Faery Folk who were said to walk with the ghosts of those who know not they are dead. I pulled to my curtains and quaked lest the ghost of Charles be abroad with the spooks but he shunned their company and mine, and first of November dawned grey and uneventful as I commenced to count the days until the weekend.

17

ON SATURDAY, Gwendolyn Haas brought her sewing kit and set about turning up the hem of my dress enough that, so long as I did not positively sprint, I should seldom trip. I stood on a stool in the drawing room and held the pincushion whilst she crouched.

"Gwendolyn, tell me about the Cowgate."

"'Tis a dodgy haunt in Auld Reekie."

"I understood none of what you just said."

"Cowgate is a questionable quarter of Edinburgh's Old Town, Miss Charlotte."

"Why 'questionable'? Wait, why 'Auld Reekie'?"

"For that folk would empty their filth pots from the upper windows onto the streets below."

"No!"

"'Gardyloo!'—then . . . *splat*. Look out below."

"Phaugh! I do hope that's nowhere near the university."

"The university's in the thick of it."

"Crikey."

"Not to worry, Miss Charlotte, 'tis a thing of the past. For the most part."

"I should hope so, Gwendolyn. The University of Edinburgh is my future alma mater."

"Ha-ha."

"I jest not."

"Oh—of course not."

"My tutor was preparing me to sit the entrance, and Father is in search of a new invigilator."

"I understood . . . some of what you just said."

"Why is Cowgate 'dodgy'?"

"For that 'tis the haunt of—it is where fallen women go."

"Fallen . . . how?"

"Fallen in the sense of . . . loose."

"I should give anything to be once more loose."

Her staccato laughter struck me as the aural equivalent of her freckles. "Forgive me, Miss—"

"Call me Charlotte, dash it."

She sobered instantly. "Really? You wish me to call you . . . Charlotte?"

"It is my name. One of them, at any rate."

"Very well." She gazed up at me. "Charlotte." And turned pink to the roots of her white-blond hair.

"Do continue, Gwendolyn."

She said shyly, "My friends call me Gwen."

I savoured the Aristotelean moment. "Gwen."

She beamed and carried on stitching. "Well, to put it bluntly, 'loose woman' is a polite term for a harlot."

"'Harlot.' The gutted fillet of my own name as 'twere. What does it mean?"

"It means . . . the opposite of a lady."

"A gentleman?"

She stifled laughter. "No, no, women only are harlots. Men are cads and bounders." She explained patiently, "The sort of men who trifle with a woman's affections. Men who love you and leave you."

To this latter, I did not trust myself to reply, and was relieved she remained intent upon my hem, tying off the last stitch. "Here, give that a go," she said, standing up.

I hopped from the stool and took an unstumbling turn about the room. "By Jove, that's better!" And on impulse, "Gwen. Have you ever angled for trout? Come, I'll teach you. We'll take a hamper for the hike across the moor."

"I'd love to, Miss—that is, Charlotte, but I—I don't know that I'm dressed for—"

"I've an extra pair of greased Wellies—"

"Please don't make me!"

"You're not . . . frightened?"

"I'm frightened of spoiling my frock and—oh dear, traipsing is so tiresome especially across a moor. I'm much happier indoors. You're taking umbrage."

"I am not, truly."

"Your nostrils flared just now."

I bid her gently, "Look out the window, Gwen. What do you see?"

We gazed out upon the moor through the rain, and I felt my breast swell with a love that was all the more tender for having been bruised by misplaced scorn. Let the world call her bleak, I loved her best in her November garb, the sky a lighter shade of ground, the horizon a charcoal smudge.

"Well. I see a good deal of grey."

"There is much to be said for grey. It is the colour of our brain matter."

"Ugh."

"And 'tisn't always grey, you know."

"Oh I know, there's the lovely heather and so on in summer, but . . . Charlotte, it's so lonely and . . . desolate."

"Gwennie, it is thronging with life. It is home to birds, mammals, lizards, amphibians, reptiles, insects, arachnids and, oh, transitional species that defy man's bid to divide and define, for as much as Nature abhors a vacuum, so too does she despise a straight line. Witness flowers that devour flies; mushrooms that spring from roots which rival the networks of telegraphic cables. The mosses, Gwennie, preserve enough water to float an ark. The moor is a great breathing, eating, living library; in its volumes we learn that nothing disappears, everything will out in some form or other . . ." Gwen's voice brought me back.

"Charlotte, would you consent to sit to me?"

I seated myself obligingly in the window.

"For a portrait," she said.

"We found a cloak. My tutor and I."

"Where? Out there?"

I nodded.

"Do you know whose it was?"

"A madwoman's."

She shivered delightedly. "What became of her?"

"They pulled her out and put her away."

"Who was she?"

I shrugged.

"I'll ask my mother, she's a right Nosy Parker."

"Is Parker her maiden name?"

"I think it may be time you saw something of the world, Charlotte Bell."

"I've seen worlds through a microscope, I've seen stars through a—"

"Are you going to spend the rest of your days peering at life through glass?"

Just then, Cruikshank wheeled in the tea cart and we fell to. "All it wants is cocoa," said Gwen, helping us both to masses of clabber.

"What is cocoa?"

"No!" she gasped, fairly flinging herself back against the cushions. "Do you mean to say you've never tasted cocoa?"

"I should not otherwise have requested a definition."

"Surely you know chocolate."

"I do not."

"Oh dear. Where to begin. Well . . . it is a dark brown substance, indescribably delicious, and when you drink it hot it is called cocoa. Maeve and I are devoted to it—"

"Maeve—?"

"Sorry, schoolmate of mine."

"Tell me, what is school like?"

Gwendolyn duly described "Miss Gourley and Miss Mellor's School for Girls" situated in "a curving wee street called Circus Lane," the building itself a former cigar factory owned by Miss Mellor's late father. "It still smells of tobacco." Instead of describing the syllabus, however, she regaled me with tales of school life, which seemed one long round of larks and reiving cakes from the kitchen at midnight in company with girls called Maeve and Aggie and Hortense, "the happy hoydens"; of slipping out their bedroom window down the wisteria vine; of bathing "nude" in St. Margaret's Loch by moonlight; of dissolving in mirth over the sentimental foibles of the head teacher, Miss Prunella Mellor— "Miss Mellor! Are you with me? *Miss Smeller*!"

"What? Oh yes, I'm with you now, ha-ha!"

"She's in love with the Angel of Cowgate."

"Is that an allegorical figure?"

"She is no less a personage than the foundress of our school, the admirable Miss Gourley."

"I thought you said only fallen women wound up in Cowgate."

"And who is more in need of an angel?"

To my mind's eye arose the image of *Winged Victory* bending to scoop a fallen woman from the reeking cobblestones.

"She does sound admirable."

"Worse luck, me."

"Why?"

Gwen groaned. "Miss Gourley thinks I have 'tremendous potential.' She's a blue-stocking of course, the lot of them are."

"What is a 'blue-stocking'?"

"A member of that 'monstrous regiment' of educated women." And she winked.

"How glorious," said I, conscious of a stirring in my breast. I imagined women in white robes and blue stockings amid Greek columns.

Gwen scrupulously divided the last piece of gingerbread, saying, "Prunella Mellor. Say it over and over quickly."

We did so.

Gales.

———

Mrs. Knox conveys to Lord Henry the glad tidings as to the restoration of his daughter's spirits, "thanks to Your Lordship's wisdom in summoning Miss Haas to the house," at which he nods serenely and returns to sorting two subspecies of plover pin feathers.

She lingers.

"Lord Henry, are you after changing your mind?"

"Mm?"

He looks up and follows her timid glance to the unposted letter at the feet of the improbable bird. "Certainly not. Do you imagine my daughter's future is not uppermost in my mind?"

"Begging pardon, Your—"

"The letter shall be posted." He clears his throat. "In due course."

She drops her gaze. "And . . . what of your own future, Lord Henry?"

"As to that. I know I am duty-bound to produce an heir," he says bitterly.

"An heir is well and good, I speak of your happiness."

"Damn my happiness." He returns to his heap of feathers.

Fayne House
November 5, 1887

Dear Aunt Clarissa,

I trust this finds you well and profiting from fine weather. The weather here is as expected in November. Father is well, as am I, especially as I have lately made the acquaintance of a young lady some two years my senior who has proven to be a salutary influence upon me insofar as I have embraced the strictures of my sex, and come to see the merit of keeping indoors and off the moors. I hope you may accept my belated thanks for the comely day dress and all its undercarriage, as well as for the tea and dinner gowns.

As *per* the subject of attire, my acquaintance, Miss Haas, has informed me that at Jenners & Co. in Edinburgh are to be found gowns which consist of one garment rather than two, and that this innovation eliminates the necessity of hoop and cage *etcetera* . . . not but what those appurtenances are delightful. If, in the course of your eventful life in town, you happen by the aforementioned shop,

I humbly beg you might acquire, on my behalf, one of these garments in a colour and fabric of your wise choosing.

I remain your dutiful niece,
The Honourable Charlotte Bell

PS Please to include a pair of stockings. Colour: blue.

On the next Saturday, Gwen had me sit motionless until I was alive with itchiness as she sketched on a large tablet of paper laid flat on Bewick's *British Birds*.

"Don't move."

"I didn't."

"You blinked."

"I must or risk blindness."

I heard the scritch and sweep of charcoal and watched as she paused by turns to rub her thumb and the heel of her palm on the paper.

"I say—"

"Don't speak."

The rapid movements of her hand were punctuated by darting glances at my face. I sneezed, she shot me a warning look. I ventured, timidly, "I've a question. Please."

"Well?"

"That is, I wonder how my brother kept still long enough to have his portrait painted, and he a bairn of two."

"He didn't, the painter would have worked from a photograph."

I rose.

"Sit!"

I obeyed. "How do you know?"

"'Tis how it's done. Especially when it comes to squirming bairns, not to mention busy aristocrats with their luncheons and wars and charity balls—"

"So there is a photograph. And I am in it."

She brushed a stray lock from her forehead, smudging her temple with charcoal, and looked up. "I see what you mean. Your mother would have a belly—pardon the expression."

"Exactly. Unlike the deceitful portrait on the stairs."

"The camera doesn't lie," she said, sketching rapidly once more, "but it doesn't tell the truth the way art does."

At last she sighed and sat back. I approached and looked over her shoulder. "Who's that?"

"Handsome, aren't you?"

"I don't look like that."

"Have you never stood before a looking glass?"

"I refer to the expression, it is . . . morose."

"'Tis sad."

"I do not look 'sad.'"

"You do, and often."

"I dare say I appear stern at times. You fail to capture the noble mien."

"If you don't like it you might try smiling."

I frowned. "Would you care to tour the stables? Hector is in foal."

"I'd rather see the false-bottom bed."

"It's no good wheedling, the answer is no."

"Very well. Here, put this on your head." She thrust Bewick's at me.

She ordered me to promenade about the room, balancing the book on my head. This she termed "comportment."

"My dear Gwendolyn, this is balderdash."

"Not according to your father."

I stopped. The book slid from my head, I caught it.

"What you want is a real governess but you're stuck with me."

"Father would never thrust a governess upon me."

"All's I know is my mother told me that Mrs. Knox told her that I'm to instruct you in the feminine graces department, and I've shirked as usual, I'll be sent packing soon enough."

I was suddenly dispirited. "Do you mean to say you are here under obligation?"

"Well of course I'm under obligation, our stations are miles apart—"

"You may go."

"Charlotte—"

"Don't let me detain you, Miss Haas."

She appeared taken aback. "At first I came because I was ordered to. But now we're friends. Aren't we?"

I hardened my gaze. Tears clouded hers. She bent to collect her sketch pad. I said, as severely as possible, "What does Mrs. Knox require that you teach me?"

"Why . . . to pour tea and to dance and be generally . . . charming."

"Well then. Gwendolyn. Shall we start with the tea-pouring?"

She smiled broadly. "No, I've seen you, you're hopeless, let's—oh, I know!"

She taught me the minuet (pleasingly mathematical), and soon we were decorously stepping about the drawing room whilst she sang the numerals one through three repeatedly. She despaired of the waltz, however, declaring I must allow myself to be led.

"Led where?"

"About the ballroom."

"Why?"

"Because the waltz is the most thrilling of dances, it allows a gentleman to draw near you without obligation or dishonour and helps him decide whether to pay a formal call."

"Why?"

"As a prelude to courting."

I waited. She explained, "A gentleman asks permission of a lady's father to court her which means visiting and conversing lightly and, oh perhaps taking a turn about the garden."

"A moor is more interesting."

"An advanced stage of courting is called wooing."

I felt my eyes narrow.

She warmed to her subject. "It entails scented letters, tête-à-têtes on the settee, pressing of fingers and such whilst the chaperone—in the absence of a mother, a maiden aunt will do—"

"I've got one of those."

"—the chaperone congenially nods off. Following which stage, the gentleman goes back to her father and asks for the lady's hand in marriage, and if the father agrees, the gentleman arranges to meet the lady alone which is how the lady knows exactly what's coming when he drops to one knee before her and, with barely suppressed ardour, offers her his hand in marriage, whereupon she gasps in surprise—"

"I thought you said she knew what was coming."

"Of course she does, but she mustn't let on to him."

"Bother that."

"You're spoiling it."

"Sorry, what happens then?"

"Well then, if she accepts his proposal, he takes her masterfully in his arms and, with a voice blurred by emotion, crushes her to his manly bosom." She was now flushed. "And that's a fair sketch of how it'll roll out." Adding, "You're lucky, he needn't be rich so he can be young, you'll have your pick."

"Pick of what?"

"Husbands, you goose." She was beaming. I was not. "Charlotte, what do you think I've been talking about all this time?"

"A hypothetical lady. Yourself, perhaps."

"Myself?! I'd be lucky to marry Murdoch Mungo!"

"Murdoch Mungo?!"

"Charlotte, you know of course you must marry."

"I know no such thing."

"Well, but . . . do you not wish to marry a fine young gentleman?"

"I'd rather discover a comet."

Her brow creased.

I added helpfully, "Did you know Caroline Herschel had typhoid as a child, and but for her father saying she was too stunted to marry, she'd've never calculated the rotation period of Mars?"

"But . . . Charlotte, sums and whatnot are all well and good but . . . have you never dreamt of 'tasting strange joys'?"

"You mean cocoa?"

"Ha-ha-ha—no, I mean . . ." She whispered, "Marital relations." Then added flatly, "Sexual congress. With a man."

"No."

"Surely you don't mean to be a spinster." She shuddered.

"Gwen, you know how you plan to lead a Bohemian life in Paris? Well . . ." I gave a smile as sly as her own, "I've a plan of my own."

"How delicious." She wriggled. "Do tell, old thing."

"I shall attend the University of Edinburgh and become a physician."

She blinked. I forged on. "I shall travel the world, learning where I may, healing where I can; my only companions, learned men of foreign parts and, mayhap in time, a staunch female friend of the sort inured to discomfort—"

"Don't move."

"What's wrong?"

"Hush."

I obeyed. And presently I heard . . .

Scritch, sweep. She had begun sketching again.

18

I DID NOT TRUST my old nurse to tell me the truth without aid of a spring-trap, thus my offhand tone as she sponged my back. "By the by, where is the photograph of Mother and Charles? The one the painter used as a guide?"

"Who told you about the photo?"

Ah-ha! "I deduced it. I wish to see it."

"We have the portrait, dearie, a perfect likeness and willnae fade so quickly."

"Aye, but the camera doesn't lie."

"Nor did the paintbrush. Well now, it empolished the truth for there was no willow in the photographic establishment, nor was Her Ladyship barefoot—"

"You were there when it was taken?"

"Why, certainly."

"Bring it me at once."

"I cannae."

"Why not?"

"It was got rid of."

"Why?"

"Och, pet, why must you know the nitting-gritting of everything?" With that, she turned away.

Dread crept over me. My mouth dried. "Was he already dead in it?" *Dead, propped up and dressed . . .*

"What? Nay, pet! No, no, no, I recollect as 'twas yesterday the making of that photograph. It was in Edinburgh shortly before they were to have set sail for Boston . . ." Here she sighed.

"Go on," I said.

"Well, the photograph-making man ducked beneath a long black hood as was standing up like a cloak on its own, and when wee Master Charles saw that he cried like the babby he was. Happen I had sweeties from his Auntie Cwissa—so he called her, for she was after spoiling him, was Miss Clarissa—and I took him round back of the hood and showed him the camera. 'Lookie,' I said, 'there's never any bodeachan, 'tis a machine, is all.' 'Machine,' he said. He was that clever."

"Hmph."

"And when the great bulb went up with a poof and a flash, he never cried but hugged his mam."

"And me."

"You?"

"I was in her belly."

". . . You were that."

"So they both of them hugged me."

"As I do now." And so she did, though I was soaking wet. "After they died, your father purged the house of all reminders. As for the photo, he couldnae 'bide the sight of it."

"But he hung the portrait on the stairs."

"That I cannae riddle."

I gazed up at my window full of stars. "A photograph is . . . a moment. But a painting is a monument. Father has no grave to visit, unless he should travel to the Alps. But he has the portrait."

Knox wiped her eyes with her damp apron. "Och, Miss Charlotte, I daresay you'll grow up to be a fine woman—"

"I'm a reminder."

"What's that, lamby?"

"I wonder he can 'bide the sight of me."

"Miss Charlotte Bell, you are the apple of your father's eye. And one day some dashing young man will come along and—"

I rose from my bath, stepped smartly over the rim and snatched my towel, surprised to see Prickle standing straight up without so much as a by-your-leave.

On Saturday morning Knox presented me with a parcel which had arrived the previous night from Edinburgh. It bore the label "Jenners & Co."

I was put in mind of the label in the muddy cloak—how long ago it now seemed—but when I parted the folds of tissue paper, the memory fled before the sight of a new kind of dress.

It was all of a piece, bodice and skirt forming one garment of serviceable serge in an indifferent fawn colour. I wrestled myself into it and Knox fastened the hooks in back, of which there were fewer. I was no longer caged, nor was I bustled or saddled with more than one petticoat. I stood before the glass and looked. I was entubed, not unlike Gwendolyn Haas, who had the trick of ambulation. I felt less like a tolling bell and more like a human being.

I hurried—yes!—down the stairs and made straight for Father's study so as to catch him before he retired for the day, keen to display my new dress, one wholly congenial to attending lectures and perching on laboratory benches. I entered, a greeting upon my lips—but the study was empty. My spirits were momentarily dampened at the sight of the letter addressed to the physician, now a fixture, it seemed, propped against the spindly legs of the laughing chimera. I was about to withdraw when my eye was caught by another letter—this one lying open on Father's desk. Were the Ancients correct after all in ascribing moral frailty to womankind? For Reader, though I touched not the letter, neither did I avert my eyes before they had taken in its contents at a glance.

Knox put her head round the door and I compounded my trespass by feigning ignorance of the answer to the question I posed: "Where is Father?"

"He's gone to Edinburgh at your aunt's request."

I withdrew, uneasily aware that had I been guiltless—or more practised at deceit—Knox's answer would have elicited from me an exclamation, *id est* "My word!" For not in my lifetime had I known Father to leave Fayne.

I had quite forgot my new silhouette when, moments later, I entered the drawing room and Gwendolyn gasped. "It's cracking!"

"At the very least it does not merit inclusion in a museum of torture."

That evening I penned a note of thanks to my aunt, renewing my request for blue stockings. And when Knox came in to douse my lamp, I asked, "Why's he gone to Edinburgh?"

"He got a letter from your Aunt."

"Yes, but why did she—that is, did Aunt bid him come?"

"I'm not to know that. Mayhap he misses his sister. 'Tis she as brought him up."

"I thought you did that."

"I was his nurse, but she was a mother to him." Her tone took on the gently chanting quality characteristic of the tale I knew so well. "He was still in skirts when Lady Catherine breathed her last."

I chimed in, "along with her two big sons afore her."

"Aye, your uncles."

"And Father was sent to Fayne for his health."

"Wee Henny-Penny was sent to Fayne and spared along with his sister."

It always tickled me to hear Father's nickname on my nurse's lips.

I snuggled against her. "I'm glad I was born when I was and not in the olden days when people tipped chamber pots out their windows."

"Edinburgh was different then."

"Auld Reekie."

Knox chuckled.

"Gwendolyn Haas taught me that. She also taught me the minuet."

"Good on her."

"And all manner of feminine graces."

She gave me an approving squeeze.

"Aunt Clarissa ought to visit now that I am well enough to mingle."

"I daresay she's content in Edinburgh."

"Does she dislike Fayne?"

"She may not love the moor nor even the house, but she loves Fayne. Miss Clarissa would lay doon and dee to see it carry on."

I closed my eyes and saw, imprinted on my inner lids, the letter written in my aunt's spidery hand . . .

November 17, 1887

My dear brother,
There is news. I beseech you, come at once.

You devoted sister,
Clarissa

And as I drifted off, I wondered, what "news" . . . ?

A gibbous moon. Like a hump-backed old woman making her way across
   the sky.
And at Charlotte's window, a face.
A child's face. Pleading eyes. Staring up.
But not at her. At someone—or something . . . just behind her.
She knows he wants her to turn round.
"No," she says in her mind.
His forehead dimples. The corners of his mouth draw down, his chin trembles.
He opens his lips and out pours a stream of gabble. He cannot be more than
   two years old. Children of that age gabble. She tells herself this even
   as cold terror steals over her with the knowledge that she is about to
   understand what he is saying—
I heard the latch and Knox was at my side.
"It was Charles. He was at my window again." My heart was pounding.
"'Twas only a dream."
"He hates me."
"Hush."
"He wishes my death."
"A baby can never mean any harm."
"Then why does he haunt me?"
She held me close and rocked me. "Pray for him. That he may rest."

Father returned from Edinburgh at the end of the week. I hurried out
onto the forecourt to meet the cart, eager to learn what had beckoned
him thence, hoping against hope that it touched my prospects. He was
subdued—unsurprising, given the journey and the disruption of his
nocturnal habits. He greeted me with a pat on my head before disappearing into the house. As I turned to follow him, I heard Byrn strike up a
song in a low chanting voice—the hairs stood up on on the back of my
neck. I turned, but the old man took no notice of me as he led Achilles
by the bridle toward the stables. I clapped my hands over my ears in sudden dread, for Reader, the nonsense words the old man was singing were
the gabble of my brother from my dream of the night before. And his
tune was the tune of the swallet that called me that day on the bog with
Mr. Margalo.

———

"Och, Lord Henry, you're forfairn."

"I shan't gainsay you, Knoxy."

His face is ashen in the low light of the great hall. She helps him off with his cape. "Is it Miss Clarissa, Your Lordship? Has she taken a turn?"

"No, she is well. That is, she is no worse."

She sees the black armband on the sleeve of his morning coat. Cruikshank appears and takes the cape away to brush it. Knox watches her master ascend wearily the stairs.

Twenty minutes later, Knox herself carries the tea tray up to His Lordship's bedchamber, where he stands warming himself at the hearth.

"Who has died, Your Lordship?"

"What? Oh, an old friend, as it happens."

"Not Miss Gourley."

"No, no."

"Mr. Baxter?"

"No," he says rather sharply. Then, more gently, "No one of note. One of Clarissa's 'causes.'"

"She is too good, is Miss Clarissa."

Lord Henry makes no reply but removes the armband and drops it into the fire.

"Don't forget to piddle afore you—"

"Knoxy, I'm not a bairn," I said, ignoring the chamber pot and climbing into bed. "Is aught amiss with Father? He seems downcast."

"There's been a death."

"Aunt Clarissa?"

"No, no, pet, some poor soul as your aunt took pity on and provided for. Your father went to comfort his sister."

I woke in the wee hours, slipped from my bed and to the pot where I duly "piddled." Thus I knew it was no dream when, up through the floor there came . . . not a cry, but a groan. Faint, yet unmistakable. I tidied myself by means of a square of paper which I recognized as having been cut from the wrappings of the new serge dress, then rose and crept from my chamber. The crescent moon cast a wan light the length of the corridor as I padded along toward the head of the stairs. I descended, feeling my way to the landing, comforting myself with the infantile notion that if I could not see the figures in the portrait, neither could they see me—and heard it again. I followed it to the study door. No light issued from within, only the soft, deep sounds of sorrow. Father was weeping.

I stole back up the stairs as fast as my legs could carry me. Not for anything in the world—not for a place at the University of Edinburgh—would I have my father find me listening at his door, and know himself violated in his private grief. It was enough that I had read his correspondence.

Shaken, but safe in my bed once more, I reflected: Father must love his sister very much to take her sorrow so much to heart. But of course—he loved her as he would have loved a mother, for so she had been to him. I conceived of a new esteem for this elderly aunt of mine: friend to the unfortunate, protector of my young Father. Defender of Fayne.

19

FATHER JOURNEYED AGAIN to Edinburgh the following week and returned, if not jubilant, then not stricken as before. Such was his devotion to his sister that he journeyed thence again the next week; and the next; returning each time in better spirits so that it seemed in lifting hers, he had recovered his own.

What with Father so oft from home, the weekdays were more than ever hollowed-out slots of time. Even a mechanical doll had the advantage of being laid in a box from Monday through Friday, whereas I had to remain animate and idle. I crept now and again into his study. In the interval since my tutor's departure, he had completed numerous specimens, and they perched now upon every available surface. For the first time, the scene struck me as something frowsty—even melancholy. In stark contrast stood our improbable bird, laughing from atop the bank of pigeon holes and looking for all the world as though it had flown through a rainbow. And propped against its legs was the letter to Dr. Chambers, gathering dust. Foolish bird. *What's there to laugh about?* I thought. And I was tempted to pitch it into the wastebasket.

But Father had a plan. All would be revealed in the fullness—or emptiness—of time.

Meanwhile, I lived for the weekends and Gwendolyn Haas's visits.

"Gwennie!"

"Charlotte!"

I marvelled at her ability to travel so swiftly between Edinburgh and Fayne as though she had wings folded between her narrow shoulders—freckled wings—but she told me that my father—three cheers for Pater!—arranged for her to be whisked by train between Edinburgh and Selkirk, where he arranged for a coach to deliver her to Aberfoyle-on-Feyn, so the entire journey took no more than three hours, during which she did what she called "home-work." I imagined dull domestic chores, but the term referred to lessons which she was required to complete over the course of the weekend, having failed to do so during "classroom-time." Thus, in the train she "fagged away" at "figures" and whilst bouncing along in the coach "crammed" Latin conjugations (thanks to the blue-stockings who believed a girl's education ought to equal that of a boy), all of which she averred "positively petrified" her with boredom. She had, for one thrilling week, high hopes of a fencing master (O, how I yearned to attend school!), for Miss Mellor and the admirable Miss Gourley did not shy from employing members of the opposite sex, in this case a lugubrious Pole with a scar on one cheek. "From a rapier?" "From a violin bow." He was also the music master. She showed me her school work—"botch-work," she put it. I tried to awaken her to the beauties of mathematics. I failed. I "fetched up" doing it for her, with one exception: she was "wizard" at geometry. I professed myself "gabberflasted," but she pointed out that she was, after all, a painter. (All in all, I proved a better student of slang than she of sums.)

I was aware that in doing Gwendolyn's homework I was party to deceit, but it saved us time of which we seemed to have less and less as the weekends flew past. And yet, what did we do? Reader, we talked. And ate. And laughed. Nonetheless, at the conclusion of each visit, I felt more edified than if I had spent the interval bent over her lessons, of which I made short work. She thrust upon me a stack of novels to see me through the weekdays, assuring me I would "adore" them—and while I could not promise to do so, I did welcome the diversion in light of Father's absence.

"He's gone to town again, has he, your dad?"

"Aye, he comforts my aunt."

"On a weekly basis?"

"Yes."

"Hmm."

"What?"

"How good of him."

"Nay, 'tis my aunt does him the world of good."

"Come now Charlotte, do you not think it likely he's courting a lady?"

I was gabberflasted.

"Sorry," she said.

"Not at all. Merely, you are mistaken."

"I'm a ninny."

"Not but what Father does have a duty to provide an heir. In due course."

"Plenty of time."

"Are you hungry?"

"Need you ask?"

She arrived the following week with divers "feminine accents" for my bedchamber, among which "scatter cushions" (which sounded amusing but were merely decorative) along with a length of chintz with which she proposed to "spiff up" my casement window.

She dragged my escritoire to the window. "There, now you may gaze out upon your beloved moor whilst confiding in your diary."

"Field notes."

"Well? How did you like them?" She patted the novels she had lent me.

"Mr. Verne's tale is intriguing, and Miss Shelley posits an interesting hypothesis *vis-à-vis* Dr. Frankenstein's monster, but *Jane Eyre* and *Wuthering Heights* are an affront to verisimilitude."

"And flying round the world in a balloon and bringing the dead to life are not?"

"Gwen, you and I may live to see man take to the skies in flying machines the like of which Leonardo da Vinci foresaw, when he wasn't busy designing waterworks—"

"And making great art!"

"What's more, science proceeds by leaps and bounds such that mortality itself may eventually be cured, but I do not believe for a moment that one might live in a house and remain ignorant of a madwoman residing in the attic." I added, trenchantly, "As for a shrieking wraith at one's window, I never mistake mine for anything but a dream."

"You dream of a shrieking wraith?"

"Everyone rides the nightmare from time to time." I cleared my throat.

She clambered onto the escritoire, taking the measure of my window with a length of string.

"Gwennie?"

"Mm?"

"I hear someone out there sometimes. At night. Someone crying."

She turned to me. "Crying?"

"A child."

"Well it couldn't be, could it."

"He haunts me."

"Who does?"

"My brother. He died. And none will tell me why. Except to say he was sickly. In dreams . . . it seems there is something he wishes me to know." I shivered. Felt my eyes water. "I fear lest he too had the Condition." My voice died to a whisper. "And that it killed him."

"But Charlotte . . . you've outgrown your Condition, surely."

"I thought so. And Father has promised to secure my future. But I cannot see that he has taken steps to do so, therefore I fear—that is, I posit: he knows my future will be curtailed. Like my brother's before me."

She crouched down and sat cross-legged before me on the escritoire. "Charlotte. I mentioned to my mother the cloak you found and she told me a secret—she was in her cups, but still, 'tis a secret she's kept for the sake of your father—or my father rather, for Lord Henry is his employer after all, but also because . . . Well, she did so admire your mother."

"What secret?"

"Mam told me she knew a lady who walked out onto the moor one night. She said it was no madwoman, Charlotte. It was your mother."

I must have blanched for she added quickly, "You see, when she was pregnant with your brother, your mam sleep-walked out onto the bog and . . . well, she ate the moor mud."

I could not speak.

"It's all right, Charlotte, Mrs. Knox told my mam *there's nowt strange* in a pregnant woman craving nutriments as are found in soil. Time was, they were even encouraged to eat it. So you see if Charles was sickly, it may be he contagioned something in the bog, and it's nothing to do with you."

I saw once more the ropy mass my tutor and I had wrested from the grip of the moor . . . laid out like a corpse. "So she—my mother—is not still in the bog."

"She couldn't be, Charlotte. She gave birth to you two years later."

"Of course." There was something amiss with my brain, for the before-and-after of it all seemed to leap-frog about and I was suddenly in danger of—

"You're coming over collywobbly," said Gwen. She slid from the desk, and guided my head to my knees.

After luncheon, much restored by steak-and-kidney pie and a sturdy tapioca pudding, I matched wits with my friend at a game of hide-and-seek, in the course of which she outfoxed me by hiding in a suit of armour from which she had to be pried free by Cook with a cleaver. Scarcely had she emerged, hot and flustered, when the great oak doors opened, admitting a gust of December air along with Father, fresh from Edinburgh.

He greeted me and nodded to Gwendolyn. "Hello, Miss Haas."

"Hello, Lord Henry." She bobbed a curtsey.

Father betrayed no weariness. He inquired pleasantly after Gwendolyn's health and that of her parents. Removing hat and gloves, he asked to know how her studies proceeded, and remarked upon the coming of Yule. Cruikshank helped him as he shrugged from his great-coat, whereupon I was not a little taken aback at the sight: Father was clad in a mulberry morning coat with a waistcoat of white quilting. And lavender doeskin trousers.

Wishing us a very agreeable afternoon, he withdrew, mounting the stairs.

Gwen turned to me and said, "He's got a lady friend, depend upon it."

This time I did not dispute her. I stood, mute.

"Listen, old thing, it may be a point in your favour."

"How so?"

"Well if he's after sorting his own future, like as not he isn't worried about yours. He knows you're well enough to sit the exam and go off to the university. And you know it too."

"Then why doesn't he say so?"

"If he's dragging his feet, well . . . Me own dad wept when I left for school."

"He grieves to part with me. How cruel of me to forget."

"Not a bit of it, just be glad he's courting. That way he'll not have you stop at home forever to look after him, he'll have a wife for that."

Although I recoiled at Gwendolyn's somewhat vulgar characterization of Father's delicate sensibilities, I did see her point.

Loath as I was to let my friend in for reproach, there remained a question only Knox could answer. I confronted her as she plaited my hair. "The cloak I found. It belonged to my mother." I felt myself trembling.

The fingers stilled and she was mute as a turnip.

"Mrs. Haas saw with her own eyes, and don't you dare get after Gwendolyn for telling me what you ought to've told me yourself, namely my brother was sickly from the bog. Because Mother ate of it whilst carrying him."

She squeezed shut her eyes and drew a deep breath, and nodded.

"Knoxy. Did she ever walk onto the bog when she was carrying me?"

She sighed.

"Tell me. Please."

"She did not, pet."

"Swear it?"

"I swear it. On her dear head."

"Only with Charles?"

"Only with Charles, pet. Only with him."

20

GWENDOLYN SURPRISED ME the following week by venturing out of doors with her sketch pad and clever collapsible easel. We got no further than the forecourt, where she tilted her head back in perusal of the façade of the house.

"The high roof attests the strong influence of the Scottish Baronial Style," I said, helpfully. But she was still looking up. I continued, "Fayne House is constructed principally of Scottish granite—"

"That's not granite." She was pointing up at the scutcheon.

"Right you are, etched in limestone is the Fayne coat of arms, a much-weathered *Salamander Rampant*."

"It looks older than the rest. Why a salamander?"

"Its origins are involved in obscurity.

"What's it say?"

"*Nemo venit ad Matrem, nisi per me.*"

"Yes, but what's it say?"

"I thought you were learning Latin, old stick, have a go."

"'No one . . . comes . . . to the Mother' . . . something . . .'"

"'except'"

"'except . . . through me.' Oughtn't it to be 'Father'?"

"Doubtless a scribal error. Carved by Celts."

She commenced sketching.

"I say, Gwen, if it's a salamander you're after drawing, I'll catch you a real one and chloroform it."

"I like that one."

"A rudimentary likeness. A child could do better."

"If you're looking for a skin-deep likeness you may as well make a photograph." She carried on sketching with broad strokes as she spoke. "But that carving up there, that's exactly how a salamander moves. I'll wager if you worked your mathematical magic on it, you'd find it follows the golden mean."

This gave me pause. I came round behind her and watched as she captured the swirls of the creature. It was true, her sketch was quick with life.

"What else've you got in there?" I asked.

She stood aside and allowed me to flip through her sketch pad. Reader, she was that good; horses, especially their legs, and the fiddly bits of people's hands along with a bowl of fruit—"I say, Gwennie, these are cracking."

"They're fine technically but look here," she said, turning the pages, suddenly shy, "I'm rather proud of this one."

It was a faun, achieved in perhaps twelve strokes of the charcoal.

"Funny . . . it looks familiar somehow."

"It's Byrn," said she. "As a faun."

Reader, so it was.

"Charlotte, would you model for a portrait?"

"I've done so."

"Nude."

I laughed. She did not. "A proper portrait," she said.

"Improper more like."

"I need to draw from life."

"I'm alive."

"Please, Charlotte, I'm sick of drawing myself in the glass, not to mention I can't sketch and hold a pose at the same time."

"Ask one of your school chums."

"Maeve's got nerve enough to do it, but there's only ever time at weekends and I'm always here."

"Don't let me keep you from your more amusing friend."

"Don't sulk, and what's the fuss? We've all the same bits."

"Yes, and some of us prefer to keep them to ourselves."

"Charlotte, all the great portraits are nudes. Why paint fabric when you can paint flesh? If I aimed to be a painter of fashion plates I'd apprentice myself at Jenners. How am I to assemble a portfolio fit for a Paris art school if I've never drawn from an undraped model?"

"Follow me."

I led her into the house and up to the marbles room.

"I say, look what you've been hiding."

"Hardly hiding. I didn't think you'd be interested."

"I'm an artist!"

"You were withering about my spot-bellied Scottish wildcat."

Here were marbles and bronzes of horsemen and dragons along with plaster reproductions of masterworks. In one corner, the David towered his full seventeen feet. Gwen looked up. "Why's he wearing a loincloth?"

"He's got to wear something, I suppose."

"No he hasn't," said she.

She fairly skipped amid the heroes and dying gods whilst I mused, "Oft have I wondered at depictions of near-naked warriors—is it not ill-advised to venture into battle shod only in sandals?"

"At least you haven't slapped a corset on the Venus de Milo."

The goddess stood bare-breasted, her robe perpetually falling about her hips—perhaps because she lacked arms with which to hold it up.

Gwen unfolded her easel and said, "Sit."

I was well-trained and kept as still as marble as she proceeded rapidly to sketch and, as rapidly, to talk. "You might navigate the Amazon, Charlotte Bell, but you'll be lost in a real drawing room and your compass will not guide you through an ordinary conversation. You're wonderful for facts, but you lack the nous to find your way to the village and back. You do realize that once he's married, your Father's going to hand you over to your stepmother and then to a husband—not a word! But I'm not handing you over to anyone 'til you've tasted cocoa and know the difference between a pence and a pound. I'll be leading a wild, dissolute life in Paris, governess by day, painter by night, leaving a trail of ignominy in my wake, after which I shall return to Fayne, penniless and shattered. You will take me in along with my illegitimate offspring and I will prove useful and diverting, foiling a plot on the part of your inbred husband to sell the moor to Mungo for a mine, instructing your children in the art of watercolour, and singing lewd songs in French when night falls o'er the fen. *Voilà!*" She tore the paper from the easel and showed me what she had so rapidly rendered: a perfect likeness of the Venus de Milo. With my head.

I was taken aback but, wishing to seem a good sport, I looked up with a smile that died on my lips at the sight of my friend in the act of disrobing.

Her bodice and skirt fell in a heap about her ankles. She wriggled her chemise over her head, exposing her slim chest—freckled, yes. Her breasts were something smaller than my own and looked to be buttoned at their respective centres with a pink rosebud. She hauled down her petticoat, followed by stockings and drawers in one go. Then she straightened and stood before me, naked but for her boots. I was shocked. Not by the presence of the silky curls at the V between her thighs—different in shade though not in kind, from mine—but by an absence. I looked away.

"I've shocked you."

"Not in the slightest."

"You look set to fall off your perch. It's the freckles, isn't it. Head to toe, so now you know. Frightful, I agree."

"Not in the least. Fetching, in fact. Like a trout."

"How horrid!"

"Trout are bonny! And so are you."

"Do you really think so?" She surveyed herself glumly. "I imagine a man's first sight of me and I die lest he laugh or flee. I ought to have said 'husband's' first sight."

"Gwendolyn," I shielded my eyes as against the sun, "if we are to converse further, I beg you re-robe."

"Oh all right." She commenced pulling up her drawers and wriggling back into her chemise. "Your turn, old chap."

"'Chap'?"

"School slang."

I attempted insouciance. "So this is what you get up to at that vaunted academy?"

"That's the trouble, we don't. Please, Charlotte, my future is in your hands. I'll give you my first-born. Fine, nobody wants anyone else's brat, let me see . . . I'll give you free governessing for your own eventual brats. Very well then," she declared, casting off her smalls once more, brushing past me, "Make way for a nude-descending-the-staircase!"

"No!" I seized her by the arm.

"Ow!"

I unhanded her. "Gwen. I may not disrobe for that I am morbidly susceptible to drafts."

"Sorry. I forgot how 'delicate' you are." She rubbed her arm where the imprint of my grip showed red.

She knew as well as I that I no longer feared drafts. But nothing could have induced me to shed my clothing. For I could not reveal my body to my friend without also revealing her defect.

21

POOR GWENDOLYN. She clearly craved the married state—or at least "marital relations" with or without benefit of clergy—and feared lest her freckles prove an impediment thereto. But how might a prospective paramour react when faced with her defect? I could only surmise that her mother had taken pains to keep Gwendolyn's condition from her; but for how long might the subterfuge be maintained? And had it been advisable in the first place? A blow delayed might not be a blow softened. *Au contraire . . .*

"Knoxy. There is something wrong with Miss Haas."

"Oh dear, luvvy, she's no took ill?" Knox was knitting nearby. I was in my bath before the fire.

"Not ill, no, that is, she . . . She is lacking."

"Lacking what?"

"She hasn't a . . ." I glanced down at Prickle, nestled innocently like the offspring of a giant seahorse between my legs. I dared not name it nor even point lest it awaken—in moments such as this it seemed cruel even to think of it as "Prickle" so soft and slumbery it appeared. I whispered. ". . . anything."

Perhaps I had spoken too softly because she made no reply. "Knox. Gwen hasn't got . . ." I mouthed the word but even so I felt mine stir, and so leaned forward and hugged my knees. "Knox?" Had my old nurse fallen under a spell?

Finally she spoke. "How do you come to know aught of her nethers, what have you been playing at?"

"We've not been 'playing' at anything. She wishes to draw me from life and so disrobed in hopes I'd do the same."

"You stood naked?"

"Certainly not. And the word is 'nude.'"

"She'd no business—"

"Shutup, Knoxy, Gwen is keen on becoming a painter, and a real painter works from an undraped model as everyone knows, like the great da Vinci—"

"You are not to disrobe before Miss Haas nor anyone else, do you understand, Miss Charlotte?"

"I am no longer a child, do you understand, Mrs. Knox?"

"Och pet, you with your Condition, you'll catch your death—"

"I haven't the slightest intention of disrobing before anyone, especially not Gwendolyn, oh Knoxy she hasn't got a—"

"Promise me, pet. I beg of you." And she clasped her hands together. "Think of your poor father."

I sighed. "Fine, I promise. But what of Gwendolyn?" I lowered my voice. "She hasn't got a prickle."

Knox drew a slow breath, as though having at last apprehended the gravity of the situation. Presently she said, "It will have fallen off."

"Fallen off?"

She nodded.

I was stricken. "How very unfortunate."

She turned to fetch my towel from the fender. "Nay. 'Tis the way of it."

I stood abruptly, setting my bath to shedding.

"You'll flood the carpet, lassie!"

"It can fall off?"

"Of course it can, it falls off everyone, every girl, that is, that's become a woman."

Her tone was tetchy, as though this were something I ought to have deduced. I stood with my hands cupped over that suddenly precarious bit of me.

"Come 'til I dry you."

"When?"

"When what?"

"When will it . . . fall off?"

"Och, well. Belike soon."

She captured me in the towel and I heard her inquire mildly, "And was she surprised to hear you still have yours?" I shielded my groin from her vigorous drying, fearful lest Prickle come away even now—for it was set to fall off, perhaps next time I coughed or sneezed! Or laughed. "I did not speak of mine lest I cause her distress."

"So you kept mum."

"Aye."

"That was wise. Ladies don't talk of such things."

"Gwennie talks of everything."

"I'll wager if you did speak of it, Miss Haas would swear she'd ne'er had one, nor heard tell of any girl who had." Down went the nightgown over my head.

"Knoxy, why didn't you tell me before?" I was suddenly close to blubbing.

"Och, lass, I ought to've before now, I know, and I'm sorry." She cradled my cheek in her broad hand. "If your dear Mother were alive, she'd've been the one to tell you. The truth is, pet . . ." She looked away. "I didn't know how to tell it."

"'Tis . . . oh, 'tis horrible!"

"'Tis normal. You'll feel differently once you're grown."

"Differently how?"

"You'll be married and forget all about it."

"You're not married. Do you still have yours?"

"Goodness, no, and that's enough now, snuggle into bed."

I obeyed.

"Knox? Does everyone call it a prickle?"

"Well I'm not to know that, now, am I?"

"What did you call yours?"

"I didnae call it ocht, what need it to be called?"

"You taught me yourself, 'this is your nose, here be Charlotte's toes,' every part of us has a name, surely Prickle is the same."

"'Tisn't, and you're no to touch it nor call it anything at all, do you hear?"

I was shocked. "Why not?"

She looked at me sternly. "Touching it may cause it to grow."

"I know," I confided. "It does that."

"Aye, but you'll worry it so it stays big even when 'tis sleeping, 'til it's the size of an ugly slug."

I felt hot in the face. "Will it hurt?" I spoke scarcely above a whisper. "When it falls off?"

"Not a bit."

"Will it bleed?"

". . . Nay."

"Will it ever grow back?" I envisioned a salamander's tail detaching in my hand.

"No chance. Now close your eyes and think on all the women as've come afore you, they none of them kept their prickle and none as would have it otherwise."

She pulled the bedclothes up to my chin, pressed a kiss to my forehead and tucked me tight as an Egyptian mummy before drawing my bed curtains against the drafts I knew I need no longer dread.

I had a new dread.

I lay staring into darkness.

Was it even now preparing to detach from my body? Would I one day rise from my bed and turn to see it curled on the sheet, already smaller, dehydrating? If I dropped it promptly in formaldehyde, might I preserve it as a specimen? Would I be the only girl to have done so? Prickle stood up.

I refrained from touching it, anxious lest it come away between finger and thumb. O Prickle, had I known I would have you for so short a season, I might have mingled pleasure with grief meted out over time; but now it was upon me with one blow! Knox, how dare you keep me in ignorance?!

I sat up, enraged—*It is never a kindness to withhold information touching one's person!* Fain would I have cried aloud but that it would bring my nurse barging back in. Prickle stood, steadfast.

Much as it was oft the occasion of inconvenience with its wanton ways, I would not willingly have parted with it for the world, and not merely owing to its capacity for gratification—Reader, it was part of me. Wayward and ungovernable, blind blunt-headed booby, it was mine. I fell back and gave in, all the while fearing lest I hasten its demise. Was that to be the means of its detachment? Its death guaranteed by its *raison d'être?* Not unlike the fate of certain insects, in which the male is killed by the female immediately upon mating . . .

Afterwards, Prickle slept, swollen but shrinking, all innocent of the fate that awaited it.

I had, up 'til then, viewed the paroxysms of Prickle as a distraction from Higher Thought, but I came in that moment to an appreciation of its power to confer clarity; for just as a storm clears the air of dullness, so my mind was similarly refreshed and it offered up now a series of scientific questions:

(i)   What is the correct anatomical term for the fleshly protuberance located superior to the feminine urinary orifice?

(ii) By means of what physiological phenomenon is derived its capacity for turgidity, increase in amplitude, spasmodic response to stimuli and subsequent diminishment?

(iii) At what point in the life cycle of the human female, and in response to what, if any stimulus/i, does it detach and fall from the body?

I drifted off.
I awoke.

(iv) Does the vacated site retain sensation?

My heart commenced to pound. I flung aside my bed curtains and, drawn by the full moon, rose and went to my window. There it hung, high and clear. Constant and, as it were, impartial. Papists and pagans saw divinity in "Her." I knew our celestial satellite commanded the tides with no need of magyk. And that cool orb must have worked on my blood too, for the pounding abated, and it occurred to me: Gwendolyn Haas no longer had a prickle. And she was happy.

She has found him in his bedchamber, retiring for the night after the manner of his new habits.

"Come in, Knox, perhaps you can help me." He holds up two ties. "Which is best to wear at luncheon?"

"Oh. The purple, I think."

Lord Henry drapes it carefully over the back of the chair where he has already laid out his mulberry morning coat. He'll be wanting a man-servant if this keeps up. Sitting open on the seat is his case of brushes.

"Are you away again to Edinburgh on the morrow, then, Your Lordship?"

"I am, Knoxy."

"Very good, sir. And might I ask if you're after taking the letter with you?"

"Which letter? Oh."

"Aye." She hesitates. But he does not remonstrate. She ventures, "Only, it comes near a concern, sir, to do with Miss Charlotte. And Miss Haas."

"Is there something insalubrious in the connection?"

"No, no. No. Happen Miss Haas is come to an end on what she can teach Miss Charlotte."

"Then it's been a success? The friendship?"

"Och aye."

He smiles.

She nods and crosses with her lamp to the door. Opens it. Turns back as though at an after-thought. "Miss Charlotte has seen a picture. Of a nude woman."

He freezes. "Where did she encounter such an abomination?"

"In a book from Miss Haas's school library."

His expression of horror gives way to confusion. "What possible book?"

"A book of pictures by a real painter, name of Vinchy."

"Da Vinci."

"Aye. From an undraped model."

"Oh dear God . . ."

"I told her 'twas customary for a painter to . . . leave out . . ."

He lets out a breath. "Quite." Sighs. "Have Cruikshank post the letter in the morning."

"Aye, Your Lordship." Knox turns with a private sigh of relief, and quits the chamber.

22

THE NEXT SATURDAY, Byrn dragged in the Yule log and laid it in the cavernous hearth of the great hall, where the charred nub of last year's log lay ready to act as a torch to ignite the new one at the solstice. He wore the wreath of holly that Cruiky had woven for him and he looked like a grim Father Christmas, but Gwendolyn curtsied, of all things, and wished him "God Yul." He made a toothless reply with a doff of his garland.

"How do you know to say 'God Yul'?" I asked.

"Miss Mellor had another of her blue-stockings in for a colloquy on British folklore. We donned Druidic hoods and danced. Apparently there were female Druids."

"Droods."

"You what?"

"That's how Byrn says it."

"I wonder you understand a single word he says, the old dear."

We stood, silent of a sudden. An awkwardness descended. In the air between us hung an unspoken word: *nude.*

"Would you care for some mince pie?"

"Much obliged, thank you."

I led her to the scullery in hopes of shaking off the pall of formality, but when Cook plunked the mouth-watering slices before us, I found I could not meet my friend's eye. I was doubly relieved to have retained my clothing the previous week, for as much as I had mistakenly pitied Gwendolyn's lack of an unmentionable appendage, I now understood she would have pitied my retention of same. Unless she had laughed.

Or worse: recoiled. And I realized I could never ask her whether the "vacated site" was capable of sensation. I shifted uncomfortably.

"I don't wonder you can hardly look at me, Charlotte, I behaved disgracefully."

I ventured a glance. She continued. "I'm sorry."

"I was a brute. I am sorry I hurt your arm."

We both looked down.

Presently she said, "I've brought you a Yuletide gift."

She reached into her schoolbag and handed me a scrolled sheet.

I opened it. "My word. Why, Gwen. I must have it framed."

"I'm glad you like it."

"I adore it."

It was the finished charcoal drawing of Byrn—that is, of the faun with Byrn's likeness about it.

"Beg of me a boon," I blurted. Then, chary lest she renew her suit for a nude sitting, I offered, "The false-bottom bed. I'll show it you. That is, if you wish still to see it."

"I'm dying to see it!"

Back on our old footing, I ushered her through a low door in the scullery that opened into the service stairs, and we wended our way in darkness up to the very top of the house.

"Not the very top, what about the attic?" she whispered.

"It's empty. Why are you whispering?"

We had emerged onto the servants' floor, scarcely better lit than the stairs by means of two arrow-slit windows at either end of the long low-ceilinged passage.

"Show me. Please."

"We've no light."

From her pocket, she took a candle stub and a matchbox and held them out to me. "Comes in handy for midnight feasting."

I shrugged and led the way to a narrow door. Lifting the latch, I pushed it open and we were met with an exhalation of dusty air. Gwen shivered. I cast her a sidelong look. "Still hoping for a madwoman, are you?"

I lit the candle and, sheltering its flame, mounted the steep steps to the opening in the floor above. Gwen squeezed next to me. I held the quivering light aloft in a sea of darkness interrupted by cracks of daylight about the chimneys. I called out, "Hello!" I felt Gwen jump, and I grinned. "Anyone home?" I cried. The stillness was broken by a whoosh past my ear that doused the flame. Gwen yelped and half slid back down the steps. I lingered in the silence, almost regretting the attic was tenantless but for the bats.

I rejoined my friend, and led the way along the passage lined with doors to servants' quarters.

"You could house an army up here."

"We have, though not in this century."

Presently, we came to the old nursery beneath the eaves. "After you."

She entered and paused, closing her eyes. "It smells the same."

"You were here, then? With him."

"Children are not long tolerated in a drawing room. Though don't ask me to remember anything but the smell and . . . yes, his—"

"Laughter."

"Aye," she smiled.

The nursery served now as Knox's bedchamber. Two dormer windows, their shutters open to the daylight, overlooked the moor. Between the windows was a shelf. Ranged upon it, like exhibits in a museum, were my old toys: a wooden giraffe on wheels, a rocking horse whose felted hide was worn to straw in patches; a doll's house, much conquered and rebuilt; blocks printed with letters and numbers, their paint chipped and faded—a locomotive engine and goods train that had been brightly painted when bought for my brother, but dulled with handling by my wee hands. And there were poppets, good as new for I never played with dollies. Surveying the scene I seemed to catch a whiff of milky porridge, and on my tongue a taste of honey. A sense of well-being enveloped me, as though I were once more crouched on the floor with my train, whilst the steady rain against the windows made of the nursery a timeless world.

"Is this it?" Gwen was waiting for me in the far corner where Knox's bed stood near the stove.

The bed was a box-like structure, and I gave a kick to its side. "Hear that? Hollow. The Duke of Cumberland scoured the premises for traitors, little suspecting the Pretender to the Throne himself lay within."

"You left off the carousing bit."

"They feasted and caroused 'til dawn, and while the Duke slept off the fumes of his debauch in a chamber directly below this one, Prince Charles Stuart rose fresh as a daisy to ride off and join his ill-fated army."

"I thought the Bells were Loyalists."

"We were. And are."

"But you hid Bonny Prince Charlie. Surely that made you rebels."

"Yes."

"Well which was it?"

"Both."

"You can't have both."

"We did. And do."

"Is that not a touch deceitful?"

"Never!"

"I take it back!"

"The Barony of Fayne is founded in Dispute and the House of Bell has ne'er made a secret of it."

"That's mad."

"I take—"

"Umbrage, yes, with your tea, I know." She knelt and set to feeling about the bed frame.

"Following the massacre at Culloden, Bonny Prince Charlie fled, disguised as a woman, in a rowboat."

"He'd have been clapped in jail for that alone, never mind the rebellion," said Gwen flatly.

"For stealing a rowboat? I believe it was lent him along with the frock, by Flora Mac—"

"For being dressed as something he wasn't, namely a woman."

"Crikey. For that?"

"For that."

"Do you mean to say 'twas a crime for a man to dress up as a woman?"

"And vice versa. Still is."

I shot to my feet. "By Jove, Gwennie!"

She toppled back. "Charlotte, what is it?"

"Father knows I mayn't enter the university unless I am lawfully attired. That is why he decreed my trial by wardrobe: to prepare me for life in Edinburgh!"

"Oh. Right then, only . . ."

"What?"

"Why keep it a secret from you?"

"As a test of my mettle of course." I took a stride toward the door.

"Wait, the bed."

"You've seen it, let's go."

"I've seen nothing!"

"I'd not be caught trespassing."

"Best be quick, then."

"'Tis a drawer full of blankets," I grumbled, but hunkered back down, feeling about beneath the mattress for the spring mechanism.

Gwen wriggled beside me. "Mrs. Knox may have a secret from her *past*."

"What 'past'? She's always been here."

"You didn't know her when she was young and nubile."

"Rum word, 'nubile.'"

We laughed.

"She may have been in love."

"With whom?"

"Well . . . there's Byrn." We laughed helplessly.

My fingers found the tiny lever, and I paused. As a child, I would insist from time to time that Knox open the false-bottom bed in order to make certain Prince Charles was not still in there. "No bones," she'd say, "no bonny bones." Just extra woollen blankets, haunted only insofar as a blanket may said to be haunted that's come from the loom of a long-dead crone in the Hebrides who sang her Gaelic weaving songs whilst shunting and shuttering. Which is to say, slightly haunted. Especially if one counts the wool that came from the fleece that was shorn from the sheep that replaced the folk who were driven from the land that was fertilized by the bones of their long-dead ancestors to grow the grass to feed the sheep . . .

"Where do you go, Charlotte?"

She was staring at me.

"What do you mean? I've not moved from this spot."

"You're off with Faery."

"Shutup."

She grinned. "What are they like? The Wee Folk."

"Like you. Freckled, every man Jack of 'em. And Jill too."

I flipped the lever and the false bottom shot forth with a *thunk*, broadsiding us both. A cedary odour wafted up and I was momentarily giddy as though with bog fumes.

"I say," said Gwendolyn, bent already over the drawer. "Look at this for fancy-dress." And she held up my scarlet tunic, emblazoned with the blue *Salamander Rampant*. "These must date back to the Crusades but they're like new. Pity you don't take as good care of your tapestries. What's the matter?"

"They're my clothes."

"Oh Charlotte, you're . . . not jesting."

Atop the promised blankets, there lay as well a pair of my suede leggings, and a cambric shirt.

"Put them on, then."

I shook my head solemnly. "Not for anything would I break faith with Father."

"I wouldn't trade my frocks for anything—well, I'd trade them for nicer frocks—but it's not fair to keep you frocked when you hate it, hell's bells, why mayn't we dress as we please? Do as we please, love whom we please." She flushed.

"Gwennie, what is it?"

She bit her lips.

In a stroke of insight, doubtless attributable to my friend's lessons in courtship, I asked, "Have you fallen in love?"

She nodded.

"With a . . . handsome gentleman?"

"I think him handsome, at any rate," she said in a small voice.

"And . . . has he crushed you to his bosom?"

"No!" she cried.

"I say, Gwen, who is he?"

She covered her face with a yelp.

"A cad," I concluded. "He dies."

She looked up. "He's a schoolmaster."

"Oh, well that sounds respectable enough—"

"He is my schoolmaster."

"Oh. I see. Unsuitable."

"Impossible!"

"The fencing master, I presume."

"Ugh! He's old!"

"Then—?"

"Miss Gourley hired him last week, oh bless you, Miss Gourley, and curse you too!"

"You've known him a week?"

"I know, it seems a lifetime—"

"What's he teach?"

"What's it matter?"

"What's his name?"

She shook her head once more. "I'm trying to forget him."

"How can you forget him if you see him every day?"

"*Exactement!*" she cried, smacking her thighs. She took a deep breath and sighed, "His given name is Isadore. And 'tis true, he is 'beloved.' By me!" The next instant she was in the drawer and stretched out on the blankets, arms folded over her chest with her eyes closed.

"I say, Gwennie, are you peckish?"

She opened her eyes. "Your Prince Charlie couldn't have been very tall. It's barely big enough for me."

"We are better nourished than in his day, speaking of which—"

"Hello, what's this?" Sitting up, she reached beneath her amid the blankets and came out with a small bundle, loosely wrapped in silk. Without so much as a by-your-leave she opened it to reveal a packet of envelopes. It was the silk, however, that drew my attention, for it was a shawl similar to . . . Nay, it was identical to the one my mother wore in the portrait on the stairs—the one that had graced her shoulders in life, the one whose fringes my brother had dandled with his fingers. I watched as, seemingly with a will of their own, my fingers reached out and touched them.

"Charlotte, look. Letters."

"Gwen, you mustn't, that is the property of Mrs. Knox."

Gwen held the packet out to me. I recognized the looping feminine hand on the topmost envelope from years of birthday and Christmas greetings—and the name in the upper left corner, *Mrs. C. Blanchard* . . .

But this envelope was addressed to *Lady Marie Bell, Fayne House, County Fayne, Great Britain*. I became aware of a thrumming in my ears.

Gwendolyn regarded me gravely. "Do you wish me to put them back?"

Upon my answer to this question hung my fate. Had Caesar turned back at the Rubicon, I would not have been crouching there, speechless before Gwendolyn Haas who sat in a drawer. And but for a finite, if forbidding, number of other contingencies, You would not be reading this.

Reader, I inclined my head toward my friend and together, we read.

Boston
April 29 1875

Dearest Mae,
Please know that I pray for you daily, and for Henry too. I hardly know what to write in this time of great loss and sorrow. Henry's letter reached us today with news of the passing of your beloved son, Charles. My heart is doubly wrenched at the realization you have been grieving these many weeks while I and everyone here who loves you so were unaware and writing you witless letters full of happy anticipation of your visit, which can only have added to your distress. Oh my dear girl, my poor sweet friend, I am making plans today to come to you. I shall write again soon, a longer letter, my darling, but for now I must see to travel plans. Carter has just rushed out to cable Henry with news of our intended visit.

Your own loving,
Taffy

May 1, 1875
Boston

Dear Mae,
I trust you are already reaping the benefits of rest and care, and in such a nice setting too. Henry has kindly promised to forward my letters to the therapeutic establishment. I admit, only a cable from your good husband asking me to postpone my journey could have scuttled my plans to fly to your side. But he is right, of course: you need absolute

tranquility. I shall therefore expect no reply, dearest, until you are better, which you will be soon (but not too soon, darling Mae, for time is the best medicine and I would not wish you a moment less of that healing balm). So, at a word from Henry, I shall come, and yes, I'll bring little Tessa with me.

Love, your true and forever friend,
Taffy

Boston
May 21, 1875

Dear Mae,

I am terribly distressed by your last letter and of course I believe you. Carter and I shall be at your side within a month (according to Baedeker, the road into the Grampians is subject to flooding at this time of year, so don't fret if it takes us a little longer). Dear, stay calm, remain tractable, it is the best way. You are not alone, and soon you shall be home safe.

Love,
Taffy

Boston
May 23, 1875

Dear Mae,

I blush even to write this because, silly girl that I am even at the ripe old age of going-on-twenty-three, I now understand your last letter to me might as well have been from someone else entirely, so please forgive me for what I wrote in reply—you must have thought I'd taken leave of my senses! Forgive me dearest girl, for even mentioning the unfortunate letter, I do so only that you might rest easy in your mind that no one else has or ever shall read what you wrote.

I have a confession to make: after receiving it, silly Yours Truly cabled a rather frantic note to your poor husband who cabled back immediately in such a way as to quench my fears . . . and quash my fresh plans to board the next liner! (Yes, I am that silly.) I have already begged and received forgiveness from Lord Henry, and I beg the same now from you because, in responding to what turns out to have been little more than a bad dream, I must have caused you pain. Henry assures me your temporary confusion was brought on by a combination of the right medicine in the wrong dosage. I only hope your head did not ache too much afterwards, sweetheart. So forget all about it, and know that I pray for you and the safe delivery of your baby as soon as next week. Yes, dear Henry let me know the happy news, and he even told me I ought to write and tell you so. He told me too that if your little one is a girl, you plan to call her Charlotte. I can think of no sweeter nor more fitting name, dearest, and I know all will be well with you both.

Henry says you will write once you are up and about again and although I am famished for a word in your sweet hand, I hereby issue strict orders of my own that you not lift a finger of said sweet appendage to answer this letter until you have been discharged and are back at Fayne House under the kind care of Mrs. Knox, and strong enough to tuck into a steaming griddle of Cook's "bannocks" with "lashings" of Gossamer's butter. In the meantime, don't overdo it with the lawn bowls and shuttlecock!

Your loving,
Taffy
Boston
June 28, 1875

Dear Lord Henry,
Our hearts are broken. What remains of them we offer up in sympathy to you and to your infant daughter, Charlotte. Please forgive me if I overstep the bounds of politeness in hereby pledging to you and your daughter my lifelong friendship. Although it may be difficult to con-ceive how a lady in Boston, whom you have never met, could be of any use or comfort to your family, I beg you file away this promise if not this letter.

At the risk of presuming further, I will be so bold as to share with you that your late wife, and my dearest friend, gave me to understand in her characteristically colorful style, that you had made her the happiest woman in the world.

I and my husband, Carter, will always do all in our power to aid you and yours. And I shall never cease to pray for your well-being and, in time, happiness.

Yours sincerely,
Timothea (Taffy) Blanchard

I sat unmoving, as though under a spell.

I felt Gwendolyn turn to me. I met her eyes. I asked, "What is a 'therapeutic establishment'?"

She swallowed. "It's a . . . kind of . . . asylum."

"For consumptives? Was she tubercular?"

"I doubt it, that sort of hospital is commonly called a sanatorium."

"How d'you know?"

"I was in one."

"My God, Gwennie."

"I'm all right now." She coughed. "Really, I am."

"Were you close to death?"

"Apparently within hailing distance."

"But you were cured?"

"I sketched my way out of it. Nothing like endless time on your own to develop the imagination."

"We have that in common."

She smiled. "I hadn't thought of that."

"Then . . . what kind of asylum was my mother in?"

"I know of only one kind."

"Tell me. Please."

She dropped her gaze. "An asylum . . . for the care of the mentally afflicted."

". . . You mean to say my mother was in a madhouse?"

"It sounds a very nice one."

"Gwendolyn . . ."

I felt her hand at the back of my neck as she guided my head toward my lap. "Breathe," she said. "Listen old thing, it isn't unheard of."

"What isn't?"

"Women. And babies. You know." I shook my head. She said, "My own mother nearly went mad herself before I was born."

"Why?" I lifted my head—and registered an odd sense that my features were somehow askew, as in a wavery mirror.

"She was after craving a babby and she couldn't have one for the longest time, so grieved she couldn't hardly rise from bed and then only to reach for the sherry. Had there been a witch next door the vicarage, Mam would've been over the wall and gorging on rape leaves if she thought she'd get a bairn out of it. Or so she's told me . . . *in vino veritas* and all that."

"And did your mother recover by means of a sojourn at a therapeutic establishment?"

"No. A vicar's living does not stretch to shuttlecock and lawn bowls. I'm afraid in her case it would've been the Edinburgh Asylum at Morningside. Not but what there are far worse places. But I came along before it came to that."

"Gwennie, was I . . . ?" I riffled through the letters. "I was born in a madhouse."

"So what if you were, you're here now and sane as sun-up."

"But . . . that means she died there too, in the asylum, in the—Here it is, 'the road into the Grampians.'" I looked up. "Not the Alps." The words died on my lips and I heard them for what they were—a flimsy lie. "She'll be buried there too. On the grounds." I felt leaden.

Tears filled Gwen's eyes. I looked away, for I felt my own grow moist, and my throat thicken. It came on me of a sudden. My mother. Had been a girl. With a friend. And she had died far from home. I kept my gaze averted while Gwen commenced to tidy everything back into the drawer. She closed the false-bottom bed, stood up and reached down a hand. I took it.

She led me back along the passage, down the service stairs and into the scullery where we surprised Knox who trod on the tail of the cat and sent it yowling—"The pair of you! I was on the point of sending Byrn out after you with Nolan!"

Gwen did not tarry but pulled me out into the yard, past the well and round back of the house to what remained of the lawn, all the drabber for December, where she flung herself onto her back.

"Lie here beside me, let's look up at the sky."

I obeyed. "Whatever for?"

"Did you know that when you cry whilst lying on your back, the bowls of your ears catch the tears and become fairy pools?"

"Stuff and nonsense."

She reached over and pinched me. I laughed.

"And everything is funnier lying down!" she hooted.

We giggled helplessly at nothing at all. We grew silent. We giggled afresh.

Presently she said, "If you are shocked by what I am about to ask, then you've only to get up and walk away and I'll never allude to it again."

"I have vivisected a frog. You cannot shock me."

"Ugh."

"Its egg sac was stirring."

"Are you looking up?"

"Yes. Are you?"

"Yes."

"What are we looking at?"

"It is not what we're looking at, it is that we're not looking at one another."

Above me, the pale moon was camouflaged by the light of day. The sky was big with clouds. In their drift I saw an elephant.

She asked, "Have you ever had a thrilling sensation between your legs?"

As I watched, the cloud took on the shape of a baby . . . It was laughing.

"Allow me to rephrase," she said. "If you have ever had a thrilling sensation between your legs, say nothing for the next ten seconds. One. Two. Three. Four. Five. Six. Seven. Eight. Nine. Ten."

After a moment, she said, "What that sensation feels like, is how cocoa tastes."

High overhead, a beautiful woman smiled down, her arms full of bog myrtle. Gwendolyn added, "Of course, unlike cocoa, it costs nothing and is always available."

Without shifting my gaze from the clouds, I reached across, found her hand and squeezed. Tears gathered at the corners of my eyes, trickled down the sides of my head and into the bowls of my ears. Fairy pools of happiness.

23

He is not at the window.
He is at her bedside.
Staring past her as before.
She says, "Go away, you're dead."
He wants her to turn around.
She starts to turn her head. Suddenly the air is full of the smell of loam
and peat, mud and decay.
Knox is there.

I woke screaming.

Knox was there with her candle.

A sip of water. A warm brick from the fire. She held me as I trembled like a poplar. "Listen to me, lass. Your brother was bonny. And he's gone. He can ne'er return. Do you understand?"

"Is it true I was born in a madhouse?"

She paled in the candlelight.

"Tell me."

"Hush now—"

"Tell me!" I hissed, setting the flame to writhing, tasting salt on my lips. "Tell me or I swear I will ask my father." I saw something new in the eyes of my old nurse: fear. Reader, it made me feel . . . strangely outcast. As though she were behind glass, and I looking in at the window.

"Who told you that?"

"Timothea Blanchard," I croaked.

Her lips parted but she was speechless.

"I read the letters."

"However did you—?"

"Gwendolyn found them—"

"The wee minx—"

"I opened the false-bottom bed—"

"So that's where you were skulking—"

"We weren't 'skulking.'"

"You'd no business—"

"What business have you?!" I shrieked it.

She shook her head. "Och, lass."

"Don't you 'lass' me, does Father know you have my mother's private correspondence?!" Shocked at the size of my anger, I was yet unable to curb it. I vibrated with violence as though about me hovered the silhouette of a raging bear, and I longed to pounce.

She hung her head. The bear dispelled. "Foolish old woman," I muttered, "he'll see you flogged and turned out."

She lifted her eyes to me. I watched them well up with tears which, rather than roll down her cheeks, collected in the tracery of lines and fanned out as on a floodplain until her face glistened. When had my old nurse become elderly? I softened. "Why did you keep them?"

"Your father wanted no reminders, but . . ." Her voice broke. "'Twas all that remained. After her pretty things were . . ." She caught her breath. "Got rid of." She sobbed into her apron. I placed a hand upon her back and patted her, as she had so oft patted me. Presently, she scraped her face with her hanky and blew her nose.

"Knoxy," I whispered, horror descending upon me like a cloak, "will I go mad?"

I fell to shivering. I felt her hands seize my shoulders. "Listen to me, child, and perpend." Her eyes, red-rimmed and wet, were once more stern. "Your mother was sad. Too, too sad. And too much of anything may whelm a body, be they never so hale."

"'The dose makes the poison.'"

"Just so. But she's long gone to her rest and ta'en her sorrows with her. They need ne'er be visited upon you."

"I am strong."

"You are that."

"Father is . . . not."

"Your father has borne much, and bravely, and all for your dear sake. But I'd no see another blow befall him lest his heart not break this time, but shatter."

"I'd sooner die—"

"You'll do no such—"

"I didn't mean—"

"Keep it close is all. He must never know that you know . . ."

"That I was born in a madhouse."

"'Twas a therapeutic—"

"By any other name."

"The place your mother went to was as far from a common madhouse as the Cowgate is from Bell Gardens."

"Why lie about it then?"

"That you yourself call it a madhouse is answer enough, I warrant."

"She is not buried in the Alps. Next to my brother."

"She is not."

". . . Then he is alone."

It pierced me suddenly. My brother. All by himself. In the cold cold ground. Of a distant land. No wonder he was restless . . .

"I'm sorry I killed her."

The old woman gathered me to herself and cradled me. "My sweet lamby you are my consolation. And your father's. There's ne'er been a bairn was loved more than you."

"Not even Charles?"

"Not even Charles."

"Knoxy?"

"Aye, pet?"

"What was its name? The therapeutic establishment."

She sighed. "Morecombe Downs."

"Morecombe Downs."

"Promise you'll nevermore speak its name."

"I promise."

In my window, the quarter moon seemed to cast a sidelong glance.

"Thank you, Knoxy."

"For what, dear heart?"

"For telling me everything."

Father had concealed it from me out of love. I would do as much for him in return. For though I was strong enough to bear it, Father was not strong enough to know I was in possession of it: the Truth.

I slept dreamlessly the remainder of the night.

24

AT THE WINTER SOLSTICE, the great hall tingled with the scent of pine boughs that threaded the banisters and festooned the hearth. The household gathered and Byrn lit the Yul log. The fire took and we cheered and toasted with mead poured hot by Cook from an earthenware ewer.

Late that night I watched from my—newly draped in chintz courtesy of Gwen—window as Byrn, according to his custom, laid elder branches before the entry to the byre to protect the livestock from harm. Then, to my surprise, he approached the house and laid several on the ground beneath my window.

On the afternoon of Christmas Eve, Father sent for me to join him in his study. I entered and noted immediately that neither the letter to the physician nor the chimera were in evidence and I wondered if this boded well or ill, for the roll-top desk itself was closed—I thought of Aunt's letter and wondered guiltily whether Father had closed his desk against my prying eyes.

Father was ensconced in an armchair by the fire, facing the window that was now uncurtained but for the slow-falling flakes blanketing the moor in white, and softening the roofline of the byre in snow. He bade me join him on a low stool by his side. I did so, and he handed me the card he had just then been perusing. I recognized immediately the lady-like loops and my heart leapt guiltily. It was bordered with holly and I quickly read the usual "warmest wishes for a Merry Christmas" along with the usual "from cousin Tess too!" I mustered the usual remark, "How kind of Mrs. Blanchard to remember us."

"A stalwart lady."

I returned the card. I knew that, later today, Father would drop it quietly into the fire. Mrs. Blanchard could not know how acutely he felt her well-intentioned reminders. And I shrank inwardly to imagine how it would pain him to know that I was privy to far more from that lady's hand.

He indicated a package on the mantelpiece, wrapped in brown paper. "From your Aunt."

I rose and retrieved it. "How very kind of Aunt Clarissa." I opened it. It was not blue stockings. It was a book. *Lives Made Perfect Through Suffering*. Father smiled—a mite sheepishly I thought. "I have a gift for you, Father."

I ran and fetched from the window seat in the drawing room a parcel gaily wrapped in floral chintz left over from my drapes. Returning to the study, I handed him the gift which I had been at—literal—pains to keep a close secret, even from you, Reader (along with my pricked fingertips). He opened it and was silent a moment before murmuring, "Oh my."

He donned them there and then. A new pair of slippers. Embroidered by me. The left: *Dear*; the right: *Father*.

"Charlotte, my own. Thank you. Never have I received a more exquisite gift."

He beamed. I basked.

He said, "I have glad tidings."

I noted the long-lost femur of the *Xenicus lyalli* sitting in a brass saucer of bits on the mantelpiece. "Oh Father, I am pleased."

"Oh that, yes, quite, but no, my treasure." He paused.

I resumed my place on the low stool, folded my hands upon his knee and gazed up at him. He stroked my head. "You are aware that your rearing has differed from that of other children."

"Yes, Father."

"And do you know why?"

"It was—is—owing to my Condition."

"Correct. It has kept you from the society of your equals; from the enlarging effects of travel; from school. In short from much that a young lady of your station might expect in regards to amusements and accomplishments."

"Miss Haas has taught me to dance. I do not care for it. Though I care for her."

"You have lately become aware too that, despite these deficiencies, few young ladies have had the benefit of your education."

"I am only too keenly aware, Father, and grateful beyond measure, even if my tutor proved a bounder."

"A—?"

"Fear not, Father, he never tried it on with me, I'd have gone taut as catgut."

He cleared his throat. "You may recall, my dear, I promised that when the time came, I would spare no effort to free you from the constraints of your Condition."

"Yes, Father."

"Those constraints I placed upon you for your good. But I must now look to your happiness."

"Father, no one could be happier than I and there is no place I would rather be . . ." Had he heard the ellipsis? Three pebbles that pointed the way to the University of Edinburgh! My heart beat faster, for I sensed it coming . . . my Future. I kept my composure—not for the world would I injure Father by betraying my eagerness to fly from his side, for all he himself held open the door to my cage.

"You think that now," he said. "But soon you will crave other scenes, other . . . society. And it is my duty—" He broke off. He coughed. Smiled, though his eyes looked sad. "It is time you saw something of the wider world."

Carefully, lest I burst with excitement, I took hold of his hand—when had he become so slight? Father was getting older. How would he manage without me? Oh how I hoped Gwendolyn Haas might be proved right and Father was even now beloved of a deserving lady. A smile was on my lips, tears were in my eyes; and in my breast, emotions ran wildly counter to one another like a riptide in the sea.

Still he did not speak. Instead, he drew from his pocket a letter, and handed it to me. I read:

Ainsley Place
Edinburgh
December 12, 1887

My Lord,
Your Lordship's inquiry does me honour. I should be pleased to receive the Honourable Charlotte Bell, with a view to conducting the indicated examination at my consulting rooms at Your Lordship's convenience.

I remain,
Your servant,
W. G. Chambers, LRCS RCSE FRCSE LRCP

"Father . . ." I breathed. "Thank you." I was trembling as I handed back the letter.

"There is nothing to fear, my dear. Dr. Chambers is an eminent physician."

"I am not afraid, Father, I am . . . slain with happiness."

He smiled. "Depending upon the outcome of your examination, we shall remove permanently to Edinburgh and reside there."

"Huzzah," I whispered.

"Three cheers."

"In the house at Bell Gardens?"

"The very one."

"I shall meet Aunt Clarissa at last," I said, with due reverence.

Far from melancholy now, Father held forth knowledgably as to the house and the city. "Bell Gardens is in a pleasant paved quarter of the New Town, with a view of the Castle, 'tis a stone's throw from the Royal Society and Princes Street, a modern avenue of shops and tea rooms, with a picture gallery and a park where the monument to Sir Walter Scott towers o'er the passing parade—"

"Is it a walk to the university, or must I drive in the carriage, or shall I take a steam-powered public conveyance?" My words accelerated as though themselves propelled by steam. "Father, I must have a velocipede!"

"Risky on the cobbles, I daresay."

Skirts and silken fetters were a small price to pay for admission to that brave new world where the sons of tradesmen studied cheek by jowl with those of princes; where stout-hearted women blazed a trail for females as yet unborn; and Scientia welcomed all who approached with an open mind. I experienced even an influx of kindly feeling toward Murdoch Mungo—let us be as equals before Athena! "When?"

"Why, in a fortnight."

I threw my arms about him. "Thank you, Father!"

"There's my happy lass. Good, good. I shall need to breathe in a moment."

I laughed and released him. "Father, what is it?"

"You are so like your mother in these moments. Happy moments. Your vigour, your . . . force."

"Did I hurt you?"

"Nothing of the kind. It is my heart that hurts when I think what we lost. But here you are."

"I'm sorry, Father."

"Whatever for?"

". . . Do I resemble her?"

He regarded me a moment. "Not overmuch. Though there is something about the set of your jaw. Definite. She was nothing if not definite."

"Don't worry, Father. All will be well." I hugged his arm and leaned my head on his shoulder.

"I too have a Yuletide gift for you, my dear."

"Oh Father, you've already given me the best gift I could hope for."

He rose and, crossing to his desk, opened the roll-top to reveal the chimera. Mounted on a handsome oak stand, fitted with a brass name-plate: *Avis Risus Bellis.* Our specimen. Our dear, laughing, unsuspecting monster. "Why Father, it's cracking."

"Fit for the Bird Gallery."

"Is it male or female?"

"Funny, I hadn't thought to wonder."

"Nor had I."

And we chuckled.

The bell tolled for dinner and Knox put her head round the study door. "Cook says the goose is cooked, Your Lordship."

I had loosened my stays and so fell to with a will. We were two but we feasted as though we were legion, and I found a penny in my Yul bread. "Good luck all year!"

"Charlotte, what's the matter? Are you in a fit?"

My eyes were wide, I stood ramrod straight, 'twas all I could do to rein in the words so as they might emerge intelligibly from my lips: "I am going to Edinburgh!"

Gwendolyn was listing a little on her heels as though at a blast from Lord Kelvin's siren.

"When?"

"First thing in the new year."

"Oh, I can't wait!" She wriggled and pranced in place. "You'll bunk in with me and Maeve—she is longing to meet you—we'll stay up 'til all hours—"

"I'm afraid not, old thing, I'm to enter the university."

"What? Not straight off."

"Aye. I'm to undergo an examination, Father has arranged it all."

"He has?"

"You doubt my word?"

"Certainly not, only . . . Well I did imagine you'd begin your school career at Miss Gourley and Miss Mellor's."

"I understand, Gwennie, but I'm beyond all that now."

"Of course you are."

"Don't be vexed."

"I'm not. I know how brilliant you are, and I am happy for you, only . . ."

She burst out crying. I was shocked. My friend was shedding bright tears, I seemed to see them like sparkly bits of crystal. "Gwennie," I said stupidly. "Don't cry." I gave her my handkerchief. She dabbed her face and whimpered, "Will we still be friends?"

"Of course we will, you ninny!" I said earnestly, "As Seneca put it in a letter to Lucillius, 'Why do I make a friend? So that I might have someone for whom to die, one whom I may follow into exile.' He wrote one hundred and twenty-four letters in all, packed with sage advice, perhaps I'll undertake to do the same for you."

"Letters to Gwenillius."

"Why, yes."

"Or you could just pop round." She laughed, and threw her arms about me.

"Nothing will ever come between us, Gwendolyn."

"'Love is not love which alters when it alteration finds.'"

"That's rather good, you ought to write it down."

She grinned. "I say, you'll finally meet your dear old maiden aunt."

"Bless her heart."

"Prepare to be petted and fussed over, I can just picture her—a plump old tea cozy of a lady. I almost envy you, especially your first sight of Edinburgh, oh Charlotte, you're going to love it."

I listened as Gwen prescribed an itinerary consisting principally of sweet shops, concert halls and art galleries, and not a word passed my lips *re* the ongoing construction of the Forth Bridge, or the exhibits at Surgeons' Hall.

A week following Christmas, Reverend and Mrs. Haas, along with Gwendolyn, joined us for a Hogmanay feast. Cruikshank carried in the haggis along with Cook's annual gourd stuffed with spiced porridge and parsnip for Father that he might enjoy an approximation of a sheep stomach stuffed with oats and tripe. Father and Reverend Haas partook of whisky and Mrs. Haas kept pace with claret. Gwendolyn and I was-sailed with ginger beer and the evening was by turns jolly and poignant, owing much to the warblings of Mrs. Haas who seemed to know every auld sang from Cape Wrath to Carlisle. Soon Knox and Cook had joined in, culminating with all of us linking arms in the drawing room in a time-honoured breach of protocol—including Cruikshank, who swayed silently along with the rest of us as we rang out the year with a rendition of "Auld Lang Syne." Everyone laughed when it was Byrn who first-footed through the door at midnight. "What's he brought?!" cried Mrs. Haas.

A lump of moss, as it turned out, the which, once he'd been coaxed over the threshold, he placed at my feet to general hilarity. Reverend Haas intoned with mock solemnity, "The question now on everyone's mind will be, 'What colour was Byrn's hair back in the days when he had some?'"

And Cook's rejoinder, "Belike he never had none!"

Later, after the guests had been ferried safely home by Byrn, and 1888 was two hours old, I was at my window when the old man emerged from the byre with his yoke across his shoulders. He loped away, buckets swinging empty in the moonlight, his silhouette playing on the pristine snow, until he was lost to the blue-black shadows of the moor.

A black-haired stranger first in the door at the stroke of a new year meant good luck. Red-haired meant ill. But Byrn was bald, nor could he be called a stranger—even if his origins, like the scutcheon itself, were "involved in obscurity."

It was the eve of our departure and I was occupied with packing when Gwendolyn called unexpectedly.

"I know you've your hands full, old thing, but I wanted to say good-bye—"

"Jolly decent of you, goodbye then, well I'd best go up and see to my trunk, I dursn't leave it to Cruiky and Knox, they're like to leave out my beetles."

"Wait a minute, I've brought you something. A good-luck gift."

She insisted on giving it me in the scullery where she bid Cook set a pan of milk on the hob.

Soon I had before me a steaming mug. Gwen reached into her pocket and produced a hard finger of . . . "Charcoal?"

"Chocolate."

She dropped it into the mug and I watched as it melted into the milk. She added a lump of sugar and stirred the lot into a thick dark eddy. Then she pushed it toward me.

I raised it cautiously to my lips and sipped. And sipped a second time. And a third.

"So?" said Gwen. "Does it?"

"Does it what?"

"Taste like the other thing feels?"

I looked away but could not suppress a smile. Under the table I felt the scullery puss slinking round my ankles.

Still looking away. Still smiling. I said, "Thank you, Gwennie."

"Don't mention it, old thing."

Indeed, I dared not mention it: the true extent, that is, of my gratitude.

Upstairs, Knox was on the point of closing my trunk.

"Have you packed my lessons?"

"What for?"

"So I may study, of course."

"What've you done with your Belgian lace bloomers?"

"Dashed if I know."

"You'll want 'em for the examination."

"Whatever for?"

"Into bed with you, now, we've a long journey ahead," she said, pressing me gently to the pillow, and planting a kiss on my forehead.

"I'll not sleep a wink."

Byrn speaks and I understand him without effort, his words as clear as
    spring water.
Ask a favour of the plover, he says. Borrow her eyes.
Then I am flying through the air, and the flying is his song, and I am
    the flying, and his words are golden ribbons scrolling about me, bearing
    me along. I see the plover's wings and I am the plover. Suspended.
    Above the moor. There is no longer any I, only All.
Simple. Vast. Known.

All to be forgot on waking, like dew on a spiderweb.

We set out in the cart at dawn when the moor looks most like a memory—and soon to be that, for I knew not when I would behold it again; veiled in mist, and silent but for Achilles's hoof-falls and the grind of our wheels.

We ascended steadily the North Fell and as I looked up, a finger of pink light touched the tip of the standing stone and I could almost fancy I heard a bell-like tone. I turned and looked back. I felt something akin to remorse. Reader, it was my brother. I thought I ought to be glad, for I somehow knew he would not follow me to Edinburgh, but . . . it was almost as though I were abandoning him . . . to the bog.

I felt the cart pause at the crest—I had never been past that point—before nosing downward. And I turned to face My Future.

Part Two

Conventionality is not morality.
CHARLOTTE BRONTË

25

THE HONOURABLE CLARISSA BELL is seated on a spoon-back Regency chair in the parlour of her house at No. One Bell Gardens, Edinburgh. The fire pops purses and coffins, banishing the chill. She is waiting.

Having laid aside her work in a basket at her feet, her hands rest folded in the pleated lap of her black watered-silk dress, and she rocks a little. Greying ringlets emerge from her lace cap to frame a narrow face, and they swing back and forth a little as though in time with a metronome. Gracing her chest is her best jet necklace.

She has sent Sanders to fetch them from the station.

Over the past many weeks Clarissa's peace has been punctuated by the painting, paper-hanging, hammering and scraping of workmen. Bales and crates have been heaved by strange men, hauled and humped up stairs. And the same men have carried and bumped all manner of moveables down the stairs. Out with the old, in with the new. All under strict supervision. "Havers, you will not suffer strangers to be one moment unattended by a member of the household." Rickety Irishmen along with primitive-looking Highlanders. What is amiss with our own Edinburghshire labourers? They have raised themselves up and out of the market thanks to public education—all to the good of course, especially as concerns the reduction in infectious disease, but no sooner is it safe to breathe the air in the kirk than another class of the poor rushes in to fill the void (largely Catholic and given to increase, the which is sapping the lifeblood of Scottish nationality).

To say nothing of the expense. Clarissa calculated it as it arrived, her head for figures as sharp as any analytical engine. The carpets (£10 per square yard) and wallpapers (15s. per piece) alone would have sufficed to raise an army in James V's day, never mind £20 5s. for drawing-room furniture alone. A hot-water tank has been installed in the attic. The Edinburgh Warming and Ventilating Company has implanted a hot-water pipe in the walls, and though it has been sealed up, plastered and painted over, Clarissa is nonetheless keenly aware of its presence; like an engorged artery running from the attic all the way down to an outsized new boiler in the scullery. A coal-fired furnace has been installed in the cellar, vents have been cut into the floors on each storey. To the tune of a king's ransom. The entire house has been plumbed for gas pipes which feed light fixtures of disconcerting brightness. A cut-crystal "gasolier" has been hung in the "foyer"—rum word, "foyer." Naturally the house, being in the New Town, was already equipped with an indoor WC, but Clarissa has followed her brother's instructions, in this as in everything, to the letter, adding a brand-new lavatory complete with ceramic basin, bath and "wash-down" convenience adjoining the marital chamber. The latter "renovation" entailed the sacrifice of Henry's dressing room. Even Clarissa's parlour has received a fresh coat of paint—mercifully with no alteration as to its shade of deep plum. The whole has cost in excess of several decades' worth of tax on the estate at Fayne. She is faint with expenditure. But the wellspring of wealth is, so far, fathomless. Wellspring? More beanstalk, judging by its provenance.

She assumed her chair by the window at nine o'clock this morning and has not stirred since. Except to place her work inside her basket. From here she commands a view through net curtains, of the circular drive—freshly gravelled—with its screen of hollyhocks at the centre. Beyond it, privet hedges flank the iron gates which stand open at her instruction. Unavoidable, therefore, the view of passersby on the pavement. A nurse pushes a perambulator—the rain has ceased, still is it wise to air an infant on so damp an afternoon? Divers silk-hatted gentlemen with umbrellas under their arms and an occasional newspaper; a hatless youth, smoking in public—Clarissa would summon Havers but that her butler is well enough occupied in preparing for the imminent arrival of Clarissa's brother in company with a young lady she is impatient to meet. Indeed, the "rumpus" (as her old nurse might put it) of the past weeks is not to be held against one whose arrival was so long-awaited, so devoutly wished. . . . *Cherish*. The word has arisen as though suspended in black and white before her eyes. Aye. The lass is to be cherished. For apart from all else, she brings with her the Future.

Across Clarissa's line of vision rides a lad on a tricycle hauling a wagonload of *The Scotsman*; he is followed by a column of schoolgirls in wide-brimmed straw hats. The schoolmistress bringing up the rear is . . . Rosamund Gourley. Clarissa used to feel sorry for her, poor thing cast upon the world to earn her living.

Clarissa's butler? Her brother's butler. Her parlour? His. Her maid— bursting in now, "M'um, Cavendish has set the meat jack, and wishes to know if you're still of a mind to serve pears?"

"Tell Cavendish that next time I am called upon to renew my instruction regarding pears, she shall herself be set upon the meat jack."

"Aye m'um."

Clarissa knows her maid will say no such thing to Cook. No one would dare.

Her brother's maid.

Her brother's meat, her brother's pears . . . *Pears!* Perish the thought. Her brother's house. Her brother's title. Of which Clarissa is custodian. She straightens her spine, lest her back touch the chair.

Here they are.

The Black and the Bay are turning in at the gates, top-hatted Sanders at the reins of her—her brother's carriage.

She rises carefully. The pain is a little less today.

"They're here, m'um!" squeals Sheehan, in the doorway once more.

Through the window Clarissa sees Havers descending unhurriedly the broad stone steps from the house toward the drive. Pugsley is already unloading a trunk from the roof whilst Sanders holds the team. Havers opens the carriage door with a white-gloved hand and stands to one side.

Trade places with Rosamund Gourley? What with the latter's "bed-sit" and penny gas ring, her poets, her pupils, her meetings of the Society for the Relief and Refuge of the Poor Irish Among Us; her Sunday treat atop Arthur's Seat where she bends to knock the mud from her hobnail boots?

She watches as Henry emerges from the carriage; like a chick from its shell, a smile on his face exactly like the one that dawned when Clarissa

fed him his first sweet—Edinburgh Rock—on his fifth birthday. And
behind him—

"Och, she's lovely!" cries Sheehan.

Clarissa forbears to scold, for the gel is a fiend for work; the grates
have never been blacker nor the linens whiter—and no one else knows
quite the way of arranging the cushion at Clarissa's back. And all for a
pittance. She owes this Irish marvel to kind Mr. Baxter who counted
it a particular favour that Clarissa consented to employ her without a
character. Plucked from the gutter, no doubt.

Clarissa twitches closed the net curtain and makes her way, bell-shaped
and rustling, to the "foyer" where she composes her features with several
seconds to spare before the door opens and Henry stands before her.

"Dear sister, allow me to present to you Lady Marie Bell, Seventeenth
Baroness of the DC de Fayne."

"Call me Mae! Oh, Clarissa, I am just thrilled to meet you!"

Her brother's bride.

Lord Henry Bell, 17th Baron DC de Fayne, has returned to his
Edinburgh residence in the New Town with his bride of six
months, Lady Marie née Corcoran of Boston.
The Scotsman, August 2, 1871

26

SIX MONTHS PREVIOUSLY, upon Henry's arrival at her palazzo in
Rome, La Principessa—"Do call me Fanny"—had given him an account
of the party. She called it a "briefing."

He had, moments before, been shown to his room—a lavishly
appointed chamber so distinctly unmasculine that he feared an error had
occurred. It was no good inquiring of the gleaming-haired servant, however, for the man had no English as he made plain by a series of ornate
utterances whilst backing from the room, bowing excessively, leaving
Henry to take in his surroundings.

He had already been taken aback—if not bowled over—by the opulence of the palace. Room after room of paintings and looking glasses

and ornate sconces, all empanelled in exotic wood or framed by gilded stanchions. His boot heels rang out on marble floors or sank soundlessly in deep pile of scarlet and peacock blue; along the upper walls, wee angels rained down fruit over whatever shipwreck or sunset roiled in oils below; urns in *bas-relief* were effortlessly held up by fig-leafed men and women. He grew dizzy gawking at crystal chandeliers.

He stood now in a sumptuously appointed bedchamber of comparatively muted peach and gold. From the oval looking glass above the marble fireplace (more cherubs, more urns) to the shapely porcelain pitcher and basin on the washstand, there was nary a straight line in the place. Glass doors to the balcony were swagged in brocade, all was tasselled, beaded and braided, each surface upholstered to the degree that Henry might have mistaken a bench for the bed had not the footman—or whatever he was—placed Henry's trunk upon it. The man had unpacked, over Henry's protestations, and now an ebony valet stand stood adorned with his blazingly new tail coat, waistcoat, shirt, bowtie and trousers, his cufflinks and studs pooled on a built-in tray. On the washstand, his dressing case sat open, displaying his likewise recently acquired combs, brushes, razor, strop and other intimate oddments, all of which added to his consternation when a smart rap at the door was followed by the entry of La Principessa herself.

"Fanny" was a handsome woman, strawberry blond, blue-eyed, a self-described "merry widow" of something in the neighbourhood of forty.

"Lord Henry, welcome!" She reached out and shook his hand before he could kiss hers. He blushed at what he understood to be his near infelicity. His hostess was American.

She bade him join her on his balcony with a view of the Coliseum. Rather than enlisting his admiration thereof, however, she lit a cigarette and, elbows resting on the marble balustrade, launched in on a survey of the field. "Count Rákóczi has three thousand acres and a mounting gambling debt but he sings like a Hungarian angel, so he is not to be underestimated." Henry felt himself blush anew. She continued, "Sir Carrington Harvey-Staines is a confirmed inebriate with rooms in Piccadilly by the skin of his teeth but he's very funny and can turn on a dime with a heartbreaker about his dead spaniel. Now, you'll want to be careful of Miss Jenkins of Ohio, she is made of money but her brother's got a club foot and no one's ever seen her from the knees down. The Russian, Prince Nicholas Nikolayevich Orlov, however, has five sisters in want of dowries and wouldn't balk at a wooden leg, so we might rest easy on that score. Miss Brayne of Scranton checks out in the sound-of-body department and her dowry is thought to be just south of three hundred thousand dollars but you'll have your hands full fending off Prince Guillaume Todiac-Fauré-de Chaume-sur-Chêne. There's absolutely nothing wrong with him, apart from his complete indifference to the female sex. And finally," she turned to him brightly, "there's Mr. Gerald Corcoran of Boston with his daughter, Mary—Marie, that is. Catholic, mind you, but she has a million dollars in hand and he's open to negotiation." He drew back slightly. Fanny smiled through an exhalation of smoke. "Don't be shy, Lord Henry, this is your chance. And don't be scared off when you meet her."

By this he took the Principessa to mean that Miss Corcoran might be as plain of person as she was rich of purse.

"Oh, and there's an old friend of yours stopping with us too."

Henry perked up. "I say, really?"

"Lord Richard Hawley."

Henry concealed his distaste, but Fanny divined his feelings. "Mmm," she chuckled. "I see your point, but I think he's your only real competition."

Henry squared his shoulders. "Thank you, Principessa."

"Fanny."

He felt himself redden yet again.

She said, "I know it means something shocking in Great Britain, but when in Rome . . . do as the Americans." She winked, stubbed out her cigarette on the railing, cupped it in her hand and carried it out, leaving him to "freshen up"—just as though she were the gentleman, and he . . . a lady. Still, one could not help but like her. Moreover, he had the reassuring sense that she was on his side.

Introductions over "cocktails" in the courtyard. Above, an azure sky was suffused with the passion of the dying day, while about, minor deities besported themselves in paint and stone between rose-veined pillars. All to the susurrations of a nearby fountain.

"Chin-chin," said their hostess.

Henry joined the others in raising his glass—a sweetish ruby-coloured beverage in which there tinkled chips of ice.

He bowed to the ladies and greeted the gentlemen, including: "Hawley."

"Henry." The signature sneer.

Hawley was louche as ever. Henry knew him well enough to know he was not actually tipsy—not yet. Hawley had affected the same languid demeanour at breakfast at Straifmore when they were still in knicker-bockers.

"I say, Penny, is that a new tail coat?"

Henry sighed. "How is your father?"

Hawley giggled. "Stubbornly *vivus*, to my elder brother's chagrin. It's all one to me, I'm actually rather fond of the old boy."

Sir Carrington Harvey-Staines had a blue-veined nose and had been at school with Henry's late older brothers. Henry listened politely. *Ditto*, laughed.

The variously titled, ribanded and medal-encrusted continentals spoke excessively or not at all and were given to an ostentatious click-ing together of the heels in greeting their hostess. The count reeked of Macassar oil and wore an expression severe in the extreme. As for his aide-de-camp (a Prussian officer so tall his valet must require a ladder to hook his collar), was it quite good manners to go about armed with a sabre among ladies?

The ladies: "Miss Brayne." Henry bowed. "I am honoured to make your acquaintance." As she minced away from him, Henry discreetly observed her gait in an attempt to discern whether she was, after all, lame . . . or was that Miss Jenkins? "Miss Jenkins, I am honoured . . ."

A hearty voice with a trace of a lilt rose above the party—"Fanny Bunker, what's a fella got to do to get a real drink around here?"

Their hostess sashayed, with open arms, toward a short rotund gen-tleman and Henry observed, like an anthropologist from amid tall ferns, as the two engaged in the modern American greeting whereby, to the fashionable kiss on both cheeks, there was added a bear hug. He braced himself as she pulled the gentleman over by the wrist. "Lord Henry, this is Mr. Gerald Corcoran."

"Well this is an honour indeed, Your Lordship."

"Mr. Corcoran, I am pleased to make your acquaintance."

And slapping his hand into Henry's, the man said, "Call me Gerry."

Mr. Corcoran had a ruddy complexion and a mane of silvering hair, his dinner jacket was immaculately tailored and as vulgarly new as Henry's own tail coat. Henry suppressed a wince. Fanny shot him a moue of amusement, then waved and called to someone over his shoulder. "Mae, darling, there's someone I'd like you to meet."

Did the fashionable assembly part at her passage across the courtyard? Did a hush descend? Henry felt the full force of Fanny's warning when he set eyes on the young lady, for she was lovely to the point of banishing speech. A raven-haired beauty; a green-eyed goddess with alabaster skin and a girlish smile.

The other ladies and gentlemen faded from his awareness. A space opened up around her like a glade in Time, affording Henry, Lord Bell, Seventeenth Baron of the DC de Fayne, a brief eternity wherein, at the sight of Miss Marie Corcoran of Boston, Massachusetts, he felt his life begin.

"I am honoured to make your acquaintance, Miss Corcoran." He bowed deeply. Before he rose he heard her giggle and it refreshed him, like water from a sacred spring. *Oh giggle again, bright angel!*

There in the courtyard, Fanny gave an *al fresco* dinner of fruit and quail and strange dainties and sparkling wine that made him sneeze, his glass perpetually full. Conversation bubbled along with the wine, the trills and titters of the ladies at one with the tinkle of silverware and china. The assembled party seemed to inhabit a *tableau vivant*, every bit as glowing as the bougainvillea that spilt from each corner and the white star jasmine that graced an archway. In the stone fountain a semi-nude nymph poured water from an endless pitcher into a pond bright with fish. Behind Henry's chair, near enough that its fruit nuzzled his shoulder, stood a pear tree in a clay pot. "Forced pears," said Fanny. "Giovanni is so clever." The scene was marred only by the braying laugh of Hawley—the self-regarding popinjay was seated directly across from him, next to Miss Corcoran.

Henry made a polite reply to a polite query from the lady to his right whilst keeping his eye on Hawley who, inclining his head close to Miss Corcoran's, murmured something at which she erupted in giggles. Henry felt his blood come up. "Quite," he said, to Miss Brayne—or was it Miss Jenkins?

But even Hawley could not spoil the bewitching atmosphere.

Exotic birds preened and lofted. Proud peacocks displayed their purple glory, only to be outshone by the entrance of a snow-white specimen. An African grey parrot suddenly burst forth, "PrettyMae-prettyMaeprettyMae!"

Miss Corcoran looked wide-eyed, her lips parted. Fanny roared with laughter, "I spent three weeks teaching him that!"

"Youbastardyoubastard!" exclaimed the bird.

"He learned that on his own," added Fanny, with wry humour.

Henry was alarmed, but the entire party laughed the more heartily, none more so than the grating Hawley. Henry caught Miss Corcoran's eye across the table—she was blushing demurely.

Conversation burbled on and the meal concluded with a remarkable "dessert" of "gelato" that quite intoxicated him beyond the wine, beyond even the fragrance of the flowers—"It's vanilla, Lord Henry, here try the pistachio." Fanny plied him with frozen delicacies and candied petals from her garden. He caught Hawley looking at him "knowingly" and realized he had been staring at Miss Corcoran, a foolish smile on his lips. He looked away and determined to water his after-supper brandy. Fanny rose, at which the gentlemen did likewise.

Under a full-bellied moon, the table had been taken away, fat candles had been lit in wax-withered sconces, and the gentlemen stood about with cigars and porto (so much for brandy). Gilt buttons shone and precious medals gleamed in light refracted by crystal-cut goblets of finest Venetian glass. More light spilt through a set of elaborately carved doors thrown open from a drawing room where the ladies sat about a card table, chattering.

The French prince was off in a corner, caught up in close querying of a young serving man. The Hungarian count and the Russian nobleman, having settled upon French as the international language, were conversing—Henry would have said "violently differing" but for intermittent bursts of laughter. From the opposite side of the courtyard came the crack of balls; through an open window, Mr. Corcoran and the Prussian officer could be seen slowly circumnavigating the green glow of the billiards table.

Henry had retreated to the shadow of the stone nymph with her pond, the better to endure the masculine interlude prior to rejoining the ladies; an interval made more tedious by his own countryman, sidling up to him now.

"It's come to this then, has it, Penny?" drawled Hawley. He clipped the end of his cigar and leaned toward an extravagantly dripping sconce to light it.

"Come to what, Dickie?"

"Why, we're both rooting for truffles."

"I shall do you the favour of failing to apprehend your meaning."

"May the best man win."

"Keep away from the lady."

"Really, old chap, you can have her. I'll take Fanny."

"Presuming La Principessa will have you, how can you dream your father would consent to a match wherein your bride is so much your superior not only in parts but in years?" Henry regretted his words instantly, not only for their implied disparagement of their gracious hostess, but because Hawley, for all he was odious, was not a worthy opponent. His father may be a marquess, but Dickie's own children and grandchildren would peter into the mists of Hon's and eventually Misters and Misses until they disappeared in the elbowing throng of a common omnibus. Or worse, Canada.

Hawley lounged against the wall, one foot crossed over the other ankle. "Ha-ha, Pater doesn't give a toss if I produce brats, that's my brother's job, poor sod. And yours!" He drew on his cigar and blew a series of smoke rings before continuing, "Miss Corcoran is an admittedly ravishing creature. Though she does strike one as . . ."

Henry's silence was taken as licence—and who knows but what Henry was curious in spite of himself as to what Hawley might say—thus Hawley went on, "Well, as the saying goes, 'One can take the Irish out of the bog, but one can't take the bog out of the Irish.'"

"Not another word if you value your throat."

"Are you challenging me?"

"Yes."

"What, pistols at dawn?"

"Rapiers if you prefer."

Hawley guffawed. "In the Coliseum perhaps?"

"As you wish."

"Dear old Henny-Penny, she is a lady of distinction and I wish you joy of her."

"Thank you."

"But you'll have no excuse in future." With this he smote Henry on the shoulder.

"Excuse for what?"

"You'll bloody well have to have the old boys up to Fayne for a shooting party once you've potted all that lovely money."

"I hardly know whether to thrash you or—"

"D'you ever come across dear Josey down there in Auld Reekie?"

"Of course. Baxter is a friend."

Hawley sniggered. Henry was about to turn away when the insufferable man continued, "Helped me out of a scrape once, did old Josey."

That could mean only one thing. Henry pursed his lips. Hawley continued, "A bit of bother with one of Father's maids a while back. A wee by-blow 'got 'twixt unlawful sheets." He snickered. "Josey sorted it for me." He paused. "She was Irish too."

Henry feinted a lunge, restraining himself at the last second. Hawley danced back. "Egad! Fisticuffs is it?" Laughing, bobbing side to side on the balls of his feet.

"You're drunk, Hawley."

He smiled insolently. "Do you know what you are, Penny?"

"Better a prig than a prat."

"You're a relic." He turned unsteadily on his heel to face the pond whose nymph endlessly refreshed the waters, and Henry recognized with horror the motions of a man arranging his flies to—He seized Hawley by the collar, the latter giggled and the cigar fell from his lips with a sizzle, "Now look what you've done!" Henry released him and the boor adjusted his bowtie, then swaggered through the open doors to the drawing room, his premature entrance welcomed by a cheer from Fanny and a general fluttering of feminine plumage. Henry fished the cigar from the pond, set it on the rim, then sought out Mr. Corcoran in the billiards room, where he allowed himself to be narrowly bested at straight rail.

There followed an interval of two days of delightful diversion during which the party visited the principal sites. At the Trevi Fountain, mighty

Oceanus presided over the taming of the turbulent waters, and Henry happened to be at her elbow. "The travertine used in the construction of the fountain, Miss Corcoran, is the same stone which was used to build the Coliseum."

"Oh my," said Miss Corcoran.

"And a sip from it ensures a return to Rome," said Hawley, bending next to him with cupped hands.

Henry muttered, "Or typhus, if your treatment of fountains is aught to go by."

Hawley appeared not to hear as he sipped with a sidelong glance at Fanny who gave him a mocking smile.

The Spanish Steps were thick with pink azaleas; Henry fell back a little, eye-drunk. All were rapt, and it seemed to Henry that the beauty of the entire scene was somehow contingent upon Miss Corcoran's presence.

They repaired for luncheon to a local *terrazzo* "for the fun of it" where a dandified proprietor fussed over the "laydees and gentlymen."

"Lord Henry," said Fanny at his elbow, "Try the artichoke, it won't bite. At least not 'til you get to the pit which is to be avoided unless you want to end up with a tongue like a cat's. Here, I'll show you." She did so. "Now you know how, why don't you help little Mae Corcoran before she learns the hard way."

Still, as the delightful two days wore on, he was forced to endure the flamboyant French prince, for whom Miss Corcoran's wardrobe seemed more an object of fascination than her person—"*Mais non, c'est une robe de la Maison Worth, n'est-ce pas?!*" "*Mais oui,* how did you know?!"—while the count's full-throated serenading to the piano accompaniment of Miss Jenkins had Miss Corcoran dabbing her eyes—indeed, Henry himself was on the point of weeping, but for a different reason. Sir Carrington had her in stitches over some high-jinks of his new spaniel, the deuced Prussian seized every opportunity to kiss her hand and the doleful Russian, with his endless acres of snow and stinging insects, played on her sympathies with an account of the plight of the peasantry. "Lord Henry, why don't you rescue Miss Corcoran, here, take her this." And Fanny placed in his hand a tiny cut-crystal glass of an emerald liquid— "Crème de menthe." These small offices with which Fanny charged him, he performed sedulously, ceding the field to his rivals whose vulgar persistence he hoped would end by wearying Miss Corcoran. Thus, "Might I intrude with the offer of refreshment, Miss Corcoran?" "Why certainly, Lord Henry, thank you. Oh, it's delicious." Whereupon, with a bow, he withdrew. Hawley alone kept his distance from the lovely Bostonian, and for this Henry was grateful, even if he was aware of owing the puppy a punch in the nose.

Indeed he was relieved, if a touch scandalized, when having risen early after a sleepless night, he crept from his room out to the gallery overlooking the courtyard and caught sight of Hawley stealing across from the ladies' wing. Retreating quickly to his quarters, Henry stepped onto his balcony, where day was breaking gold and rosy. He looked off to his right, and there, at the far end of the palazzo, likewise leaning on her marble balustrade, was Fanny, in a loose wrapper of crimson. She was smoking and gazing into the dawn. As though she felt his eyes upon her, she looked over and lifted her chin in greeting with a suave smile. He nodded. He knew he ought to be shocked, but really she was rather splendid.

On the third day the entire party toiled up the Palatine Hill. All about, immense marble fragments lay strewn; collapsed arches, buckled floors and toppled columns, at once grand and desolate, were over-mantled by vines, fissured with grass. Prince Nicholas Nikolayevich quoted *The Marble Faun*. "'The firmest substance of human happiness is but a thin crust . . .'" Sir Carrington inclined his head toward Miss Brayne and graced her with an account of his spaniel's final moments.

Henry contrived to find himself next to Miss Corcoran—rather, Fanny managed it with a sleight of social know-how. And as they strolled amid the ruins, it struck him that Miss Corcoran's youth and beauty shone all the brighter against the sombre backdrop. Beneath the faded umber of the Church of San Bonaventura, they paused.

"Charming, would you agree, Miss Corcoran?"

"Oh Lord Henry, it's scrumptious," she breathed, conveying to him the pleasing sense that he was somehow responsible for having designed and built it especially for her.

"And the view," he said, turning to indicate in the middle distance the crumbling slope of the Coliseum. "Rather fine, would you agree, Miss Corcoran?"

"Oh yes, I adore Rome, it's so . . . old."

He pointed out the Arch of Constantine, "And there in the distance, the Basilica of San Giovanni."

"Daddy always says the art is the best part of being Catholic," she remarked, blushing. Henry was not a blurter, but he blurted now, "I am of course Church of England and Scotland, notwithstanding those denominations do not commonly reside within a single breast." He barely understood his own words and hastened to add, "I am, however, a confirmed agnostic." She cast him a look of alarm. But before he could compound their mutual confusion—

"Ha, not very likely." *Hawley!*

"You demur, Lord Richard?"

"It's a contradiction in terms, old man."

"What is?" Really, the fellow was not be borne.

"'Confirmed agnostic.'" Hawley smirked.

"Oh," said Miss Corcoran to Henry, "I thought you said 'confirmed bachelor.'" She giggled, bit it back, and dropped her gaze charmingly. Henry swallowed and steered her effortlessly by the elbow toward where Fanny was in conversation with Mr. Corcoran in the shade of the convent wall.

A bird sang nearby. He stilled their steps. He said, bashfully, "A calandra lark. Rare. In my native clime, that is."

"What a sweet song."

"I am pleased you agree."

"Oh, listen, it's saying *pretty-girl*, over and over again." She flushed. "Silly me."

He listened. He tried to hear what she had heard . . . One thing, however, was certain: the bird was not calling *teacher-teacher*. He prevaricated, "By Jove, I believe you're right."

He spoke to her father that evening.

"Mr. Corcoran, might I have a word?"

"Call me Gerry. Fanny tells me you Bells go back to before the Flood."

"I don't know that I can claim so biblical a provenance—"

"I'm just kidding. But you're an old family."

"Only upwards of some four hundred and fifty years, although if local lore is to be credited, there was a Pictish yeoman name of Beal who, following the Roman invasion—"

"Well look who's invading Rome now, Your Lordship!"

Henry elevated his eyebrows politely; the intensity of the man's joviality was somehow a disquieting intimation of the opposite humour.

They were in the library, a room which boasted more busts than books.

Henry said, "It is my hope you will take no umbrage at my applying to you for permission to make an offer of marriage to your daughter, Miss Corcoran."

Mr. Corcoran frowned, shifted his jaw to one side, raised an eyebrow and his chin, and gave the impression of looking down on Henry from a superior height, despite his being head and shoulders the shorter. "So it's a hereditary title, no bones about it?"

"That is correct." Henry was standing very straight, his own expression serious, even severe, as he offered, as if it were a sword laid across a sacred tablet, Fayne.

"And your son will be a baron."

"He will. Eighteenth Baron of the DC de Fayne." Henry's chest swelled almost painfully—*is this what a pigeon feels like?* The oddest thoughts at the most inapt moments.

"With a seat in the House of Lords."

"Yes."

"By the seat of your pants."

". . . I'm afraid I do not take your meaning."

"Well a baron just squeaks by when it comes to a peerage, am I right?"

"There are degrees of rank, but none of merit."

"That's just my Yankee ignorance talking, no offence meant."

"None taken." *Lie.*

"All right, then."

"Is that . . . ? Do you mean, sir, to say—?"

"That's a yes."

"I hope I might prove worthy of your daughter."

"She's Catholic, you know."

"I do not foresee religious variance posing an impediment to marital felicity. Is it your wish the children be raised as Papists?"

"You fellas can decide that on your own, so far as I'm concerned the good Lord doesn't give a hoot one way or the other. What're you going to do with an Almighty who smites you with a famine one minute and five million bucks the next, huh? Fickle bastard." And he grinned good-naturedly.

"Quite."

"You know something?"

". . . Er."

"I'm a baron too."

". . . Really."

"I sure am. A bean baron!" Mr. Corcoran laughed and walloped Henry on the back. "Now, let's talk turkey."

"'Turkey.'"

Mr. Corcoran produced from the inside pocket of his crimson smoking jacket a document which he spread on the leather-inlaid table. "This is in case she says she'll have you." There, overlooked by the busts of Seneca and Cicero, the Irish-American captain of industry laid out his terms. They were generous. "There's just one little thing, Yer Lordship."

"Yes?"

"A codicil."

"I see."

Henry signed without hesitation, for even if Miss Corcoran were not the most exceedingly lovable woman in all Creation—the which she was!—Henry would never sully his honour with divorce. Thus the codicil "*In the Event of the Obtaining of a Writ of Divorcement*" was moot.

Mr. Corcoran signed, then hailed the count, who was passing on his way to the billiards room, and commandeered him as witness.

"It's a deal," said Mr. Corcoran, and thrust out his hand. "Let's shake on it."

Henry took his soon-to-be father-in-law's hand and, returning the unaccustomed pressure, allowed his own to be pumped.

"She's a good girl, Lord Henry. Don't make her cry."

"I would not dream of it."

Upstairs, in Mae's boudoir, Fanny sat, one leg crossed over the other, behind Mae who was brushing her hair in the mirror.

"You'll have to learn to say 'looking glass' once you're Lady Bell," said Fanny.

"I beg your pardon?" Mae blushed.

"And say 'what' not 'pardon' or they'll think you're a peasant."

"Don't tease, he doesn't care a fig for me, Fanny."

"Don't be silly, that's just his way."

"The count is so handsome."

"The count lives in Transylvania, do you know how far that is from Paris, never mind London?"

"Europe's so tiny, it can't be that far."

"That depends how many miles you have to cover by sheep-track."

"I don't know . . . Can't you just imagine all those romantic evenings in his castle in front of a roaring fire?" The girl hugged herself and giggled.

"Yes I can," said Fanny flatly.

"What about Lord Richard Hawley?" said the girl with a saucy elevation of her untroubled brow. "He's amusing."

"He's mine."

Mae shrieked with laughter and Fanny chuckled. "He suits me, darling, but I wouldn't wish him on you."

"What on earth can you mean?"

"Now listen to Fanny, buttercup. Lord Henry is smitten—"

"Could've fooled me."

"He's speaking to your father right now."

Mae gasped and whirled on her stool to face Fanny, both hands over her mouth.

Fanny continued, "The count is handsome, Hawley's amusing but Lord Henry is nice. I don't expect you to understand how important that is when it comes to . . . marriage. And I hope you never find out."

Just then came a tap at the door which promptly opened, and Gerald Corcoran put his head in.

"Oh hi, Daddy."

Mae turned to Fanny. The older woman cupped the lovely face in her hand and gave the girl a look both fond and . . . Mae saw something else but couldn't put her finger on it.

"I'll leave you to it," said Fanny. And withdrew.

———

The next morning Fanny informed Mae, "You have a headache."

"I do?"

"You do if you know what's good for you." And she winked.

The rest of the party set out for the Basilica after breakfast and Mae descended to the courtyard, where she seated herself on the fountain's edge and trailed her fingers in the water. She heard Lord Henry arrive but waited until he spoke.

"Good morning, Miss Corcoran."

"Oh, Lord Henry," she said, turning. "Good morning."

He made to stride toward her but bumped his head on a low-hanging pear. She giggled. He reddened but smiled and, owing to whatever Muse it was that breathed into the psychical ear of Henry Bell, he reached out, plucked the pear and handed it to her.

"Oh, why thank you."

He dropped to one knee. Nearby, the parrot erupted, "Shutupshutupshutup!" He shooed the bird with his brushed silk hat, and spoke. "Miss Corcoran, I have your father's permission to make you a proposal of marriage."

"Oh my goodness, Lord Henry, oh my . . ."

"Please do not feel obliged to answer immediately. Or indeed at all. The prerogative is yours. The privilege of offering a lifetime of devotion is mine."

He looked at her steadily. This amber moment will last forever.

She fairly sighed it, "Okay."

He let out the breath he had been holding, too light-headed to rise immediately. He frowned. She faltered. He said, "You have made me the happiest man in Christendom . . . and beyond."

She smiled shyly. "Me too." And looked down at the fruit in her hands.

He gazed up at her. "Forgive me, perhaps you are not partial to pears." And he held out his hand to relieve her of it.

She looked straight at him and bit into it. A little juice dribbled toward her chin. He rose, offered his handkerchief, and watched, helpless with desire, as she patted dry her mouth.

The evening before, upon entering her room, Mae's father had made himself comfortable in the one large channel-back among the boudoir chairs, while she perched on the stool, swivelling a little back and forth.

"Do you like him?"

"He seems nice."

"Well he's not like that greasy Robespierre who can't keep his hands off a deck of cards."

"Do you mean the count or the prince?"

"The prince? I don't care how many hyphens he's got in his name, I'll not be marrying you off to a pansy."

"Daddy!"

"And the Russian's got consumption, I'd put money on it."

"He's delicate."

"My foot."

"The baron's a bit old."

"He's thirty-two!"

"Like I said."

"Come here, lass." She did, and he settled her on his knee. "Now I don't think there's any skeletons in his closet, I've asked around. He's going to pop the question tomorrow." She bit her lip and looked away. "I promised you, didn't I, and Pappy always keeps his promises. Look at me now." She obeyed. Tears filled her eyes. He took her chin between thumb and forefinger. "Sure I wish your Mam were here too." She buried her face in his shoulder and he hugged her. Father and daughter stayed like that for a moment, neither trusting themself to speak. Then he took her by the shoulders and had her face him square on. "Now you're not to be saying yes to him for my sake, even if he is a baron, do you understand?"

"Yes, Daddy. I like him, I do."

"And you're not to be liking him only for my sake, even if my grandson will be a British lord and no one in Beantown will dare shut me out of the State House again." He grinned and winked.

"No, no, Daddy, I do want to marry him, I think he's . . . well he's nice, isn't he? I mean he's a real gentleman and I think he . . . well Fanny says he cares for me."

"He's head over heels, lass, he's paralyzed!"

She smiled. "I guess I know that," and she looked up from under her lashes.

"Of course you do. As for him, he knows he got the better end of the bargain even if you were flat broke. So it's settled. You can tie the knot at the end of the week."

"Oh Daddy."

"What is it?"

"It's just . . . I wonder if maybe we should wait."

"What for?"

"Maybe he should come home with us and . . . I could be married in Boston. Maybe a fall wedding. And Taffy could be there and dear Annie and, well just everyone." She wiped a tear. "Even Bonnie. I know you think me silly."

"I think you grand."

"It's just, I always pictured a big wedding, Pappy. With my friends."

"And your old dog."

She laughed, "Yes!" Then burst into tears. He dug out a handkerchief. She blew her nose. He patted her hand. "I'd love nothing more, sweetheart, but you see the election's only three months off now, so it is. And it'll be four years afore I get another kick at the can, so . . ."

She nodded. "I understand, Daddy."

"You're sure now?"

She nodded.

"Just think, when you waltz back home with your high-falutin' husband, we'll have a right shin-dig and the governor himself will be beating down the door. All my hopes and dreams, everything I've worked and slaved for from the day I docked half-dead in that stuck-up town. All your Mam's sacrifices—" He broke off. Mae folded the hanky and handed it back to her father who likewise blew his nose and collected himself. He spoke solemnly, "None of it amounts to a hill of beans if you're not happy. You know I'd do anything for you, my girl, cut off my arm, so I would."

"I'm happy, Daddy."

"Can I have a smile?"

She smiled.

"There's my good girl. Or should I say 'My Lady'?"

Then he brought out the contract, recently signed in triplicate by himself and Lord Henry—"Daddy, you didn't!" she exclaimed—and he made sure his little girl understood every word.

The engagement party took place next evening in the grand dining room of the palazzo (in out of the rain). There were toasts, speeches and tributes and playful but respectful elegies of regret from the gentlemen, Hawley jesting that Henry had "succumbed to the Roman fever." There was song in the drawing room where even the Prussian and the Frenchman linked arms, there was dance—Henry noted with guilty gratification a slight halt in Miss Jenkins's gavotte. Or was it Miss Brayne?—bother, it no longer signified. All that mattered was his bride-to-be was a vision. More captivating every moment. Henry found excuses to leave the room only for the pleasure of returning to behold her once more; to see her feel his gaze upon her and turn, unfailingly, to smile at him. *To the victor, the spoils!*

"Lord Henry, more Champers?" Fanny herself was circulating with a magnum.

"Thank you."

"Bottoms up."

He seized her wrist, startling them both and occasioning the spillage of a few droplets on his sleeve. He released her and in low but urgent tones, "Forgive me. I mean to say, thank you. Fanny."

"Dear Lord Henry," she said. "The best man won." She smiled and topped up his glass which fizzed over in his hand.

At the end of that week, Mr. Gerald Corcoran gave his daughter away. Lord Henry Bell and Miss Marie Corcoran were joined in the eyes of God by a Roman Catholic prelate in the chapel of the Palazzo Montesilvio; and in the eyes of man by a member of the British legation in a brief civil ceremony immediately following—"May's well cross the t's and dot the i's, huh, Your Lordship?" said Mr. Corcoran. The Bride wore a gown of ivory silk (purchased at twice the price, hastily altered and equipped with a train by La Principessa's own seamstress) and a veil of silk *réseau* (at thrice) and carried a bouquet of orange blossoms with silver leaves and white ribbon. The Bride was attended by La Principessa della Montesilvio von Badenkreuzer as Matron of Honour. Lord Richard Hawley served as the Groom's best man. (The alternative being a foreigner.)

"You may now kiss the bride."

Henry kissed her cheek.

Lady Marie Bell, Seventeenth Baroness of the DC de Fayne, tossed her bouquet directly to La Principessa who caught it in one—"I say, well done," smirked Hawley. Then Mae pulled off the lapis lazuli ring and pressed it into her friend's hand. Fanny said, "Keep it as a wedding gift."

"No, that's bad luck, considering it was both borrowed and blue!"

"What was your 'something old,' then?"

"It was Henry!" piped Hawley, and even Henry laughed.

"No need to inquire as to the 'something new,'" Hawley added. Then, bowing over Mae's hand and lightly kissing it, he murmured, "Lady Marie. Your servant."

Henry squared his chin in approval. Breeding. It will out.

Fanny tied a pair of slippers to the carriage that whisked Lord and new-minted Lady to their honeymoon suite at the Hotel de la Minerve in the piazza. And Mr. Corcoran set sail for Boston the next day.

Perhaps the less said about the first night of holy matrimony, the better. (Nothing to do with the hotel room which was, as one might imagine, something more than adequate.) Henry would rather die than discomfit her in any way. He withdrew to the adjoining room. They had a lifetime ahead of them. What was the deferral of a night?

As for the second night.

On the third . . .

"Henry, please don't go."

"My dear?" He affected a vague distraction so as to spare her . . . any . . . further . . . well, one might imagine.

"Come here."

"Certainly." And he returned to sit on the edge of the bed. The room was in darkness save for a little moonglow through the balcony doors that stood open on the soft Roman night.

She drew him to her and, this time, placed her lips on his and held them there until her lips became her mouth . . . She reclined. And gently pulled him down. On top of her . . . And this time . . . "Ohhh," she sighed.

"Mmm."

"Ow."

"I'm sorry!"

"Don't go. Wait. Just. Mmm. Just. Can we just stay like this for a bit?"

"Anything."

Kissing again.

"Oh." Not pain in her voice this time, but polite surprise.

He drew back. "So sorry."

"No, come back."

. . . He suppressed a moan.

She said, "Is that . . . ? Oh my goodness . . ."

He gasped.

"Oh did I hurt you?" she cried.

He fumbled for his voice, "Not . . . in the slightest, on the . . . contrary."

"Okay . . . Oh. Oh my goodness."

"Oh my darling."

"You sure you're okay?"

"Oh!"

"Ow!"

"I'm sorry!"

But she sank her fingers into his back with a force that would not be out of place in an eagle's aerie and—"Oh! Oh, my . . . oh . . . Ohhh."

He groaned—shocked at the sound—as he slipped suddenly so easily inside her—*don't talk.*

She made small sounds but kept hold of him. His heart fairly beat out of his chest and he shuddered. Before he could catch his breath, he felt his whole being yield to sleep.

She stroked the back of his neck and whispered, "Lord Henry."

He said groggily, "You must call me by my Christian name."

She giggled ever so softly in his ear, and he felt himself stirring once more despite his heavy lids. "Henry, you're crushing me a little."

He sprang aside, "I do beg your pardon, Miss—that is . . ."

She laughed. And so did he. They laughed until . . . "Why don't you come a little bit closer, Henry?"

One morning toward the end of that first week, they were basking on their balcony with a view of St. Peter's when the bellboy delivered a gift box along with the fruit and the rolls and the—so strong!—coffee. "*Prego*, Mi-lord."

"Open it, Henry."

"Hadn't you better open it, Marie, it being from your father?"

They were still somewhat formal with one another in the light of day—she feeling rather "eggshelly" about saying his first name, he pronouncing hers gingerly as though handling an item of intimate feminine apparel. These were the early days of blushes and awkward brushes of fingers that kindled to fire.

She tore the bow from the box—"I love presents!" she cried. He chuckled. She was not merely charming, she *was* Charm.

"What is in it?" he asked.

She lifted the lid and burst into tears. He shot to his feet, "My darling, what is amiss?" She thrust the box at him and he looked inside. Elegantly printed on durable parchment were two certificates *Entitling the Bearer to One Trans-Atlantic Passage, Saloon Class, Liverpool to Boston.*

She sobbed, "Isn't that just the nicest present Daddy could've ever given us?"

". . . Indeed."

"Oh Henry, I love you!"

He hadn't time to wonder how he'd merited such a tribute before she threw her arms about his neck; he held her and inhaled the fragrance of her hair—"And I love you, my Marie."

She melted into him, he rose with her in his arms and carried her back to the bed in the broad light of morning. Another first.

Through five countries and more hotels, she saw the tickets under lock and key. Curious, thought Henry, as she was not overcautious with her jewellery, which she left scattered on the various vanities and dressing tables. Not to mention gloves and bonnets and parasols which she strewed for the maids to see to . . . Indeed, her—his, now—wealth was such that the purchase of a passage to Boston would not count so much as a drop in the ocean to be crossed, thus her particular care regarding the tickets struck him as noteworthy. He finally asked her about it in Capri.

"Oh Henry, of course we're drowning in dollars, darling, but those tickets were given to me—us—by Daddy himself, and those are the ones I want to hand over when we walk up the gangplank and I take you home with me."

By Munich, weary of the Continent, he was ready to return home. His home. "In town."

But she insisted on seeing Paris, even though he told her, "I'm afraid they've had a spot of bother there recently." They arrived to find the City of Light still reeling from Bloody Week.

"I know it's gloomy, here, Henry—"

It was rather more than that. Henry knew but did not say the inhabitants had, until recently, been reduced to eating rats in order to survive the siege.

"—and these ruins aren't nearly as nice as the ones in Rome, or half as old," she added.

But in truth, Mae found it gloomy for another reason entirely . . . one her husband had no need to know. One that would stay between her and the chambermaid who cleaned the mess and got the stains out from Mae's body linens.

Still, this was no time to quit Europe entirely. "Henry, I thought we'd take a villa in the South of France 'til end of August. Won't it be awfully hot and sticky in town?"

"Oh as to that, I shouldn't worry, darling."

27

THE DRIZZLE OF AFTERNOON persists into the early Edinburgh evening. Fires are lit. In the dining room of No. One Bell Gardens, the bronze fire screen shines before the blazing hearth. The walls have been newly hung in flocked damask paper and the curtains recently aired. The dinner plates with their residue of mutton are lifted from the table by the white-gloved hand of Pugsley (pressed into house service for the occasion, an odour of the stables clinging to him), as Havers stands by with the decanter.

Clarissa has spoken little throughout the meal, but now she announces, "I have, through the kind offices of Mr. Josiah Baxter, been vouchsafed some half dozen pears."

"Oh Clarissa!" exclaims Mae, half reaching a hand across the table, "I have an absolute passion for pears, how did you know?!" She casts a sly glance to her husband, adding, "Money may not grow on trees, but thank goodness pears do."

In Mae's estimation, this first supper—*dinner*, that is (thank you, Fanny)—has been, if not a triumph, then not a failure (leaving aside for the moment the matter of the food itself). She has curbed her inclination to chatter, observing as early as the fish course that her husband and his sister are content to dine in virtual silence—a custom no less strange to Mae than would be the offer of a sheep's eyeball were this a heathen banquet, complete with a polite belch at its conclusion. Oh well, when in Rome and all that . . . At least her sister-in-law speaks English. After a fashion.

"Havers. Pooding," says Clarissa.

Mae giggles. Silence.

"Clarissa, I adore your fire screen with that darling dragon, wherever did you find it?"

". . .'Find it,' Lady Marie?"

"Oh, um, purchase it, then. Or . . . acquire?"

"Ah. That distinction belongs to your husband's great-great-great-grandmother."

"Henry's great-great-grandmother?"

"His great-great-great—"

"Oh of course, I only meant to say, would she not have been your great-great-great-grandmother too, Clarissa?"

"That is of no consequence, Lady Marie."

"Um. Golly, have I . . . ? Don't tell me I've put my foot in my mouth. Henry, you didn't tell me you and your sister had different . . . mothers, is it? Not that it matters a fig, of course." She looks from her husband back to her sister-in-law.

Finally Clarissa says phlegmatically, "We had no such variance, Lady Marie."

"Oh, I'm sorry, I—" A gay little laugh. "I'm lost."

"My dear," says Henry gently, "Clarissa is correct in privileging me with reference to our matrilineage."

"Oh. I see."

Clarissa's tone is not unkind. "It is as well, Lady Marie, that you beg clarification of this custom, for it is now your own, going as it does to primogeniture."

Mae sits silent. Henry touches her hand. "It means inheritance, darling, by heirs male of the body."

Mae is shocked to feel herself blushing.

Havers sets down, with all solemnity, a covered sterling-silver dish. Mae watches as the butler lifts the lid on a mass of pallid . . . blobs. He spoons one up and it appears to slither onto her plate—surely not more fish for dessert—*pudding*, rather. He then proceeds to serve her sister-in-law and husband. Mae regards her plate doubtfully. Is this a Scottish delicacy? On the order of haggis?

"It is a salamander, Lady Marie," says Clarissa.

Mae looks up, alarmed.

"The fire screen," murmurs Henry. "It is a salamander, not a dragon."

Mae smiles and returns her attention to the mystery on her plate.

"Delicious, Clarissa," says Henry.

Clarissa raises a fragment to her lips. Tastes. Her brow stirs. She eats. Henry smiles at his older sister, "I told you so."

Mae nearly bursts into tears—*silly chit, brighten up*—upon realizing that there, on her plate, swims a pear, stewed to annihilation.

In the kitchen, Cavendish is on the point of tipping the dish into the slop bucket. "Hold," says Clarissa.

Luckily for Cavendish, the fierce stones of her gaze are powerless to quail Miss Clarissa—for despite skill with knife, pot and fire, the cook has been dismissed from lesser Edinburgh houses for no crime other than scarifying its lady with a look. She hesitates. "Cooks have hung before now for pysoning their employers. That'll no' be my fate, ma'am."

"No one's going to hang you for stewing pears, Cavendish, unwholesome though they be."

Cavendish sets the dish before her mistress. She has done her best to stew the poison from the fruit, and if the lady chooses now to gorge herself upon it, let her pay the consequences (or let Sheehan pay, for 'tis she who will empty Madam's close stool come morning).

Here, in the privacy of the scullery, Clarissa takes up her spoon. The pear lies cut-side-up on her plate; the dim concavity at its centre retains the impressions of the seeds which Cavendish entrusted to the fire. No good comes of eating fruit. Ask Eve.

Clarissa knows her Bible back-to-front, however, and nowhere is there an interdict against consuming pears *per se*; such is merely common sense if one values one's digestion. Common sense, however, does not preclude pleasures of the palate taken in moderation; they stimulate the appetite, not only for wholesome food, but for the duty of remaining in this world. Besides, Mr. Baxter himself went out of his way to obtain the pears as a special favour to her—to her brother, that is.

Cavendish watches, wary lest her mistress turn blue and die.

Before retiring for the night, Henry seeks out his sister in her parlour.

"Well?" He raises his brows expectantly. Smiles. "What do you think?"

Clarissa folds her hands. "She smiles a good deal."

He clears his throat. "Is that all you have to—?"

"Now Henry, take no umbrage, Lady Strathallan is just the same, she too is an American."

"Well then, goodnight, sister."

"Brother. You have done well by Fayne. Lady Marie is the picture of health and comeliness."

Henry goes to his sister, kneels and squeezes her hand. "Thank you, Clarissa. For everything."

She watches him leave the room; hears his tread on the stairs—accelerating toward the top. Then she reaches down—carefully, favouring her shoulder—lifts her work basket onto her lap, and allows her back to rest against the chair.

Upstairs in the bedroom, Mae has changed into a peignoir set and now she starts a letter—

No. One Bell Gardens
August 2, 1871

Darling Tiff,
"Town" as in Edinburgh, alas, not London

At the sound of her husband's approach, she folds it away and quickly unpins her hair before the mirror—looking glass—so that she might be discovered brushing her tresses when he enters.

He leans down and kisses her shoulder, she gives him a smile and he withdraws to undress for bed.

The Irish maid has managed to lay out Mae's vanity set but hasn't got far with her trunk. The girl is pretty, though—full set of teeth at any rate. We'll have to do something about those hands of course—shocking fingernails.

"What was that, Henry?"

He addresses her now in the glass from where he lies stretched out on the bed in his nightshirt. "I said, my darling, we might politely mention figs. Just. But never is it polite to mention money."

Mae pouts her lower lip and puckers her forehead in a show of feminine consternation which she knows he finds irresistible. "Who said anything about money?"

"You did, my treasure."

"When?"

"At table. In connection with its refusal to 'grow on trees.'"

". . . Oh, that! It's an expression, Henry."

"Nevertheless."

"All right, Mr. Nevertheless, can you explain to me why you leave out so many articles?"

"My dear?"

"'At table.' It would kill you to say, 'At *the* table.'"

"I've never given it a thought. I dare say you're right. Come to *the* bed."

But she continues brushing her hair in languid strokes from crown to past her shoulders, setting the folds of her peignoir stirring where it is unfastened at the cleft of her breasts; aware of his eyes upon her. She tosses the words, as negligent as her nightgown, "You Scots are even stingy with articles. Spend them, Henry, like they're going out of style. They're the pocket change of the English language. Oh," hand to her chest, "so sorry, darling, there I go talking about *money* again. But you can't tell me the subject didn't come up between you and Daddy."

"You are mistaken, my darling."

"Bunkum. Gerry Corcoran can't so much as go to confession without giving the priest a stock tip. 'Buy pork bellies, Father.'" And she is gratified by his inability to suppress a laugh at her spot-on mimicry.

"Your father and I did come to a mutually beneficial arrangement."

Here she swivels the stool to face to him. "I'll say you did." She rises, dropping the brush to the table behind her, and advances upon the bed.

Her husband says, "The mistake to which I refer is your use of the term 'Scots' in reference to me." He reaches to one side and douses the lamp.

"What on earth are you talking about?" She is next to him, lying against the length of him.

"I am not, strictly speaking, a Scot."

"Mmm, okay, what?"

"I am . . . oh . . . oh my dear, wait, oh . . . I . . . am . . ."

"Shutup now, darling, oh . . . oh, I'm yours, Henry—"

". . . Oh. Oh Mae."

"Mmm-hm."

It is her smallest moan which unfailingly sets off his paroxysm.

"Ohhh Henry," she sighs, her fingers tracing the fine hairs of his chest. "Again."

Across the passageway, Clarissa suffers the Irish maid to brush and replait her greying hair. Although Clarissa usually performs this function for herself, it has of late cost an effort that rekindles a discomfort which, for the past several years, has simmered in her shoulders but which more recently, as though by dint of gravity, has extended to her hips. Tonight, therefore, along with the pears, she permits herself the pleasure of feeling the bristles rake across her scalp. Sheehan has the way of it.

"That will be all."

"Aye m'um."

Her door closes.

It needs no resorting to the "mind's eye" to know her brother's haste-to-bed betokens that—Nature taking its wonted course—Clarissa's work will soon be done. And she will be free to retreat from the world with a modest sufficiency.

She has long envisioned it.

She would require but one room. With one adequately sized window. Bright but spare. And her spoon-back chair. She is not Roman Catholic, therefore this is no cloister-dream—no fuss of robes and incense. Hers is a secular vision of unmolested tranquility. Save perhaps, from outside and of an afternoon, the *crack* of a cricket ball. Distant laughter.

28

A BIT OF A FALSE START the next morning. When the maid finally showed up, she hadn't the first clue how to confect a basic chignon. Taffy would be impressed: Mary Corcoran demonstrating the patience of a saint while the girl fumbled with pins—"That's my scalp, not the comb."

"Sorry, m'um!"

"'Sorry Your Ladyship.'"

At breakfast in the dining room—"Don't look at me 'til I've got a hat on, Henry." Good gracious, what's that he's eating? Never mind, there's toast. And marmalade, thank God. And here's the butler . . . with tea. "Any coffee?"

"'Coffee,' Madam?"

"That's what I said," she sing-songs to take the sting out of it. Oh my, she can still smell last night's mutton. She wrinkles her nose accusingly at the hideous flocked wallpaper.

Henry glances up from *The Scotsman*. "You look lovely as ever, my dear."

Mae announces her intention to "brighten up the place. If it's all right with you, of course, Henry dear." He gives silent thanks that his sister has already breakfasted and so is not present to hear his wife pass sentence on the "quaint wallpaper" not to mention the "charming old gasolier in the foyer. "I saw an ad for a really smart one in *The Englishwoman's Domestic Magazine* . . ." He listens, speechless, to his angel's plans for a scorched-earth campaign on his recently refurbished house.

Havers returns with the regrettable news that coffee is not presently to be had but that plans are even now afoot to rectify the omission on the morrow, but Her Ladyship has flown from the room.

Henry follows his wife to Clarissa's parlour in time to hear ". . . so cozy, but don't you think it could use a fresh coat of paint? There's a simply divine colour I saw at Fanny's, 'Tuscan Sunset,' you'll adore it, Clarissa. And we'll have to get you a new chair. One with arms."

Henry says, "The carriage is ready, darling."

"We'll talk later, Clarissa, so long for now!"

They leave. Clarissa finds she is clutching the handle of her work basket. She loosens her hold. Collects her thoughts. Her parlour, surely, is exempt. For all that it is her brother's.

The carriage leaves the New Town, with its parks, its treed avenues and Georgian dwellings of smooth sandstone arranged in symmetrical "Circles" and "Places," its banks, its shops and colonnaded public buildings, and rolls onto North Bridge, which spans a gorge of grass and tracks and time—the buried swill of secrets ever more firmly compacted by the trains passing to and fro. The carriage is headed toward the jigsaw skyline of the Old Town with its tall tilting "lands" of stone and timber, crowned at the high end by "Edinburgh Castle up there on your right." "Oh my," says Mae. And away to the left, starkly visible beyond the roofs and blackened spires, is an imposing hill. "That imposing hill is Arthur's Seat," says Henry. "Legend has it, 'twas the site of King Arthur's Camelot." "How romantic." "On its flank there may be seen—just lean out a wee bit more, darling, that's right—the Salisbury Craigs which, taken together with Duddingston Loch, offer some of the finest bird-watching in . . ."

Mae leans obligingly out the window (despite the rain) so as not to miss a single thing. "Henry, let's buy a landau. On fine days you could drive it yourself with the roof down and we'd see ever so much more of the sights." The carriage turns down the cobbled clatter of the High Street and her voice wobbles along with the wheels, as she asks, "Are there many fine days, Henry? I mean to say, when does Scotland experience summer?"

The carriage pulls up at a palace but before Mae can ask upon whom they are to pay a call at this hour of the day and panic somewhat as to her hair, he says, "Here we have Holyrood Palace, where our own gracious Queen Victoria resides when in Scotland. Charles X lived here in exile, and the Pretender to the Throne likewise sought refuge within its walls."

"Well I suppose if you're going to be exiled it may as well be to a palace."

"Queen Mary herself lived here. In exile."

"Bloody Mary?"

"That was Mary Tudor."

"Poor girl."

"You see that window up there?"

Mae looks up at the many windows. Says, agreeably, "Yes."

"'Twas in that chamber Mary's alleged lover, David Rizzio, was murdered in the midst of a game at cards when—"

"I thought Mary was a nice Catholic girl."

"I speak now of Mary Queen of Scots. Also Catholic. Perhaps not so nice."

"Oh."

"She was mother of James the Sixth of Scotland and James the First of England and Ireland."

"She called both her sons James?"

"No. She had but one son . . ." Here Henry launches into the tale of his forebears who fought on the side of Mary Queen of Scots against forces loyal to Elizabeth I. "They were defeated in battle, but Mary's son, James, acceded to the throne of England and Ireland."

"So she won in the end."

"To him we owe the King James Bible. He was, as well, a great burner of witches."

"You don't still do that here, do you?"

He chuckles. "You are quite safe, my enchantress. Shall we alight and inspect the chapel ruins?"

"I don't think I'm dressed for it, Henry." Her husband seems not to have noticed the steady thin rain and Mae senses it might be somehow impolite to mention it.

"Of course," he says gallantly and taps the ceiling with the butt of his cane. The carriage lurches forward and follows the hunched, winding ascent of the Middle Ages, all the way up the "Royal Mile."

He points over her shoulder. "There is the home of John Knox. He who railed against the 'monstrous regiment of women.'"

"Let's not visit him."

"He is dead."

"All the more reason."

He laughs.

Past the Tron, "where false notaries and malefactors were nailed by the ears."

"What's a false notary?"

"A blackguard."

"What's a—? Never mind, oh that's impressive, what's that?"

"St. Giles' Cathedral."

"Is that where Clarissa goes to 'kirk'?"

"No."

"Gosh, it's all every bit as old as anything in Europe."

"It is medieval, darling."

"It's not that bad, is it?"

He clears his throat.

She laughs. "I'm joshing you, Henry, I know what medieval means. Oh, but of course you know so much more than I do about—well, just everything and, oh my, look at that decrepit old house, I'm just falling in love with Edinburgh."

"Then you will be pleased to learn Edinburgh is known as the Athens of the North. Home to feats of engineering, great advances in the natural sciences and medical arts."

Mae widens her eyes and pinches a yawn between her lips.

"It is called a land," he adds.

She nods, torn between feigning understanding and risking enlightenment.

He explains, "Your 'decrepit house.' Fourteen storeys some of them; the Great Fire took care of a good deal of the blight, of course." She cranes her neck out the window, trying to make out the carving on a noble old scutcheon through a flapping line of washing.

"Look, Henry, 'Fleshmarket Close.' Fancy that for a name."

He hurries them past the Cowgate which, after all, is not such as to invite inspection by a lady.

In the Grassmarket, the carriage plies a sea of hawkers and shoppers amid stalls piled high with produce, and he points out where the condemned "were conveyed in the hangman's cart to the place of execution."

"They're not hanging anyone today, are they?"

"What's today, Wednesday? No hanging, 'tis market day."

She pales.

"I jest, darling. 'Tis almost a century since the last neck was snapped in the market square. To your left is the White Hart Inn where Robert Burns and William Wordsworth slept. Not in the same bed of course, heh-heh."

So far as Mae can tell, it's one imposing, spooky old building after another. "Samuel Johnson slept there. And of course Boswell. David Hume slept there also. And here slept Mary of Guise."

"Queen Mary?"

"Queen Mary's mother."

"I thought her name was Catherine."

"Mother of Mary—"

"Queen of Scots, I've got it."

Mae puts her foot down when it comes to Greyfriars Kirkyard— "I'm not joking, Henry"—and closes her eyes against the looming stone angels and menacing marble scrolls enumerating the wages of sin.

All the way up to massive Edinburgh Castle, perched atop an extinct volcano, the indestructible Castle Rock.

They stroll along a line of cannons, and Mae pauses to look over a parapet at the sheer drop. "Oh my, so is this where you made your last stand against the English? I can just picture them falling down the cliff, serves them right."

Henry launches into a tale of his forebears having fought on the side of "Elizabeth I to preserve the Union with England."

Mae is a tad confused. "I thought you said they fought for Mary Queen of Scots. Are you saying they were traitors?"

"Certainly not," huffs Henry.

"Oh dear, sorry."

"Not to worry. How were you to know?"

Suddenly, a cannon blast! Mae cries out and seizes Henry's arm.

"The firing of the one o'clock gun!" He beams, exhorting her urgently to look all the way across to a spot in the New Town. Mae pretends to see the ball falling from the flagstaff of Nelson's Monument.

He suggests they venture beyond the city to the "Lochleven Castle ruins, scene of Mary's captivity."

"I thought she was locked up in Holyrood."

"She was in exile at Holyrood."

"All because her father wanted to get rid of her mother."

"That was Mary—"

"The bloody one, right."

"Also a prisoner for much of her life."

"Of course they were, they were queens."

"You are my queen. Do you feel yourself in any way a prisoner?"

"That depends. I don't suppose there's a dungeon at No. One Bell Gardens?"

"Not to my knowledge." He raises his eyebrows teasingly and earns a playful punch on the arm. "Shall we drive out? A mere twenty-five miles."

"I'd love to, Henry, but I'm a mite chilly."

He fusses with a rug about her knees, and tilts his head out to direct Sanders.

Down the cobbles they rattle once more, and Mae loses track of the bends and turns until the carriage slows before the Edinburgh Museum of Science and Art, where her husband proposes to show her the Bird Gallery and "a skeleton entire of a whale suspended from the ceiling."

"I'd love to, but I wouldn't for the world make Clarissa wait luncheon."

The road surface smooths as they roll over North Bridge back toward the New Town, which appears even smarter to Mae's history-dimmed eyes than it did this morning. The sun has come out and that makes all the difference, the rows of tall buildings fairly gleam, in fact she just might miss this place once they've moved to London. West Princes Street Gardens is a vision of symmetry and colour—if you look past the stone tower that appears to have mislaid its cathedral, ". . . the magnificent Scott Monument, wherein each and every one of the author's fictional characters is to be seen, while straight ahead you have a fine example of neoclassical architecture in New Register House wherein the records of all marriages, births and deaths, and the courts of session—"

She perks up. "What's that big building there?"

"Oh that. Jenners and Company."

"Let's go in there."

"Merely a linen draper's and purveyor of ready-made—"

But she has already leaned out the window—"Hey there, Sanders, hold your horses!"

Some three hours later, Sanders follows them into the foyer at No. One Bell Gardens, carrying a tower of parcels. "Wait, I'll take this one," says Mae and heads for the parlour.

She contains her delight as Clarissa pulls the string, undoes the brown paper wrapping, lifts the lid on the box, and surveys the contents.

"It's a casquette. Put it on!"

Clarissa hesitates. Lifts the confection of mauve and silver from its bed of tissue paper and places it gingerly on top of her head—*As though it were a bird's nest!* thinks Mae, saying kindly, "It's meant to tilt down over your eyes a little. Here, I'll show you." She makes the adjustment to the adorable little pillbox, stands back and claps her hands. "Utterly beguiling!"

Clarissa says, balefully, "Thank you, Lady Marie."

"I'll get the maid to bring you a hand mirror—glass, that is."

Mae pops into the hall and nearly collides with Sheehan who is on her way upstairs with a pair of Henry's boots freshly blacked. No wonder the girl's fingernails are a fright. Mae hikes her skirts and runs upstairs herself, returning moments later to the parlour with her own hand mirror.

"What have you done with your new *chapeau*?"

"I have restored it to its box. For safekeeping."

"Don't go hiding your hat under a bushel, Clarissa, here—" Mae lifts out the hat and settles it perfectly on Clarissa's head. Then she holds up the mirror. Her sister-in-law winces. Mae is perplexed to see the corners of Clarissa's lips rise in what is, technically, a smile.

29

MAE HAS RISEN from an afternoon nap—the past is so exhausting—and, despairing of the Irish maid who has yet to appear after three tugs of the bell cord, has begun dressing herself for dinner(!) "Henry, where's the rest of the household?"

"Why, I believe you've seen them all. With the possible exception of Cook, of course. And whoever Cook's got in the scullery and," he adds vaguely, "one imagines, the wash house."

She pauses in the assessment of a gold bangle with black enamel tracery. "Do you mean to say there's just the one maid? For upstairs, downstairs and"—prettily, by way of countering any hint of complaint—"in 'my lady's chamber'?"

"Is there? I suppose there is."

"Poor Clarissa," she says generously. "Well we'll fix that, won't we?" She shoos him from the room before he can answer because the maid is here, *finally*.

"Sorry, Your Ladyship, I were—"

"What are you wearing?"

"Sleeve protectors, 'Ladyship, I were helping Cook—"

"Oh dear, I see, well take those off and, um . . ." The apron. Mae hardly knows where to look. Can't be helped. Must be dressed.

The girl is unschooled but nimble-fingered; buttons yield to her touch and she doesn't need to be shown twice about the placement of the pearl-cluster pendant in Mae's décolleté.

Havers removes the soup bowls, empty but for Mae's.

"What kind of soup is that, Havers?"

"It is white soup, Your Ladyship."

"Really, I had no idea 'white' was a flavour."

It is not silence *per se* that greets Mae's remark—they have been eating in silence just as they did yesterday evening—rather, it is the suspended quality of that silence: a sort of restrained bemusement. She smiles. No one smiles back because no one is looking at her. Clarissa cleared her throat and averted her gaze the moment Mae appeared in her pearlescent dinner gown with its plunging but entirely apropos neckline. Even Henry trained his gaze toward the stodgy surface of his soup, as though lest he scandalize his sister by looking at his wife. Mae forms a serene smile and Havers serves the fish.

Turbot. Which is all one can say about it.

Followed by the meat. Remnants from last night's breast of mutton. Having been cooked grey throughout the first time, the fragments have now been pressed into mounds and somehow . . . boiled?

Followed by:

"Havers, pooding."

Little distinguishes it from the main course apart from a thick layer of treacle weighing down whatever mass of flour and lard lies beneath.

Next morning, the Irish girl appears—cheek smudged, but without the soiled sleeves and unspeakable apron—and Mae is successfully laced and petticoated. She has plumped for a jaunty Emile Pingat on a nautical theme, and now the girl reverently holds out the striped navy-and-white underskirt with its ruched panel and double row of pleats.

"Don't forget the balayeuse," says Mae.

"The . . . ?"

Mae points to the length of ruffled fabric in a heap on the floor. Really, she needs a boudoir, this is ridiculous!

"Och, I thought 'twas a bed skirt."

Mae laughs.

The girl gets the underskirt over Mae's head with no damage to her coiffure, then she hooks the dust ruffle to the hem without a hitch. Next, Mae lifts her arms while her maid wraps the navy silk overskirt round her waist and fastens it in front to fall in a wide V, exposing the stripes of the underskirt and framing it with frills and bows. With her maid's help she shrugs into the bodice, likewise ruffled and bowed, and shoots her hands through the complex cuffs that spew lace like sea foam. Mae looks straight ahead while Sheehan fastens the buttons of the bodice, each embroidered with a tiny anchor, before affixing the final bow to Her Ladyship's waist. Maid hands mistress the straw boater hat with the white and navy ribbons twinned in back. Mae takes it and positions it saucily atop the rigging of her chignon. Sheehan hands Her Ladyship the diamond hatpin, but takes over when it fails to cooperate with Her Ladyship. Mae surveys the result in the mirror.

"Will there be anything else, Your Ladyship?"

"Call me Lady Mae. And close your mouth, flies'll get in," she adds with a wink.

Mae descends to the foyer, calling out gaily, "I'm ready, Clarissa." At the door, she pulls on a new pair of kid gloves from Jenners. "Feel them, Clarissa. Soft as love's first kiss." Sheehan hands her her fan.

Clarissa has succumbed to the "casquette" and now, mindful of her duty, she embarks with Lady Marie upon the first of several "at-homes" in the New Town.

Together, over the next few days, they make the rounds; Clarissa in her customary black silk, slope-shouldered and bell-shaped from the waist down, progresses up the various pathways with a slight tolling motion. Mae plies the pavement like a sleek corvette, her "cargo" borne fashionably astern in the form of a bustle. Mae has high hopes of the ladies she is to meet, and is keen to see within as many handsome Georgian dwellings as possible.

The dwellings are handsome without. Within . . . they are a study in indifference to fashion, united with a passion for modernity. Case in point being the Farquhars, with electricity throughout their otherwise frumpy abode. Mae knows that shabbiness often signifies good breeding, especially in the Old World, still . . . would a cheerful chintz curtain bring down the Empire?

She does, however, warm to the Farquhars; Sir Ian and Lady Nora are a kindly couple in their fifties who make a proper fuss over her. He has caterpillar eyebrows and is something in bridges and lighthouse beacons. She is (oddly) adept at mathematics. They press delicate shortbreads upon her and quiz her about Boston and America—albeit venturing outside her ken when it comes to dams and the manufacture of steel. They have a married son in Glasgow who is in . . . oh dear, something to do with vessels. "How jolly!"

Next stop, Colonel MacOmber's; a thoroughly masculine if not musty milieu of deep-buttoned leather upholstery and weapons cases. The gentleman is a portly veteran of the Battle of Balaclava, godfather to Clarissa and boyhood friend of Henry's late father, the Sixteenth Baron Bell of the *etcetera*. To Mae's eye he resembles a whiskered iguana, and he blinks with about the same frequency, leaving her to wonder whether he has mastered the art of sleeping with his eyes open. Given to bluff outbursts. "What's that on your head, Clarrie? Newfangled hat, is it?"

A bright spot in the Heatheringtons. He is a professor of something at the university and heir to an old established—scientific, but even so— publishing house, his wife is mercifully uneducated and their daughter pretty. "I am charmed to meet you, Miss Heatherington, you must come for dinner at Bell Gardens," says Mae warmly, "With your parents too, of course." But the Heatheringtons are off to London next week in advance of the Season and their daughter's debut. "Why then, we're sure to meet there!" She catches a look from Clarissa and tempers her enthusiasm.

From Georgian square to Georgian circle, Mae's smile never flags, even if she droops a little inwardly. No more young ladies. Not even a young man. And among the remaining houses at which they call, several are absent their proprietors who are from home for the day. Clarissa leaves a card, seeming neither perturbed nor surprised.

And then, the calls are returned.

It is not that Mae is keen to converse about lighthouses or the weather, but guests pay calls of such brevity they leave nothing in their wake that might so much as provide grist for gossip, some declining even to be divested of hats and cloaks, while others merely leave a card to show they've called. Which suits Clarissa perfectly. "I thought they would never leave. Feared they'd put down roots."

She does wonder what Henry can be getting up to while she's out trailing from one house to another or seated in her own drawing room tipping the china teapot over cups and passing them to stuffy old dowagers and . . . well, she has no wish to be unkind. Still, it isn't easy being anchored in this rather sober city, soon to be bereft of what little amusing society it would appear to boast at the best of times. Mae is good at making friends, a natural hostess by temperament and training, but she lacks here the raw materials with which to practise her art—whatever Henry might say about the glorious "Scottish Renaissance," so far as she can tell it's all bridges, beacons and engines.

. . . Taffy, it seems someone famous slept or was born or imprisoned or murdered in every second house. And Queen Mary lived everywhere at some point. Which Queen Mary? Well might you ask!

Everyone I have met is old, intellectual or pious. I refuse to believe that Edinburgh, alone among European capitals, boasts not a single personable young lady who shares a taste for pretty things and lively conversation and . . . fun. They can't all have fled to London, it's the middle of August! Oh, but I fear Clarissa will be so lonely—you should've seen the look she gave me when I mentioned the Season. I don't think she's in a hurry for us to go. Still, unless all the amusing people have emigrated to the New World, I refuse to believe I am the only one. Right about now, I'd settle for a Katie Buxton! Send gossip. I don't care if it's true and I've no one to whom to repeat it anyhoo.

Not to mention, for all their technological superiority, Mae has yet to set foot in a single Edinburgh home—including her own—in which she does not feel chilled to the bone. "Henry, I wonder if we mightn't invest in a furnace? Much as I love a cheerful fire."

He beams. "I had Clarissa install one prior to our arrival. Runs on coal. Forged in Glasgow by—"

"You're so thoughtful, darling." She kisses his cheek. "Let's have it lit, then, shall we?"

". . . In August?"

30

SHE IS IN A WARM wrapper, waiting to dress for dinner—although, considering it's just the three of them again, why bother? She instantly upbraids herself: there is her husband and it is for his eyes alone she takes pains over her toilette. Not that he wouldn't think her lovely in a smock and mobcap—a girl should be so lucky! A trunk sits open in the middle of the room, frothing with lace and silk.

"Henry, we need to hire another maid, it's not fair to either of us."

"I agree, it puts a burden on Sheehan."

"Not Sheehan, silly, I'm talking about me and Clarissa."

"Oh, quite."

"I'm still not properly unpacked and I can't find a thing. Speaking of which, have you seen the tickets?"

"'Tickets'. . ."

"The steamer tickets from Daddy."

"Oh. No."

"Oh no!"

"My dear, they're bound to turn up."

Mae tugs the bell cord then goes straight to the door, sticks her head out and hollers, "Sheehan!" She turns back to her husband, "Dots or floral?"

"What?"

"For dinner."

He looks blank. She gestures—'impatiently' is too strong a word—to the dinner dresses laid out on the bed. "Oh," he says. "Doesn't matter."

She holds back a sigh.

The Irish maid arrives, breathless. Mae poses the question. The girl replies, "Och, Your Ladyship, them dots is gorgeous so they are but not much longer will you be wanting to wear a flower print what with autumn round the corner."

With a pert look to Henry, Mae says, "The floral it is. Now see to the trunk."

Henry is about to slip away to his dressing room—as the cramped old garderobe is now called—when:

"Where will you be wanting this, Lady Mae?"

He turns. "You will address your mistress as Lady Marie."

The girl quails, bobs. She is holding a bonnet the size of a man o' war, ribbons trailing like tentacles.

"It's all right, Henry, I asked her to call me that."

Out from the bonnet drops . . . the gift box.

"Oh you found them, thank goodness!"

The maid quickly retrieves the box and hands it to her mistress.

"You'll never guess what's in here, Sheehan."

Henry watches his wife lift the lid and withdraw the two certificates, *Entitling the Bearer to One Trans-Atlantic Passage* . . .

"Are you planning a voyage to America, then, Your Ladyship?"

"Hold your tongue, girl," says Henry.

Mae turns and, brushing the air with both hands, "Off you go, now, Henry, I'm dressing."

He retreats. Mae turns back to the maid, "What's your name?"

"Why, Sheehan, Your Ladyship."

Mae laughs. "Your first name."

The girl goes crimson, but she manages to say, "Maggie."

Mae drops her wrapper and lifts her arms for the underskirt. Yes, Maggie will do nicely.

At table (as they say), Mae sits resplendent in the floral which poofs and blooms about her. And lifts her spoon.

Aristocrats will skin you for saying "supper" but they see nothing wrong in audibly slurping soup. Mae consumes hers silently, but perhaps that is just another vulgar middle-class habit she picked up along with friendliness, warm rooms and nice things. Is it a harbinger of her coming "monthly" that she is being driven batty by the sound of her sister-in-law swallowing? Another monthly, another . . . well you can't call it a "failure." It's early days yet.

"What kind of soup is this, Havers?"

"It is economical soup, Your Ladyship."

Within Mae stirs the sort of vexation that leads to frown lines. She smooths her brow. Don't judge an entire meal by the soup course.

Or the fish.

Henry says, "Oh Clarissa, Mr. Baxter asked me to convey his cordial regards."

Clarissa frowns.

Mae is surprised. She thought Clarissa approved of this Mr. Baxter. "Isn't he the one who gave you the pears?"

Her sister-in-law nods almost imperceptibly.

Henry offers, "He and I had the pleasure today of two unbroken hours at the Museum in the ornithological wing."

Mae laughs.

No one else does.

Henry looks at her quizzically. She changes tack, saying, mock stern, "So that's where you spend your days."

"'Spend my days'?"

Why do they repeat everything as if they haven't understood? Is it to make you feel you have an inferior command of the language?

Henry says solemnly, "I am a bird-fancier. I don't know that I made that plain."

Now she really wants to laugh. Don't.

The Meat.

Mutton. Can it be the same one? Minced this time and blanketed in a viscous brown sauce. There is a sheen to it. Mae's fork sinks unresisted into a disk of boiled carrot. A potato crumbles at the touch of a tine. In contrast, the mutton, despite being minced, is as tough as it was last week and monopolizes the mouth to the exclusion of conversation—not that there is any to be had. Worst of all, every single dish is set upon the table at the outset, letting one know exactly what one is in for. All except, however:

"Havers, pooding."

A bowl containing a blob which is growing a skin.

"It is tapioca, Your Ladyship," replies Havers smoothly.

The texture is . . . the less said.

By the end of the meal Mae is—let us just say she is the teensiest bit miffed. And hungry!

Afterwards, in the parlour, Mae sits on a pressed-back chair by the fire, across from Henry who takes up the newspaper. *Scrunkle*. Clarissa takes up her needlepoint. *Sclicket*.

There is not even a piano in this house. Mae is schooled in the feminine arts; she can stitch a sampler while brightly chatting or discreetly eavesdropping. She can play charades, she can accompany herself in a sweet air on piano, and she has a light foot for a gavotte. Above all, she can facilitate sparkling conversation.

Sclicket.

Scrunkle.

Sustaining Mae is the knowledge that she and her husband shall, certainly before Christmas, decamp to the house in London and the social whirl. She looks forward to looking back fondly on the peaceful evenings by the parlour fire at No. One Bell Gardens.

Sclinkle.

She knows her sister-in-law must, at some point, repair to bed, but every night Clarissa keeps to her chair as Mae admits defeat. "Well, nighty-night."

"Lady Marie, I bid you goodnight."

She says it without looking up. Indeed, her sister-in-law rarely looks at her unless it is to steal a glance at her midsection. And Henry, lest he betray unseemly eagerness to join his bride, will, Mae knows, linger an extra twelve minutes before: "Dear sister, I bid you goodnight."

"And I you, dear brother."

Back home the above exchange would mean brother and sister hated one another. But here it means they really are dear to one another.

Upstairs, the door to their bedroom is ajar, but Henry waits without until the maid shall have finished with his wife's evening toilette. He hears them chattering. "Och, you've a head of hair, Lady Mae."

"Like a horse's tail!"

They laugh.

Eventually, he is admitted to his chamber. The maid bobs on her way past him. Henry says it not by way of reproof, but out of a concern for his wife's welfare: "It does not do to be familiar with the servants, my dear."

"She's my maid, Henry, not yours."

"All the more reason she ought to remember her place."

"Henry? I wonder if we mightn't vary the menu a little?"

"The 'menu'?"

Her smile does not falter. "I know mutton is a national dish, but . . ."

"Oh, are you not partial to mutton?"

"Only in the way I'm not partial to shoe leather."

"Hm, it is rather . . . toilsome."

They laugh.

She says, "I think I'll have a word with Cavendish."

Henry looks alarmed. He is wearing a nightcap. He's reverting, the dear. He has even acquired a slight Scottish burr since arriving in Edinburgh. "I wouldnae advise that, dear."

"Henry, she's an employee."

"A . . . servant, quite."

"We—you pay her. She does what you tell her to do."

"Hm."

"Oh my. Are you . . . ? You are! You're scared of the cook!"

"I am no such . . . Perhaps somewhat."

They laugh.

"So it's settled, you'll speak to her."

He douses the lamp. As he pulls her close she asks, "What's Clarissa got against Mr. What's-His-Name, the one with the pears?"

"Baxter? Why nothing. They are the best of friends."

"Oh." And it dawns on her. *Taffy, they frown when they are happy.* Mae recalls her sister-in-law's upward rictus when she saw herself in the cas-quette. *And they smile when they're not.*

In the middle of the night she wakes up ravenous and pads down to the kitchen where she rummages and clatters in search of food. Cavendish appears brandishing a knife, and while Mae's chipper "It's just me, Cavendish" seems not to allay the woman's suspicions, she nonetheless lowers the knife and produces a "wee lunch." *Taffy, have you ever tasted bloater paste? My advice: don't.*

She eats it all up, though. She feels enlivened. Excited. Something has still not happened. Something is two and a half weeks late. *I've said too much already!*

The following morning, Mae is violently ill. Maggie holds her hair back and pulls the flush chain. Tidies her. Puts her to bed.

"I'm fine, Henry, just indisposed."

He flees at the word.

She checks. But her "friend" has yet to come.

She counts in her head again just to be sure.

By afternoon she feels much better, and positively ravenous by evening. She devours everything on her plate. Including . . .

"Did you talk to Cook?"

"'To Cook.'"

"Henry."

"Ah."

Late that night, she avoids the bloater paste in favour of plain bread and butter.

But next morning . . . a galleon-worth of sea-sickness!

August 11, 1871

Dear Taffy,

My "friend" has yet to arrive. Yes. That "friend." Don't tell a soul, but I think I'm pregnant . . .

31

AS THE SUN SLANTS lower in the August sky and the leaves of the wych elm at her window filter a light of an older gold, Mae's certainty grows . . . The only sour note: the mornings. She wakes each day to an overwhelming nausea that—better not to dwell. Thank the good Lord for Maggie Sheehan, who is unfailing and unflinching.

"I feel like I'm going to die," she says, drooping over the basin after a particularly exuberant bout.

She hears the maid say, "It never took me that way."

She looks up. "You have a baby?"

The maid turns away, fetching a cool cloth.

"Maggie, I didn't know you were married."

Silence. The girl looks down.

"Where's your baby?" asks Mae.

"I'm not to know, Your Ladyship. Only he's got a home, and that's more'n I could give him."

"What about your husband?"

No answer.

Mae swells with the sense of her own benevolence—after all, she could dismiss the girl on the spot—but deflates a little at the thought which follows: *There but for the grace of Daddy's money, go I.* It strikes her now she has as good as confided the secret of her pregnancy. "Maggie, not a word of this, do you understand?"

"Och no, Miss Clarissa would sack me if she—"

"No, you goose, I'm talking about me." And she strokes her belly.

"Ahhh, oh, o'course not, Lady Mae, I can keep a secret, I can."

"Listen, Maggie. Have you ever crossed the ocean?"

"I crossed the Irish Sea to—

"I'm talking about the Atlantic."

"No, Your Ladyship."

"Well, would you like to?" Mae asks it tartly—and a little conspiratorially. The girl's big brown eyes grow wide. "Look here, Maggie Sheehan, I'm going to need someone on the crossing to look after me and . . ." She glances down. "Little You-Know-Who."

Maggie Sheehan clasps her hands and drops to her knees before Lady Marie. "I promise, Lady Mae, I'll take care of you and your babby like it was me own."

Over the next couple of weeks, Mae takes her mind off that which must not be spoken to a living soul—save Maggie Sheehan—by throwing herself into domestic improvements. A new crystal gasolier is hung in the foyer and new gas fittings in bronze and ormolu are throughout the house. In the course of a single day, thanks to a liberal application of cold hard pounds sterling, the dreary lavatory off her bedroom is ripped out and replaced with matching lily-of-the-valley ceramic fixtures and rosewood enclosures. The principal rooms have been repainted or repapered—good riddance to flocked damask!—with the exception of Clarissa's parlour, which Henry has given Mae to understand by means of a wistful look, is not to be touched lest a tragedy of Greek proportions ensue should his sister be forced to sit in a cheerful room. Henry's sombre study with its oak panels is also off-limits— "But Henry, that old stuffed pigeon looks so sad." She muses aloud, "What about tartan wallpaper and matching upholstery?!" To which he replies, "It is a red grouse."

She commandeers the former bedchamber of Henry's second-eldest dead brother ("Poor Finlay") and, along with the cholera-contaminated bedstead, expels whatever spooks might be lingering with "rosebud everything," all under cover of "doing up a guest room." Mae is yearning to shop for baby clothes but will not risk tipping her hand, mindful as she is of . . . well, *splat*.

"Henry, how are we doing with the hunt for an extra maid?"

"'Extra maid.'"

Her smile does not falter. "I only ask because nice Lady Farquhar has gone out of her way to recommend someone."

"Has she indeed?"

"I told her you were seeing to it."

"Ah."

"So she knows I'm having to check with you first."

"Quite right." He clears his throat. "What do you think, my dear?"

She shrugs prettily. "You're the boss."

"I have every confidence in Lady Nora's judgment."

"Oh darling, thank you, I knew you'd take care of everything!"

Mae acquires the new maid and makes a gift of her to Clarissa. A plain thing with small eyes and a prematurely ropy neck—*thank heaven I snatched up pretty little Maggie Sheehan from the cinders!* Not that Clarissa seemed all that pleased.

"Och, she was, Lady Mae, very pleased."

"How could you tell, Maggie? I didn't see so much as a frown of pleasure."

"'Tis the pain, Your Ladyship."

"Pain? Goodness me, is she ill? What's she got?"

"I'm not to know, only she be sore of a morning especially. And evening."

"Clarissa, have you seen a doctor?"

The family eyebrows. "Whatever for?"

Mae is in the parlour, seated on the unupholstered tub chair usually occupied by Henry. She leans forward a little and speaks gently, as though to a child. "I can't help but notice that sometimes you appear to be in some discomfort." In fact, Mae had put her sister-in-law's rather stiff movements down to the poor thing's old-fashioned garments.

"I am fine well, Lady Marie. I only hope I've not drawn attention to myself by means of my . . . retiring manner."

"I don't believe you."

Clarissa looks up, shocked.

Mae smiles sincerely. "My friend's mother had something perhaps similar."

"What did she 'have'?"

"A painful growth in her—on the inside of her female parts. She had it out. She died—but not of that, it was—oh it doesn't matter, only just to say the physician cured her pain."

"I do not know that my trivial complaint is exclusive to the female sex, all normal men and women being equipped with shoulders and hips. And knees. I thank you for your solicitousness, Lady Marie, but what can't be cured must be endured."

"Clarissa, would you do something for me?"

"I will do all I can."

"Would you call me Mae? Or at least Marie?"

Her sister-in-law reddens. Mostly about the neck. Unfortunate how some women don't flush so much as blotch.

Mae is kind-hearted and it hurts her to see her sister-in-law in pain; a worthy response which is not incompatible with her awareness that *if Clarissa becomes an invalid, she might have to live with us forever.*

With September close upon them, it is not too soon to begin preparations for the move to London. Thus, dressed for dinner and strolling about the bedroom, she chats with her husband who is in the lavatory, shaving himself. "We need to get you a proper valet, Henry."

"What's that, my dear?"

"And I need to know whether to order a winter travelling costume or if you intend we should set out before the end of October, I need at least three weeks notice either way."

"'Set out'?"

"I'm just longing to see the house, dear." She adjusts the tri-fold looking glass of her new vanity, and spears home a hairpin.

He puts his head round the door, wiping his cheek with a washcloth. "Truly?"

"Don't tell me you've been waiting for me to say so?"

"Why, not for the world would I rush you."

"Silly, I can't wait to see it!"

"My darling, you please me more than I can say." He enters in his vest, suspenders hanging down—"We shall set out as soon as ever you please"—catches himself and retreats back into the lavatory.

"Oh Henry, I'm so glad," she spins on her stool to face him. "I'm just dying to get out of here! That is, Edinburgh is charming, of course, and Clarissa's friends are . . . Golly, what would we do without bridges and . . . I intend to use the word 'hypotenuse' in a sentence at the first opportunity."

He laughs and re-emerges, buttoning his shirt.

She waxes solemn. "I'll miss Clarissa, of course."

"Clarissa will visit, my darling, as often as you like." He feasts his eyes upon her as she ties his cravat. Really, she is fetching in that frock. More fetching out of it, of course—he blushes at his own brazenness.

"Well, it's a bit of a trek," she says.

"Scarcely a day."

He shrugs into his tail coat.

"Really? Has Sir Ian invented a super-velocity train, then?"

He laughs again. Embraces her.

"Henry, my hair."

"Darling, I hardly dared hope. I promise you, we will be happy there."

"Oh darling, who wouldn't be happy in London?" She rests her hands on his lapels.

"'London.'"

"Poor darling, I know you told Daddy you wished you could spend more time there."

"I did?"

"You most certainly did, you said you wished you could spend more time in the house in London, well now you can afford to!" With a playful pat of his chest. "I can't wait to meet the Queen, I've been practising my curtsey."

He regards her, puzzled. She puckers for a kiss.

He says, "We—I haven't got a house in London, Marie."

It is Mae's turn to be puzzled. "But Henry . . . you told Daddy . . ."

He chuckles as it dawns on him. He is, however, unprepared for her words. "You lied to Daddy."

She is not play-acting.

He is shocked.

He regards her a steely moment. Removes her hands gently but firmly from his chest.

"Henry, I'm sorry. Henry, please look at me. Please, I'm just. I guess I'm a little confused. I . . . seem to recall . . ."

"I do not doubt your recollection, Marie. Retention, however, is not comprehension. I did indeed refer to 'the house.' The House of Lords." A wintry smile.

"Ohh." She covers her mouth with her hand—she has heard the squeal in her voice and it is funny and Henry is funny because when men get mad it's funny in a nerve-wracking sort of way especially if you're their adored little girl in which case Daddy is going to take it out on Donny the horse or Donny the stable boy, whichever he sees first and Mae will be in a torrent of tears if it's the former, but. Marie is a married woman. And this is her husband. And he is not amused. She composes her features. Then bursts out laughing.

Henry has no rejoinder. He regards her, at a loss.

"Oh Henry, I'm sorry. Just give me a minute." She tilts her chin up and fans her chest with her hand. "All right, I'm fine. No I'm not!" Even to Mae, the wave of hilarity is of unusual force—there is an undertow to it, so to speak. All right. There. She has got hold of herself. She bursts into tears, "Now you hate me!"

"My darling! I love you!"

In his arms. Sobbing. The hairpin, his cheek. He produces his hand-kerchief—for her, not his cheek. Guides her to a chair. Kneels before her.

She whimpers. "Then, what did you mean?"

"By what, my own?"

"When you said, 'My darling, you please me more than I can say.'"

He is momentarily nonplussed for she has mimicked him precisely.

She explains, "When you came out of the lavatory just now with your braces down and were so happy about setting out 'as soon as ever you please.' I know you didn't mean the House of Lords, you should know I'm not an idiot, Henry, I read the Baedeker on the train. Quite a lot of it."

"Ahh, it was to Fayne House I referred."

"Your country house?"

"Aye." He smiles. Touches a fingertip to the end of her pretty nose. "My darling, you are anything but an eediot, why you exceed my late terrier, Hamish, for intelligence, and that I may say of few men and fewer women."

"Horrid boy."

He laughs.

"But Henry . . . why would we go there in the middle of autumn?"

"Fayne is most congenial at any time of year."

"All right. But is there anyone there?"

"Why certainly, there is the household. And. There's the vicar. And his wife, if memory serves. Not to mention an entire village full of . . . villagers."

"Of course I'm longing to see it, Henry, and I'm sure it's divine, but what's the good of a country house without friends? Oh I know, we'll get up a shooting party, you must have grouse."

He suppresses a shudder.

She surveys him calmly. "Henry, I want us to buy a house in London. I have honest-to-goodness friends-of-friends there and I'll bet you know just everybody."

"One can hardly avoid it."

"I know for a fact Fanny's going to be in town and she's just crazy about me, and there's that amusing Lord Richard Hawley."

"Quite."

"Your name will open every door in the best circles, and you can leave the rest to me, we'll have lots of friends and loads of fun."

"'Fun.'"

She speaks kindly, and for a moment it is as though she were the elder of the two. "While we're still young, Henry." She strokes his brow. "And I want to do it sooner than later because in a few months . . . I won't be wanting to travel."

"Whyever not?"

She drops her chin and looks up at him through her lashes.

He clasps her hands, breathes, "Mae."

She nods, suddenly bashful.

"Oh my darling. Really?"

She whispers, "Really."

"Oh my own, my love, my treasure. My forever." His lips pressed to her hand. His head in her lap.

She runs her fingers through his fine hair. He will be noticeably balding within a few years. The observation serves only to reinforce for Mae something which—like a building, brick by brick—is taking shape within her; but which is still so fresh an undertaking that it retains the power to surprise her. It is her formidable capacity for love. He is hers. This mild man. This potent, kind, harmless Henry. There are many reasons why many women might love Henry Bell, and why many more might at least try to love the Seventeenth Baron of the DC de Fayne. But Mae loves him because he is hers.

Time expands—perhaps to accommodate the heir not-quite-apparent, multiplying even now, inches from Henry's dear head.

They lose track of time. Allow me an eternity in one moment with you, my love, for what is time? We are in it. Are we of it? We know not what it is. I know only that time stops for Love.

Time resumes with his spoken words. "How are you feeling, my darling? Is there anything at all I can get for you?"

"A house. In Mayfair."

Life is cream and dream and beauty. Simple.

The dinner bell.

Mutton.

———

That night in bed.

"Henry, I'm pregnant. And I'm hungry. And if I'm hungry, so is the little Eighteenth Baron."

32

NEXT EVENING.

A sirloin of beef. Pink at the centre.

Mae is somewhat tipsy with her second helping, though she has left her wine untasted, mindful of old Annie's warning that women who over-indulge when they're expecting risk giving birth to dipsomaniacs—a glass of stout is excepted, but Mae isn't about to swill black beer at the table.

"Yes please, Havers—no, the big piece. Thanks."

Clarissa surveys the remains of 2s. per lb. on the platter. And waits for Lady Marie to finish eating. As does Henry.

Finally—"I don't know what you said to Cavendish, Henry, but it worked." Mae sits back. "I'm tempted to sop up every last drop."

Clarissa raises a finger and Havers appears at Mae's side with the loaf.

"Really? You won't think me barbaric?" Mae takes a slice of bread and mops a smear of red from her plate.

Clarissa says, "Certainly not, Marie."

Mae's heart sings at the sound of her first name. She shoots a triumphant look to Henry.

Clarissa adds, "Nothing is barbaric which sustains a gravid woman." And folds her hands.

"'Gravid'?" Mae looks from Clarissa to Henry who goes pink as the roast. "What does that mean?"

"Havers, more bread for Her Ladyship," says Clarissa.

"No, thank you. Henry?"

He looks up affably, as though momentarily distracted. Mae looks over her shoulder. Perhaps she ought to ask Havers.

Clarissa speaks. "It means welcome news. For the continuance of Henry's line."

Mae's lips fall open. She looks at her husband.

"Havers. Pooding."

Mae rises. Leaves the table.

———

In the bedroom:

"How could you?!"

"My dear, do not distress yourself."

"I'm not distressing myself, you are!"

"I shan't pretend not to comprehend your meaning."

"Well that's nice for a change!"

"Marie, whyever oughtn't I to . . . share the glad tidings with our sister?"

"Your sister, not ours!"

"She is your—"

"Sister-*in-law*, Henry, and I know the difference—" She bites her lips between her teeth and plunks onto her vanity stool. Catches sight of herself in the mirror ("looking glass" be darned!). Her forehead is contracted and she is put in mind of a rhyme, *There was a little girl, who had a little curl*—she strikes her brow with the heel of her hand.

"Hold!" cries Henry, seizing her wrist. Her face crumples. "Oh, Mae, dearest . . ."

She wails, "I want to go home! I miss Taffy! I want my Daddy! I want . . . I want Annie, and . . . and Bonnie!" She wails this last, he fears her heart will break.

"There, there, my darling . . . Who is Bonnie?"

"My dog!" She sobs with all her might. He holds her. "There, there. There. Dearest, please you mustn't, that is, I'm so sorry and I do not blame you for hating me—"

"I don't hate you!" Redoubled weeping. "I love you, you stupid!"

"Listen to me dearest, I've—I've had a thought just now. What would you say to . . . How be if we invite Taffy—Miss Weaver—to visit us?"

The wracking ebbs. She makes thorough use of his hanky. Hiccoughs. "Really?"

"Why, yes."

"She'll have to stay for a good long time." Blowing her nose. "Maybe forever."

"So be it. Tell her to bring Bonnie, and . . . the other person—"

"Annie, my old nurse."

"Quite, bring Annie, bring . . . good Lord, I was about to say bring your father. Well I shall say it, bring Mr. Corcoran."

She laughs and flings her arms round his neck. "We'll never get Daddy on a ship again, we'll have to visit him once the baby is born."

"Of course we shall."

"I'll write and ask Taffy to come and stay for my 'confinement.'" She catches herself before she lets slip Taffy's knowledge of her "gravid" condition. It wouldn't do for Henry to know she told Taffy first. Oh, and the maid.

"Henry, I just realized, if Taffy comes we'll have to put off London."

"Oh."

"Do you mind very much?"

"'Mind'?"

"There wouldn't be time to find a house and do it up before she arrived."

". . . I should think there wouldn't."

"I want to be able to spend all my time with her. And you, of course."

"Of course."

"I'm sorry to have got your hopes up."

"Not at all, I don't mind in the slightest."

"Henry, can I ask you one teensy question?"

"Anything."

"Why did you go ahead and tell Clarissa our news? And all on your own, too?"

He flushes. She presses her advantage. "Is it because you figure it's really only yours to tell since I'm just a prize cow?"

"My dear, you shock me."

"I can see that."

"If you were a man and said as much with reference to my wife, I would . . ."

"Run me through with your rapier?"

"Yes."

She laughs, but he remains stern. She sobers. "I know what I signed up for, Henry. You're the boss, and not in the same way as any old husband, but in an ancient kind of way. My life is in your hands. You have complete power over me. You may do with me what you will, and . . .

Well, Your Lordship . . . if I weren't already 'gravid' . . . I'd be angling for it right about now."

"Mae, really, we've only just dined."

"Okay, then answer the question."

"The . . . ?"

"'Why did you tell Clarissa our news?'"

"Ah. As to that. Why, in point of fact, I really can't say."

She narrows her eyes cannily. "Did you talk to Cook about the meat?"

He is looking overly attentive. "What has that to do with . . . ?"

"You were too scared to talk to Cavendish so you asked Clarissa to do it for you, am I right?"

"In point of fact—"

"You said that already."

"Matters domestic are, of course, Clarissa's bailiwick, thus I quite naturally may have . . . that is, I did. Suggest she might broach the subject." He swallows. "With Cavendish."

"And Clarissa didn't want to provoke Cook either, so you brought out the big guns and told your sister our news."

He squares his chin and looks to one side.

She says, "You would walk through fire for me—"

"Now you speak truth!" he booms.

"But you're scared of the cook, and you won't stand up to your sister."

He clasps his hands behind his back, executes a quarter turn.

"Henry? Henry, unpuff your chest, you look like one of your pheasants. I don't blame you, and don't worry, I'll protect you from the cook." He cradles his forehead. "Henry, look at me."

"Marie, I intended no breach of our intimacy. I am, however, guilty of thoughtlessness. Forgive me. I beg you."

"You are hereby forgiven, Your Lordship."

In her smile is the promise of compensations for the strictures of this mortal coil the like of which Henry, Lord Bell, Seventeenth Baron of the DC de Fayne, had never imagined until setting eyes on her last April.

She reaches out and hooks her fingers in the waistband of his trousers, pulling him toward her.

"And please know, my angel, that Clarissa wishes only your happiness. She would lay down her life for—"

"Oh Henry, shutup and lay down your wife."

August 30, 1871

Dear Taffy,

The best part of a conjugal quarrel is making up afterwards. That is not why I'm writing, but if you wish to know more, you will have to board a ship of the White Star Line to Liverpool, thence by train to Edinburgh's Waverly Station and into a waiting carriage emblazoned with the Bell family crest ("Salamander Rampant"—a cute little blue dragon) which will convey you to No. One Bell Gardens and your own Lady Mae. Say yes! Henry wants you almost as much as I do, and won't take no, and it's on his dime, and he's a lord so look out! Oh Taffy, say yes, yes, yes, yes, yes. I'll take you shopping at Jenners and to tea at the Douglas Hotel and give you a proper tour of all the jolly morbid sights, and one day they'll point to No. One Bell Gardens and say, "Timothea Weaver slept there."

Love love love,
Mae

PS Still pregnant. "Gravid" by any other name . . . I'll explain later. See above re "quarrel."
PPS Bring your dear sweet mother if you like, bring Bonnie if you can bear it.
PPPS You'll stay for the "babby," then we'll all go home to Boston for the summer, say yes!

33

"I'LL BE TWO TICKS," cries Mae from the landing.

Forty-five minutes later, Clarissa feels prickles of perspiration beneath her bonnet band. To remove it now, however, would be to invite a chill upon finally exiting the house. Clarissa Bell waited years for a sister-in-law. She can wait a little longer. Especially under the circumstances.

This morning she surprised herself by agreeing with alacrity to her sister-in-law's proposal that they "go shopping." Perhaps less surprising, if more welcome, is the recent abeyance of the pain which, having come, Clarissa feared might fail this time to go. And while she might not be equal to clambering up Arthur's Seat—even should she wish to do so—she does feel she might manage a carriage ride and a brief tour of the shops along Princes Street. Thus this morning did she reach, painlessly, for the bell cord to summon her maid, set down, in one fluid motion, her work basket, then rise from her chair without recourse to gripping the table's edge and walk effortlessly across to the foyer, where she lifted her arms without a thought and thrust them through the sleeves of her black crape mantle which now rests lightly on her shoulders.

"I'm ready!" announces her sister-in-law, descending the stairs.

She is not ready. She is a vision in carmine and gold; she is buttoned, bowed and hatted but she is struggling to put on her kid gloves which are soft as . . . the rest escapes Clarissa. She flinches as Marie hollers, "Maggie!"

Clarissa hasn't time to wonder aloud who "Maggie" is before Sheehan appears with a parasol.

"Help me on with these," says Marie.

The costly gloves are no sooner on than Marie will have them off again—"Pull!"

Clarissa waits as Sheehan is dispatched and returns quickly with a different pair of gloves.

"That's more like it," says Marie, surveying a freshly gloved hand with fingers outstretched.

Clarissa is quite as startled as the maid when Marie flaps the kid gloves at the girl and says, "You can have these."

In the carriage, Clarissa does not so much admonish as dutifully observe, "The gel will get above her station."

"Oh Clarissa, why shouldn't she have a few pretty things?"

Clarissa can think of many reasons. But she steals a look at the pert and pretty profile beneath the fetching—if foreign—hat; at the extravagant gown, beneath whose layers there beats a tiny new heart. Her sister-in-law reaches across a gloved hand and pats Clarissa's own and she reflects, "One cannot help but like the lass."

Indeed, as the carriage pulls out of Bell Gardens and into George Street, Clarissa is suffused with a long-dormant well-being. She points out the sights to Marie, not omitting "the handsome New Register House, where—"

"Oh, I know, ever so many documents!"

"Across the way is the Auld Toun, I'd fain show you—"

"Oh yes, I've seen it, ever so fascinating."

The carriage pulls up to West Princes Street Gardens and stops.

"I thought we might begin with a turn about the gardens."

"Sure, if you like," says Mae, with a longing look toward Jenners on the corner.

The ladies are handed down from the carriage by Sanders and, upon paying the entrance fee, commence, along with members of the gentry, to stroll amid autumnal beds of fuchsia and sunset-coloured roses that remind Mae of Rome and love.

Clarissa is keen that Mae should admire in detail "the Royal Institution, built in the classical style by . . ." Against the buzz and burr of her sister-in-law's inventory, Mae gives herself over to the soft September day and a reverie inspired by nursemaids pushing prams. "Clarissa, do you hear that?" There is music coming from somewhere. Mae follows it to its source.

A young man has stationed himself by the gates and is playing a penny whistle. A broom leans against the fence nearby. He taps his heel in time with the music. He has a face full of freckles and his ginger curls blow free, for his cap sits on the pavement, weighed in place with a few coins.

"Best not encourage vagrants," says Clarissa, catching up.

"He's working."

"Begging by any other name."

Mae tosses a shilling into the young man's cap. He bows and gives her a big smile, then snatches up his broom and rapidly sweeps the street before them as they cross to the opposite pavement. Mae is by now laughing with delight. He retreats to his post with a spring—even a little jig—in his step, and the lilting music of his whistle strikes up once more and follows them into Jenners.

Upon setting foot in the emporium of soaring windows, towering palms and gleaming display cases, Clarissa pauses. Purses her lips lest she gape.

"Clarissa, don't tell me you've never been in here before."

"I have not had occasion to acquire . . . ready-made goods."

"Well follow me, you're in for a treat."

Department by department.

Swatches of silk and satin. "Send the lot, I'll think it over."

Ladies' Foot-wear. Clarissa averts her eyes as the male shop assistant holds, in his bare hand, the ankle of Lady Marie, Seventeenth Baroness of the DC de Fayne.

"I dare say Henry will love me in these." Red high-heeled slippers with pearl-encrusted clasp and silk ties. A month's wages at Fayne. Per shoe.

Clarissa suffers herself to be stood on a stool and draped in bronze silk from a massive bolt. It is tugged and tucked about her person by a seamstress who mumbles instructions through a line of pins between her lips. Clarissa raises (painlessly!) her arms, lowers them, and turns about obediently. She meets her own startled gaze in the looking glass, whilst behind her: "Clarissa, if you fail to order this in a dinner gown, I'll never speak to you again. And don't ask me if that's a promise!"

It is no doubt a trick of rosy lampshades and burnished fabric, but even Clarissa cannot fail to see that the glass reflects a face and form quite . . . "rejuvenated" is too strong a word.

Mae devotes the balance of the afternoon to trying on hats. She selects one. "Well, Clarissa, what do you think?" It is loaded with plumes of snowy white egret and pink flamingo amid which peeps a ruby-throated hummingbird. The corners of Clarissa's mouth rise. "I don't know that your husband will be partial to it, Marie."

"Sure he will. Henry loves birds."

They restore themselves over a "pot of India" in the public tea room. Marie claps girlishly at the arrival of a tiered tray of tiny sandwiches and cakes. Clarissa opts for a bowl of cock-a-leekie soup which arrives scalding and over-salted. She reaches for a minuscule cucumber sandwich, more to poultice her scorched tongue than to satisfy hunger and finds it quite . . . "refreshing" is not too strong a word.

As they emerge onto the street, Clarissa, seized by an impulse, directs Sanders into Melbourne Place where she purchases a tin of Ferguson's Edinburgh Rock. Ginger flavour. She has purchased it for Henry but somehow, between her and her sister-in-law, the tin is empty by the time they arrive home. Clarissa proceeds immediately upstairs and naps until dinner.

Mae models her new hat for Henry who pales at the inventory of slaughter.

"Well I'm not taking it back, Henry, they're already dead, do you send your plate of chicken back to the kitchen?"

Mae grows restless. She has redone the house. She has toured the shops. She has logged miles about the little private park across the road. "I wonder if there's time to have a fourth storey built onto the roof before Taffy arrives."

Clarissa freezes, her fish fork halfway to her lips.

Henry clears his throat, and with a slight perturbation of brow inquires whether Marie might wish to consider obtaining livery for the serving men of the household.

"Henry, you're a genius, why didn't I think of that?!"

Afterwards, in the parlour, Clarissa asks her brother, "What made you suggest livery?"

"God did. As the lesser of two evils."

Clarissa laughs.

Mae catches him on his way out to a meeting of the Ornithological Society.

"Don't take this the wrong way, Henry, but don't you have any friends?"

"Why, of course I do. There is Mr. Baxter and . . ."

"Who else?"

"Why, no one of note."

"Poor darling, just the one friend."

"As such, yes. One alone whom, as the Ancients said, I would follow into exile." He pecks her on the cheek, adding, "One has, of course, a wide acquaintance." He dons his hat and—

"Wouldn't you like to introduce me to them?"

He replies vaguely, "Why, certainly."

"It's settled then."

"What is?"

But she has turned back into the house.

She steps into her sister-in-law's parlour. Clarissa is absorbed, poking and plucking away at a taut tambourine in her lap.

"What are you sewing, Clarissa?"

Her sister-in-law looks up. Frowns happily. "I am making a *broderie anglaise* collar for your son."

"Oh that's so nice. What if it's a girl?"

Clarissa does not answer right away. Mae falters. Quails, even. But her sister-in-law's tone is not unkind when she says, "I daresay 'twill do as well for a lass."

Mae could hug her. And after all, the first baby is just for openers, as Pappy might say. "Clarissa, I so awfully enjoyed meeting your interesting friends last month, especially . . . what are their names again? He's something to do with bridges . . ."

"Sir Ian Farquhar. When complete, it will be the longest continuous suspension bridge in the world."

"And his wife, poor thing."

"'Poor thing'? Why, Lady Nora is a mathematician in her own right."

"Like I said."

Clarissa's head tilts quizzically, but she returns to her work.

"Clarissa, what say we throw a jolly dinner party?"

"'Throw . . .'? Ah. You wish to give a dinner."

"That's right."

"Have you applied to your husband?"

"This is women's business, Clarissa, Henry will love it, invite all the best people."

Clarissa's brow furrows.

Encouraged, Mae goes out on a limb. "Have you got any girlfriends?"

Her sister-in-law looks up—but not with the show of incomprehension Mae has come to expect from her new family. No. Mae senses she has touched a nerve.

34

MAE PLUNGES INTO preparations for the dinner party. It is the nicest few weeks since their honeymoon, what's more she is eager to vet the friends before inflicting them on Taffy. Clarissa continues to be downright spry, lingering "at table" after dinner. Henry too is spending less time sealed up at the museum and more out traipsing after birds with his "one true friend" Mr. Baxter whom Mae has yet to meet. Henry has tried to get her to join them, "We saw—heard rather, truth to tell—a sedge warbler, I've no doubt he was exhorting every female within hearing to join him on his imminent flight to Africa, oh Mae, just consider, those wee wings take them halfway round the world then back to the selfsame stand of reeds in an Edinburgh loch."

"That's sweet of you Henry, but you and Mr. Baxter don't want a woman tagging along."

"Nonsense, we often—that is we have, on occasion, been accompanied by an old female acquaintance."

"Really," Mae raises her eyebrows. "An old female or an old acquaintance?" She laughs.

"A Miss Rosamund Gourley, herself an avid bird-watcher."

"How nice for her, run along now, I'm going to have a little lie-down."

"Why of course, my dear, you must rest, I'm a brute."

"You're an angel."

He trundles off happy, returns ruddy and, yes, ready in a certain department which has, if anything, become even more compelling to Mae in her not-so-delicate condition. She is over the morning sickness and feeling quite indomitable—not that she meets much resistance. Even Cook has waved the white dishcloth in surrender. Mae quickly understood that a charm offensive would be worse than useless in that quarter. Instead she captured Cavendish's loyalty with a ruthless assertion of rank and a withering reluctance to be pleased. "You call that cake?"

She damned with faint praise. "You surprise me, Cavendish. I wouldn't have thought you had a soufflé in you."

She cowed her with condescension. "You do know what a French whisk is?" With the result that Cook's fearsome energies have been lined up and let fly on butchers, florists and greengrocers, all in aid of a "social triumph." Mae set the bar with a copy of *Mrs. Beeton's Book of Household Management*. And after a trial run of *côtelettes de volailles*, followed by a successful jelly with whipped cream, Mae smacked her hand down on the book and pronounced sternly, "Yours to keep, Cavendish."

Even Clarissa's maid—whose name Mae never learns, for Clarissa never calls her by one—looks a little less ligatured about the neck in a new collar with just a touch of froth. As for Maggie, her nails are clean, her breath is sweet, she smells of soap and looks pretty in her new uniform. Mae conducts an inventory of her own wardrobe.

"Come here, Maggie. Try this on."

The girl has practised not gawping, so it is with only a seemly amount of reluctance that she strips down to her skivvies, steps into a crinolette and tries on the floral-print Worth gown.

"You can have it," says Mae, and is gratified to see the girl is properly speechless. "By the time I fit into it again it'll be last season's."

Truth to tell, she has tired of the floral and it's diverting to dress up her pretty little maid in her cast-offs. "Now take it off and put your uniform back on."

She has left the guest list to Clarissa on condition she have "final approval" (as Daddy would say). The one note of discord, if one can call it that, is between Henry and Clarissa. Mae is not eavesdropping, merely pausing outside the parlour door so as not to interrupt what sounds like a more than usually terse exchange between brother and sister.

He: "Miss Gourley? Is she even in town?"

She: "She is."

He: "We cannot invite her."

She: "We can hardly invite Josiah Baxter without inviting Rosamund."

He: *Sigh* of acquiescence.

Mae shivers with pleasure at this hint of intrigue. The elusive Miss Gourley and the mysterious Mr. Baxter clearly share a "history". . .

Two extra kitchen maids have been hired from the Douglas Hotel for the occasion and, together with Cavendish and a new scullery maid, have been chopping, simmering, setting and skimming for days. The new livery has been fitted and an extra footman has been engaged. At last, the great evening arrives.

Mae is glamorous in an evening gown of gold silk jacquard and pale pink taffeta. Her hair is piled in several finger puffs atop her head whence loose waves ebb into perfect curls that frame her face—clever Maggie! And nestled in her décolleté, as if it had just now alighted, a bird pendant, its silver wings and tail feathers set with an array of rose-cut diamonds— four and a half carats, but who's counting? The whole effect is stunning against the new chinoiserie wallpaper in the dining room with its cherry blossoms and white parakeets.

If, so far, the evening has fallen short of "jolly," Mae counts it a minor victory that four ladies and as many gentleman are now seated at her table. Forming the centrepiece is a large and elegant epergne, each silver arm of which supports a crystal bowl of pink rose blossoms, crimson dahlias and white freesia.

They have just now come in from the drawing room. There they par-took of sherry served by a white-gloved Pugsley whom Mae has trans-formed, fairy-godmother-like, into a footman—now if he could only stop tugging at the collar of his handsome new livery.

Mae has managed to browbeat Henry himself into a white waistcoat, and he and she were perched on the new lime-green settee awaiting their guests when Henry began fretting, "What can be keeping Clarissa? I do hope she has not fallen prey to one of her spells." At this, Mae winked at (otherwise nameless) Maid, who skedaddled out and upstairs. Moments later, Clarissa entered the drawing room wearing the new bronze dinner gown, with its overskirt of embroidered vines and under-skirt of pale ruched silk, and its "natural-form" silhouette (and very clever about the neck, thanks also to Mae, who knows that when a woman reaches a certain age, she develops wattles best concealed by a looser and frothier collar).

Henry rose, speechless. Clarissa stood, chin level, eyes lowered.

"Well?" said Mae. And pinched her husband's arm.

"My word, Clarissa. I must say. Quite the attire."

Clarissa looked up with . . . neither a scowl nor a smile, but a degree of . . . uncertainty. It was an open look. And it struck Mae: Clarissa must have been quite pretty once.

The Farquhars were, mercifully, first to arrive. Sir Ian fell immedi-ately into genial conversation and Lady Nora out and out hugged Mae— who was taken by surprise at her own sudden impulse to cry. The older woman smiled kindly and told Mae she was a vision and the dearest thing ever to have trod the earth—and it occurred to Mae that a woman might in fact pine for a daughter.

"Miss Gourley, Madam," announced Havers. And Mae turned to acknowledge the new arrival who—and this was odd—had been waylaid in the foyer by the maid of all things. Maggie Sheehan, that is. Mae could not hear what briefly passed between them, but she saw Miss Gourley pat the girl's hand before Maggie bobbed and withdrew. A glance to Clarissa told Mae that her sister-in-law, too, had witnessed the encounter. As for her husband, well, he wasn't paying attention—after all, there were no birds flying about in the foyer.

Miss Gourley entered and Mae swept graciously over to her, hand outstretched. Miss Gourley took it firmly in a mannish grip. Mae immediately took the measure of this vigorous spinster whose mousy bun and dowdy dinner dress—one could not call it a gown—of serviceable bombazine in a muddy purple, not to mention shoes which bordered on the sensible, struck her as better suited to a governess than a lady; but Miss Gourley was, after all, a school-teacher, poor thing. "Miss Gourley, I am delighted to make your acquaintance."

"And I yours, Lady Marie." The voice too was forthright, even strident. But Mae was, by now, accustomed to Scottish good manners and was therefore not put off. She did, however, note that her husband was a titch remiss in his attentions, and she nudged him with a word: "Henry, do tell Miss Gourley about the lovely ruins we saw in Rome." Admittedly Mae had spoiled him, but that was no excuse for a gentleman to neglect a lady just because she had taken so little trouble over her toilette.

"Colonel MacOmber, Madam." Havers looked even more patrician in his new black waistcoat and tails.

The Colonel entered, leading with his chest, emblazoned as it was with a red silk tartan waistcoat, one end of his bowtie jauntily extended as though loosed by a stiff breeze. At the sight of his middle-aged god-daughter radiant in bronze, he planted his feet and bellowed, "Well now, Clarrie, I'm deuced!"

Mae tittered charmingly and guided him to sit next to her on the settee, where she could keep him contained.

And at last, "Mr. Baxter."

"You're the one who sent the pears!" exclaimed Mae. The pale dark-haired gentleman bowed over her hand—which he, unlike Miss Gourley, forbore to mangle. Miss Gourley herself greeted the mysterious Mr. Baxter as warmly as did Henry—a fact not lost on Mae. While Mr. Baxter was clearly every inch a gentleman, his degree of shabbiness seemed to owe more to a state of prolonged bachelorhood than to breeding, judging by his wilted bowtie and rather crumpled collar of doubtful white. Mae felt the immediate urge to take him under her wing.

"I have also to thank Mr. Baxter for my maid," said Clarissa, positively genially. "Your maid now, of course, Marie."

"Oh, she's a treasure, Mr. Baxter, thank you. Although," Mae turned generously to include Miss Gourley, "I suspect Miss Gourley had a hand in that brilliant acquisition."

Silence. Sensing a *faux pas*, Mae quickly added, "Oh, I noticed her greeting you in the foyer."

Miss Gourley replied, "Yes, Lady Marie, Miss Sheehan and I are acquainted."

And Miss Gourley being Scottish, Mae found it impossible to tell whether this was a good thing or a bad thing or . . . any thing.

"Are you indeed, Miss Gourley," said Clarissa with some asperity. "Pray tell."

"We were able to offer her guidance at the Refuge."

Clarissa turned then to Mr. Baxter, who looked a little sheepish, and said, all trace of asperity gone, "You will be glad to know, Mr. Baxter, that Sheehan is indeed a treasure."

He inclined his head graciously and a hank of jet hair flopped into his eyes.

Now Mae surveys her guests from the end of the table; to her left is Lady Farquhar, to her right is Mr. Baxter. Next to him is Miss Gourley (to whom Mae has determined to be especially kind in compensation for Henry's neglect).

Henry is at the head of table. To his left is Sir Ian, to his right the elderly Colonel. Next to the Colonel is Clarissa, seated directly across from Miss Gourley. Like duelling spinsters.

Mae has opted to serve *à la Russe*. Thus, rather than a table littered with every last covered dish and platter, there is room for the epergne with its blossom-laden bowls along with the silver candelabras and their white tapers, lit now and setting all to glittering.

"I'd love to keep you in suspense as to the menu," announces Mae, "but I feel it only fair to warn you to keep room for the main course, which will follow the soup, the fish and three light entrées." Muted "mms" and "ahhhs." Mae is unperturbed to see Clarissa looking pained at her little pre-prandial speech—just so long as her sister-in-law is not in actual pain.

The Soup. A satiny *consommée à la royale*, with succulent custards.

Followed by *chaud-froid* of salmon.

Havers glides about with Burgundies and Bordeauxs (pre–French blight, another triumph!). Mae herself is nursing a well-watered glass of the former.

"Grub's first-rate, Clarrie!" says Colonel MacOmber, tucking into the pigeon pie. Mae laughs good-naturedly. Lady Nora protests at the appearance of the chicken *côtelettes*—"Well I can't say you didn't warn me, Lady Marie!" to general laughter.

Sweetbreads with peas, croquette potatoes and new carrots.

"How was your sabbatical, Miss Gourley?" asks Sir Ian heartily.

Miss Gourley's tone is dry. "It was most fruitful, Sir Ian, thank you."

Henry clears his throat. Havers refills His Lordship's water glass.

Sir Ian continues, for the benefit of his young hostess, "Miss Gourley left us for a spell in order to pursue studies in . . . ?"

"Pedagogical Science," says Miss Gourley flatly.

Lady Farquhar leans forward earnestly, craning a little to see past the trailing freesia. "Really? How fascinating."

So much for witty repartee. Still, people are chatting and enjoying the food.

"We were so very relieved when, when she returned, weren't we, Henry," says Mr. Baxter. His speech betrays a slight hesitation which only enhances his endearing waifishness. Really, the man ought to be married. Mae's match-making wheels begin to turn, for what is stopping Miss Gourley from uniting with her old bird-watching friend Mr. Baxter?

"We were," replies Henry, a little curtly. "Quite relieved."

"I for one could not be better pleased to see the Ornithological Musketeers reunited," says Sir Ian, and beams like one of his lighthouses.

Mr. Baxter turns to Mae by way of explanation. "We three were birding companions, I've, I've been at loose ends as you might imagine."

"I'm the culprit," says Mae, gaily, "I stole Henry away from you"—and adds, over Mr. Baxter's blushing remonstrations—"but Miss Gourley, what's your excuse for deserting poor Mr. Baxter?"

Miss Gourley is evidently not one for badinage. Mae shrinks a little under the schoolmarmy gaze and braces herself to hear her last words repeated, but dear Mr. Baxter steps into the breach, saying, "High time we returned to Salisbury Craigs, Henry, you've not been up there since your near-miss."

"What near-miss?" asks Mae.

"Henry would have tumbled from the Craigs had it not been for, for Rosamund's quick reflexes."

"Good show, Miss Gourley," says Sir Ian.

"Oh dear," says Mae, "is that the fierce-looking cliff over by Arthur's Throne?"

"Arthur's Seat," murmurs Clarissa.

"It is," says Henry with a thin smile.

Mr. Baxter says, "We, we spotted a dotterel just before it happened."

"Fascinating species," says Sir Ian. "Am I correct in thinking it among the few in which the female is brighter than the male?"

"You are," says Henry somewhat tersely.

Mae says, "Speaking of the female of the species, it looks as though we have Miss Gourley to thank for . . . well, golly, just everything! Now, I insist the three of you grab the first fine day and go bird-watching together. What do you say, Miss Gourley?" and Mae bestows a kind smile on that drab female.

Miss Gourley replies dourly, "I'm afraid I've my hands rather full these days."

Really, I don't know that I'd wish her on poor Mr. Baxter.

Asparagus and a French salad.

"How are things at your school?" asks Lady Nora, craning the other way round the roses.

Sir Ian interjects, "Miss Gourley is foundress of Miss Gourley and Miss Mellor's School for Girls."

"Really, how very important," says Mae.

"You've hit it exactly, Lady Marie," says Lady Nora. "The pupils, rather than being confined to their desks, undertake regular outdoor excursions by foot and omnibus such that one might almost say the world is their classroom."

Sir Ian observes sportively, "Edinburgh, being the Athens of the North—perhaps it ought to be renamed 'The Peripatetic School for Girls.'" A table-wide chuckle to which Mae hastens to add a titter of her own.

Lady Nora asks Miss Gourley, "Are your lasses taught mathematics?"

"They are indeed."

"Is that wise?" asks Clarissa.

"What could be wiser?" asks Lady Nora kindly.

"Really, Nora, can that be wise which unfits a gel for marriage?"

"It did not unfit me, Clarissa," says Lady Nora.

Mae jumps in with the social salve. "I'm afraid I have to take my sister-in-law's side on that point. Even the sturdiest girl can be made sickly by sums."

Sir Ian says pleasantly, "It appears not to have harmed Miss Gourley." And turning to that lady, "I observed you only last Sunday, scampering up Arthur's Seat like a young nanny-goat."

Mr. Baxter says, "I have heard tell there be those, those on the Old Town Committee for Technical Improvement who clamour for a, a funicular up the slope."

"They can't be serious," says Miss Gourley.

"A simple matter of a counterweight pulley system," says Lady Nora.

Sir Ian adds, "A simple steam engine would serve."

Lady Nora finishes his thought: "And would have merely to move the cable the difference in weight from one car to the other."

Mae catches Henry's eye, stifles a giggle and sees Henry bite his cheek. They look quickly away from one another.

"I strenuously object," says Miss Gourley. "A mechanical conveyance for those who shirk the effort yet would reap the benefit of the view? It cannot edify such souls, and would spoil it for the rest of us. Surely just because we can do a thing, it need not follow that we must do it."

"Would you deny an edifying view to the objects of your charitable work, Miss Gourley?" asks Sir Ian. "For though their flesh may be weak with privation, thereby unfitting them for the climb, their souls may be ever so edifiable."

"Point to Sir Ian," Miss Gourley declares heartily. "I stand rebuked and rightly so." She smiles, and Mae notes her teeth—horsey.

Beef-steaks and oyster sauce.

"I say, any more of that Bordeaux?" says Colonel MacOmber.

"Hear, hear!" cries Sir Ian.

"Colonel," says Henry, "What odds do you give the Iron Chancellor with his German unification?"

Mae is gratified to find the conversation has finally splintered off into twos and threes. She basks amid the convivial hum and soon finds herself chatting with Mr. Baxter, to whom she has taken a tremendous liking. He asks about her family and listens so sympathetically. "We have the nicest house in the Back Bay. My cousin Taffy—her real name is Timothea, she's a Peabody on her mother's side, oh and she's not really my cousin, we call each other that because our fathers are like brothers, Taffy's daddy hired mine when no one else would have an Irishman, and when war broke out between the states and Taffy's big brother was killed—oh, it was terrible!—"

"I am sorry."

"Thank you!" Mae dabs her eyes. "Daddy somehow got himself down to Virginia and brought the poor boy home, otherwise he'd've been buried there because no one could get through and Lord knows how Daddy managed it—he bought a whole tannery while he was at it—and well, Mr. Weaver—that's Taffy's father—he never forgot it."

"Your father sounds a remarkable man."

Mae's eyes shine, she presses her lips together in a smile but manages only a nod.

Sir Ian joins in, "Boston is an acknowledged locus of progressive ideas and pedagogy. Quite your bailiwick, Miss Gourley."

"Indeed, Sir Ian, education is the great thing. It is the first 'E.'"

"Really, Miss Gourley?" says Mae. "What is the second 'E'?"

"The second 'E,' Lady Marie, stands for Emancipation, principally as regards Woman."

"Emancipation from what?"

"Slavery."

Mae is not alone in being taken aback, but she is the only one to gasp and, struggling to keep her smile in place, "We just fought a whole war over that, how can you say—?"

"Lady Marie, I do not draw an equivalency between the oppression of the female sex and the atrocity visited upon African peoples by your own country and mine, but I pose the question: How is the human race to continue its upward climb when one half is bound upon the wheel of childbirth which, compounded by the marriage laws, guarantees their economic enslavement?"

"That's four 'E's," says Clarissa.

"What? The last two don't count, Clarissa, that is they do, but . . ."

"I take it you are an in favour of woman suffrage?"

"I am, Sir Ian."

"Hmm. I confess I can marshal no rational argument to the contrary."

"Except that it is wholly irrational," says Clarissa. "A wrong and peril such as threaten the fabric of civilization."

"I have to agree with my sister-in-law," Mae says, folding her hands. "Can you just imagine how topsy-turvey the world would be if women started smoking cigars and fighting wars?"

Colonel MacOmber laughs.

Mr. Baxter says gently, "I incline toward Miss Gourley's view. Especially as concerns a vote cast by, for example, Miss Clarissa, in whom I have more confidence than many men."

Mae sees Clarissa blush—and revises her match-making plans.

Henry says, "While woman suffrage may be an inevitable outcome of education, I would not wish the burden of equality on any lady of my acquaintance."

Mae smiles. *He can be so gallant when he wants to be.*

"Do go on, Miss Gourley," he adds, chivalrously.

"Thank you, Lord Henry."

Mae notes the slight reddening of Miss Gourley's lean cheek and a fluttering of lashes that bespeak confusion as that worthy woman says, "Where was I?"

"The third 'E,'" says Mae with an air of rapt attention.

"Thank you, Lady Marie. It is: Equality. At present, in strictly legal terms—and you'll back me here, Josiah."

"I will," says Mr. Baxter modestly.

"A woman is the property of her father until her rights are transferred to her husband. In short, she is chattel, with scarcely more rights than common livestock."

Turban of veal.

Sir Ian says, "One hears tell of ladies of advanced views who dispense with husbands altogether in favour of throwing in their lot with a member of their own sex in what is termed—correct me if I err, Lady Marie—a 'Boston marriage.'"

Mae groans. "I can't think of anything more dreary, it's bad enough being a spinster"— she brings herself up short, shocked, and, uncharacteristically floundering—"not that a state of single blessedness isn't itself a noble calling." *Oh dear.*

Henry—*bless him!*—says, "Some would say there is no higher calling than that of school-teacher and, insofar as Woman is concerned, marriage is an impediment to that noble profession."

Clarissa says, "In point of fact, Miss Gourley has reduced her teaching duties in favour of gathering alms for the poor."

Miss Gourley is looking a little wind-blown, but rallies. "I don't know that 'alms' is quite the word, Clarissa."

Mae is galvanized by Miss Gourley's use of Clarissa's first name. There is definitely *history* there. She shoots Henry a look but he is swirling his Bordeaux.

Clarissa explains, "Miss Gourley labours selflessly for the betterment of the Poor Irish Among Us. Is that not so, Rosamund?" *Rosamund!*

"Not exclusively the Irish, surely," says Henry with an apprehensive glance at his wife.

Just then Colonel MacOmber comes to life and in sonorous tones says, "Perhaps the most notorious Irish immigrants of the nineteenth century were the murderers Hare and Burke, who in 1828 killed at least sixteen people and sold the bodies for dissection at the University of Edinburgh. To quote our own Walter Scott: 'Our Irish importation have made a great discovery in Oeconomicks, namely that a wretch who is not worth a farthing while alive becomes a valuable article when knocked on the head and carried to an anatomist.'" He laughs almost to apoplexy. Havers steps forth with the decanter.

Lady Nora inquires, "Where is your charitable establishment, Miss Gourley?"

"In the Cowgate."

"The same building where you had your bed-sit," says Mr. Baxter.

"Yes, I still live there."

"Above the shop, as it were," says Clarissa.

"Clarissa," murmurs Henry. Mae hears the warning in his voice and is about to change the subject to Edinburgh's fascinating new tramways when all at once the Colonel thunders, "Cowgate! One hardly likes to mention that quarter in mixed company!"

Lady Nora chides him gently, "Now Colonel, Miss Gourley can hardly expect her needy clientele to follow her to the New Town."

"They are in need of improvement, certainly, many of them," says Clarissa.

"Pitiably backward, through no fault of their own," says Lady Nora. "I am told they arrive in our midst with nowt but their wee ones."

"Several lack husbands," says Clarissa.

Colonel MacOmber rumbles, "Many a fine lad is got on the wrong side of the blanket, Clarry, look at Heriot's."

A brief pause. Clarissa says, "Why ought we to look at Heriot's?"

Henry clears his throat. "Heriot's Hospital School for the orphaned sons of gentlemen."

The Colonel breaks in with, "Orphans be damned, they're bastards most of them, and a good sturdy lot too!" He laughs and waves his glass at Havers.

Clarissa continues, "If the poor in general were to be restrained from procreating willy-nilly, the whole of the race might grow stronger."

Lady Nora asks, "Clarissa, do you mean to say, with the help of modern hygienic methods, we might choke off the defectives among us from perpetuating their flaws?"

"Well, Nora, I fail to see why we deny our own human race that which we grant our 'livestock.'"

Mae says suddenly, and somewhat to her own surprise, "How can I help, Miss Gourley?"

That lady appears taken aback. "Lady Marie." She rallies. "That is generous. We do, of course, survive on subscriptions."

Mae rescues her guest before she can veer any closer to the forbidden topic of money. "Sign me up, Miss Gourley." Then, as though opting to upset the apple cart herself, "Henry will write you a cheque."

Miss Gourley flushes unattractively. "Thank you, Lady Marie, you are too kind."

"Nonsense, how could I refuse? After all, I'm Irish."

Silence.

"Rich Irish," adds Mae with a winning smile.

The Colonel laughs.

Henry says, "Claret, I think, Havers."

"Don't worry, Miss Gourley," says Mae breezily, "I'm not offended, I'm American." Then, addressing the table at large, "And we all come from somewhere. Even if it's a bog in County Leitrim."

Sir Ian says, "If Mr. Darwin is to be believed, as indeed I see no reason to doubt him, we all trace our origins to a primordial bog."

"Yes, but some are still splashing about in it," says Clarissa. "Present company excepted of course."

Mae laughs.

Henry looks positively tragic.

Miss Gourley says, "Fill the bellies first. Put a slate into their hands and lead them to letters and learning. Then we shall see who is truly defective."

Henry smiles. "I suppose if an ape can learn to drink tea and wear a bonnet, any savage can learn to read."

All laugh except for Miss Gourley, who frowns—and not in a happy way.

Having steered the conversation from choppy waters, Henry cedes the helm to Sir Ian. "Lord Henry, I wonder if I might enlist you—and you too, Mr. Baxter—in the service of a population of cormorants that seems to have taken a suicidal liking to the pharoscopic beam at Bell Rock?"

They respond simultaneously: "Why, gladly, Sir Ian." "Name the day." The two old friends laugh and Mr. Baxter turns to Clarissa, "Miss Bell, why don't you join us." Mae sees Clarissa smile. An actual smile.

A downright American smile. Mae lifts her chin and says, "Havers. Pudding."

Compote of fruit, a marbled jelly, iced orange and a positively lethal trifle work their magic and by the time the gentlemen are filling the dining room with cigar smoke, Miss Gourley has pleaded an early morning at the Refuge and departed, leaving Lady Nora, Clarissa and Mae to a lively hand of widow whist in the drawing room.

Mae is at her vanity, having changed into her peignoir—"That'll be all, Maggie"—and bent happily over a letter.

. . . Lady Nora is a dear but I feared she would pull out a slide rule right there at the table. And there was a bony old maid called Miss Rosamund Gourley, a blue-stocking of the first order, devoted to good works. Taffy, have you ever noticed that a woman's charm reduces in proportion to how admirable she is? On the other hand, I am convinced Clarissa is sweet on Mr. Baxter and I think they'd make a splendid couple . . .

Downstairs, Josiah Baxter has lingered with Henry and the Colonel, and now he takes his leave. The two men clasp one another in a bear-hug and Henry slaps his friend's back soundly. Clarissa bids him goodnight, her hand enclosed in both of his. "I don't know that I am up to the outing to Bell Rock, Mr. Baxter. But I thank you for the invitation."

"Of course, Miss Bell."

"Perhaps you will visit again soon. Now that Henry is home."

It is approaching midnight when Colonel MacOmber, having retreated with honour in the face of an empty decanter, pulls on his gloves in the foyer and bids Lord Henry goodnight. "Off wi' you lad and get skeppit, I'll just look in on Clarry and give her my thanks."

Having dismissed Henry to bed, the Colonel steps into the parlour and, squaring his shoulders, renews his offer of marriage to Clarissa, assuring her, "I can wait. You're hardly more than a gel."

Clarissa smiles wanly. "You are too kind, Fuzzy." And, setting aside her work, she rises (utterly painlessly) to see the old warrior out.

Henry, nightshirted, weary and longing for bed, is surprised to find his wife has waited up for him.

"Well? Aren't you going to congratulate me?"

He bends and kisses the top of her head. "Good show, Lady Marie. I don't know that I shall be able to eat another morsel for a week."

"Not too shabby, huh?"

He smiles. "Not too shabby."

She draws him down for a proper kiss. "I'd rather be your chattel than trade places with poor Miss Gourley."

"'Poor Miss Gourley'?"

"That's what your sister calls her."

"Does she."

"She's sweet on you."

"How absurd!"

"Don't be too hard on Miss Gourley just because of her 'advanced views.'"

"I am not aware of having been in the slightest hard on—"

"Well you weren't exactly a model of courtliness—"

"I should be sorry to learn I'd given the slightest offence to that lady, regrettable though her views assuredly are."

"She's a little toothy, don't you think? Perhaps a little horse-faced."

"All women pale next to you, my love."

"Silly boy." She smiles and takes up her hairbrush. "And really, we ought to be grateful, she saved your life, if it weren't for her we'd never have met."

"She saved me from a nasty fall. In point of fact."

"You're blushing."

"It's the port."

"What's Clarissa got against her?"

"'Got against her'?"

"Why doesn't Clarissa like Miss Gourley?"

"Ah. In point of fact—"

"Whenever you say that I know you want to wriggle out of something."

"'Wriggle out'—?"

"Please don't repeat everything I say."

"I say—"

"You just did it again."

He knits his brow.

"Henry, you can't tell me you didn't notice when I put my foot in my mouth at the very start of the evening."

"I am afraid I *can* tell you that. To what, my darling, do you refer?"

Men discover continents but they miss what goes on under their noses. She explains patiently, "In the drawing room, when I mentioned seeing Miss Gourley and Maggie—"

"'Maggie . . .'"

"My maid!"

"Of course, do go on, darling." He blinks hard once or twice.

"I saw Miss Gourley and Sheehan greet one another in the foyer—which would be odd in any case for a guest to be pressing the hand of a maid, but doubly odd because I realized not only did Clarissa have no idea they knew one another, she was none too pleased to see they did."

He stifles a yawn. Is brought up short by the realization that he is expected to reply. "Quite."

"Darling, please unknit your brow, I beg of you. Thank you. Well?"

"Ah. As to that, I dare say Sheehan is one of Miss Gourley's causes."

"You mean she'll have been at the 'Refuge for the Poor Irish Among Us'?" Mae has imitated Miss Gourley's accent to a T.

Henry smiles.

"What's wrong with coming from the Refuge?" she asks. "Even if it is a haven for unwed mothers—"

"My word."

"Now Henry, Clarissa made that perfectly clear—"

"I'm afraid she did."

"—and what do you call the mother of the Baby Jesus, for that matter? I say if Miss Gourley helped Maggie out of a jam like that, then Miss Gourley is a saint. Not to mention kind Mr. Baxter, who got Maggie the job."

"Well, my dear. The Refuge, being in the Cowgate, is also the redoubt of . . . purveyors of . . . the social evil."

"Oh dear. You mean typhoid?"

"No. I refer to . . ." Lord, but he is tired. "A trade practised since time immemorial by fallen women." He waits. "Prostitutes."

The blood drains from Mae's face. Such an ugly word. "You don't think Maggie . . ."

"What? No, my dear, compared to practitioners of that ancient profession, the girl is dewy as a rose."

An unwed rose . . .

"Then that doesn't explain why Clarissa was so miffed."

"Very well, if you must know, it was dear old Josey who agreed to do
Miss Gourley a favour by recommending Sheehan to my sister's employ."

"'Josey'? Oh, short for Josiah, how sweet and it suits him perfectly,
don't worry I won't call him that 'til we've been acquainted for twenty-
five years, but anyhoo do you mean Clarissa wouldn't have taken on
Maggie if she'd come with Miss Gourley's recommendation instead of
Mr. Baxter's?"

"Perhaps not."

"Because Clarissa might think her a . . . prostitute." Terrible-tasting
word.

"Certainly not, Miss Gourley would never make an infelicitous recommendation, as Clarissa knows fine well."

"Of course she wouldn't, so we're back to my question, what's Clarissa
got against Miss Gourley?"

"You are every bit as tenacious as dear old Hamish."

"That's the second time you've compared me to your dog, three
strikes and you're out."

"What?"

"Well?"

He draws a breath and, with an obliging air, says, "Miss Gourley and
Clarissa were great friends. Once." He makes for the bed.

"Don't go to bed."

"Whyever not?"

"You'll fall asleep, I want to know what happened with your sister and
Miss Gourley."

"They . . . grew apart."

"Over a man?"

". . . In a sense."

"I knew it!"

"What . . . did you know?"

"Clarissa's in love with Mr. Baxter—"

"What?! No!"

"Dear sweet naïve Henry."

"You cannot genuinely believe—"

"Don't you see how she looks at him? Haven't you noticed how she frowns whenever his name is mentioned?"

Comprehension dawns on Henry's features. "Blimey . . ."

"That's right. But he's sweet on Miss Gourley."

Henry looks freshly bewildered. "Is he?"

"Come now, you knew that part."

"Did I?"

"Why else didn't you want to invite Miss Gourley to the dinner party?"

"Did I not . . . ?"

"No need to look shifty, Henry, I heard you—that is, I overheard you by accident when you and Clarissa were discussing the guest list."

"And what did you, 'accidentally,' hear?"

"I heard you being a prince of a man as usual in the face of your sister's self-sacrificing determination to invite her rival to dinner." She smiles saucily. "Even if Miss Gourley's affections are elsewhere."

He shakes his head. "I am doing my best to keep up."

She laughs. "You can't fool me, you know perfectly well she's in love with you."

"She is no such thing!"

"You're blushing again."

"I am not."

"You blush at the mention of Miss Gourley."

"Do I? Well, I dare say 'tis embarrassing to have been rescued by a woman. No doubt such a view renders me hopelessly old-fashioned, very well then, I am old-fashioned."

"You're adorable."

"I am nothing of the kind."

She slinks past him, douses the overhead light and climbs into bed, reclining luxuriantly in the moonlight. "I may not be emancipated but I've got the boss wrapped round my little finger."

He surveys her, fists on his hips. "You think so, eh?"

"Come here, I command you."

It is all the invitation he needs. He joins her. She gives him a chaste peck on the lips. "Not tonight, Henry, I have a head."

It is all the rebuff he needs. He gets to his feet. "Forgive me, my dear."

"I blame the Farquhars and their funicular."

He laughs in spite of himself.

"You'll be all right down the hall, won't you?"

"Of course I will."

"Oh Henry," she sighs, turning onto her side, her peignoir falling open at her breasts, hand trailing toward him, "You're sure you don't mind?"

"Not at all," he says, and bends to pull the coverlet over her. And to conceal the front of his nightshirt.

"Give me a kiss," she says sleepily. He does. "You're just the nicest husband. I'm so glad you didn't fall off the cliff that day." And with closed lids, "Thank you, Miss Gourley."

His late eldest brother's bedroom has been aired and made up for just such this sort of circumstance, and as Henry feels his way in the dark, he reflects that his young wife's gratitude to Miss Gourley is not misplaced, for it is true he was spared a possibly fatal fall from the precipice that windy day. It seems a lifetime ago, whereas in reality it is scarcely a year and a half since that afternoon in spring . . . He lies down on the bed in which the erstwhile heir to Fayne died over thirty years ago—poor Bertram. As for Henry having gone on to meet his future bride, however, the credit for that is due his sister; for it was she who insisted he travel to Rome.

Henry curls onto his side and reflects that—his readiness in the conjugal department notwithstanding—it is just as well he skep here tonight, for he wishes to be alone with his thoughts; if only to quell them.

Everyone has secrets, and Henry Bell is no exception. Herewith, one of them, kept from his sister: he never minded the Bell family's impecuniosity, for there were marked advantages to it. For example, because he was not in a position to reciprocate, he was not long obliged to attend shooting parties at the country estates of his—one must not call them "friends"—old school fellows. He never came out and said it, but he felt it and keenly: deplorable as it was to shoot other people's birds, he could not have borne the slaughter of a single Fayne pheasant. Bear it, however, he must needs have done, for it would have been his duty to help his sister to a suitable husband had he the means to furnish her with a suitable dowry. And suitable husbands are to be found among gentlemen who make the sky rain death . . . not to put too fine a point on it. But now his sister is past the age when a woman might reasonably expect to become a mother—that sounds brutal, he doesn't mean it to—thus Henry is under no obligation to find her a husband. And, thanks to the wondrous creature in the marital chamber down the hall, Henry's newfound wealth means he need ingratiate himself with no man over the limp bodies of feathered innocents.

Moreover, if his wife is right—and she has a knack for these things—Clarissa has ideas of her own in that department. *Fancy Josey becoming my brother-in-law* . . . He smiles in the darkness. His wife is mistaken in one respect, however, for Henry has known Josiah Baxter long enough to know he is not "sweet on" Rosamund Gourley. The two are friends. In the true Aristotelian sense—uncommon enough in a man, vanishingly rare in a woman. Indeed, there was a time when Henry counted Miss Gourley as such a friend, and he registers a pang—not of jealousy, he does not begrudge Josey his continued friendship with Miss Gourley. The pang is to do with a falling out, which began with a near falling down. But that is all in the past. He closes his eyes.

35

AS A YOUNG MAN, Lord Henry Bell had gone on the Grand Tour. He dutifully visited the great collections and cathedrals of Europe, but found himself inclined to spend less time with the Old Masters and more time in the open air. In the Alps were busy spotted nutcrackers who mated for life and re-sowed their own forests. In the Caucasus he saw a great rosefinch, painted by the hand of God Himself. In the Dordogne he all but wept at the tender notes of golden orioles. And in Gibraltar he laughed at lavishly crowned hoopoes taking dust baths.

He amassed calling cards from museum curators and bird-fanciers and spent many a day and evening too in their knowledgeable and often pleasant company. To his sister's dismay, Henry returned with not a single card from a suitable young lady or parent of same—let alone a bride. Clarissa had beheld the clutter of ornithological lithographs, to say nothing of an entire cabinet of stuffed and mounted specimens—"It cost much less than one might think, Clarissa."

"It cost time, Henry."

And time is money.

Clarissa had already been impatient. Now she grew fearful. She forbore to elaborate for her brother the workings of compound interest as pertaining to debt; it was not for his quiet nor for his good. Matters fiscal were her domain. His was to remain an aristocrat of easy manners and unassailable pedigree, innocent as Parsifal in his matrimonial quest.

Tempus, however, *fugit*. It was all very well for Henry Bell to bask in the reduced circumstances of his nonetheless exalted station in life, insouciant and free to marry for love if and when the spirit moved him. But Henry Bell's freedom, Clarissa knew, was enjoyed at the expense of Lord Bell, Baron of the DC de Fayne; for the wind beneath her brother's wings was the same which blew through the crevices and cracks of Fayne House, removing crumb by cornice that which was only on loan to him, entrusted to him by his father, held in trust by Henry for his son in turn. Henry Bell is one man. But Lord Bell is many; a yet-to-be-born succession rising up one by one as in a looking glass, before falling back into eternity, a message in their mute gaze: *Do not deny me.* Aye, Henry Bell might die happy and penniless—even childless—a gentleman bird-fancier married to an equally impecunious bird-besotted woman. But what of the quashed succession of never-to-be Lords Bell—legion of the betrayed? Henry is not merely associated with the vasts of Fayne and the name of Fayne and the ancient right of title to Fayne. He is synonymous with it. The Queen is a European mongrel, dignified by majesty in the same way Cavendish dignifies Sunday's mutton with an ermine of sauce. Victoria is a tenant of Buckingham Palace. Henry *is* Fayne.

The Bell title is land-entailed, thus though the manor house might be left to return to dust, the land itself must remain in the possession of the family to ensure continuance of the title. And that land bears a significant burden of tax in exchange for the perpetuation of the Oral Claim (*circa* 1300) upon which rests the title.

Clarissa was not the heir to the peerage—at least not on the English side of the border—but to her fell the duty of assuring its continuance. A sacred trust. She would see the line of succession live on through her brother. This she had pledged to Lord Bell, Sixteenth Baron of the DC de Fayne. *Papa*. And she would not be forsworn.

She shielded her brother as long as possible while he, as it were, gloried in his waxen wings, flying sunward among his beloved birds. But he was bound to come back down to earth. "It is for you to choose whether you wind up drowned in the Aegean or preening your plumage before your own fire," she told him after that first foray when he returned wifeless.

She had saved Henry from himself more than once. There was the daughter of a textile merchant in Manchester, a Miss Maud Smedley. She was modest and not stupid. "Is that all you can say of her, Clarissa?" asked Rosamund—Clarissa and Miss Gourley were still close at the time. Clarissa answered, "Her father is in trade."

Henry himself had been, as a child, sweet on Miss Gourley, his older sister's great friend. She was a lofty five years his senior and had always with her some treasure—a shell, pebble, feather—which he reverently added to his very own curio cabinet, duly labelling and categorizing each one, from childish "fether" and "pwitty wock" through adolescent "shed skin of smooth snake" up to young-manly "swift mandible."

Clarissa had looked on with concern as Rosamund, the daughter of a younger son of a younger son of an earl, lost her own chance at even a reduced form of womanly fulfilment when her brother emigrated to New Zealand and took with him the hope that he might have assumed the living at St. Foy in Aberfoyle-on-Feyn along with its charming vicarage, thereby providing his sister with a home. Instead, Rosamund was obliged to earn her bread. Clarissa was full of admiration for her friend's uncomplaining application of shoulder to wheel and went so far as to encourage an alliance between Rosamund and Mr. Josiah Baxter. Much as the prospect privately pained her, Clarissa was aware she herself could not marry until her brother was settled, and in the meantime Rosamund was fast losing her youth to study and work; better one of them should marry than both wither on the vine. But nothing came of Clarissa's match-making efforts, and she was secretly relieved. And as the bothersome pain came more frequently and sojourned longer, she joined her friends less and less on the windswept cliffs and lochs about Arthur's Seat, and even on excursions to Fayne. She had never been as avid a bird-fancier as the other three; it was the comradeship she enjoyed. Friendship. The three people she most cared for in all the world: her brother, her friend and her . . . *He was never your intended.*

Her brother and Rosamund continued on as companions in their own right, venturing forth together when Mr. Baxter became increasingly wanted elsewhere, that diligent gentleman having established himself as a solicitor in an Albany Street firm. Though no impropriety attached to these outings, they did contribute to her brother's foot-dragging in the matrimony department, for so long as he was scrabbling over hill and dale, he could not be courting. Moreover, "There can be no friendship, properly speaking, between a man and woman, Henry."

"That may be true of most women, but Miss Gourley is a new sort of woman." Clarissa sighed, her brother continued, "One who transcends sex, one with whom it is possible to commune on a high platonic plane. One of whom the Ancients might say—"

"'Tis time you got on with your real work, Henry," she snapped.

"And what is that, Clarissa?"

"Getting an heir."

He winced. "Must you put it thus baldly?"

"This is what comes of consorting with the middle classes—"

"Miss Gourley is not—!"

"She may as well be. She is *employed*, Henry. I begin to mourn your Miss Smedley."

"Surely you jest."

"You have fiddled while Rome burns!" Clarissa was not given to hyperbole, and felt for an instant all trace of discomfort flee her frame such that it was as though she stood suddenly in a cool glade, astonished by the bodily reminder of how well she had used to feel. "You must find a wife to give you a son. Then you may gaze into the skies and peer into the bushes and the bracken all you like, with whomsoever you like." And it flared once more: the pain, which had installed itself within her like a furnace.

He thought she was chafing him as was her wont when she was feeling out of sorts. He thought he had time.

"You have had a great deal more time than is granted any woman, Henry."

"Do you advise I renew my acquaintance with Miss Smedley?" And he came as close to sneering as he had in his life. "'Twas you soured on the match despite her fortune."

"Her fortune comes with her family, Henry."

"By the terms of your own mercenary argument, any woman worth marrying comes with a family, the origin of whose wealth might not bear scrutiny."

"Yes, but not every worthy woman with a wealthy family resides within these British Isles."

". . . I'm not sure I follow."

"An ocean goes some way to cleanse the grime from even the most vulgar pedigree. Don't gawk, Henry. Have you never desired to journey to America?"

"Never."

"Why then, don't trouble yourself. America comes to Europe in the springtime of every year."

Still, he was in no hurry. And while he owed his sister love and respect, he would not be ruled by any woman, for he was Henry Lord Bell, Seventeenth Baron of the DC de Fayne. It was a fact as immutable as the cliffs of Salisbury Craigs where he spent so many stimulating and harmonious hours with Josiah and Miss Gourley. It was a fact as timeless as the moors of Fayne some fifty miles to the south as the crow flies; his vast lands which, though sparsely treed and all unploughed, were anything but barren. As for blood, his was as noble, if not bluer, than any in the House of Lords, where it seemed every ruffian with a railroad, mine or mill could purchase a seat. Henry *was* Fayne and the notion that this could be altered via the vagaries of a ledger somewhere beneath the pen of a lowly clerk in the employ of a mere banker . . . well it never crossed his mind.

Even while it traversed, with increasing urgency, the mind of the Honourable Clarissa Bell.

Henry was not without experience. He had had, to date, carnal knowledge of four women: a Galician tart, an Alsatian widow, a barmaid in Pitlochry, a touring music-hall acrobat in Leith—not unpleasant, if perfunctory, affairs of divers duration and frequency. In the arena of courtship he counted himself fortunate to have been refused by no fewer than three suitable ladies—Honourables all—whose fathers opted for sons-in-law of more means than breeding. It chilled the blood to consider what a connection with such people might mean to a man's future happiness.

"Dodged another bullet, did you, Henry?" said Josiah with a sheepish grin. The two men laughed. Miss Gourley did not. "Really, Josey, you are his friend and oughtn't to encourage him. He must marry and marry wisely."

It was some eighteen months prior to Mae's jolly dinner party. The three friends had scaled Arthur's Seat and scrambled to a vantage point at the edge of the Salisbury Craigs overlooking the footpath of the Radical Road far below. Henry, propped on his patched elbows, spyglass in hand, was lying between Rosamund and Josiah, observing the gulls wheeling and crying and . . . aye, laughing.

Away off to their right, atop Calton Hill stood stone tributes, starkly spaced, among them the National Monument like an unfinished Parthenon; farther to the north and wrapping round behind them to the east, lay the heavy blue flank of the Firth of Forth—the wind up here carried a whiff of salt. And before them, majestic in the sunset, were spread the topsy-turvy roofs and piercing spires, the thrusting smoke-stacks and crookedy chimney pots of the Auld Toun, all sloping gently upward to the great jutting Castle. They were on a level with the birds and it seemed to Henry he drifted and wheeled along with them . . . It was only when Josey nudged him that he roused himself from a reverie in which, uncanny as it might seem, he had quite lost himself . . . suspended and effortless amid the gulls, he had seemed no longer to exist and yet . . . all was so vivid. How could that be? He was almost cross with Josey as he passed him the field glasses.

Beside him, Miss Gourley had been jotting notes with a stub of pencil. She thrust them at him, saying, "You take over, Lord Henry, I can't feel my hands." He did and they tarried, the three of them indefatigable in the face of cold and damp until forestalled in their observations by the sinking of the sun behind the Castle.

They shared a round of tea from Josey's double-walled flask before rising rather stiffly—"I say, I'm being vouchsafed a premonition of old age," said Henry, straightening, reaching down a hand to Miss Gourley who, eschewing it, popped nimbly up despite seniority. They set out, half sliding down the path, grasping here a bit of scrub, there an outcrop of stone to steady themselves—until Henry stopped short, causing Miss Gourley to all but collide with him from behind. "Hark," he whispered. They paused. And they heard it: a dotterel. They listened, silent. Reverent. Until the sound retreated. At which point Henry whispered, "It's calling, '*teacher-teacher*'!" and gave Miss Gourley a grin. She chided him as of old—"Silly mannie."

"All for one!" he cried suddenly, resuming the descent, stumbling— just in time, Miss Gourley seized an outcrop of stone with one hand and shot forth the other to grasp Henry's wrist before he could tumble to his death onto the Radical Road below. They all three froze for a long few seconds, hearts pounding, before she scolded him, "Don't you dare fall over the edge, Henry, Clarissa would never forgive me!"

The remainder of the descent was uneventful. Then they strode along, swinging their arms as they skirted Holyrood Palace and the moss-gleamed Chapel Ruins to cut across the darkening emerald of the Cricket Ground. Their shadows leapt long and lively 'til they came into the South Back of the Canongate and were swallowed by the gullet of the street, where the tops of buildings all but met overhead. It was colder here too, and they quickened their pace until just past the Free Church where Josiah, never voluble at the best of times, turned into his wynd without a word, leaving his companions to smile after him and call out, "Much obliged for the pleasure of your company, Josey!" To which he responded with a raised hand but not so much as a look over his shoulder. Too happy to bother.

"You called me Henry," he said, as they proceeded up the Cowgate— here it was more than faintly malodorous, doorway shadows were thickened by slouching shapes . . .

"I did no such thing."

"In the mortal moment of my near-demise, you did."

"Nonsense. Well," she said briskly, stopping before a teetering five-storey land, this is me then, ta-ra."

"Wait."

"What?"

"I'm froze." And he shivered with no need of feigning, for owing as much perhaps to his brush with death as the raw evening air, he was indeed chilled.

"Very well then, but only 'til you thaw, then it's home before dark, don't you be worrying your sister, *Lord* Henry."

He followed her in and up the dark narrow zig-zag and wondered if she was quite safe lodging here—ruffians without, dubious timbers within—"I say, you don't live at the very top," he said, pausing to catch his breath.

"I do."

"Is that wise?"

"It is cheap."

"You do realize Number One Bell Gardens is far too large for Clarissa, and I am seldom in residence, being much involved with the management of Fayne." (This latter was an exaggeration insofar as "management.") "You might make digs there 'til you find your feet."

"I never misplaced my feet. They are reliably beneath me."

"Still." He followed her up round the fourth turning. "Rather a rum neighbourhood. Not to mention the premises themselves."

"Tosh. Boswell slept here."

"Cold comfort, that."

She chuckled. "Come now, in you go and off with your boots."

Henry was pleasantly surprised to find Miss Gourley's garret quite congenial. At the apex of the sloped ceiling a porthole window admitted the last of the evening light—"One advantage of being on the top floor." Tucked in the alcove beneath the window was a divan with a sateen coverlet of pale pink, a sturdy bolster at one end and a heap of lumpy cushions at the other, presumably in lieu of arm rests. Close by, a straight-backed chair was pushed up against a deal table decked with lamp, ink pot, pen, and a litter of nibs and papers. On the opposite wall an open cupboard held a few bits of crockery but mostly books. Below it, on a small dresser were a washing-up basin and pump, while close by—everything was close by—a single gas ring was affixed to the wall. In the corner squatted a small pot-bellied stove. What more did a body need, really? He did not allow his gaze to linger on the striped curtain in the corner which must conceal Miss Gourley's dresses and . . . well, other garments.

Miss Gourley stuffed her gloves into the pocket of her coat which she now shrugged off and tossed onto a peg in the back of the door. Henry had pried off his boots and stood with his coat folded over his arms.

"Sit. Your Lordship."

He grinned and obeyed. "Why haven't we done this sooner?"

"Because you have been on your Grand Tour and I have been governessing." She was crouched before the stove, busy screwing up pages of yesterday's *Scotsman*.

"I like your . . . is it called a flat?"

"Not by half. Bed-sit is rather too grand."

She opened the flue, lit the fire, and set about filling the kettle from the pump.

"I don't see a bed."

"You're sitting on it."

"Ah"—he rose reflexively—"hence the term." He laughed. "Allow me," he said, crossing to her, taking from her the kettle, placing it on the nifty gas ring, and then he was kissing her and she was kissing him back— the intervening seconds with their series of small actions such as the brush of a forearm, any bridging event or scent such as damp wool, soap or smog are lost to time, and Lord Henry and Miss Gourley are simply standing there, kissing. Passionately.

He is thirty-one. She is thirty-seven. She possesses nothing but her education and her good name. He has a debt of four thousand seven hundred and thirty pounds, three shillings and sixpence, increasing at a rate of four percent per annum compound interest, a name of incalculable price, a crumbling country house and a good address in the New Town where the roof leaks and the maid is reduced to half days. They stand kissing, and kissing. Their arms encircle one another's bodies. His hand presses the small of her back, her hand finds the nape of his neck . . .

Meanwhile, at No. One Bell Gardens, the Honourable Clarissa Bell has sent Havers out on the pretext of having him fetch the *Edinburgh Evening News* so he will not know her to be bent over, gloved and aproned, blacking her own grate. Small economies.

They cling to one another on her divan—bed, rather—Lord Henry is lying on top of Miss Gourley. Lord Henry is unbuttoning his flies, Miss Gourley is hiking up her tweed walking skirt along with her knees. She reaches down, takes his member and guides it into her. She holds him tenderly, as though comforting him, he is indeed wracked with urgency and she is biting her lower lip. She clasps him. Cries out. He sobs his paroxysm. They lie still. The kettle steams like an engine.

He falls asleep. She frees herself out from under. Rises. Shakes down her skirt.

Over in the New Town, Clarissa rubs and rubs relentlessly back and forth. Thrift. Victories are made of this.

He opens his eyes. Reaches for her. She places a hot mug of tea in his hands. Brushes back the fine hair from his eyes. "Rosamund," he whispers. She shakes her head. "We must draw a veil."

With that, she passed her hand down his face, turned and left the room. He heard her footsteps descending. He knew it would not be easy. He would have a hard case to plead with his sister, but he was his own master after all—Clarissa's too, come to that. He expected Rosamund herself would pose the greatest obstacle to their happiness, invoking his "own good." All this he knew as he rose and buttoned his breeches.

In the parlour at No. One Bell Gardens, the grate gleamed jet.

36

THE MORNING AFTER the glorious dinner party, Havers enters the now-cheerful morning room and brings Mae her "post" on the silver salver. She opens it there and then with a squeal of excitement that Havers has come to take in his stride, ecstatic to receive word from Taffy that she is coming! She rings for Maggie and begins to make plans. Another dinner party, that's for certain, a redecorated bedroom complete with *en suite* WC for Taffy and not a moment to lose . . .

No. One Bell Gardens
October 2, 1871

Dear Taffy,
I am over the moon and fending off fits of vapors! You are coming! You will be here when he (of course it might be a she, which wouldn't be a tragedy) arrives. Dear, I shall soon be big as a house—a country house! Here's the plan . . .

———

Clarissa reflects that her sister-in-law, in addition to an imminent heir, has brought unlooked-for comforts to her lot; witness Cavendish— whom Lady Marie plans on taking away with her to London in due course. While Clarissa had no truck with matters gustatory before, the thought now of returning to minced mutton strikes, if not quite "despair," then something akin to resignation into her heart. Not to mention Sheehan who, regardless of having been surreptitiously inserted into the household by Rosamund Gourley under cover of kind Josiah Baxter, will be missed; for although Clarissa can tolerate Maid and does not, these days, require Sheehan's deft way with a cushion, she does still, of an evening, when she knows Marie has retired for the night, ring for Sheehan and have the girl comb and replait her hair. It is soothing. She straightens her back, and spears the fabric she holds in her lap. The aforementioned sacrifices are a small price to pay, for her work here is nearly done. In a little less than a year Clarissa shall retreat with a modest sufficiency. The single room. The window. Her chair.

Now that the prospect is solid, however, the words themselves ring hollow to her. Not the "modest" bit—notwithstanding that there is no longer need for economies, small or otherwise—but the "retreat."

Mae has the renovation of the third-eldest dead brother's room (Poor Donal) well in hand and turns her attention to Clarissa, pressing upon her two new tea gowns. Having staked her sartorial claim, Mae turns her attention to Clarissa's coiffure, gratified to see her sister-in-law puts up no great resistance to Sheehan's new arrangement of bun and modest finger puffs. She contrives to have Mr. Baxter as a frequent spontaneous dinner guest—even if he does spend most of his time holed up with Henry in his study—and considers her efforts crowned when Clarissa says with the hint of a sly smile, "Josiah, I believe you remarked on the meringues when last you joined us. Havers, pooding."

Round about this time, Mae "begs a boon" of Henry. It has to do with their son's name. He listens. He agrees. "Oh Henry, that is the nicest present you could ever give me." All in all, Mae has grown accustomed to her new family. (But never will she grow accustomed to fish for breakfast.)

Clarissa has started on a set of *broderie* cuffs. Mae watches as she spears the fabric methodically with a lethal-looking . . .

"'Tis a stiletto, Marie. Here. You try."

Clarissa shows Mae how to stitch a tiny circle, then pierce it in the middle. "'Tis called eyeleting."

Mae then carefully goes round the hole with another series of stitches . . .

"Well," says Clarissa. "Not a complete failure." High praise.

The two of them pass several such evenings in companionable silence as the fire crackles and purrs.

Thus, peace and tranquility reign at No. One Bell Gardens.

Thank goodness Taffy will be here next month because, really, there's a limit to how much peace and tranquility a girl can stand. As October draws to a close, Mae begins to chafe a little, having discovered "confinement" to be something more than a charming Old World term. Thus one night after dinner:

Husband: "You mean to walk out of doors?"

Sister-in-law: "At this hour?"

Husband: "Keep to the garden."

Then her own maid wrapped her in a woollen cloak of such weight, Mae shuddered to think what might happen should she encounter a drop of rain.

Not permitted to walk in the morning dew nor the evening chill, and between times only briefly and never alone and never beyond the gate. Clarissa considers it unseemly (*because a woman who is "big with child" ought not to be seen in public. Taffy, I'm not actually at all big yet*) while Henry pronounces it "unwise. What if you should be run down by an omnibus?"

"Henry, why is it more likely I'd be run down when I'm pregnant than when I'm not? Surely my increased size means I'm more easily spotted by the driver."

Bonnie, if you were here, I'd take you for a walk and no one could stop me.

"Talkin' to yourself, Lady Mae? My gran told me, 'When you find you're talking to yourself, talk to Our Lady instead.'"

"I'm not talking to myself, Maggie, I'm talking to my dog." Tears. At which the girl coos and sings and undoes Mae's hair, combing it out with her fingers, playing Mae's tresses like a harp.

Everything will be all right when Taffy gets here.

November is two weeks old when Havers brings Lady Marie her post in the morning room. She tears open Taffy's letter with the usual squeal, then bursts into tears. Maggie comes running and ducks a flying teacup. Luckily Henry is in his study at the time. Mae is careful to throw the rest of her fit in the privacy of her bedroom.

By the time the dinner bell sounds, she has composed herself. Finding her upper lip capable of stiffening with the best of them, she descends with dignity, determined to be henceforth every inch Lady Bell. After all, it won't do to give way to temper in her condition—"A woman carrying new life must think nice thoughts." Her old nurse Annie from back home again.

Henry takes a forkful of fowl—Cavendish has outdone herself. Who knew that behind the basilisk there lurked a Continental chef?

"Henry," says Mae in regal tones, "where shall we reside once our wee Scottish laird is born? I know Clarissa must be anxious to know our plans."

Henry is chewing.

Clarissa says, "Marie, it is not my place to contemplate your domestic arrangements, except insofar as I might be of use."

"Surely you'd like us out from underfoot?"

"Dear sister, it is I who reside here on sufferance."

"Dear Clarissa, this is your home as much as ours."

The fleeting rictus. Mae is touched. "Henry, why don't we sign Bell Gardens over to Clarissa? After all, we'll have a house in London soon enough."

Henry says, "My son and heir will not, strictly speaking, be a Scottish lord."

"I beg your pardon—I mean, what?"

"He will not be—"

"He'll be a British lord, of course, silly me!" Feminine titter. Adding, with due gravity, "Peer of the Realm, Eighteenth Baron of the Distinguished County de Fayne."

Clarissa looks up.

Henry is bemused. "'Distinguished County'?"

"It sounds better when you say all the words, makes the title longer." She catches the look that passes between the other two. "Oh dear, was that gauche?"

"Not at all, my dear," says Henry with a light touch of his hand on hers, "a slight misapprehension as to the initials 'DC,' merely."

"Really? Daddy told me what they stand for."

"Did he? I imagine he misheard."

"Then what do they stand for? Wait, let me guess . . . Designated County?"

"They stand for Disputed County."

". . . What does that mean?"

"It means precisely what it says."

"So . . . but your title isn't disputed."

"It is a Disputed County, hence the title is as well disputed. Clarissa, my compliments to Cavendish."

"Brother, it occurs to me Sanders might be well advised to re-spring the carriage in deference to Lady Marie's condition."

"Capital notion, sister, thank you."

"Are you a real baron or not?" It has come out coarsely, not what she intended.

"What a question," blurts Clarissa. Henry rebukes her with a look and she lowers her eyes.

Henry addresses his wife patiently. "The designation 'Disputed' goes to the provenance of the estate, in that it comprises a county which, straddling the border of England and Scotland, is acknowledged 'Disputed' at Whitehall, where there is no written record." He reaches for his glass—a good sturdy claret.

"So there's no proof," she says.

"'Proof'?"

"Yes, 'proof.'"

"There is an OC, which—"

"A what?"

"Sorry, of course, there is an Oral Claim"—enunciating now as though she might not understand English—"which has ensured the continuance of the Dispute these upwards of four hundred and fifty years."

She shakes her pretty head. "Um. Just so I'm clear. Are we welcome at Court?"

"Why of course." Incredulous chuckle, echoed by his sister. "That has never been in dispute."

"And my son will be Charles, Lord Bell, Eighteenth Baron of the Disputed County de Fayne."

"If it is a son, yes. Otherwise, she will be 'the Honourable.'" And he smiles.

"Until she marries an earl," says Mae.

"I have not met the earl to whom I would entrust a daughter of mine."

"Is there anything else I should know?" she quips. "Any skeletons in the family closet?"

Something passes between her husband and sister-in-law—less than a look, more a faint perturbation of Bell brow. Mae's smile tightens. "Henry? What is it?"

Clarissa clears her throat. "Your husband may have already recounted to you the story of the Blighted Heir."

". . . I don't think so, no. Henry?"

He pooh-poohs it—"Mere legend."

"I'm all ears," says Mae.

He sits back. Steeples his fingers. "Round about a century and a half ago, there was born an heir male of the body who was found to be . . . unsuitable." He steals a glance at Clarissa. Their eyes twinkle.

Mae smiles uncertainly. "In what way, 'unsuitable'?"

Henry gives her an ominous look.

Clarissa says, "He had a tail."

Henry bursts into laughter. Clarissa joins in, the two of them overcome by mirth. Mae feels tears in her eyes. Manages, "Surely you jest."

Henry says jovially, "Family lore, my dear, but even if true, you need not fret, the miscreant was driven off and out of the bloodline."

"That sounds kind of . . . sad."

"Nowadays of course, such an individual would be encouraged toward a useful avocation in the Far East."

"Papa was a great one for telling this tale." Clarissa's mouth clamps in an upside-down smile.

Henry regards his sister wistfully. "I have very little memory of my father but what my sister has kept in trust for me." And he places a hand on Clarissa's.

Mae says brightly, "How soon can we get this pesky 'Disputed' off our backs and out of the title?"

"Not soon, I think, nor is it to be wished." He takes up his fork once more and falls to with a will.

"Why not?"

"Why, because then the title would disappear."

"What?"

He answers with his mouth full, his tone pedantic. "It is rooted in Dispute. Were the Dispute to be settled, the title would dissolve and the estate would be absorbed by the prevailing side or else severed in two." Another forkful. Roast pheasant, but Henry has managed to close his eyes to that.

"Golly. Pappy never did buy a thing on the up-and-up."

He chuckles, "Marie, really."

"Yes really, even my pony, Donnybrook, could turn in only one direction."

He sets down his fork—as it happens, the fowl is cloying after a third mouthful.

"I take umbrage, Marie."

"Take what you like!" She rises abruptly, knocking Havers back on his heels, and sweeps from the room.

Clarissa folds her hands and refrains from mentioning to her brother the muffled caterwauling that issued from the upper floors earlier today. The monthly function is known at times to take a woman in that way—but Marie is temporarily exempt. Still, what does Clarissa know of the ways of a gravid woman? She does wonder, however, if it be not too soon to send for Mrs. Knox.

There is nothing to get fussed about, she fell prey to a fit of pique brought on by the provoking news that Taffy will not be coming after all—and for an unimpeachably good reason which just makes it worse. She is dressed for bed and her maid has warily approached her with the hairbrush—"It's all right, Maggie, I won't bite." She'll make it up to Henry tonight. It's been ages since they quarrelled . . . Not since the night she told him he was about to become a father. She softens.

A low knock at her door. Her husband's voice. "May I enter?"

"Of course!" And to Maggie, "Shoo!" But the maid is already retreating.

His look to her in the mirror is more sorrowful than angry. "I would not for the world rebuke you, my darling, especially in your—"

"Taffy's not coming!" She bursts into tears.

He drops to his knee.

"She's . . . she's . . ."

"She has let you down."

She punches his chest. "How can you say that?!"

"Forgive me."

She weeps. He takes her in his arms. She soaks his shoulder.

Finally she says, "She's engaged."

Cautiously—". . .Oh."

"I'm so happy for her!" She sobs afresh.

Sniffing. Composing herself. "It just makes us more special, doesn't it?"

He realizes his mouth is agape. He closes it. Opens it, hazards, "What does?"

"The Dispute thingamajig."

"Why, yes."

She nestles against him.

And later, in the dark, whispers, "Take it. Take what you like."

No. One Bell Gardens
November 14, 1871

Darling Taffy (or shall I say "Miss Weaver," as opportunities to address you as such are now numbered!),

Of course I forgive you . . .

37

WHEN HENRY ANNOUNCED to his sister his intentions regarding Miss Gourley, he watched the blood drain from her face. Undeterred, he hastened joyfully to the Cowgate and took the higgledy-piggledy stairs two and three at a time up to her bed-sit. She was not there. He waited on the steps. She did not return that evening. Nor the next, nor . . .

When it became clear that Miss Rosamund Gourley had quitted her attic quarters in the Old Town. When he learned that neither Clarissa nor Josiah had received word. When her employers confirmed that she had abandoned her post with a note of apology but no forwarding address. When Henry had searched the brush beneath the Craigs and scoured the beach at Leith. When Clarissa adjured for the umpteenth time that she had received no letters; when Josiah Baxter shook his head and kept pace with him quart for quart at the White Hart. When none of their mutual friends, including the Farquhars, the Heatheringtons and even the Colonel, could shed light on her movements, and three fruitless months had passed, Henry, ill-shaven, hair in disarray, croaked to Clarissa, "What if some ill has befallen our friend?"

"Which friend?"

"Why, Miss Gourley of course."

"Really, Henry, if such were the case we should by now have been apprised."

"How do you reckon?"

"Her godfather, Mr. Moore—"

"Does the good doctor know where she is gone?"

"As I say, Mr. Moore is the party whom the authorities would alert in the event Rosamund be discovered dead at the bottom of a well."

"God!"

"Or cut in two by a steam locomotive." He covered his ears. She continued, "But Mr. Moore assures me she has met no such fate."

"Does he say when she might return?"

"He does not."

"But how could she desert her friends, her post, her . . . ? I don't understand."

"Henry. Conspicuous by its absence among your queries is the word 'why.'"

"I don't follow."

"You ask 'what,' you ask 'where,' you ask 'how' and even 'when,' but you do not ask 'why' she left."

He swallowed. Felt his chin quiver. He looked away. He was not obliged to answer to her. Presently he heard her mutter something. He turned. "Forgive me, sister, did you say something just now?"

". . . Nothing of consequence." She straightened her back.

They dined in the parlour to save heating the dining room. Small economies.

He spent the winter in London at his club.

Haunted the British Museum where he sought to forget himself amid the wealth of specimens. But it was as though he perceived all at a remove. Through the veil which she had drawn. A veil of tears.

Duty dictated his presence in the house once or twice. Her widowed Majesty's protracted mourning mirrored his own—though he reflected bitterly that whereas Albert had been sundered from Victoria by death, Rosamund had fled from Henry of her own accord. *Rosamund, why hast thou forsaken me?!* Out of a misguided belief in his "best interests"? Some skewed sense of honour? *"I could not love thee, dear, so much, Loved I not honour more."* Lovelace be damned, Henry loved Rosamund more than honour. There in the Lords' Chamber, in his scarlet robe and ermine cape he smote his forehead in time with the slamming of the Commons door as it struck him: the possibility of a sequel to their union. Well, what of it? If there were a child, all the better. He would claim it! Love it, along with its mother! And as his Gracious Queen sat in sombre silence whilst the Lord Chancellor welcomed Her "Lords and Gentlemen," Lord Henry Bell, Seventeenth Baron of the DC de Fayne, wept. And not for Albert.

He dined with his fellow peers of the realm, stood and drank "To the Queen!"—but what cared Henry for empire? No more than did the birds of the air who neither tilled nor toiled . . . nor received statements of account from their estate manager, Ramsay Mungo—nor, come to that, an allowance drawn from air as thin as that plied by the Arctic tern. Naïve Henry may have been in the ways of commerce; privileged certainly; but spoiled? A nobleman cannot be spoiled, he can only be ruined. If it should prove no longer possible to have Everything, Henry would choose Nothing.

At No. One Bell Gardens Clarissa rolled a bit of candle wax between her palms, squeezing and shaping it into soap.

One afternoon, coming on springtime, while her brother was still in London, Havers brought Clarissa a letter. It was addressed to her in Rosamund's hand. Clarissa would not have the lamps lit before dinner, so she brought the letter to her rain-dimmed window and, squinting, braced for the worst: notice of illegitimate issue, expectation of an annuity to support mother and child, assurance of discretion. But the letter was an apology. If Rosamund had occasioned anxiety on the part of her friends— "*If*"?!—Clarissa nearly cast it onto the embers there and then. The letter went on to explain that Rosamund had been obliged "of a sudden" to attend an ailing relative in a remote northerly corner of the kingdom. The relative had died and Rosamund, thanks to a modest legacy, had removed to London where she had embarked on a course of teacher training at Whitelands College. "Please convey my cordial regards to Lord Henry and assure him he is, no less than yourself, included in my nightly prayers. I would also enjoin you, dear friend, to keep close for the time being the intelligence of my whereabouts, as I fear there be those among my friends who might seek to assuage their (needless) anxieties on my behalf by means of seeking me out."

Clarissa folded the letter, tucked it into the bottom of her work basket, and sank with relief onto the armless Regency rocker where she was ambushed by tears which, by dint of self-discipline, she staunched at the lids.

The words did not bear repeating aloud—the ones she had muttered some months ago to her brother as he struggled to compose himself before the fact of Rosamund's flight—but they arose now to her mind: *She was my friend too.*

Luckily, Lady Strathallan was to be "at home" next afternoon and would be delighted to receive the Honourable Clarissa Bell. Lady Strathallan, née Adeline Coakley from Rhode Island. *Sigh*. Clarissa donned her best watered silk and called for the carriage.

At Clarissa's urgent summons, Henry left London and returned to No. One Bell Gardens where she greeted him in her parlour and presented him with a lump of soap. "If you please, Henry, shave."

"It isn't Pear's."

"It will serve."

After dinner, she handed him a letter of introduction from Lady Strathallan to La Principessa della Montesilvio von Badenkreuzer, née Fanny Bunker of Yonkers.

"You are to arrive at the Palazzo no later than the twenty-fifth of April."

"But Clarissa, the spring migration of turtledoves to Wales commences in the first week of May."

"As does the migration of American heiresses homeward."

He cradled his forehead. She spoke to the patch of scalp which was lately become visible through his hair. "You have a title, a good face and a pleasing manner to recommend you."

"How does my face come into it?"

"We shall be ruined before the close of the year. Time waits for no man, Henry, even a nobleman. I do not reproach you for my single blessedness—"

"Dear Clarissa, you might yet marry—"

"Shutup, Henry."

Shocked, he obeyed.

"Listen to me, brother, for I cherish you beyond my life which I hold cheap beside your well-being." She paused. It was her own want of flint that threatened just then to upend her self-possession—she oughtn't to have used the word "cherish" when "value" would have served. She lifted her chin and addressed the fireplace, gleaming and cold. "You must marry money before your title is in tatters and your person has deteriorated, for what woman of means wants an eccentric old bird-fancier with egg on his cravat?"

"I haven't egg on my—oh."

"Henry." She reached across and took his hand; smooth—not so much as a gun callus, for her brother shrank from sport. If only the elder brothers had survived, Henry might be a bishop now—and married for love, and Rosamund would be her dear sister-in-law . . . But the brothers had died of the cholera. Thus, needs must. She let go his hand.

"I am pledged elsewhere."

"You are not."

"I wish to be." His voice cracked.

"Govern yourself, Henry."

He wept. She handed him Miss Gourley's letter. Watched him read it.

"You see she gets on quite well without us."

He bowed and quitted the parlour.

He set out for Folkstone three days later, having left behind his field glasses. He was after birds of a different feather.

38

THEY HAD PUT OFF going to London because Taffy was supposed to be coming. Now they're stuck in Edinburgh over Christmas and all winter. Cheer up, Mae, Taffy will come in spring with dear, handsome Carter—"Henry, you and Carter will get on like a house on fire, I just know it, you're both so reserved." And fingers crossed, Taffy will be here when the baby is born in May!

Christmas draws nigh and everyone is very kind and the food is lovely and Mae is tired. Of course that is to be expected, as everyone tells her—including the Bell family's kindly old doctor, Mr. Moore. But Mae knows she is not only physically tired. She is tired of her clever maid, her lovely house, her kind sister-in-law, the nice friends, she is even tired of . . . Well, she hasn't much of a chance to tire of Henry because he is so often busy with his bosom friend, Mr. Baxter, what with all the birds that need watching and rescuing. Clarissa, at least, is the picture of contentment—no more wincing and limping—and Mae expects from one day to the next to hear that "Josey" has popped the question. Not exactly the love story of the century but at least Mae could start planning the wedding. All told, she does her best to keep up a cheerful demeanour—even if she seethes inwardly whenever she thinks of Katie Buxton's oyster party. She is even piqued at the thought of Daddy swanning around town boasting about her while here she sits, like a big festive-looking lump. Henry gives her a darling *bijou*. She puts it with the rest.

Christmas is a trial because it's just so lovely. *Ditto* Hogmanay—which is what they call New Years. Haggis, however, is a revelation—*not at all nasty, Taffy*. She links arms with the others and sings the Robbie Burns anthem, swaying in time to "Auld Lang Syne," counting the days 'til her "due" date . . . !

Drab January. The house is overheated. She is in the morning room next to a growing pile of imperfect lace. She has pricked her finger. He is reading one of his periodicals; it has no pictures. *Or conversations*, she's willing to bet. She sucks her fingertip.

"Henry, what if there's something wrong with it?"

"'Wrong'?"

Really, he can be exhausting. "It happens in the best of families."

He lowers the page. "Do you mean to say, my dear, there is reason for doubt on your side?"

"Not my side, I have no idea about my side before Daddy—except that if they survived they had to've been tough as nails, and Mam too—she came from a long line of spinners but . . . She was never strong in the lungs, so . . . Never mind, I'm talking about your side."

"My side?"

She fights vexation and tries for girlish confusion. "What about the one you 'drove off'?"

"Oh." He chuckles. "That is mere legend, my dear, a family jest."

All at once he mirrors her grave look and says solemnly, "If it has a tail, we'll dock it."

"Henry!"

"I'd do the same with a spaniel in gorse country."

"Hush, you."

He laughs. And for a moment it's fun again. *Oh Taffy, I miss fun!*

"My dear, permit me to tuck this rug about your knees."

"Thank you, darling." She is roasting.

Henry relishes the respite from socializing, and profits from it by finishing his essay on the Arctic tern. He submits it, fingers crossed for luck, to *The Journal of the Edinburgh Ornithological Society*, and attends a lecture with Josey at the Royal Society.

February, the shortest month and the longest.

The bigger she gets, the more he fancies his birds.

"There you are! I was about to send out a search party."

"Whatever for?"

"You've been gone all day."

"Hardly. 'Tis tea time." And he gives her a peck on the forehead.

"You'd rather spend time at your Ornery Logical Society."

Not a flicker.

Havers averts his eyes from her entirely.

Henry slurps his soup. "It is in deference to your condition."

"You mean my 'gravidity'?"

"Quite."

"It makes me feel like a ghost."

"It ought to make you feel like a Lady."

"What's that supposed to mean?"

Henry appears at a loss. Clarissa steps into the breach. "It is no more than your due, Marie. To feel you are that which you are." She performs the fleeting facial rictus that is her smile. Henry achieves similar evasive action with his eyebrows. Mae wants to . . . scream? Sing? Dance a jig? At any rate, she finds she's feeling quite . . . Corcoran at the moment—perhaps on account of the wee chip off the old County Leitrim kicking up his heels in her womb. "Havers!" she hollers toward the service door and sees Clarissa flinch. Mae knows better than to holler from the table, of course, but there must be some imp-of-the-perverse at work, goading her in the face of her new family's habitual restraint—as though she were trapped in a play and compelled to act the foil. She'll be after lilting a tune any minute! She giggles.

Clarissa gives her a look. Mae gives it right back. "Confinement" is their idea, and they can deal with the consequences.

"Mae?" he ventures, cautiously.

"What?"

"I wondered, merely, what had struck you as amusing?"

"Nothing at all, Henry, and that's the truth."

He blinks in quick succession.

Not to mention this wallpaper has got to go, she's sick of those ruddy parakeets.

The next day her edginess is replaced by an unaccustomed . . . lethargy. She stays abed. Cries for no reason. Declines to descend to breakfast. Picks at luncheon in her room. Ignores tea time. Even the baby is lazy. She feels beached. Huge. Over the next couple of days she rouses herself only for letters from home.

She fails to appear at dinner. Henry abandons his soup and goes upstairs to find her lying on her side, shoulders heaving. "Mae, darling, what is it?"

In her hand is a crumpled letter. He glimpses Miss Weaver's ladylike loops.

"My darling, what has happened?" He steels himself for mortal news of Mr. Corcoran. Will they be required to make the crossing to attend a death-bed or funeral, he wonders? She garbles something—he bends close and listens. Replies, "My darling, I am deeply sorry to hear of it." He sits on the edge of the bed and takes her hand. "Who was Bonnie?"

"My dog, you idiot!" she cries, sitting up around her belly, red-faced—here is he put in mind, rather disquietingly, of Mr. Corcoran.

But her rage is fleeting and gives way to tears. Henry rings for Sheehan.

Several days pass with Mae in an eerie sort of stillness, speaking little, staring out her window. He does his best. "Mae? Darling? I wonder if we oughtn't to acquire a dog? A dear wee spaniel?" Fresh tears.

By week's end, he is concerned. Seeks out his sister in her parlour.

"I should think Marie's new-found serenity a boon, brother."

"I'm not certain 'tis serenity."

Clarissa orders the carriage made ready.

"She has offered to take you for an airing, dear," says Henry.

As if I were a set of curtains.

She dresses grudgingly.

But as the carriage crunches from the drive onto the smooth bricks of George Street, Mae feels her spirits lifting in spite of herself. The sun is shining, the crocuses are cropping up and while she has no desire to negotiate the aisles at Jenners, she wouldn't say no to a turn about Princes Street Gardens. What's more, she is pleased with her new wide-waisted dotted Swiss day dress—perhaps a tad early in the season, but she is perishing for a sign of spring, and she might as well be it.

Meanwhile, Henry is wending his way home from the Museum with a copy of *The Journal of the Edinburgh Ornithological Society* under his arm, wherein appears his essay on the Arctic tern. He wonders if Josey has seen it yet—too early in the day to call on him, he'll be in his office, up to his ears in writs and wills. And perhaps because he was just now thinking of Josey, Henry finds himself in Cowgate where he slows his steps—not only so as to be careful where he treads, but to see if he can't pick out Miss Gourley's—Aye, there it is, the teetering five-storey land. It now bears a painted sign: SOCIETY FOR THE RELIEF AND REFUGE OF THE POOR IRISH AMONG US. If he is not mistaken, the building is also the source of an appetizing aroma and he suddenly realizes he is famished. The White Hart is nearby, he could nip in for a solid luncheon, but he is here now and may as well pay his respects to Miss Gourley who earns her bread by sharing it with those less fortunate. And he has, after all, at his dear wife's insistence, pledged a not inconsiderable sum to the charity.

"Stop!" Mae orders with a rap of her parasol on the ceiling.

A parasol, and not yet March! Clarissa has said nothing of this of course, grateful only that her sister-in-law consented to the carriage ride; it won't do to have a melancholy mother-to-be on Henry's hands. Clarissa even donned the "casquette" in a bid to cheer Marie but it drew no comment.

"Are you all right, Clarissa?"

"I am well, thank you, Marie, why do you ask?" The question has slipped out and Clarissa braces herself to withstand the resulting prattle, so injurious to clarity of mind. Not but what the lass is a treasure.

But today Marie merely says, "I'm so glad you're feeling better."

Yes, one cannot help but . . . "Cherish" is not too strong a word.

They have stopped amid the cabs and brakes near the Scott Monument and Marie is adjusting her own little spotted cap and collecting her copious skirts about her. "You do not mean to alight, surely," says Clarissa. *In your very apparent condition!*

"Of course, why else did we come out?"

"I thought we might make the circuit of Queen's Drive round Arthur's Seat—"

"Yes I know, such an imposing hill, no wonder Miss Gourley is so gristly, she's forever clambering up it." Mae sees the corners of Clarissa's mouth twitch. "Come on, Clarissa, you know you love the Gardens. Let's take a turn."

Clarissa descends and walks alongside her flagrantly expectant sister-in-law, head held high with the dignity of a doomed queen on her way to the place of execution.

Henry knocks, waits. Tries the doorknob. And enters a dim vestibule. As his eyes adjust, a cloakroom takes shape. Articles of outer-wear, variously lumpy and dingy, are piled two and three to a hook. A low din reaches him through a second door. He cautiously opens it and finds himself in a large makeshift refectory. Several rows of trestle tables run the length of the room where, hunched cheek by jowl over mugs and bowls, the various owners of the mean garments in the cloakroom are eating. They appear to him to be somewhat smudged, as though shading one into another. Amid the clatter of spoons against crockery, the buzz and hum is shot through by a spear of rebuke here, a burst of laughter there, and from all sides, the squeals of children, the crying of babies. Down the middle of the room, a queue of drab women and scrawny children, along with a few emaciated men, proceeds, bowls in hand, toward the far end where, stationed at right angles another table supports an immense blackened cauldron. This, then, is the source of the homely aroma that drew him. And behind the cauldron, dipping and dispensing with a great ladle, stands Miss Gourley.

Henry removes his silk hat, aware already of an alteration in the texture of sound—a slow gathering tide of attention until all eyes are upon him and the room has fallen silent but for a bawling infant. Too late for retreat, Henry stands as though caught out in an absurd biblical reversal: *And he knew he was clothed.*

Miss Gourley's voice rings out. "Lord Henry, welcome!"

A general scraping and shuffling. Several are on their feet, men clutching at actual or phantom caps, some women bobbing would-be curtseys. Others, oblivious.

Miss Gourley hands the ladle to a thin-cheeked girl in a dirty plaid and, wiping her hands on her apron, comes out from behind the trestle table and up the length of the room to Henry. "Thank you so much for stopping by, Lord Henry. Are you hungry?"

Henry hesitates before answering, "I am, rather. Untoward though it may be to admit as much amid such a gathering."

"Nonsense. We are all of us human, prey to the same appetites and needs. Let us satisfy yours, then once I've finished here, allow me to give you a tour. If you've time, that is."

"Thank you, Miss Gourley, I would be most grateful on both counts."

He follows her and sits, acutely self-conscious, at one end of the table before a steaming bowl as, before him, the slow pageant of the poor is satisfied. And he eats. A hearty beef barley soup and a hunk of decent bread. Delicious. Satisfying.

Miss Gourley joins him. "How did you know it was my day for soup?"

"I cannot say as I did."

"Well that's lucky, because otherwise Miss Elliot would have had the pleasure of serving you and showing you round."

"Craving your pardon, Miss Gourley, but had it been Miss Elliot, I am unlikely to have tarried."

Miss Gourley says with a tartness just this side of Clarissa, "Follow me, Lord Henry."

Henry blushes like the boy he was when Miss Gourley first admonished him in the art of holding—not too tightly—a tree toad, and obeys.

A ruckus greets them one floor up. In a spacious white-washed room, a havoc of freshly fed children is under the would-be supervision of two young ladies, one of whom hugs a striped ball to her chest against a siege of small hands whilst the other, more hearty by half, places a whistle between her lips and blasts it. Henry backs out and Miss Gourley closes the door in time for it to absorb the *thwack* of the ball. "Where are their mothers?" asks Henry. Miss Gourley answers by leading him across the narrow landing to the opposite door.

This room is as silent as the other is raucous and given over to long tables in the manner of the refectory below; but the shawled and kerchiefed women crowding the benches are bent over slates and, threading among them, a poker-thin woman pauses here and there to correct and instruct. "Miss Elliot," says Miss Gourley in hushed tones. "Lord Henry is here to observe." No, Henry would not have lingered had he encountered Miss Elliot first. All beak and beady eyes. Miss Gourley is saying, "The alphabet, Lord Henry. Each letter is a handhold on the ascent from poverty." Henry's legs are tired. He has walked an awful distance today, and though he would not for the world admit as much to his companion, he is longing for a glass of sherry and his slippers. "This has all been most edifying, Miss Gourley, I thank you."

"Lord Henry, there is one other thing."

"Oh?"

She steps from the room. Henry nods at Miss Elliot—who looks implacably back at him (singular lack of charm)—before following Miss Gourley out onto the privacy of the landing. She smiles and, obliged by the close quarters to do so, she raises her face to him—he is suddenly less tired. Thanks, no doubt, to the soup.

"I am in the process of compiling statistics . . ."

She speaks and he squints as though through the glaze of former days, those happy hours spent with Rosamund and Josey perched on a windswept craig . . .

"Although by no means complete, my observations indicate that once a woman is literate, she goes on to bear fewer offspring over the following two years for which I have so far kept records. And of those offspring, fewer go on to die within those two years than those of her unlettered counterparts."

"Offspring," nods Henry, a tad too attentive.

"You and Lady Marie have already pledged a generous sum, but the Refuge is presently soliciting subscriptions."

". . . 'Subscriptions.'"

"That is, a regular contribution—"

"Quite, yes, hebdomadal or—?"

"Periodically," she says and goes crimson, "That is, monthly—"

"Monthly, why certainly."

She turns quickly away, and descends the narrow staircase. He follows. He wonders if she still lives in the bed-sit upstairs. There can be no question of asking her, of course.

Downstairs a wiry woman of indeterminate age and intermittent teeth—"This is Moira, Lord Henry"—briskly takes his particulars for the subscription and he signs a promissory note on the spot. He seeks out Miss Gourley to bid her good afternoon and to thank her, "for a pleasant and dare I say most edifying interval—" But his leave-taking is cut short by the arrival of a rough-looking woman, staggering and bawling something unintelligible. Miss Gourley takes the creature's filthy hand in her own and Henry draws back at the sight of Rosamund leaning close to the woman in an effort to make out the slurred words. Then Rosamund turns back to him. "I'm afraid I'll have to let you see yourself out, Lord Henry, it appears we've got another Brigid."

He emerges onto the street, rather shaken if he is being truthful, and never so glad to see the sun—even if it is shining on the reeking cobbles of the Cowgate.

———

Now that they are strolling, Clarissa is surprised by a singular note of joy which it seems her sister-in-law's particular gift to bestow. The pink hyacinths are in bloom, and the braw wee crocuses dot the green slope with purple and yellow. She draws a deep refreshing breath.

Mae walks, a ship in full sail with her pregnant prow. She squeezes Clarissa's arm, suddenly full of affection for the old stick. "Oh look, there's the penny whistle man again!"

The freckled ragamuffin. With his tinker hair and tin flute. "Let us toss him a coin, shall we?" says Clarissa.

As they draw nearer the music, Mae is seized with the urge to dance. "Daddy insisted I learn Irish dancing. The whole idea is you're dead serious from the knees up but all jiggedy from the knees down. Taffy and I used to dance upstairs in our nightgowns and we'd be in fits and gales, do your people do the Highland fling, Clarissa?"

"Not to my knowledge, Marie."

"Don't worry, I won't disgrace you by dancing in public." Mae laughs, Clarissa smiles, Mae doubles over.

"What is it?"

". . . Nothing." She straightens. Smiles. "He kicked."

Mae registers a moistness between her legs. Is she making water? She knows from Annie back home, a baby can press on a woman's bladder such that "accidents will happen." This is just a little bit of, yes—goodness me, no need to spoil the outing over a little leakage, after all she is swathed in twenty-five absorbent yards of cotton and linens. The point is, it isn't blood. Blood feels different. Thicker. Blood would be worrisome. She promenades on without a word to her old-maid sister-in-law who would never admit to possessing plumbing, never mind discuss Mae's.

The freckled young man, clad in a tattered russet coat, with his broom leaning to one side, his grubby cap set on the pavement, taps his foot in time with his tune and smiles at them through puckered lips—*the Irish cheek of him!* But Clarissa dips into her reticule for a shilling—she is stopped by a sudden grip on her wrist, Marie has seized hold of her. Annoyance converts to alarm when Clarissa sees the girl's face; blanched, mouth agape—Clarissa totters, Marie will have them both flat on the ground in a moment—"What is it?!" It comes out as a hiss, she looks about—*we are making a spectacle!*

A cry.

"Hush!"

Bellow of a sick cow.

The blow smites Mae from within. Heavy. Another cry escapes her with the force of a cannon. Her insides contract, gather power then surge forth like a great wave—"*Oh my God!*" Trembling, shuddering, she is a ship about to split.

Clarissa has braced her spine, made of her forearm a post for her sister-in-law, but even now the girl is sinking to her haunches. "Help," says Clarissa.

And people do.

Mae is down. Not pee. Not blood. Water. Her waters.

Something muffles her. She is borne aloft. Howling.

Clarissa watches the freckled beggar-boy lift Lady Marie bodily from the pavement, "That's it, m'um, up we go." He has wrapped her in his filthy russet coat which he threw over her as though she were on fire, but it cannot fully obscure her shame—head lolling, foolish *chapeau* hanging from her hair, coils loosing—a crowd has gathered, a woman cries, "Someone fetch a doctor!" Where is Sanders with the carriage?! The young man carries her toward a hansom cab parked nearby. He lifts Lady Marie into the cab with the help of the driver who seizes hold of her legs—silk calves for all the world to see. The screams are frightful.

"Are you her mother, m'um?"

Clarissa does not reply to the young rascal who she supposes expects a tip for carrying Marie and putting her into the cab—she catches sight of blood on his sleeve. "Bell Gardens!" she bawls at the cabman, embarking, pulling tight the door against the young wretch where he clings, yammering something—"Drive on!" she cries with a stab of her cane at the ceiling. The cab lurches forward and has turned up St. Andrew Street at a canter before the ruffian is shaken loose. Clarissa looks behind to see him picking himself up from the street, limping, waving, shouting something. "Faster! Faster, I say!"

Mae is on her hands and knees on the floor of the cab, lurching with its movements. Her cries shred the air.

If the baby is to be born in a hansom cab, so be it, and Clarissa is no midwife but—phaugh, the stench—it is early, is it not? "Is it early?" she hears herself ask, idiotically. She thrusts her head out the window, fearing she may be sick.

———

Henry walks back toward the New Town, a spring in his step—after all, he has everything he could desire. On his way across the bridge, he passes a freckled young man who, shivering and coatless, is using his broom as a crutch, hobbling toward the Old Town. Henry directs him to the Refuge and continues on his way, feeling the world is all the righter for his having dispatched a needy young man to benefit from his own largesse by way of Miss Gourley. He spots his carriage parked near the Scott Monument and, smiling, directs his steps thither to find Sanders a tad bewildered, still waiting for the ladies to return from their stroll. Henry waits a while. Decides the ladies will be wrapped up at Jenners, then happily walks home, determined to approve of anything Mae will have purchased, be there never so many feathers and claws.

The cab turns smartly into the drive at No. One Bell Gardens and the horse—as much as a hansom horse can—prances up to the entrance.

"Havers!" calls Clarissa, opening the door before the conveyance has quite come to a halt. He is there immediately and seizes the bridle. "Let go o' that!" cries the driver. Havers does so, not in obedience to the brute at the reins, but at the sight of Miss Clarissa, stumbling from the cab. Havers catches her, takes her by the arm and round the waist before she can collapse, but she snaps at him, "See to Her Ladyship! And send for Mr. Moore!"

Havers disappears into the cab. The cabman jumps down, looks in and says, "I'll have double for my trouble and the muck and shite on my upholstery."

Clarissa is in her chair in the parlour. She sent Maid away and called for Sheehan who came and deftly tucked the cushion, just so, at her back—bless her.

Sheehan unstoppers the smelling bottle and is about to wave it under Miss Clarissa's nose when the commotion in the foyer draws her attention. It is Havers, carrying Lady Marie across the hall and toward the stairs.

"Oh my Lord, miss, is she . . . she's no dead?"

"Eediot. She's having the baby. See to the mess. And lay the fire."

Sheehan wavers between the two commands, then runs from the room and up the stairs.

Lady Marie is groaning, curled on her side. Maggie is alone. She bends to Her Ladyship and goes to work on the twelve ivory buttons of her bodice—"Mrs. Cavendish!" She has tried not to scream it. Blood, thick, not just blood . . . *black pudding*—she tries not to think it—and all-over-everything smeared with shite—Cook is here, thank Jesus, Mary and Joseph—

Cavendish barks, "Basin!"

There is no basin because there is no washstand because there is a lavatory, therefore Maggie Sheehan runs from the room, swings round the door frame, down the back stairs and all the way to the kitchen for a basin.

Cavendish has rolled Her Ladyship onto her back, pushed up her knees, her skirts, and parted the slit in her silk drawers, soaked bright red now. "You'll want to be pushing, Your Ladyship. That's it."

Her Ladyship cries out fit to be tied, and when the maid arrives with the basin—"Take hold of her," Cavendish commands.

Maggie has her pinned at the wrists. "And again," Cook orders Her Ladyship. "Once more and . . . there we are."

Maggie stares, shaking.

"Ring for Maid," says Cavendish.

Henry arrives home in time to see Maid streak up the stairs. He smiles in amusement and even a little sympathy for the girl, who will be run off her feet with untying parcels and finding space for yet another silk extravaganza. He chuckles at the thought of the latest "abomination" to which his sister will have acquiesced, what new "casquette," what "*marin anglais*"—aye, for all Henry's seeming absent-mindedness, he does listen.

He listens now, hand on the doorknob of his study, as an exclamation of some kind reaches him from upstairs. He ducks in. Out of the line of feminine fire.

Cook leaves with the basin.

"Where's my baby?"

Maggie is terrified. Her Ladyship has sat straight up, her hair is matted, her face is pale, and her baby is dead.

"Give me my baby," says Her Ladyship, fierce of eye.

"Aye, Your Ladyship, Cook just took it . . . to be cleaned."

"I know he's dead." Her voice disintegrates, crumbles. Maggie is weeping too. Mae turns her face to the pillow, keening.

"Och Your Ladyship . . ."

Maid arrives and sets about stripping the fouled linens out from under Her Ladyship. "Don't just stand there," she grumbles. "Help me."

Clarissa sits, her work basket untouched, the fire unlit. Where is Havers with the doctor? Where is Maid with the tea? Clarissa rings. No one comes. A good sign, surely.

Henry puts his head out the study door, having thought he heard something. He pulls his head back in and closes the door, reminding himself, rather foolishly, of a cuckoo-clock.

In the kitchen, Cook sets the basin on the draining board, and washes up.

In the heart of the Old Town, at the five-storey land in Cowgate, the coat-less young man has undertaken to mend a pot in gratitude for the bandage Miss Gourley has wound snugly about his ankle.

Mr. Moore has been busy with yet another Brigid—too young, this one, even by "country" standards, and not far along by the look of her. He turns now to Miss Gourley and says, "The lass is after keeping the child, Miss Gourley."

"Well," says Rosamund, "We can help with that too."

A hammering at the door. She opens it to a breathless serving man in livery—behind him is the carriage with the Bell crest. "Miss Gourley?"

"How can I help?"

Realizing he has read the same paragraph in the *Alphabetical Synopsis of British Birds* several times, and despite the peace and quiet—perhaps because of it—Henry abandons the volume and leaves his study altogether.

He crosses the foyer and puts his head round the parlour door to see Cook standing with her back to him, blocking his view of Clarissa. Cavendish bobs, turns and hurries past him without a word.

His sister is white as a sheet. He inquires cautiously, "She's not given notice, has she?"

"No."

"That's a relief." He enters, sits, reaches for the decanter. "Miss Gourley sends her regards."

Stony silence.

"Really Clarissa, time to let bygones be bygones, you ought to visit the Refuge."

Another sound from overhead. He looks to the ceiling. "I say, what . . . ? Did you not hear that?" He rises.

"Sit, brother. There is news."

She is shaking. He is about to ring for Havers to send for Mr. Moore, but she sobs something. He turns back to her.

She is stricken, her whisper is dry as tinder. He bends his ear to her mouth and she tells him.

Upstairs, Mae is still crying.

It is to be wondered whether any woman ever finishes crying about this.

Maggie Sheehan is stroking her head, herself in floods of quieter tears.

Mae moans into her pillow, but Maggie understands the garbled words, for it is not the first time Her Ladyship has said, "I want to see him."

This time Maggie says, "It was a girl, Your Ladyship."

Her Ladyship sits up, and clear as a bell, says, "I want to see her."

"Och, you can't, 'Ladyship, she—Cook took her away, she's . . ."

"Away where?"

Maggie Sheehan shakes her head. Weeps.

Mae vomits sorrow.

Perhaps this is why Maggie forgets herself enough to say, "I lost me *leanbh beag* too, m'um. A boy."

Lady Marie's weeping abates. After a moment, she says, dull-voiced, "Go away."

Maggie hesitates. Obeys.

Mae feels the girl get up. Hears her leave.

She curls onto her side once more, and cradles her empty belly.

39

HENRY STEPS ASIDE as the maid exits the bedroom, and hesitates. He is assailed by a sense that he is somehow watching himself. *If I do not go in, it will not have happened.* The thought has peeped out from some atavistic chamber in his brain; the echo of a child who believes in magyk. He taps again, a little more firmly this time. Silence. *Be a man.* He enters. *Don't cwy.*

The room is dark with the curtains drawn. A stench lingers. He crosses the carpet, eyes downcast—his sober shoes, his trousered legs, a seeming reproach in their reliable carriage of him over to the bed.

She looks so young lying there, curled on her side. *Is she . . . ?* He leans down. Of course she is breathing. He is set to *run away*—to slip away without waking her, but she opens her eyes. They blur with tears. Overflow. Her words are blurred too. "I'm sorry, Henry."

He sits. His voice is thick. "My darling." He feels his brow furrow. He squeezes shut his eyes and finds her hand. Presses it, not too tightly, careful not to compound her grief with the slightest indication that tears are leaking through his own lids.

"It hurts," she whimpers. Wracked now, she weeps.

Havers has stationed himself outside on the broad stone steps, watching for the carriage, and now he opens the door for the doctor. "If you would please to follow me, Mr. Moore."

Henry rises with relief, carefully extricating his hand from his wife's grip. "Ah, Mr. Moore, thank you so much for coming."

His wife appears scarcely conscious of his withdrawal, she is as though abducted by pain. He cedes his place at her side to the doctor.

Out back in the wash house, Maid stuffs Her Ladyship's soiled body linens and petticoats into the tub. Maggie watches as they release a swirl of scarlet sighs before the squat scullery maid spears the billows with the laundry stick.

Cook marches in, carrying at arm's length a bunched-up rusty brown . . . Cook thrusts it at Maggie who recoils—the stink of it! She sways on her feet. Cook says, "Make yourself useful."

"I'm to wash it?" Maggie looks queasily into the cauldron of blood and suds.

"Burn it, eediot."

Maggie Sheehan takes the reeking bundle from the wash house but stops halfway across the yard. She places it on the ground and gingerly lays it out. It is a coat. Not a fine one, even without the filth smeared on it. She carefully reaches into one of the pockets. A disgusting hand-kerchief. A penny whistle. She reaches into the other one. A greasy peaked cap, folded over . . . a small fortune in coins. And at the bottom, a roll of notes. She looks over her shoulder, but there's only steam coming from the wash house. She knots her apron around the money and heads back into the scullery with the horrible coat. From the corner of her eye she sees the basin that Cook carried from Her Ladyship's chamber; it is now on the cutting board, full of carrots and leeks. She crouches at the hot stove and opens the door. The smell is like—never mind what is like, it is what Maggie Sheehan sees that prompts the cry from her throat and she quickly stuffs the reeking bundle into the flames.

She jumps at the sound of her name, and slams the iron door of the stove. "You're wanted upstairs," says Pugsley.

She hurries to the pump and, as she scrubs from her hands to her elbows the way she's seen old Mr. Moore do, she ponders a hiding place for her windfall.

Having scrubbed his hands and pulled up a chair to the young woman's bedside, Mr. Moore now lightly holds an ether-moistened cloth over her mouth and nose. "Breathe it in now, there's a good lass." Thanks to his colleague, Mr. Simpson, there is no longer need for a woman to suffer bodily pain on top of heartache in a case like this. Satisfied the drug is taking effect, he looks about for a—"I've clean cloths here, Mr. Moore," says a soft Irish voice behind him.

"Ah, Maggie, is it?"

She nods, bobs.

"Well now, look at you"—he too speaks quietly.

"Landed on me feet thanks to you and Miss Gourley, and Mr. Baxter and—"

He has placed a finger in front of his lips. She bobs. She bends over the bed and draws back the sheet; then draws up Her Ladyship's nightgown; then carefully tucks several layers of cloth under Her Ladyship's bare bottom.

Satisfied his patient is deeply asleep, Mr. Moore places his knowledgeable old hands on her belly, kneading and massaging it like bread.

In his study, Henry stands, as though stranded halfway to his chair.

In the parlour, Clarissa sits straight-backed and motionless in her chair.

Maggie Sheehan sponges Her Ladyship. She and Mr. Moore have taken away the soiled bedding, bundling it over the blood and human tissue. The afterbirth has been safely expelled and, thanks to Joseph Lister, there is no danger of sepsis—the room smells now only of carbolic acid. Together, doctor and maid skillfully dress Lady Marie, limp and dead to the world as she is, in a fresh nightgown.

As they work, Mr. Moore asks Maggie, in his customarily calm tone, "Where is the foetus?"

"The . . ."

"The babby."

"Oh, 'twas—" Sheehan finds she cannot speak without sobbing—or worse. Mr. Moore gestures for her to follow him out into the passage. There the girl hiccups but manages to tell him, "I was after burning an old coat so I was, Mr. Moore, when I opened the stove and I saw . . ."

Twenty minutes later, Mae awakens to a heavy sort of pain, dull but for jagged blades when she tries to move. She once saw the scrap heap behind Daddy's can factory. Rusty peels of tin that hadn't become proper cans, piled willy-nilly; that is what it feels like inside her.

Mr. Moore shakes the mercury and consults the thermometer.

"Am I dying?"

"Not a bit of it."

"I want to."

He places a cool dry hand on her forehead. "It feels like the end, my dear, but it is not. You are in company of a great many women. That will not comfort you now, but tuck it away in your mind for the days and weeks to come." He reaches into his leather bag which sits hinged open on the floor, and withdraws a small blue bottle. "You are a normal, healthy young woman, and hard as 'tis to hear, 'tis far from rare to lose a first pregnancy. Now I'm going to give you a little medicine for the pain—"

She whispers. "But it wasn't my first."

"Oh?"

She tells him. He nods. "Even so, Your Ladyship, 'tis by no means unusual, and you're no to fret."

She looks into his kind eyes, a sob escapes her. "I'm sorry."

"Och, Lady Marie, I too am sorry." He holds her hand in both his own.

She cries, frankly and freshly into his woollen shoulder, reactivating the must of innumerable Edinburgh rains. He pats her back. There is one word she wants very badly to say . . . *Don't even think it or you'll never stop crying.*

Finally, she says, "They took her away . . ."

"I know, my dear."

"Where is she?"

"She is gone, lass."

"I want to see her."

"You cannae."

"Why not?"

"My dear, one of the household erred in—"

"What did they do to her?" Screaming, "Sheehan—!"

Mr. Moore speaks quietly, "Mrs. Cavendish had the remains of your dear daughter conveyed to the Royal Edinburgh Infirmary—"

Mae is wracked. "I want her back!"

"It cannot be."

". . . No." A child's voice, a woman's comprehension.

"It was wrong, my dear, but I can tell you she was handled with care and respect."

He turns his steady gaze to Maggie where the lass stands trembling by the vanity table and she nods: *Not a word . . .*

Mae pleads, "Where did they bury her? I want to see her grave."

He shakes his head. She understands. No baptism. No burial. *Disposal* only. At the hands of strangers. She disintegrates into moaning. "My baby, my baby . . ." No one ever finishes crying over this.

Mr. Moore unstoppers the small blue bottle. "I am going to place a drop of this under your tongue, my dear. Now, it is laudanum, and it will not taste very nice, but it will take away the pain."

He takes the glass dropper with the single drop of reddish brown liquid, and slips it under her tongue. Then he stoppers the bottle and sets it on the nightstand. And waits a few moments.

Mae is in a cloud that is pulling her unresistingly back and away from anything that hurts, from everything. Now the word slips out so easily, the one she held back from saying to the doctor, and she sees it floating away, *Daddy* . . .

Turning to Maggie, Mr. Moore speaks softly. "There are two drops remaining in this bottle. If Her Ladyship should wake in the night, unable to rest for pain, you're to give her one drop at a time, four hours apart. Otherwise, I'll expect to find them here when I return."

Only when Lady Marie's breathing has become deep and regular and her body relaxes completely does Mr. Moore take his bag and leave the room, careful not to wake Maggie who has likewise fallen asleep, head on her folded arms at the vanity table whose looking glass reflects the shadows and sorrows of the room.

Mr. Moore is with Henry in his study. He has accepted a glass of brandy.

"Has your wife friends and family nearby, Lord Henry?"

"We are her family, and of course she has made . . . numerous friends here . . ."

The doctor nods kindly. Henry clears his throat, adds, "Her people are in Boston." He studies a corner of the carpet. While he was in the Old Town indulging in the fanning of an old flame, his wife was suffering a miscarriage. No. A *still-birth*.

Old Moore is saying something about Mae's mother—

"She is dead," says Henry—more abruptly than he intended. "Passed away when Mae—Lady Marie—was a young child. Consumption or . . ."

"Ah. Well, a sea voyage might do Lady Marie the world of good."

"We are in possession of certificates of passage, we can leave at any time. When she is well enough, that is."

"She is not unwell physically, Lord Henry, 'tis her heart needs lifting. Familiar sights, old friends and family—"

"My sister has been most attentive."

"Och, I've no doubt."

"So . . . there is nothing, physically, wrong. In terms of . . ."

"Lord Henry, I assure you, Lady Marie needs only sleep, good food and, soon enough, fresh air and gentle amusements."

"And. As to. At what point might it be advisable to seek to . . . renew her hopes?"

And in the same gentle tones, "There is no impediment to a full married life as soon as ever your wife is disposed."

"Might that have . . . ? That is, might the . . . might it have—?"

"By no means, Your Lordship. A miscarriage, never mind a still-birth, is not caused by conjugal relations of the ordinary kind."

"Entirely ordinary."

"I bid you set your mind at rest, for as I told your dear wife, there is nothing unusual in a second loss. Even if this one occurred later than one could wish."

"'Second'?"

"Ah." He nods. "'Twould seem I've spoken out of turn."

"Nonsense, Mr. Moore, she is my wife. What, precisely, did she tell you?"

"Be assured, Lord Henry, the first pregnancy was so brief as to, in her young eyes, merit mention only in light of the second."

Henry elevates his brows.

Mr. Moore explains, "An early miscarriage is sometimes mistaken by a woman for her monthly—"

"Quite." He clears his throat once more. "So it was nothing."

". . . Very nearly."

Henry tops up the doctor's glass. Rings for Havers. "Tell Cavendish we'll be three at table." Turning to Mr. Moore, "You'll stay to dine?"

"Thank you, Lord Henry."

Havers withdraws.

Mr. Moore sips. Says carefully, "Your Lordship. In a case like this, it is well the young woman be allowed to hold her baby in her arms, however small it be."

"Is it." Henry sounds eminently reasonable, even to himself, even when he inquires, "Do you mean to say, there was—is—an actual. Body?" The latter word exerts a strange force. A sort of plush undertow to it . . . He is going to be sick. He sits back and fixes his gaze on a corner of the ceiling.

"Small, as I say. But quite recognizable. In this case, I am told, it was a girl."

Henry slumps forward. Head in his hands. Presently, "I shall have it seen to." He reaches for the bell cord.

"Your Lordship, I'm afraid 'tis no longer possible. The remains have been removed."

"Removed . . ." He swallows. "Where?"

"They were cremated, Your Lordship. Here, in the kitchen stove."

Henry's collar tightens. "By what—by whose . . . ?"

"A misunderstanding, Your Lordship. The cook—"

Henry shoots to his feet—Mr. Moore continues calmly, "Cook was but following an instruction of Miss Clarissa, you see, for when Cook asked what ought to be done with the—and here she used the term 'mess,' for so, Your Lordship, it would have appeared to her—your sister, understandably, ordered all to be burnt."

Henry is numb.

Mr. Moore says, "Your sister grew up in the time of the cholera, Lord Henry. Well do I recall wee Miss Clarissa to-ing and fro-ing from your brothers' sick-rooms, and in those days, you see, all was burnt and rightly so for fear of contagion."

Henry looks away.

Mr. Moore waits. The gentleman will feel better for having cried.

Mae could not reasonably have expected a proper funeral for her still-born daughter much less burial in sanctified ground. She knew she was already heretical in her belief that the Blessed Virgin Mary would look after her child, for the Church Fathers teach that unbaptized babies are denied Heaven, being consigned instead to everlasting limbo. But Mary is a Mother. And there is something in the very word that says, "Come to me, my child, and I will give you Rest." So Mae prays now in her strange sleep, *Dear Mother Mary, never was it known that any who implored your help were left unaided* . . .

Havers ladles a second serving of soup into the doctor's bowl at a nod from Clarissa. Mulligatawny. "You are partial, Mr. Moore, if memory serves."

He smiles and nods.

There are some who would have had the old surgeon served his victuals in the scullery for he is, in terms of rank, a little above a craftsman. Mr. Moore, however, went above and beyond for the Bell family back in the days of the Irish Affliction (as the cholera was known); and when nine-year-old Clarissa's mother lay dying, it was Mr. Moore who made sure to call Clarissa into the sick-room in time to say goodbye. Thus, although the sight of him rekindles feelings which she might as soon leave like ash in a neglected grate, Clarissa would never deny the doctor a place at her—her brother's—table. He has been like a—well he is nothing like her father was, but so the saying goes.

Now, as she nods to Havers to top up Mr. Moore's glass, she reflects that it is a shame he finds himself reduced to tending Rosamund Gourley's guttersnipes and harlots, when he might by now have become a physician with a proper surgery. Clarissa leaves her own soup all but untouched, having found her hand too unsteady for the task.

Henry likewise has scarcely touched his.

Nor does he eat the chop on his plate, instead picking at the turnip and potato.

Following the meal, Clarissa sees the doctor to the door. She finds herself a touch weary but does her polite best to attend as he conveys to her what he has already told Sheehan, ". . . One drop as needed at four-hour intervals, and I've left as much to hand."

"You have left medicine?"

"Laudanum. A tincture of opium mixed with alcohol."

"Is that quite safe?"

"I have left a very little, only to see her through the worst."

"I am glad to know that." The thought, unbidden, *A drug fiend. 'Tis all I need.*

He surprises her with a question. "Are you in some discomfort, my dear?"

Clarissa is embarrassed. She is not a whinger. Not one to draw attention. "I am tolerably well, Mr. Moore."

"Last we spoke, it came and went."

". . . What did?"

He smiles so kindly, speaks quietly. "The rheumatism."

She sighs, smiles in turn as though discussing an old friend. "It still does. Come. It is less inclined to go."

"And have you had recourse to the waters at Leith?"

Nettled now—"Thank you for the reminder, Mr. Moore, that I may at any time repair to Leith." *And make a spectacle of myself at the local public baths.*

"There are foreign spas, Miss Clarissa. In the Alps. Well regarded, and now that your material circumstances have altered—" She purses her lips in warning but he continues, "you might consider a sojourn of some months. The baths promise relief. Even, in some cases, healing."

In spite of herself, her mind's eye throws up a wholly new prospect: herself and Maid. Parasols. Travelling costumes. Alighting at a spa amid snow-capped mountains. Light. Quiet. *Healing . . .*

He tilts his head and smiles. "It seems like yesterday I was listening to your Latin verses, Miss Clarissa."

She smiles back. "*Mens sana in corpore sano.*"

With a promise to return on the morrow, Mr. Moore dons his hat, its band moulded about his head, and steps through the front door into the night.

Scarcely has she lowered herself onto her chair when Henry puts his head round the parlour door.

"What is it now?" she says, regretting immediately her tone. "Come in and sit, Henry."

He does so, wearily.

"Sister. It is a matter of . . . the remains of the . . ."

"Set your mind at rest, brother, it—all was seen to."

"That's it, you see . . . Mr. Moore is of the view Mae ought to have . . . That is, in cases such as this it is well the mother should be allowed to hold the . . . baby."

She appears shocked anew. Henry reflects he may have erred in assuming his sister would know more than he of these matters by virtue of her sex. He reproaches himself now as it strikes him she could know but little given her unmarried state.

Brother and sister regard one another.

He says quietly, "It was a girl."

She raises her eyebrows. For a long moment. Blinks. Lets out the breath she has been holding.

He rises. Pours her a glass of sherry, and a whisky for himself.

They gaze into the fire.

Clarissa asks, "How is Marie?" Her voice cracks—this is why it does not do to dwell.

"She is sleeping. Moore gave her something for the pain."

She nods.

He pours more sherry into her glass. Whisky into his own.

After a moment, Henry says, "It was not her first . . . loss."

Clarissa looks up from the flames.

"Apparently there was . . . a negligible episode in Paris."

She reaches down—too quickly, and is assailed by a *twinge*—for her work basket. Somewhat more deliberately, she sets it in her lap.

Her brother's tone is aggrieved, and a little steel creeps back into Clarissa's spine along with the pain as he—*whinges* is too strong a word. "Does it not surprise you, sister, that my wife kept from me, her husband, news of her first . . . mishap?"

"Henry. Women do not tell their husbands everything. If they did, an abyss would yawn at the feet of men such as would unfit them for war, piety, profit, in short their duty. And who would build our precious bridges then, eh?" It is a particular sort of pain. Specifically, soreness. Like the soreness of a sore throat. But elsewhere in the body. Clarissa tries for a deep breath but is restricted as though by a band about the rib cage. Notwithstanding, she has sufficient breath to add, "Unless you mean to cede the day to a regiment of blue-stockings, I suggest you count yourself fortunate your wife had the good sense not to burden you with woman's troubles."

Henry drains his glass—perhaps his sister knows more than she lets on. He rises, reassured. "Goodnight, Clarissa."

She softens her tone. "'Tis a set-back is all, brother."

He smiles sadly, sways a little on his feet, suddenly exhausted, and turns toward the door.

"Bear in mind it was only a girl," she murmurs, uncertain as to whether he has heard.

She watches the flames reflected in the windowpane and listens to his slow tread up the stairs. Then, as coffins and purses pop in the fire, she opens her work basket, removes her squares of fabric, and proceeds to pick and pull at the lace until all her work is undone.

Late, very late that night, Clarissa rises from her bed. Her bed has become stone. Lying down is the worst. This is not new. Just more.

She exits her room. A little bluish light from the window at the end of the hallway suffuses the passage. She walks haltingly, one hand on the wainscotting, until she comes to the bedroom of her eldest dead brother. She opens the door carefully, soundlessly. Yes, Henry is asleep within. She retraces her steps and enters, just as quietly, the marital chamber. Darker in here. She pauses until she discerns her sister-in-law's steady deep breathing. She advances with some difficulty across the thick pile of the carpet toward the darker mass of the bed. Slowly, slowly, she reaches out her hand and, by degrees, lowers it toward where the night-stand must be until—*stop*. She feels the top of a very small . . . bottle. She picks it up. Unstoppers it.

She tilts back her head. Two drops on her tongue—*bitter*.

Clarissa replaces the bottle.

The effect is swift.

By the time she has crossed back to her own room, she feels she is gliding. She lies down. The pain seeps away. Blessed. Blessed sleep.

"The best medicine," says Mr. Moore the next morning, pleased to learn his patient slept through the night. Noting that the small bottle is empty, he returns it to his bag.

"How is the pain, Your Ladyship?"

"Gone," she says, trying for a smile.

"There's a good lass. Now I want you to eat up every morsel that Maggie brings you. I'll be back to see you soon enough, and sooner if you send for me."

Henry has slept poorly. But he is shaved. He has waited outside the bedroom door, in his hands a vase of forced blooms from the conservatory. And now, after a brief, reassuring exchange with Mr. Moore, he takes a deep breath, squares his chin, and enters.

His wife is, if anything, prettier what with her pallor, the shadows beneath her lovely young eyes. He sets the vase on her vanity table.

"Mr. Moore tells me there is no reason you mightn't enjoy a carriage ride in a day or two."

She does not answer. She starts crying. He moves to leave. She stays him with an outstretched hand. He goes to her, takes her hand. Understands what she is telling him. *Stay with me.* He does.

Downstairs, Mr. Moore is waylaid by Cavendish who insists on fixing him a wee by-bite whilst detailing the peculiarities of her gammy knee. She is decidedly miffed when Mr. Moore delivers his diagnosis, "Housemaid's knee."

"I'm nae housemaid!"

"'Tis a manner of speaking only, Mrs. Cavendish. A duchess may develop it, though not from scrubbing nor, as in your case, from twisting and turning with heavy pots of tasty broth and good stew and great sides of meat."

Mollified, she presses an extra Eccles cake on him.

Mr. Moore does not wish to leave without looking in on Miss Clarissa, but not finding her in her parlour, he seeks out the housemaid in the pantry where she is polishing silver.

She starts at his entrance and all Mr. Moore can get out of her is that her mistress has yet to emerge from her chamber. "Is she poorly, then?"

Maid appears stumped by the question, but luckily Mr. Moore is able to catch Maggie on her way to the service stairs with a tray. "She's not poorly, Mr. Moore, only she's after having a lie-in."

"Is she, now?"

The girl adds brightly, "Up in the wee hours, she was, come into 'Ladyship's room to check on her, I heard her, so I did, for I were curled up on the day-bed."

It crosses Mr. Moore's mind to wonder whether it was Maggie herself who administered the remaining drops to Her Ladyship last night, but he is forestalled by the butler:

"Sheehan. You are wanted upstairs."

Henry stays. Steadfast, holding his wife's hand and staring past the flowers to the window, he stays 'til morning turns to afternoon and the Irish maid has come and gone with the untouched tray. Marie weeps and slumbers by turns. Evening descends and the flowers grow dim and still he stays. It costs nothing. It is no more than what he vowed to do back in Rome not quite a year ago. It seems much longer—is that what tragedy does? Come now, one can hardly call it a "tragedy." Mr. Moore has assured them both of that. And, as though she has read his thoughts, she says, eyes still closed, "Mr. Moore says I will have another and that it's not unusual."

"Of course you will. Of course it isn't."

She trembles. He bends and holds her close. *I love you.* He does not trust himself to say it aloud. There will be time later. They have so much time, after all. They have the rest of their lives. He holds her close.

February, 1872

Dear Taffy,
It was a girl. Dead.

Your,
M

40

WITHIN A FEW DAYS, Mae is able to sit up and eat without crying. Dear Mr. Moore has been in and says she'll be up and about in no time; he's told her to eat a plate of black pudding and drink a glass of stout every day for the next few weeks. After a week or so of this, she gets up and goes to her vanity. Combs and plaits her own hair. Runs her own bath. Calls for her maid to help with her corset, then dismisses her, saying, "I can put on my own wrapper, Sheehan." Soft mauve with wide copper cuffs and matching sash. She descends and finds her husband in his study, looking about as glum as the stuffed pigeon. But he brightens, and she sees him shed ten years at the sight of her. He opens his arms. She goes to him, and settles in his lap.

She tells him what she wants. He nods. He is happy that she wants anything at all. Especially something he can easily provide.

"Of course, my darling, I shall see to it promptly."

"You were right, Henry. Be sure to give her a good character, though. It's my own fault she was familiar, I encouraged her."

He kisses her. "You are too good, my dear."

Mae would never, even inwardly, refer to Sheehan as a wee Irish *you-know-what*. But Sheehan is, for all her pluck and prettiness . . . unwholesome. Annie back home would say she's "bad luck." Superstition aside, Mae needs a fresh start and that means a fresh maid. Besides, it would not do to return to Boston with exactly the kind of girl Daddy sacrificed everything to prevent Mae becoming.

In the butler's pantry, Havers places a guinea in Sheehan's hand along with a written "character" from His Lordship. "You ought have no trouble finding a new position."

Maggie Sheehan stands, rooted to the spot.

"Be off with you," says Havers.

Next morning, as Pugsley clears the breakfast things, Clarissa places both hands on the dining table and levers herself to standing. She walks, stiffly, but with head erect, into her parlour. She steadies herself on the occasional table—setting a china shepherdess and a lost lamb to rattling—turns slowly, grasps the back of her chair, and lowers herself carefully. Ruddy Maid has removed the cushion. She reaches out—yes, painfully—and tugs the bell cord.

Maid answers the summons.

"I want Sheehan."

"I don't know where she is, Madam."

"Well find her!"

Moments later, Henry himself appears and explains that Sheehan has been let go.

"What? Why?"

"Marie asked that I dismiss her."

"On what grounds?"

Henry inclines his head and, with a gracious half smile, looks away. Clarissa shifts, with difficulty, in her chair. She realizes, of course, that she has overstepped. She presses closed her lips before she can say, *She was my maid too.*

Over in the Old Town, at the Refuge, the freckled young man has made himself useful, turning his hand to all manner of chores. Mending pots, splitting wood and, more surprisingly, filling the margins of yesterday's newspapers with caricatures of the residents and even Miss Gourley herself.

"They're as good as anything in *Punch*," observes Miss Elliot.

"Sadly, it is an apt likeness," says Miss Gourley. And to the young man, "You're lucky I don't turn you out."

He plays the spoons and gets the bairns singing every evening. It calms them. Miss Gourley sees no harm in his staying 'til his ankle heals. "But you're not to sketch me anymore, do you hear, I'll have your hide." He laughs.

Clarissa does her best to dissemble the pain if only to fend off her brother's well-meant and increasingly irksome query, "Why not lie down for a spell, Clarissa?"

The other night. The night of the dreadful day. Having availed herself of the drops in the blue bottle, Clarissa found herself indulging in fancy. There in the dead of night, a forgotten propensity to daydream bloomed afresh like a lotus on a Chinese mountain lake. As a child she had entertained fancies of foreign travel; of speaking strange tongues with dusky peoples, some of whom went about armed with scimitars. She would see the pyramids.

Fresh and fleeting like springtime clouds across her unfettered mind were these memories. And in their wake, a new fancy. Closer to hand. Foreign skies, but not so exotic. She is at a spa on the Continent. She enters an airy dining room; its doorway is framed by fat, gleaming leaves of potted palms; all along one side, a glass wall affords a view of snow-capped mountains while, in the foreground, coils of steam rise from hot springs. She looks up at the sound of her own name being spoken from across the elegant room. And she replies, "Why, Mr. Baxter. What brings you to the Alps?"

A couple of weeks later, Mae is up and about and bored out of her wits. "I can't do without a lady's maid, Henry, and that beanpole of Clarissa's doesn't count." Mae has done her own hair again *and it shows!*

"I've already had a word with Havers, darling."

"Of course you have, darling, I'm such a nag!"

"You are anything but. Are you coming down to breakfast, darling?"

"I'll be two ticks." *I wouldn't miss the haddock for the world!* She suddenly sets down her hairbrush and right there, in the midst of a gathering squall, she flags—as though the wind whipping her sails had suddenly dropped. She says solemnly, "I want to go home, Henry."

"'Home.' Ah yes, Mr. Moore did say it might be advisable. A sea voyage."

"I want to go soon." She has tried to say it lightly, even petulantly, anything to shake the strange weight of what feels like premonition. A grey, low-bellied cloud . . .

"As soon as ever you please."

"Do you mean that?"

"Of course I do."

She smiles as girlishly as ever. But for the first time it feels like a "face" she is putting on—that's what Fanny always said in Rome when applying her "paint," *I'm putting my face on.* Is this what it feels like to be a grown-up woman?

"You go on down, Henry, I'll be right there. Save some finnan haddie for me."

Clarissa stirs her tea and cautions her brother, "Henry, marmalade will spoil your digestion."

Havers removes a plate—His Lordship hasn't touched the kippers this morning—and murmurs, "The new girl has arrived, Your Lordship."

"Good show, Havers."

A scream from upstairs. Henry is on his feet and away, his chair caught by Havers with his free hand. Clarissa closes her eyes, draws a deep breath. As deep as she can manage.

Henry enters the bedroom to find Mae on the floor in the middle of her daisy-print dress, like a raging undrowned Ophelia, brandishing one of the Certificates of Passage. The other is gone. "She stole it!"

"Who did, darling?"

"Sheehan, that little—*argh!*"

"Not to worry, darling, I shall purchase a new ticket."

"I don't want a new ticket!! I want *my* ticket!!!" She smites the carpet with her fists, a coil of hair comes loose.

He draws back a little, as though from an electric eel. "Of course you do, darling."

"Daddy gave us those tickets." She cries inconsolably.

He crouches next to her. "My darling, you shall soon see your father. And Miss Weaver, and . . ." He narrowly avoids mentioning Bonnie who is dead, *you idiot.*

She clings to him, mutters something. He registers the strength of her fingers digging into his back. He finds he is aroused in spite of himself. "What's that, my darling?"

Mae bites his tweedy shoulder to stop herself repeating the horrible words she said just now. Of all the terrible things that have happened in the past little while, she doesn't want to add a shocking vulgarity to her list of wrongs.

He helps her from the floor. Embraces her. She kisses him back. He takes her to the bed—whispers, "Is it all right?"

She nods, moans a little. He lays her down.

He takes her for the first time since—don't think about anything, just . . .

"Oh Henry . . ."

Afterwards she is doubly grateful she did not repeat the horrible phrase.

But Henry heard it the first time. Even now, as he lies next to her, the weight of her dear head on his chest, it seems to mock him like a sigh, prompting him to harden once again: *That little Irish whore.*

Leaving her to freshen up, he slips away. Down and across the hall to his late brother's room where, hating himself, he quells himself.

March 21, 1872

Dear Taffy,
We're coming home to Boston! I'll write more in a trice, no time now, too excited!

Love,
Mae

PS Mr. Moore says a second miscarriage is not dire. Certain doctors are called "Mr." here—so confusing!

———

At the Refuge, a roomful of women sit in rows, eyes on the blackboard where beaky Miss Elliot wields a pointer and a piece of chalk. Among them is the freckled young man. He listens and watches as the marks become letters and the letters become words.

41

IS IT DUE TO HER YOUTH that Mae does not question it? The sense that everything is going to be all right. The dining room seems brighter the following morning, and the breakfast service less unappealing than usual—it might even be possible to acquire a taste for smoked fish—*let's not get carried away.*

Henry, having risen at her entrance, "You're looking bonny this morning, my dear," resumes his seat, and his *Scotsman*.

Mae basks. Savours the sound of butter scraping onto her toast. The dazzle of orange marmalade in the crystal dish. The gleam of table linens. She is reminded of their honeymoon and all those balcony breakfasts. The crossing to Boston will be like that. She reaches over and strokes the back of his hand. Just the two of them . . .

"Where's Clarissa?" she asks.

"I'm afraid she is indisposed."

"Oh dear. Has she taken to her bed?"

"She has taken to the garden."

Mae looks out through the window. Through the bare spikes of the hollyhocks may be seen the jet figure of her sister-in-law, ramrod straight and still as a statue—like the ones in Greyfriars Kirkyard. Mae shivers.

"Are you chilly—?"

"Not at all—"

He rings for Havers.

While the butler banks up the fire, she folds her hands demurely and waits for her husband to look up. The new maid has done something really rather chic with Mae's hair this morning. Henry reaches for his teacup without taking his eyes from the page. She refuses to be piqued this morning, however—*I'm in too good a mood. Think of others for a change, Mary Corcoran.* "What's wrong with Clarissa, Henry?"

He looks up, apparently nonplussed. "'Wrong'?"

She swallows a sigh. "What ails her, Henry? What is the nature of her complaint?"

His eyebrows migrate north, spring must be in the air—*That was not very nice, Mary Corcoran.* She tilts her head prettily.

"My sister has always been prey to—that is, since I can remember, she has been prey from time to time to spells of what I suppose one might call . . . discomfort."

"I think she's in pain."

The eyebrows again.

"Have you asked her about it, Henry?"

"I would not dream of doing so."

She persists. "Darling, what if she's really ill? Maybe we can help her."

"She will assuredly have consulted Mr. Moore."

"It doesn't seem to have done her much good. Don't get me wrong, I love Mr. Moore—" Her voice catches. She brightens. "Only sometimes it pays to get a second opinion."

He turns a page.

"Henry?"

Absently, without looking up, "Warmer now, darling?"

"Tell Cavendish to prepare a roast of beef for dinner this evening. Rare. And bring me my cushion, it does not belong on the other chair."

Maid stands motionless and gapes like a lamped hare.

Clarissa sighs inwardly and revises her order. "Tell Cook."

The creature bobs and retreats. Without having handed Clarissa the cushion. Which is eight feet away. Slowly, she rises to her feet.

Cavendish has, of course, been let go. By Henry. He told Clarissa in a would-be offhand manner at the parlour door, "By the way, I've let Cavendish go."

"What? Why on earth?"

Hands clasped behind his back, he studied the carpet just long enough for Clarissa to supply the answer to her own question. Of course one could no longer have the woman in the house after what she had done—in obedience to Clarissa's order. Thus, with her brother's announcement, Clarissa understood that no more would be said on the subject. For the which she was grateful.

Clarissa has retrieved the cushion and returned to her chair, but the cushion has not cooperated. It lies where it fell just now on the floor. She rocks a little—the motion does nothing either to ease or exacerbate the pain, but it accompanies her prayer. *Lord in Heaven. One son. I beseech You.*

Mae steps into Clarissa's parlour. "I'm sorry, I should've knocked."

"Nonsense, come, sit, Marie."

She does.

"Clarissa?"

"Mm?"

"I just want to say . . . I know things have . . . I just want to say thank you for everything you've done. Keeping the household running smoothly even with all the servant trouble and . . . everything that's happened. And I want you to know I'm—Mr. Moore says I'm all better now and," mimicking him jauntily, "'brighter days ahead.' So I'm right as rain, but. Clarissa, are you ill?"

The eyebrows.

"Only, I know you're sometimes uncomfortable and I worry about leaving you here on your own when we go to Boston."

"You need not."

"Well, good. That's really good. Um. What have you got?"

"'Got'?"

"I mean to say, what is your illness called?"

"If you must know, Marie, I suffer from a discomfiting but by no means life-threatening infirmity."

"Have you talked to dear Mr. Moore about it?"

Clarissa thinks of the contents of the tiny blue bottle. "Rheumatism does not admit of cure."

"Oh . . . I see." Mae's heart swells with sympathy. "Well, you know Mr. Moore has been an absolute angel, I don't know what I would have done without him, but . . . Well he can't know everything, can he? And one of the marvellous things I've learned about Edinburgh is that along with the amazing lighthouses and bridges, it's known for medical advances, so I'll bet you dollars to doughnuts I can find you a physician as good as any in America. Worth a try, don't you think?"

Mae sees Clarissa nod—unless it was simply the motion of the rocking chair.

"Clarissa, wouldn't you be more comfortable in a nice armchair?"

"No. Thank you, Marie."

After a seemly interval, Mae retreats.

In the morning room she summons Havers.

"Send this note to Mrs. Heatherington."

Next morning, Havers brings in the post on the silver salver and bows as Mae takes up an envelope addressed to her from Mrs. Heatherington. She reads it, then skips across to Henry's sacrosanct study.

He has received a letter too. She kisses the top of his head as he hunts for a letter-opener amid the clutter of periodicals and papers and stuffed birds—really, his "lair" is getting frowzy, if Henry isn't careful he'll wind up like old Colonel MacOmber.

She waits as he opens his envelope, in which there is a second, smaller envelope, in which there is an engraved note card. He reads silently.

"Hmph."

"What is it, Henry?" And reading over his shoulder, "Oh look, it's addressed to both of us."

She plucks the card from his fingers and reads aloud, "'William, Lord Hawley, Marquess of Camberleuch'—How do you pronounce that?"

"Camber*loo*."

"You're kidding me, anyhoo, he 'cordially requests the presence of Lord and Lady Bell'—" It is the first time she has seen it in print and she squirms a little with pleasure. "—'at the nuptials of his son, Lord Richard George William Hawley, and La Principessa della Montesilvio von Badenkreuzer, to take place on Saturday, the 29th day of June at 9 o'clock in the morning at St. George's Church in Hanover Square, London.' Oh Hank, how thrilling! Fanny and Hawley! It will be the event of the Season, I cannot wait!"

"What—? I thought we were to set sail for Boston."

"We can do that after." She regards him, aghast. "Don't tell me you don't want to go to the wedding?"

He cradles his forehead.

"Don't cradle your forehead at me, Henry, we're going and that's that."

He looks up, incredulous. She regards him mock-imperiously. He laughs. Gives in.

Bell Gardens
March 23, 1872

Darling Taffy,

I'm afraid we have to delay our arrival the teensiest bit. Fanny Bunker from Yonkers and Lord Richard Hawley from Camberleuch (last syllable pronounced like the English slang for water closet) are tying the knot and Henry and I are to attend the June nuptials in London!

It's just as well we're leaving because I don't think Clarissa can put up with me much longer. I'm always saying the wrong thing. She is a martyr to rheumatism, poor soul, but won't do a thing about it and is glued to her Regency rocker—Taffy, it has no arms so yes, it is a *nursing* chair. I asked Henry if his sister had ever wanted to get married and have children and he looked at me as if I had two heads. So I said, "Then why in the world is she so attached to that nursing chair?" Turns out that was the chair in which he and Clarissa, and all the dead brothers, were nursed (!). . .

Pugsley's white-gloved hand removes the platter with the grey remains of last Sunday's mutton. The vegetables are pallid spectres of their former selves. Mae pats her lips with her dinner napkin. "Well I suppose word got out about Cavendish and she was snapped up." Clarissa does not meet her eye—poor thing, she's taking it hard. "Never fear, Clarissa, dear, we'll train up this cook just like we did the last one."

"I daresay we shall, Marie."

They watch Henry, complacently spearing his cauliflower.

After dinner, Mae enters the parlour and discreetly hands Clarissa the note from Mrs. Heatherington.

Clarissa waits until Mae has left before reading it. Then she folds it and tucks it into her sewing basket.

Now Mae and Henry, arm-in-arm, are taking an evening turn around the gated park across the way. The days are getter longer; the cherry trees that line the path are studded with tight green buds, and ranks of yellow tulips shine in the gloaming.

"Henry, I meant to tell you, I've found a physician for Clarissa."

"Do you mean to say you . . . ? Broached the subject? With her?"

"I did, Henry. I used full sentences and I spoke just as kindly as I feel toward her which is very kindly indeed. She's my sister now too, after all." She hugs his arm and he returns the pressure.

"And she has agreed to consult a . . . a physician, you say?"

"She did not refuse."

He gives her an admiring look. "Good show."

"I got a name from Mrs. Heatherington who says he completely cured her sciatica and another lady of her acquaintance swears by a vibratory-type thing he did with some kind of electrified wand and a great big battery."

"Sounds ominous."

"He's very forward-thinking. Especially known for female maladies."

Henry manages not to cringe. "But rheumatism is not exclusive to the female sex."

"So you did know what was wrong with her."

"I surmised."

"You're just as clever as any physician."

He smiles and lifts his chin. Truly it is a lovely evening.

His wife says, "His name is Dr. Chambers."

꙳

At the Refuge, up in her own room and away from the melee of the common areas, Miss Gourley is listening to the freckled young man read aloud. The bed-sit has not much changed but for less crockery and more books. He stumbles upon a word. They are seated side by side on the divan with its pink satin coverlet. She inclines her head over the page. Two people, one book. He turns to her . . .

42

MAE IS "SPRING CLEANING," conducting an inventory of her wardrobe.

"A June wedding, how charming . . ."

The bed and all available surfaces, including now the floor, are piled high.

"Even if the bride and groom are in the autumn of their lives," she adds. The new lady's maid either registers nothing or dutifully maintains a neutral demeanour. "Fanny's actually close to the first frost." The girl is about as expressive as the dressmaker's form which stands stripped and waiting. Which is to say she's perfect. "Not there, silly, hold it up so I can look at it." It doesn't take a couturier to see Mae is in need of a new gown to wear to a London society wedding.

She turns now to Henry, hands on her hips, "Well?"

"You would look like a queen in any one of these garments."

"You're no help at all."

The maid knows her way around a ribbon and a towering chignon—Mae has taken to wearing a rat, and the girl is able to position the net pad invisibly so as to lend the impression that Lady Marie possesses tresses of Rapunzel-like bounty. Stripes versus florals, and the relative merits of a pagoda versus a puff sleeve, however, appear lost on her. Whether tongue-tied or devoid of opinion, she is about as far from "familiar" as Henry could hope. Nor is she from the Refuge, and if she has borne a whole passel of fatherless brats, Mae needn't know a thing about it. All for the best since it's high time she started acting like the Lady she is. And the Mother she will be.

She sweeps past her husband.

"Where are you going?"

"Into your dressing room."

". . .Why?"

Muffled, from the haberdashorial crypt, "Just as I thought!" And returning, dusting off her hands. "You haven't got a thing to wear."

"I am, if anything, overprovisioned when it comes to—"

"We're going shopping."

Henry has endured greater privations than standing in various awkward positions whilst a stooped little man measures him stem to stern. He eyes

Mae pleadingly, but she ignores him, absorbed as she is in bolts of mulberry worsted, lavender doeskin and snowy white quilting.

Bell Gardens
May 23, 1871

Dear Taffy,
Mr. Moore said the first two were practice runs. Third time the charm?
I hope. Especially as things appear to be heading in the right direction,
after all, the second one got a whole lot further than the first. Yes dear,
I am once more "*en ceinte.*" Don't tell anyone yet!

I'm terribly happy of course, but something is niggling at me . . .
Taffy, what if I can't give him an heir? What if this one turns out to be
a girl too? Not that I wouldn't be over the moon and terribly grateful
to have a healthy baby—not to mention a darling little Honourable
Miss Bell! But what if I keep on having girls? Do you know what
happens then? A big nothing. They get married off and the whole
estate dissolves when Henry dies. In a way that's worse than no child
at all. Lucky for me, my Henry is nothing like a previous one known as
"the Eighth"—ha-ha! But how unfair it would be to him. He hasn't said
a word but I can't help feeling he must worry, and that makes me worry,
and that can't be good for whoever is being concocted inside me.

Love,
Mae

"Havers, where ought I to address a note to Mr. Moore? I wish to convey my thanks to him." Mae does not need to explain herself to the help,
but she is keen to cover her tracks when it comes to confiding the
renewal of her hopes to Mr. Moore. And she just knows he'll be pleased
for her.

"Your Ladyship may write to him care of the Refuge for the Poor
Irish Among Us, Cowgate."

"Oh." A little moue of distaste. Oh well, fiddley-dee, Mae knew
from the start the old doctor was hardly *accoucheur* to the Queen. She
reminds herself that her own Daddy taught her not to be fooled by airs
and graces (mastering them for himself and his daughter was merely

"good business"). When it comes to childbirth, Mae does not flatter herself that she is any different from a peasant or an empress. Mr. Moore is experienced. And that counts for more than fashion. *I may have a pretty head on my shoulders, but it's a pretty good one too.*

The weeks speed by and her principal trunks are packed. Henry is keen to take the express train to London, otherwise known as the "Flying Scotsman," but Mae objects. "Really, at ten and a half hours, it's neither a day nor an overnight, I'll be a dishrag when I stagger onto the platform at King's Cross." All she need do now is decide which pretty little sacque to wear before bedtime.

Her new gown arrives in the nick of time. Jenners has sent a seamstress along to Bell Gardens to perform the alterations. The sinewy woman stands behind Mae, her hands on the laces—"Not too tight," says Mae. And with a wink in the mirror, "Precious cargo." The woman nods, and backs off the stays.

Bell Gardens
June 17, 1872

Dear Tiff-Taff,
I am closing in on the three-month mark and all is well. What's more I won't be showing 'til after the wedding-of-the-decade (We're off to London day after tomorrow!!!) so no need to dress around my delicate condition. Confession: I still haven't told Henry about said condition (or Clarissa, needless to say). I just can't bear to get his hopes up, poor lamb. I figure I'll keep the happy news under my (loose) corset 'til it's too big to fit . . .

This time it starts mid-morning. It is Cook's half-holiday, Clarissa has gone to church and taken Maid with her, and the new girl is off to purchase lace-edged handkerchiefs for Her Ladyship as the ones that Jenners sent were plain. So there is no one to help her. But neither is there anyone to take it away and burn it—and at twelve weeks there is so much less to push out.

The day is so bright it seems to blare in at the window. She lies, as though pinned by the sun to the bed, in a ball on her side with the corner of her pillow between her teeth like a bit, she knows this pain. Can see the edges of it. It is not infinite. Only God is that. Only Mary Corcoran is that, in her immortal soul. Up on her haunches, squatting now, gripping the headboard. Don't cry out.

The last of it leaves her . . . jelly, mercifully soft. She turns. Looks at the mess. And reaches in.

The curtains have been drawn. Mr. Moore rises from the chair at her bedside. Mae is still leaking at the eyes. But she is calm—clean too—and he is so kind.

"Thank you."

"Not at all, my dear."

"Don't tell my husband."

"He'll know by now, my dear."

She cries. Piteously, like a child past hoping anyone will hear.

He sits once more. "All will be well."

And he makes her a promise.

He has administered laudanum once more for the pain. It has begun to work. He sets the small blue bottle on her nightstand with instructions to the maid as to the use of the remaining two drops—he had rung for Maggie Sheehan but a new lass answered the summons. She nods, and Mr. Moore slips from the room.

The butler is in the passage.

"His Lordship awaits you in his study, Mr. Moore."

"Thank you, Havers."

"She is resting, Your Lordship, I've given her a dose for the pain, and I'll look in tomorrow to see how—"

"Am I to understand, Mr. Moore, that you were aware of my wife's condition?"

His Lordship is seated behind his desk. The doctor has not been invited to sit. "I was indeed, Your Lordship, Lady Marie took me into her confidence some weeks back, a good sensible lass is your wife, rest assured."

"I require no assurance as to Lady Marie's character, Mr. Moore, rather I require intelligence touching her health."

"Her health is excellent, Your Lord—"

"If it were, she would still be with child." His voice has wobbled. He clears his throat and all but chokes. The doctor steps forward, Henry rises, hands clasped behind his back.

"All in good time, Your Lordship, as I assured Lady Marie, I find no physical impediment to—"

"Henceforth you will report her every 'confidence' to me." He has spat it.

"Why, Lord Henry . . . that I cannot promise to do."

"Why not?"

"Lady Marie is my patient."

"She is my wife."

A hint of regret creeps into Mr. Moore's kindly expression as he looks at Lord Henry, but he does not speak.

Lord Henry tugs the bell cord.

"Havers, take Mr. Moore to the scullery and see he is given a meal before he takes his leave. And his fee."

Mr. Moore reaches into his coat and takes from the inside pocket a fountain pen. Uncaps it, pats his remaining pockets, comes out with a small ringed pad of paper. Setting it on His Lordship's desktop, he leans over and writes. Tears off the page carefully and hands it to His Lordship. "I don't expect Her Ladyship will require it, but in these cases it is as well to be prepared should there be severe cramping in the next few days."

Henry glances at the doctor's scrawl before dropping the scrap to his desk, resuming his seat and his book. He does not look up until he hears the click of his door open then close.

Mr. Moore had hoped to look in on Clarissa before leaving, but her parlour door is closed and the butler is hovering. He presses upon the doctor a pouch of coins, informs him that Miss Bell is otherwise engaged and escorts him to the scullery. There Mr. Moore chats with the new cook about her nephew's catarrh but does not stop to eat. He dons his old hat, leaves by the tradesmen's entrance and walks away up the paving stones of the mews where the wisteria cascades over garden walls on either side, carrying his medical bag.

———

Slow persistent tears. Her limbs are lead. Her inside is a stagnant pond choked with long grass and debris like hair caught in sticks.

A knock at the door.

"Darling? May I come in?"

She turns her face away.

"Did I wake you? Forgive me."

So pale.

"Mae. Darling." He sits in the chair lately vacated by the old quack. "Why didn't you tell me?"

She weeps. Speaks into the pillow. Slurred. "I didn't want to . . . disappoint you. Again."

"Oh my dearest."

"I'm sorry." She sobs.

"You have nothing for which to apologize."

She is back asleep almost immediately.

Henry retires to his brother's room. He will not ask Clarissa, and Clarissa will not ask Maid, and Maid will not ask Cook, and no one will ask Mae, what became of the "remains." Such as they might be.

Late, very late that night, Clarissa rises from her bed of stone.

She exits her room.

By the bluish light from the hall window, she walks with short, halting steps to the door of her late brother's room. Yes, Henry is asleep. Thence— it seems a longer way down the passage than it did those months ago, pain plays tricks with time and distance. She enters the marital chamber. Listens for her sister-in-law's breathing. Traverses the endless carpet toward the darker bulk of the bed . . . the nightstand. The bottle. *Bitter*.

Bliss.

Under cover of darkness, in a corner of Greyfriars Kirkyard hard by the high wrought-iron fence, Mr. Moore, his medical bag sitting open beside him, is on his knees with his back to the implacable angels, the marble scrolls and listing gravestones, inscriptions slowly filling with grime, shoaling with time. He sets aside the trowel with which he has dug a small hole, and lays to rest a tiny bundle wrapped in a new lace-edged handkerchief.

43

HENRY LOOKS IN ON HER the next morning. She appears . . . she is not worse. She is sitting up, she is tidy—her maid has been in—but her look to him is . . . slack. She is drawn with weeping. He has scant knowledge of such things and their aftermath—though more now, perhaps, than his sister would think fit. "How are you feeling, my darling?"

"I'm . . . I'll be fine."

He remembers the prescription. "Are you in any . . . discomfort?"

"'Discomfort'?"

"Pain."

"No. At least . . . Please send for Mr. Moore."

Alarm in the pit of his stomach—more acute for having become more frequent. "My dear, what is—?"

"I just want to talk to him."

"Ah."

"I'm not sick. I'm sad."

"Well then. I shall see to it."

Has he been hasty? Why shouldn't his wife have recourse to whatever comfort the old sawbones can provide? Henry had thought to seek out Clarissa's counsel but his sister has slept late again. He is glad. The rest will do her good. And after all, she is not called upon to weigh in on a matter involving husband and wife. That is up to him.

He repairs to his study to reflect and is on the point of relenting and sending for Mr. Moore but stays his hand in the act of reaching for the bell cord behind his study chair . . . What if Marie should once again confide in Moore, but this time something rather more grave? Is it possible Marie could descend to such depths of sorrow that she might contemplate . . . doing away with herself? Henry draws a deep breath, lets it out through his lips. It is unlike him to indulge in morbid fancy, and after all Moore has served the Bell family for decades, he would never keep such dire signs to himself. Besides, to whom will they turn next time if not to Mr. Moore? And there will assuredly be a next time. Unless . . . He straightens in his chair: what if his wife and her doctor have kept from him the fact that she is wholly incapable of producing a child? Shocked, he thrusts the thought from his mind and clenches his fists. Indeed it is just this sort of vile suspicion that germinates when the natural order of things is disrupted. Moore was wide, wide of the mark—*nay, he deceived me.* Henry smites his desk with the flat of his hands, setting the doctor's script to fluttering. He is Marie's husband. She belongs to him in the eyes of God and man. He it was she vowed to obey. She it was he vowed to cherish. He pulls the bell cord.

"Havers, tell Her Ladyship's maid to tell Her Ladyship, when once she wakes, that Mr. Moore is unavoidably detained at the Refuge."

"Very good, Your Lordship."

There are other doctors in Edinburgh. Physicians. As his wife well knows.

Mae opens her eyes. "Clarissa. How kind of you to look in on me."

Clarissa forms a smile. "Is there anything you require, Marie?"

Mae shakes her head. Tears. Reaches out, takes the narrow hand, careful not to squeeze too tightly. Whispers, "I'll do better, I promise." Tears.

Clarissa sits at the bedside until her sister-in-law falls asleep. Then she takes the tiny bottle and raises it to the light. A drop, perhaps two, remains. She closes her hand over it and leaves the room.

June 21, 1872

Dear Timothea,

I am no longer pregnant. Please encourage Daddy and everyone there to take it lightly. I will have another. There is nothing wrong with me, says the doctor.

Your Mae

❧

The freckled young man boarded a merchant vessel to Nova Scotia in late May, grateful and carrying the good wishes of all, including Miss Gourley.

Now that lady sits at the refectory table, writing. About her, several residents along with Miss Elliot and Moira—herself a former resident, now all-round sergeant-major—are tidying away the evening meal while children run wild prior to being rounded up, washed up and settled in bunks upstairs. Miss Gourley likes to work here amid the din, she finds it soothing and it helps her to focus when she has a particularly tricky bit of writing to do. As now. She is writing to Mr. Moore. She has worked shoulder to shoulder with him in the nearly two years since the Refuge got up and running. Discretion is the better part of valour, and Mr. Moore is valorous. From him she has learned to care for the women who come, all destitute, some drunk, some heavily pregnant; others in the early stages and clear-eyed enough to choose the path that best accords with their means and circumstance. She and Mr. Moore, Miss Elliot and Moira, help the women regardless of what they choose. In this the four of them break the law and risk penal servitude for life. Worst of all, they risk closure of the Refuge, for few if any subscribers to its upkeep would countenance the procuring of abortion. Many women choose to bear their child in the full knowledge they will part with it. Miss Gourley and Mr. Moore are practised in finding homes for "foundlings" and "orphans." There is no shortage of couples who crave to be parents but lack the biological good fortune. Now, however, she is writing to Mr. Moore about a particularly pressing case. Regarding a woman of her own age. And of similar station in life—

She tears up the note and starts again.

The Refuge
The Cowgate, Edinburgh
June 21, 1872

Dear Mr. Moore,
I have fallen pregnant and wish to bear the child with a view to placing it in a loving home, in the seeking out of which I would be most grateful for your assistance at the soonest . . .

~◦

Clarissa looks in on him. He failed to appear for dinner.
"You must keep up your strength, Henry."

He hasn't the energy to quibble. "I'll have something here. Tell Cook."

"Very well." She backs carefully through the doorway, leaning a little on the knob.

"Sister. Are you well?"

"I am tolerably well, brother."

"Is it your . . . rheumatism?"

She colours. He regrets instantly the intrusion.

She asks, "How is Marie?"

"She is. She is poorly."

"What does Mr. Moore say?"

"In point of fact, Moore says there is no cause for concern. In the long term. No need for him to return in fact. In the near term."

"Ah. Good."

"Aye."

"And she is not . . . in any . . . discomfort?"

"No."

"Good. I believe Mr. Moore was able to relieve her discomfort quite effectively on this occasion. As on the last."

"Quite."

"I suppose at the first sign of any discomfort, we might send for Mr. Moore."

"That will not be necessary. He left this." Henry lifts the script between two fingers, lets it drop again.

Clarissa nods. Frowns. "I'll tell Cook to make you a plate."

"No meat."

"As you wish."

The door has almost closed on her when he says, "Sister. Thank you."

"Of course, I have observed your late aversion to flesh—"

"No, Clarissa, I mean, thank you for your kind concern. For my wife." He swallows.

She smiles. "She is my sister, Henry."

When he looks in next morning, she is . . . he hardly knows how to describe it—"inert"? She is as though insensible to his presence. Still abed, and staring at the wall opposite.

Her maid enters. Fails to entice her Ladyship with a sip of honied tea or a taste of scone. Leaves.

"When is Mr. Moore coming?" she whispers.

"As to that. Mr. Moore has his hands full . . . with the less fortunate."

"He's given up on me."

"What can you mean?"

"He'd rather spend his time looking after dirty little . . ."

"Hush, now."

Mae can't seem to fully wake up. She does not wonder what day it is. Or whether it is night-time. Does not look in the mirror. Does not dress. Nothing matters. It doesn't hurt. It doesn't anything.

She is young, she will recover. Mr. Moore said as much—for all Henry dismissed him, the man knows his subject. And as his sister pointed out, it is a set-back only—at least that is what she said the first time—the *second* time, that is, devil take it. Surely it is a good sign that Marie is in no physical discomfort—primarily for her sake, of course, but for Henry's too as it saves him writing to Mr. Moore—the scrap of paper has disappeared from his desk and he cannot for the life of him remember the name of the drug. No doubt swept into the dustpan along with a dear speckled fragment of plover egg by the overzealous Maid.

Clarissa is prudent. One drop, no more. Under the tongue at bedtime. Every other night.

Weeks.

She hears him enter but does not turn her head on the pillow.

"My darling."

She turns. He looks flushed—has he become ill while she's been wrapped up in her own misery? "Are you all right Henry? Why don't you go out and get some air. Take Mr. Baxter and go bird-watching."

He strokes her brow. It is the longest sentence she has uttered since . . . A little colour has entered her cheek. He ventures onto a limb, "I have a notion."

She reaches, listlessly, for his hand. "Mm?"

"Let us go to Boston."

Her eyes fill, overflow. "I can't."

"My dear, whyever not?"

"I can't go home a failure."

He resists the urge to retreat for fear of setting off her grief. He squares his shoulders. "You are no such thing. But if My Lady refuses to go to Boston, then Boston shall come to My Lady."

He discerns the hint of a smile. She is still a lass, after all, and wants guidance and gay prospects. They missed Hawley's wedding (it is not lost on Henry that his wish in that regard was granted as though by a spiteful genie) but: "As your lord and master, I hereby command you to write to Mrs. Carter Blanchard, also known as 'Taffy'. . ." She smiles outright. ". . . inviting her and her esteemed husband to visit post-haste at our expense by way of belated wedding gift. Send a cable if you like."

This time when he leaves her room, she is sitting up with her desk on her lap, writing.

Taffy will be tickled pink! Mae has decided a letter will do fine. After all, she'll need time to prepare—for one thing, she'll have to train up that new cook or find a replacement. And this is a perfect opportunity to get another hot-water pipe put in. There is so much to do, she cannot believe how much time she's wasted!

Clarissa endures the return of the builders to No. One Bell Gardens. The noise they make is joyful insofar as it heralds a return to the field on the part of her sister-in-law (O Lord hear my prayer). Clarissa might quail at the thought of the upcoming American invasion but begrudges nothing that conduces to her sister-in-law's well-being. As for her own well-being, Clarissa's increasingly frequent absences at breakfast draw little notice, and what with overseeing the latest round of upheaval, Marie appears to have forgotten her insistence that Clarissa consult a newfangled physician. Clarissa has been careful to give her family no cause to fret. They know her rheumatism comes and goes and, if they think about it at all in these heady days, may content themselves in observing that it appears for now to have gone . . .

Never more than one drop. Nightly.
Why, Mr. Baxter, what brings you to the Alps?

Over the next couple of weeks two letters arrive from Taffy, borne in by Havers on the silver salver, and, knowing her friend wrote them before receiving the invitation, Mae reads them with the relish of dramatic irony. At the end of the fourth week she stations herself in the foyer and when Havers enters with the post, snatches Taffy's letter and dashes upstairs, for she knows this will be the one!

Henry has seen her flash past his half-open study door. He gives her a few minutes' privacy with her correspondence, then mounts to their room, already drawing up in his mind an itinerary of points of interest for their American guests—and of course they shall wish to meet the Farquhars and Josey and . . . why not a reprise of the jolly dinner party? He rubs his hands together, pleased with himself, faltering only slightly over whether or not to invite Rosamund—Miss Gourley, that is—but of course they must invite her along with the rest of "the gang" as Mae would put it and, smiling, he enters the room, "Mae I've had a thought."

She is slumped in her chair, weeping, the letter trailing from one limp hand. He is alarmed. The death announced in this letter will be human, her dog is already dead, it will be her father this time, unless . . . hold on, was there not a pony . . . ?

"My dear. What is it—?" He has nearly added *this time.*

"Daddy got elected to the state senate."

"Oh. Well done, he. Darling, are not these glad tidings?"

"It's Taffy."

With the wind knocked from him, he drops to his knee, reaches for her hand.

Weeping, Mae says, "She's pregnant."

Within only hours, Mae is able to write an affectionate letter of sincere congratulations to her dearest friend. And to assure her that any need on Mae's part for consolation has been more than answered by this wonderful news of Taffy's pregnancy.

———

Quiet descends once more as Mae sinks along with her hopes.

Clarissa supposes she ought to be relieved now that the prospect of visitors has been quashed. But the renewed silence upstairs makes the recent racket seem, in retrospect, like a reprieve. Her brother, too, is silent. There is nowt to do but wait. Clarissa is practised in the art.

Sherry. "Thank you, brother."

Whisky for him.

"How is it with you, sister?"

"Tolerably well, brother."

"Only 'tolerably'?"

"In fact I am quite well, brother."

"I am glad."

Clarissa sent Havers with Mr. Moore's script to the chemist in Princes Street to fetch the second bottle of laudanum "for Her Ladyship." A doctor's note is not required to purchase opiates—even so, Clarissa dispatched the butler to Leith for the third bottle, "lest any form a misapprehension as to Her Ladyship having developed a dependency." "Very good, Madam."

She never imbibes directly from the bottle, even when a single dose remains. Small proprieties.

And never more than two drops.

Why, Mr. Baxter . . .

August draws to a wet and chilly close.

44

SEPTEMBER DAWNS with a golden warmth as though in compensation for its grim predecessor. But in Henry's wife's bedroom—for so it is, he having essentially removed to Bertram's room. (Funny, that. After a lifetime of thinking of it as "my eldest late brother's room" it has become "Bertram's." As though Henry's late trials have caused a comradeliness to spring up between him and his dead brother. He is put in mind of stories about prisoners of war who befriend sparrows or spiders in a bid to retain sanity.) Point being: in his wife's bedroom the curtains remain drawn against lambent September.

Marie will recover her spirits, she always has. And Henry would not be the first gentleman whose wife is prone to bouts of invalidism and therefore indisposed for prolonged periods when it comes to certain aspects of a full married life.

He is frequently from home during the day, making the most of Josey's scant free time and . . . In point of fact, Rosamund—Miss Gourley, that is—has been kind enough to receive him on a couple of occasions whereupon he has attempted to make himself useful, manfully transporting a scuttle to the ash heap out back, lifting an urchin from the bowels of an old flue in the floor of the attic.

But when he called last week he was told Miss Gourley was "off on a sabbatical." Henry was moved: Miss Gourley, tirelessly improving her mind yet again, that she might decant its contents for the benefit of those less fortunate. Really, is any woman—apart from his wife of course—Miss Gourley's equal?

He was donning his hat, on his way out to consult a taxidermist when his sister summoned him from within her parlour.

He entered affably with no show of impatience but for his hat revolving in his hands . . .

Only to find himself agape at Clarissa's opening salvo. A "suggestion," she called it, before thrusting at him a circular for a certain establishment.

"She requires a complete change of scene, Henry."

"Of course I am in favour of a change of scene—"

"Of the sort to be had at a private hospital."

"I was thinking more along the lines of a jaunt to the Lake District."

"You have denied her a doctor."

"I have done nothing of the—"

"She has begged to see Mr. Moore."

"Damn Mr. Moore."

"He is not the only doctor in Edinburgh, in fact I have it from Marie herself, a physician just round the corner in Ainsley Place—"

"Moore said there is nothing physically wrong with her."

"Weeps morning to night. Keeps abed round the clock. Glittering of eye, pale of cheek. This is your portrait of health?"

"Out of the question."

"A stay at a therapeutic establishment—"

"A madhouse by any other name." He tosses the circular onto the occasional table.

"I could hope as much for myself."

"What? Why?"

"A rest cure, Henry. You need not tremble and look pale."

"Then why not avail yourself of this remedy, why seek to foist it—?"

"Until my work is done, there shall be no spa holiday for me in the Grampians or—anywhere else. Your wife, on the other hand, may benefit. And return to you restored and ready to resume her own work."

A pause. He knows what she means by "work." He rises.

"Brother, forgive me, you may think I exceed my brief but your wife is the future of Fayne, and she is failing. In more ways than one."

He quits the parlour.

Clarissa tucks the circular away in her work basket. Feels for the small blue bottle. Grasps it. Lets it go.

In the foyer Henry shoves his hat at Havers and climbs the stairs.

Braves the bedroom.

She has listened to his idea and exhibited the first sign of life in two months in the denouncing of it. He reflects that his raising of ideas, like the sending up of clay birds to be shot, appears to be a reliable remedy where his wife is concerned—he must merely withstand the report of her gun.

Mae has gotten out of bed, plunked onto her vanity stool and taken charge of her hair, gutting each braid with a finger. She takes up her silver tail-comb and, with its point, changes the part in her hair from centre to left, then, swivelling, flings the comb across the room where it spears into the wall. He waits. Blinks. She has made it plain she does not wish to remove to Fayne.

"How could you even suggest such a thing?!"

Wrathful tears—he decides this may be a good sign.

"You said yourself there's no one there and it's in the middle of nowhere!"

"It is situated on upwards of twelve thousand acres of—"

"If your country seat is anything like your 'house in town'—especially the state it was in when we first got here—then why don't you just bury me alive?!" The brush, the vanity stool, the commode (empty). Crash, bang, smash.

In her parlour, Clarissa hears the ruckus overhead, followed by abrupt silence. Perhaps he has murdered her. Not but what it would clear the way for a new Lady Bell.

"Oh Henry, I'm sorry." Weak with spent temper. Face in her hands. "I'm horrid."

"You are nothing of the kind."

"I wouldn't blame you for hating me."

"I love you."

"Look at the state of me." Mae has of course spared the mirror—seven years bad luck, as if the past year hasn't been enough. "I look like the wreck of the *Hesperus*."

"You are beautiful. And brave."

She weeps. Cooler tears now. "I don't know how you can ever forgive me."

"There is nothing to forgive."

He opens his arms.

A break from Bertram.

Henry's demeanour at breakfast the following morning might reassure the most exacting sister. But Clarissa no longer takes that meal.

October 14, 1872

Dear Taffy,

I haven't told Henry. I'm even scared to tell you. I feel as if with each one, there's less to hold on to in there. I thought I'd be happy to be expecting again, but I'm scared. I'm sorry, sweetheart, you should only be reading pleasant things in your happy condition. Like Annie says, *Think nice thoughts*. Oh pray that it lives, Taffy. Pray it's a boy. Pray that I

She crumples it and drops it into the fire.

———

After yet another dinner alone with his sister, Henry sits in her parlour with the circular in his hands. Clarissa betrayed no hint of smugness when she produced it at his request. Thoroughly decent, is Clarissa. A brick. She and Rosamund both. Place the world in their hands, why not? His own are weary.

"'Morecombe Downs,'" he reads aloud. "'A well-appointed house in the Grampians near Perth. Formerly the estate of the Eighth Duke of Margrave.'"

"And much nicer than ever it was when he was in residence, judging from the literature."

"Hmm. 'Shuttlecock'. . ."

"And therapeutic waters."

"'Electric bathing.' Is that quite safe?" His lips form half a smile. "The alienist's name is Finch."

"Marie," says Clarissa.

Henry looks up at the *non sequitur*, then turns round. His wife is in the doorway. She is in her nightgown, her hair is . . . in some disarray, but her demeanour is calm. She holds his gaze with her deep green eyes and places a hand on her belly. "Henry, I'm scared."

He goes to her. Enfolds her. Feels her trembling. He places his lips close to her ear and, because he knows she believes him, he is able to say and to believe in turn, "I promise you, my darling. We will have a son. And we will have a daughter. And they will be healthy and beautiful, and grow strong and proud, and live to honour our memory after we are dust."

Clarissa watches the lovers retreat from the parlour.

She rings for Maid. "Bring me my writing desk."

Clarissa pens a note to Mrs. Knox.

45

PREPARATIONS FOR THEIR DEPARTURE have resembled more those for a flight before Napoleon's army than a retreat to his country seat, but Henry knows better than to query the inclusion of Mae's three trunks.

In the dining room, Havers sets out a light travelling breakfast of oatmeal, rolls and preserves. In the scullery, Cook packs a hamper as buttress against "train victuals." Outside, Sanders holds the team as Pugsley lashes the last trunk to the roof of the carriage.

Fayne House
October 16, 1872

Dear Miss Clarissa,
We are well as I pray you be well also. In the case of Her Ladyship it is well a young woman as has had several miscarrys to rest. Not only that, but there be in the water at Fayne or mayhap the soyl or the ayr or mayhap all three that which helps the womb to hold. Byrn has nayr lost a calf nor lamb nor kid nor any other such and begging pardon for not meaning to give offence we are no so different when it comes to it and I do not know but what it may help to bring Her Ladyship here.

Your loyal servant and loving nurse,
Tabitha Knox

Clarissa showed Henry the letter the moment it arrived three days earlier.

Henry broached the subject with his wife as to the merits of country air and pure water, leaving aside any mention of calving or lambing. He gave her the choice. Edinburgh, London or Fayne.

She chose Fayne.

"My darling, I would not for the world insist."

"When can we leave?"

"Howsoever soon you wish."

"How many words is that?"

Women are variable and fathomless. As is the sea. Henry knew better than to resist a favourable tide and a fair wind.

Now Clarissa draws aside the net curtain and watches from the parlour window as Henry hands his wife up into the carriage. It pulls away with a spray of gravel. Silence. Were it not for her rheumatism, she would lean gratefully back against her chair.

Never more than three drops.

———

Mae did not so much choose Fayne as reject London and Edinburgh. Bell Gardens was already the scene of repeated failure; as for removing to London, well . . . just imagine fitting up a house and hosting the cream of society, many of whom would come to know of her condition, only to—*think nice thoughts.*

Mae is young, but her body is engaged in an ancient undertaking. Complex beyond comprehension. Wise beneath wisdom. And who knows but what the cells of her body, having consorted with all matter across time as do everyone's, managed to sway her waking mind. In any case, Old Wisdom won out.

Now the train leaves behind the Edinburgh skyline, its spires, battlements and monuments, and soon enough is chugging south-ward. They pass in and out of beautiful valleys, and Mae passes in and out of sleep. Henry is solicitous, waking her only to ensure she is well, under the pretext of admiring a castle ruin or nestled village. Finally they disembark at a sleepy station in a small town and board a post coach, all seats in which Henry has purchased, and the scenery com-mences to pass more slowly. Mae takes a polite interest and ceases to inquire, "Are we there?" All grist for a cheerful letter to Taffy, for Mae has pledged inwardly to write nothing gloomy to her friend. Taffy is "due" early in the New Year. As Mae is carried farther and farther away from civilization, she nestles ever closer to her husband. And it occurs to her it wouldn't hurt if she were a little more chipper for poor dear Henry, too.

Thus, once out of the hills and through a patch of woodland Henry called a "forest," into yet another charming village—this one couched on a riverbank—and after the coach clatters over a bridge and labours up a slope toward a tall white stone; as it emerges onto the crest of a wind-swept expanse of heather and bracken and brush, and there comes into view on the stark horizon an old stone mansion, it is on the tip of her tongue, as the house looms closer, to exclaim, "What a lovely old ruin, shall we stop and look?" when Henry says, "We're home."

Sanders pulls up on the cindered forecourt. Henry alights, turns and hands her down from the carriage. The household has gathered.

Mrs. Knox and Cook curtsey, Cruikshank bobs, Mrs. Mungo, big
with child, does her best to follow suit, Mr. Mungo bows, a stable hand
shuffles and snatches off his cap.

Mae surveys the meagre rank—*That can't be everyone, can it?* Henry,
as though hearing her thoughts, smiles and says, "Byrn will be about
somewhere."

Fayne House
October 21, 1872

Dear Taff,
I have barely removed my hat, having been whisked directly up the
grand staircase and into the "family wing" by the housekeeper whom
I judge to be somewhere between forty and one hundred years of age.
Yes, I am at the vaunted Bell family seat . . .

Over in the stone bothy with the ramshackle thatch, Mrs. Knox seeks
out Byrn.

"He's brought her."

"Why?"

"For her health."

"Sickly?"

"Nay. 'Tis bairns. She cannae keep them. I reckon the air might do
her good."

"Air be nowt to do wi' it." He turns back to his seedlings. Commences
humming.

Henry had hardly expected Marie would join him for dinner the first
night, but here she is, a vision of freshness in the baronial dining room
where she takes her place at the far end, suppressing a giggle as she does
so, and shading her eyes, "Henry, is that you way down there?" He
laughs and hails her from the head of the table. "Your Ladyship is welcome to sit at my right hand, no protocols will be breached, no heads
will roll."

"Your Lordship, I would not dream of it. This is my place, is it not?
At your exalted foot?"

He wants her more than ever. "Claret, I think, Cruikshank." And luxuriates in the knowledge that he can wait. They have their whole lives ahead of them.

Mae watches the serving girl pour and once she's retreated, leans forward a little—as if those extra few inches of proximity might do anything to close the sixteen-foot distance between them. "Henry, it isn't decent."

He flushes. Has she read his mind? She continues, "We'll need to engage a man to serve at table."

"Oh. If you like," he says.

Cruikshank returns with a cauliflower cheese for Henry and a plate of black pudding and a glass of stout for Mae. "Mrs. Knox's orders, m'um," the girl squeaks before scuttling off.

Tonight, Henry's happiness exceeds that which felled him in Fanny's courtyard. After dinner he envelops his wife in a tartan rug and settles her by his side on a bench before the blazing hearth of the great hall— "In former days, we roasted whole venison here."

"I can believe that."

He strokes her cheek, murmurs, "Well, Your Ladyship, what do you think of Fayne?" And is enchanted by her answer:

"Oh Henry, it's like a fairy tale!"

Taffy, it's like a fairy tale, complete with a drafty castle, a motherly woman who might be a witch, and a dreary landscape that appears to be slumbering under a spell . . .

She thinks better of it, however, and starts over on a more positive note.

Fayne House
October 25, 1872

Dearest Taff,
There is no running water except in the scullery. Need I say more? Probably not, but just try and stop me. . . .

In keeping with her pledge to write nothing gloomy, Mae leaves out the portrait of the "Blighted Heir" because it is really quite sad when you think about it, for all Henry laughs. The poor man driven off for the crime of having been born with a tail. They call it a portrait, and it is framed, but it's completely blank.

On the whole her resolution serves her well, for it is soon apparent she will need all the good humour she can muster to weather the ways of Fayne. Case in point, Cruikshank.

"Cruikshank, go scrub your face then come back and show me the result."

"Aye, Your Ladyship."

The creature ruckles off out the door. And returns ten minutes later looking the very same.

Henry, meanwhile, is happy. He is no longer afraid of his wife. He is once more loving. Even playful.

"Oh my, Henry, this butter is so good, is it from the old white cow?"

"'Tis from the bog."

Mae gets busy. She explores the village. There is little to purchase, and the Inn at the Kenspeckle Hen isn't exactly the Douglas Hotel. Moreover, no one will speak to her except in a humble mumble. There is not a single social equal within fifty miles. In desperation, she attends both churches on a single Sunday. Both are Protestant, alas, but the minister is a widower and the vicar is not. "'Twas the vicar's Missus left the card, Your Ladyship," Mrs. Knox reminds her. "Will I send Cruikshank with a note?"

Fayne
October 27, 1872

Chère Taffée,

I told Hank I would stay on condition I be given free rein—and wallet—to spruce up the place. He agreed, the lamb. My lord and master can deny me nothing, even the freedom to return to town, so you see I am far from a prisoner, and healthy as a horse. Still, say a little prayer for me, dearest, a novena if you can manage it. There's no darn church around here. Not a real one. Not an alabaster Mary in sight.

How I wish I could lay eyes on you, especially now, sweetheart, that you are a ship in full sail. I just know pregnancy becomes you.

Although I giggle when I try to picture you with a belly!

There isn't much Mae can do at the moment about the house's grim exterior—the cinders, alone!—but for now she orders the front steps to be swabbed and the great funereal urns to either side of the portico, scrubbed. Cruikshank and the stable hand go at them with brushes and lye but, as with Cruikshank's own visage, the grime seems to be permanent.

She turns her attention to the interior and establishes a stronghold in the drawing room which hasn't seen a lick of finish since Elizabethan times; which is to say it is a nightmare of indigo and heraldry. A team arrives from Edinburgh and is quartered on the fourth floor in the disused servants' wing. Henry retreats from the line of fire into his study. He trembles when she announces her plans to open a new front in the dining room. "Henry, since when is drabness synonymous with masculinity? Look at peacocks! Look at Sicilian men!" "Quite," replies Henry, his first and last word on the subject; defeat with honour.

. . . The back of the house seems to occupy a geographical zone all its own. I know that sounds cuckoo. There is a willow tree, despite the absence of a stream into which to weep. There is an actual lawn; soft, and freshly rolled by some serf or other whom I have yet to clap eyes on. But the garden is the real jewel in the crown of Fayne. And now I understand why the deer might clamour to get past its walls. The vegetables are delicious. It must have something to do with the fertilizer used by the phantomly serf. It works, even if it does smell disgusting when freshly spread. Whatever it is, it produces the sweetest carrots and peas, the zestiest radishes and the creamiest mashed potatoes. I am growing fat around the central fatness which is my baby . . .

46

FALL CLOSES IN, the fires are kept going and Mae savours the sense of being marooned with her husband whilst her baby grows inside her. The garden is harvested, much of the bounty put up in jars and cooked down into jellies and jams and relish, and for days a homely heavenly aroma pervades the "manse."

On the last night of October, Mae is drawn from her bed by a dancing amber light at her window. In the yard below, just off the forecourt, she sees a blazing bonfire. Round it are gathered several shapes—she makes out Mrs. Knox and Cruikshank, Cook, a stable boy, Henry is there too, standing a little apart, and . . . a tall figure. Human, to be sure, but somehow uncanny in its movements. Supple as a reed, it capers before the flames, elbows flaring, knees kicking up. She watches, strangely lulled, until she grows drowsy and the fire subsides.

In the morning, she is surprised to feel beneath her pillow, something stiff and . . . She draws it out. A leafy twig. "Henry, wake up. You need to speak to the maid."

"Hm? Oh." He takes it and twirls it between finger and thumb. "A rowan sprig."

"What's it doing under my pillow?"

"She'll have put it there a-purpose."

"Why on earth?"

"To guard against the Wee Folk." Taffy, I'm not kidding you. And Burn is the name of the old gardener who must toil day and night, considering he is also in charge of "stock and flock." I fear he is senile, for when I wished him "Good morning" today, he bade me "God even." And vice versa this evening when I sought him out again just to be sure. Not to mention those were his only intelligible words, the rest is gibberish, poor soul. He lopes from "byre" to "bothy" singing nonsense songs. Did I say "old," Taffy? He looks to be going on dead. He is bald as a cue ball, toothless, and doesn't look as though he'd stand up in a strong breeze but I saw him dancing like a pagan round the fire on Halloween night—they call it something else, I forget what. And he is terribly strong. He carries a yoke with buckets full of muck he dumps on the garden. I hold my nose when I see him coming. I told Henry that whatever he's paying old Burn—sorry, "Byrn," as Henry corrected me (he claimed he could hear the difference!)—he ought to double it, for I've never tasted such vegetables, not to mention milk, butter, cream and cheese. All this on a barren moor. Apparently he gardens according to "the old ways" whatever that means. I'll bet the estate could support itself if Henry were to muster a pinch of agricultural science, add a dash of economics and expand the garden to a farm, the cattle to a dairy, and the henhouse to a barracks. I've just now heard the supper bell—I fly!

So far so good. And Mae should count herself lucky to be still pregnant but it is perhaps a measure of her recovered spirits that she chafes a little inwardly. Really, there are only so many excursions with wicker hampers and field glasses a girl can undertake. Even—or especially—in a tweed walking ensemble. On each occasion Henry promises a treat which turns out to be some bird or other—"See it? Just to the left of the alder."

"Oh, I see it now." Her first real lie to her husband.

Yes, there are trees. They grow in "copses" within "dells"—sounds prettier than "gullies." And once you get pine sap on a skirt, it's fit for the poor box.

Henry has helped her over numberless stiles, and she has learned neither to fear nor hope for rapport with sheep. Nuala, the pregnant blue-eyed border collie, is apparently not for patting, and seems constantly to be nipping at her hem and—"She's trying to herd me, Henry!"

"She is keeping you to the path, my darling."

"What path, I don't see a path."

"Just so. A foot wrong in some stretches might result in a nasty soaking. Or worse."

Whole huge tracts of the fen are strangely like a desert, you can lose your way if you're not careful because apart from the tall white stone that has a habit of sinking behind the heaving landscape, there are no landmarks.

"It is a moor, my dear."

"Mrs. Knox calls it the fen."

He smiles indulgently and continues in that pedantic way she is having more trouble enduring because it makes her feel claustrophobic— like one of those bugs he's forever catching in jars. "These vasts are, strictly speaking, moorlands. They encompass, of course, bogs of one sort and another and at one time there were indeed fens—"

"Oo, I just caught a whiff of . . . Oh dear, that's quite a strong smell."

He chuckles. "I suppose I no longer notice."

She wrinkles her nose. "That's what he puts on the garden."

"I shouldn't wonder."

"He gets it from the bog?"

"Byrn calls it *sùil-chruthaich*."

"What does that mean?"

"'Eye of Creation.'"

She shivers. "Let's go back to the house, I can smell rain now."

He offers his arm.

His wife was right. The skies open soon after they step through the great doors.

The reverend's wife is pretty, though some years older than Mae— at least Fanny's age—and childless. Never a happy fate, but at least Mrs. Haas's entire future does not turn upon her fruitfulness, unlike Mae's. The first visit was almost too congenial, warmed as it was by a potent cordial of Mrs. H's own making; which Mae declined. Mae reciprocates with tea in order to try her out, so to speak, on the premises. She then invites the Reverend and Mrs. Reverend for luncheon with Henry present. It goes off without a hitch but there can be no question of a real friendship.

Mrs. Haas is perfectly nice, in fact really rather sweet with a tinkling laugh and sparkling eyes, and if they had met under other circumstances they might very well have become friends. But Mrs. Haas is too conscious of Lady Marie's status; and Lady Bell expects no less, which puts Mae in a bind because she is dying for a friend. Thus, Mae bites back giggles and Mrs. Haas struggles to subdue her Northumbrian accent until the state of the weather, the forthcoming church jumble sale, and the wisdom of Mrs. Beeton have been exhausted. The women cannot talk about children, because neither has any, and Mae discourages Mrs. Haas's impulse to fawn and query as to plans following "the great event"—for more reasons than one. Still, the pretty little woman unfailingly brings Mae a "posy" from her own garden and an extra rosebud for "the future wee one."

She passes the twelve-week mark.

Henry is perched obligingly upon a newly acquired chair of spinal dignity but doubtful comfort and Mae is waxing lyrical about the new

Turner yellow of the drawing room when she stops suddenly, wide-eyed, and places both hands on her belly. He shoots to his feet.

She says calmly, "He kicked." And starts to cry.

"Shall I—? I'll ring for Knox, I'll order a carriage—"

"Henry, no, it's all right. I'm crying because I'm happy."

He sags with relief.

She smiles at him. "Aren't you?"

"My darling, I could not be better pleased."

"'Pleased' is what you are when Cook serves you those awful mushy peas."

"I am happy." He holds her close to cover the catch in his voice—turns out it is rather a tricky word, *happy*.

Henry ceases to sleep with her for fear of "disrupting things" and goes off at dawn with his specimen case and field glasses. He doesn't invite her along anymore—not that she'd go, but a girl likes to be asked. When he is in, he tiptoes about. Hushed voices prevail. There is no one to talk to. Cruikshank is hopeless, Mae can't understand a word Mrs. Mungo says, Knox is old and Cook doesn't come into it.

She finds him in his study, bent over a magnifying glass.

"I want my maid after all, Henry, send for her, would you?"

"Of course, my darling, though you might make inquiries for a local girl, lest your maid decline to remove permanently to Fayne."

". . . We haven't removed permanently to Fayne either."

He looks up from his magnifying glass, trained on the wing of a big green bug.

"Do you mean to say you do not desire to reside at Fayne?"

"Henry, I love you. And I love . . . that you love this old house—"

"It is not merely the house, it is—"

"Oh I know, it's the whole swamp too—"

"Bog."

"And the lovely fields you can't walk on."

"I shouldn't dream of insisting, darling, but you might come to love it as I do."

"I know I will, I can't wait to have a jolly house party."

He smiles through the urge to wince.

"You know, this room is even gloomier than your study at Bell Gardens."

"Is it." Back to his magnifying glass.

She looks about at the heavy wainscotting, the time-darkened oak panels, the coffered ceiling, it's like a great big coffin—*nice thoughts*. "A cheerful picture or two might spruce it up."

"I've ordered a stuffed kestrel."

As November draws to a grey and rainy close, Mae feels a morbid weight settle on the house like the cloud that seems never to lift from the moor.

"Knox, I'm just about ready to get the vicar's wife back up here with her bottle of cordial. I need a friend!"

Mrs. Knox has taken to helping Her Ladyship with her evening toilette, and now she replaits the girl's thick dark tresses. "Why there's His Lordship, and perhaps Miss Clarissa might—"

"A friend in the American sense, not in the Jane Austen sense of an ally or relation, an honest-to-goodness girlfriend."

"Of course, Your Ladyship."

"You know what I mean."

"Och aye, Madam, Miss Austen is most unsuitable, being herself dead."

Mae laughs. "Oh Knoxy, shed fifty years or so and you and I would be bosom friends!"

Mrs. Knox twinkles. "I thank Your Ladyship, but I hail from peasant stock, whereas you—"

"I hail from cattle thieves and potato farmers, and a Daddy so ornery even the typhoid didn't want him on the ship to America."

Perhaps it is the Moon which wakes Knox from solid sleep a few hours later up in the old nursery. She rises more from habit than apprehension, accustomed as she has been to taking any opportunity to ensure the well-being of her charges. She lights her lamp and descends to Her Ladyship's chamber.

Entering, she crosses to where the great bed sits moored in the middle of the room, draws aside the bed curtain and raises the lamp. She is taken aback by what she sees. The young face is beautiful, certainly, but ghastly too and beaded with perspiration.

The eyes open. Green as emeralds. They focus. "Knox? I feel funny."

"All's well, My Lady."

Knox sets down the lamp and presses her cotton sleeve to Her Ladyship's brow, not only to absorb the moisture there but to deter Her Ladyship's gaze from following her own as, with the other hand Mrs. Knox draws back the bedclothes—*blood*. Dear God. She draws the blanket up once more.

"Tut, tut, My Lady, you're drenched with a night fever, so you are, I'll make you fresh in no time."

"Knox?" The young woman holds her hand up, fingertips glistening red.

"'Tis nowt, M'Lady, only a wee bit of blood."

The lovely face crumples, she emits a whimper on the way to keening.

"There, there, My Lady. Only a spot, do you hear?" Wiping Her Ladyship's hand.

Mae grapples onto Knox's gaze. "How much?"

"Blood always looks like more."

"Blood only?"

"Blood only." What prayer can Knox say to make this so? "Had you any pain in the night, My Lady?"

"No."

"That is a very good sign."

The girl wipes her tears.

Knox removes the sheets from the bed with minimal disturbance to its occupant, bundles them in one motion and places them on the floor outside the ring of lamplight. From the armoire she fetches a linen, from the fireside a basin of water, and sets to sponging the blood from the thighs, careful to keep the girl from turning over and incurring even the least abdominal strain.

"You've done this sort of thing before, Knoxy."

"Aye, Your Ladyship."

"Who for? For *whom*?"

"Why for His Lordship's mother."

The girl takes this in. Then reaches up and pulls the old housekeeper down into a hard hug.

At length free to rise, Knox allows her hand to rest on the swell of the young woman's bare belly.

It is a strong hand, trellis of bone wound with veins, well-clothed in flesh; fingers clever, each tip of which is like a head packed with skill and discernment—the whole hand is listening for life.

"There, there, My Lady, all will be well. But you must remain all night, and for the next while, here in your bed, and I shall do for you, do you understand?"

She nods.

"Lady Marie . . . I've seen a woman bleed as much and more yet be delivered in due course of a healthy babe."

"Really?"

"Aye. 'Really.'" Knox strokes her brow. "I'll be straight back, Madam."

The girl closes her eyes.

Knox bends to retrieve the soiled bundle. She is at the door when Lady Marie says, "Knox, I love you."

Mrs. Knox stops, turns halfway and gives a nod before pulling the door softly to behind her. The girl has gone straight to her heart.

Mrs. Knox passes through the scullery and out to the wash house. Oft has she accomplished a full day's worth of work thanks to an implacably white moon, badgering stains from linens and dirt from corners that escape scrutiny in the light of day. Thus she needs no candle by which to read the sheets that she spreads on the floorboards. Blood—darkened now and crusting with exposure to air—but blood only. Just to be sure, she goes over the immense stain with her fingers. She closes her eyes and gives thanks to Brigid—not *Saint* Brigid, this Brigid is older than the saints. She follows with a hasty sign of the cross so as to placate any divine Christian emissary as might be watching.

. . . Taffy, I am in bed. I have had a very little bleeding. Mrs. Knox tucked me in last night and says not to worry or get up. The former is much harder to obey than the latter. She said all would be well, and sure enough I felt the baby move again this morning. My husband and his ancient—and aromatic!—old man-of-all-work carried me downstairs on a chair and I am presently supine on a new silk divan in the (delightful Turner-yellow!) drawing room. And I learned the nicest thing: Mrs. Knox delivered Henry, and Clarissa too. This puts her in walking distance of sixty!

———

Lord Henry takes a mug of willow-bark tea from the hands of his old nurse. She has brought it along with the reassurance that his wife is still with child.

"Knox, I know it is happy news, but . . ." That word again.

Mrs. Knox waits for him to collect himself, before speaking. "Fayne has bred strong Bells for better than four centuries. Look at you, Lord Henry. Born and weaned at Fayne House. And survived when your town-bred brothers did not. There's a blessing in the land."

He speaks into his hands. "But my mother never suffered as my wife does now. Never lost a child before it was born, never mind twice. Nay, thrice."

"She be yet young."

"She is not strong, Tabby, in her nerves. Not like us."

"More's the reason to trust to Fayne."

Mae stays supine all the next week, her feet, fairy-tale-like, forbidden to touch the floor. She is compliant. Uncomplaining. She has made peace with chamber pot and bedpan. Henry reads aloud to her for hours, and she sleeps like the baby she is determined to have.

47

I followed a smell which felt like a song 'til I came to a moonlit dell . . .

ALL AT ONCE she is at her window. The moon is immense, all breast and belly, low in the sky. Summoning her. Surely this is a dream. If she looks behind her, she will see herself lying in her bed asleep. She shivers, recalls Annie at home telling her, "When you see your double, whatever you do, don't look it in the eyes, wait for it to slip back inside you." But how are you supposed to know which is the double and which is the real you? She turns and looks back at her bed but it is empty. She is here at the window. Awake.

At the foot of her bed on a low couch sleeps the old nurse, attuned to any hint of distress. But Mae is not distressed. Barefoot, she slips out.

Down the marble staircase and across the cold slabs of the great hall, she glides as though weightless despite the precious load she carries—but if Moon is potent enough to move oceans, ought we to wonder at its power to draw a young woman from her bed and buoy her steps? Out through the front doors and onto the forecourt where the cinders glint like diamonds.

All at once, the smell. Big, rolling and dark. It is coming from out there. Faint strains of an old song waft as though borne along by the smell, a song she knows she cannot know and yet . . . Now a feeling. In the pith of her. Hunger.

Famished, she follows the smell like a siren song, out and into the dark and glistening swells of the moor.

Above, the moon sails through sapphire clouds. Mae walks and walks. The hem of her nightgown is sodden and caked, mud clings to her ankles; a sucking sound as one foot after another gets born again and again. She is beyond sight of the house. The smell is big and embracing now, the song has become the sound of water flowing underground, growing louder until the ground ripples beneath her feet, caressing her soles, it is arousing, irresistible. She follows.

Water seeps up from the ground. A black seam has opened in the earth, gushing softly. Night seems to gather more thickly here, and here is her treasure. She lies on her belly—no fear for her child and its accelerating cells, this ground is all give. Her arms are outstretched as though in flight, and the dark elixir holds her, caresses her. The smell is intoxicating—more powerful than a spell, for it is older than words, older than song itself. She lowers her face to Earth . . .

Does she know, deep down? In the knowing way of ants and ocean waves and grass—what it might mean?

. . . And she drinks.

When Mrs. Knox arose at dawn to find her mistress from bed. And nowhere in the house or garden. When she roused Lord Henry. When Henry stumbled down the stairs, pulling on his boots. When Cruikshank was sent to the vicarage in the cart lest Her Ladyship. When Knox found Byrn in the midst of his milking song. When Henry plunged onto the moor and set off running—impossible to run across moorland.

Staggering, he cries, "Mae! Mae!" Hoarse and sobbing, he blunders through the grey dawn.

The old man overtakes him. Lopes on past. Disappears amid the browning heather.

Henry falls, rises, presses on. He ought to have ridden into the village. But if she is in the village she is safe, whereas if she has sleep-walked onto the moor. If she has miscarried and fled. Bleeding—He jams his fist against his mouth. How much time? How long has he been? The sun full out. He shields his eyes, turns about. Here comes the cart along the track. Two figures. Is it she? Running, stumbling. It is my lady, oh it is my love—! It is Cruikshank with the vicar's wife. Damn them, damn all women who are not she.

He stumbles on, crawls, rises. Spies a figure to the east, etched against the raw morning, plodding as though in place—a bulge at its middle. Henry sets off at a run once more. Turns an ankle, limps forward, eyes on the figure, drawing nearer now—it is the old man, with something draped in his arms, a muddy sack—"Does she live?!" Henry bawls. "Byrn!" he screams.

Byrn carries the mud-cloaked figure into the hall and sets it down— "On her side," orders Knox, already kneeling, taking hold of Lady Marie's jaw, hinging it open, determining that, though black with mud, the mouth is empty, throat unblocked. A chirruping of distress. Knox glances up to see Mrs. Haas, hand at her lips, with Cruikshank trembling nearby.

Henry arrives, breathless, hopping on one foot.

"She lives, Lord Henry," says Knox.

He drops to her side. "She fell into a sinkhole."

"Nay," says Byrn. "She were eating."

Henry turns to the old man in disbelief. "'Eating'. . . Eating what?"

If Henry had not repeated the old man's assertion by way of querying it, Mrs. Haas would not have learned what Lady Marie was doing out on the bog that night, unaccustomed as she is to old Byrn's garbled speech.

"Go home, Mrs. Haas, if you please," says Knox. And the chirruping retreats.

Knox, still holding the jaw, inserts two fingers into Her Ladyship's mouth and presses the back of her tongue. Lady Marie gags but fights, head thrashing, and Knox narrowly escapes with a full hand of fingers.

Henry looks on. His wife's face is a mask of mud, parching now into a thousand wrinkles . . . He finds he cannot look away as she transforms from damsel to . . .

Knox rises. "Cruikshank, light the copper."

Cruikshank scurries off in obedience. Byrn carries Lady Marie up the stairs. Then he returns and carries up Lord Henry.

On the bedside table rests a jar and a dropper. Knox has administered the warm mustard water between Lady Marie's lips and is waiting for it to work: if Her Ladyship swallowed aught, 'twill soon come back up. She stations an empty basin on the floor beside the bed.

She has cleaned Her Ladyship as well as she can but a proper bath will wait. The lass has fallen into a deep slumber. Knox has bolstered her head and shoulders with pillows to prevent choking should she upthrow in her sleep. The forehead is damp, the cheeks are flushed, but the basin remains empty. And the mound of Her Ladyship's belly remains firm. And quick. Mrs. Knox keeps vigil, relieved for brief spells by Cruikshank and Cook, all through that day, into the night and through the next; at intervals, drawing back the covers to check for blood. But the sheet remains snowy, the legs streaked only with the fine black powder of moor mud. Thanks be to Brigid. And all the saints.

Henry paces the corridor with the help of a stout walking stick. He ought to be resting his ankle, letting Byrn's poultice do its work. He has attempted to pray. But what is the use of petitioning an omnipotent God who, if He does exist, saw fit to fashion us first as apes, then raise us up to a level of intellect such that, as with a man who clings to the last spire in a flood, we cannot escape knowledge as to the enormity of the deluge which must at last engulf us? Not to put too fine a point on it. He hovers outside the bedchamber door. "Is she still . . . ? Did she . . . ?"

"I see no sign of trouble, Lord Henry, the lass is still with child."

"Oh, thank God." He could weep. He does so. Hears his old nurse murmur, "Poor Penny."

Gets hold of himself. Whisper-shouts, "What in God's name was she doing on the bog?!"

"Belike sleep-walking. 'Tis no uncommon for a pregnant young woman to—"

"Sleep-walking or no, I should think it dashed uncommon for anyone at all to . . ." He lowers his voice to a grimace, "Byrn said she was 'eating.'"

". . . Byrn says all manner of falderal."

Knox is there when Lady Marie opens her eyes on the third morning. The lips are dry but so is the brow, and the eyes are clear.

"How are you feeling, My Lady?"

"I'm . . . Gosh, I feel fine." With that she flings aside the quilt—

Knox restrains her before she can swing her legs over the side. "Stay!"

"Jeepers, Knoxy!"

Knox looses her grip. "Begging Your Ladyship's pardon."

But Her Ladyship lies back obediently, and laughs.

Och, if only Lady Catherine were alive to see the lass, the bonny daughter she never had—excepting Miss Clarissa, of course.

"Bring me food! All the food in the house! I'm famished . . ." A faraway look enters her eyes. Knox follows her gaze to the window. Suddenly the lass turns back, "Knox, I've had the strangest dream. If it was a dream . . ."

". . . Aye, M'Lady?

"I dreamt . . . that I went away out onto the fen and . . . And I got to this place, oh it was very dark but warm and so safe-feeling and . . ." Tears course down the girl's cheeks, but her expression remains unchanged. "My mother was there, waiting for me. And she . . ." Her lips are parted, in her streaming eyes is the same distant look. "That is, I . . ." She blushes and looks down. "I can't say it."

"No need, Your Ladyship."

"But I want to tell you. It was . . . so real and . . ."

"I'm listening, 'Ladyship."

"Come closer, Knoxy."

Knox obeys.

The girl cups her hand around her mouth and whispers into the old woman's ear . . .

———

Henry summons Byrn to his study and commends him for his rescue of Her Ladyship. The old man accepts the offer of a dram. Demurs in the face of praise, for many's the time he's done the same for the ewes, and even Gossamer in her day when she was took by the "honger." Henry nods. Does not remonstrate. Byrn has his ways.

"Not a word to Her Ladyship, Byrn."

"Nay."

"That will be all."

Byrn withdraws. And takes the stench of the *sùil-chruthaich* with him.

As for the notion his wife obeyed a morbid appetite for moor mud, the empty basin on the floor next to her bed has quashed that notion. Anyone might believe that a pregnant woman could sleep-walk across the moor onto a bog and, mistaking its softness for that of her own bed, lay herself down in the mud. But only a superstitious old relic like Byrn, bless him, could believe that any woman, let alone Lady Bell, Seventeenth Baroness of the DC de Fayne, would thereupon proceed to feed like cattle . . . His wife's belly is not swimming with swamp spawn; she is the incubator of his child, not the offspring of the fen.

Still, while Henry certainly does not believe it, neither can he quite forget it.

Knox knows that pregnant women sometimes crave nutrients straight from Mother Earth, but she sees no reason to tell Lord Henry so. His Lordship has judged it best that Her Ladyship not be told she sleep-walked onto the moor, thus Knox tells her only that she slept through a critical fever. Nor does Knox worry Lord Henry with the dream that Lady Marie confided, for as she told Her Ladyship, "Pregnant women are given to vivid dreaming."

In his bothy, Byrn chants softly to his seedlings.

Od y tayse en drow ny hawse,
Od y mayse en trow ny mawse,
Bryg en braw,
Bryg en yd,
Bryg en braw,
Na Caylyx yd

48

IT SNOWS, draping the swelling moorland. Fayne is far from the lights of Edinburgh, farther still from the twinkling candles on Christmas trees in windows all along Beacon Street in Boston. But Mae does not feel homesick. "How could I, Henry? I'm home."

She watches, enchanted, as Knox and Cruikshank deck the great hall with boughs of holly, and she claps as Byrn carries in a whole fir tree he cut from a copse—only to yelp when, instead of setting it up in the drawing room to be decorated, he tosses it into the huge hearth and sets it on fire. "God Yul!" exclaims Henry, and hands her a cup of warm punch. One sip only she takes, lest the baby grow tipsy in her womb.

Reverend and Mrs. Haas join them for Hogmanay, and the Reverend pipes in the haggis, borne aloft by Cook. They sing, arm in arm.

Winter settles in. And Mae gets bigger. In February, she receives the happy news that Taffy's child has been born. A girl. Theresa. *Little Tess.*

She passes the six-month mark.

"Henry, give me your hand."

He obeys—draws back in some alarm. "Are you—is that—?"

"He kicked."

In April it rains incessantly but with a freshness that banishes hoary Old Man Winter—even if Mae is a touch sorry to see him go, he's been such cozy company. Standing out on the forecourt, she turns her face to the sky to catch the drops and laughs when she hears Knox clucking after her to "keep out of the damp!"

Fayne House
April 9, 1873

Dear Taffy,
After a journey of some months' duration, Mrs. Haas has materialized with a baby! I am convinced she found it under a cabbage leaf, for unless I have fallen once more prey to the "vivid dreaming" of pregnant women, that lady gave no indication of being in the family way at New Year's—certainly she imbibed like a sailor! A sweet little thing, though, a girl called Gwendolyn—a little fanciful for a vicar's daughter

who's destined to become a governess, but perhaps she'll live up to her name and marry a handsome prince . . .

By May she is a ship in full sail and busies herself filling every urn, vase and visored suit of armor with buttercups and bunches of gorse and stalks of bright-red sheep's sorrel. And perhaps Beltane is to blame when Lady Marie cheerfully takes a sledgehammer to the dining-room wall, making way for a set of French doors.

June.

Cries hang in the air. In the baronial bedchamber there may be seen, from the foot of a four-post bed, the bare knees of a young woman, her modesty spared by the broad back of an older woman, busy between those knees.

The older woman straightens.

In her cupped hands, the infant. Stricken-looking and ancient too in the way of newborns.

"Your Ladyship. You have a son."

Mae reaches up. Takes the baby. Folds it to her, slick and warm. "Charles," she whispers.

～◉

Tabitha Knox is a solid woman, barrel on a box. She is past the age of flushes, though there was a time . . . Her legs are piles like the ones holding up the wharf in Glasgow where a branch of her forebears set sail a hundred years ago and forgot to pack her great-grandmother. That is why Knox is here. Contingency is grand. What are the trickle-ways of Chance and how strong a force is Fate and its soignée sibling, Destiny? Mrs. Knox seems born to bake and brew, to fetch and carry, stolidly to serve; she would be doing so no matter where, no matter how—whether serving up charity balls in New York or bullets in the Outback.

And she can keep a secret. Such as the one Lady Marie confided to her after that night on the moor.

I got to this place, oh it was very dark but warm and so safe-feeling and . . . my mother was there, waiting for me. She smiled at me and opened her arms and I went to her and she held me close and warm and safe. She was dressed in white and in my dream I didn't wonder how her nightgown had stayed clean out there on the fen. Then she opened her gown and put me to her breast. And I drank . . .

This morning Mrs. Knox exits the house by the scullery door and crosses the earthen yard through rain that does not so much fall as descend like a veil, skirting the byre and the lean-to where the peat stacks are drying, and enters the dimness of the bothy, carrying a bundle wrapped in oilcloth.

In the gloam, tools take shape, some on hooks, others upright between nails; pitchfork, hoe, blade shears, yoke and buckets. Herbs hang drying from the low ceiling. In the one dim window, a row of clay pots. A work table is crowded with more pots and saucers of seeds. A muttering thickens the air—rhythmic, rote like prayer or incantation. Knox pays it no mind. She sets her bundle on the table amid the clutter. "Her Ladyship has borne a son."

Byrn says, "Bairn belongs to Brigid."

"Foolish old man." But she makes the sign of the cross and leaves him to his seedlings, knowing the old man will take the bundled afterbirth and bury it just as he did with Lord Henry's. To keep the lad safe and attached to the land. She hears him humming and the sound persists, like an after-image, until she is well away and back in the house.

These plants grow in darkness
Others in the light.
To each its own, my lovelies,
To each of you what's right.
Grow, grow, wax and wane,
Some to heal, some to bane . . .

~◉

To Lord Henry Bell, Seventeenth Baron of the DC de Fayne, and Lady Bell, a son, the Honourable Charles Henry Gerald Victor. *The Scotsman, June 1, 1873*

~◉

Part Three

In these matters, the only certainty is that nothing is certain.

PLINY THE ELDER

49

WE CLATTERED ACROSS the bridge over the Water of Feyn and for the first time I entered the village. Goose-flesh skittered up my arms and sides. The colour, the industry and variety! There were shops purveying all manner of goods—candlesticks, paper, cakes! I was agape at teeming humanity, counting fifteen people on the High Street alone! We stopped at the Inn at the Kenspeckle Hen where we boarded the waiting post coach, all the places in which Father had purchased. We rolled through farmland, neat stone byres and cottages tucked in its lush folds; the very air smelled softer. I remained glued to the window, glorying in the rounded hills to either side as we passed through valleys, over streams and across moorland altogether new to my eyes, craning so as to miss not a single village or distant peak, fairly breathless as we passed through Ettrick Forest and whole tracts of trees.

Thus we wended our way through the beauteous green Borders, those contested lands of yore, their still-dubious frontiers so unlike the civilized concordance with contradiction contained by Fayne.

I refused to so much as look at Knox for the duration of the journey to Selkirk, for she had neglected to pack my lesson books and now they were miles behind me. I dealt her old carpet bag a kick, "You managed to pack your own rubbish. What is the point of meeting the doctor when I am so ill-prepared?"

"What need have you to prepare?"

"Blockhead! The doctor is going to examine me."

"Aye. And what need have you of your lessons for that?"

She was right of course: I had every word of those lessons by heart. I was on the point of retorting, "'Tis the principal of the thing!" but stopped short: my old nurse was out of her depth, and it behooved me to be kind. "Knoxy, I'm sorry I've been so obstropulous." (Another serviceable bit of "slang" courtesy of Gwendolyn Haas.) I smiled kindly, but she looked a mite sorrowful, and it struck me she was sad at the prospect of losing me to the wide world. Dear old Tabby Turnip. I flung my arms about her.

Selkirk snatched away what remained of my breath for it dwarfed Aberfoyle-on-Feyn with a population of over six thousands souls!

We passed through the market square and I yelped at the sight of Sir Walter Scott himself, in stone! At the train station I was set to hop down from the carriage but Father preceded me, then turned and extended his hand.

"Father, I am not an invalid."

He smiled, "No my dear, you are a lady."

I took his hand and allowed myself to be needlessly assisted in disembarking the carriage. Bless dear kind sweet Papa, but following the examination I would eschew such distractions which, however well-meant, interrupted the flow of thought thereby impeding its conversion to action—at this rate it was a wonder females got anything done at all. We waited on the platform in close proximity to other people (!) and, heralded by a distant rumbling that set my blood to humming, the great iron horse hove into view. With a screech of its whistle it grew larger until it rolled relentlessly in a cloud of steam and a cacophony of brakes and gears to a stop before us. It was thrilling!!! I could have stood gazing up at its metallic majesty for hours. But I felt Father's hand beneath my elbow and we repeated the performance of assistance in boarding the first-class carriage.

I yearned to walk as though drunkenly up the swaying aisle and out between the cars, through the coal-filled boiler room where men stoked the furnace, all the way to where the driver sat atop the roaring engine itself. But Father insisted I remain seated as the locomotive catapulted us at eighty miles per hour (!) up the North Sea coast, and I was soon lost to my first view of the ocean which, up to then, I had only ever seen depicted on maps with puff-cheeked zephyrs. The great grey slab of sea stretched to meet the sky and I yearned to sail upon it, just as I yearned, in peering out the opposite window, to scale the wild treeless hills and to run alongside the brooks that creased their beckoning valleys. I wished to be every place at once, but mostly I wished myself in Edinburgh—portal to all places.

And after a mere hour, I watched as the lights of the city itself twinkled into view on either side of a gorge as we slowed and joined the shuntings and leviathan sighs of not only our own engine, but ranks of others to either side—I could have stretched out an arm and touched them. "Close the window, pet."

Waverley Station put Selkirk to shame and I clung willingly to Father's arm through the echoing throng as we made our way across the platform and up stone steps and emerged into the wintry evening.

I saw, on the far side of a great bridge, the jagged skyline of the Old Town sloping upward to meet the parapets of Edinburgh Castle atop its rock of timeless basalt. Somewhere amid those eaves and eyes was the University of Edinburgh—"This way, pet." A bewildering number of curiously shaped conveyances stood ranked along the roadway—"hansom cabs," supplied Father—in their midst, a carriage, its side emblazoned with the *Salamander Rampant*. A liveried driver opened the door and we boarded. I heard Father murmur, "Thank you, Sanders." We rolled toward a bank of modern and magnificent buildings wrought of smooth sandstone that seemed to glisten in the lamplight—

"Keep your head inside the carriage, you're like to lose it to an omnibus!" clucked Knox.

I gasped and pointed.

"The Sir Walter Scott Monument," said Father.

I swivelled and spied what looked like the Parthenon.

"The Royal Society of Edinburgh."

"I shall be its first female member," I murmured.

I scarcely knew where to look as we passed buildings, many bearing signs and insignia—"Jenners!" I cried, recognizing the name from the long-ago cloak. "And just there," said Father, "is New Register House where all Scottish births are recorded."

"Even mine?"

"Especially yours."

Along with deaths and marriages and who knew what else. "Only imagine, all that knowledge, cram-packed into one building, Father."

We turned into a wide and gracious street, I saw another Parthenon—
"'Tis a bank." And another! "Likewise a bank." There were people and
churches and verdigrised monuments—"George the Fourth." We followed arcing "Circles" and curving "Places" with many a wee park girded
about by wrought-iron fences, and I kept an eye out for Circus Lane,
hoping for a glimpse of Gwendolyn's school. Presently, the carriage
slowed and we came alongside a privet hedge where a brass plaque in a
stone post announced: NO. ONE BELL GARDENS. We turned in through
a set of open wrought-iron gates.

"We're here! Wake up, Knoxy," and I thumped her arm.

I heard the crunch of gravel—instantly and thenceforth for me, the
aural *sine qua non* of sophistication—as we proceeded along a lamplit
circular drive, and I beheld the handsome Georgian house. "Oh Father,
it's lovely."

Its portico and columns were aglow, and as we drew up I had the
strangest, strongest sense that, despite setting eyes on the house for
the very first time, I had come Home.

No sooner had we halted than the polished oak door opened, and a
grey-haired gentleman in black waistcoat and tails emerged from the
rectangle of light and descended, with a blend of formality and efficiency,
the immaculate stone steps.

Father placed a hand on my arm as I reached for the carriage door
and I understood I was to wait for the gentleman to open it. This he did
with a white-gloved hand. He then stood discreetly aside as Father
alighted with a murmur, "Thank you Havers." My first butler.

Father held up his hand to me. "Come, my dear, and meet your aunt."

A movement at a dim ground-floor window drew my eye—the twitch
of a net curtain.

Aware that I was in all likelihood being observed by no less a personage than my Aunt Clarissa, I placed my hand upon Father's and entered
into the pantomime of assistance. As Gwendolyn Haas might put it,
"So far, so good." I was determined to make a favourable impression
upon that lady who had herself taken pains with my breeding. Thus, on
Father's arm I processed with *dignitas* up the broad steps toward the
open door and crossed the threshold into a brilliantly lit vestibule. Its
walls were papered in crimson and gold stripes and hung with ranks

of paintings of flowers, lapdogs and fruit—pears, principally. Overhead a crystal chandelier shone with gas jets (!). All was dazzlingly augmented by a great oval looking glass mounted above a marble-topped table upon which sat a vase of hothouse blooms. Reader, I was aware of having stepped, at last, into the nineteenth century.

Father dropped his ivory-topped cane into a porcelain umbrella stand painted with storks, and tossed his gloves onto the table. A long-necked maid in crisp cap and spotless apron appeared and curtsied. She relieved me of my mantle and hated bonnet and Father of his coat and hat, and vanished them into a built-in cabinet which had seemed part of the wall until a panel was revealed as a door. She swiftly withdrew and, with an alacrity suggestive of a conjuring trick, her place was taken by a lean woman of upright posture and superior years. She had iron-grey ringlets and was clad in a black silk gown, bell-shaped from the waist down. Her parchment hands were folded before her.

"Welcome, brother."

She turned on me a blue gaze, the pallor of which I suspected belied its power. If a girder of the Forth Bridge were to adopt human form, it would be this lady.

"Charlotte. Niece."

"Aunt Clarissa, I am honoured to meet you at last."

Did the blue gaze flicker? Like a gas jet at a draft . . . Aunt had never 'til now set eyes upon her brother's only child. Indeed, being childless herself, she must be the more moved to welcome, at long last, Me. I smiled, intending to put her at her ease, notwithstanding she was of course in her own home. (Notwithstanding it was my Father's property.)

She did not answer but looked past me and I witnessed an abrupt alteration in her lineaments. The sallow cheeks took on tint and pliability, the eyes shone, her mouth contracted in a frown. I heard Knox behind me, her voice breaking with emotion, "Miss Clarissa."

"Don't stand there, Knoxy, come in. Maid will show you to your room."

"I need no showing, miss," said Knox, her own eyes brimming.

My aunt's frown intensified. As did the glistening in her eyes. She turned and exited. Knox was smiling through tears. Father was inspecting the chandelier.

He too now quitted the vestibule and I followed into an even brighter and more lavishly papered entry hall. At its centre a carpeted staircase mounted to a landing overlooked by nothing more imposing than a half-moon window and a swan table bearing more blooms. I glanced to my right in time to see a door closing. "Your aunt's parlour," said Father.

The very doors of No. One Bell Gardens closed with a plush sound. All was plumb and fitted, there was no pitch nor roll to the floors, no doors of crypt-like recalcitrance. All was fresh.

I was shown by the grim-faced maid upstairs to a chamber which in no wise resembled my quarters at Fayne save for the presence of a bed. Even so, this object was provided with no curtains, nor did it stand in the middle of the room, rather its headboard was snug against the wall. I was unsurprised at the room's comparatively modest dimensions—Fayne had, after all, been at one time a castle—but its appointments came near to beggaring my store of vocabulary. The window was curtained and the walls were papered in matching pink rosebuds and pale gold ribbons against a cream backdrop. I paused for breath before looking up.

Overhead, more rosebuds in what I would come to know as a "medallion." At the centre of the medallion was an opaque glass fixture within which a gas jet softly illuminated the room. The bed itself was clothed with counterpane and pillow slips—so many pillows!—all in the selfsame rosebud-gold-ribbon pattern, and the floor was carpeted, if not positively *pillowed*, in pale pink. Its pile seemed to cup one's foot with each step so that I was reminded of the ominously spongiform terrain of the moor. My dresser—"vanity," Knox corrected me—was topped by a looking glass with hinged side wings. I appreciated the utility of this in ascertaining whether one had a spider crawling up one's back, but Knox said it was to aid in the preparation of "a lady's toilette, especially her *quaffer*"—the latter being another French term, this one for the arrangement of a lady's hair. Fussy as it sounds in the describing, the whole effect of the *décor* (French again!) was tranquil, even . . . tranquilizing, for I felt sleepy soon after entering. Most striking, however: "Knox, all the furniture is clothed."

The vanity table, the vanity stool, the *boudoir* chair, the night stand, the bed, all were skirted and valanced in rosebuds and ribbons. In the midst of so much textile I could not but speculate as to the proliferation of *Dermatophagoides pteronyssinus*.

"What's that?"

"Ferocious six-legged creatures, Knox, with powerful pincer jaws, devourers of human flesh, we are surrounded by them."

"Where?!"

"In the fabric. Depend upon it. Billions of dust mites feasting on the dead skin particles of the household. Soon to batten on mine own."

In contrast to the microbial magnetism of drapery was the porcelain sheen of the Water Closet. I had heard of such marvels. Gwendolyn Haas had regaled me with tales of a "flush-down" convenience at her school, the which was operated by means of pulling a chain suspended from an overhead cistern. The "lavatory," which adjoined my bedroom, contained a convenience with just such a pull-chain fitted at its end with a porcelain rosebud, but no visible cistern. I grasped the rosebud and immediately pulled the chain. Water cascaded into the porcelain bowl and whirled about before disappearing down the hole. I did so again. A third time, deducing a cistern behind the wall. The porcelain bowl itself was painted with rosebuds. They rioted up and over the rim just as though the convenience were itself a vase rather than . . . It was fitted with a hinged rosewood lid and seat, varnished against splinters. Beside it stood the wash basin, at one with a porcelain pedestal and likewise covered in rosebuds. It was equipped with two matching enamelled taps which released a flow of hot and cold water respectively through a faucet and which drained at the centre of the basin, indicative of a pipe concealed within the pedestal. I left the water running while I turned to the *pièce de la résistance* (bother French!): a great porcelain tub—rosebudded—encased in a rosewood cabinet . . . like an open sarcophagus, but cheerful. The faucet here produced a torrent of water. Leaving it to run, I pulled once more the chain above the convenience. Three waterfalls at my command.

"Are you all right in there, pet?"

I emerged, rather damp, glad of the cheerful fire now dancing in the hearth, as the effects of the journey began to tell. I yawned and Knoxy had me stretch out on the bed, removed my boots and bid me, "Snooze, so's you'll be fresh for dinner."

———

Knox produced a new dinner gown of—"I match the curtains!"

"Nay, pet, they be peonies not roses."

"Try not to mistake me for the lavatory."

"Och!"

Dinner was taken in near silence.

The room was papered in fuchsia with a blizzard of white parakeets. The only sound was the low hiss of the jets in their sconces. I came over giddy at the thought of the parakeets suddenly squawking all over the walls—the which I suppressed and put down to the possible effect of gas.

Mentally dull, I was yet keenly aware of every clink and sip and chewing sound as Father worked his way through his parsnips and my aunt picked at the mutton in brown sauce. The butler hovered with the decanter. Weary as I was, I longed to venture out of doors and onto the pavements of the New Town. I hankered for the morrow and the one after that, which was the appointed day of my examination—I jolted with excitement as though at an electrical shock. Aunt and Father appeared not to notice—to my relief, for I would not have Aunt think me a fidget.

I waited for her to quiz me as to my avocations, tastes and ambitions, and to remark upon the degree to which I favoured either Mother or Father. I was equally ready to oblige should the conversation consist of nothing but dross. But my aunt directed to me no word, nor look.

I spoke. "It is my ambition, Aunt, to traverse the desert on camel-back."

She did not look up but made a sound which might have been "Indeed."

A white-gloved footman removed plates.

"Father, at what o'clock is to be my examination by Dr. Chambers on Thursday?"

Aunt Clarissa looked up as though surprised. I hastened to clarify, having learned it is ill-mannered to discuss matters with which not all are conversant. "Aunt Clarissa, I do not know whether Father has shared with you the happy intelligence that I am to be examined by an eminent physician."

"He has. Though I wonder you refer to it at table."

". . . I beg your pardon." I felt myself redden. "Only, I thought it might please you to know Dr. Chambers—that is the physician's name—shall ascertain my eligibility to attend the University of Edinburgh."

She looked up, but not at me. "Henry?"

"What's that?" said Father. "Oh, quite. In point of fact, Charlotte is something of a scholar." He smiled and directed his own gaze, opaque behind his spectacles, to the centre of the table where a plate of cheese had been uncovered.

"Fear not, Aunt Clarissa," said I with aplomb, for I had guessed the source of her misgivings. "I am aware of the risk of being pelted with sheep, but I am not faint-hearted in the face of livestock, moreover there have since been ladies who obtained their degrees and I intend to swell their ranks."

"Havers," said Aunt. "Pooding."

Hardtack with currants in hard sauce.

After the meal, I took a turn about the garden under the eye of the butler, who stood sentinel behind the wavy glass of the conservatory. And for the second time in my life, I felt confined—the first having been when I was inserted into the cornflower-blue dress and its under-ruckle. The paradox struck me: both occasions were milestones on my way to freedom. About me were high limestone walls o'ergrown with wisteria, its vines winter-bare and tough enough to climb even in skirts—I could "o'erleap" this garden wall in a trice and make for the Old Town and the University of Edinburgh . . . I upbraided myself for the childish thought. I squared my shoulders—as far as my bodice would permit—and made my way back up the garden path and into the house, intent upon taking myself off early to bed thereby to hasten the morrow. At the foot of the staircase I paused. Aunt's parlour door stood open. I approached. Within, on a low armless chair, sat my aunt. Her eyes were closed. Behind her stood Knox. She was slowly stroking my aunt's head and humming softly. I drew back—*shocked* is perhaps too strong a word. I knew Knox had been Father's nurse and it must therefore follow she had been Aunt's too. But the sight discomfited me.

I sought out Father in his study—an abridged version of its counterpart at Fayne, boasting only a stuffed kestrel and a red grouse in a bell jar.

He was writing a letter but put it aside when he saw me, and smiled. With that I was back at Fayne, aye back many months before when Father and I would pass the evening hours peaceably amid his specimens . . .

"What is it, my treasure?"

"Why does Aunt hate me?" My words were out of order and I knew it the moment they left my lips.

He winced.

"Forgive me, Father."

"You are forgiven."

"Only, my aunt seemed . . . unmoved by news of the entrance examination."

"Oh, that, well . . . quite, hm."

"Does she perhaps not approve of higher education for females?"

"In point of fact . . ." His voice trailed off.

"Not everyone is as forward-thinking as you, Father."

He cleared his throat. "Your aunt was something of a scholar herself."

"Was she?"

"A head for figures. Knack for Latin. Bested me though she hadn't a day's tutoring nor any school of course." He removed his spectacles. Polished them. "If it weren't for blasted primogeniture, my sister would have inherited Fayne and I don't doubt but that she would have managed it better than ever I did." He smiled, as though to take the sting from his words.

"Father, do not say so even in jest. Fayne could not have a better master nor I a better father."

He smiled once more. And I broached a subject as delicate as snow on a stream. "Father. If, upon examination, Dr. Chambers recommends me for a place at the university, it is my fondest hope that you should . . ." I could not speak.

"What is it my dear?"

I whispered. "Marry."

He drew me to him. In my father's embrace, my face against the fine worsted wool of his shoulder, I wept yet could not have said why.

50

NEXT MORNING Father took me on a tour of Edinburgh. At Holyrood I beheld the scene of royal exile and queenly captivity, and explored the chapel ruins in a drizzling rain that showed them to advantage. We hiked up the "lion's haunch" to the summit of Arthur's Seat where, standing on a level with the gulls, our exhalations the only clouds in sight, I took in a three-hundred-and-sixty-degree view of the city and environs, from Leith to—in the distance on this cold clear day—the Forth Bridge! At the base of the Salisbury Craigs I stood before the same rock that James Hutton had when he formulated his Theory of the Earth, and like him I gazed deep into time with "no vestige of a beginning, no prospect of an end."

In a bustling marketplace I saw the scene of execution. "I say, Father, we missed the last hanging by a mere century." There were horses in pens and stalls piled high with pyramids of produce. There were bare-headed fishwives in striped petticoats singing out the catch they carried in dripping creels on their backs; some went about on bicycles—"Father, I shall ride daily to the university on a bicycle!"

I longed to lose myself amid shadowy "wynds," dank "closes" and beckoning stone stairways. "Cowgate!" I cried, at the sight of the word on the corner of a grimy building. I scanned the street for a fallen woman, but all were upright, some selling flowers, others huddling in doorways with children . . . "Father, why do they not keep to their homes?"

He cleared his throat. "I daresay they prefer the fresh air."

"But it isn't fresh, is it."

"Drive on, Sanders."

Up the High Street.

Past the Tron—"I daresay those false notaries and malefactors got what they deserved!"

St. Giles' Cathedral, and the pedestal of the Mercat Cross—"Look up there, Father, the Scottish unicorn!"

At Castle Rock I leaned over the parapet and whooped at the sound of the one o'clock gun and the sight of the ball dropping from the flag-staff of Nelson's Monument.

We rode out to the Lochleven Castle ruins where I seemed to feel the ghost of Mary Queen of Scots emboldening me, and I wished it had been I who rescued her and tossed the keys into the loch.

We returned to the city in the gathering dusk of the winter's afternoon and as we drove past the Royal Edinburgh Asylum, I shivered. "Is that where they lock up the lunatics?"

"In point of fact, the Royal Edinburgh Asylum at Morningside is a world-leader in the humane treatment of the insane."

I had expected our outing would be crowned with a tour of the university—and, time permitting, a visit to Surgeons' Hall where I knew there were numerous human specimens preserved in jars. Bits of folk in formaldehyde. But Father declared these merited a day unto themselves and I concurred. Still, I did wish I might have the chance to at least glimpse the Medical Arts Building before sitting my examination the day after tomorrow. "Might we return in the morning?"

"We might."

We took a turn round Greyfriars Kirkyard and carried on to the Museum.

It was the best day of my life.

"I saw the skeleton of a whale, entire, Aunt!"

This elicited a slight movement of brow. I took it as encouragement. Havers ladled soup from a tureen. "Ah, white soup. My favourite."

Silence. But for slurping.

"Father has promised an excursion to the Bell Rock Lighthouse. Perhaps you would join us, Aunt."

"Perhaps."

I did not wonder Father was subdued; he had after all effected a wholesale inversion of his waking and sleeping hours, and must be utterly fagged.

"We hadn't time to visit the Medical Arts Building, but we shall do so following my—that is, at the first opportunity. After all, as Hippocrates said, *Ars longa, vita brevis*, and 'tis time I got on with the long process of learning the medical art, for life is indeed short."

"Havers. Pooding."

———

I found myself alone at breakfast next morning.

Knox forbade me to stray from the premises.

Aunt appeared at luncheon.

I mustered dross. "Aunt, I do so admire your domestic arrangements."

"They are not mine."

"Oh . . . ?"

"They were your mother's."

"Of course, I thought they looked familiar."

She looked at me sharply and seemed to live-pin me with her tiny pupils.

I explained, "My mother decorated our drawing room before she . . . Before I was born. The *décor* is perhaps not to your taste."

"My taste does not come into it."

I seized on common ground. "I myself am indifferent to the vicissitudes of fashion."

Silence.

I pressed on. "I am of a more scientific bent. Father tells me you had—have a head for figures."

Silence.

"I am glad to know such acumen runs in the Bell line. Personally I would trade all the frippery in the world for a crack at Babbage's Analytical Engine." I chuckled. "I refer to a machine designed to calculate mathematical—"

"I care less for your talking like a scholar than for your looking like a lady."

I was stung silent. With that, she rose—the which appeared to cost an effort—and quitted the room with a halting gait. Was she lame? The thought went some way to mitigate my shame—aye, and anger too, my cheeks were aflame. And yet . . . I was more bewildered than anything. The rebuke was not only unwarranted but unprecedented and it took me a moment to collect my thoughts. My aunt was immune to my—not "charms," for I aspired to none—no, Reader, she was numb to my *intelligence*. It dawned upon me that I had just now been treated with something utterly foreign to my experience, before which I was as defenceless as a blue-footed booby: contempt. Why, even Murdoch Mungo respected me.

I rose and followed.

I found the door to her parlour closed. I rapped upon it and opened it, set to enter. She shot me a look from her chair and I stopped as though at a physical barrier. Her work basket was in her lap, and her hand, having been in the act of retrieving something from it, now quickly withdrew. "What do you want?"

The elderly were known to be irascible. Perhaps she was in her second childhood—though if this one were an indication, her first did not bear contemplating. I summoned grace under fire and altered my battle plan. I determined to be agreeable to the old cross-patch, perhaps even a comfort in her dotage. "Dear Aunt. Have I done aught to discomfit you? Pray tell me, that I might make amends."

She did not answer.

"May I enter?" I sallied forth.

"You may not," said she.

I froze.

"You may go."

I withdrew, closing the door with its cushiony exhalation, my heart pounding.

As the afternoon dragged on and Father had yet to emerge, it became clear that a tour of the university was not "on the cards" today.

"Knox, why does Aunt hate me?"

Knox was lacing me back into my corset for dinner. "She doesnae. Breathe out now."

I had the trick, learned from Achilles, of pretending to exhale fully while the girth was tightened.

"She does, she gives me nothing but stick and won't let me in her parlour."

"Well now that's as may be, pet, your aunt is . . . set in her ways.

"What 'ways' are those?"

"Och, well . . ."

"Is she dotty?"

"Dear me, no."

"Then tell me. Why can she not love me?" I caught her eye in the looking glass.

"Well now, happen she were that fond of wee Charles."

I groaned.

"He was the apple of her eye, so he was. She used to feed him sweeties from her work basket." The old woman smiled mistily at the recollection.

"So that's what she was hiding when I came in. Well it's not my fault he's dead."

"Nay, 'course not, only . . . Your Aunt Clarissa let her heart melt for him, you see. And when he died, it froze back up."

". . . Father says she held promise. As a scholar."

She tsked and nodded. "Some clever she was, like you in her day."

"So I'm to hide my light under a bushel because she hid hers? I'd like to see anyone try to douse my light, I'd burn the ruddy bushel to the ground! Let her keep her stuffy old parlour, it stinks of camphor!"

"Is it your woman's time again, pet?"

"No!"

But it was. As a trip to the lavatory presently confirmed.

Knoxy insisted on the peony gown with the addition of a torturous lace collar. "Why not simply apply brambles to my collarbone?"

And Maid—it seemed she had no other name—was unrelenting with my hair, drawing a part along my scalp with the pointed tail of a silver comb—"Why not sever my *corpus callosum* while you're at it?"

This ratcheting-up of my *toilette* was in honour of a dinner guest. "A particular friend of your father's."

"A fellow bird-fancier?"

"You're to be on your best behaviour."

"When am I otherwise?"

Nothing could dampen my spirits, however, for tomorrow was Examination Day.

I sat in the drawing room with Father and Aunt, waiting. And not without pleasure, for here at least was the prospect of intelligent conversation, however grizzled the guest. Perhaps the Curator of the Bird Gallery himself. Or was he dead?

Father said, "My dear, you are very prettily turned-out."

He was rather handsomely turned-out himself, in the lavender coat and doeskin trousers.

"Thank you, Father."

"I should say she is," said Aunt.

I looked at her in astonishment.

Havers appeared in the archway. "Miss Llewellyn, Your Lordship."

Father rose.

In the doorway there appeared a slight creature with chestnut ringlets and a cream-coloured dinner gown that matched her bare shoulders. Father went to her. "Miss Llewellyn, allow me to present my daughter, Miss Charlotte Bell."

I supposed she was pretty. She entered and murmured a polite greeting, first to me, then to Aunt. Who pressed her hand. And smiled warmly.

Dross.

Sherry. Sarsaparilla cordial for me. (Cracking.)

Miss Llewellyn scarcely lifted her gaze beneath fluttering lashes, but the corners of her mouth rose with every word Father spoke. And she listened modestly as Aunt Clarissa, with the precision of Debrett's, informed me that Miss Llewellyn was a daughter of the Bishop of St. Someone-in-the-Something, now deceased, and had been educated at Somewhering-in-Somethingshire by the Misses Someonely, adding, "Miss Llewellyn has French and Italian, along with a little German."

"A little German what?" I pictured a diminutive Alsatian. There was hope for her yet.

Her eyes widened. She looked to Father who cleared his throat. "I believe the reference is to the German language, Charlotte."

"Dinner is served, Your Lordship."

Father offered his arm and escorted Miss Llewllyn into the dining room mere steps away, where he pulled out a chair for her whilst Havers hovered, perhaps lest the manoeuvre should come to grief.

Soup.

Aunt said, "White soup is not to everyone's taste, Miss Llewellyn."

"Oh Lady Clarissa, I am particularly fond of white soup."

Aunt Clarissa smiled.

"I for one intend to have a great deal of German, Miss Llewellyn," I said brightly, in a burst of good-will, for this was the eve of my examination and I would not allow Aunt Clarissa's preference for a dead nephew and a live dinner guest to dampen my spirits. "Bound as I am for a scientific career, and Germany being at the forefront, as doubtless you know, of chemistry and bacteriology. Indeed a drop of your soup beneath the lens of a microscope would reveal a riot of animalcules the which, were they of a size to be perceived by the naked eye, would provoke cries of terror along with vows to forswear soup—or any nourishment—forever more. Not to mention your eyelashes, Miss Llewellyn, the infestins of which nightly creep forth to feed helpfully upon dead skin cells. And what recompense do they receive? Why in the morning, we wash them away. Cleanliness is, in this case, next to mass murder." I perceived a deepening of her colour.

Fish. Leeks for Father.

Dross.

Chops with brown sauce. Welsh rarebit for Father. Really, Bell Gardens had nothing on Fayne when it came to cookery.

Aunt Clarissa said, "Miss Llewellyn is a governess."

"I'm afraid you've come to the wrong place, in that case," I said waggishly, but I was the only one to laugh.

"Claret, I think, Havers."

"Not but what Father oughtn't to keep you in mind for the future, for you see I am the eldest of an as yet incomplete family, Miss Llewellyn, being not in fact my father's heir." I put up a hand. "I anticipate your objection that a female may inherit in Scotland, but Miss Llewellyn, she may not do so in England. Why"—chuckling ruefully—"any claim I might bring—the which I would never!—would pit Scotland against England and rather than attenuate the Dispute would, by means of a legal decision for one side or the other, *end* it, thereby dissolving the estate. Would you be so kind as to pass the sauce." Whereupon I playfully repeated my request in Morse Code.

"Havers, pooding."

After supper Father invited Miss Llewellyn to accompany him on a turn about the conservatory to inspect the various tropical cuttings. I mounted the stairs, grateful to have been spared the social chore even whilst smarting that my presence was evidently neither required nor desired. Between Miss Llewellyn's simpering smile and Aunt's closed door I felt for the first time something of an outsider. *I*, Charlotte Bell of Fayne! "Knoxy," said I, entering my chamber, "Why do you suppose

Father—?" But Knox was not there. The fire was lit, my bath steamed in the lavatory and hemp-faced Maid was loitering.

"Shall I help you into your bath, miss?"

I quitted the chamber, clattered down the back stairs and looked in the scullery, the kitchen, the pantry—I even opened the parlour door and glimpsed Aunt reaching for her basket. I pulled it to before she could look daggers at me, and ran up the stairs all the way to the top of the house and Knox's room, where she was not. "Knoxy! Where are you?!"—aiming a kick at her bed leg. I could have wept there and then in that mean low-ceilinged cell, so vexed was I, for the morrow was momentous; I was to be examined by an eminent physician. I was to enter the holy orders of Science, did no one in this house care for anything other than cuttings or confectionery?! I turned on my heel, set to return the way I'd come, when my eye was caught by a light at the far end of the passage.

It issued from a half-closed door. I walked quietly toward it. Candlelight, unmistakable, and suddenly I was homesick for Fayne. I looked through the opening and saw Knox, perched on a wee bench. I pushed the door wider and she started as though I had waked her from a trance. "What's the matter with you?" I asked roughly, for I loved her and was frightened. My eyes adjusted as I peered into the room. "Was this . . . the nursery?"

She nodded.

The toys were not neatly ranged, but scattered. A wooden locomotive—like the one at Fayne but for its unfaded paint—lay on its side. A rocking horse, its felt worn but intact. An abacus. Bright blocks—some with letters, some with animals—set one atop the other, as precarious as the lands of the Old Town. It was as though wee hands had only just left off playing, perhaps at the summons for tea, a nap, a cuddle . . . Knox wiped her eye. I said, "Lot of rubbish now," and left the room.

More than anything, I longed for the morrow. Longed for a world into which he could not follow, one where he'd never been. Even here in Edinburgh in this modern house he haunted me; tainted with guilt my ambition, smeared with shame my joys, supplanted me in my aunt's affections—*I did not dead you!* The infantile syntax had risen unbidden to mind. Clearly I was no better than a child of two.

I returned to my chamber, oddly grateful for the pale rosebuds and creamy gold ribbons, the skirted silliness of it all. Maid had taken herself off, so I stripped down before Knox could descend upon me and stepped into my bath—tepid now—watching as Prickle rose up as though in shared umbrage. I scrubbed myself, not even sparing Prickle—if it was to fall off, so be it and the sooner the better.

Relenting later that night, mindful that Prickle had only ever lived to serve . . .

51

I WAS UP AND BREAKFASTED well before dawn which in winter at this latitude did not occur before eight-thirty. When the sun rose it was on a lucky sky of brilliant blue and I rejoiced even whilst registering a certain solemnity. For I was at a turning point. A hinge in my life. Time itself would henceforth be measured in accordance with BE and AE: Before Examination and After Examination.

The one blemish on an otherwise ideal morning: another new dress.

With ceremonial assurance, I exited the house, descended the steps and allowed Havers to hand me up into the carriage, aware of demonstrating to Father—and Knox—how well I had taken to the new protocols. It was the least I could do in light of Father's untold sacrifices on my behalf—especially considering I should soon be free of said protocols.

We drove along George Street and, to my surprise, rather than turning onto North Bridge, carried on straight past it. "Father, is the examination not to take place at the Medical Arts Building?"

"Ah, in point of fact, it will take place at the physician's private surgery."

"Ah. Quite right." Next thing I knew I was head and shoulders out the window, ladylike manners thrown to the wind, crying, "Gwennie!" For there she was, walking in a line of girls, two by two, in matching broad-brim hats and navy-blue cloaks behind a generously proportioned schoolmistress who could be none other than Miss *Smeller*! Gwen saw me and bounced up and down in a frantic silent *halloo*, setting off a stir

among her fellows and alerting Miss Mellor at the head of the squad, all
in the space of the few seconds it took for us to pass them and turn the
corner into Ainsley Place. I spoke over Knox's flusting and huffling—
"Father, I wish to invite Miss Haas to dinner at the earliest, may I?"

"I can't see why not."

"Thank you, Father."

I gave Knox a pitying look. From today, I should require no Nurse.
I was already experiencing an agreeable sense of my own benevolence
in cultivating a kindly condescension toward the old tuber, when the
carriage pulled to a stop before a rank of tall terraced townhouses.

"Here we are," said Father.

"Already? We might just as soon have walked."

I waited patiently for Father to hand me down whilst inwardly I
snorted and pawed the ground. Knox, bless her, looked positively pickled
with woe but I refused to allow her to cast a pall on the best day of my
life. "Come on, gloomy guts," I whispered so as Father might not hear.

Father himself looked rather more vague than usual—even pale. My
new-minted maturity supplied the explanation. He too was on a verge.
I was not quite thick as a gourd when it came to surmising such things,
for I'd had an able teacher in Gwendolyn. I smiled now to think how
she'd be pleased as Punch when I told her she'd been right in saying,
"He's got a lady friend, depend upon it." For the penny had finally
dropped and I realized that Father's festive attire, Miss Llewellyn's
presence at dinner, and their subsequent turn about the conservatory
in fact constituted wooing. And while I chose not to dwell, I did
acknowledge that if Father looked fair to derive a morsel of happiness
after his self-abnegation of the past nigh on thirteen years, I was the
last to begrudge him. These thoughts and innumerable others flew
through my mind before my foot touched the pavement, so swift is the
human brain.

I passed between low wrought-iron gates and followed Father up a
path of square paving stones to a black lacquered door beneath a striped
half-moon awning. In the top panel of the door was a brass plaque:
W. G. CHAMBERS LRCSE RCSE FRCSE LRCP. Knox stood behind me on
the step as Father reached out and pressed a brass button affixed to the
door frame. After a moment the door opened and a tidy little woman
with a tight grey bun stood before us. "Lord Henry," she said.

52

THE SUN, THE MOON and the stars revolve around wee Master Charles. He laughs, he toddles, he chatters, he has several wee pearly white teeth—"Ouch! Naughty Charlie, don't bite Momma." Mae taps his nose playfully. They are snuggled in the nursing chair in her bedchamber at Fayne. He giggles, milky and sweet, and she shifts him to her other breast. He is a year and a half old.

"Madam, Nature cannae bless you while your bairn is at the breast."

"Be a dear and fetch my diamond hairpin, Knoxy, it's there on my vanity."

"Och aye." The old woman obeys. But: "'Tis no here, Your Ladyship."

"Oh for goodness—" Rustling impatiently over to her vanity with the child still latched on, Mae snatches up the hairpin and subdues an errant curl. "Really Knoxy, it was right under your nose."

Knox has drifted along for the most part, as who could ask for anything more? What with a lighthearted Lady Marie, a contented Lord Henry and a healthy beautiful child. Well . . . one could ask for another child. Once Lady Marie has provided a second son—if not a third—what need anyone worry lest wee Master Charles not grow up to provide an heir himself? Or fail to grow up at all, as witness Lord Henry's own brothers—banish the thought! Knox frets but keeps mum lest the fear be named into existence. And after all, perhaps Brigid—that is, Mary Mother of God herself—or indeed Her Ladyship's own mother, really is taking care of the bairn.

As fall turns to winter, however, Knox has been at pains to remind Lady Marie oh so delicately that she is less likely to "cleck" so long as she continues suckling wee Charles. What's more, does Her Ladyship wish her own father to meet a bonny laddy come springtime? Or a babby mewling for the teat?—or nicer words to that effect.

"I know you mean well, Knoxy, but I'm not going to deprive Charles of his best chance at rude good health just so's I can rustle up a spare to go with the heir. I'd rather have one sturdy little boy than three weaklings. And I've got loads of time, you've said so yourself."

". . . Aye, Madam."

"Then what's the problem?"

"Nowt, Madam.

"Here, I got you a present."

Knox opens the small package. "Spectacles, are they, m'um?"

"Put them on."

Knox dons them and jumps back. Mae can't help but laugh.

It is the last Mae sees of them.

"Your Lordship?"

"What is it, Knox?" Henry looks up from *Birds of America*.

"'Tis I'm only after wondering about wee Master Charles's . . . diet."

He removes his spectacles. "His diet? Is aught amiss?"

"Not as such, Your Lordship, but you see, so long as Her Ladyship continues to nurse the bairn, she'll no . . . That is, only I wonder if Your Lordship intends the bairn might have a brother or sister?"

"Of course I do, what's that got to do with his 'diet'?"

Knox explains . . . Henry blinks rapidly.

Mae so loves her baby, it is as though the two of them and anyone who enters their sphere, even dear serrated Clarissa, is enveloped by a softness, impermeable to strife—they have been to Edinburgh with the baby baron-apparent, but never for more than a few weeks because at the first sign of a sniffle Mae has Henry spirit them back to Fayne.

Yes, fear has from the first pawed at this cloud of love. Whenever baby Charles has cried out in pain—"'Tis wind is all, Madam," says Knox, teaching Her Ladyship to lay him over her shoulder and pat his back 'til he emits a belch and sometimes more—"You may as well do that part, Knoxy, you're good at it." Whenever he has appeared to sleep too soundly—"No need to wake him, Madam, but let's have him on his side, like this, you see how I tuck the bolster at his back. Faery cannae snatch him if he's no facing heaven." With each cough—"'Tis natural, making mighty his chest and swallowers so as to take good solid food one day. Soon."

Mae watched in wonder as her son took to gobbling pap with a tincture of beef broth, boiled carrots and peas; and in delight as his plump little arms and legs grew sturdier every day, carrying him farther and farther from her 'til he crawled right across the nursery—"Charlie, come back!" Whereupon he'd pause and let loose chuckles that Mae fancied she could see dancing about his head and catching in his curls, before bestowing upon her his rosy pearly toothed smile, "Momma!" Only to sally forth again. At first scampering on all fours, then before long running, like as not tripping on his own tiny boots, crying, clinging to her as she'd lift him up, hold him close, rock him and croon, "One day you'll get on a great big ship and sail around the world but you'll always come back to Mammy, always, always, always." No sooner would her neck be damp with dew from eyes, nose and mouth, than he'd be wriggling—"Down!"—emboldened and off to the opposite pole of the drawing room, the dark heart of the conservatory, the dusty reaches of the library; thus has he circumnavigated every room, scaled every staircase, traversed every parquet prairie and stone desert, acquainting feet and sometimes face with the rude shock of gravity, growing stronger, reaching for door latches, becoming more and less hers every day.

"Your Ladyship, I caught Master Charles at the brink of the laundry tub," says Cook, with the child tucked squirming under her arm like a prize piglet.

"He's all boy!"

"He is that, Madam."

He laughs helplessly whenever Mae pretends to chide him—"Charlie, Charlie, Charlie!"—his very name a tickle. Why should she wean him before she absolutely must?

They are in the midst of dinner in the Gothic twilight of the dining room. The food, however, is as good as ever thanks to the old gargoyle of a gardener.

Henry says, down the length of the table, "Darling . . . Do you never wish for another child?"

"You mean . . . more children?"

"Of course. What else might I have meant?"

"Nothing, it just sounded funny, almost as though you were asking me if I wished for a different child."

"Ha-ha. Of course not. Only I do wonder, if it may be the case, that you wish for *additional* children—"

"You're at me to stop nursing him. Jealous?"

He flushes. "Of course not."

"I'm teasing you."

"I'd rather you didn't."

She sighs and sets down her knife and fork. "Henry. Can't you all just let me enjoy my baby for a little while longer? After all . . ."

She looks fair to weep. "Of course, my darling."

She smiles again, tilts her head back so as not to let her tears fall. "My own little Bonny Prince Charlie."

Of course Mae knows she must have another child. And another after that, and more besides, but . . . Perhaps it has to do with the loss of those might-have-been children, Charles's older siblings—a thicket of death through which he had to pass in order to be born alive . . . Enough of that now, Mary Corcoran, think nice thoughts. Or perhaps it is because she knows she could never love anyone as much as she loves her son. Knox says, "Och, Madam, there's love enough in your heart for twelve bairns and more."

Fayne House
February something-or-other, 1875

Dear Taffy,
Wait 'til you see Charlie. He has green-gray eyes, by turns merry and grave, curly strawberry blond locks and the most fetching grin which I just know will be roguish one day, four teeth, a dimple and a laugh to melt your heart. He is far from being breeched of course, so I have him decked in the cutest little dresses—Daddy will be gratified to see how well he looks in emerald green! He is a very pattern little boy—which reminds me, we've commissioned a portrait of the two of us. We'll sit for a photograph in Edinburgh prior to boarding the train for Liverpool then setting sail (!) and the artist can paint from it while we're in Boston. It's going to be <u>big</u> and I know just where I'm going to hang it too. In generations to come people will gaze up in awe at the wee baron-to-be and his Irish-American mam! Thank you, Daddy, thank you, beans and cans and factories, carts and railroads.

Henry and Knox are at me to stop nursing so I can "cleck." Yes, they intend that I should produce a "spare" to go with the "heir." You remember Mrs. Haas, the vicar's wife, and her miraculous baby (and by that, I don't mean an immaculate conception, more like <u>no</u>-conception) well the itty-bitty thing has proved a jolly playmate for Charlie. Gwendolyn gives far better than she gets, pinching Charlie and chasing him about the drawing room. You'd think he'd cry and run away from her, but he only ever laughs! He'll be thoroughly "broken in" and ready to play with another little girl once we get to Boston—O, I am dying to set eyes on dear little Tessa!

I'm in a tizzy as to what to wear to your first tea party. I have a passel of new gowns. I'll bring them all and you can choose. I am afraid that, despite my angelic intentions, I will end up putting Katie Buxton quite in the shade . . .

53

HENRY IS DOZING in the armchair of their first-class carriage. Mae is a titch put out by the raspberry hue of the upholstery which has clearly been chosen without ladies in mind, for she is today dressed in a travelling costume of burnt orange. She doesn't know where to look.

"Have you got the tickets?"

"What tickets?"

"Henry!"

"Ha-ha."

She slugs him in the shoulder.

"Ow!"

"You deserve it!"

"I deserve a kiss! Of course I've got them, what do you take me for?"

She purrs and burrows into his lately pummelled shoulder. "Both, right? The original, plus the new one?"

"I've yet to purchase the new one."

She sits up. "Henry, what are you waiting for?"

"There is no urgency, darling, I'll see about wiring for one from the station."

"Don't forget to purchase one for Knox too."

"I shan't."

"And you've still got the remaining one from Daddy, you're sure?"

Henry opens his frock coat and draws from its inner pocket the certificate *Entitling the Bearer to One Trans-Atlantic Passage* . . . somewhat less crisp, given its peregrinations, but no less authentic.

"And you are leaving that old coat in Edinburgh."

"It is perfectly serviceable."

"Henry, don't tease, you promised."

"I have, of course, kept my promise. My newly acquired garments are packed away in my trunk for the crossing."

"Your new clothes don't belong in your trunk, they belong on your back. I want you in full fig from the moment we get to Bell Gardens."

"As you wish, my darling."

And nuzzling back into his shoulder, "I'm sure Havers will appreciate the gift of a perfectly serviceable frock coat."

"No doubt."

Suddenly taut and trembling—"Henry, I'm so happy I could bust."

"I can tell, darling."

Seizing the lapels of the despised frock coat, she whispers, the better to compress its power, "I love you."

From the adjacent compartment comes the battle cry of little Lord-in-Waiting Charles, answered by the tempering tones of Knox. The train whistle pierces the air and at the window Mae laughs to see a herd of "hairy coos" retreating as fast as their shaggy legs can lumber, while lambs bounce off in all directions across the cropped pasture. Along with lovely ruins, the fields are of course full of sheep. She knows she is looking at part of the reason Daddy was starved out of Ireland, but they're so pretty! And aren't I lucky he was starved out! Better a lovely ruin than a ruined lovely.

Henry is sound asleep with *The Scotsman* splayed on his chest. Mae herself is drowsy and allows her eyes to rest on the page . . . She sits up suddenly, "Henry!"

"What is it?" He starts awake, flinging out his arm to brace her—a derailment?

"Fanny's had a baby!"

"What? Who?"

"Fanny and Hawley, look, never mind I'll read it to you. 'To Lord Richard Hawley and Lady Frances, a son, the Honourable Ebeneezer George William Francis Hawley.'"

"Oh," says Henry, rubbing his jaw, "well, capital news, of course."

"How lovely for them. Imagine Fanny having a baby at her age! She must be forty!"

———

The carriage, drawn by the Black and the Bay, is turning now into No. One Bell Gardens and Master Charles is all for trying to climb out the window. "Here now, you wee scallywag," says Knox.

"Give them to me for safekeeping, Henry, I trust you with my life but not those tickets."

"Dash it, I forgot to purchase the extras."

"Don't tease!"

"I really did forget this time."

"Well where were you for twenty minutes in the station while I was gasping for air on the platform and your child was exposed to the great unwashed?"

"Why, seeking out a porter of course."

She sighs, but leans out the window. "Clarissa! Hi! Wave to Auntie Clarissa, Charlie, wave! That's right!"

"Where are you looking, I don't see her," says Henry.

"Of course you don't, neither do I, she'll be hiding behind the net curtain."

"Mae."

"Well."

He suppresses a smile and secures the brim of his silk hat—

"I forbid you to wear that ugly old hat onto the ship!"

The carriage door opens and Henry ducks out, turns and puts up a hand to his wife, who takes it and descends with an almost comically haughty air.

In the foyer, the child is suffered to approach its aunt who has not set eyes on it these six months. It looks up solemnly. Its aunt looks down, equally solemn. Extends her hand. The child takes and hugs it to his chest.

"Hmph," says Clarissa. "Fine boy."

Clarissa experiences a scintillation. Not given to fancy—at least not during waking hours—it strikes her nonetheless as somehow silvery . . . It ripples through her and pain ripples away with it. She says, "Come into my parlour, Charles, and let us see if I can't find you a sweetie."

Mae shoots Henry a look. *Can you believe it?* He smiles back.

The child toddles after his auntie into her parlour and watches, enchanted, as she lifts the lid on her wicker sewing basket.

54

CHARLES CHARMS THE HOUSEHOLD. Havers himself is seen to smile. The scullery maid plays Ring-Around-the-Rosie with him, the stable boy tosses him into the air and catches him, Pugsley amazes him by taking off his nose, and Sanders holds him atop the Bay, whose name is Nellie. Maid alone is immune. Her indifference to Charlie's charms almost makes Mae miss Sheehan. Almost.

In the kitchen Cook, arms crossed over her wooden spoon, grins down at him and says, "Into the pot 'til I cook you for dinner." Charles screams in terror, Cook laughs approvingly and gives him a spoonful of strawberry jam. Knox appears, out of breath, "There you are! Now don't be botherin' Cook or we'll none of us have a morsel tonight."

He toddles back into the kitchen at the first opportunity.

"You want me to put you in the pot, is that it? Spit you on the meat-jack?"

"Nay!"

A hearty cackle. A handful of currants.

Mae brings Charles, in company with Knox, to a photographic studio on Princes Street. She has had him dressed in his new sailor suit— "Who's Momma's handsome boy?!" She drapes a silken shawl about her shoulders and lifts Charles in her arms, but he is skittish at the sight of the black hooded camera on its spindly cane tripod, and refuses to settle before its great glass eye. Knox takes him by the hand and shows him round the back of the contraption. Peace reigns. Mother and son pose before the *poof* and flash. The artist will paint from the photograph. The portrait ought to be finished and framed by the time they return from Boston in the fall.

In the interval before their departure, Henry basks in the harmony that holds sway in Bell Gardens. Marie has not uttered a word against Cook's traditional—and toothsome—white pudding, and Clarissa has entered willingly into his wife's plans for a series of at-homes.

"Be sure to invite the Heatheringtons if they're in town," says Mae, with a touch of her fingers on Clarissa's hand. "Oh, and the dear Farquhars of course."

Clarissa enthuses, "I believe Sir Ian has, in the interval since last we met, devised a new type of weather-impermeable pitch."

"You don't say," says Mae.

Clarissa looks bemused. "I just did."

Henry tops up Clarissa's sherry.

For her part, Clarissa is smitten with her nephew. She teaches him a fencing pose with a knitting needle. Teaches him to count. She gives him an abacus. And at the bottom of her work basket she keeps, in place of the blue bottle, a sweetie. He forages for it whenever he invades the parlour.

"Ye wee reiver!"

"Weever!"

"And what is the name of your favourite sweetie, Charlie?"

His marble-mouthed garble, complete with a glimpse of the candy in his wee gob with its perfect pearly teeth elicits Clarissa's laughter, refreshing her whole being, just as though a spring had gushed from a stone at the touch of a willow wand.

"Ed-in-burgh Rock.' Say it."

"Embuhwok."

She laughs.

How she dotes on the wee mannie, how she loves him, just as she loved his father before him, but with the blessing that her love for Charles is unburdened by care. Not to her fall his upbringing, education and continuance of title. Not for her the duty of mother and father combined, for the lad has one of each. He is nestling in her heart, rather than weighing upon her shoulders, for the future of Fayne is assured. Not but what a spare is to be desired, if only to remove from her nephew's curly crown the weight of fate, for *uneasy lies the head* etc. . . .

"Dinnae swallow it whole, ye dafty wee skellum. Here, have another, and one for Auntie Cwissa."

When the laddy clambers onto her lap Clarissa experiences no discomfort in her hip sockets, nor when she embraces him is there so much as a twinge in her shoulders.

Half a drop. Every other night. *Why, Mr. Baxter, I should be delighted to accompany you up Arthur's Seat . . .*

———

Mae throws herself into the planning, ordering and altering of her wardrobe. She engages a new lady's maid. A plain little thing but a dog for
work. Mae has decided to arrive in Boston in a sassy frock of Bell tartan
with Charlie in a cute little kilt to match.

"Very bonny, Madam."

Mae decides to bring the new maid to Boston. "That's another ticket
we'll be needing, Henry."

Up in the nursery Mae is playing quietly with Charles. Having tumbled
twice from his rocking horse, he is now absorbed in his abacus. "My
little man."

She hands him, at arm's length, to Knox. "Someone needs a fresh
nappy."

Knox takes the child and Mae adds, "Call me when he's in his bath."

Mae never misses bath time. After all, the days are numbered when
a mother can bathe her son.

At dinner Henry, venturing back into carnivorousness, finds himself
working dormant mandibular muscles on the minced mutton, which
bears a mournful resemblance to many a meal at Straifmore School.

"Henry, I'd like you to line up some nursemaids for me to interview."

He discreetly palms a bit of gristle into his dinner napkin. "Does
Knox require assistance?"

"Knox requires a rest."

He ponders this.

Clarissa glances up.

Mae adds, "I think the journey might be a little much for her. At her
age."

"Really. I hadn't thought. Is Knox pleased at the prospect of a respite?"

"I haven't told her about the respite, I was hoping you would."

Mae is "sensible" of the aristocratic code of loyalty that entails feeding and housing servants until long past the latters' ability to return a lick
of work on the dollar; nor does she begrudge it, goodness knows there's
plenty of greenbacks—pounds, that is—to go around. Of course Charles
is attached to his old nurse but Knox herself is keen for him to outgrow
babyish habits, and he'll soon get used to a new one who can run about
and play. And can Mae be blamed if she'd rather take a sprightly young

lass home to Boston instead of a ponderous old woman, however beloved? One who never leaves off reminding her of her duty to "cleck"?

"Would not Charles miss his Knoxy?" asks Henry, sounding regrettably effeminate to his own ears.

"Well of course, but he's small, he'll forget her soon enough."

"As like to forget his own mother," mutters Clarissa.

Mae pretends not to hear. *I'm not telling you to send her to the glue factory, just put her out to pasture.*

At week's end, Mae is unsurprised to find her husband has yet to make inquiries as to a new nursemaid.

That evening before dinner, Knox brings Master Charles, dewy from his bath and dressed for bed, into the drawing room as usual to bid his parents goodnight.

"Oh Knoxy, he dropped a half-eaten oatcake on the carpet earlier, would you mind terribly?"

Spotting it, Henry moves to pick it up but Mae places a hand on his arm.

The old nurse shifts Master Charles to one hip and squints about at the carpet. "I dinnae see an oatcake, Madam."

"What's the good of spectacles if you won't wear them, Knox?" says Mae, and rings for Maid.

"Och, Master Charles'd have 'em off me in a trice, M'Lady, and what good are they broken?"

"You spoil him. Teach him not to grab what isn't his."

"He'll never be a proper nobleman in that case," says Henry with a chuckle.

Knox bends the child toward his mother and she kisses him.

"Henry, kiss Charlie goodnight."

"Oh, quite." It is a custom to which Henry may never become accustomed.

They watch as Knox withdraws with the little sleepy-head and Mae says to Henry, "Not to mention, she's blind as a bat."

55

THE FARQUHARS, Colonel MacOmber, the Heatheringtons, Josiah Baxter—Clarissa has even invited Miss Gourley—all pay a call.

Mrs. Knox brings in the child by the hand to a chorus of "ooh's" and "ahhhs." The little boy is in a green tartan dress, trimmed with *broderie anglaise* lace at his collar and cuffs; on his feet, stout wee boots topped with matching tartan socks leave his dimpled knees bare, one of which sports a plaster.

"Ohhh!" exclaims Lady Nora, captivated to the point of tears, "goodness me for a bonny wee laddy!"

Mae whispers to her, "You know, Lady Nora, my own mother is no longer with us and a lad cannot have too many grandmothers." And receives a warm handclasp.

Sir Ian too is more than usually animated and manages even to make cement sound interesting. The Heatheringtons see in the child the promise of their own future happiness, their daughter being newly married in London. Colonel MacOmber knits his brows, mock-fierce, in an attempt to frighten the bairn but succeeds only in making him laugh which provokes a guffaw in the old man which frightens Charles to tears, which could not be more delightful. Josey is gentle, offering the child his pocket watch to play with. Mae watches, deeply gratified, as her son wins them all over.

All, perhaps, but Miss Gourley. At least so far as Mae can tell. The spinster has sat quietly and, though not frowning (even with pleasure), nor is she quite smiling.

"How was your sabbatical, Miss Gourley?" asks Henry.

"Most edifying, thank you," replies that lady with a flush that does not go unnoticed by Mae.

Sir Ian jests, "Colonel, if you keep roaring and smacking the armrest like that, the child will take you for a bear and run away." At which the party laughs, as does the amiable child who submits to a great rustling hug from Lady Nora, at which point Miss Gourley murmurs thanks and an excuse and shows herself out.

Henry watches her go. And wonders, not for the first time, whether she really did visit "an ailing relative in the north" some four years—and a lifetime—ago.

Mae is speaking brightly of their upcoming visit "home to Boston," and of her dearest friend—"Henry, I won't blame you if you fall a little in love with Taffy, in fact I'll blame you if you don't!" Laughter.

Clarissa makes plans with Mr. Baxter to walk out into Queen's Park on the first fine Sunday. With field glasses. "I should be delighted, Miss Bell."

"Do, please, call me Clarissa, Mr. Baxter."

"Clarissa. Would you honour me by calling me Josey?"

Clarissa experiences a sharp pain in her chest as the over-wintered tulip bulb of her heart puts forth a green shoot.

Of course Henry loves his child. One does not suppose there exists an instrument which, hooked up to a dial, might gauge the rate at which his father's heart produces paternal oscillations. Neither by breeding nor by temperament is Henry wont to ask himself what he *feels* for his child. Rather, it is a matter of what he is duty-bound to *do* for his child. The latter, surely, is the true measure of paternal love. If there be those who derive amusement from their intercourse with the child—for he is merry and pretty, Henry must give him that—then all the better for the lad's prospects of survival and the acquisition of a superior mate; the ultimate end being the continuance of the House of Fayne. Clarissa was right all along. About everything.

Thus does Lord Henry buttress himself with the knowledge that if, of late, his wife lavishes more of her affections on her son than on her husband, it is to the good. And there are birds who need him.

He repairs to his study.

Mrs. Knox has no need of hawkish vision to change a wee laddy's nappy, merely deftness to cover his loins afore he can strinkle his nurse. In her time she has tended enough such—including Lord Henry and his brothers—that she knows to keep handy a linen to drop over a pizzle at the first sign of stiffening.

This evening, however, once she has Master Charles on his back on the nursery table and has opened his napkin—"No you don't!" she chides as he tries to wriggle free, for he does love to run nakit, "You wee wiggle-waggle!" which always makes him laugh—she bends, the better to peer at the fleshy pouches either side his safely sleeping pizzle. She presses gently with her thumb, feeling for the wee bollocks as are still too shy to show theirselves—mayhap the only shy part of Master Charles who, like his predecessors, now takes hold his pyntle with glee, tugging and giggling like the tiny Tartar he is. It stands stiff as a twig and this is the moment to drop the linen so as to avoid a dousing but Mrs. Knox does not drop the linen. No dousing ensues. And yet . . . the child is making water. She reaches into her apron, finds the spectacles. And dons them.

She knocks. And enters.

Waits for him to look up. He does not.

"Lord Henry."

"Mm?"

"My Lord, it concerns wee Master Charles."

Henry looks up from *Proceedings of the Society for the Preservation of the North American Carrier Pigeon.* "Is aught amiss?"

"Nay, Your Lordship, the bairn is fine well, only . . ."

He removes his pince-nez. Rather tersely, "What, then?"

"His cods, sir. "

"His . . . What?"

"The knackers."

"You've lost me."

"He . . . Well, 'tis not uncommon at first for a male infant to lack them."

". . . Do you refer to my son's testicles, Mrs. Knox?"

"Aye, sir, those. They've yet to come down."

"Whence?"

"Why sir, happen sometimes they lodge in the belly 'til they be fully baked, then they drop."

"I see. Is this dangerous?"

"Not a bit of it."

"Good. Let me know when they've dropped." He resumes the pince-nez. The bird will be extinct within a decade if—

"My Lord."

"Well?" Removing them yet again.

"I have wondered at the . . . his wee pyntle . . .'Tis wee, My Lord."

"As what on earth ought it to be in a child of scarcely more than year?"

"Nigh on twenty-two months, My Lord. Even so."

His brow furrows.

She hastens to add, "Not but what many's the man with a pizzle no bigger than my thumb and they get bairns."

"Well. That is reassuring." He resumes his pince-nez.

"There is something else, My Lord."

"Dash it, what?"

"He makes water from . . . another place."

". . . What 'other place'?"

"Not but what there be men whose water comes from further down the . . . shaft."

He takes this in. Swallows. "There are?"

"Och, aye, but . . . Mayhap best ask Mr. Moore for a look-see. In case his cods be overbaked, you'd no wish him to take sick with fever on the voyage."

Pleading headache, Henry sleeps in Bertram's room. The next morning he looks in, expecting to find his wife still asleep, but the bed has sprouted a riot of spring colour and his wife stands, hands on hips, surveying it.

"Good morning, my darling—"

"Tell me honestly. The dots or the cherry blossoms?"

"The . . . ?"

"For our arrival. I want Taffy to see me at my prettiest and I want everyone else to die of envy."

"I thought you had in mind a tartan—"

"That was last week, darling."

"Oh. Well. They're both lovely."

"Off you go now and ring for my maid."

"My dear, I must speak with you. Knox has brought to my attention—"

"Oh all right, Hank, I promise."

"What?"

"I'll stop nursing Charles just as soon as we make Boston Harbor, and you and I can get busy on son number two." She winks. "He'll be an 'Honourable,' am I right? Not so bad. A handsome rake and rich to boot, then we can try for a girl for me." Turning to face him suddenly—"When am I getting my new nursemaid?"

"Ah, as, as to that, soon."

"You haven't even spoken to Knox yet, have you."

"I shall see to it."

She turns to her open armoire and methodically empties it onto the bed. "Are you still here, Henry?"

"Mae. Have you, of late, had occasion to bathe our son?"

"Of course I have, and you don't know what you're missing."

"And have you . . . had occasion to make fresh his napkin?"

"No, well yes of course I have at some point—what are you saying?"

"No, no, that is quite as it ought, uh, I'm sure, only . . . Have you had occasion to be present when he . . . ?"

She tilts her head with a little shake in a manner that used to be charming but which now strikes him as a bit . . . convulsive. "When he what?" Her voice too small. Too harmless.

"Nothing, darling, just . . . It would seem . . . there may be some question concerning whether his . . . male parts be quite in order."

"Oh that, Knoxy says it's not uncommon for testicles to take their sweet old time."

"Ah." He smiles. Blinks.

"What's the matter?"

"Not a thing, darling, merely a normal matter of his, uh . . ."

"Testicles. It's okay, Henry, you can say it." Her minxy smile.

He smiles. Plays his part. "Rum word, 'testicles.' Oddly aquatic."

She laughs. But her cheeks are flushed. "What is it, Henry? What are you thinking?"

". . . The dots."

Clarissa has resumed her early-morning habits and Henry joins her now at breakfast. He scrapes butter onto a rusk and asks, as though by way of an afterthought, "What's the name of that physician chap? The one Mae recommended to you?"

"I bid you rest easy, brother, I am not unwell. Indeed, I plan to walk out into Queen's Park with—"

"It is Charles of whom I speak."

"Charles? Is there aught amiss with the lad, is he ill?"

"Not in the least, sister, it is a matter merely of . . . well, his . . ." He looks about for the marmalade. "His male parts. Aspects of which have yet to . . ."

"The cods, is it?"

He parts his lips, closes them. Parts them.

"You look like a guppy, Henry. And don't be shocked, I had four younger brothers in a time of straitened means and a mother who was indisposed, thus it fell to Knox and me." She gives him a wry smile. Almost a chuckle.

Henry has a sudden hankering for a dram of whisky. He chooses his words carefully. "Knox has given me to understand his cods are in danger of 'overbaking' as it were. The which may place him in danger of developing fever on the crossing to America."

"I see. I take it you still nurture an animus toward Mr. Moore—"

Henry draws himself up, "I'll not be gainsaid in my own—"

"Nobody's gainsaying you, brother, come with me."

She rises in one motion and precedes him to her parlour, where Henry watches her bend with ease, retrieve her work basket, and take from it a notecard.

Henry looks in on his wife. The bed is a shipwreck of silken cargo.

"My love—"

"I'm busy," she singsongs, a warning in her voice.

"Mrs. Knox has brought to my attention that, owing to his testicles being harboured within the heat of his little body, our son might be at risk of fever."

Her hands fly to her cheeks. "I'm a terrible mother!"

"You are a marvellous mother."

"What if he gets sick on the crossing?"

"It did occur to me."

"We have to take him to a doctor."

"Do you think so?"

"Of course I do, my goodness, Henry, this isn't the Middle Ages!"

"I suppose you're right."

"There is no way I am boarding a ship until—darn it all, Mr. Moore has dropped us, who can we see?"

"Leave it with me, darling."

56

THE BLACK LACQUERED DOOR bears a brass plaque: W. G. CHAMBERS, LRCS RCSE FRCSE LRCP. Henry reaches out and presses a brass button affixed to the door frame. After a moment the door opens and a small woman with a tight greying bun worn low at the neck stands before them. Henry says, "Lord and Lady Bell, to see—" But the woman is already turning, "Follow me, please."

Henry and Mae, with Knox carrying Charles, are shown up a staircase and through a sliding panel door into a sort of truncated morning room where two ladies and a gentleman are seated separately. They spare the newcomers hardly a glance. The gentleman—presumably Chambers— half rises and Henry looks askance, about to speak, when the grey-bun woman says, "The doctor will be with you soon. Please wait here." Then she leaves, sliding closed the door behind her.

If not downright insolent, the expectation is certainly skewed that he, Lord Bell, should await an audience with a physician in his employ— in the midst of strangers to boot. Ah well. Can't be helped. The march of democracy and all that. Not to mention Henry is here with his wife and child because the physician declined to call in at the house. Scarcely to be borne. So be it, however, if it means peace of mind on the cross- ing. Especially for Marie.

In the centre of the room is a low table upon which are fanned sev- eral periodicals. Mae takes up a copy of *The Englishwoman's Domestic Magazine* and leafs through it while Knox allows Charles to unravel a ball of yarn from her carpet bag. Henry remains standing, hat in hand, his gaze having settled on the portrait of Queen Victoria on the near wall. It looms suddenly closer and he steps back—a concealed door, likely an old service door, has swung open to reveal the small woman. "The doctor will see you now, Your Lordship."

Hmph, will he indeed? Henry steps aside that his wife might precede him. Knox follows with Charles.

Mr. Chambers is a tall man, his demeanour as grave as his linea- ments are gaunt. He stands before his desk. Bows. "Your Ladyship, Your Lordship, you do me honour."

Henry unbristles somewhat.

Mae chirps, "Thank you for seeing us on such short notice, Dr. Chambers."

Framed diplomas on the wall behind the oak desk proclaim the man a Licentiate of the Royal College of Surgeons, Edinburgh and England; Fellow of the Royal College of Surgeons, Edinburgh; Licentiate of the Royal College of Physicians, Edinburgh and England. And there is one in French from the Hôpital de la Salpêtrière, Paris.

This room is not so different from Henry's study—what with its glass-fronted bookshelves, its Turkey carpet—excepting of course the enamel basin and tap. And the white linen towel folded over the rail of a sort of end-table-on-wheels . . . And the smell. Reeks of carbolic. It occurs to Henry to wonder what might be housed in the large cabinet. Cherry wood. Altogether decent.

"How might I be of assistance, Your Lordship?"

"We are here with regard to my son."

Charles is babbling, Knox is keeping him busy with the abacus she thought to bring from the nursery.

Henry adds, "The Honourable Charles Bell."

The physician directs his gaze to Charles, who looks up and dissolves in tears.

Chambers redirects his gaze to Lord Henry and inquires, "What is the nature of your concern, Lord Bell?"

"It concerns a slight anatomical . . . quirk, brought to my attention by his nurse, Mrs. Knox."

Knox looks up in the act of preventing the wee Honourable from tugging open a cabinet door, and reddens as though caught trespassing.

"What is the nature of the 'quirk'?" asks Chambers.

Henry answers, "It is in regard to the child's . . . as regards his—"

Mae pipes up, "He's got shy testicles, Doctor." She smiles, "I'm American, Dr. Chambers, you can get straight to the point, I won't faint."

The man's expression does not alter as he turns now to Mae. Men like him activate a switch in her—she gets flighty and flirty, compelled either to flummox or to fascinate—and her eyelashes commence batting. "Anyhoo, we're leaving for Boston on Wednesday and I want to be sure Charlie doesn't get a fever on the crossing. Mrs. Knox has been using warm compresses for months and frankly I wonder if that's part of the problem. I'd like to know if I ought to have his new nurse put cool compresses on his groin, what do you think, Doctor, do you back me up?" Mae can see by Knoxy's expression that Henry hasn't broken the news, well if that isn't the limit—! "What was that, Doctor?"

"Merely, I was suggesting that with Your Ladyship's permission, I shall reserve judgment until I have examined the child."

"Of course!" And Mae plunks herself down on the couch.

A pause.

"Lord Bell, you and Her Ladyship may wish to take a turn about the park while I examine Master Charles."

"Oh no you don't, I'm staying," says Mae.

Henry colours.

"That is, of course, Your Ladyship's prerogative," says Dr. Chambers. "It is my experience, however, that while a child rarely submits to a physical examination without protest, its distress is increased in the presence of its mother."

"What are you going to do to him?"

"I shall examine the child with particular attention to the scrotal sac which I shall manually palpate with the greatest care in order to form an opinion as to the presence and position of undescended testicles."

Henry looks as though he might faint.

Dr. Chambers adds, almost congenially, "It is the least uncommon defect of the male genital tract."

Marie pales. "'Defect'?"

"Minor," says Dr. Chambers. "Commonly self-resolving."

"You mean . . ."

"The testicles eventually descend on their own without medical intervention."

"Oh well, good, wonderful. Um . . ."

"Your Ladyship may wish to leave your nurse in company with the child."

"All right, then."

"Henry, how could you do that to me?"

"'Do' . . . ?"

She has waited until they are out of Ainsley Place altogether. "You were supposed to have spoken to Knox by now."

He strikes his forehead with his palm.

"You forgot, didn't you. Poor Knoxy, what a horrible way to find out you've been fired."

"'Fired.'"

"Sacked, then!"

"As to that—"

"Never mind we'll take Knoxy with us too, Henry, buy another ticket, I don't know what I was thinking, she can help the new nurse and Charlie just adores her and so do I." She bursts into tears. "I'm sorry!" Henry strives to collect his thoughts. He steers Mae into a small park whose gate is unlocked. Pigeons strut about. On a bench sits an old woman feeding them from a paper sack. The path branches in three directions. Mae inclines her head to his shoulder. He tilts his own toward hers and guides them rightward. Beneath a heavy overhang of cherry trees, buds held tight and safe against the coming of April, they stroll in silence until they have completed a circuit and are back within view of the pigeons and the now-empty bench.

"What a long face he's got, that Dr. Chambers. I was sure he was going to tell us something awful even before he looked at Charlie."

"Bears rather a resemblance to the Grim Reaper."

"Henry!"

"I jest."

"You and your Scottish sense of humour. You don't think there's anything really wrong, do you?"

"Not in the slightest."

She squeezes his arm. They turn back into Ainsley Place and Henry remarks, "There is something to be said for an habitually grave demeanour in a physician: one need search his face for no sign whatever, good or bad."

Mae mimics Dr. Chambers's compressed Edinburgh speech, "*Leddy Bell, Um afreed yoor chylde is pairfectly weyl.*"

Henry laughs outright. And for the first time, he looks forward to the voyage. Standing on deck before a mahogany railing, his Irish-American beauty at his side. Off to the New World. The cry of gulls overhead both transports him and returns him to the present moment.

"What's the matter, Henry?"

"Nothing whatever, my dear, I'm . . . I am happy."

She laughs. "I might've known. You look positively tragic."

——

Meanwhile, in his consulting room, Dr. Chambers instructs the child's nurse, "Lay the child on its back."

The small grey-bunned woman has wheeled the utility table over and spread it with the linen towel. Knox lays Master Charles on it with a tickle at his armpit which induces a chuckle.

"Remove the child's napkin."

Knox obeys.

"Hold the child's wrists."

"Aye." Knox stations herself at Master Charles's head.

"Nae," says Charles.

"Nonsense," says Knoxy, gently enclosing the wee wrists.

The small woman takes up a position to the side where she grips Master Charles's ankles, bends his knees, and pins his feet apart. He screams.

"Now, now, Master Charles," says Knox, her mild admonition at odds with the passion of his protest.

The doctor bends forward and proceeds, over the child's cries, gently, to knead with his thumbs the pouches of flesh to either side of Master Charles's wee pyntle . . . which stiffens. The doctor withdraws to the other side of the room. There is the sound of a drawer opening. He returns with a pair of tweezers with which he grasps the tip of Master Charles's penis.

Charles screams. Writhes, but is powerless.

"Hush-hush," says Knox.

Hush-hush is for a scraped elbow, a sweetie dropped in the dirt. *Hush-hush* invites a child's mind to re-categorize dropped sweeties and scraped elbows such that either dropped sweeties and scraped elbows are much worse than he thought or this is much better, so that even as he howls he is reorganizing his experience.

Knox watches as, with his free hand, the doctor places a small ruler alongside the penis which he now stretches with the tweezers.

Still screaming, the child kicks, but only his dimpled knees convulse, for his ankles are held fast. He flails, but only his shoulders flinch, for his wrists are likewise pinned.

Without letting go of the tweezers, Dr. Chambers lays down the ruler and takes up a magnifying glass—the child's crying now takes on a hiccoughing quality, and Knox says sternly, "That's enough now, Master Charles," which is how Knox knows she herself is frightened. She dares to say, "How much longer, Dr. Chambers?"

He does not answer her, the small woman does not look at her. He is peering through the magnifying glass at the tip of Master Charles's penis.

Charles strains to raise his head—it is more difficult to breathe like that but the child needs to see. He sees: the huge grey-blue eye. He snaps his head back, and side to side to side. Blur of the strange woman at his side. Blur of Knoxy overhead, she is saying *hush*. He tries to clutch his pizzle, "Momma, ma, ma, ma, ma . . ." in a bumpy voice, the kind that comes out when they ride over cobblestones and he sings and Momma laughs but Momma is not here—

Dr. Chambers takes up two steel probes—one resembles a file, the other a tiny spade. Knox watches as he runs the file between the pouches, parts them, then, with the spade, holds one pouch aside and takes up the magnifying glass once more. He looks. He sets it down. Now, with the blunt edge of the file, he parts the pearlescent seam and inserts his little finger.

It looks like sleep, but the child is not asleep.

The child is here and not here. It has been snatched out of Time by Mercy, and is experiencing the Present as though it were a Memory, and is suspended, watching as through a window. The child does not know that he is not dreaming, and when he wakes up from what was not sleep, he will not remember remembering. But he may, one day, remember that he has forgotten.

Knox waits. The doctor remains still, as though listening like a robin for a worm. Finally he withdraws his finger, rises and crosses to the far side of the room. Knox fears more instruments, but the small woman releases her grip on the ankles and clears away the instruments that have been used. Knox watches the doctor's back as he washes his hands at the basin. She releases the wee wrists ever so gently. The red impressions of her hands have faded by the time she has dressed the child. Who is unusually compliant.

"Dr. Chambers." It must be due to the strangeness of the whole proceedings, for Knox knows it is not her place to speak. "Begging pardon, sir . . ."

He looks up from his desk where he is writing. "Yes, Mrs. Knox?"

"I knew something were amiss wi' the bairn, but I . . . ought I to've . . . noticed sooner?"

"Are you schooled in the medical arts, Mrs. Knox?"

". . . My mother were a midwife, sir, and she passed the art on to me."

"I see. Then what makes you think yourself qualified to diagnose a pediatric anomaly?"

The fact Knox does not answer does not mean she did not understand the question. But Dr. Chambers is not to know that. His tone is reassuring: "You have nothing with which to reproach yourself, Mrs. Knox."

Mae and Henry are shown directly into the consulting room, where Knox has Charles nestled in her lap on the couch. He's been crying but sucks on a sweetie. He shoots out his arms at the sight of his Momma. "Charlie-boy, Momma's brave soldier, look at you, who's got a sweetie?" She tickles him and he giggles. "Who's the big strong boy?" She peppers his face with kisses and he laughs. She sits. The gentlemen sit. "Well?" she says.

"I am pleased to assure Your Lord and Ladyship that your child is in excellent health and well able to weather an ocean crossing."

Mae claps her hands, then so does Charles. "I'm so relieved, thank you, Doctor! And I'm sorry I was such a fraidy-cat, I'll send you a post-card from Boston." She rises. The gentlemen rise. Mrs. Knox gathers up Master Charles's cape and cap and the contents of the carpet bag, Marie scoops up Charlie and spins him round, and Henry bends to retrieve his hat, catching as he does so a gesture from Dr. Chambers—a raised forefinger.

"Let's go, Henry." Mae sweeps toward the door with her bonny bairn, followed by her laden nurse.

"I'll be right there, my dear."

"What is it?"

"A word, only, with Dr. Chambers."

"Why, what's wrong?"

"Nothing at all, Marie, only . . ." He clears his throat. "I wish to consult Dr. Chambers in private."

". . . Oh! Sorry." She retreats, "*Au revoir*, Doctor."

Henry turns to Chambers. "Well?"

———

Mae has been waiting in the carriage, her eyes on the lacquered door, having sent Knox ahead on foot with Charlie to give him an airing—he was an absolute jumping bean the moment they got out of the doctor's office.

At last the door opens and Henry emerges. "Finally!" she cries. Then, contrite as he approaches, "Are you okay? You look like you've seen a ghost."

He climbs into the carriage. "I'm fine well, fine well."

"You're ill."

"Certainly not." He settles beside her. "Where is—?"

"Knoxy's airing him, what did he say, Henry?"

"Nothing, I'm . . . I expect I'm famished."

"You skipped luncheon again, didn't you."

"I may have done."

"Holed up with your mouldy old birds."

"Mm."

It's not like him to take an anti-bird remark lying down. "Why did you want to see the doctor, Henry?"

"For goodness sake, Marie, you are my wife, not my nurse."

"Not yet. Just you wait, you're way older than me."

He cringes reflexively—*older than _I_*. Grammar. My refuge.

"Henry?"

"Mm?"

He rouses himself, raps the ceiling with his cane, and the carriage pulls away. "Let's stop at the Douglas Hotel and get you bolstered, then you can watch me try on tea gowns at Jenners."

"I'm not certain I'm up to it, my dear."

He sinks into silence.

Whatever it is, nagging him won't help him. And it's such a lovely day, last but three before they set out—she watches it flash by like a zoetrope through the window. To cheer him up she chatters about the wonderful sights and people she'll introduce him to in Boston. "Daddy will take you on a tour of the State House and there's bound to be bird-fanciers at Harvard, and you may as well know that Gordon Peabody, he's Taffy's cousin on her mother's side, asked Daddy's permission to court me, but I . . ."

They come alongside the park. "There they are! Yoo-hoo, Charlie!" she cries, waving madly. "Henry, wave!"

Henry leans over his wife's shoulder and raises his cane to his child who, mirroring its mother's waving, scatters a paper sack of seeds to the delight of the pigeons that flap and swoop about him, whilst Knox does her best to shoo them.

Henry leans back, knocking his hat to the floor, in the reaching for which he experiences a fleeting light-headedness. He feels her hand on the back of his neck, cool, soft. "Darling Hank, let's get you home and fed and 'fettled,' like Knox would say."

As Knox would say.

MARCH 12, 1875

W. G. CHAMBERS, CASE NOTES

2:00 P.M. _Lord Henry and Lady Marie Bell entered consulting room with patient: the Honourable Charles Bell, aged twenty-two months._

APPEARANCE: _Colour wholesome, features regular, moisture on brow and upper lip due to over-bundling in accordance with custom._

HISTORY: _Lord Henry Bell is 17th Baron of the DC de Fayne. Lady Marie, née Corcoran, of Boston is of Irish stock . . ._

The carriage pulls up in time for them to encounter Clarissa in the foyer, herself just in and removing her outer things—"Where have you been, Clarissa?" asks Mae with a saucy smile.

"I've been for a walk." Clarissa looks away in the act of unpinning her casquette.

"All by your lonesome?"

"Josiah Baxter accompanied me."

Mae prompts Henry with a sly look and a wink, "Look at your sister, Henry, doesn't she look perky?"

Clarissa can tell immediately that her brother has sustained a shock.

He says, "Why, yes, what a very fetching bonnet."

"It's not a 'bonnet,' Henry—!"

"_Chapeau_ of course, silly me." His smile is wistful.

"Havers, tell Cook to fix a tray for His Lordship."

"Very good, Your Ladyship."

Clarissa has escaped to her parlour, but Mae sidles round the door. "Did you have a nice walk, Clarissa?"

"What is amiss with Henry?"

"He's just hungry. I'm seeing to it." She lingers expectantly but her sister-in-law has clammed up. That tells Marie the outing has been a success (*whee!*). She discreetly withdraws, leaving the parlour door ajar.

Clarissa rises to close it but a renewed kerfuffle in the foyer announces the arrival of—"Cwissa!" Yes, in he runs on his sturdy wee legs, straight to his Auntie Cwissa. "Och, ye wee scallywag, where've you been all the morning?"

"Bowds!" Jumping up and down, flapping his plump wee arms in their velvet sleeves—his lace cuffs all agrime, well that's our wee laddy and no matter, there's more cuffs where those came from, right here on Auntie Cwissa's tambourine. "Birds, is it? You're like your father, lad."

"Sweetie," says Charlie.

Knox objects, "Here now, don't you be rifflin' your Auntie's basket."

"Leave him be, Knoxy, the wee reiver." And Clarissa chuckles.

Knox smiles in what she hopes is the usual manner, but if her smile is unconvincing . . . well, no one is looking at the old woman anyway, for which she is grateful.

Alone in his study, Henry sits, staring unseeing at the painting of his Highland terrier, Hamish, above his desk.

There is no question at the moment of coming to grips with what transpired this afternoon when the doctor bid him linger in the consulting room.

How does one come to grips with a bottomless opening in the Earth?

There is nothing to grip.

57

"WELL?" SAID HENRY.

"If Your Lordship would care to be seated."

Henry remained standing. So did Chambers, his weighty gaze unwavering. *I suppose that is the new medical mien*, thought Henry, suddenly impatient with a man who appeared to be getting above his station—imperturbability being the province of the ruling class. It was enough to make one pine for Mr. Moore.

"I asked you to remain, Lord Bell, that I might inform you further as to the results of my examination of your child."

"Go on, then."

"Lord Henry, it would appear your child has been misapprehended in its sex."

Henry waited. More was not forthcoming. "Speak plain, man."

"Your child's external genital organs exhibit characteristics of both sexes."

Did the earth shift just then? A slippage and correction such that blink and you miss it . . . "What's that you say?"

"Your child appears to be both male and female."

Henry was now sitting, with no awareness of having done so, his gaze still fixed on the doctor, although directed upward now. He was perfectly calm. Calmly aware that he had no power of speech.

The doctor was holding out a glass of water. Henry watched his own hand take it. Raise it to his lips. He drank. Breathed finally, it having slipped his mind to do so for some moments. Spoke, "You mean to say . . . Do you mean he's a . . ." His throat closed.

"Your Lordship. Permit me to reassure you: there is no such thing as an hermaphrodite."

Henry flinched. Stood. "Then what the devil."

Chambers did not alter his stance or his gaze—the latter seemed to Henry somehow palpable, as though it were holding Henry upright. Chambers was saying, "It is a belief which persists among a, by no means small, portion of my medical brethren. Advanced scientific thinking, however, has relegated the term to the annals of myth. There are no hermaphrodites, Your Lordship, there are merely mistakes of Nature. Mistakes which, in many cases, admit of correction."

Henry was sitting once more. The doctor was now holding out a glass of whisky. Henry shook his head. Then took it and swallowed it. "I don't understand, what, what, what are you, what. What is amiss?"

"Your child's external genital organs exhibit both male and female sexual characteristics. But this condition admits of correction."

Henry shook his head, as though awakening from . . . "What do you mean, 'correction,' what will you . . . ? What . . . ?"

"Your child's phallus is imperforate."

"'Imperfect'? 'Tis small, to be sure—"

"The urinary opening is situated—"

"Yes, yes, my nurse told me."

"What did she tell you?"

"My son's member is small, his testicles as yet undescended, and he makes water from . . . from further down the, uh . . . the member. You speak of a cure."

"Correction."

"Well out with it, how soon might you proceed? My wife and I are to sail with our son to America in a matter of days."

"As to that—"

"We can of course delay departure if you deem it prudent."

"Lord Henry, I think it well I first provide you with my diagnosis in detail, the better to inform your decision regarding treatment."

"Oh. Quite. Go on, then, Chambers."

"Your child is afflicted with a condition we now term pseudo-hermaphroditism."

"Confound it, man, you said not moments ago—"

"There are no hermaphrodites, Your Lordship. Only pseudo-hermaphrodites, 'pseudo' meaning—"

"I know what it means, man, I wish to know what *you* mean."

"The condition of pseudo-hermaphroditism consists in the occurrence in one individual of characteristics of both sexes."

"How does that differ from . . . the other?"

"Every person is of one sex only, Your Lordship. Never both. There are, however, cases in which the line between the two sexes is less than distinct. The reasons for this are varied and not entirely known. But however indistinct, there always is a line, and each individual is situated on one side or the other of it. It is the task of the medical professional to discover, by means of measuring and assessing the preponderance of characteristics, on which side of that line an individual falls, and thus to determine its true sex."

"I see. And how do you propose to perfect his phallus?"

The insufferable man continued as though Henry had not spoken. "Cases of pseudo-hermaphroditism are of two types, My Lord. On the one hand, there is the Pseudo-hermaphrodite of the Male Type. On the other hand, there is the Pseudo-hermaphrodite of the Female Type. Your child is the latter."

Henry chuckled mirthlessly to himself at the thought that this must be how he sounded to the untrained ear when it came to matters ornithological. "And the treatment? In plain terms, if you please, Dr. Chambers."

"Fortunately your child is so young as to retain no memory of its infancy, nor of the proposed treatment. And, as an infant of less than twenty-four months, neither will it feel any pain associated with the procedure."

"What . . . procedure?"

"Amputation of the phallus."

"What?!"

"I find no indication of testicular tissue, the which I view as a positive sign."

"How can that be positive?!"

"As to the internal organs, it is impossible to say in a living child this young whether there be uterus and ovaries."

"Why the blazes would there be, you said yourself, he has a phallus!"

"Your Lordship. A penis is a phallus. But a phallus is not necessarily a penis."

". . . Then what in God's name is it?"

"My examination points toward it being a monstrous clitoris."

"A . . . what?"

Dr. Chambers refilled the glass of water. Henry took it, blindly.

"Clitoris," said Dr. Chambers. "A small structure, no larger than a pea, embedded in the feminine genital suite and corresponding to the penis in the male, though of course inferior and without perforation. Whether 'tis purely vestigial or serves some purpose is the subject of medical debate."

"What did you call it?"

"Clitoris."

"And . . . it . . . What is it?" It sounded like . . . What were the sea monsters Odysseus sailed between . . . They were female too, weren't they? He raised the glass to his lips but it was empty.

"Lord Henry. Your child may or may not be a complete female. But your child is without doubt an incomplete male."

Henry waited.

"Lord Henry?"

"I'm listening. He is incomplete. How do you propose to complete him? Certainly not by cutting off his . . ." He covered his eyes with the heels of his hands.

"Your Lordship, in cases of doubtful sex, it is advisable to raise the child as female."

"Poor chaps."

"In this case, My Lord, the preponderance of sexual characteristics point to your child's true sex as being female."

"Yes, yes, his true sex is obscured by female characteristics."

"Your Lordship, your child has a vaginal canal."

Henry stares.

"Lord Bell, your child is female. You have a daughter. Not a son."

His voice, when he found it, sounded plaintive in his own ears. "But he runs and plays and roisters about, he . . ."

The doctor drew a deep breath. His tone was not unkind. "We come now to secondary characteristics. More complicated and perhaps more crucial, for if not stemmed early they confound any hope an individual might find fulfillment in either the male or female domain, but remain stranded, as it were, in between." He refilled Lord Henry's water glass. "Or worse, they deceive others and perhaps themselves; fall prey to accidental simili-sexualism, enter into wrongful occupations, even disastrous same-sex marriages. Deceit, however unwitting, leads to depravity, broken lives, even suicide . . ."

Henry tried to raise the glass. He was shaking. He set it down. Listened.

"There are reports of those who, owing to diagnosis later in life, resort to emigration in order to resume life as the opposite sex. Now, thanks to modern medicine, no such fate need await the sufferer."

"My God," said Henry, his voice a wisp. "You are . . . You're certain."

"At present we can be certain of nothing."

"Damn you!" He rose, spilling the water.

Chambers remained unperturbed. "I can create certainty, My Lord. Where Nature has left blurred a line, I can redraw that line straight and true such that the child may lead a normal life up until puberty. And possibly beyond."

"Possibly?"

"At worst, they may remain childless or even unmarried, owing to the absence of a full complement of reproductive organs. But no opprobrium will attach, no hint of shame, scandal, or confusion. No sorrow, beyond that which attends the childless lot of those many normal men and women whose hopes in that regard are dashed."

"And . . . at best?"

"Full function."

Henry breathes, very nearly pants. "As . . ."

"As a female."

Henry's face dropped into his hands.

The doctor continued, "I can remove the fleshy appendage today in this very room—and safely, as infants require no anaesthetic, being immune to pain. After which you will take your daughter home and rear her according to her entitlements, including the prospect of marriage. She need never know. Nor, and this is germane, need her future husband."

Henry raised his head. "How in God's name . . . ?"

"Your Lordship, these things happen. And they will continue to happen so long as human beings gestate within Woman's womb." His tone grew graver. "Nature's mistakes tend toward devolution: a blurring of lines—between species, between sexes, such as is more commonly found among animals and the lower races. This devolution is like a reverse tide which threatens to pull us back to our undifferentiated primordial past. To a swamp, as it were. Woman, with reproductive organs capable of supporting life both male and female, is the mutable sex, and thus most in danger of slippage. Backward . . ."

"She is . . . Irish."

"Lord Henry, bear in mind the majority of defective births are idiopathic and occur at the highest levels of society, such that we need look no further than our own Royal Family and its European cousins. You and your wife are not related to one another by blood, which bodes well."

"So you don't think it . . . likely to . . . recur?"

". . . Did Lady Bell sustain a shock during her pregnancy?"

"None whatever. She was content. Of course she was anxious—even at times fretful—until it appeared a successful outcome was likely."

"Had it been in doubt?"

"Yes. She had suffered, you see. With the loss of two—three previous."

Chambers nodded. "And how did her suffering manifest?"

"She went from melancholy to . . . well, a degree of ill temper, even . . . anger. Then at times she seemed calm. At others . . . well, quite the opposite."

"Hm. And during the course of her successful pregnancy which resulted in the birth of your child, did you know her to eat or drink anything out of the ordinary? Any patent medicines, tainted water?"

Henry coloured. Surely that night on the fen did not signify . . . He sank to the couch once more. In a strangled whisper, "She dotes on him, she . . . What am I to tell her?" He looked up, wild-eyed. "'Give me your son, and I will return you a daughter?' 'Mutilated'?"

"Restored."

"She will not bear it." He all but sobbed it.

"Your Lordship, I am keenly sensible of the delicacy of the situation—"

"'Delicacy'!" On his feet once more, pacing.

"But I bid you cast your mind forward to the effect upon your wife when, the child having attained puberty, it displays none of the secondary male characteristics, and instead develops enlarged mammary glands, retains its high piping voice, achieves, as is not unlikely, the menarche."

"The . . . what?"

"The monthly function."

"Better he should be put away!"

Chambers spoke firmly. "Your Lordship, I will not be party to the putting away of a child whose condition admits of correction and whose prognosis is positive."

"Teach me my duty, will you?!" Henry made to stride toward the doctor but doubled over as at a blow, hands on his knees, gasping. He got hold of himself. Straightened, turned away, dragged his handkerchief across his face.

"Your Lordship, the child is young enough that it will take on, like candle wax, whatever form is impressed upon it. Thus do I urge you to act promptly in your child's best interests."

"Chambers?" All the fight had drained out of him. "What if you are mistaken? What if he is . . . more male?"

"Your Lordship. Better a blighted female than an inadequate male."

Henry groped for his hat—Chambers held it out for him. ". . . What are we to . . . What are we to tell the world?"

"That is not for me to say, Lord Henry. But people have been known to go abroad with one infant and return with another."

Henry closed his eyes. Reeled. Opened them. Walked toward the door.

Chambers said, "I am, of course, prepared to take it upon myself to inform your wife of my diagnosis."

"I shall myself inform Lady Bell."

Henry left the room. Exited the building. And rejoined his wife in the carriage.

Now in his study, he is roused by the dinner bell. On his desk sits a plate of sliced beef, untouched from luncheon.

He quits the study.

Clarissa encounters him on her way downstairs—she is in her bronze silk. "Henry? What is it?"

He passes her without a word, mounting the stairs like a man on his way to the gallows.

Mae sees the door open in her mirror. "I heard the bell, Henry, I'll just be two ticks." She picks up her silver tail-comb.

"Marie, dear, I have determined that an ocean voyage is not wise at this juncture."

"What?"

"'Tis meet we delay our departure."

"'Meet' what? Who? Why?"

"Because I think it best."

"That's not an answer."

"It is my answer."

"What's wrong, Henry, what's happened?" She pivots on her padded stool to face him, tail-comb in hand.

"Need there be aught wrong? I have thought better of the voyage, and there is an end on it."

"Not by a long chalk, there isn't—"

"Mae. I know you are disappointed, but—"

"I'm more confused than anything else, Henry, what is going on?"

"Please. Trust me."

"Not when you won't tell me what's wrong."

He is silent.

"Henry . . ." She quavers. "What did the doctor tell you? Is there something wrong?" Whispering, "Are you ill?"

"Of course not."

"Then why don't you want to come to Boston? Are you ashamed of having married me?"

"Certainly not!"

"Too high and mighty to mingle with the hoi polloi of Beantown?"

"Really, Marie."

"Well?"

"I . . . am thinking of our child."

"The doctor said he's fine—"

"Mae, he is wondrous and the best we can do for him is give him a brother—"

"Ugh!" Smack goes the tail-comb onto the vanity.

"Darling—"

"What am I, a brood mare?" She takes a breath. More calmly, "I know what my job is, Henry, but can I please have one measly minute to enjoy the baby I have? You saw what I . . ." She is crying.

What she went through. Yes. He saw. He is seeing. "Mae."

"Go away."

"Darling."

"Don't touch me!"

He dodges the flying tail-comb.

"No more babies!" she screams. "Do you hear me? No more babies for you and your precious Fayne!" Sobbing.

"Mae! Forgive me, it's my fault, it's . . . I'm a brute."

She gets hold of herself. Pats her tears. Bites her lip.

He swallows. "I ought to have said, I . . . I stayed behind to consult the doctor . . . with regard . . . With regard to my tendency to fall sea-sick."

"Ohhh. Oh sweetheart, and you were ashamed to show any weakness in front of me. Don't you know it only makes me love you more?" She goes to him and reaches up, encircling her arms about his neck. "I forbid you to leave our stateroom or stray farther than twelve inches from a bucket for the whole crossing. And you'll be on a strict diet of soda crackers and seltzer."

"What is that?"

"Yankee home remedy." She melts against him. "Oh Henry, I love you so."

EXAMINATION: *Growth of tissue anterior to vaginal and urethral openings. Two inches stretched. Turgid upon stimulation, absent either urethral or seminal perforation at tip.*

Finger exam inconclusive as regards presence of uterus.

Vaginal crypt/canal not inconsistent with norm in female of this age.

Presence of ovaries impossible to affirm in vivo. (Cadaveric bequest in event of infant's death?)

Labia not fused. No evidence of testes by palpation.

DIAGNOSIS: *organogenic scaffolding indicative of feminine preponderance conducive to categorization as per Pseudo-Hermaphrodite of the Female Type.*

AETIOLOGY: *Inconclusive as to iatrogenic versus exogenous causes.*

INDICATED: *Surgical removal of deceptive organ.*

58

THERE IS NOWHERE Henry can go because everywhere he will meet himself as he was and that man is as though dead. And yet he walks. Blindly between the street lamps, his breath mingling with the fog, onto Waverley Bridge. Below are the railway tracks. To his right, the Scott Monument stands two hundred feet high. Not to mention the towering tenements of the Auld Toun, some of which loom over the gorge, adding to their height. Then there is Castle Rock. How very vertical is Edinburgh. Not forgetting Salisbury Craigs where he was once already nearly killed . . . Henry shakes his head. He is not himself. Because his son is not his son . . . He somehow endured dinner, then left the house without his hat. There is no one whom he can tell. Everyone, his family, his friends, the entirety of his acquaintance, all yet dwell in a world from which Henry Bell was exiled this afternoon.

From Waverley Bridge to Cockburn Street, into Fleshmarket Close past the Halfway House Pub, into a nameless wynd, he walks he knows not where . . .

A small sign out front says simply, THE YARD. It appears derelict, its windows boarded up, but it is a soldier's refreshment room as evidenced by the kilted bear who brushes past him and in through the door. Henry follows.

Within it is dark and cramped—the fug suits him, made of whisky, beer and sweat and smoke. The rumble of masculine voices is pierced by a high-pitched laugh—any woman in this establishment will be of a low type. The floor is sticky underfoot as he makes his way to the bar where oil lamps at either end throw shadows on the patrons—a mix of soldiers and working men. He glances at the man next to him in whose two-fisted grip are a glass of whisky and a pint of bitter, and says to the elaborately moustached barkeep, "I'll have the same." His neighbour looks up with a smirk—"Evenin' toffey." A clerk, by his grimy cuffs . . . and something odd in the man's bloodshot gaze . . .

"Henry?"

Henry turns round to see, "Josey!"

He clasps his friend's hand in one of his own and claps the other on his shoulder. Josey looks taken aback, as well he might. "True, I do not frequent such haunts, but tonight is . . ." His throat catches—he tries to laugh. Fails.

"Will you join me, Henry? I'm, I'm over to the back."

Henry turns to pay the barman, who says, "You're treated," with a jerk of his sleek head at the clerk, who stares strangely up at Henry. "*Slainte*," says Henry politely.

"Come, Henry."

Henry follows his friend through the smoke, brushing past rough sleeves and a pair of sloping white shoulders—two or three women here as it turns out, and of precisely the sort one might expect. Surely Josey has not recourse to harlots—Mae is right, he must marry—and for the second it takes him to think this thought, Henry forgets his misfortune. It reasserts itself the next instant with redoubled force and he is glad Josey cannot see his face as he gropes after his friend toward a small table against the wall, where a candle flickers next to an empty glass and a half-full bottle of whisky. The table is scarred, the plush all but worn from the chairs. But his friend is here. *One whom I would follow into exile. Would he follow me?* Josey's pallor is more pronounced than ever against a day's growth of whiskers; there is a sheen upon his high brow, dark circles beneath his intelligent eyes. Henry is suddenly concerned lest his friend be drinking much and eating little. "You frequent this place, Josey?"

Josey pours them each a dram. "I'm afraid so, Henry. But you . . . ?"

Henry downs his, Josey pours him another. Henry drinks, then rests both hands flat on the table. "I am . . ." His voice breaks, "Dear God, I must tell someone or go mad."

Josey leans forward. "It's all right, Henry."

"Promise you'll tell no one."

"I promise."

"Josey . . ." Henry's sorrow erupts, he weeps, forehead in one hand. Josey reaches across and takes his free hand. Henry returns the pressure of his friend's grip, applies his hanky with his other hand and is about to speak when—"Josephine, dear heart, who's your braw bonny friend?" One of the young women. Heavily painted, obviously a prostitute. Henry looks away. Poor Josey, reduced to this.

"Off with you now, Davey," says Josey.

Henry looks up again. She leans into him, reeking of scent—inches from his face, Henry sees the fuzz on her upper lip, at her throat an Adam's apple. He recoils with a jerk. "She" laughs and weaves away into the crush of men.

Josey says, "Pay him no mind, Henry."

Henry gapes.

Josey leans forward, his kind gaze full on Henry. "I will always be your friend, and I will never betray your secret."

"I've told you no secret." He rises.

"Henry."

"Stay away from me, do you hear? Come not near my family." He looks about with new eyes. "This is a cesspool." He leaves.

Back through the dismal wynd he staggers, though not with drink—he trips on a loose cobble, steadies himself with a hand on the damp wall, then emerges from the piss-reek—a rat scuttles past, then another, are there more than there used to be or is it that he is looking down? To think what has lurked behind Josey's "friendship": sick, degenerate—enough. At school there were boys who—why even Hawley—no need to dwell. Like other childhood disorders, it is not deadly unless it persist to adulthood—he stops. He is on the bridge. The air is clearer here. He place his hands on the railing. Leans over.

"Sir? Are you poorly?"

The young constable watches the gentleman turn and stride away over the bridge. You never know when someone will take it into their head to leap. This one is wearing no hat—a red flag, perhaps. Even rich gentlemen have their worries, much as most of us would trade ours for theirs in a heartbeat.

He pauses in his study to fortify himself with a drink. Another.

He slips through the door to their bedroom to find her brushing her hair. Without missing a stroke she smiles at him in the mirror. Sniffs. "You're gingered up, naughty boy."

"Mae, my love." The whisky is converting already to headache. "In point of fact . . ."

She laughs. "You're drunk."

"I'm shattered." Has he spoken those words?

"Why? Where've you been?" She turns. In her eyes, concern. Love.

"The Auld Toun, in point of fact."

"Where in the 'auld toon'?" Her eyes narrow. "Not the Cowgate?"

"Near enough."

"Isn't that where Miss Gourley's Refuge is?"

"Is it?" He flings himself onto the bed.

"Henry, you're scaring me."

"I'm scaring myself." *Get a grip on yourself.* Deep breath. The ceiling spins. Up on one elbow. "My darling, I have received news."

She blanches. "Who died?" Rising, "Daddy!"

"No, no, not your father, darling."

"Taffy!" Wailing—

"No one has died!" *Not yet. Lord and Lady Bell are grieved to announce the death of their son, Charles . . .*

"Then what is it? Jesus, Mary and Joseph, out with it, Henry!" Smacking her tears away. "Have we lost money? Have you gone bust?"

He leans on truth—"I received news today . . ."—which bends like lead—"of an old friend whose child is . . . afflicted with . . . a certain condition."

"Who? What condition? Why are you so upset?"

"It happens I feel responsible. Having been instrumental in the formation of the attachment. Between its parents."

"Henry . . . I understand, oh poor darling, you're in your cups," taking his hand. "Feeling a little 'tired and emotional,' huh? And here I am making a big fuss over nothing—I mean, over something really sad. Go ahead and tell me all about it now, I'm listening." She resumes her stool, folds her hands in her lap and tilts her head sympathetically. Swallows a yawn.

He sits up on the edge of the bed—in the nick of time, for it tilted just now as though with the roll of the sea. "It concerns a young—very young child. Of just about the same age as our Charles, in point of fact." A riffle at her brow—he hastens to add, "But there the resemblance ends. Notwithstanding, the child is of noble birth. Said child . . . A son—did I say?"

"Mm-hm? I don't know. Go on."

"Well, as luck would have it. Luck or . . . in any case, it transpires that the child was misapprehended in its sex."

Her expectant expression has not changed. "What does that mean?"

"They . . ." He clears his throat. "What they thought was a son, is in reality a daughter."

Her eyebrows lift, her chin drops. "What on earth?"

"It . . . apparently, it is less rare than one might suppose."

"How could anyone possibly make a mistake like that?"

Henry shakes his head.

"No really, what kind of idiot—what kind of *mother*—Oh my God, Henry, what did it have?"

"It hadn't anything in the way of disease, it quite simply—"

"No, I mean what does it have. Down there."

Henry closes his eyes. This is Hell. One cannot know when, on an ordinary day, the air will open—slit, like an invisible screen, to admit one into a wounded world of no return.

"Henry, I'm only asking, I mean the child must have *something*." She shudders.

"Apparently there is, was, something."

"What do you mean, 'was'?"

"Well. They had it removed. Surgically."

"Oh I feel sick."

"It was . . . for the best."

"Of course, but still, oh God, is it okay? I mean the child."

"Yes, no harm done."

"Wait, how did you hear about this?"

"In point of fact, I . . . well, Josey told me."

"Josey? So that's who you were with tonight."

"Did I not say?"

"You did not. And don't tell Clarissa he was leading you astray."

He looks sharply up, but she is smiling.

"Poor Josey needs a wife and I know just where to look." She winks. "Well? Who told Josey?"

"Ah. In point of—as to that it, it was a friend—a mutual friend confided in Josey who, being in his cups, waxed indiscreet with me. As do I now with you."

"Who are we talking about? Some old inbred family, who?"

"You don't know them." He colours.

"You're fibbing, who is it?"

"I'd rather not say."

"A couple you helped to get together, people I know—well, that narrows it," she says rather tartly. Then suddenly, "Fanny and Lord Richard Hawley, I knew it!"

"What did you know?"

"Well she's so old! And he's so . . . oh, he doesn't matter, she's the one. Oh, poor Fanny." She heaves a great salacious sigh. "What are they supposed to do now? The whole world thinks they have a son—the Honourable little What's-His-Name."

"Their physician has advised them to . . . go to the Continent. After all, people have been known to go abroad with one infant . . . and return with another."

"They have? Lordy, how do they pull that off?"

"They . . . announce the death of the, of their heretofore supposed son."

"Ebeneezer."

"Who?"

"That's the poor thing's name."

"Quite. Then, following a suitable interval—"

"And they stay in Europe the whole time?"

"Yes."

"Some spa town in the Alps that no one's ever heard of."

"Whence they announce the birth of their . . ." He swallows. "Daughter."

"I want to faint just hearing you say it, oh God, Henry."

"They'll have more children."

"Fanny? Don't count on it. Don't wish it on her. They're lucky the child's not worse off, at her age."

"Even if such a misfortune were to befall us—"

"Please, God, don't even say it."

"Only I was going to say, we at least could look forward to having more children."

"Now you're jesting."

"Nothing of the sort."

"Henry, I wouldn't want 'more children.' No one could replace Charles. And what if it happened again? Oh my God." She picks up her hairbrush. "Poor Fanny, I'll write her this instant."

"You mustn't! You must not let them know we know, for Josey told me in the strictest confidence. Give me your word."

"I promise." And, when he continues to look doubtful, "All right then, I swear. Jumpin' Jehoshaphat, Henry." She resumes brushing her hair. "So what about their two-year-old 'newborn' daughter?"

He marvels at the speed of her shift in mood. "Well. They are further advised to confine—rather, shield from general view—the child, the daughter—the erstwhile son—until it reach such an age, round about—oh how should I know?" He sags.

But she is nodding now. "Yes, round about the age of five or so, and then they can say, 'She's a big girl, for three.'"

He nods. Swallows.

She heaves another sigh, sail-emptying and sincere. "Poor Fanny. I even feel sorry for Hawley, no one deserves that."

He looks beaten. She thought the Scots could hold their drink, but Henry's half-English and thoroughly blue-blooded. She goes to him. "Hank, honey, it's not your fault. Fanny was bound and determined, a regular von Bismarck, she set her course for Hawley, he never had a chance."

"Funny. I thought he bagged her."

"How very vulgar of you, Lord Henry." And she settles herself astride his lap. "I'm sorry, darling," he says, "I have a head."

"My husband, the drunkard," she giggles. "That's okay. You go to sleep now."

He lies back, closing his eyes. She pulls off his boots—fine-creased leather. Real gentleman's boots. "Why didn't you tell me right off the bat you were with Josey? Instead, you let me think you were sneaking off to Miss Gourley."

"Silly of me."

"No, silly of me! As if you could ever see anything in poor Miss Gourley."

She douses the lamp. And gets in next to him. She listens for his slow sleep-breathing. Then, subtly . . . soundlessly, almost not stirring, does for herself that which dear Henry less frequently of late is apt to do for her. Sometimes, however, it's just as well . . . She purrs.

Sleeps.

Henry lies still, eyes closed. Shocked afresh.

59

February 13, 1875

Dear Taffy,

Henry gave me quite a turn yesterday. He hung back with the physician after our appointment (we took Charlie, nothing wrong, just a look-see before the journey) after which he came down with a case of the doldrums that had me worried, then positively alarmed when he announced we'd have to cancel our trip (!). Such is ancient Bell pride, he moped all day before 'fessing up to sea-sickness. So the crossing may not be quite the "second honeymoon" I envisaged, but by the time you get this, I'll be sitting in your boudoir, you with little Tessie and me with wee Charlie, and we'll be laughing about it—there's nothing like a dash of alarm to leaven love. And I do love Henry. I was fond of him before, but I truly love him now because he gave me Charlie. I used to wonder what my life would have been like if I had married Gordon Peabody (jug-eared children for one thing). But now I can't imagine life beside any man but my Lord and Mild Master Henry. Last night he reeled in after a "quaffing" session with sweet Mr. Baxter, all but weeping at a misfortune that has struck

friends of ours who shall remain nameless—if it weren't so sad, and if it
hadn't happened to someone I like, I'd call it a juicy tidbit. But it is and
it did so I won't, but I'll give you hint: tonight say a special prayer of
thanks for your darling baby <u>girl</u>, and I'll say one for my <u>boy</u>. We are
so lucky! *Ça suffit!* Must away now to "post" this, my last letter to you
before we see one another. You'll barely have had time to read it before
I'm at your door. Is the porch swing still there? It better be! And how's
the dear old chestnut tree? Oh, I can't wait to see you again, sweetest
friend in the whole wide world!

Love from your own forever,
Mae

He has opened the door to see her at her escritoire, head tilted, pen
moving rapidly. He taps lightly. She turns and smiles at him.

"Darling, I've received word that Dr. Chambers proposes to prescribe
a certain remedy, something we might employ in the unlikely event
Charles should become feverish on the crossing."

"Oh good, have him send it along." She turns back to her letter—he
sees the girlish loops dancing across the page.

"I think he means to explain its use in person. It is, after all, a medicinal . . . embrocation."

"When's he coming?"

"He is not coming here—"

"The nerve of the man, all right then, will you be back for luncheon?
I'm craving lamb." Swivelling in her chair, she winks and pats her tummy.

Henry is so tired.

"Don't worry, Henry, I'm not expecting."

"'Expecting'—? Oh, I see. But if you were, how joyful."

"Are you joshing me? It's enough you're going to be upchucking all
the way, we don't need to be two on a bucket across the Atlantic." And
she laughs.

He is so tired.

"My love, in consideration of my anticipated indisposition, might it
not be desirable that you accompany me to Dr. Chambers's surgery to
learn first-hand how to administer to our child the . . . embrocation?"

"You want me to come with you? Why didn't you say so?" She hears her own fishwifey tone, but if he wants a sweeter one he knows what he can do . . . "It's just, there's so much to do before we leave, Henry." And bending once more to her escritoire, "I'll be right down."

He moves to withdraw as she says without turning, "Why do they call it a 'surgery'? As if all they do in there is cut people up." He sees her shiver—ringlets like bells tinkling at the back of her neck. His wife is still scarcely more than a girl. They will have more children. He retreats, pulling the door softly to.

PS Off to doc. again for medicine in case Charlie feverish on crossing— and must find seltzer for poor H., looks like a ghost this morning, green at thought of weighing anchor! Tough ole Boston will do him a world of good.

"Mae?" Her husband's too-tentatively elevated voice from the foot of the stairs.

"I'm coming!" She has all but shrieked it. *Really, Mae, temper down now*, as Pappy would say.

Henry consults his timepiece. He has been waiting, perspiring, for twenty minutes in the foyer. The sweat trickles down his spine and into his smalls, last night's whisky and this morning's fear collecting uncomfortably in the crease of his buttocks. He badly wishes to scratch. He squeezes shut his eyes, then opens them wide.

"Are you okay, Henry?"

Here she is at last. "I am fine well, Marie."

"Don't be mad."

"I am . . . neither 'mad' nor in the slightest peevish."

"Coulda fooled me."

"Shall we?"

She brushes away Maid's hand which remains unschooled in the tilt of a petty boater, and suffers herself to be helped into her plum velvet mantle. "Well?" she says to her husband.

". . . Forgive me, what?"

"How do I look?"

"We are simply to pay a call upon the physician, my dear."

"I give up."

"You look . . . as lovely as ever. Indeed, lovelier. Is that a new *chapeau*?"

"It is." She beams.

Let her smile. Let her pout and primp and—oh, for a little while longer. For the time it takes to ride to Ainsley Place . . .

Mae fairly skips down the broad steps to where Havers is holding open the door of the waiting carriage. She reaches up to Sanders, "Mail this, would you, Sanders? 'Post' it, that is."

"Aye, M'Lady."

She springs up into the carriage on her own steam, turning to call laughingly, "Hurry up, slow-poke!" Look at him dawdling down the steps—"And you thought *I* kept *you* waiting!"

The carriage pulls up before the handsome townhouse in Ainsley Place.

Henry steps from the carriage, squinting against the brightness of the day. His palms are moist, his mouth is dry. He turns. "Come, my dear." He proffers his hand but she hesitates—like a calf that gets wind somehow of the axe and fails to follow . . .

"Henry? I just want to say I'm sorry."

"Whatever for?"

"I . . . Come closer, I don't need the whole street to hear."

He remounts the bottom step and leans in, knocking his hat askew in the process, and she giggles. He rights it, feels her hand on his sleeve, looks into his wife's eyes. Her lovely green eyes. Her young unsuspecting face. Her rosebud mouth. He has seen that bud swell, open, breathing, sighing . . . *"Nevermore," quoth the Raven*—Don't be ridiculous, our life together has hardly begun. The best is yet to come. The worst, soon to be over. "What is it, my darling?"

"I've been . . . uncongenial with you. Worse, I've been saucy. Even downright—"

"You've been an angel."

"I haven't and you know it and I want you to know I know it too, it's just I've been so excited about our trip and all, I just sometimes want to jump right out of my skin and the only thing that calms me down is . . . your attention." She blushes and drops her gaze. Then, looking back up at him, "But also . . . in addition to how pleased I am to be going home—going to Boston, that is—with Charlie and you, my two lords a-leaping—well . . ." Solemn once more. "I also realize I maybe hadn't really let myself miss Taffy until now, when I'm about to see her in two short weeks." Her eyes fill. "Oh no, silly me," fanning the air rapidly about her face, tilting her head as though to drink back the tears into her eyes.

Henry holds out his hand. "My darling," says the prisoner. "Come now," adds the jailer. "It will be over and done before we know it," promises the executioner.

The same sawed-off female with the ugly bun. Mae suppresses a moue of distaste. The same ugly "waiting room" with the dog-eared magazines. Different but equally dull strangers.

"Dr. Chambers will see you now."

"Charmed, I'm sure," says Mae under her breath to Henry.

Mae sweeps in and plumps onto the sofa. "Well, Doctor Chambers, why don't you tell us about this 'embrocation' of yours."

"Marie," says Henry.

The lantern-jawed man regards her gravely. Who does he think he is, Abraham Lincoln? Let's get the gripe water and get going.

"'Embrocation,' Lady Bell?"

"I think my husband meant to say 'medicine.'" She smiles winningly.

Dr. Chambers looks from Lady to Lord, then back again, unhurried as a tortoise.

"For my son. For the crossing." *Cripes*.

"Might I inquire, Your Ladyship, what Lord Bell has told you regarding his private consultation with me of yesterday?"

"He told me—"

"I told Lady Bell that I consulted you with regard to my propensity to become sea-sick." Her husband has gone chalky, as though at the very thought.

"I see. Lord Bell, is it your wish that I should apprise Lady Bell of the nature of our private consultation?"

"If you please," says Henry curtly.

"Lady Bell, the matter concerns not your husband, but your child—"

"Charlie? . . ." A catch at her throat. Her hands float up, she rises, eyes dart to her husband—but her husband is looking away. She is off her mooring. "What's wrong with him?" she says to the air.

The doctor replies, "Your child is healthy, Lady Bell, save in one readily curable respect."

She settles somewhat. "What respect? Tell me what's wrong."

"Would Your Ladyship care to be seated once more?"

She sits.

"Your Lordship and Ladyship consulted me as to the question of undescended testicles—"

"You said his testicles were fine, they wouldn't cause a fever—"

"There is no risk of fever. As to the question of testicles—"

She gasps, her hand flies to her mouth. "Oh God, are you going to have to . . . ?"

"'Have to' what, Your Ladyship?"

"Operate?" She is already wiping away tears—*Be brave, Mary*. "That's going to hurt him . . ." *Be strong for your baby*—"I'm sorry, go on, Doctor, is it dangerous? I mean if you don't operate? How dangerous is it if you do?" His expression has not changed—there is, after all, something reassuring in that.

"As I told His Lordship, your child's condition admits of correction by means of a minor surgical procedure which, I hasten to reassure Your Ladyship, will be painless to your child."

"Are you going to . . . chloroform him?" She is trembling, as with cold.

"Anaesthetic is not indicated—that is, it is neither safe nor necessary, the pain response being not fully developed in an infant prior to the age of two."

Bewilderment clouds her fear. "But . . . he cries when his finger gets pinched by the what-d'ye-call-it of his rocking horse."

"A surgical intervention is quite another matter."

"It is? Henry?"

Her husband gives her a wan smile. Clearly Mae will have to be strong enough for the both of them—he looks set to faint at the mere thought of blood. "So. We'll have to postpone the crossing." She has said it so that Henry need not—she realizes with a dawning sense of maturity that he must have been in torments anticipating a tantrum on her part at the prospect of delaying—yet again—the journey home. But she is no longer a flighty bride. She is a mother. "Don't worry, Henry, we'll leave when Charlie's in fettle and not a day before." She smiles, her use of Knox's word the cherry atop the gift of reassurance. "Poor you," she says, reaching for his hand. "You could have just come out and told me." *Instead of scaring me half to death.* And to the doctor. "So you'll make a little . . . cut?"

"A small incision."

"Very carefully of course, so as not to slip and hurt his little . . . willy."

"There is nothing to fear in that regard, Your Ladyship."

"How soon can you do it?"

"I can perform the procedure today."

"Well then." She rises. "Let it be done," she says, like the Lady she is. But her husband stands motionless. Wait a minute . . . "Have you done this operation before, Dr. Chambers?"

"I have performed many more complicated procedures."

"I'm talking about this one in particular."

"I have not, Your Ladyship."

"Then I'll thank you to send us to someone who has. Henry, I don't wish to be rude, but I'm not letting an inexperienced surgeon anywhere near our son's testicles."

Silence.

Marie looks from her husband to the doctor, then back to her husband. Who says, "Dr. Chambers. Please tell Lady Bell what you told me."

"Lady Bell, the surgical procedure which I propose to perform upon your child has naught to do with testicles."

"Well what in Sam Hill are we talking about if we're not talking about his testicles?"

"Lady Bell. Your child does not have testicles."

A moment of incomprehension—devoid of emotion, as the centre of a whirlpool is devoid of water when it winds deep enough to expose a patch of ocean floor.

"Of course he does, they're tucked up inside, that's the whole point of the operation."

"Your child, Lady Bell, has neither testicles nor penis."

She blinks. She blinks a second time, her brows contracting. Lips part with the slow descent of the jaw-bridge. She turns to her husband.

Henry sees his wife, slack-jawed—the temporary idiocy of shock smearing her features. He looks away.

"Lady Bell, it is my duty as a physician, regretfully to inform you that your child has been misapprehended in its sex."

Dr. Chambers observes Lady Bell rise, and turn to her husband, who says, "Marie."

Lady Bell screams. It starts as "No" but dilates rapidly.

Lord Bell says, "Marie, please—"

Lady Bell flies at Lord Bell. Lord Bell reflexively raises his hands against the rain of blows.

Prudently positioned behind, Dr. Chambers closes his hands around Lady Bell's upper arms. Lord Bell pivots, clapping a hand over one eye. Lady Bell's head snaps back, catching Dr. Chambers on the chin—it is no worse than a graze in a Rugby match and the reflexive outrage is short-lived, for Lady Bell is his patient—swiftly he adjusts his grip, embracing Her Ladyship firmly about the rib cage, achieving thereby with his grasp the effect of a short-waistcoat. Her feet now slightly off the floor, she kicks his shins with the heels of her boots—not unlike cleats. He positions his feet either side of hers, immobilizing her legs in the manner of a vice.

The inner door opens, the small woman enters, goes to the cherrywood cabinet, opens it, returns promptly and presses to Her Ladyship's face a wad of gauze. Lady Bell's body slackens. Dr. Chambers lowers her to the couch.

Mae is unconscious. Henry is bleeding from below the left eye. The woman sees to him without a word. He speaks through her deft fingers, "What have you done to her?"

Chambers answers, "Lady Bell is under the influence of a light dose of chloroform. She will soon awaken, Your Lordship."

"Oh God."

"I can, with Your Lordship's permission, administer a dose of chloral by injection such as will induce sleep 'til morning. Indeed, I strongly advise she be granted respite from the shock."

"And . . . then what?"

"Some time away, perhaps."

"Aye, the Continent, so you said. She'll not board a ship bound anywhere but Boston."

"I speak, in the short term, not of the Continent but of an accredited asylum."

Henry rises, brushing aside the woman's hand. "Shall I cut your throat for you, sir?" The doctor is calm. Henry commences to shake like a willow. To weep too. It feels like weather, as though it were happening to someone else.

Chambers is speaking. "Much has altered in the treatment of those afflicted in their nerves. Time, Your Lordship. An interval of tranquility. These will assist Her Ladyship in reconciling herself to the truth."

"You don't know her." Henry finds he is slouched in a chair.

"I know Woman, Lord Bell."

A glass of water is held to his lips. He sips. Moves to rise. Thinks better of it. "I know not what to say, Chambers. I have never known my wife to—she has not been distressed to anything approaching this degree since . . . the loss of—You see, she was with child . . . more than once, and . . ."

"She miscarried, so you said. Thrice."

"Aye." For the first time, Henry speaks of how he found Marie on those occasions, "quite . . . having taken leave of her . . . usual demeanour. And . . . habits of grooming . . ." *Her matted hair, eyes wild, nightgown gaping . . . laughing and weeping in quick succession.* Henry does not say precisely those words, but it would appear from Dr. Chambers's grave expression that he is seeing precisely what Henry saw on those occasions. Henry concludes with a shuddering sigh, "Normally, of course, she is happy, high-spirited."

"A spirited nature, especially in Woman, is prone to becoming one that is high-strung when subjected to shocks or repeated nervous strain. In these cases, previous experience, far from lessening the blow, serves to exacerbate it. It would appear Lady Marie's fear of losing another child has been rekindled."

"She's not mad."

"'Madness' is a term so general as to be of little use. The medical diagnosis is 'puerperal dementia.' It normally strikes close upon the birth of a child. But it may lie dormant, only to strike later with redoubled force in response to a shock of some kind. Especially a shock concerning the child itself. Once in its grips, a mother cannot be held accountable for the ensuing harm, whether to herself. Or her child."

"Marie would never harm Charles."

"Your Lordship, there is no Charles."

A chill runs down Henry's spine. "Dr. Chambers. My wife, when she was pregnant with Charles—with my child—walked out from our country house one night and . . . and . . ." He can scarcely get out the words his voice trembles so. In a ragged whisper, ". . . was found. Face-down in the bog."

A glass of whisky is in his hand. He drinks it.

Mae moans a little, but does not wake.

Henry says, "I told her 'twas a dream."

Chambers's gaze does not waver. "You say you found her face-down on the bog."

"Aye. That is, my man did. He claimed she was eating mud. Absurd, I know."

"Such is not unheard of, Lord Bell. Pregnant women—and others—are known to evince morbid appetite."

Henry sees once more his wife's face fading into a thousand wrinkles of drying earth, her open mouth still black with it. "You mentioned others who are driven to eat . . . 'morbidly' did you say?"

"Yes."

"What others?"

"Why, lunatics."

"Lunatics?"

"Unsurprising insofar as pregnancy is viewed, in advanced scientific quarters, as akin to insanity."

"What?"

"Temporary, of course."

Mae stirs.

Chambers's voice takes on new resonance. "Not only is it misguided to hold Woman to the same standard of mental hardiness as Man, it is cruel. Her whole being is focused on the healthy evolution of her reproductive system. A blow to her reproductive system is a blow to her person. And to the race. Your wife has already sustained more than one such blow."

"You say she suffers from . . . what did you call it?"

"Puerperal dementia. A form of hysteria."

Henry rises, casts about as though for some means, a switch, a lever, to right this cursed scene—

"Lord Bell, hysteria is today so widespread as to remove any taint from the diagnosis. Our society is in a state of critical error when it comes to Woman. I do not pretend to know best how to resolve demands for suffrage, for admission to the halls of higher education including even the medical arts, but I do know that Woman today is in peril. And we deny her help at peril to us all."

Henry takes a deep breath and looks down at his wife. Her eyes open. Drift closed. Is it unfair to note here the thought which rises to his mind like the mist of oblivion? *I envy her.* "Go ahead, Chambers. Give my wife the gift of sleep."

Henry watches the gaunt man cross to the cherrywood cabinet where even now the odd little woman is busy preparing what must be an injection. A sort of metal plunger affixed to what looks like a darning needle. She hands it to Chambers who holds it up to the light. Henry sees a drop of clear fluid emerge from the tip of the needle—and turns away. He hears Chambers approach Mae. Hears a rustle. Followed by a familiar moan. How strange that pleasure and pain should share the selfsame sound . . .

The grey-bun woman is pressing a packet into his hands, wrapped in brown paper and tied with string. Chambers is explaining, "She will sleep 'til morning. But in the event she awakens and exhibits distress, apply a few drops to the gauze . . ." Henry nods. Pockets it.

The woman opens a panel door behind the desk and together they lift Marie from the sofa, Henry at her head, Chambers with her legs, and carry her down a narrow set of service stairs. Her form is slippery with silk, treacherous with tassels that catch at the posts, her hat hanging by a pin from her hair. Out the rear entrance and into the blaze of midday where the carriage waits and Sanders looks smartly straight ahead.

Who could have predicted that, having entered by the front door, Lord and Lady Bell would exit by the mews?

60

THE CARRIAGE PULLS UP to the tradesmen's entrance of No. One Bell Gardens and Lady Marie is carried quietly up the back stairs.

After he has seen her laid out upon the bed. After he has sent Havers away. After he has summoned Maid—"Tend to your mistress. She has been given a sleeping draft for her . . . health." After he has left the bedroom. After he has stood, at a loss, in the passage outside the bedroom.

He descends the stairs and opens the parlour door.

"Sister, a word."

"Henry? What is it?"

And he tells her.

Clarissa sits unblinking.

At length, she speaks. "What do you propose to do with it?"

"With . . . ?"

"The child. Where do you propose to house it?"

"Clarissa . . ." He pours her a glass of sherry. She appears not to notice. He places it on the table next to her.

Her voice is eerily conversational. "In a home, I presume, for defectives."

"Clarissa, shutup."

She looks at him as though surprised to find him seated across from her. He rises and puts the glass into her hand. She sips. He watches the strained movements of her throat. The tight lines at her mouth. She draws a deep breath and returns her gaze to him. He says, "It admits of a cure." He tells her the rest. The prescribed procedure. The proposed subterfuge. His wife's reaction. Then he sits back. Blanched.

"What am I to do?"

"You must do as the physician advises."

He drops his forehead to his hands, a heavy bulb of bone. "I know."

"And you must beget another child."

He heaves a great, shuddering sigh.

She stares straight ahead. "Pity you did not leave the telling 'til after the getting, a fortnight would have done it, judging by her linens."

He drops his head between his knees.

The parlour is quiet but for the purring of the fireplace.

"She flew at you."

He looks up. Touches his cheek. "It's nothing, the doctor insisted on a plaster."

"As well he might, a human scratch, nothing filthier save a cat's."

"She was understandably distraught . . ." He whispers, "Hysterical."

"What did you expect?"

"What am I to say to her when she wakes?"

"I shall not presume to advise you there."

"You advised me to marry her!"

"I advised you to marry. You did so. And well, I might add."

"How can you say so in light of . . . My God."

"The blight may well be on our side, Henry. There is hardly a noble family without an eediot or . . . worse. Including our own line."

He sighs, "Aye, the 'tail.' That is legend—if not merely an error in spelling."

"Legend often conceals truth behind a veneer of the fabulous. More likely the man was an imbecile."

He buries his face once more.

She rises. Pours sherry into two glasses this time, and hands him one. She remains standing, her back to the fire. "If it's to be done, 'tis best 'twere done quickly." He looks up sharply. "Today," she continues. "Before she wakes."

He nods. Then squeezes shut his eyes and shakes his head in a mildly convulsive manner that puts Clarissa in mind of her sister-in-law. She drinks.

He opens his eyes. Parts his lips. "'Twill make her run mad."

Clarissa bends, glad somehow of the pain, and takes up her work basket. She withdraws from it the brochure, which she sets on the table. On its front leaf is an engraved illustration of a handsome country house. *Morecombe Downs* . . . Henry puts up a hand. "Never."

"Where then? The Continent?" says Clarissa.

"I shall take her home to Fayne."

"What? Do you propose to chain her to the bed? Confine her to the—?"

"Of course not."

"Make a drug fiend of her?"

"Clarissa."

"You dream of removing to Fayne with your child in her arms?"

"Best begin as we mean to go on."

"She'll tear it to pieces."

"She'll do no such thing."

"She tried it on you."

"She was understandably—"

"She'll be more distraught when you've taken her son and returned to her a daughter, Henry, think!" Clarissa pauses. Gets command of herself.

"What you propose is not a kindness. Lady Marie has . . ." *Cherish*. She is suddenly in danger of . . . She draws a breath. "Your wife has endured a shock. She requires help. And you require time. Enough that you may announce the death of your son. And the birth of . . ." Her voice withers. "Your daughter."

"Henry?"

It is Marie. She is in the doorway. *How long has she been standing there?* Hair down, barefoot, in her nightgown. Eyes glassy, roving. "Where's Charles?"

He rises . . . "My darling. Let me help you back to bed."

"Where's Charlie?" More urgent.

"He's well, my darling, he's—"

She fixes on him as though suddenly recollecting, "Don't let them cut him, Henry—"

"Marie, don't upset yourself—"

"He's done it already . . . Has he done it already?" Pitch rising.

"No. No, no, of course not, no one has laid a hand—"

"Tell me where he is." Agony.

"He's in the nursery with—"

Clarissa says flatly, "Knox is bathing her."

Henry looks at his sister, shocked.

Marie's brow furrows, her chin retracts as she slowly shifts her gaze to Clarissa. "Bathing . . . who?"

"Your daughter."

Before the howl can journey from the misted isle of Mae's mind to the rocky shore of her body, Clarissa says, "Best begin as we mean to go on." And rings for Havers.

Henry rises and slips an arm around her shoulder. Mae is slowed by chloral but the drug is receding before the tide of terror, the superhuman strength that visits us *in extremis* coursing now through her body—she breaks from her husband's embrace like a titan from her bonds, eyes aglitter. She is waking up to a nightmare—"Where is he?" Maid appears, arms outstretched to subdue Her Ladyship, and receives an elbow to the chin for her efforts. "Charlie!" Her features slack, shoulders sagging, nightgown gaping—"Mae, please—!" She flies at him with a blood-curdling cry—Havers seizes her.

Together they carry her, thrashing, up the stairs.

Above, in the nursery, Knox sets to singing to the bairn in his bath to drown out the sound.

Locked in her room, Mae hurls herself against the walls like a great bird trapped in a house, blundering from door to window.

Down in the parlour, Maid is shaking like a stray. Behind her, her mistress: "Close the door, gel."

Henry enters the bedroom. Protects his head from the rain of blows, diverting attention from Havers who comes up behind her with the wadded gauze of chloroform. She slumps.

They lay her on the bed.

"That will be all, Havers."

"Very good, Your Lordship."

Her lids open, eyes roll back. "Don't kill my baby."

She falls back onto the pillows. The pillowy pillowy pillows . . .

And Now is all there only ever has been. Life is but a dream. Who is that drunken slut slurring her words? It is herself. Mary Corcoran. "My baby. My baby muh baby mumbaybem mabaym, mabem . . ." Slow leakage from the corner of each eye.

Henry does not appear for dinner. Clarissa goes so far as to tap at his study door and look in.

"Did you take any dinner, Henry?"

"Do not speak to me."

He will thank me.

Charles has broken free of Knox in the kitchen where milk is warming on the hob, and raced in his nightgown, laughing, damp curls flying, to the parlour.

Clarissa does not look up at the entrance of the child—"Auntie Cwissa!" She turns away. The child pounces on the work basket, opens the lid, thrusts in its hand in search of a sweetie—"Oww!"

Charles is scooped up, crying, by Knox who hustles him from the parlour, kissing his reddened fingers even while remonstrating, "Well, what do you expect, reiving your Auntie's basket!"

Clarissa's heart is clacking uncomfortably. It was reflex, her turning away. For the sight of a counterfeit beloved was more than she could . . . It was too much. Her shutting the lid on the child's hand, however, was intentional. Neither was a deliberate unkindness. Children must learn to keep their hands to themselves and to respect another's property—a female child especially, whose hand must be given away in marriage and who, far from laying claim to another's property, must hope herself to become the property of another. Clarissa may no longer love the blighted child but she is duty-bound to protect it. Shunting sideways now, is her heart—it has lost its customary rhythm. It will pass. Everything does. She raises a hand to reach for the bell cord but is stayed by the weight of pain.

Her heart clutches. She clutches back. An empty space opens up within her—not a clearing, but a clearance at the centre of what she had only recently discovered was the great green glen of her heart. Where a little boy once played.

Up in the nursery, Knox lays the child in its crib, its cheeks flushed with sleep and health. The son who rose this morning has settled to sleep this night a daughter, swift and sure as any Faery changeling.

"You are wanted in the parlour, Mrs. Knox."

She is startled to see Mr. Havers filling the doorway of the nursery.

At the door to the parlour, Knox steels herself. If she is to be turned out, so be it. She will undertake whatever her charges require of her, even if it be exile. She enters and stands with her hands folded on her apron. Awaiting sentence.

"Rub my head," says Miss Clarissa.

Knox comes round the back of the chair, unplaits the greying braids and sets to rubbing the scalp with practised fingers and thumbs.

Clarissa sighs. "Nobody blames you, Knoxy. After all, it took a specialist to see what was under everybody's nose. Including its mother's."

If Knox, from that moment, ceases to blame herself, it is not because of Miss Clarissa's words of absolution, nor those of the doctor yesterday. It is because she knows she will need her remaining strength to care for the bairn that Byrn called Brigid's child.

61

IT REQUIRES MORE STRENGTH than she knew possible, but Mae is fighting her way up through the undertow. Her mind, thrashing through drowny darkness. Struggling to bridge the gap between her thought and her finger, willing it to . . . *move*—it is the switch that sparks the rest of her and she opens her eyes. "Charlie."

Hush. Up. Yes, sit up. Shhh. Am I at Fayne? Is this that dream? Across the room, the shadowy reflection of the vanity mirror—I'm still at Bell Gardens, but—Hush, Mary Corcoran, you are awake and you must move quickly and silently. I am the Moon, I am here to help you. Get dressed. Now go to the hiding spot and take that magic piece of paper that will speed your bonny boat home to Boston. Good. Now slip out, and ever so softly up the stairs. To the nursery . . . I will bathe the old woman in my glow so she will not awake. Bend now to your child.

He does not wake up when he is lifted from his crib, for he knows the feel of his mother's arms. The warmth of her breast.

Downstairs she wraps them both in her woollen cloak with the ivory buttons, and steals out the back through the tradesmen's door into the darkness of the mews. Her little boy is heavy, no longer a baby, almost a child now, but Mae is young and she could carry him across County Leitrim and onto a famine ship if she had to. We find out what we are made of. All Mae has to do, however, is walk to Waverley Station and purchase a North British Railway ticket to Glasgow, thence to Liverpool, and onto a White Star ocean liner. "Then we'll be home, Charlie, my bonny prince." He chuckles. Reaches up and strokes her cheek before falling back asleep, lulled by the rhythm of her footfalls.

The city smells different at night. Especially as she approaches the bridge, reflecting that she can smell the Old Town—not foul from this distance, but dank with the exhalation of ancient masonry and wood, the mingling of mortar and mortality—grateful she need go no closer than the station. A knot of figures beyond the next lamp, darker against the night sky—people out on the bridge in the wee hours. Have they too chosen this night to run away? *But I'm not running away*, she thinks, *I'm going home*.

"Well now, queanie, what do you say to a drap?"

Mae ignores him. He plucks at her cloak. She quickens her pace.

Male laughter. Indistinct words behind her but no footsteps following. Her heart is beating hard but Charles has not made a peep. She ducks through an archway and hurries down winding stone steps to the cavernous hall, where she stops and looks about. Dim and deserted. Shadowy pillars, the stench of coal.

"May I be of assistance, Madam?"

She jumps, relieved to see a member of the Edinburgh Constabulary. "No thank you." Charles wakes up and whimpers. "Look, sweetheart, we're here."

"This is Waverley Station, ma'am."

"Yes and there's the ticket window, excuse me." She raps at the shuttered wicket.

"Opens at five, ma'am. Best return home 'til then, I'll take you."

"That's all right, I'll wait—hush now, Charlie, we're going to get on a big train, *Woo-woo! Chugga-chugga.*" She heads for a stone bench on the platform near the filthy tracks, overlooked by a huge placard for Nestlé's milk. Uncannily on cue, her little boy nuzzles and slips a hand beneath her cloak.

"You may not wait here, ma'am."

"Why not? It's not against the law, is it?" She smiles.

"Aye, ma'am, 'tis."

"That's ridiculous." Her son is fussing. She jiggles him, cooing, "Then we're going to get on a great big ship—"

"I cannae allow it, Madam."

Charlie starts crying in earnest—"Now look what you've done. Why don't you go away and chase those bums off the bridge up there."

"I am in charge of seeing off vagrants in the station."

"How dare you?"

"Does your husband know you're out in the nicht, ma'am? Time to go home—if you have one."

"Of course I have one. I have several."

"What is your name, ma'am? Is that your bairn?" He approaches.

"Out of my way." It is as though Clarissa herself had said it, and it works well enough that Mae is able to swish past him and back up the stairs.

The Constable follows at a distance and watches as the woman continues across the bridge toward the Old Town and is swallowed by the darkness. Many of them look like ladies. He was on to this one, however, for she did not sound like one. Can't help but feel sorry for the bairn, though.

Once over the bridge, Mae slips into the nearest wynd. It is pitch-dark but mercifully short, and presently there appears a dim patch up ahead. She walks slowly, taking care not to turn an ankle on the slippery cobbles. Lord, it really does reek in here . . . oh dear this must be what a public convenience smells like. A fat wet drop falls on her neck and she pulls up the hood of her cloak. She emerges into the comparative twilight of a street. She is walking now just to pass the night, and goodness knows she's safe enough for who would look for her here? Besides, all the residents of No. One Bell Gardens are still fast asleep. She comes to another of those mouse-hole streets and, looking up, makes out faded letters on the sooty brickwork, HORSE WYND. *It smells worse than horse if you want to know*, thinks Mae, her nose wrinkling yet again—

"Well if it isn't the Queen o' the May." Female voice. Harsh.

"How much you be wantin' then, darlin'?" Male this time. Irish.

She is pushed against the slimy wall, another voice behind her, "She's got a brat"—there are two men. The woman's face close to her own, foul breath, rasping, "I'm only after holding him for ya, love, I'll give 'im straight back after."

"Take your hands off him!" Mae swivels. The man is there, pressing up hard against her, "I'll have a wee taste first," he says, and the other is wrenching open her cloak, rucking up her skirts—"There's coin," says the woman, having left off trying to snatch Charlie in favour of plucking at Mae's handbag. "Och, aye, she'll have it and pay for it too," he says gruffly and Mae does not have to look to know that he has taken his— yes, from his trousers—he grabs her hand, she makes a fist so only her knuckles brush against—Charlie is screaming, she hangs on to him with her free arm. The other man has her dress up—she is going to scream. She cannot scream. Filthy palm over her mouth and nose—her baby, hoarse with terror, *Oh don't touch him, please, I'll do what you want, I won't make a sound*—"Stop it! Stop it, and get out, all of you!" A light. A woman. "I know you, and you know me well enough to scatter!" A shrill, piercing sound as she blows a whistle.

It is far from the first time Rosamund Gourley has broken up a scene like this. And it is far from the only scene of its kind being played out across the city—but one must count the small victories and leave the roll-call of defeat to the Almighty or one might just as well pack it in. It is, however, the first time Miss Gourley has been personally acquainted with the would-be victim. "Lady Marie?"

Miss Gourley conducts Lady Marie and little Charles into the Refuge and up the five flights to her garret. Miss Elliot puts her head out from her own door across the landing. Her hair is down, she's been asleep but you wouldn't know it from her alert tone, "Can I help?"

"No need."

"Who've we got here?"

Miss Gourley ushers the lady and her child into her own quarters and gives Miss Elliot a shrug over her shoulder by way of answer.

"Fair enough, Roz. Sure you're fine?"

"Never better, get some sleep, Edna."

"Thanks, you."

At the deal table in her bed-sit, Miss Gourley has set a mug of tea before Lady Marie and now she tips a bottle of whisky over it. Wee Charles is awake and wide-eyed and chewing on an oatcake in his mother's lap. Lady Marie takes up the mug but her hands tremble so that she cannot safely lift it. Rosamund Gourley puts her hands around Lady Marie's own and lowers the mug to the table. She takes a spoon, dips it into the hot liquid and raises it to Lady Marie's lips. Lady Marie sips. Closes her eyes. Presently she is able to raise the mug to her own mouth. The child falls asleep. Only then—and quietly, does Rosamund Gourley ask, "Lady Marie, what has happened?"

It comes out in a flood—"Miss Gourley, he's trying to take Charles away from me, he says Charlie has to die so we can turn him into a girl, they're crazy, they're trying to kill my baby!" Taking from the pocket of her cloak a folded document, thrusting it at her. Miss Gourley opens it on the table. Certificate *Entitling the Bearer to One Trans-Atlantic Passage, Saloon Class, Liverpool to Boston* . . .

Mae struggles to catch her breath, to catch her thoughts, to seize the events of the last twenty-four hours and stick words onto them. But the words, rather than itemizing and sequencing, do the opposite— like the blocks in Charlie's nursery, stacked one atop the other, tumbling down over and over again.

Miss Gourley listens. Nods. Until Lady Marie, by turns crumpling with distress and brightening with laughter, runs out of words and sits, drooping, over her mug. Now Miss Gourley shows Lady Marie and wee Charles—he is fast asleep—to her own bed with a promise to wake her in two hours. In time to make it back to Waverley Station when the ticket window opens at five o'clock.

Then she crosses the landing and taps on Miss Elliot's door.

A half hour later, Cook opens her eyes, then the back door to a tall lean woman who is stood next to a bicycle and requires to see Lord Henry urgently. "Who shall I say?" says Cook, eyes narrowed.

"Tell His Lordship Miss Gourley sent me."

Even as it unfolds, Miss Gourley is aware there is no alternative to her witnessing the scene that transpires between Henry and his wife whilst their child cries convulsively.

Miss Gourley is not given to regret. Regret is an indulgence, a gooey-centred self-pity. Remorse is different and there are remedies: atonement—for most deeds are redeemable. Such is the backbone of hope and it is not for the merely cheerful. Miss Gourley was a cheerful girl and she is not a gloomy woman, there being far too much to do to waste God-given time and energy on wishing something had turned out otherwise. That is a sin; "sin" meaning, simply, *waste*. Thus, though she knows it to be a waste of time and tantamount to regretting having entered Horse Wynd last night—which she would do over again to the end of time—she cannot help wishing she were not witnessing:

Henry, leaning over his sleeping wife and child who are nestled in Rosamund's own narrow bed—the divan, yes—within the gabled alcove where she and Henry—She blinks hard. Hears his murmured endearment. Sees his wife's untroubled gaze upon opening her eyes to behold him. The terror that breaks in on her the next instant, followed by howls of "Noooo!" His snatching up of the child into his arms, shielding its eyes from the sight—and his own from the swipe—of her nails. Lady Marie springing up, shrieking, flailing, impotent—for she will not, even with a fit upon her, lay a hand on her husband whilst he holds her treasure and it is this which cuts Miss Gourley with the keenness of pathos: the self-control of a woman gone mad with fear for her child.

Miss Elliot has entered, stands next to Miss Gourley, the two of them keeping clear as Lady Marie sweeps the tea and crockery from the table, overturns the latter, tears books from the shelf, sends a chair flying, exhausting herself on all that is insensate in the room, while the child screams and clings to its father, until she sinks, exhausted, to the floor, sobbing. Miss Gourley prays, *Lord, I know not what has befallen this young woman and deprived her of her wits, but grant that I might comfort her and any who suffer in this way.* It is more a command than a prayer, for Miss Gourley is feeling what she not infrequently feels for God: disgust.

Now Lord Henry is speaking to Lady Marie. Her face is stricken. But she is listening. "No one will lay a hand on him, I promise, Marie. I will take you and Charles to London for a second opinion. Tomorrow. Do you think you can be ready to travel?"

She looks up. Weeps afresh. Nods.

"Good. But now you must come with me."

She nods.

Miss Gourley and Miss Elliot help her to her feet.

"And you must take this. It will help you to rest."

Lady Marie accepts from Lord Henry's hand a dropper half-full of liquid from a blue bottle. "This time tomorrow we will be in London. With our son."

Miss Gourley picks up the certificate of passage from the floor and hands it to Lord Henry. Lady Marie looks groggily round. Henry says to his wife, "I'll keep it safe, don't worry."

When Miss Gourley has seen Lord Henry and Lady Marie and their baby off in the carriage, she climbs back up the five flights to her room where Miss Elliot has already set about putting it to rights.

"What's wrong with the child, do you reckon?"

"Who can say, Edna. He looks hale enough."

"Poor souls."

"Aye."

The women bid one another goodnight—tomorrow is another day and their days are full.

Miss Gourley douses her lamp and stretches out on her divan-cum-bed beneath the pink coverlet. She says a prayer for Lady Marie Bell whose fantastic fears of her husband's murderous designs on their son are the stuff of mental distress unimaginable to the unafflicted. Then she says a prayer for the child who may or may not be ill. But who has certainly been terrified this night.

Henry's wife is asleep—if one may call it that. In the plush darkness of the carriage, he holds her and she holds their sleeping child as they spring over the cobbled street, then sail across North Bridge.

He becomes aware of a respite. He knows he is travelling through Time, toward events that must be got through like threshers. But if he leans out the window now and says, "Sanders, the station," the man will obey. What would that detour signify in the great scheme of things? Even now a flock of birds is rising from a rock in the ocean, ancient turtles ply the seas, oaks outlive empires; and below the bridge, a train is releasing steam, at its terminus a ship awaits to carry them over the sea to . . . anywhere . . . Australia. California. Tears sting his eyes. He allows them to run down his cheeks in the dark as he feels the carriage wheels roll from the bricks of North Bridge onto the cobbles of Princes Street, where even now a gas lighter is busy dousing the lamps . . .

62

A FEW HOURS LATER, in the circular drive of No. One Bell Gardens, Sanders and Pugsley are fastening a good-sized trunk to the rear of the carriage.

Meanwhile, up in the house an invalid odour greets Henry as he opens the door to the bedroom. The window is closed. The fraught-looking lady's maid is even now removing the commode. "Begging Your Lordship's pardon." His wife is slumped in a chair facing away from him. He withdraws, satisfied she is calm, and being made ready for the journey.

Maid and the lady's maid wash her. Her head lolls. She drank down all her cocoa like a good girl. They dress her. Her tongue is thick. "You're pinching me." Now she is being carried downstairs, giggling. *This is the way the ladies ride, clippety-clop, clippety-clop*—Out the door and down the steps.

Pugsley and Havers have her, "Havers have 'er Havers, have 'er, ha-ha . . ." Sanders is sitting atop the carriage, whip in hand—*This is the way the gentlemen ride*—and sddenly, perfectly clearly, she cries, "Where's Charlie?!"

"He's coming, darling, Knox has him."

Sleepy.

Henry stands aside as the butler and footman boost his wife's bustle up the carriage steps and Knox's hands reach out from within. And as he watches he reflects, thank goodness Clarissa had the foresight to preserve the blue bottle of sedative Mr. Moore left for Marie more than two years ago now.

Hoop-la. Mae plumps onto the seat. Her head drops, so heavy. Eyelids are sandbags . . .

Henry embarks, pulls the door to behind him, raps on the ceiling and the carriage pulls smartly round the drive, sending the dead weight of his wife against him. He holds her fast. Like cargo.

She has screamed it this time, but of course Knox and Henry are not to know that. No one can hear her from in here . . . From way down in her body . . . But she has screamed it: "*Where's Charlie?!*"

It is a lovely journey from Edinburgh up into the Grampians. Lovelier still in 1875 if you possess a well-sprung carriage. There is poverty but it is picturesque. And the further north one ventures, the fewer people there are and the more sheep; the former having been driven off to make way for the latter. The lambs in particular are as endearing as they will be delicious, bouncing as though shod with springs of their own. If the above were Mae's faux Baedeker recitation, and if Taffy were here, they would both be laughing, but Taffy is a world away and Mae is unconscious.

Henry peruses in relative tranquility the brochure.

Instead of being a place to be avoided, as asylums were in times past, Morecombe Downs is a resort for recreation and the judicious care, treatment and cure of a limited number of Patients suffering Mental and Nervous Afflictions, as well as Chronic Cases of Lunacy in the better classes of Society.

The general aspect of the house is that of a Private Residence of a person in affluent circumstances. Healthily situated in the centre of thirty acres of Pleasure Grounds, Flower Gardens and Water Features that conduce to therapeutic pursuits, the estate boasts unrivalled views of the majestic Grampians, and is a short ride to the prettiest village in Scotland. Extensive and costly alterations have been completed which render the house at once an Efficient Hospital and Comfortable Home that has been well reported of by the Commissioners in Lunacy and Visiting Magistrates.

Considerable pains have been taken such that the noise of an asylum is eliminated without entailing any objectionable features suggestive of restraint. Morecombe Downs is among the first asylums in which the abolition of restraint has been successfully tried and carried out.

Proprietor and Resident Medical Superintendent: Dr. Hitchcock LRCPE
Chief Alienist: Dr. Finch LRCPE

The carriage drawn by the Black and the Bay rolls up the stately tree-lined drive. Henry watches as the house comes into view. Dominating its roofline is a stone cupola in the shape of . . . a pineapple. Henry alights and is met immediately by a porter. "Take me to Dr. Hitchcock."

The porter bows and bids His Lordship follow him.

In the carriage, Knox waits. Lady Marie's head is in her lap. She tenderly strokes the girl's hair with one hand, while with the other she holds the dropper, replenished and at the ready.

Some thirty minutes later, Henry has received a tour of the residence and grounds conducted by Dr. Hitchcock, a reassuringly grey-whiskered gentleman for whom the unannounced nature of His Lordship's visit was no impediment to a reception commensurate with His Lordship's status. Henry stands now in the pleasant ground-floor corner office belonging to Dr. Finch, the Chief Alienist; a younger gentleman, though suitably grave and bespectacled. Henry has been assured of superior accommodations and treatment for his wife, who is suffering from a temporary delusion brought on by the death of their child.

Henry looks out a side window onto lawns where several ladies and gentlemen stroll in twos and threes or recline on chaises beneath rugs in the afternoon sun with books or newspapers, some sipping tea. It would be impossible for the casual observer—and certainly Henry—to say with certainty who might number among the patients and who the staff. Or indeed, to discern whether the premises itself be spa or asylum.

Henry makes a quarter turn to face the front window and, with his hands clasped behind his back, watches as two white-clad female attendants lift Mae expertly down from the carriage and place her in a high-backed wheeled wicker push-chair. One of the attendants takes hold of the handles and wheels his wife up the walk while the other follows until they pass from Henry's line of sight. Two burly male attendants appear and follow with Mae's trunk.

En route home, Henry has Sanders drop him at the Edinburgh Museum of Science and Art. He ascends to the Bird Gallery where he is shocked to encounter a custodian in the act of tipping a dustpan of feathers and bones into the bin. "Hold!"

Upon his return to No. One Bell Gardens, Henry goes directly to his study where he deposits his trove of salvaged bird bits on the desk. Setting them carefully to one side, he takes up pen and notepaper.

It is scarcely a paragraph, but it takes him until the dinner bell to compose it.

Pugsley answers the summons.

"Where is Havers?"

"On an errand for Miss Clarissa, Your Lordship."

"See this cable is delivered post-haste to the telegraph office."

"Very good, Your Lordship."

"I'll dine in here. Tell Cook."

"Yes, Your Lordship."

His sister never remains chastened for long. She sends for him after dinner. He obeys, reporting as though for duty in her parlour like a wretched subaltern.

He is in no mood for her questions.

"What of the child?" she demands.

"All in good time."

"What are you waiting for?"

"To catch my breath."

"Finish it."

"You sound like an English officer on the field of Culloden."

"The English were never so merciful."

———

Henry dispatches Sanders to Ainsley Place with a message instructing Dr. Chambers to make space in his schedule for the prescribed procedure first thing Monday morning. Sanders returns with a reply. Henry is piqued to see the note has not been penned by Chambers himself, but presumably by his female assistant.

. . . Dr. Chambers will perform the procedure Friday next at two o'clock. Please make note of same and advise Dr. Chambers's Surgery of any change . . .

Henry will not indulge in a display of temper even in the privacy of his study. No whispered vulgarity regarding the unappealing female assistant or the arrogant doctor. Such poison would only recoil upon himself and drive him to imbibe a third glass of whisky when he knows fine well two will do. Thus, he merely crumples the note and sighs. *Sufficient unto the day is the evil thereof . . .*

His wife will come home, cured. They will have more children. And their daughter . . . A whimper escapes him. He clamps his hand over his mouth. He must not think of—dear God, just now to his mind's eye— the tendril of flesh . . . *Innocent.* He pitches forward at his desk, his head in his elbows.

While Henry is content to believe all manner of things so long as the social contract of decency and birthright be not breached—at least not so noisily as to impinge on his peace of mind—he finds there is one thing he is unable to believe: that when Chambers cuts off the bit of flesh, his child will feel no pain.

Havers knocks and enters Clarissa's parlour. He hands her a small packet wrapped in brown paper.

"That will be all, Havers."

The blue bottle bears the stamp of a chemist in Leith. Lest any in the New Town should take note.

In the post office at the intersection of Princes and Leigh Streets and North Bridge, the telegraph operator taps at a metal key, sending electrical impulses racing along a wire that runs first underground, then above ground, trapezing pole-to-pole all the way to Glasgow; thence into a cable that drops into Atlantic depths and stretches more than two thousand miles along the ocean floor, while high above it, whales swoop and soar and sing, oblivious to the words passing through the belly of the man-made snake below; all the way to St. John's, Newfoundland, thence to a post office in Boston where the dots and dashes are received and jotted down in English.

DEAR MRS. BLANCHARD REGRET UNABLE COME BOSTON CHARLES UNWELL TAKING HIM TO SPECIALIST ON CONTI-NENT CORDIALLY HENRY BELL BDCDF

63

CHARLES WOULD BE in frocks 'til age seven in any case, his curls kept long and flowing. And if he registers the difference between "There's a handsome laddy!" and "There's a pretty lassie!" they are no more than variations on vocabulary, for which the child has a voracious appetite. After only a matter of days it is as easy to answer to "Charlotte" as it is to "Charles." He is, however, unprepared for his Auntie Cwissa's closed door. Her averted gaze. Her basket, suddenly forbidden. He cries and turns red a good deal but children do, then they forget. And soon it is as if Auntie Cwissa never was, or else belongs to a shimmering other-world. In the real world there is a woman called "Aunt," who must be avoided.

Poppa is something else entirely. "Come here, Charlotte."

And Charles does. He climbs onto Poppa's lap, which takes some doing for he's never had occasion to practise, those paternal peaks having been 'til now debarred. "Up we go, that's it, Charlotte." The wool is scratchy but the waistcoat is velvety and—"That is my watch and chain. Can you tell time?"

Tell it what?

"Look. The long hand tells the hours. The short hand tells the minutes. And the fast little hand tells the seconds."

The child points to the three hands in turn. "Poppa, Momma, Chaws."

"Can you say Charlotte?"

"Shahwot."

Poppa is better than Aunt. Poppa's lap, Poppa's spectacles, Poppa's whiskers. The word *Charlotte* has turned out to be a magic word that opens the delights of Poppa—looping watch chains, winding dials, sparkling tie pins, nibbles of tea-dipped biscuits and pretty feathers. *Charles* is like an erstwhile favourite toy, left with increasing frequency in the corner of the nursery until it is forgotten altogether—where it gathers cobwebs and sheds memory . . .

At first he cries for Momma. Hurls the feeding bottle whose rubber teat cannot replace the breast. Then he forgets, unless speared by a scent—lilac water from her cloak in the foyer—he screams, thinking she has been wrapped up in it and hung on the peg, though he has no way of explaining this apart from *Scream!* Maid takes the cloak and puts it away "in a chest." *Whose chest?* The more *Charlotte* he becomes, the less he misses Momma.

"Poppa!"

The arms open, the foothills are scaled and Mount Olympus receives Charlotte.

All this inside of a week. Only God can do as much in so little time.

Clarissa takes a glass of sherry from the tray in Havers's hand. The house is peaceful once more now that her sister-in-law is safely off recuperating. And the child has learned to keep out of Clarissa's way. The minor surgical procedure is scheduled for tomorrow, after which they can put this ordeal behind them. It seems the worst is over.

She picks away at the lace with the seam ripper and asks her brother, "Where will you go following the procedure? Biarritz? Baden?"

"Hm?"

His sherry sits untasted. His eyes rest on a corner of the parlour ceiling.

What with her brother having already cabled his wife's people in Boston, it remains only to inform their Edinburgh set of Marie's sudden indisposition requiring an immediate spa cure abroad. Their friends will, of course, surmise Lady Marie is pregnant. All the better. "When shall you depart for the Continent?"

"I shan't. I shall return with Charlotte to Fayne." He downs his sherry.

She inquires carefully, "And what might the vicar and . . . why, Mungo and sundry, make of the child's return? On the heels of its supposed demise?"

"They shall think nothing because they shall not be apprised. Charlotte shall be sequestered in the nursery with Knox. While she recovers."

Clarissa sees the wisdom of this. Better the child should convalesce at Fayne, rather than languish at the mercy of foreign physicians in the event of complications. Although if the child should die . . . An unpleasant thought, but thoughts will arise of their own accord. She continues sedately, "I take it we shall, nevertheless, put it about that you and Marie and . . . 'Charles,' so-called, are off on the Continent."

"Quite."

The fire pops. Clarissa works, *tug, snip* . . . "Henry?"

But her brother's gaze remains on the ceiling . . . as if there might be a rare bird nesting up there.

"Henry?"

"I'm sorry, what?"

"It occurs to me we might be at home to friends one afternoon now that Marie is . . . resting. If only to give them to understand that Her Ladyship is indisposed, thus lending credence to any assumptions as to her . . . gravid condition. We might send cards to the Farquhars, the Colonel, Josey, Miss Gourley of course, and—"

"Under no circumstances is Josiah Baxter to set foot in this house."

Heat blooms in Clarissa's chest. Her throat dries. "May I ask why?"

"You may not."

The seam ripper falls from her fingers which have grown suddenly clumsy.

He retrieves it. "I'm sorry."

"You are of course within your rights."

"It grieves me to tell you, the man is a degenerate."

". . . Do you refer to a suspected alliance—dalliance—with the erstwhile Irish maid?"

Henry sighs. "He would be more like to dally with the footman."

She looks down.

She resumes her work.

In the hearth, a log collapses softly with a spray of embers.

"Clarissa . . . There is now a good deal of money. Enough for you, more than enough for me and my descendants. Indeed I could purchase a new estate in a pleasant quarter of the kingdom. Have you ever imagined what it might be like to be free . . . of Fayne?"

"No."

Snip, tug . . .

At length she rises—carefully so he will not see what it costs her. "Well that's me away to bed."

He rises. "Goodnight, sister."

Two drops.

A third.

A single room. Bright but spare. An adequately sized window. And her chair.

Henry lingers in the parlour. The butler enters for the drinks tray. "Leave the decanter."

"Very good, Your Lordship."

Tomorrow he will hand his child to the grey-bun woman. She will lay her on the surgical table. Henry drinks. Pours. *The pain response being not fully developed in an infant prior to the age of two* . . . Drinks, pours. A bit of flesh. Like Hamlet's patch of contested ground, too small to hold the bodies of the soldiers who will die fighting over it. He drinks. Pours . . .

The bairn has held out flat its wee hand with a sugar lump each for the Black and the Bay and squealed its fearful pleasure at the great snuffling lips. It is all Knox can do to bundle her into the carriage over her clamouring to ride "atop!" And now Knox turns to the window and watches as her father exits the house and walks toward the carriage.

Seating himself across from nurse and child, Henry allows his eyes to close, surprised by the intensity of his headache—why is sherry a lady's drink when it is in fact a hammer? Perhaps it is more to do with the fact he is tired, so tired. He is downright knackered—*As to the knackers, My Lord* . . .

"Poppa!"

He reaches across and takes his child from Knox, settling her beside him—attempting to settle her, rather, for she does not remain where she is put. He raps the ceiling, the carriage jolts into motion and the child tumbles against the backrest before bouncing forward against the opposite bench, mercifully likewise upholstered—"Lord, miss!" cries Knox, reaching to gather the lass to her bosom against gleeful protests. But Henry secures the bundle of curls and limbs on his lap—like a trout she is, with her wriggling. She swivels to face him, seizes his side-whiskers and kisses his face. He jerks his head back and the child laughs. He repeats the movement. More merriment. She fairly head-butts him with another kiss. He digs out his handkerchief, for the kisses are as wet as a trout's—"'Tis a game for you, is it?" In a bid to dodge the next moist volley, Henry pulls in his chin like a pigeon. Gales. He coos.

"*Rrroo-rroo*," the child answers.

"*Teacher-teacher-teacher*," he tweets.

"*Teacher-teacher-teacher*," she repeats.

"Charlotte."

"Poppa."

The carriage stops. Through the window may be seen the neatly paved path to the black lacquered door with its brass plate. Before Sanders can climb down, Henry thrusts his head through the window. "Drive on, Sanders. To Fayne."

"Aye, Your Lordship."

At No. One Bell Gardens an envelope arrives. It is from a photographic studio on Princes Street. It is addressed to Lady Bell. Clarissa opens it. She looks at the photograph of the beautiful young woman. And the bonny wee laddy. She goes to drop it into the fire. And instead puts it at the bottom of her work basket.

Part Four

No coward soul is mine.
EMILY BRONTË

64

WE ENTERED A BRIGHT, high vestibule where we were relieved of our outdoor things by the grey-bunned woman who all but disappeared beneath their bulk. The walls were painted a plain creamy white, adding to an overall effect of modernity the which was amplified by—what I hardly dared hope when I spied a button set in a small brass plate on the wall—electrical light! I pressed the button. Immediately the vestibule was plunged into gloom. I pressed it again and watched the milky glass fixture overhead instantly illuminate. "Don't be messing, pet," whispered Knox. I could have brained her. Eager for the main event, however, I followed her and Father up a set of stairs then through a sliding door into a pokey room fitted out in more domestic style, not unlike a parlour. Several chairs and a sofa were arranged about a low table on which were fanned numerous periodicals as well as nonsense magazines for ladies. "Please wait here, Lord Bell." I smiled to myself. Mistress Grey-Bun could not know that Father was unaccustomed to wait on anyone except the Queen, whose portrait hung on the opposite wall.

We were not the only occupants of the "waiting room." On the sofa sat a lady whose fingers were busy with something in her lap. Beside her a gentleman, presumably her husband, was absorbed in his newspaper. Knox plumped onto a chair, giving the impression of being quite at home, and commenced knitting, the yarn regurgitating slowly from the mouth of her carpet bag whilst Father stood, hands clasped behind his back, staring at Queen Victoria. I was revisited by the interesting feeling of familiarity which had greeted me on my arrival at Bell Gardens—perhaps unsurprising, given my years of having imagined just such a moment.

I sat so as not to pace, and turned my attention to the lady of the busy fingers, curious as to what bit of lace or ribbon she was worrying into a "pleasing arrangement"—only to see her lap was empty. Whatever she was tricotting was imaginary. Without taking his eyes from his newspaper, the gentleman next to her reached across and stilled her hands.

I stole a look at Knox but she was absorbed in actually knitting, and I was on the point of rising if only on the pretense of perusing the periodicals, so restless was I, when Father stepped back adroitly before the portrait of the Queen, which had swung to with the opening of what turned out to be a door and the grey-bunned woman announced, "Miss Bell, the doctor will see you now."

I rose. Knox followed, but Father merely stepped aside. I had presumed he would accompany me, perhaps sitting off in a corner whilst I puzzled through sheafs of questions—but of course this was no mere schoolgirl's quizzing, rather it was University Business. We followed Mistress Grey-Bun into the room and I suddenly "came over queer" as Gwen would say. It was the smell. Not in itself remarkable—*carbolic*. It was of course far from out of place, indeed reassuring in a modern physician's surgery. But it elicited in the pith of me a hot and fluttering sort of disquiet . . .

"Are you feeling poorly, pet?"

"Don't be ridiculous."

I mastered myself and drank in my first sight of a medical consulting room. On one wall stood a white enamelled sink with a steel towel rail. Next to it, a floor scale. Next to that, a tall sort of end-table-on-wheels upon which rested another scale, this one cradle-shaped. On an enamelled table of normal height, laid out like silverware, was a range of metal instruments. I drew near. There were nickel-plated prongs, probes, tweezers and tongs, and several which resembled shoehorns—one was shaped like the bill of a duck—there was a lone slim rod of glass.

"Don't touch," whispered Knox.

"Shutup," I whispered back.

I noted with disappointment what there was not: (1) skeleton suspended from stand, (2) anatomy chart, (3) shelves crammed with specimen jars of bits of folk. Although, perhaps it was all in the great cherrywood cabinet which took up the rest of the wall.

On the other side of the room, upholstered in quilted maroon leather, was a sofa. It looked new. Everything did. With the possible exception of the great oak desk and swivel armchair at the far end of the room, above which hung a series of framed medical diplomas. I advanced to the desk and settled into the chair behind it.

"What are you doing, Miss Charlotte?" said Knox.

"I am sitting in preparation for the examination."

Behind Knox stood wee Grey-Bun with my cloak folded over her arms and pressed against her—something affronting in that, as if the woman were presuming to hug me or . . . somehow restrain me.

"Miss Bell, I am Dr. Chambers."

I started. And turned. Behind me was an open doorway and standing in the doorway was the doctor himself. A tall imposing figure, his face framed by greying whiskers the texture of a rough-coated terrier. He wore a suit and waistcoat of no-nonsense tweed. He was neither smiling nor unsmiling—the scientific mien. I composed my own features accordingly, convinced we should get on famously.

"Dr. Chambers, I am glad to make your acquaintance. Do be seated."

"Do you wish the nurse to remain, Dr. Chambers?" importuned Grey-Bun, with reference to Knox as though to an object. But the doctor directed a polite nod in Knox's direction. "Do please stay, Mrs. Knox."

"Much obliged, Dr. Chambers." Knox bobbed.

How does he know her name?

Silly question. Father would have given Dr. Chambers to know that I would arrive in company with my servant, Mrs. Knox.

There was a pause.

"Well, Dr. Chambers, let us begin, shall we?" Emboldened by the ring of command in my own voice, I placed both hands flat on the desk before me—wondering a little at the absence of pen and paper. Perhaps it was to be an oral examination.

"Miss Bell, I invite you to take a seat on the couch where, I venture, you might be more comfortable."

"I am quite comfortable here, Dr. Chambers." This must be what it meant to lead: inwardly trembling, outwardly steady. I would do brilliantly on this examination.

"Miss Bell, I bid you be seated the better to examine you."

"As you wish, Dr. Chambers." I was right: oral.

I made to stride but stumbled, thanks to the new dress. Dr. Chambers's hand was at my elbow but I dared not shake him off lest he take out the rebuff in docked points. I sat on the sofa . . . "Are you all right, pet?"

"Yes, of course, it's only the smell."

"What smell?"

I became aware of Dr. Chambers's gaze upon me. *Nerves.* I would have to get used to them if I hoped to weather the rigours of the University of Edinburgh School of Medicine. As for the sudden nausea, I blamed my corset as, unbidden to my mind's eye, there sprang the image of this morning's kippered haddock now reconstituting itself into a fish swimming frantically back up my throat . . .

"Miss Bell, do you understand what is involved in a medical examination?"

I swallowed the fish and straightened my spine. "I have a tolerable grasp of anatomy and the circulation of the blood including its chief constituents, red corpuscles, white globules and—"

"That will do for the moment." His voice was calm. Lulling, even. "I hope to quiz you more closely on your medical avocation."

"It is not an avocation, it is a calling."

He smiled. "Therefore, as an aspiring Galen-ess, it will not surprise you to learn that a medical examination may also refer to the examination of a patient by a physician as to the state of their health. You being the patient."

I reddened. "You mean . . ." Of course, what had I been thinking? "You mean first to pronounce upon my Condition. Naturally."

He nodded.

I hastened to oblige, briskly unbuttoning my collar, batting away Knox's fingers. My neck bared, I lifted my chin to facilitate glandular palpation.

Dr. Chambers said, "I will now leave the room, Miss Bell, that you may disrobe completely. When you have done so, pray lie down on your back and cover yourself with the sheet." He withdrew the way he had come.

I sat, agape.

"Pet?"

I looked at her. I felt incomprehension crease my brow. I was going to upthrow. The basin was there, as though in response to my thought. Up it came. All of it. Foul, fish mess, mucus, bile. "Better now," said Knox. The woman whisked away the reek, returning with a glass of water and a clean basin. I rinsed. Knox patted dry my mouth. Said, "Arms up pet."

I obeyed. Raising, then lowering my arms by turns in the familiar procedure rendered disorienting by context, as tractable as though I'd been stunned by a blow. Limbs in motion, thoughts suspended. I looked down at the growing heap of fabric ringing my feet. I was briefly roused from this quasi-catalepsy by a sudden movement of the sofa, which had begun to rise as though in obedience to a conjurer. The grey woman was crouched next to it, working an unseen crank, her elbow pistoning with surprising vigour. It had attained chest-level when, by means of a concealed lever, she caused it abruptly to revolve, exposing an underside of smooth steel. Rimmed with a gutter. She flipped down the now-upturned sofa legs and levered up in their place at one end two steel rods fitted with what resembled nothing so much as stirrups. *Presto*, a metal table now stood where moments before there had been a quilted sofa. I half expected the woman to turn and take a bow.

I could leave. Ridiculous thought, again involuntary. I could walk out in my petticoat and camisole. Past Grey-Bun who waited with a white sheet folded over her arms in place of my cloak—had she conjured the one into the other? Through the door, past the lady of the fitful fingers, out the electrified vestibule and into the street where people kept their clothes on. But Knox hadn't finished. Up went the camisole. I commenced to shake like a sapling. Petticoat down, stockings down, hated split drawers—"No."

"Pet, you must."

"But he'll see," I whispered urgently.

"He needs to see the whole of you in order to—"

"No, he'll see." My voice grew tiny. "That I've still got my . . . you know."

"Och pet, 'tis nowt he's not seen before."

"Really?"

In her eyes was a depth of—I knew not what. She spoke gently, "'Twill all be over afore you know it."

"But . . . it's my time." I heard my voice quaver. Felt water in my eyes. Truly, I was undone.

"I know, love," Knox murmured, stroking my cheek. "That's as it ought to be. He's after making sure you're well in every department."

I squeezed back tears and clenched my jaw.

Drawers down. Along with the arrangement of folded linen, wrinkled and stained, releasing its odour of earth and iron. Knox rolled it and tucked it into her carry-all.

Naked, I stepped from the ring of fabric, climbed onto the cold steel table and lay on my back as the white sheet, held like a great blank page by Grey-Bun, descended and covered me to my chin. I felt the table begin steadily to pitch up beneath my legs, and the pulse thickened in my neck with the lowering of my head. Once more I failed to hear the door open, but I felt his presence behind me. For such a large man he was soft-footed as a cat. This was my last thought before the mask was over my nose and mouth, whether by his hand or Grey-Bun's, I could not say. My saliva ran bitter and I swallowed, then all was as red and dark and finally black as the back of my own throat.

In the waiting room, Henry sits upright, hat on his knee, eyes trained on the low table. Obscured by an overlying periodical, a partial caption, "spotted near Willow Brae." The phrase enters and repeats in his mind, meaninglessly.

Up from death. If this is all death is made of, why fear it? Absence with no awareness of being absent. We fear death but not the vasts of time that preceded our birth. Were we not then equally dead? And did we mind it?

But I was once more above the surface of oblivion. Eyes closed, I felt beneath me, steel. Atop me, the sheet . . , pushed up and gathered about my waist. My legs splayed, knees bent, my heels in . . . the metal cups that had resembled stirrups. I stirred. About my ankles were restraints of some kind. I opened my eyes and saw the light fixture in the ceiling slowly revolve. I closed my eyes. I searched my mind for my hands and found them at my sides, strapped by the wrists to the table. The carbolic smell was back and stronger now, filling my nostrils. I opened my eyes once more. Lifted my head. Saw. At the foot of the table. A black-cloaked figure. At its centre a blank eye. A flash of light together with a soft shattering of sound. The hunched cloak hobbled away on stick legs. Its hump split and disgorged the grey-bunned woman. I saw, standing between my legs, Prickle. Tears slid from the corners of my eyes and pooled in the bowls of my ears.

Scritch, scritch. I turned and saw Dr. Chambers, his back to me, his jacket doffed, sleeves pushed to the elbows. He was standing at the enamel table, writing. Next to him was the array of steel instruments, among them the rod of glass, now glistening with blood. He took up the tweezers. Sensing him about to turn, I closed my eyes. I felt his proximity. His breath between my legs. I fought the urge to gasp lest he know me to be awake and witness to my own shame, for he had hold of it! He was stretching it. It would detach presently and perhaps that was what he wished to determine—I panicked, for much as I knew it must come to pass one day, I was wholly unprepared—! But he released it.

Scritch. Scritch scritch. I felt the flick of . . . it must be his finger—*flick, flick.* I felt Prickle stiffen painfully once more. Felt fingers palpating the soft flesh to either side of it. "Cough for me, please," he said.

He knew I was awake.

I obeyed.

Scritch.

My face burned.

Then he was out from under the sheet and across the room with his back to me. I heard water running. He was washing his hands. In a moment he was gone, out through the door behind the desk.

Grey-Bun wheeled away the enamel table. She returned and released the bindings at my wrists, my ankles. Presently I heard the door to the waiting room opening. For a moment I was terrified lest Father enter. But my field of vision filled with the whiskery underside of Knox's chin.

"It's all over now, pet, let's get you dressed."

I wept, Reader, but with no more sensibility of sorrow than has a rain-blurred window. Thus was I reassured to note my capacity for objective observation remained intact.

I sat up and registered a stabbing sensation in . . . Reader, I here convert to laboratory format in order to drain the facts as far as possible of emotive residue, herewith:

anus: stabbing sensation subsiding to dull ache, spotting blood

vaginal canal: searing sensation, cessation of menstrual flow

Prickle (sic): shooting pain, persistent turgidity

Clutching the sheet, I slid from the table and, trembling, stepped back into the circle of garments set out by Knox who bent before me. Drawers up, stockings up—"What about . . . ?"

"Right you are, pet." She rummaged in her bag and drew forth a clean folded linen. Behind me I heard the *thunk* of the steel table flipping over once more, followed by the working of the crank. Petticoat up, camisole over, underskirt up, corset, bodice, skirt, collar, buttons, ties, boots, bonnet. I looked behind me to see the steel slab transformed once more to an ordinary sofa. Grey-Bun had vanished.

"Knox . . . he had hold of Prickle and . . . He put something in me—up me in . . . both places, I know he did. Why did he do that?" As I spoke the words aloud I awakened to the realization that Dr. Chambers was mad. And I had lain there meekly whilst a demented doctor committed an outrage upon my—"Knox, he must be apprehended, Father must be told—!"

"Och, pet, I ought to've warned you, only . . ."

"You knew what was to occur?"

"Aye, pet, 'tis normal. Woman's business."

". . . He is not a woman."

"Nay, but he be a woman's doctor, a—och, there's a name for it—"

"What have my—what has any of that to do with my Condition?"

"He'll have made sure all your parts are in fettle, including your female parts."

"He didn't examine my other parts."

"Mayhap he did whilst you slept."

I recalled the mask, the bitter taste, the black descent . . . "Why did he put me to sleep?"

"To spare you pain and . . . embarrassment."

"Well I woke up," I said fiercely.

"I warrant he'll give you a stronger dose next time."

"What next time?"

She sighed and bit both her lips, appearing to gather her thoughts. "For females of quality as are fortunate enough to be in the care of . . . whatever he is called—there is oft a next time. Come, pet."

"I'll wait here."

"For what?"

"The results, of course. I wish to hear him say I am cured." I turned to face the door behind the doctor's desk even as I shrank inwardly from facing the doctor. But was I a squeamish girl petticoated in the white flag of surrender? Or was I a scholar? I fixed my gaze upon the rank of diplomas hanging on the wall.

"The doctor will say nowt to you, pet."

"What do you mean?"

"He'll speak to your Father."

"He'll . . . tell Father . . . what he did . . . to me?" The last word came out as a squeak.

"Pet. The doctor does nowt but what your father bids him."

I covered my face.

"It is for your good, child. And there is no shame in . . ."

I nodded.

Presently, I spoke through my hands. "Then, I am not to sit the written portion of the exam today?"

". . . Not today."

I became aware of a strange metabolic admixture of excitation and fatigue. A postponement was perhaps as well, and I determined to take an optimistic view. A stoical view: I was through the worst. Compared with the physical examination, the written examination would be easy. Bolstered by visions of framed diplomas, my name followed by qualifications so numerous they would weary a herald, I turned round and took a step toward the door to the waiting room—then hesitated. "Why did Grey-Bun take a photograph of Prickle?"

"Did she? Well I'm sure the doctor has his reasons."

"What reasons? He'll have seen plenty, you said so."

"Saints preserve us, child, what's to say she didnae photograph every inch of you whilst you were dead to the world?"

"It wasn't just because of Prickle, then?"

"Och, there's more to you than that."

I flushed. "I thought he might have had it off me today."

"Aye, well. 'Twill come to pass sooner or later."

I strode from the room as from the scene of a medieval chivalric ordeal.

Except that knights were never required to prove their mettle on their backs.

65

HEAD HIGH, I re-entered the waiting room.

"Charlotte."

"Father." I was suddenly scarlet. Rooted to the spot.

Father rose and spoke easily, saying, "Why don't you take a turn round the park with Knox? I'll just tarry on the chance of a word with Dr. Chambers."

I mumbled something and followed Knox, past the woman whose fingers worked a phantom skein, and her husband who was fast asleep.

In a nearby park, Knox purchased a paper sack of seeds from an old woman—older even than Knox. She handed it to me and I scattered some among the pigeons who gathered about my feet, strutting and cooing. Then, possessed by what imp I knew not, I flung the contents in an arc over my head, setting off a mad flapping and swooping that made me laugh. I demanded a fresh sack and repeated the exercise, wondering at my own taste for this sport, all the while Knox regarded me, disapprovingly I thought. Bother her, I'd earned a bit of fun. I chased and fed and tormented the birds until finally our carriage hove into view and I cried, "Poppa!" Funnily enough. For I had not been wont to call him that for ever so long. Not since I was a wee tot.

He raised his cane in greeting from the carriage window. I could not see his eyes for his dark spectacles, but his side-whiskers were silvery in the noonday sun. I climbed in and kissed his cheek.

"Well what did he say?"

Father answered in his usual tone of mild amusement, "The good doctor is satisfied that you have outgrown your Condition."

"Father!" I exploded from the seat, striking my head on the carriage ceiling, eliciting a cluck of alarm from Knox.

Father chuckled. "Steady on."

"How soon may I begin?"

"Begin . . . ?"

"My studies! At the university!" I had shouted. "Forgive me, Father!" I shouted. "I did not mean to shout!" And I laughed like Gwendolyn Haas.

"Oh, why, as to that, in point of fact, there remains an intermediary step."

"Of course, the written exam."

". . . That will not be necessary."

"Really?" I cocked a snook at Knox.

"The step in question involves a procedure."

"What sort of procedure?"

"Oh, as to that. It is a, it is, the procedure in question is of a surgical nature."

"Is it. My word. I have to date dissected nothing higher than a frog."

"As to that, to be quite plain, my dear, the procedure is to be performed by the doctor upon your person."

I quailed. I summoned equanimity. Father must not see misgiving on my part lest my hopes be scuttled by his desire to shield me. "Upon what part of my person, Father?"

"Upon . . . a glandular structure."

"Of course. He means to open up my neck." It sounded so reasonable when I said it, I quite reassured myself.

"In point of fact, I believe it to be more of an abdominal structure."

"Abdominal?"

"Though you are not wrong to cite the neck, the glandular structure in question being not unlike a tonsil, insofar as I am given to understand it is of no functional consequence. Vestigial. In fact."

I was silent. For I knew suddenly the precise structure to which Father referred. I dared not look at Knox. I looked away from Father, grateful for his dark lenses.

He continued. "Dr. Chambers has diagnosed the structure as a locus of illness, not unlike the tonsil again, such that should it remain *in situ* it might cause a relapse of your Condition. And whereas relapse in a child is not grave, in an adult it is life-threatening. Not to put too fine a point upon it."

"I see."

"Good."

We drove in silence. I noticed a parcel wrapped in brown paper stowed beneath the seat opposite. Presently Father asked, "Have you had a bite to eat?"

"I'm afraid we were rather busy with the pigeons."

"So I saw."

"I say, Father, what's that you've got hidden under the seat?" Knox made to shush me with a look. "Who's it for?" I demanded, as a child might of Father Christmas.

"All in good time." Father smiled, leaned back and closed his eyes.

Father went directly into Aunt's parlour and I mounted to my room to freshen. "They mean to have it off me, don't they, Knox."

She paled. Licked her hard lower lip. "Have what—?"

"Prickle. Don't lie, I know 'tis for the best." I saucered my bonnet onto the bed with a show of insouciance meant to flush out the truth— after all, I might be mistaken, there being numerous glands in the human body.

". . . Aye."

The breath shot from me, I sat heavily on the bed.

How is it possible, Reader, that shock may follow upon a wholly expected piece of intelligence?

Knox held a glass of water to my lips. I sipped.

"Breathe," she said.

I did so.

"I'll tell them to send luncheon up to you."

"Don't be silly," said I, rising.

At luncheon, Aunt was, if not cheerful, then not positively dour. Father, too, was in good humour. For once 'twas I who was subdued. I managed a smile in response to Father's. Pugsley served. The food lodged like sawdust in my throat. I chewed interminably. I drank a good deal of water—

"You'll spoil your digestion," said Aunt, not unkindly, and offered me a glass of sherry. Her own luncheon lay mostly untouched. Truly, she ate like a bird. A sparrow.

"Are you quite well, my dear?"

"Father, I'm fine." I was surprised to hear in my voice a sharpness which 'til then had been reserved for Knox, and hastened to add, "In fact I am in fettle."

Luncheon ended.

An interval before dinner.

I passed the day as though in a daze. I could not read. I could not decide upon a walk out of doors. It was a state akin to that which may be induced by a heavy afternoon nap, when one knows one is asleep. But cannot awake.

Dinner.

Father was absent.

"He dines this evening with Miss Llewellyn," said Aunt, as though conveying glad tidings in which I ought to rejoice. I felt a pang of guilt for having shown insufficient gratitude to Father for my own glad tidings. Namely the procedure, which would be the last "stop" as it were, en route to the university.

I could not, however, muster joy outright, aware as I was of a . . . aye, a sort of caesura in my near future. A chasm to be got over. A cut. Why it was that the prospect of Prickle's surgical removal should disturb me more than that of its inevitable detachment, I could not say. Surely the former was kinder because swifter. Not to mention essential to my health! Still, irrational though I knew it to be, I grieved silently. As at the prospect of a loyal dog that, gazing up as one strokes his ears, knows not he must be put down.

I was undressing for bed when Knox entered with the brown paper parcel.

66

HENRY ENTERED CHAMBERS'S consulting room on the heels of his daughter's and Mrs. Knox's departure. His daughter had appeared shaken. That was to be expected. He himself had sought to conceal his anxiety when he bade them await him in the park.

Now, finding himself alone, he paced and cursed Chambers for keeping him waiting. Soon enough, however, the door opened behind the desk.

"Lord Bell, I pray you be seated." He indicated with a gesture the quilted leather sofa.

Henry remained standing. "Your verdict, sir."

Chambers smiled. "I am a physician, Lord Henry. I deal in diagnoses, not judgments."

Henry might be mild by temperament, but Lord Bell was not to be trifled with. "Out with it, man."

"Your Lordship, your daughter's condition admits of correction, moreover she is merely a few inches or so of flesh away from developing, for all intents and purposes, into a normal woman."

Henry sinks to the quilted sofa. "Oh thank God." Clasps his knees, composes himself with a deep breath. "I thought as much, of course, only . . . So you are quite certain she will be capable of . . . leading a full married life?"

"Apart from the anomaly, I find nothing to contradict that expectation."

"And she may bear children."

"As to that, pregnancy alone proves the existence of functional ovaries."

"You mean to say any marriage I contract on my daughter's behalf might be . . . ?"

"My Lord, no one can say for certain of any intact female that she is either fertile or barren before she is tested in matrimonial relations."

"But you find nothing to . . . contradict."

"Nothing, Your Lordship."

Henry nodded. Heaved another breath. "Well then. Let it be done." He rose.

"Lord Henry, I could amputate the anomaly here, today."

"So be it, Chambers."

"The effect of the surgery on the body will be benign. But the effect on an unprepared mind could be grave."

Henry stared. "You do not mean to acquaint my daughter with her true nature?"

"My Lord, allow me to assure you, I shall neither do nor say anything whatever to distress your daughter. As to her true nature, that is what the procedure will go some way to reveal and restore, but it cannot do so on its own—"

"You told me that was precisely what it would do twelve years ago in this very room." His fists were clenched.

"As it would have, in a child of scarcely two years. It is my Hippocratic duty to impress upon you that a girl of your daughter's age, having recently achieved menarche, is already prone to nervous instability. Your daughter's anomaly renders her mental state more precarious still."

"That's where you're wrong, Chambers, my daughter is an exception. Mentally strong, mathematical even, loves bridges, engines, birds, has a formidable capacity for learning." He smiled in spite of himself.

Dr. Chambers looked grave. "'An exception.' Just so. In Woman, Your Lordship—all the more so in the adolescent female—overstimulation of the brain can only be at the expense of the womb. With the result that she is tipped into an unbalanced state as surely as if she had sustained a grievous blow. Lord Henry, you have seen first-hand the toll that may be taken by hysteria."

The blood had drained from Henry's face. "You mean to say her . . . her mental vigour, her . . . yearning to attend the university . . ."

Chambers looked at the floor and shook his head.

Henry's voice grew faint. "It is my doing. I plied her with learning. Quizzed her, provisioned her with books, a tutor—"

Chambers looked up. "A tutor, My Lord?"

Henry's forehead found his hand—*Don't cradle your forehead, Henry.*

Chambers poured a glass of water from a carafe on his desk and handed it to His Lordship. "Lord Henry, it is not your rearing alone that has engendered in your child confused tendencies. The anomaly itself is responsible for stimulating masculinizing secretions."

"Then off with it! Enough parley!"

"In this case, My Lord, it is advisable first to constrict the tendencies, that they may shrink, rather than suddenly to amputate their fleshly counterpart and risk brain-shock."

Henry placed the empty glass upon the desk. Squared his shoulders. Looked the man in the eye. "Had I heeded your advice twelve years ago, my child would have been spared the strictures of secrecy. Would today be walking the length of West Princes Street Gardens with her schoolgirl companions rather than yearning to join you in your macabre métier, and my wife would—" He turned away. Mastered himself. Turned back. "How am to I part my daughter from her . . . tendencies?"

"By means of a brief interval during which she may begin to adapt to habits more compatible with her future than her past. Requiring strict abstinence from scholarly books, intellectual conversation and physical exertion. Aided by a therapeutic appliance."

"What . . . appliance?" He turned to see the grey-bunned woman holding a parcel wrapped in brown paper.

"A garment designed to enforce a particular abstinence which is bound to excite a degree of opposition in your daughter."

"Abstinence from what?"

"Autonomous stimulation."

"Auto . . . what?"

Chambers hesitated, as though to afford His Lordship the opportunity to work out the answer for himself, before saying, "The solitary vice."

Henry inquired calmly, "Shall I cut your throat for you, sir?"

"I beg Your Lordship's pardon for the distress which is an unavoidable side-effect of the discharge of my duty; by which I am bound to urge you to listen closely to what I am about to say: When excited, the anomalous fleshy appendage draws a surfeit of blood which causes it to become turgid. The consequent spasm releases not only the diverted blood, but a host of masculinizing secretions. These secretions renew in the appendage the urge toward turgidity, thus driving the cycle of release and masculinization—with the corollary effect of a malignant increase in the size of the appendage, even when flaccid. Left uninterrupted, the cycle must lead to anemia, melancholy, wasting. And finally, dementia praecox. In layman's terms, adolescent insanity."

Henry took the parcel.

67

I BRIGHTENED AND TOOK the parcel from Knox's hands. "I knew 'twas for me!"

But Knox commenced to unwrap it herself.

"Give over, 'tis my gift."

Heedless, she laid open the wrappings to reveal . . . "Lederhosen?"

"Step in, pet." And she lowered the short leather pants before me.

"Are we off on a spa holiday in the Alps, then?" And it struck me Father might bring me to visit my brother's grave.

"'Tis a type of corset."

"I have enough corsets, surely."

"'Tis a French corset."

"I don't care if it's Greek or Russian, I'll not wear it at this hour, I'm dressed for bed."

"'Tis to wear to bed."

"You're dafty, Knoxy."

"Please pet, step into the appliance."

"'Appliance'?"

"Och, you'll be the death of me."

"I doubt that, you're a hundred if you're a day, if you croak tonight 'tis none of my doing."

"Miss Charlotte, doctor's orders!"

"Balderdash."

"'Tis a thera . . . something. 'Tis for your good."

"'Therapeutic'?"

"Aye."

"Really." I examined it more closely. There was a belt to it, and a clasp and a . . . keyhole. "What's it for?"

She closed her eyes. "Dr. Chambers would have you wear it."

"Is this to smother the prickle so it will fall off? But why, if he means to have it off me in any case?"

"'Tis to stop you . . . worrying it."

I looked away, my cheeks ablaze.

Knox said, "Worrying it can make you take sick."

"It never has."

"It may yet."

I trained my eyes on the rosebuds in the carpet, and turned over the facts in my mind: "worrying" Prickle stimulated the locus of illness. How long had I been playing with fire? A lifetime. And now, because I was no longer a child, the shameful habit threatened mortal consequence.

I stepped into the appliance. I would not court relapse. Not when I was so close to my goal. Knox fastened the belt round my waist and produced a small key. "Why lock me into it?"

"Because it might be uncomfortable at first. Girls cannot be trusted to keep it on through the nicht."

"I am not 'girls,' I am the Honourable Charlotte Bell and I'll not be locked into a pair of fancy French underpants."

"Pet."

I pitied her suddenly. I stood, tractable, while she turned the key in the lock at my back. "How am I to . . . heed the call of nature?"

"You've but to ring the bell and I'll come."

"Knoxy, it feels . . . uncongenial." I was horrified to feel my eyes welling up.

"I know, pet. And you're a brave lassie." She pocketed the key in her apron.

I climbed into bed.

"Knoxy?"

"Aye, pet?"

"How did he know your name?"

"Who?"

"Dr. Chambers. That odious little woman referred to you only as 'the nurse.'"

"Did she? Well now, I wonder."

I sat up. "You'd been there before."

She looked away.

". . . With Mother? Was it he who consigned her to the madhouse?"

"'Twere no—"

"Morecombe Downs, then."

"He recommended a rest cure."

"And. Was she? Cured?"

"She looked fair to recover, 'til . . ."

"I was born."

She stroked my brow. I closed my eyes. Then opened them and sat up. "Knoxy, bring me pen and paper."

"Whatever—?"

"Do it. I forgot to write to Gwendolyn—"

"You may do so in the—"

"Now."

She obeyed and I wrote.

January 11, 1888

Dearest Gwennie,

I have begged and received permission to request the pleasure of your
company at your earliest convenience, which I fervently hope will be
no later than three days from now, at dinner. I have tidings to share
with you such as are cause for celebration. Do come, I perish without
you! Do not disquiet yourself, I am well, and soon to be even better.
I "perish" only for want of your delightful intercourse. I am bored as
a stuffed stoat, if you must know! Among the delights of No. One Bell
Gardens, prepare to meet my invalid aunt, Miss Clarissa Bell. She
is tough as teak and greeted me like death on a doily. Suffice to say,
I need fear no petting nor fussing.

Yours cordially,
The Honourable Charlotte Bell, DC de Fayne

PS Upon reviewing this missive I am put in mind of Mother and Taffy.
Funny, that.

I folded the letter into an envelope, addressed it to Miss G. Haas care
of Miss Gourley and Miss Mellor's School for Girls, Circus Lane,
Stockbridge, Edinburgh and thrust it at Knox. "See it is carried thence
first thing in the morning."

"Yes, miss."

She bobbed. *That's more like it*, I thought. I felt myself again—
notwithstanding the stiff leather chafing my thighs—and, tumbling into
bed, fell instantly into a heavy slumber.

In the Dead of Night.
At the foot of the bed.
Stands the cloak. Empty hood upright, empty arm slits upraised.
She is aware the cloak is trying to convey an urgent message. But of course
it cannot speak. Because it has no head. In her mind the words bloom, dark
and distending, "No one comes to the Mother except through me."
She awakes with a cry.

I awoke with a cry caught in my throat.

I sat up. I could feel Prickle alert and straining against its confines—vestigial gland, rather. I stopped my ears, as it were, against its smothered pleading, every bit as importunate as the child crying out on the moor. I concentrated instead on its function as bacterial host. Locus of illness. Impediment to Destiny. And presently it abated.

Next morning, Knox turned the key at my back and I stepped from the "appliance." Moments later, in the WC, I observed Prick—the gland, lying chastened, withered between my legs. Perhaps it would have the decency to drop off and save the physician his effort. A sharp knock at the door and Knox's voice inquiring as to how much longer I would be at my ablutions. I pulled the cord, washed my hands and emerged. "You needn't worry, Knox. I'll not play fast and loose with my prospects." And she locked me in once more.

Breakfast. Father did not appear. Nor did Aunt.

Luncheon.

Tongue in aspic.

Aunt was there at tea time. I was by now in torments for Father to appear, on tenterhooks to know when the Procedure was to take place.

"Your father is out driving with Miss Llewellyn."

"I thought . . . That is, he and I had made plans to tour the university—"

"You are to undergo a minor surgical procedure in a week's time. Until then you are to keep within the house and avoid exertion. Of any kind."

I felt the now-familiar flaming of my cheeks. She knew. I had at least been spared a mincing of words.

She bit into a liberally marmaladed slice of bread and butter.

As soon as I could decently do so, I excused myself and headed for Father's study intending to select a book with which to pass the time—I had earlier spied a slim volume entitled, intriguingly, *Metamorphoses*—but his study door was locked. I turned to see Havers . . . hovering. "I bid you unlock the door, Havers."

"I may not, Miss Charlotte."

"Why not?"

"It is His Lordship's wish the door should remain locked."

I returned to my bedroom to see, mercifully on my nightstand, a book. I snatched it up. *Etiquette for Ladies: With Hints on the Preservation, Improvement and Display of Female Beauty.* I set it aside, lay on my back and commenced to re-read, with my mind's eye, Father's library. Beginning with *"Achilles was son of Peleus, king of Pythia in Thessaly, descended of Zeus . . ."*

JANUARY 11, 1888
W. G. CHAMBERS, CASE NOTES RE CHARLOTTE (FORMERLY CHARLES) BELL

Subject is fourteen years of age, intact virgin. Examined on third day of menstrual cycle. Overall robust appearance, broad of shoulder, small of breast, narrow of pelvis, but not outside boundary of feminine type. Face and nipples show no hirsutism. Voice is agreeable, no hoarseness of male type.

EXAMINATION
Ether administered.
Internal exam, rectal, pelvic.
Vaginal opening nearer than average to urethral opening, but within normal. Vaginal canal of normal length and width as measured by glass stem through hymen; cervical crypt likewise. Labia majora more than usually textured, uniting at a higher level but not fused.
Tumescent tissue three and one half inches erect. Imperforate as before.
Cough test: no indication of testes.
Patient professes desire to attend university, train as medical doctor etc. Spurious masculine mentality; absent feminine modesty.

DIAGNOSIS
Pronounced hypertrophy of clitoris.
Pseudo-Hermaphroditism of the Female Type.

INDICATED TREATMENT
Clitoridectomy via amputation with cautery knife.

PROGNOSIS
Cure.

68

SOLITARY BREAKFAST.

I began to fear lest Father had come to harm. "Knoxy, tell me the moment Father wakes up, I wish to speak with him."

"He's awake and gone, miss."

"What? Where—?"

"He's out—"

"Driving with Miss Llewellyn, damn her."

"Miss Charlotte!"

"They're to marry, I know it, I wish it, but she'll have him to herself for the rest of her life, whereas I shall shortly be gone to the ends of the earth."

"Eat your porridge."

"Pass me the marmalade."

"This come for you, just now."

I snatched the envelope from her hand. "Gwennie!" I cried, tearing it open. "She's to come to dinner Sunday."

"You'll be having to beg leave of your—"

"He gave it already!"

She took a step back, for I had roared it and pounded the table. "I'm sorry, Knoxy. I don't know what came over me."

She regarded me sadly. ". . . The corset chafing you, is it?"

"Not in the slightest." I resumed my stoic composure.

"Only, Sunday is the nicht afore the . . ."

"The Procedure, yes. And what better way to mark the auspicious occasion?"

Practised though I was in the art of patience, the rest of the week was an eternity. Each day the vestigial gland slumbered, and each night it awoke entombed in leather—I blessed Knoxy for locking it out of reach, otherwise I might be in no fit state to undergo the Procedure, for where there was infection there could be no incision. As it was, I was frequently out of humour because I was out of sleep. Plagued by dreams, chafed by leather, hounded by the gland and forbidden to so much as walk about the garden. No conversation. No books worthy of the name. Father, alive and well as I saw when he made a point of looking in on me as I sat across from Aunt at another funereal luncheon, was daily taken up with driving out with Miss Llewellyn to points of interest, the which he must by now have depleted, the abundant wonders of Edinburgh, Leith and environs notwithstanding.

Sunday at last!

I prevailed upon Knox to grant me a holiday from the "corset" for the space of the evening, and the many layers of underclothing felt suddenly like feathers. I fairly floated down the stairs.

Havers entered the drawing room—"Miss Llewellyn, Your Lordship."

She simped in, Father rose and bowed. She joined me and Aunt on the sofa. Dross, sherry, titters. A rustle in the foyer. I sprang to my feet and deserted the drawing room—there she was, my dear skinamalink—"Gwennie!" I cried.

"Charlotte!"

We flew into one another's arms. I released her that she might shrug from coat and bonnet, then pulled her by the wrist into the drawing room where, breathless with the unaccustomed exertion, I announced, "Aunt, Miss Llewellyn, may I present my friend, Miss Gwendolyn Haas!"

Gwennie curtsied and proceeded to do Miss Smeller proud. Speaking demurely and with lowered chin, she answered my Aunt's queries *vis-à-vis* her "prospects." "I hope to merit a position as a governess, Miss Bell."

"Hm," said Aunt. High praise. Flying colours!

Gwendolyn of course said nothing of Paris, nudes, wine or trails of ignominy. She drossed beautifully with Miss Llewellyn, "who is in fact a governess," I put in helpfully. That lady tittered, "Indeed, I was, until . . ." And with a lowering of lashes, "Recently."

Father stepped in. "I have encouraged Miss Llewellyn to take a sabbatical, as it were."

Havers appeared. "Dinner is served, Your Lordship."

Gwen and I comported ourselves admirably throughout the meal, faltering only when our eyes met simultaneous with Aunt's pronouncement, "Havers, pooding."

Afterwards, in the privacy of my chamber, we fell about laughing on the carpet.

Finally, wiping her eyes, Gwennie said, "So, your father's engaged."

"He hasn't come out and said it yet, but—"

"I knew it!"

"Yes, you did, clever-boots."

"When do you start?"

"'Start.'"

"University!"

"Ah. Soon."

"Have you not done the exam yet?"

"Ah. As to that. I have."

"And? Oh dear, how'd it go?"

"Splendidly."

"Good on you, I knew it would." She smiled. I smiled back. "What is it?"

"What is what?"

"You're staring."

"Am I?"

"You've noticed, oh goody, I was hoping you would."

"Noticed what?"

"My face."

"What about it?"

"Do I not look different to you?"

"Now you mention it, you've a charcoal smudge there, at your temple."

"What? Not that." She licked her palm and rubbed away the spot— "I'm talking about my—oh for criminy sake, my freckles."

"What about them?"

"Can you not tell they've faded? A bitty?"

"I shouldn't worry, they're as vivid as ever."

"Argh!" she cried in vexation, digging from her pocket a bottle which she thrust at me. I perused the label: *Rowlands' Kalydor* ≈ *Freckles fly before its application.* ≈ *Beware the party offering imitations.*

"Gwendolyn. If there existed a potion capable of imparting freckles to my face, I should unhesitatingly apply it."

"You're . . . not lying."

"You are my friend. I would follow you into exile. And freckle-dom."

She hugged me. "I've missed you, old stick." Her eyes were wet when she released me. "What is it, Gwennie?"

"Nothing."

"You're lying."

"I'm in love."

"With what's-his-name, Ichabod."

"Not Icha—"

"I know, Isadore—well?"

Her eyes danced and she pressed her palms together at her lips. Then, in a quiet voice, she confessed, "I declared myself."

"You didn't!"

"I couldn't bear it anymore, I was going to explode."

"I understand. So it is with me and intellectual passion."

She looked momentarily bemused, but continued, "I was set to write to him but I thought, no, any love-sick schoolgirl might pen a silly pash-note to their schoolmaster, so I decided to do it in person and risk scorn or reprimand, either of which might at least cure me. So I waited in the classroom 'til the others had left and he was cleaning some horrid Latin conjugation from his slate, and I told him."

"Whatever did you say?"

"I said . . ." —here she closed her eyes and I witnessed her summon a gravitas of which I had not known her capable. "'Sir. I wish to tell you that I harbour tender feelings for you.'" She opened her eyes wide, squeezed her face between her hands and looked at me agog, adding, "Or words to that effect. I was petrified."

"And what did he say?"

"He was very gentlemanly and assured me we need never mention the subject again and that he had the utmost regard for me as a pupil with great potential."

"Good show."

"I told him in that case I would leave school, and I was sorry to bother him and all that."

"Oh Gwennie, you haven't, have you?"

"He said he would resign his post, that I must stay at school. And I said, 'There's no need for us both to suffer' and he said, 'I shall suffer if you do.' And that's when I knew." She had blushed to the roots of her freckles. "Then he apologized. And pledged to leave the country so as not to put either of us in the way of . . ."

"Ignominy?" I whispered.

"Near enough."

"And did he? Leave?"

"I begged him not to, but he wouldn't hear of me sacrificing my education—I may as well tell you, Charlotte, he's every bit as passionate about learning as you are. How on earth did I wind up violently in love with a bookworm?! 'Tis enough my best friend is one!"

I grinned. Pleased.

"So we made a pact. He is making application for a teaching post abroad. Meanwhile we promised not to speak again of our feelings nor to find ourselves alone with one another until my sixteenth birthday. A sentence of almost a year."

"It will fly by."

"On wings of lead, I know."

"Who is this honourable gentleman? I wish to make his acquaintance before he leaves the country."

"You can't. Not yet."

"Of course not, but tell me his name."

"I . . . mustn't."

"I see."

"I'm sorry, old thing."

"Pshaw, I'd not for the world ask you to break a promise."

"I didn't promise."

"You didn't?"

"Not in so many words, that's part of what's so wonderful, I didn't have to promise for him to know I'd never—"

"You don't trust me."

"Of course I trust you."

"Then why not tell me?"

She had no rejoinder. "You have no rejoinder."

"Charlotte, I trust you with my life. But I don't have the right to decide whom to trust when it comes to his life. Surely you understand that, with your chivalric codes of honour and so on."

"I stand corrected."

"You're miffed."

I yawned. "I'm knackered, and I've an early start—"

"Don't sulk!"

"I'm not sulking!"

"You are!"

"Yes I am, because you're right and I'm wrong and I hate that!"

She laughed. "If you really want to know, I'll tell you."

"Don't you dare, I forbid it."

"I'm going to tell you."

"Stop!"

"You can't stop me—"

"I'll not be the occasion of your being forsworn!"

"I didn't swear anything, I don't go about swearing—"

I commenced to remove my collar.

"What are you doing?"

"Have you a bit of charcoal?"

"Always."

"And paper?"

"Ditto."

"Well then. In exchange for not telling me the name of your beloved, I shall allow you to sketch me from life."

She laughed outright. Then, as she saw me squeeze the halves of my corset together and single-handedly undo twelve hooks at one go, she dove for her satchel.

Presently she stood poised and peeping round her easel as I, stripped like a pirate from the waist up, pulled the drawstring of my split drawers with a flourish. They dropped to the floor, and I stood before her nude as a newt. She stared.

"What's the matter?" I'd no need to follow her gaze to know what had given her pause. "You look as though you'd never seen one."

"I . . . haven't."

"Pish-tosh, what of your own, what of others', old chap?" I was flustered but determined to live up to the brash and dash of Gwendolyn's schoolmates.

"I haven't got one."

"Of course not, it'll have fallen off."

"I never had one."

"It's no good dissembling."

"Charlotte. I have never seen one."

"I thought you bathed nude, the lot of you, in St. Margaret's Loch."

"We did."

"I suppose it was dark."

"There was a moon."

"They'd already all had 'em drop away."

She spoke slowly. "Charlotte, girls don't . . . Girls do not generally have a bit like what you've got."

I felt myself redden. "You know very well they do, and like the tail of a tadpole, it drops away—usually before now, I grant you."

"No Charlotte, they have something more like a pea—"

"Which is why I'm to have it taken off tomorrow, happy? Now, how do you want me? Standing? Lounging? How's this?" And I struck a David pose.

But Gwen had yet to sketch a stroke. "Does it work?"

"What do you mean?" But I knew very well what she meant. I grabbed my drawers and hauled them up.

"Charlotte, wait, you needn't be ashamed."

"I am not ashamed!"

"Charlotte." She offered up the words carefully—crystal amid cattle. "Is that why you've been kept shut in?"

I whirled on her. "How dare you?!"

"It's all right, I'm your—"

"Knox said you would deny it—"

"I'm telling you the truth."

I went cold. "This then is your mocking revenge for my daring to surpass you and your ilk? To scale the heights of Academe whilst you toil as a governess and, and, mistress to a mere schoolmaster. This is what comes of mixing with the lower classes!"

"Your father has lied to you, Charlotte."

"Get out! And take your worthless scribblings with you!"

Gwendolyn Haas did not move. Pale and tear-stained, she looked at me. "Don't let them take your extra bit off you, Charlotte."

I turned my back and pointed to the door.

69

AT FIVE MINUTES TO EIGHT the following morning we pulled up in Ainsley Place. Father descended from the carriage, turned and offered his hand. I took it.

Knox followed as we walked up to the black lacquered door. Father pressed the bell and stood back. The door opened and the grey-bunned woman said, "Miss Bell. Please follow me." I made to do so but Father lingered on the doorstep. He smiled and said, "Well now, my dear, I'm off to the museum. By the time I return, it will all be over. What shall I bring you as a convalescent treat?"

"Cocoa," I said without thinking, and turned away before he could see my cheeks suddenly flushed.

"Charlotte." He regarded me through the dark lenses of his spectacles. I could hear the warmth in his eyes, however, when he said, "My own." His voice thickened. "I wish you to know that afterwards . . ."

"Yes Father?"

". . . You shall thank me."

"I already have."

In the doctor's examination room, the table was prepared. Knox undressed me, then left. Grey-Bun held up the white sheet. I lay down on my back. The sheet descended. My heels found the stirrups. The table rose, tilted, blood shunted to my head. Leather straps were fastened round my wrists and ankles. I became aware of an electrical humming. Then Dr. Chambers was there. His back to me, in waistcoat and shirt sleeves, scrubbing his hands at the enamel basin. I smelled something burning. I turned my head and saw the doors of the cherrywood cabinet standing open. I saw a rank of jars, wires sprouting from their lids—batteries. The wires ran to a large machine bristling with dials and more wires. Dr. Chambers was standing at my feet. He appeared calm. He did not acknowledge me. Grey-Bun reached up and tied a white mask across his face, leaving visible his eyes. Then she strapped to his forehead an electrical lamp. Clearly, he was in the vanguard of surgical practice. I knew how lucky I was. It was the last thing I knew before the mask was pressed over my nose and mouth, the bitterness found the back of my throat, and darkness engulfed me.

Chambers has consulted the newest edition of *Guide to Surgical Treatment in Diseases of Women* with special recourse to Chapter V, "Thermocautery as Pertains to Deformities of the Vulva." "When the cautery knife glows red, the surgeon may be certain it will incise efficiently the prepared tissue. In this case, the cautery loop attachment is indicated: its cutting surface being obloid, it may be looped about the base of the tissue in the manner of a snare. Said snare is tightened by means of a well-oiled screw at the base of the cautery post to ensure a clean, nearly bloodless amputation once the loop closes entirely, pinching off the tissue at its base. Thus are stabilization, cutting and cauterizing achieved in one simple swift procedure, using one instrument."

It goes just like that.

With the surgical tweezers, Dr. Chambers drops the bit of detached flesh, its base singed and pinched, into the enamel pan held by his assistant.

Then he sits at his desk to write up his notes.

JANUARY 16, 1888
W. G. CHAMBERS
Patient, C. Bell.

SURGICAL NOTES
10:03 A.M. *patient anaesthetized.*
10:04 A.M. *mons pudenda shaved.*
10:07 A.M. *cautery loop applied to base of clitoris.*
12 turns of screw, tissue severed at base simultaneous with cauterization of wound.
10:08 A.M. *clitoris detached.*
Negligible bleeding at stump.

Dr. Chambers has joined Lord Henry in the waiting room which has been reserved, today, for His Lordship's sole use. The physician, being taller, inclines his head and, cradling one lightly closed fist in the other, murmurs his report to the patient's father. The father stands, gaze averted, one wrist loosely clasped in the other hand before him. He nods once. Twice. Thus, the men confer.

I awoke. It hurt. Knox was there. My throat was dry.

"I thought it was supposed to be painless."

"The doctor did say to expect some abominable discomfort."

"He said nothing of the kind."

"He'll've told your father."

"And Father told me 'twould be painless."

"Och, so he did, what was he thinking—"

"Hold your tongue, he was reassuring me."

"Of course he was."

"Don't tell him I whinged."

I lifted my head. My body was still covered by the sheet. I lifted it. I was swathed in a white linen dressing, like a loincloth, secured with safety pins. It was bundled round the pain.

"Can you sit up, pet?"

"I'd rather stand under the circumstances."

"Slowly—"

I rolled onto my side. Raised myself on one hand. Slid from the table, stood up and vomited.

Presently. Cleaned, rinsed, woozy. "I wish to go home."

"We are going home. Arms up now, pet."

Grey-Bun showed us out through the door behind the desk. Down a set of service stairs. Out into the mews. Where the carriage waited. I walked slowly. Every step an excruciation at the surgical site. Such a tiny proportion of my body, such outsized pain. I mounted into the carriage. Father was not there. I looked out the window into the cold rain. My eyes commenced to cry.

"Your father is speaking with Dr. Chambers."

"He was going to bring me some . . ."

"What, pet?"

"Nothing."

The carriage pulled away.

In your place, Reader, I too should wish to know: How could she sit, much less endure a carriage ride? Answer: I knelt on the floor, facing the upholstered bench, on which I leaned my torso, my arms spread out as though clinging to a spar.

There are gaps in my recollection, a side-effect, I surmised, of an advisedly strong dose of anaesthetic. Thus it seemed to me I went from the carriage to my bedroom with no intervening actions. Likewise the abrupt shift to my bed, where, now clad in my nightgown, I lay whilst Knox slipped a dropper of evil-tasting stuff between my lips. I slept.

———

Through luncheon, tea, dinner, and into next morning.

When I awoke, the pain was gone.

I sat up gingerly. Still no pain. Nothing. I arose. Stood, one hand on the bed post; light-headed from a sleep—not to mention a fast—of some twenty hours, for so the clock on the wall told me with its rosebud hands. Rain thrummed at my window where the curtains admitted a stripe of dull light. I thought of the smell of worms at Fayne, of moss, of Gossamer's stable, Byrn's peat fire in the bothy, and experienced a stab of homesickness. As for pain at the site, however, I felt none. I walked carefully across the carpet to the lavatory.

The gas light was on. I raised my nightgown and, bracing myself for the sight of blood, removed the safety pins and opened the dressing—to find it sour with urine. I was shocked, but soon reasoned that the contents of the dropper might be implicated in my incontinence, itself anticipated by the napkin—for so it was, there being no call for a dressing as there was no blood. I gave thanks that incontinence had taken liquid form only. I lifted the lid of the commode, sat on the rosewood seat, curled forward and surveyed the surgical site.

Reader, the principal shock was the hairlessness of the triangle between my legs. It had been shorn such that it now resembled the skin of a naked mole-rat. As for the site. A charred nub.

Shocking, not insofar as the absence itself, for the which I had mentally prepared, but insofar as the manner by which said absence had been effected. I had thought to behold a tiny, stitched, seeping wound, even now scabbing overtop a pea-sized remainder of flesh.

I touched the nub. It fell away like charcoal from a spent log. And into the commode. No pea-sized bit of flesh was revealed. Rather, there was an indentation. Pink. Puckered—as though it had been pressed by a baker's baby finger before being place in the oven. There was a sheen to it.

I released a stinging stream of urine into the porcelain bowl of rosebuds—the site, being raw, was of course sensible to uric acid. I patted myself dry. I noted the burning sensation described a tiny circle—

like the still-steaming rim of a crater. And at the centre of the crater? I placed my middle finger in the pink depression and felt . . . nothing.

Prickle was gone. Pea . . . had yet to emerge.

Knox entered, taken aback to see me up and dressed.

"Tell Father I am ready to meet the Dean of Medical Arts."

But Father was from home. Paying a call upon Miss Llewellyn.

His study was locked. Aunt's parlour door was closed. The drawing room was too large. The morning room, too cold.

I mounted to the top of the house and sat on the floor of the nursery as rain drummed on the dormer window. Idly, I took up the abacus—gift of my aunt to my brother. I slipped the beads back and forth, then set it down once more. I felt curiously peaceful here in the scene of my brother's infancy. What might it have been like to have an older brother? He would be at school now. Would he ridicule my hopes? Or, like Father, champion them? He might even be kind. *Hello*, I thought. There in the stillness of the abandoned nursery. Surrounded by his well-loved toys. *Hello, Charles.*

Reverie was interrupted by Havers of all people. He appeared like a giant in the low doorway. Balanced on the palm of his hand was the silver salver. On it, a letter.

I returned to my room before opening it. I knew the hand, of course, and forced myself to open it slowly as though loath to betray, even in my solitude, any eagerness.

Miss Gourley and Miss Mellor's School for Girls
Circus Lane
January 17, 1888

Dear Charlotte,
I wish you to know that I have not told, nor will I ever tell, anyone anything of what transpired between us on Sunday evening. You may trust me to the antipodes of the Earth.

Enclosed please find a letter addressed to your father. I know it will come as a shock to you to learn that the letter is from your former tutor, Mr. Margalo.

My heart beat faster and fairly sideways, I forced myself to breathe through my nose and, gripping the page with both hands, I read the words as slowly as I could.

That gentleman is a schoolmaster at Miss G. and Miss M.'s. When you and I spoke on Sunday night, I did not know that he had been your tutor, for you never told me his name. How I discovered this to be so must await another occasion. I can tell you that I confronted Mr. Margalo with his having abandoned you. Suffice it to say, he denied the charge. I could get from him nothing beyond his word that he was dismissed without warning or explanation, in the middle of the night, and taken from Fayne to the post-chaise in the village with instructions never to return nor seek to communicate with you or Lord Bell. He asked me for news of you. I have told him nothing of your circumstances beyond the fact that you are alive and in good health. The which he was glad to know.

Your friend, always,
Gwendolyn

I crumpled it and pitched it into the fire. Heaped now upon the outrage of her having mocked and taunted me was the realization that her beloved "Isadore" was very likely none other than my blackguardly tutor—a fact doubtless known to her from the start despite her claim to the contrary. For a long moment, I could not stir and did not breathe.

My eye strayed to the floor where the enclosed envelope had dropped. The sight of the handwriting was like a dear friend's face after a long parting—there before me was the fine, efficient hand I knew so well from field notes and jottings in the margins of my laboratory reports. And in the upper left-hand corner of the envelope, his name: *I. Margalo*. I squeezed shut my eyes against tears as I stooped to retrieve it, and I would have cast it too onto the flames, but that it was addressed to my father.

No doubt it contained a plea of innocence, an attempt to ward off damage to his reputation when Father should learn—as he shortly would, from me—the whereabouts of the miscreant and that he could now count the seduction of a schoolgirl among his crimes.

I had the envelope in my pocket as I entered, with icy calm, the dining room—but Father and Aunt were in company with Miss Llewellyn so I kept mum. Father wore a crimson cravat. He looked like a red-throated diver. He rose. "My dear, oughtn't you to be . . . resting?"

Miss Llewellyn asked, "Are you not well, Miss Charlotte?"

"I am quite well, Miss Llewellyn, and on the point of enrolling at the University of Edinburgh." I favoured her with a serene smile.

Father surprised me by flushing.

Miss Llewellyn surprised no one by tittering.

Aunt Clarissa levelled a Medusa stare at me and I dropped the subject, mindful of her jealousy in matters academical. "Havers," said I. "Set another place."

"Very good, Miss Charlotte."

As I sat through the meal, I became aware of . . . That is, I realized I was no longer aware of . . . Reader, not only had pain retreated but all feeling else, it was as though a mist had settled over the surgical site, obscuring in this case not vision but sensation. I waited for it to clear.

Later, I watched from my bedroom window as Father escorted Miss Llewellyn from the house, sheltering her with an umbrella, handing her up into the carriage and waving her off. I raced downstairs intending to give him the envelope. I put my head round his study door just as he was donning his spectacles.

"Charlotte, my treasure, it gladdens my heart to see you so well recovered from . . . yesterday."

"Who would not recover swiftly with so shining a prospect, Father?"

"As to that . . . My dear . . . I fear I owe you an apology."

"Oh?"

He removed his spectacles and cleaned them. Put them back on. "I promised to bring you a mug of—chocolate, was it? And I forgot."

"Don't worry Father, I hate the stuff."

"Are you . . . quite well, my dear?"

"I am capital, Father. And now that Aunt is safely out of earshot, let us make a plan for the morning."

"'Plan.'"

"To meet with the Dean."

"Ah, in point of fact we shall have to work round the, what's it called now, the follow-up appointment."

"'Follow-up'?"

"Standard medical procedure."

"Ah."

"Aye."

"In the morning."

"First thing."

"Then I suppose the Dean might wait 'til afterwards."

"I suppose he might," he said, taking up a document on his desk. My eye was drawn reflexively such that, without intending to pry, I read upside down, "... *nuptial agreement shall be considered binding whereas both parties* ..."

I withdrew quietly. "Goodnight, Father."

"Goodnight, my own," he said without looking up.

I was halfway up the staircase when I recalled the envelope in my pocket. It would wait until the morrow.

I went to bed. I reached down. Still numb. But of course, it was only yesterday that ... I closed my eyes, reflecting that this interval of peace between Prickle and Pea ought to be savoured.

I could not, however, help but wonder, where was Prickle now?

70

CLARISSA TAPS at the crown of a boiled egg with her knife. Henry spoons marmalade onto his plate.

"Are you to drive out with Miss Llewellyn following Charlotte's appointment this morning?"

"Yes, as it happens."

"Shall I tell Cook to expect a guest for luncheon?"

"I should think we may picnic. If it is fine."

"Henry, marmalade will spoil your—"

"Not a word to Charlotte, she believes we are to visit the Dean of Medical Arts."

"Why would you tell her that?"

"I did not tell her so much as I . . . did not disabuse her of her assumption."

"No good will come of it, Henry, she must be put right on the subject." Clarissa reaches for the marmalade, stops herself.

"She's had enough shocks," he says.

"What shocks?"

"Why, the nature of the Procedure of course."

"She knew very well its nature beforehand."

". . . What makes you say that?"

Clarissa takes a spoonful of boiled egg. "She guessed and Knoxy admitted it."

"My God. Then . . . does she know?"

"She guessed the whereabouts of the offending 'gland,' nothing more, believing it to be a standard feature of the female anatomy, abnormal only insofar as it has not, before now, fallen away of its own accord." Having said all this in one breath, her voice, as it were, runs aground. She takes a sip of tea.

He cradles his forehead.

She sets down her cup. "Henry, you think you can draw a veil and have life proceed in an unruffled way. No doubt all is unruffled on your side of the veil, but on the other side—the seamy side, Henry, all is tiptoes and whispers. Exhausting. As Charlotte will soon come to know." She seizes the marmalade.

It rushes in on him, the abject helplessness—aye, horror—of the female estate. He thanks God that his own beloved daughter has him for a father. And the next instant, he envies his sister. She has neither to toil nor to spin, merely hector him from time to time.

I lay once more on the table, sheeted and with my feet in the stirrups, but clothed this time—except for my drawers—and fully conscious. Dr. Chambers addressed me from beneath the sheet.

"What do you feel at the site, Miss Bell?"

"Nothing."

"Any pain?"

"No."

"And now?"

"No."

"Anything?"

"No."

"Numb?"

"Yes."

"Entirely."

"Yes."

Dr. Chambers straightened and I heard the metallic click of an instrument being placed in an enamelled pan. Knox hovered.

"Am I cured, Doctor?"

"Not only are you cured, Miss Bell, you have made an excellent recovery."

"Thank you, Dr. Chambers." I felt myself once more. I had excelled. I would go on excelling. I would win the Anatomy Prize, the Medical Arts Medal—

"You may, in the days to come, Miss Bell, experience a sewing-needle-type pain at the site. It is merely phantom, and will abate in time."

He rose and crossed to the basin, his back to me, washing his hands. I seized my chance, speaking quickly, "Dr. Chambers, what is likely insofar as the duration of the present state of numbness at the site?"

"Allow me to reassure you, Miss Bell. The numbness is permanent."

Then he withdrew.

FOLLOW-UP

Accelerated healing at site. Attributable to efficacy of electric cautery loop.
(May now oblige with testimonial regarding same in upcoming edition of
Tiemann and Co. Catalogue of Surgical Instruments.)

I wished to walk.

"Father, I wish to walk."

"Really. It looks like rain."

We were in the carriage, jouncing within view of the Scott Monument. I experienced again the curious sense of time having jumped. I knew I had to have risen from the doctor's table, donned my many layers of clothing and crept in this petticoated pace down the stairs and out to the carriage, but I had no memory of any of it.

"Shall I direct Sanders to the Gardens?

"I shall descend here," said I gaily. And I did so, over Knox's protestations, hardly waiting for the carriage to halt. It kept pace beside me as I walked along the pavement. But Reader, it was the moor I craved beneath my feet, the rebound of moss, the hampering heather and slippery stones—

"Charlotte!"

My father's cry behind me. I stopped. I had left the footpath and been running. Amid the dormant beds and naked trees of West Princes Street Gardens, my skirts bunched in my fists. "I'm sorry, Father, I'm just so happy!"

He smiled, his spectacles blank amid the drizzle. I returned to the footpath, and slowed to a walk. I seemed to have the energy of a jumping bean—it was as well I should discharge some of it before we carried on across the bridge to the university—as I had no doubt was our destination, the "follow-up" having gone off without a hitch. I wondered idly whether anyone had ever hurled themselves from the top of the Scott Monument. I saw ladies on the arms of gentlemen, hurrying from the rain; none of those ladies was bound for the School of Medical Arts. I saw nurses trotting toward shelter with their prams, I saw a governess dragging her ringleted charge by the hand—none of them would likely earn a Bachelor of Science then cross the Sahara on a camel, keeping warm at night by means of burning its dung as fuel. As for Fayne, had it not been my prison? And Prickle my jailer? But now I was free. Thanks to Father. I was on the ground at the base of a thick holly oak, its evergreen branches shielding me from the worst of the downpour, and found myself of a sudden—Oh distraught! It was as though I knelt at the grave of a loved one, freshly mounded before me. I bent over my knees and sobbed, I knew not what nor why, it made no sense and but for rain sheeting down would there have been by now a crowd about the strange sight of a young lady weeping into the mud—*dear mud, dear Earth!*—wracked with grief, I cried, I moaned audibly, I did not know myself. Was I mad? Was my mother's blood rising to claim me?

ENOUGH.

ARE YOU A GREAT BABBY? OR ARE YOU BOUND FOR GLORY?

I struggled to my feet.

I did not blame Father. How could he know, why should he? Even Knox could not have known and of course I had never asked. Oh if only it had fallen off of its own accord, I would still be able to . . . Witness Gwendolyn Haas . . . My false friend was at least true so far as that, for she'd had no call to lie about—

DESIST.

I smacked the tears from my face. What was done was done. I looked myself "in the eyes" as it were, and posed a solemn question: *If you had to choose between your future as a scientist and the retention of sensation at the site of the diseased gland, what would be your choice?* I squared my chin. I chose my Future. I walked out from behind the evergreen oak and toward Father who, followed by Knox, had descended to search for me on foot.

I was back in the carriage. Knox had, without a word of reproach, wiped the mud from my face. I said, in my usual tone of good sense, "Father, would you mind very much if we went straight home rather than to the university? I fear I'd make rather a poor impression turning up with my skirts muddied from having slipped on the footpath."

"Not at all, my dear."

And indeed, Sanders had anticipated Father, for the carriage, as I now noted, was already turning left into St. Andrew Street. "I shall be clean as a whistle and sharp as a scythe tomorrow, Father, I promise."

"Charlotte, I have news."

"Oh?"

"Happy news."

"I know, Father, I am cured. Dr. Chambers told me."

"Of course, that is happiest of all." He patted my hand. "The news to which I refer touches upon an addition to our family. I am to acquire a wife. And you, a mother."

To my mind's eye sprang the image of a life-size doll with glass eyes . . . I blinked it away. "By Jupiter, Father, that is capital news, who is the fortunate lady?"

"Why . . . Miss Llewellyn."

"Of course."

"Are you not . . . pleased?"

"I am most pleased, Father."

"Only, for a moment you put me in mind of my sister."

We laughed heartily.

He recovered, adding, "Not but what Clarissa has been Miss Llewellyn's champion in this campaign."

"Campaign?"

"Aye," he sighed. "Fayne of course. And its future."

"Of course."

Enough said. I was to acquire a stepmother, and Father a brood mare—I repented of this latter, even whilst reflecting that Father was right and I was perhaps more like my aunt than I might care to admit.

"When is the happy event to transpire, Father?"

"The nuptials are to take place in three days' time."

"Well."

"Quite."

Upon re-entering the house I was felled with fatigue. I clamped onto the newel post at the bottom of the staircase. It was all I could do to haul myself up that Matterhorn by the railing—"Leave off, Knoxy."

Upon gaining my bedroom: "I'll just have forty winks before luncheon."

I woke next day at noon (!) to the provoking news that Father, having been loath to disrupt "the soothing balm of sleep," had gone out driving with blasted Miss Llewellyn. I wondered there remained an inch of Edinburgh roadway unscathed by the wheels of our carriage in conveyance of that lady.

Another day wasted.

At last it was time to dress for dinner—a crinkling in my pocket reminded me of the dashed letter. Oh how I longed to be free at last of any reminder of my former life! I slapped the infernal skirts into submission—they would be first on the ash heap when once I had earned my medical degree.

I entered the drawing room and took my place at the opposite end of the settee from Aunt. Father resumed his armchair. Tonight was to be a celebratory dinner in honour of Father's engagement to Miss Llewellyn— "Soon to be Lady Bell," said Aunt. It rang oddly in my ear.

I thrust my hand into my pocket, and instantly Aunt's talon-like grip was on my wrist to forestall my unladylike action. Before I could protest, Havers lowered the drinks tray before me. A small crystal goblet contained a blood-thick ruby beverage. "Raspberry liqueur, Miss Bell."

I took it. Sipped. Drained it.

"Steady on," said Father with a smile, "It is a spirit. If a mild one."

"'Tis well you should learn the proper way to sip a fortified beverage," said Aunt, demonstrating with her sherry through pursed lips.

"Why?" I demanded, flatly. Hastening to add politely, "I mean to say, how intriguing, Aunt. And why might that be advisable?"

I saw Father swallow a smile and I took heart.

"Etiquette."

I nodded sagely.

Aunt continued, "Such as stands one in good stead on the Grand Tour."

"Really. I had not anticipated being offered spirits by the Dean, thank you, Aunt, for your guidance." Indeed, I was pleasantly surprised to find her suddenly so well disposed toward my academic prospects as to refer to tomorrow's tour of the university as "grand."

"The Grand Tour of Europe," she spat, as though suddenly at the end of a rope, the existence of which had escaped my notice. "Following the nuptials."

"Clarissa," said Father.

"Ah." I turned to Father. "Forgive me, Father, of course you and Miss Llewellyn shall embark following the happy occasion of your nuptials." Rum word, "nuptials." Like "nipples," and before me arose the laughing face of Gwendolyn Haas.

"My dear girl," said Aunt, "you shall accompany your father and your stepmother to the Continent for a tour of some eighteen months' duration."

I chuckled. I waited for Father to set her to rights, even as I felt a lump forming in my throat—I was to be parted from Father for a year and a half? How would I bear it? And why had he not told me? I bowed my head to conceal my emotion—and instantly forgave him, for if he had withheld the intelligence, it was because his grief matched my own. I awaited his words. They did not come. I looked up.

"Charlotte," he said, a wistful tinge to his voice, "I had thought to share the happy news with you following upon your full recovery." Here he looked meaningly at Aunt.

"Oh Father, I have made an excellent recovery as you know." I came near now to chiding him—"Though I cannot deem 'happy' a separation from you of such long duration." Salt stung my eyes.

"Well you see, my dear, that is the happiest bit, we needn't be parted at all."

"Dear Father, I wouldn't for the world have you cancel your post-nuptial tour."

"Your aunt is correct, you shall accompany us."

"But . . . I am to enrol at the university."

"Charlotte, my treasure, the University of Edinburgh will still be standing in year or two."

"A year—what?"

"And if, at the conclusion of eighteen months you harbour still a wish to—"

Aunt and I ejaculated simultaneously; I: "Father!" She: "Henry!"

He cradled his forehead. I could not have said in that moment which was more shocking: Father's assumption that I should drastically postpone my education, or Aunt's objection which seemed to bolster my own.

I tempered my tone. "Father, it is splendid of you to invite me, really it is, but much as it grieves me to be parted from you—"

"Cease to badger your Father, girl!"

My cheek smarted as though at a slap. "Really, Aunt. I'm afraid you've got hold the wrong end of the stick, if you'll pardon my slang."

Her eyes were steely with anger. "Your stepmother shall take you in her charge as governess and see to the completion, if not rehabilitation, of your education."

A laugh escaped me.

She continued. "Your father has no intention that you should attend the university, now or at the conclusion of eighteen months. You are to put it from your mind."

The laugh yet alive on my face, I looked at Father.

"Tell her, Henry, and put an end to this charade."

"Tell me what? Father?"

"Tell her or we shall have no peace."

But Father's gaze was fixed on the far corner of the ceiling.

I spoke carefully. "Dear Aunt. It is Father's wish that I should join that glorious regiment of educated women. Why do you suppose he engaged a tutor for me?"

I was reaching into my pocket once more when she said, "And why do you suppose he dismissed him too?"

I froze. I looked at Father.

He did not speak.

He did not shift his gaze.

There would be an explanation. He would put all to rights. I handed him the envelope. He took it with an air of mild surprise. Pocketed it absently. Turned to me with his wonted gentle gaze. Addressed me with his wonted reasonable voice, the voice I knew so well. But the words. Reader, the words . . . "Charlotte. Dear heart. The doctor assures me that, what with the successful cure of your Condition, these . . . ambitions of yours, these . . . tendencies will, in time, fade and . . . fall away."

There are states of distraction which mimic calm.

"You never intended I should go to the university," I said, my voice oddly flat in my ears. "You lied."

"Govern yourself," said Aunt without looking at me.

"Why?" I asked.

But Father gave no sign of having heard me. A sense of unreality crept over me. "Father? Look at me, Father, please. Please. Please." I had commenced moaning. Unable to keep in the gouts of sound. No holly oak nor rain to shield my shame. I was wailing—rather, the wailing was something that was erupting from me. Issuing forth like a siren, filling the room. But, as in a dream, it seemed my father could not hear it.

Aunt said, "The doctor warned of this."

Father looked past me.

"Don't dead me, Poppa," I whimpered, a stranger to myself.

Aunt sipped her sherry. "Perhaps a spell at Morecombe Downs."

"No!" Shocked onto my feet, my throat shredded.

Havers appeared in the archway. "Miss Llewellyn, Your Lordship."

Miss Llewellyn, in a shimmering dinner gown of pale gold, entered. Father rose and turned to her with outstretched hand. I stumbled from the room.

Behind me I heard Aunt. "Please excuse my niece, Miss Llewellyn, she has been unwell."

———

I would rather be dead.

"Never say it, pet."

I want to die.

"You dinnae, you're young, you've your whole life ahead of you."

My ragged sobs. The drops. Slow, cloudy cushion . . .

71

I AWOKE IN THE NIGHT. Convinced I had heard a cry. My own? It had seemed to reverberate up from the floor beneath my bed. I was put in mind of the groan I had heard at Fayne. Last autumn. It had been Father, grieving a deceased friend of Aunt's. Had there been tonight another bereavement? Or had Father cried out in remorse for having lied to me? I was smote afresh, as though a wound had opened and was seeping hot within my breast. *Father lied to me.* How could this be? It was unfathomable—as though the man in the drawing room this evening was and was not my father. As though my father had been snatched away and replaced by a simulacrum of himself. And was it my real father who had cried out just now for succour? Held captive by the evil replica? I clapped my head between my hands as though to still the wild fancy that racketed about within my brain like a bird trapped in a house.

I listened. All was silent. I became aware of a familiar—but impossible—sensation. No need to reach down to know Prickle was standing straight up as of old, demanding to be quelled. At once joyful and horrified, I slipped my hand beneath the covers and took hold of . . . Nothing. Still it persisted, an urgent ghost of itself. Oh what would become of me?! I prayed for numbness, even the "sewing-needle-type pain"—anything but this! I curled into a ball on my side.

How I dreaded the morrow. No more had any ancient seafarer dreaded sailing past the edge of the known world. How was it possible I could ever again be in Father's presence with anything but grief. Confusion. *Rage!*— No! Father lied, yes, but he . . . I could find no fit ending for the sentence. I groped inwardly for Logic, ever my staff and guide. Thus: either Father had in mind this outcome from the start—*diabolical!* No! I smote my forehead with clenched fists. Begin again: Either Father had in mind this outcome from the start, for good reasons which for the moment remained dark to me, or . . . Aunt! Yes, Aunt had persuaded Father of this course hard upon our arrival at No. One Bell Gardens, plotted it, executed it— *viper!* Though the latter possibility reflected poorly on Father's firmness of mind, I could not but prefer it to the former, for did it not hold out the faint hope of recourse . . . ?

I must have slept, for I awoke, suddenly—out of bed and on my feet, spurred by a craving which, though every bit as compelling, differed from the phantom one in that it admitted of being slaked. Reader, I craved sweets. And I knew where to find them.

I slipped from my room and along the dark passage to the stairs where a thin gruel of light trickled in at the half-moon window. I descended, following my shadow into the ghastly blue pallor, drawn by the promise of sweeties.

At the bottom of the staircase I saw a crack of light at Father's study door. Had he resumed his nocturnal habits? Was he indeed consumed by grief even now? I took a step toward the door . . . I stopped. It occurred to me to wonder whether—if indeed he had cried out—it had been with rage . . . at my conduct. *Rage.* An alien notion as applied to my father. And yet, what could be more alien than *deceit*? I shrank back without a sound.

Slowly, I turned the knob of Aunt's parlour door. In the gloom, the outline of her armless chair took shape . . . empty. Boldly I entered the forbidden chamber. Navigating the litter of end tables with their trembling bric-a-brac and this-a-that, I alighted on the work basket. I sat cross-legged with it in my lap, lifted the wicker lid and reached in. Wary of lurking needles, I felt about among balls of yarn and spools of thread for a sweetie in a twist of waxed paper . . . I could almost taste it . . .

I was about to withdraw unsatisfied when my fingers encountered, at the very bottom, something smooth . . . a square of paperboard—and I was dazzled by sudden light—like the flash of a camera. For a moment all I saw was a yellow orb. I blinked. There in the doorway was Aunt. My heart commenced to pound. She stood stock-still and spectral in the lamplight, her iron-grey hair in two long braids past her shoulders. She said, "I hope you're satisfied."

Even if I had been able to find my voice, to this strange greeting I had no reply. I looked down at the square of paperboard in my hand. It was a photograph. Of my mother. And my brother, in her arms. With his halo of curling locks. He was smiling merrily at the camera—his fingers laced in the fringe of my mother's silk shawl. There was a date written at the bottom. He was not yet two. And fated to die, not three months hence—within weeks of my birth. This, then, was the photographic study for the painting on the landing at Fayne. Identical in pose. Identical too, in silhouette . . . For while a painter might alter an outline in deference to his subject's modesty, the camera had no such power to lie. My mother's skirt hung straight down from her bodice. Her belly was flat. There was no sign she was big with child. Big with . . . *me*.

My head swam.

"Aunt," I croaked, for my voice was hoarse. "It would appear that Mother was not with child at the time of this photograph."

"She was not."

"Then . . ." Logic. "Am I . . ." I drew a breath. "A foundling?"

"Hah." The ejaculation was as mirthless as it was brief.

"Tell me, Aunt, I beg of you. Do I bear the taint of . . . illegitimacy?"

"You bear a taint. But not of that kind."

"Of what kind?"

I cast about for an answer denied me by her silence. ". . . Who was my mother?"

"The woman in the photograph of course. The late Lady Marie Bell." The last three words were dipped in acid.

"Then . . . I must already have been born at the time it was taken."

"Aye." Her lip curled in a sardonic smile.

My reason threatened to dissolve like salt in a stream of thoughts.

"I don't understand . . ." I closed my eyes in an effort to keep my balance, seated though I still was. My brother and I had been alive at the same time—if only for a matter of weeks. A transitional moment. Charles and I had shared Time. Shared our mother.

"Then . . ." Logic. "I did not kill her?"

Aunt Clarissa regarded me a moment. "You did not."

"Then why tell me I had?" I summoned rage, it shrank to sadness. Then something worse. "Does she yet live?" Horror nipped the heels of sorrow—my mother, alive but put away in a madhouse, ranting and restrained, her beautiful face disfigured by fury . . .

"Don't be ridiculous."

"Then . . . how did she die?"

"She killed herself."

"No!"

"And she would have killed you—"

"No."

"—drowned you in the bog. Stole away in the night with nothing but her child."

A floor gave way beneath me and I dropped into a dungeon. Then, like a giant stepping over the rubble, came the question, "Is that what happened to my brother?"

Her lips contorted.

"Foolish creature," she said. "You never had a brother."

"Then . . . if the child in her arms is not my brother, who is he?"

"'Tis you."

She turned away, taking her light with her. "Now go to bed."

My voice shook. "I don't understand."

She whipped round, setting the flame to writhing. "Idiot. They thought you were a boy."

". . . Why?"

"Because of that which you have between your legs. Had."

"The . . . gland."

"The deformity."

"No, they took it off to make me well."

"They took it off to make you marriageable."

"No—"

A keening sound.

"Silence," she hissed. "You'll wake the household."

My brain had frozen but my body was in motion, rocking.

"Better you both had drowned that night on the bog." She was white with rage. "But for you, my brother would have a wife and Fayne would have an heir. Know yourself, Charlotte Bell, for the blighted female you are. Cease to torment your father with demands against Nature. Leave him his private sorrow; spare him public shame. And be grateful there is a place for you at his hearth."

I looked up at her in wonder. For in that moment, I remembered. "You gave me sweeties."

"Monster."

There are states of distraction which mimic calm.

I rose, walked past my aunt, and exited the parlour. I know not whether I would have left the house or returned to my room if it hadn't been for the triangle of light spilling from the now half-open study door. Like a moth to a flame, I entered.

And froze. He was slumped over his desk.

"Father—"

"Hush, pet," said Knox. "He's had a blow."

In his clenched hand was a sheet of parchment—with a wrench of guilt I thought of the nuptial agreement. Had Miss Llewellyn called it off because of me? But the paper in Father's hand was soiled. And on the desk nearby lay a note in Mr. Margalo's hand.

January 17, 1888

Dear Lord Henry,

I crave your pardon for having delayed in sending you the enclosed, over-mindful as I may have been of your proviso that I refrain from communicating with you. I beg you may excuse my doing so now.

The enclosed document was found by me in the pocket of the cloak which Miss Bell and I unearthed from the moor at Fayne, and is, therefore, your property.

Respectfully,
I. Margalo

I reached out and drew from Father's grasp the crumpled parchment—his hand retained its phantom shape. I smoothed it open and saw, still legible through stains of mud and time: *Certificate Entitling the Bearer to One Trans-Atlantic Passage, Saloon Class, Liverpool to Boston.*

Knox said, "'Twas in her cloak."

I heard him sob.

I looked at Knox. She hovered over him protectively.

"My mother's cloak."

Her old eyes amid their latticework of lines were red-rimmed, her broad cheeks scored with salt.

"Aunt said she meant to kill herself and . . . her child."

Knox made no reply.

"But she was . . . running away."

A shudder wracked my father's frame.

"With me," I whispered.

The old eyes overflowed.

Father spoke not a word, nor did he turn to look on me—as indeed, what right had I to expect he should? Had he not borne sufficient on my account? Blighted creature that I was.

I left the house. I wished to walk.

∾◦

Part Five

The terrible patients are nervous women with long memories.

SILAS WEIR MITCHELL

72

THE GROUNDS AT MORECOMBE DOWNS are gently rolling and discreetly manicured. On a spring day such as this may be seen ladies and
gentlemen strolling its treed walks, some in company with white-clad
attendants. Nearby may be heard the *pock* of a tennis ball. On a green sward
in the distance, a lady follows through with a swing and a golf ball arcs
through the air. Best not to cut across the croquet lawn lest one trip on a
metal wicket. Along the east wing, a colonnaded terrace shelters a rank of
lounge chairs, their occupants tucked round with rugs, some reading, others napping or cloud-gazing, the therapeutic benefits of wool-gathering
being thus acknowledged. The house itself is of serene sandstone in a style
more playful than imperious, featuring as it does a great carved pineapple
at its pinnacle in place of crenellated tower. The starched nursing sisters
threading amid the loungers or here and there wheeling their charges in
comfortable push-chairs only reinforce the impression of a luxurious spa.

Inebriates of a passive temperament are admitted, likewise a small number of quiet delusional patients; otherwise, nervous complaints are chief
among the infirmities treated here—melancholia, mild mania, neurasthe-
nia and the like. In the west wing is a locked ward for certificated lunatics;
and a secure ward for full-blown hysterics. Mae is in the secure ward.

The rooms of the secure ward are among the numerous themed
guest-rooms of house parties past. Mae has been made comfortable in
the Chippendale Room.

Located on the first floor, directly above Dr. Finch's office, it overlooks
the croquet lawn. While indistinguishable in terms of opulence from the
regular guest-rooms, in Mae's room the heavy furniture is unobtrusively
affixed to the floor; there is an absence of potential projectiles, of anything

sharp or apt to be used as a ligature, of any structure capable of supporting the suspended weight of a body; there is no looking glass; there is, on
the window, a delicately worked screen of wrought-iron vines. And there
is of course the locked door.

Mae wakes to sunlight. A sound . . . *claque. Claque, claque.* That is not the
sound a heart makes. It is more like the sound a brain makes. *Claque.*
Except that it is coming from outside. Her eyes rove the room. Hideous
flocked wallpaper in crimson arabesques. Dark furniture. Clunky
Chippendale. Smell of lye. It clashes with the *décor*. Sleep. Wake.

Same light. Same day?

Claque.

Nestled at her shoulder, its eyes closed, head smooth and hairless, a
wax baby doll. Sound of a key turning in a lock. To her left. A woman in
a white cap and bib apron, smiling down at her. Dream? Too bright.

"I see you've rejoined the land of the living, Lady Marie, and how are
we feeling?"

Mae has no answer, she is parched in any case, tongue fused to the
roof of her mouth. The nurse puts a dropper to her lips—Mae clamps
shut her mouth, turns her head even whilst registering it is water, then,
turning back, parts her lips to receive the cool drops. "Where am I?"
Shredded voice.

"You are at Morecombe Downs, Lady Marie, where we shall nurse
you back to health."

"Where's my—what is this?"

"It's your baby."

"It's a doll."

"Just so, Your Ladyship, and much solace it brought you too, shall I
remove it now?"

"Where's my son?"

"Och, Your Ladyship, he's with Our Lord in heaven."

"That's a lie." She sits up.

"Madam—"

"Out of my way!" She is strong, she is up—down with a crash—

"Oh dear—Orderly!"

Barrelling now on hands and knees across the slanting floor toward
the door—caught. Her arms fast against her sides, she is lifted, not

roughly—"No!" It's no good thrashing, she is carried, placed gently but firmly onto the bed, more drops. Bitter this time. Sleep.

MARCH 20, 1875
R. FINCH, CHIEF ALIENIST

NOTES:
Lady Marie Bell labours under delusion her deceased infant son, Charles, is alive.
Further, she believes her husband to be plotting to "turn him into a girl." Evinces acute anxiety lest her husband "cut him" *re* her fear that her "son's" penis is to be amputated.

ASSOCIATED SYMPTOM: HYSTERICAL LACTATION.
Ovariotomy not indicated considering patient's marital obligation as *per* heir male of the body, as well as degree to which restoration of patient's sanity depends on latter.

INDICATIONS FOR TREATMENT:
Chloral hydrate in solution as needed.
Hydrotherapy.
Invalid diet, chiefly koumis, beef lozenges etc. . . .
Airings when sufficiently recovered.

Same light.
  Room.
  Claque.
  Drops.
  Blank.

Same light.
  Room.
  Food. "No."
  Drops. "No."
  Blank.

———

Same light.

Room. Ugly.

Food. Yes, or go blank again.

"What's that you said, Your Ladyship?"

"Wazzis?"

"It is called koumis, Your Ladyship, and very nourishing it is too."

Tastes like cow piss.

"And a wholesome beef lozenge tea."

Blood.

"I'm sorry, Your Ladyship, I can't make out what you're—oh! Oh dear, now that was naughty. Don't worry, there's plenty more."

Let me go.

"The way she mumbles, can't make out a word." Different voice. There are two of them.

"Hush, she understands everything we say."

She wakes to feel a hand stroking her breast. *Henry.* And yes, she wants it. Reaches down. Mmm . . . "Tut-tut, Your Ladyship." Her wrist is grabbed, hand wrenched up and rapped. "Filthy pig," says the second voice.

Mae forces her eyes open a slit. The nice one has her hand on Mae's breast—in her other hand, she holds a cabbage leaf.

"'Twill stop your milk and you can begin to forget," says the nice one. She is nice, but she is crazy. *Claque.*

Drops.

Blank.

Different light. How long have I been here?

"You have been our guest for a fortnight now, Lady Marie."

"Let me out."

"Would you like to go for a nice walk?"

"I want to go home."

"We'll soon have you well and home with your husband."

"I want to see Charlie."

"You'll see him again, in time, Your Ladyship."

"When?"

"Why, when you're called home by Our Lord."

". . . Lord Henry?"

"Oh dear, no, Your Ladyship, by our Saviour in heaven where your wee bairn is safe in the arms of Jesus."

Moaning sound.

Drops.

"Poor thing. All inveigled in her mind."

Claque.

Claque claque.

Darkness. Someone is pummelling her head with their fists. Her fists.

Her wrists are seized, she fights, loses, is forced down, bound.

The nice one, "There, there, My Lady, you mustn't hurt yourself now, all is well."

Cool cloth on her brow.

"I'd've hit her back." The mean one.

"Hush, you."

Moments repeat and leapfrog. Just as she catches hold of one, it detaches like a tail from the body of a tadpole and a new one grows out of sequence.

"Am I here?"

"What kind of a question is that?" The mean one.

"Is it still today?"

"Daft."

"Hush, I'll tell Matron."

She is sitting up in the ugly room. Her wrists are strapped to a metal rail hidden between the mattress and the mahogany bed frame. She has to wee. She shifts. Her bottom stings, as though . . . like salt in a wound. Did she . . . ? Oh it smells as though she has. Smells like that cow piss they force-feed her. She kicks off the satin coverlet, kicks up her night-gown—no, not her nightgown, but a nice one all the same. Is this a dream? She is wearing a "nappie." It is wet.

"Help!"

The lock, the kind nursing sister. Bustling in with an armload of linens. "Let's make you fresh, Your Ladyship."

If she wishes her hands freed, she must not use them to hit herself or anyone else, nor allow them to venture below her waist. "Can you do that, Lady Marie?"

She kicks out. Pulls madly at the restraints, arches her back—*prick* in her arm. Blank.

APRIL 1, 1875
R. FINCH, CHIEF ALIENIST

NOTES:
Wrist restraints pursuant to auto-erotic stimulation, violence toward self and nurse.
Attacks of hysterical rigidity, posation.
Administered, intravenous chloral hydrate.

Different room—no, not room, corridor, whizzing past as though she were on, yes, wheels, she is in a chair with wheels, *whee!*

"'Tis a push-chair, Your Ladyship." Different nurse voice, also kind. How many nurses are there?

HYDROPATHIC ROOM

"That's right, Your Ladyship."

"She can read."

"Of course she can read, she's mad, not an eediot." The mean one.

"Hush, you."

Echoey.

Shock. Water so cold it feels hot. A humming sound . . . the water is trembling, its surface all ripply—is there an earthquake happening?

"Electric bathing, Your Ladyship, relax and enjoy it."

A cacophony of echoes. Women's shrieks. Moans. Ceramic tiles. Steam. Like a Roman bath. She is in Rome. I wonder if I'll bump into Fanny. Poor Fanny, something terrible happened to her baby, what was it now . . . ?

"Upsy-daisy, Your Ladyship!" She is pulled out.

Shapes in the steam. Women—some are old, *ugh!* That will happen to me one day—not if I kill you first. Who said that?

She is sprayed with a hose, held upright so she isn't knocked over by the force. It stops, she hugs her knees, naked.

"In you go."

A warm pool. Heaven. Salty. Pool of tears?

Lying flat on her stomach now, firm hands on her back, kneading her like dough, grinding her into the cushioned table, oh that's good, that's so good, oh, oh, oh Henry . . .

"Don't worry, that happens to some of them."

"Nymphomaniac."

She is sitting up in bed. Dressed. Like a doll. Is someone playing with her?

"How old am I?"

". . . Your Ladyship, do you no recollect your age?"

The nice nurse is seated on the edge of her bed, brushing her hair. Plaiting, coiling . . .

"I was twenty-three when I got here."

"Well you're only five weeks older now."

Mae looks around as though for the first time. It is, in fact, her first time seeing the room with something akin to her usual faculties. Horrible wallpaper. Furniture bolted to the floor—as if anyone would want to steal it, ugly old Chippendale. Metalwork over the windows. And something missing . . . what is it?

"Am I in jail?"

"You're in hospital, Madam."

"Where?"

"You're at Morecombe Downs in the Grampians, Madam, north of—"

"Everything." The mean one.

Mae looks at her. Pudgy often equals kind. But this one is mean. Thinks she's funny. "You're not funny," says Mae.

Pudge retreats behind *The Scotsman*.

Mae knows she sounds drunk. It's the blue bottle. "That's the name of a fly."

"What is, Your Ladyship?"

"Daft," says Pudge under her breath. Turning a page.

"There, now," says the nice one, pinning up Mae's hair.

"Where's the looking glass?" That's what's missing . . .

"All tidy and pretty for your visitors."

They leave.

A male attendant enters. Ropy-looking arms. He stands aside and two gentlemen enter. One old—grey whiskers, rumpled tweed, waist-coat straining over belly. The other is young. Horn-rimmed glasses.

"I am Dr. Finch," he says.

"Did Henry choose this place because of your name?" She has asked the question in earnest, her funny bone being decommissioned by drugs.

Dr. Finch's therapeutic demeanour does not alter. "Lady Marie, your husband chose Morecombe Downs because he knew you would receive here the kind and judicious care that will see you restored to health and your family in due course."

"I'm ready to go home, Mr. Bird."

"I am pleased to hear you say so, Your Ladyship," says the older one, seating himself on the edge of the bed. His face too close.

"Be so good as to send for my husband, Mr. . . . ."

"Hitchcock." He smiles. "Might I inquire," he leans closer. His breath. Hairs in his nose. "To what do you look most forward upon your return home?" His spectacles need cleaning.

"Well, Charlie of course."

"Charlie?"

"My son . . . Charles . . ." A sick feeling, creeping into her tummy . . .

"Your Ladyship. Do you not remember? Your son died. In Switzer-land."

"That's a lie."

"Now why do you think your husband would lie about a thing like that, hm?"

The moan. Rising. Now she is rising too, running—the attendant catches her round the middle with his ropy arms.

She sees the ugly old one writing on a note pad. She doesn't see Dr. Finch come up behind her with the hypodermic needle.

The attendant relaxes his hold which was never more than the mini-mum required to prevent Her Ladyship harming herself.

73

SHE WAKES UP. Sees the iron vines. She is in front of the window in a chair. The chair has her by the ankles, and . . . *Where are my arms?* Mae looks down. She is wearing an ugly gingham cotton blouse, and she has no arms . . . *Panic.*

She does not know how long it is before the nurse enters in company with the matron and the ropy man. The drops. A promise not to kick if she is released. The man gets down on one knee. *But I'm already married.*

She rises. Promises not to hit. Behind her, the man undoes the terrible blouse. Her arms fall, limp, to her sides in sleeves so long they trail on the floor. And which are sewn closed at the cuffs.

In his study at Fayne, Henry is bent over his desk, pen in hand. It is scarcely two sentences, but it takes him the better part of the afternoon. Finally, he blots, folds and slips it into an envelope with his seal, and addresses it to *The Scotsman* in Edinburgh.

The dinner bell has sounded before he summons Knox.

"Have Cruikshank go immediately to the village and post this."

Claque. Claque. She sits up. Hands folded. Wide awake.

Pudge is in the comfortable chair, reading *The Scotsman.*

Mae opens her mouth, forms words. "I would like to use the commode, please." Her voice has cleared up.

"Why, Lady Marie, of course." A new one. A nice one. Standing.

Mae swings her legs over the side of the bed and stands, her fall broken by the new young nurse who has anticipated her collapse.

"What's wrong with me?"

"It's only bed rest, ma'am, come to that there's more right with you now than was wrong when first you came to us."

Mae hobbles, leaning on the young nurse, over to the revolting "close stool." Sits. Evacuates her bowels. *Phaugh.*

These people won't believe her. "I'm not crazy, I have a son. His name is Charles. My husband and that lunatic doctor want to cut off his willy and turn him into a girl."

Pudge snorts.

The nice one says, "Och, Your Ladyship, why would anyone wish to do that?"

"They're pretending he's dead."

Pudge says, "He is dead, for heaven's sake."

"Shutup, you ugly bitch," says Mae.

"Now, now, Your Ladyship. Have you finished your business?"

"If you don't believe me, look at this." Pudge tosses the newspaper at Mae's feet. The nice nurse offers Mae a wad of hygienic paper as though to forestall her using the newspaper to wipe herself. But Mae's eyes have alighted on the page, snagged at the name and . . . she's . . . staggering, thrashing—

"No, Madam!"

Flailing down the corridor, crying, screaming, stinking—

It takes Matron, a nurse and the ropy man to capture her—"It's a lie!!"—and bring her back to the room, kicking, screaming—*prick*.

She is still screaming but no one can hear her.

There is no way now to tell them, "Next time when you come with the injection, wait until I have stopped screaming, otherwise it keeps going in my head." But soon enough even her thought is drowned out by the stuck scream. Well, next time, Mary Corcoran, don't start screaming at all.

They have cleaned the patient and put her into bed. They have cleaned the floor. Matron is seated at the bedside. She retrieves the newspaper from her pocket and in that instant the patient sits bolt upright— the dead are known to do this—eyes wide. Matron calmly passes the bottle of salts under the patient's nose and, when the pupils contract and the eyelids flutter, she follows it with a spray of opium from an atomizer. She waits, and supports the patient's swoon back onto the pillows. Then Matron sits and reads.

> *Death notice.* BELL. The Honourable Charles Henry Gerald
> Victor, age twenty-two months. Of fever, abroad. Son to Henry,
> Lord Bell, Baron DC de Fayne, and Marie Lady Bell.
> *The Scotsman, April 15, 1875*

MATRON'S NOTES:
Apprehended patient, Lady M., running distraught in corridor.

Patient flew at staff. Overturned commode and contents. Threw self against walls, onto floor.

Chloral hydrate administered intravenous.

Fit was pursuant to Nurse J. showing patient distressing newspaper item.

Mae experiences an island of clarity subsequent to the shock of having seen Charles's obituary—perhaps she ought to thank Pudge, but Pudge has been sacked. On that blessed island, Mae sees clearly: her son has been maimed. The false obituary is proof. She must go to him. She has wasted too much time fighting people who have themselves been duped. Her heart has broken, bled white, and now it is dry and tough. There will be time to weep for her baby when she has him once more in her arms. And here she wishes—oh she can taste it . . . the desire to kill her husband. To drive a dagger into his heart—Stop, stop, Mae, don't you see? You must not indulge, either in fantasy or the act. You must get out of here. And you must save your son.

She is quiet for . . . she does not know for how many days. Tractable. Please and thank you, chew and swallow. Commode. Hydrotherapy. The chair at the iron-vined window.

Until, with force of will, Lady Marie raises the "wreck of the *Hesperus*" from the bottom of her silty brain and, with elocution that would do Miss Jolly proud, says, "If you please, Nurse, I should like to take the air."

"How wonderful, let me just check with Matron, Your Ladyship."

Along the corridor in the push-chair to the head of the stairs where two male attendants appear, lift the chair and carry her down the grand staircase to the great, airy and generously carpeted foyer.

"I shall, with your kind assistance, walk."

This is greeted as though she has just announced the cure for colic.

And she does walk. On jelly legs. And lounges on a colonnaded terrace overlooking the croquet lawn—*Claque—so that's what that sound is, it's not in my head, I'm not crazy.*

"Then what are you doing here?"—a male voice.

He is in the lounge chair beside hers. He wears a dandyish chequered waistcoat and flamboyant silk tie. "I don't belong here," he says forlornly. He is pale as straw, his hair a faded ginger. He says, "They told me I was going to a hydropathic establishment, and they brought me here."

She tells him nothing of the horror that brought her here. He asks if that's a "genuine House of Worth you're wearing?" His name is Archie.

"Would you care to dine downstairs this evening, Your Ladyship?"

"Oh, yes please," says Mae. And suffers her hair to be done and her body to be dressed and is it really so different from the ministrations of a lady's maid?

A pleasant airy dining room with lofty windows, and portraits of languorous ladies and bewigged gentlemen.

"Are you going to eat your Victoria sponge?" asks Archie. She slides her slice of cake across the table to him.

Before long, Mae is taking turns about the grounds with Archie. "I'm witty, you're pretty, we're a match made in heaven, dear heart." He calls her "Victoria Sponge" and makes her laugh. But she can only manage a degree of light conversation before the darkness descends and she is helped back to her room.

Archie is permitted carriage exercise. Once a day he embarks for points picturesque. She asks him if he can smuggle her paper and ink.

"Before you can say Twinings Tea by Appointment to Her Majesty, Queen Victoria."

Mae writes a letter to Taffy, telling her of Henry's crime and the doctor's complicity, of her incarceration at Morecombe Downs in the Grampians, and begging her to come.

"Are you driving out today Archie?"

"I am, Victoria Sponge, shall I bring you a bon-bon?"

"Will you be going by a post box?" She hands him the letter addressed to Mrs. C. Blanchard of Chestnut Street, Boston, Mass., USA.

He takes it. "I shall post it from the prettiest village in Scotland. For the prettiest madwoman in Scotland."

Later in the gracious dining room.

"I'm not mad, Archie, I'm sad."

Pudding is served. Trifle.

"Darling, when you get out of here—and you will because you're still young and pretty—be sure to smile a good deal. No, not like that, more like a vacant idiot—that's better. That's right, smile and be gay and give in. Got it?"

"If you know so much, why are you here?"

He looks suddenly wistful. ". . . I was told I was going to a hydropathic establishment."

"So you've said."

"I'm a nancy boy, darling, or didn't you gather?"

"What's that?"

"Oh you lamb. Well, in practice 'tis nothing out of the ordinary, but you see I smiled rather too much, too gaily. I flounced and failed to marry. Or to take up books and butterflies. Or a sword. Not to mention I was caught with the footman's cock up my bum." He smiles. "Let's do something about your hair, shall we?"

"Why, what's wrong with it?"

"The mere fact you can ask, dear girl . . ."

Mae waits. But Taffy does not come.

74

AT NO. ONE BELL GARDENS, the bell-knob of the front door is hung with white crape tied with white ribbon.

Inside the house, the parlour door stands open to facilitate the quiet entry and exit of the few callers who know themselves to be welcome. Clarissa receives them in her armless chair. She wears mourning— admittedly the black crape dress entails no marked departure from her wonted attire. Next to the window stands a simple wreath of white roses with the name strung across it: *Charles*.

Chairs have been drawn up to either side of Clarissa. From one, Mrs. Heatherington murmurs her condolences. From the other, Lady Farquhar presses, ever so gently, Clarissa's hand. Tears flow. The ladies dab their eyes with black-edged handkerchiefs. Mr. Heatherington and Sir Ian stand, hands clasped behind their backs. Chins squared. Such a shame. What can be said? Poor Lord Henry, ". . . quite shattered." Dear Lady Marie, ". . . taken to her bed." Hushed tones.

Dear little Master Charles has been buried abroad. Lord Henry and Lady Marie remain on the Continent, there being no question of Marie's travelling—and here Clarissa 'lets slip'—"in her delicate condition." Discreet nods. In the midst of death, we are in life . . .

Even Colonel MacOmber is subdued. "If there is anything," he says in his low growl. "Anything at all, Clarrie."

"Thank you, Fuzzy."

At last they have gone.

Then, another gentle ring of the front door-bell.

"Miss Gourley, Madam."

Sigh. "Show her in."

Miss Gourley is a tad discomfited to find herself alone with Clarissa. She and Josey had timed their calls together.

"Clarissa. I am so terribly sorry for your loss."

"Thank you, Rosamund."

Silence.

"Are Lord Henry and Lady Marie to remain on the Continent for the foreseeable?"

"They are."

Silence.

Clarissa derives a degree of satisfaction from Rosamund's evident discomfort, however stoically borne. This, after all, is the woman—erstwhile friend of her youth—who came near to scuttling the House of Fayne. But the next instant Clarissa endures a twist of the heart at the thought of whatever bastard "foundling" might even now be running about in the home of strangers—a boy, perhaps. Whole and hale. *Damn Rosamund Gourley.*

Absorbed in her brief, bitter reverie, Clarissa is alerted to the soft ring of the door-bell only by Rosamund's having turned her head in that direction.

"Mr. Baxter, Madam."

No sooner does Miss Gourley register relief than Clarissa says, "Tell the gentleman I am indisposed."

"Very good, Madam."

Miss Gourley is taken aback. Half rises, "I'm sorry, Clarissa, are you poorly? I'll be off then myself, shall I?"

"I am perfectly well, Rosamund, sit."

Miss Gourley falters, "I don't understand . . ."

"Nor need you."

"Has there been a falling out?"

"You would need to ask my brother. If, that is, you continue on intimate terms."

Miss Gourley feels her face burning. Old friends—like, at times, family members—retain the way of cutting one off at the knees. The death of Clarissa's cherished nephew would seem to have stirred up old rancour—the which Miss Gourley had thought long ago laid to rest. She rises and takes her leave, pausing in the doorway. "Clarissa. If you need anything. If I can help in any way. You've only to send word."

But Clarissa's eyes are on the window, through which she is tracking Mr. Baxter's unhurried retreat on foot, along the curve of the drive and out through the gates between the privet hedges. If anyone—including Rosamund Gourley—should observe her tears, they are no more than what might be expected, considering there's been a death in the family.

She feels in the side pocket of her dress and closes her hand round the blue bottle, which she has taken to keeping on her person.

No more than one drop, hourly.

As Rosamund Gourley walks out between the stone gate-posts and onto the pavement, she is visited by a misgiving. It hardly bears putting into words, but . . . something does not sit right. Quite apart from Clarissa's cruelty just now—or indeed perhaps prodded by it—is the thought that . . . On that night those months ago, when Rosamund rescued Lady Marie and her baby from Horse Wynd and brought them back to the Refuge, Lady Marie was adamant that Henry was intent upon killing the child. And now that child is dead.

She sees Josey up ahead, just past the statue of George IV, and quickens her pace.

On the other hand, although Lady Marie laid not a finger on her child even with the fit upon her, Miss Gourley's work has taught her that, in extremis, a mother might kill where she loves if she believes she is doing so to protect her child from worse harm.

"Josey! Hi, Josey, hold up!"

Miss Gourley dismisses both thoughts as unlikely if not beyond the pale. Still, something does not sit right.

Josey has heard her and turned. "What's happened, Josey? Why wouldn't she let you in?"

He shrugs.

"You must have an inkling."

He shakes his head, smiles sadly. "It's all right Rosie."

"Tell me."

He looks down at the pavement. "Henry."

"What about him?"

He looks up. "He knows . . . about me."

"Oh."

"Mm."

She takes his arm. "I'm sorry, Josey. It's his loss." She feels instantly the infelicity of her words in light of Henry's bereavement—but still, something does not sit right.

The two friends walk together arm in arm on this fine spring day as far as North Bridge, where Josey continues to his law offices in Albany Street, and Rosamund turns toward the Old Town.

Clarissa has the curtains drawn in her bedroom. Darkness takes longer to descend at this time of year. She suffers Maid to unpin her hair and to plait it but not to brush it. The creature does not have the way of it.

But for her brother's proviso, Miss Clarissa Bell would happily turn a blind eye and become Mrs. Josiah Baxter. Should the opportunity arise. A gentleman's private affairs are his own. Mr. Baxter's predilections in no way alter his need of a home. Or Clarissa's desire to provide him one. Nor pose any impediment to a marriage of true minds. *He was my friend too.*

No more than four drops at bedtime.

At Fayne, Henry opens a letter addressed to his wife. It has been forwarded to him by the Chief Alienist at Morecombe Downs. A thoroughly sound fellow.

He reads it. And hastily pens a cable.

DEAR MRS BLANCHARD ALL IS WELL DO NOT COME MARIE MISTAKEN LETTER TO FOLLOW HENRY BELL BDCDF

He rings. "See this cable is dispatched immediately."

Cruikshank bobs. "Aye, Your Lordship."

Then he takes a fresh sheet of notepaper, takes a long breath, and writes.

May 29, 1875

Dear Mrs. Blanchard,

I thank you for your kind condolences subsequent to the death of my son.

I entreat you may forgive this intrusion upon the private correspondence between you and your dear friend, my wife, Lady Marie, on whose behalf I write, she being presently indisposed.

I have had occasion to peruse your recent letter to her, wherein you express a degree of alarm as to her well-being, with a promise to come to her side. I surmise that your letter was in response to one from her wherein she expressed distress.

Permit me to assure you that Marie is recovering her health and that you may rest easy knowing your fears for her are, happily, unfounded. A condition of nervous exhaustion brought about by the death of our beloved son, Charles, has necessitated for my wife a course of rest at a private hospital where treatment includes an array of modern therapies including a pharmacopeial medicament, the dosage of which was, in one instance, misjudged such as to induce the mistaken beliefs of which, I presume, she wrote to you. The medicament itself did her no physical harm, and her recuperation proceeds apace such that I anticipate her return home in the near future.

I remain your servant,

Henry, Lord Bell, Baron DC de Fayne

At Morecombe Downs, Dr. Finch and Dr. Hitchcock are visiting the patient in her room. She is dressed, coiffed and seated in a chair.

"How are you feeling, Lady Marie?"

"How kind of you to ask, Dr. Finch, I'm feeling ever so much better."

Dr. Finch consults a clipboard. "You have been taking regular exercise, I see."

"The grounds are most pleasant. I'm almost sorry to leave." Demure smile.

"And you . . . feel your departure to be imminent, Lady Marie?"

She sighs. "I'm afraid so, Dr. Finch. I wonder if you might be so kind as to send for my husband, Henry Lord Bell, to fetch me home."

The two gentlemen exchange a look.

Dr. Hitchcock smiles at her over his spectacles. "May I ask, Lady Marie, what prompts this latest request?"

"Dr. Hitchcock. Thanks to your kind and judicious care—and that of Dr. Finch of course and—oh just all the wonderful nurses . . ." She touches her handkerchief to the corner of her eye. "I wish to reunite with my husband. And together with him, travel to the Continent, and visit the grave of our infant son."

Open sesame.

JUNE 1, 1875
R. FINCH, CHIEF ALIENIST

NOTES:
Patient cured.
Discharged into care of husband.

She is sedated, but able to smile at the man who comes to collect her. "Hello, Henry," she says.

"Mae. My darling."

"Goodbye, Archie."

"I don't belong here."

She takes her husband's arm and walks toward the carriage, balancing her head on her neck like a tea tray—one false thought and the whole thing will fall, *smash*. She is aware of moving toward sanity and horror at the same time.

"And you, my darling, belong at home," says her husband.

Home. Where her child has been—*I told you not to think of that, Mae.*

She is in the carriage next to him, he is saying something. She smiles.

"Wait 'til you see her, my darling."

"See . . . who?"

"Why, Charlotte of course."

Brightly, "Of course."

He squeezes her hand.

The carriage pulls away, drawn by the Black and the Bay, and she watches until the stone pineapple is lost to view amid the trees of the pleasant walks.

75

THE CARRIAGE PULLS UP and she sees him through its window. Cloud of Titian curls. Green-grey eyes, sober and merry by turns. His perfect little cupid-bow mouth. His perfect little nose. Momma's perfect little boy. She clamps down on her heart. Her head is still level thanks to the drops, able to think certain things without losing control. Her son is alive. Soldiers came home, less than a decade ago, terribly wounded, some of them in their male parts. If her son were a soldier and came home wounded like that it would make him no less beloved. No less her son.

Henry hands his wife down from the carriage and together they take a moment to acknowledge the household gathered on the forecourt. Knox has his daughter by the hand. They are flanked by Cruikshank and Cook. Next to Cook is Mr. Mungo, at his side his pregnant wife, scrawny Mrs. Mungo, holding the hand of their young son whose name escapes Henry. He feels his own wife leaning tractably on his arm. He pats her hand. His sister was right. Marie needed time and professional care.

Mae drinks in the sunshine, the sweet smell of clover. A moth flutters by—emerald, like a flying leaf. From the barn, a lowing from the great white cow. She's a mother too, she understands—Mae feels the tug of her own milk all of a sudden, and stifles a gasp of pleasure. No one will keep her milk from her bonny Prince Charlie—Don't think it. Mae has learned how Mae works: don't let Mae think certain things, because certain things make her go crazy and get lost in the monkey-puzzle where no thought or moment stays where she puts it. There will be time to think the thing she is not thinking now, later. She knows what "now" is, and that is a good sign. But the drops are wearing off.

The child watches the progress of their father and . . . who is that with Poppa? Coming nearer . . . Like a big life-size doll. With glass eyes.

"Say hello to your Mam, Miss Charlotte," says Knox.

The name, Charlotte, has settled on the child like a mist, absorbed now and invisible. Charlotte is already older than Charles will ever be. Except that Momma is here.

"Momma!" cries Charles, and would run to her but that Knoxy has him by the hand no matter how he twists and yanks to be free—

Momma says, "Hello Charlotte."

And Charles cries.

"Hush, now, Charlotte, what'll your Mam think?" says Knox, more for the benefit of Lord and Lady than the bairn who clings to her leg, face buried in her apron, screaming. "Here now," Knox scoops her up—best get her indoors.

Mae watches them disappear into the house. The drops help with the not-thinking, but Henry has the bottle in his pocket, they don't trust her with it. A tingling of her scalp heralds the return of cruel clarity, she is going to break something in a minute . . . She whispers to her husband, "Henry, I need to lie down." *I need to kill you and save my son.*

Henry looks worriedly at his wife. But her brow is serene. He says, "She's missed you terribly."

"I've missed her," smiles his wife. A mild invalid smile. Henry's breast fills with a protective passion. From this day forth he will dedicate himself to her peace of mind, for he sees now how desperately she needs him and always has.

Upstairs, he lingers in the doorway as Knox settles Marie onto the bed. He beckons the old nurse discreetly. Taking a blue bottle from his coat pocket he hands it to her with whispered instructions. Then he withdraws.

Knox removes her mistress's pearl-buttoned boots. Lady Marie is thinner. The lovely green eyes are larger. "We'll soon have you fettled up, Madam. You'll be ruling the roost and frighting Cook in no time." Lady Marie receives the drops as meekly as a chick receives nourishment.

The lovely falling-leaf sensation . . . Mae looks up into the kindly face. "Knoxy?"

"Aye?"

"Are you my friend?"

"Of course I am."

"Would you follow me into exile?" Heavy lids . . .

Sleep.

Knox turns Her Ladyship onto her side, slips fingers into the seam along the spine where the hooks-and-eyes hide and undoes the bodice; then she reaches into the breach and loosens the corset. Her Ladyship gives a wee sigh. Knox takes from her apron pocket a sprig of Brigid's wort and slips it beneath Her Ladyship's pillow. It will take off a charm—according to Byrn, any road. Then she goes to the window and kneels, her hands folded on the ledge. "Please, dear Mary, Mother of God, intervene on behalf of Lady Marie and take the sickness off her mind and heal her soul." Two remedies. One is bound to work.

She leaves the room.

Mae sleeps.

Out in the barnyard, Knox hikes her skirts and hollers, "Byrn!" Whenever the child cannot be found, she's sure to be with the auld one; in byre or bothy, dogging his steps through stables, garden—or, God help us, onto the moor—gabbling and singing along with his nonsense words. Impossible to keep her clean. Lord knows what the codger feeds her—goat's milk and mush and berries and seeds and all manner of wild stuff. Knox lives in fear the child will pluck and eat a poison mushroom. Byrn says, "Bairn knows better." And each night, Knox washes the mud from the wee hands and face and gives thanks for the rude good health of bonny Miss Charlotte. Today, however, there was to have been no mud-frolicking, and Knox is in no mood—"Byrn!!"

The old man emerges from the byre, his "duckling" in tow. Knox slips a sugar lump into the child's filthy fist by way of bribery, then scoops her up and barrels into the scullery, making Cruikshank jump. "Don't skook about, Cruikshank, fetch a ewer of hot."

Cruikshank sets the sad iron down on the trivet so as not to scorch the linens. "Aye, M'um."

"Hi Cwooky," says Charlotte.

"Hello Miss Charlotte," says Cruiky, skittering off.

When did I wake up? When did I get dressed? Mae blinks, smiles. She is in the drawing room. This keeps happening. It's the chloral. It helps and it hinders. She is in the drawing room. She is wearing a tea gown. Therefore it must be . . .

"More tea, my darling?"

She has to have been here long enough to have drunk from the bone china cup in her hand—she can see the painted white lily at the bottom through an inch of amber liquid. There is a seed cake. There is shortbread. There is Henry. Smile. Ladies smile and no one knows the difference.

The room is all creamy white and Turner yellow. "I did that," says Mae.

"Did . . . what, my darling?"

"All the pretty things, that was me."

"Anything pretty is your doing."

PrettyMaeprettyMaeprettyMae—she giggles.

Henry regards her intently. This beautiful, fragile creature has only ever needed him to take charge of her. He has. And now: peace. He pulls the yellow bell cord with the buttery silk tassels.

At the end of the room, the door swings open and Knox brings in the child.

"Poppa!" comes the joyful cry. Henry smiles, looks nervously to Mae. But she is still smiling, and has not so much as turned her head at the piping voice. Except that now— "Mae? Don't cry, my dear, all is well."

"It's only, I forgot to blink," she says brightly.

Knox brings wee Charlotte into the room. The child, having greeted her father, has eyes only for the tea tray and grabs a triangle of shortbread.

"Here now, naughty lassie," says Knox, but does not confiscate the biscuit.

Charlotte steals a look at the doll lady. She is sitting down. *Can't get me.*

"Hello, Charlotte. Come to Momma."

"No."

"Charlotte," says Henry. "Give your mother a kiss."

"No fank you, Poppa."

Mae's trilling laugh, "That's all right, he—she doesn't have to." His hair is the same, his eyes, his voice, his—Mae is aware of a terrible sound—

"Take her upstairs, Knox—"

—a no-good, unladylike sound, someone is howling, oh this is a terrible way to behave at a tea party—

"There, there, Madam . . ." The strong arm around her shoulders, the smell of starch and hair and beeswax, Knoxy . . . ?

"No harm done, Madam, lie right down now, that's it . . ."

Mae falls back on the great bed where she gave birth to her son. "Knoxy . . . ?"

"There you go."

The bitter drops.

Evening. Dining room. Lamb on her plate. Is this the same day? Don't ask.

Henry gazes down the length of the table at his lady wife. Glowing in the candlelight. She has joined him. She is eating. She is recovering. She is . . .

"My darling, what is amiss?"

"Nothing in the world, Henry, I'm just so happy is all."

She wipes away the tear. And is rewarded with a smile from her husband.

The tear was for Morecombe Downs. For all its fear and blear, the memory is streaked with sunshine . . . a chequered waistcoat, a sunny walk, "You look positively ravishing today, Victoria Sponge." She had a friend there, Alisdair . . . ? "Archie."

"Who is Archie, my dear?"

Her husband looks worried, *don't act crazy, they'll send you back. Claque.*

Mae has a plan.

Her plan is that she will take money from Henry's billfold and the remaining certificate of passage. She knows it's in his study. But not until they're back in Edinburgh. That is when she'll take money—*wait, are we here or are we in Edinburgh? We're here, of course, just look at the size of this room.*

Drops.

"Can you keep a secret, Knoxy?"

"Aye, my lady. What secret?"

"What was I saying?"

"A secret."

"Don't tell."

"Tell what?"

Pretend-sleep so she can think: Once they're in Edinburgh, she'll take Charles out for a walk in Princes Gardens, which is right next to the train station and—everything will be easier if Knox helps her . . . "Knox . . . ?" Sleep.

Cruikshank's duties have not altered. She walks to the village and back for the post once a day. Sometimes twice. Like the rest of the small household, she has been told Master Charles is to be known henceforth as Miss Charlotte, and that Master Charles is to be thought dead. She has been told to keep mum on pain of dismissal. All of which she has understood, to all of which she has replied, "Aye, Mrs. Knox." She has not, however, been told to deliver Her Ladyship's post to His Lordship.

It is morning. Do not seek to know which morning. How many mornings? Still no heather blooming on the moor. Unless it bloomed and now it's next year . . . Silly girl, it's still last year. You know you won't get anywhere with your head full of chloral.

She is propped up in bed when there is a knock and Cruikshank enters.

Mae receives her post, not on a silver salver but direct from Cruikshank's fingerless-gloved hand. A letter. Boston postmark. Her heart leaps.

But it is not Taffy's hand—Taffy abandoned her. *How can you say that?!* Taffy's letters will have been kept from her is all. Taffy herself has been kept from her. Maybe Taffy has been locked up too . . . ! Mae looks about for the blue bottle and is on the point of ringing for Knox—but she presses her lips together and takes a deep breath. No drops. Not just now. She opens the letter. There are two pages.

The first page is scarcely legible:

20 May 1875

Deer Laydy Mary,
I em sory I stold from you. Inclost by way of restitooshun, plees fynd a noo ticket.

Yors trooly,
Maggie Sheehan

The second, printed on parchment, is a crisp new certificate, *Entitling the Bearer to One Trans-Atlantic Passage . . .*

A knock at the door. Knox enters, balancing a breakfast tray, and Mae slips both pages beneath the bedclothes . . . as if she knew, already, how it would be.

And as though this small act of deceit—or autonomy—has triggered new wakefulness, Mae's heart commences to pound with terror at her near-miss. The thought—chloral-cloaked—that she might have confided her intentions to Mrs. Knox, sought to make of her a companion in exile. Mrs. Knox, who waited with empty arms in the carriage as Mae was lured by the lie that Charles was in there too. Mrs. Knox, who sat by when Henry climbed in and closed the door and Mae's baby was left behind. Mrs. Knox, who colluded when Henry took Mae, not to London for a "second opinion," but to Morecombe Downs for a "rest cure." And who but Mrs. Knox would have undressed Mae's baby, and held him down while the doctor took a scalpel and—?

"Good morning, Madam, did you sleep well?"

In the full knowledge that she is stepping in front of the answer as much as if she were stepping in front of a speeding train, Mae asks, "Did he cry? When the doctor cut him?" Weeping now. *Don't run mad, they'll send you back.*

"Och, dearie . . ."

The broad hand strokes Mae's cheek—*bite it*—but Mae hears, just in time, "They've no done it yet."

She looks up. Joy unfurls through shock, like a crocus in filthy February. "Why not?" she whispers.

"I cannae say why, only . . ."

"What?"

"Well . . . we was on the way to the . . ."

"The surgery," she whispers.

Knox nods. "And Lord Henry heard the call of a bird. And Miss Charlotte—och she was wonderful for copying it, she had the chirruping of it just so and the two of them . . . Well. He—His Lordship said to drive on to Fayne."

Mae is staring past the old nurse. Like a poisoned dart is the tiny word. It takes on form, as though suspended in air before her like a dagger: *yet.*

"When?" she whispers.

"I know not, Your Ladyship, mayhap—"

But the child is here, in the doorway, cries "Knoxy!" Cook has him by the hand. In his other hand is an oatcake.

Mae sits up. Smiles. A real smile. "Charlie?"

He smiles. He has a new pearly white tooth. That makes a full "china closet" as Pappy would say.

"Momma." His tone is both soothing and gently reprimanding; as though she had played a trick on him, but he'll not hold it against her.

"Madam, you mustn't," murmurs Knox.

Cook swiftly withdraws.

Mae's baby boy toddles to his Momma.

Knox watches as the mother scoops the child into her arms. And unbuttons her nightgown . . .

76

MAE FEIGNS SWALLOWING. Holds it in her mouth until the broad back is turned, then lets it seep into her bed linen, her sleeve, her teacup— spitting out half a dose at first . . . weaning herself, as she never weaned her child. A simple matter for a woman practised in girlish stratagems. The hard part is resisting the desire to swallow the liquid nettles, so soft once they have slipped past the palate guards. Oh the craving for bitterness followed by bliss . . .

The Body screams for it, drowning out the Soul that whispers, "my poor beloved, all will be well, let me hold you."

But Mae can be hard. Harder than her husband. Hard enough to smile, to join him at table, to take nourishment despite her silent-screaming veins. Hard enough to smile at her son when in company and call him Charlotte.

On her third drug-free night—she is able to count again—there comes a diffident knock at the bedroom door. It opens.

"Mae, darling. Are you awake?"

"Mmm?"

He is at her bedside. "You're trembling."

"Am I?" *With craving.*

"You are." *With desire.* "Let me warm you."

Yes, there is much she can endure.

She makes it a game. She whispers, "Charles," in his little ear and he melts into her arms, her everything-me-want-arms. "Charlie," whispers Momma and it makes him feel so good, *like me bath and soap all over.* She tickles him and he laughs and she puts him to her breast, and within three days he longs only for that secret world unlocked by the magic word, *Momma.*

Chairs and a table have been carried by Byrn and Cruikshank out onto the grass near the garden wall. Lord and Lady have lunched "*al fresco*" with their child who besports herself under the watchful eye of her nurse.

"I confess a poor likeness to Fanny's *terrazzo* in Rome," says Henry, "but I dare say we'll make do 'til you're well enough to travel."

"How divine."

"You're shivering."

I'm shaking. "Just a mite chilly, Henry, would you mind . . . ?" And he jumps to fetch a rug for his beloved invalid. He has never wanted her more. That too, she has been able to feign. She, who used to crave only that.

But she won't cleck, no fear of that, for Knox has not stood in her way when it comes to nursing her little one. Even the pain of his baby teeth is pleasure to her.

Now, while her husband peers through his field glasses, and "Charlotte" chases a moth, Mae forms a serene smile and examines the dagger: *yet.*

"Henry, dear?"

"Mm?"

"When did you have in mind taking Charlotte back to town for the Procedure?" There. She sounds perfectly normal.

He lowers his field glasses. Clears his throat. "Ah. As to that . . . yes, I'm afraid I put it off, rather."

"Silly boy."

"I shall write to Dr. Chambers forthwith."

"I want to be there, Henry. So she won't be frightened."

He grasps her hand. "That is precisely why I put it off, my love."

It is accomplished now, the first part of her plan. And when they arrive in Edinburgh, she will take Charlie—and her brand-new certificate of passage, no need to hunt for the other one, God bless Irish hussies everywhere—and fulfill her original plan, in broad daylight this time. But . . . in the clear light of mind, doubt creeps in, for Henry is bound to pursue her. All the way to Boston. And what's to stop him bringing her home again? She and her child are, after all, his property . . . *I should never have left Beacon Hill . . . except that I wouldn't have my baby boy*—Charles climbs onto her knee and slips a hand inside her bodice. "Now, now Charlotte," she admonishes him with a tickle.

Her husband couldn't follow through with the mutilation of their child, but he put her in a madhouse and let her think he had done the deed already. He's a coward. And cowards are cruel. He has brought her home only to dangle her son before her like a mouse in the paw of a cat. Unless he is a sadist . . .

He is peering through his field glasses. He straightens suddenly. "Oh my. Well, well, I shouldn't believe it, were I not seeing it with my own eyes." He turns to her excitedly. "Darling, have a look through the glasses, and see if you can't spot a smudge of dull red right at the tip of the tallest larch, there in the copse beyond the garden wall."

She raises the glasses to her eyes and the trees leap forward.

"You'll need to adjust the focus, darling . . . That's right. Do you see it now?"

"I sure do, Henry, oh it's lovely, a lovely . . . dull red."

Coward or sadist . . . ? There is a third possibility. He hasn't done it "yet" because he doesn't believe Charles is a girl any more than she does. A chill runs the length of her spine. But why would he pretend? Is he crazy? Is Clarissa? And Dr. Chambers too?

"Me see," says Charles.

Mae steadies the field glasses in the little hands.

Henry looks on approvingly. "Can you say Scottish crossbill?"

His heart is full. With Marie by his side he can face anything. And so might their child; for in the absence of anaesthetic, might not her mother's presence mitigate any . . . discomfort occasioned by the surgical procedure? For the first time since the dread day of the diagnosis, Henry feels all will be well.

"Mae, darling, if it is fine tomorrow, let us take sketch pad and paint box and venture onto the moor, I'll have Cook make up a basket. What say you?"

"Henry, darling, there's nothing I'd like better."

Here comes truth on amphibian feet, creeping up on her—no, it rams her like a galleon: they're not crazy, but they want people to think she is. That's why they put her away. That's why he brought her home: to drive her crazy once and for all with the sick pretense of "Charlotte." How long before he locks her up again? For good this time. A galleon, yes, and laden with treasure. Her Daddy's money—her money. That is what Lord Bell wanted from the start and now he's got it, he need only rid himself of his wife. She watches him, leaning down, showing Charlie the way to adjust the lens. He loves Charlie.

But he hates her. Has always looked down on her, she knows that now, her sister-in-law at least had the decency to be honest. Mae has fallen among the worst type of thieves: aristocratic ones, and she a little Yankee lamb to the slaughter. He'll lock her up now she's given him an heir, divorce her and marry . . . the one with a face like a horse. The spinster of Cowgate who lied to her and sent for Henry to take her away the night she fled. Mae's heart is hammering, she fears it will disturb Charlie, but he climbs onto her lap and lays his head in the crook of her neck.

Henry beholds his wife tenderly cradling their child, and turns away, in danger of weeping like a woman. They are over the worst. They have a daughter. Very likely, they will soon have a son. Just as he promised her. A gentleman always keeps his promise.

"My love, are you still cold?"

"Not a bit, Henry dear, the air is doing me good."

He's going to put you away and pretend you're dead. *Oh Taffy, don't believe them when you hear it, Taffy don't you grieve!* Every man has his price, Daddy always said so and she thought him a boor but he found out Henry's price—No. Daddy put a price on her, his only child. Funny how she was so proud of that price . . .

"He's off again," says Henry, following a speck in flight with his glasses.

Her heart lurches. They have already announced Charles's death— *Oh God!*—what's to stop them making it true? She feels faint. He'll remarry—and not the old maid—a young blue-blood, one who'll give him an heir with no taint of Irish. Oh Charlie, oh my baby boy . . .

The sun has reached the noon meridian and Henry leans back in his chair, envying no man. A flight of curlews overhead. "Listen, Charlotte . . . Do you hear that?"

She cocks her curly head. The birds call *Cur-lee? Cur-lee? Cur-lee?* They have returned and reunited with their mates. Soon their nests will yield a new generation . . .

How do they plan to kill her child? Will they get Byrn to do it? Drop him in the bog? Gone without a trace. Come to that, what need your husband put you away, Mary Corcoran, when he can take you for a walk "on the moor, my dear," with his field glasses and hamper full of final victuals . . . He will be able to tell himself it was an accident when he watches her tread onto an especially green patch of grass and sink into the earth.

Mae is suddenly calm. And it is not as though she formulates a plan; rather, the plan arises, fully formed. This is what thought can do when liberated from fear. Part of the plan is behaving as if there is no plan. "Charlotte," Mae chirps, "what does the owl say?"

"*Hoo, hoo, hoo!*"

Mae claps.

There is the rest of the day to be got through.

She dresses for dinner. Dines with her husband. Nods, smiles. Eats. Leans on his arm as he escorts her from the room at the conclusion of the meal. Allows herself to be steered toward the great front doors where he taps the barometer. "Tomorrow bids fair, my love."

"I can't wait."

Her husband beams at her. In return, she . . . oh, it hurts her heart—easier by far to open her legs to him in the dark than to smile at him now.

He has seen the hesitation. "I shan't rush you, my darling, if you'd rather—"

"Don't be silly, darling, I'm longing to go."

He smiles once more. "Why then, let us bring Charlotte with us. And Byrn too, in case of a mist."

So it is to be tomorrow. Therefore it must be tonight.

77

SHE HAS GIVEN Henry to understand that the monthly indisposition is upon her. And Knox has agreed to let her child sleep with her tonight. As why not? She has been so well of late.

High in her window, the gibbous Moon. Up she rises. All but humming along to the song in her head, *"Rise you up in the morning, altogether ear-ly . . ."* It will be dark for another couple of hours.

Pen and ink and notepaper from her escritoire. She writes. She waves the page to dry the ink, then places it on her pillow.

She dons a travelling costume, folds the certificate of passage and slips it into the pocket of her heavy cloak. No money, no matter. She bends over her sleeping son—warm and burgeoning, he is flowers, he is birds of the air, fish of the sea, crown of creation—lifts him tenderly, enfolds him within her cloak and fastens the ivory buttons. Of course he does not awaken, he is in his Momma's arms. *"You need not be at all afraid, indeed I love you dearly . . ."*

Out and along the passage. Descending the marble stairs to the landing where she had intended the portrait be hung, and down into the shadowy valley of the great hall, stone underfoot like mortuary slabs, she reaches the doors—push. Ah, the night!

The hump-backed Moon hangs gauzed in mist, a few spilt stars like specks from a paintbrush. She breathes in deeply of darkness. Sets out across the cindered forecourt.

Her little boy is heavier than he was last time they fled—and she is physically weaker. But all she has to do is follow the cart track—it glims with the stored light of day, guiding her safely across the moor and up toward the white stone beacon at the crest of the fell.

In less than an hour, she'll be in the laneway next to the Inn at the Kenspeckle Hen. She will hear the clatter of hooves and wheels before she sees the light of the carriage lamp that heralds the arrival of the postchaise to Berwick-on-Tweed. She hasn't a penny, but she has her facility for mimicry, her finishing-school French, and the sparklers on her fingers—*"Ah, monsieur le cocher, desolée, mais je n'ai pas les pound sterling, non plus un sous,* but I have ziss." Fanny would approve. "A woman's jewels are her rainy-day fund." Apparently Fanny had a perfectly normal baby—"And so did I," she says aloud. He stirs. She sings softly, *"Charlie's neat and Charlie's sweet, Charlie is a dandy, Charlie is a nice young man, he feeds his girls on candy . . .*" She walks steadily on. The stone seems to grow no closer, but she is used to the moor and knows its tricks.

By the time the alarm is sounded at Fayne House, she and her child will be at the station. *All aboard for Liverpool!* By the time the search party's hopes dim with the sun, she'll have turned her diamond ring into pound notes. She hardly cares what she wears—*Mae, is that you?!*—but Charlie must have a new sailor dress. Then it's *Weigh anchor!* He reaches up and strokes her cheek before falling back asleep.

Behind them the house has shrunk to a hulk of darker darkness. Soon it will disappear from her sight forever. They will be at sea, crossing to a world braver than this one, and newer than ever.

Knox is awakened by . . . silence. As why should the night be otherwise? The bairn is with her mam. No reason why a body oughtn't stay nestled in her warm bed and fall back to sleep . . . But being Knox, she rises, lights a candle, hauls on her wrapper and, sighing, nudges her feet into her felt-bottomed clogs.

At the head of the service stairs she chides herself, "Hold tight the railing now, that's all Their Lord and Ladyship need is a foolish old woman broke-backed at the bottom of the stairs because of a babby who didnae cry in the nicht."

An owl hoots in the distance. Charlie wakes.

She starts to run, as much to make Charlie laugh as to quicken her pace, for she has energy to burn. Chanting with the rhythm of a train, "Hasten-to-the-station, hasten-to-the-station!" Giggling with her babykins. "Wait'll Taffy hears about this crazy night, huh, Charlie? Can you say 'Taffy'?"

"Taffy."

"Good boy!"

Knox slips into Her Ladyship's bedroom. The moon is clouded but she can see by the light of her candle the bed curtain is closed, just as she left it. *Now, old woman, leave before you wake the bairn and he—she—sets to bawling.*

But Knox puts down her candle, approaches and opens the bed curtain a crack. The baby does not stir. Nothing does. Not a breath. Heart leaping, Knox puts out a hand, fearful of finding a cold brow, and touches . . . paper.

Darker now, clouds obscuring the moon, but she can still see the white glow of the stone and it is definitely closer. In less than three weeks she will step from a hansom cab and, with her child on her hip, sashay up the flagstone walk, past the glorious chestnut tree, up the broad wooden steps to the veranda with its porch swing, and rap on Taffy's front door . . .

In the adjoining bedroom, Knox looks down at her master's sleeping face. This is the last time he will sleep unburdened by horror—"Lord Henry."

His eyes spring open. She hands him the note, and holds steady her candle so he might read it.

First come the cries from the house, far behind her, not far enough. Her name. Her husband's voice. "Mae!"

Charlie starts to cry. "Hush, my darling, hushabye." She breaks into a sprint, stumbles. "Mae, where are you?!" Closer now. She leaves the track. And now the barking of the dog. She runs. But it is difficult to run across moorland.

The child clings to her with the strength of a monkey, as if determined, having once lost her, never to let her go. Sobbing for breath, she sings, *"Charlie's neat and Charlie's sweet, Charlie is a soldier—"*

Knox stumps blindly along, nightgown bunched in her fists, having lost her clogs to the mud.

"Marie! Mae!" cries Henry, his voice swinging as wildly as his lantern, blundering through gorse—and now Nuala is circling his ankles, "Get gone!" *I am not the one needs saving!* "Byrn!"

Mae falls, the moss embraces her—it is difficult to rise, her child wrapped in her arms, the two of them wrapped in her cloak, wet now, "Hush!" stifling his cries in the folds, the moss bidding her, *Bide a wee. Up, get up, Marie!* She's up. Yes, the child is still breathing, hold him less tightly lest you . . . "There, there, my darling."

"Mae!"

Turning without stopping, she sees, a way's off but drawing closer, a light swaying. She falls a second time—mud! Still, no harm—set down your child. Now stand up, stumble back, get your footing, good. "Hush now, Charlie, stop crying." He cries harder.

"Lady Marie!"—croak of the child's nurse, not far off. The child turns its head.

Mae attempts a step toward her child, her boots squelch, mud grips her ankles. Stop. Better he should come to her, easier for him on this quaking turf. "Charles," she says, and stretches out her arms.

He toddles toward her.

The ground shifts suddenly beneath her feet, she regains her balance, but . . . "Charlie, no."

He keeps coming.

One of her legs plunges suddenly to the knee. "Go away, Charlie!"

The mud swallows her other leg. It's got hold of the hem of her cloak, dragging it down . . . Her child keeps coming.

"Stop!" He does not. "Charlotte," she says.

And he stops.

She feels the earth relax to receive her.

The child watches their mother growing shorter. Sinking . . . into the centre of her cloak . . . as if a hand were being withdrawn from a puppet . . . Sinking lower. Lower. Until her head is a nub, level with the ground. Before it disappears. Then the cloak turns in on itself and follows her into the earth with a sucking sound. The child moves to follow the mother. But the door that admitted her has closed.

"Lambie!" cries Knox. "Come to me, now, come to Knoxy!"

The child turns. Sees the nurse through the gloom, and toddles toward her. Knox hurries toward the child but sinks to mid-shin. "Stay, child," she says calmly. She sinks to her knees, her nightgown and wrapper conspiring with mud. "Come not near."

But the child will not be barred twice and, being light, does not sink. The child flings themself at the big woman, clings and only then lets loose a scream. The nurse sinks to the waist, struggling to free the child from her arms. Suddenly she is hooked by the armpits and hauled painfully up and out with her precious charge. She is dropped to safety on a hummock and from there, with the child safely in her arms, Knox watches the old man dive like a spear into the earth.

Henry staggers along, the world black beyond his lantern. "Knox!" The collie girdles his ankles, hobbling him, nimbly avoiding his kicks.

"The child is well!" cries Knox to spare Lord Henry a moment's more anguish.

"Give her to me, oh thank God!" He trades the lantern for his child and clasps her to his heart. "Where is Mae?"

Knox closes her eyes. Henry's face contorts, a ragged cry escapes him but he holds his child close. Knox lights the way, and together, they trudge toward the house.

Nuala remains behind, circling the spot where Byrn disappeared.

Cruikshank stands in the open doorway of the house with a candle, its flame trembling not with a draft but with her grip for there is trouble afoot out there on the moor, shouts and barks . . . She sees a lantern approaching . . . Mrs. Knox . . . And the master. He has Miss Charlotte. They are all over mud.

"Don't gawk, fetch His Lordship a dram and light the copper."

Cruikshank's flame gutters and goes out.

"Now!"

Cruikshank turns and hurries across the pitch-black hall, through the service door and along the passage to the kitchen, where Cook clings to sleep like a pirate to his booty.

In the great hall, Henry hands Charlotte to Knox, takes the lantern and makes to plunge back out into the night. "Nay!" commands Knox. He stops and turns to his old nurse. She continues, quietly, in deference to the child, who has gone to sleep—or somewhere like it—"There's nowt you can do, Lord Henry. For either of them."

Henry watches Knox mount the stairs with his child.

She carries the child up to the nursery and lays her in her crib. She leans close and listens for the warm breath. Whispers, "Thank God. Thank Jesus, Mary and Joseph and all the saints. Thank you, Brigid." There will be time enough tomorrow to bathe the bairn. A tear rolls down Knox's muddy face. Is it for Mae? Or old Byrn? Or for the poor child who'll wake to find her mother gone again—and the old man too, with his songs and wandery walks and bits of wild stuff.

She sinks to the floor and weeps for them all.

Henry appears not to register the shattering of crystal behind him, where Cruikshank has dropped the dram of whisky. He is himself frozen at the sight: The old man, black from head to toe with moor mud, carrying Lady Marie, likewise enrobed, into the great hall and laying her on the floor. What faery tryck is behind this reprise of horror? His wife, borne by Byrn, rescued from the bog and laid mud-sodden on the floor of the great hall. But this time his wife is dead. He watches, speechless, as the old man turns her onto her side and thrusts his filthy fingers down her throat.

"Stay with us!" cries Knox, quaking down the stairs.

A retching sound as the late Lady Marie vomits the moor. Henry falls back, transfixed as the old man bends over her limp form and, like a demon lover, seals her mouth with his own. Her bosom heaves with a great convulsive breath—she's alive! Henry is jolted as though by an electrical charge, as what was moments before Sorrow transforms to Tragedy.

Byrn rises. Now that he's got the bog out of her stomach and the life back into her lungs, he leaves to get himself clean. He has resuscitated larger animals, and smaller, before now. Keltie, the best collie that e'er cornered at a whistle, for one. It is easier to breathe back humans, as the snout fits snugly.

Henry approaches. Knox is on the floor, cradling the encrusted head and shoulders. "There, there, M'Lady."

He looks down. The green eyes look up at him. She says, "Where's Charles?"

Henry says, "She's dead."

It is merciful to follow a death-blow with a hastener. It is what the Duke of Cumberland denied the Highlanders who'd been stupid enough to rally behind a bonny prince. Thus, he adds, "You drowned her."

Knox tightens her hold on her mistress, bracing for the cry that must come—but it seems the sound is snatched from Her Ladyship's throat and she faints. Might this blow do what the bog could not, for how can she go on living?

"Nay," says Mrs. Knox to the insensible girl, shaking her, "'Tis niver so, he lives, she lives, M'Lady."

Lord Henry says, "Another word on pain of exile, Knox."

"I care nowt for your exile."

"Then for God's sake, have a care for . . ." His voice catches. It is too much . . . He fights to get command of himself—every word, a shudder suppressed. "She must not know the child lives lest . . . she try again to kill it." That is all. That is enough.

Out in back of his bothy, Byrn has drawn the hump-backed Moon from behind the curtain of cloud, snagging her with a song; a peep from Her is all he needs. There. He thanks Her, lets Her go and She springs back behind Her veil. She'll not be pleased and there'll be peas to pay and perhaps a kid, but he is clean now in the way that counts most. Now he crosses the barnyard, past the henhouse, out back of the kitchen to the well. He bends to lower a bucket—and looks up as the cry soars overhead. The one Marie did not utter. He follows its trajectory across the night sky. The cry will change into something else—a gust on a leaf, a caterpillar dislodged, and thereby hangs a world. The Old Man hauls up the bucket and commences to strip off his garments . . .

Lady Marie must be carried upstairs, "Where's Byrn?" Knox sends Cruikshank to find the Auld One. Henry does not wait for Byrn. He lifts his wife and carries her up the broad staircase, pausing on the landing to adjust his grip.

Cruikshank, her candle raised before her, passes Cook ladling water from the steaming copper, opens the door from the kitchen onto the yard and emerges to see Byrn in the act of tipping a bucket of water over his naked form.

But she does not call to him.

She cannot.

When Cruikshank finally returns, Mrs. Knox exhorts her, "Mind you say nowt of what you've seen nor heard tonight to anyone lest you be whipped and turned out without a character. What is it, gel? Cat got your tongue?" By signs and squeaks Cruikshank reports that she could not find the Old Man to give him the message. Then she flees, back through the service door, along the passage, into the kitchen and across to the door to the service stairs and up—Cruikshank, wait. Here in the safety of the service stairs. Tell us. What did you see out back by the well just now?

But even if she were to turn to us and try, Cruikshank would be unable to answer. For she has lost the power of speech.

Marie's cloak is missing. It is all she took with her, except for the child. She chose a heavy garment, the better to drink up the bog. In his bedroom, Henry leans over his washstand, smashing water into his face— he straightens. He strides, dripping, from his bedroom, out along the passage and down the stairs in darkness. It has just occurred to him. If it is not where he put it . . . If she took it with her . . . Then the note she left was a lie and she never intended to—He enters his study, rolls up the top of his desk and feels for the pigeon hole, desperate to find it empty. But the scrolled certificate of passage is still there. He crumples it, and drops it into the wastebasket. He rings for Knox.

Byrn, clothed once more in leggings and smock, is in his bothy, gumming his mash. Mrs. Knox folds her arms across her bosom. "Now," she says.

He rises.

Mutters something.

Knox replies, "Of course she's no dead, you dotard, you brought her back yourself."

He rises. He goes to the stable and hitches Achilles to the cart.

Mae is moving now. She can feel them carrying her. She is laid down on something hard. She killed her child. And she is alive.

78

HARD SURFACE RATTLING under her body . . . Comes to a stop. She is lifted. Carried. Laid down on something softer. She is in a coach. Rolling. Bouncing. On. On. On . . .

Daylight—the blow of a broadsword.

She is lifted.

Beneath her now, a mattress.

She opens her mouth. Something comes out. A broken-winged word.

"What did she say?" Her husband's voice.

"She said, 'Why'?" Her sister-in-law's voice.

"Why did you bring me back?" Her own voice. A full sentence.

Sister-in-law, sharply, "You've been brought back to Edinburgh for your good."

"Clarissa," Husband. "I think she means, why did I . . . bring her back from . . ."

Sister-in-law, "From death. Aye. Why indeed, Henry?"

Bitter drops.

Door closing. Key turning.

Clarissa has read the note that Mae left on her pillow. She folds it now and hands it back to her brother. He sits across from her by the fire, blanched. Bleary-eyed.

"You did the right thing, Henry." He has shown mettle. More is required. She takes up her work. Fingers busy, thoughts reporting for duty. There is something to be said for knowing where things stand at last. "While she believes her child to be dead, the child is safe. It wants only to make that child whole. The which you ought to have done before now."

He nods.

She sews. *Puncture, tug.* "And you must remarry."

"What?"

Her brother looks half-crazed. The Irish-American catastrophe upstairs will make us all run mad. She rings for Havers.

He enters with the drinks tray.

"Leave the decanter."

"Very good, Madam."

Henry drinks. Refills his glass. Rubs his face. "I suppose there is not a court in the land would deny me a divorce."

"Out of the question," says Clarissa.

"Forgive me, sister, but 'tis not for you to say."

"I overstepped. Forgive me."

He draws a haggard breath. "She may . . . recover . . ." His words die in the air.

Clarissa takes her time—pulls free a snag—proceeding by rhetorical increments. As Socrates said, *Understanding a question is half an answer*. As a girl, she used to sit, sewing, through the long hours of her younger brother's tutelage—just one example of a sisterly devotion which earned her the approbation of her father and extra hugs from Knox. Day after day in the library-cum-schoolroom at Fayne, when Henny-Penny could hardly hold his eyes open except to follow the flight of a goshawk out the window, Clarissa stitched. And listened. And every evening picked free her work, resuming next morning with a blank linen slate, imbibing, amid Euclidean geometry and the Gallic Wars, Cicero's principles of rhetoric . . . *You must conceal your intention of defending the point you wish to defend*. Courtesy of Henry's tutor who reeked of cabbage.

Now she asks, "And if she does recover?"

"Why then . . . She is young. We'll have more children."

She rests her work in her lap and indicates her glass. He refills it. "We speak here, Henry, not of a woman with a bodily ailment, but one who, when she most appears to be in the bloom of health, is most . . ." *Sigh*. "Henry, your wife is mad. You get more children of her at their peril."

"You intend I should put her away."

"Is that then your view?"

"Divorce is my view."

"Divorce means destitution."

"I care not, Marie can take back her fortune and return to Boston."

"With the child."

"Of course not."

"What is to prevent her?"

"There is not a court in the land—"

"You are right, of course. You would keep your child. If not your fortune."

"Damn my fortune."

"Your daughter will, I am sure, be a comfort to you in your old age. But who, I wonder, will comfort her when you are gone?"

". . . Why, her husband, of course."

"No dowry. A divorced father. A mad mother. What husband?"

Henry colours, aware of treading on his sister's . . . well, on something within her that remains crushable. He refills his glass. "You're right, of course. Insofar as divorce."

"I merely state fact."

"Well then. What do you propose?"

"I? I propose nothing. I but pose questions, following on logically from your—Ah, forgive me, I now take your meaning, brother. Much though it takes me aback."

"What 'meaning'?"

"Why that, in ruling out both divorce and incarceration, you free your wife to slip away and fulfill her suicidal intention. Leaving intact her fortune and Fayne. As well as your daughter's prospects."

He has gone white. "That is not my meaning."

"I am relieved to hear it, brother." Scalloping the edges now . . .

His head is in his hands. "I don't know what to do."

"Really? I should think you've made quite plain what it is you plan to do, as there remains but one avenue open to you."

He looks up. "And what is that?"

"You must remarry."

She notes his bewilderment. A masculine luxury.

"Then you do see the wisdom of divorce," he says, with growing exasperation.

"I do not."

"I begin to despair of you, sister." He drinks. Pours. "I cannot remarry while my wife lives."

"Then she must die . . ." Her pause is vanishingly brief, but as Zeno would have it, infinite, therefore sufficient to admit the spectre of murder. But we are in a parlour of the New Town in 1875, not a reeking wynd of long ago when Burke and Hare trundled their gruesome wares in a barrow through the Auld Toun to the Anatomy Hall—"There's many a woman dies in childbed. You are about to announce your daughter's birth. Announce her mother's death." *Snip.*

"You mean . . . put it about that Marie is dead, and take another wife?"

She commences the over-stitching, achieving a satin effect.

"You counsel me to commit bigamy? Are you mad?"

"It is no more than your duty."

"My duty is to live an honourable life."

"Henry, there is your honour, and there is Fayne. Closely allied though they be, they are not one and the same. Do as you will with your daughter, as is your right—even if she, being born and bred a Bell, might hope for better of her father than the millstone of a mad mother. But what of the unborn Bells? Is it right to deprive them of land, of treasure, of life? You are one man. Fayne is many. Do you think your title was won by men who feared to stain their hands with blood? Or who shrank from deceit in the cause of defeating an enemy? Did they fight and die and kill and lie, that you might sit in your sister's parlour and consign their sacrifices to the ash heap? For the sake of your 'honour'?"

He stares into the fire. Each leaping flame like a signal of distress.

He draws himself up. "Speak no more of this preposterous notion. Nor presume to teach me my duty." He drains his glass. "I shall have my wife removed indefinitely to the locked ward of Morecombe Downs. For her good and the good of my child." He rises, signalling an end to the discussion.

But Clarissa has not done stitching. "Aye. Once you have yourself written the Lunacy Order—for we speak here of no mere rest cure. And arranged for consultations by two physicians heretofore unconnected with the patient as required by law. And had them sign the Certificate of Lunacy. And submitted it to the asylum as well as to the Commissioners in Lunacy, such that Marie Lady Bell of the DC de Fayne may be certificated insane and committed indefinitely to custodial care on grounds she attempted the life of herself and her child. No doubt discretion is possible even with so many interlocutors." She ties off the thread on the underside. "Unless discretion is rendered moot by Messers Hitchcock and Finch, who may decline to admit an attempted murderess into their locked ward—that is, if those gentlemen are even given the choice by the aforementioned authorities who alone will determine whether your wife be referred to Morecombe Downs . . . or reported to the Edinburgh Constabulary. Thence charged, publicly tried and jailed—or committed to an asylum for the criminally insane. I do not pretend to first-hand knowledge of such an establishment but I surmise that croquet, cricket and a pleasant view do not form part of the prospectus."

Henry's mouth is slightly agape. She does not reproach him. He says, "What shall we do?"

"I shall make inquiries."

He lists a little on his feet.

"Go to bed, Henry."

He obeys.

Clarissa drops the note onto the fire and watches as it darkens at the edges and curls in the embrace of flame, its girlish loops and flourishes fading . . .

Dear Henry,

Today I am happy once more. And while I am happy, I must do what is right, before melancholy gets the better of me again. I have taken Charles and walked onto the bog. We shall soon be in a better place. We are free. And now you are too.

Your first wife,
Marie

Then, by the light of the dying fire, Clarissa unpicks her stitches.

79

THE CARRIAGE, drawn by the Black and the Bay, rolls slowly up Leith Walk with Sanders at the reins. Within, Clarissa ventures a look out the window, impatient of their start-stop progress, to see the rear end of a horse-drawn tram. A placard affixed there seeks to persuade one and all of the merits of Bovril. She withdraws once more and leans back in an attitude of patience, shifting slightly in a bid to find the least uncomfortable position. The carriage creeps along between rows of factories and workers' tenements, but at the stench of rubber she draws the blind. When the pace picks up, she opens it again in time to see, between the

Gas Works coming up on the left and the grimy Glass Works to the right, the Firth of Forth—a V-shaped slab of the North Sea, grey as granite today.

At the reins, Sanders turns right into Salamander Street, paralleling to his left the noisy docks with their forest of masts. Onward the carriage rolls, past a stretch of open water, past the Chemical Works and a strip of waste ground, before drawing up in front of a three-storeyed house of quarried stone. It stands on a patch of defeated grass, girded about by a low wrought-iron fence nibbled by rust. It looks to have been stranded in the wake of the Industrial Revolution, originally home to perhaps a judge or a magistrate. Bars on the upper windows—sole clue to its current function.

Sanders descends and opens the carriage door. Clarissa steps down.

Clarissa never had recourse to *The Daily Review* with its thickets of advertisements, until today, when she sent Pugsley to purchase a copy. She turned its pages, seeking the sort of establishment not featured in an illustrated brochure . . .

A licensed private establishment in Leith. Kind care of chronic sufferers in the proprietor's home. Quiet cases only . . .

Now she walks up to the front door of the soot-grimed house, formerly genteel, now respectable. Respectability is what the middle classes possess in place of honour. And while she despises to hear them bleat of it, Clarissa relies upon it to stop them cutting the throats of the aristocracy in the night. She takes hold the brass knocker—a Scottish terrier head—and raps. A twitch at the shutters in a ground-floor bay window to her right is followed by the opening of the door a cautious six inches. And then a full body-width, to reveal a thickset man of more than middle age and in need of a barber—especially about the brows—in the act of swallowing. He pats his mouth with a knuckle and inclines his head—bald on top. "Beg pardon, Madam, how might I be of assistance?"

"Reverend MacGilvary?"

"As was, Madam, retired now."

"I believe you take in private residents?"

His shaggy brows rise over watery blue eyes—he smells the prize, she thinks. *Is that fair, Clarissa?* The man must make a living, he and his wife—for that will be she from within, "Who is it, Ewan?"

"Madam, I thank you and would bid you enter, but I'm bound first to inform you we accept quiet cases only."

"It is a quiet house I seek."

"Step in, Madam, if you please."

Clarissa steps into the fug of Tuesday's stew.

She is seated now in a dark pokey room, what do they call it? Not a morning room, surely. It is certainly no parlour. She has declined a cup of tea. Not a blessed breath in this house. "How many lunatics do you house here?"

"We refer to our residents as 'guests,' Lady Esther, for so they are, poor souls." The man's demeanour is a commingling of the mildly quizzical and the deeply sympathetic.

"What are your terms?"

"As to that, Lady Esther, I fear you may find us steeper than many, but we take care to provide the best-quality victualling—"

"We subscribe to the Doctrine of Fatness," puts in Mrs. MacGilvary, a sturdy woman who had performed something approaching a curtsey when "Lady Esther" introduced herself.

"Just so," says Mr. MacGilvary, "as *per* the distinguished Superintendent of the Royal Edinburgh Asylum in Morningside, an institution watched by the world for its innovations in the treatment of mental patients. And as for physicking, all our tonics, tinctures and injectables being bona fide medicaments, steering clear as we do of patent medicines and any and all nostrums."

"I am a trained practical nurse," states Mrs. MacGilvary.

Mr. MacGilvary continues, a note of apology in his voice, "I ought to have mentioned right off, Lady Esther, we discourage dipsomania cases as well as morphine and the like, for we are not equipped—"

"We are not equipped," states Mrs. MacGilvary.

"There be many as claim to be equipped, but—"

"They're not, nor do we claim to be."

Clarissa says, "The lady in question is neither drunkard nor drug fiend."

Mr. MacGilvary appears pleased, nodding, looking to his wife, who nods provisionally and asks "What is the nature of the lady's nervous complaint?"

"She is afflicted with . . . an array of . . . false beliefs."

"Delusions," pronounces Mrs. MacGilvary.

"Quite."

A tour of the house. Up the carpeted staircase to the first floor where doors off the landing are all shut. And quiet reigns. Up another flight to the second floor where linoleum has been laid in place of carpet. It smells less of food up here than of wax and lye. Mr. MacGilvary, puffing a little from exertion, hangs back as Mrs. MacGilvary takes a ring of keys from her belt and opens a door opposite the top of the stairs.

Clarissa is unprepared for the airiness of the room, and the light which reflects off the lemon-coloured wallpaper. A single room. Bright but spare. An adequately sized window. A chair.

And a bed of course. The window overlooks a walled garden. Along an embankment beyond the garden run the tracks of the Leith Branch Line. And beyond the tracks lie the heavy waters of the Firth of Forth.

Behind her, Mr. MacGilvary explains sympathetically, his very words seemingly softened by his moustaches, "We get a goods train twice daily, but Mrs. MacGilvary and I, and I dare say our guests, never hear it anymore, so accustomed are we."

"The bars are not to be argued even in the quietest cases," says Mrs. MacGilvary, evidently no stranger to dissent on this point.

Clarissa, having scarcely noticed the bars, turns from the window and observes that the legs of the bed are bolted to the floor, likewise the nightstand and armchair. "On the contrary," she says. "Miss Corcoran must on no account be permitted to slip away. She is a suicide case."

"Ohhh," say both Mr. and Mrs. He continues soothingly, "You've come to the right place, Lady Esther; if I do say, we have never lost a case, indeed it is a spec-i-ality of sorts. These poor souls need the keenest vigilance coupled with a gentle but firm—"

"Very firm—" interjects his wife.

"—routine, no exceptions, for when they seem most well is when they are most in peril."

"Mid-morning is their witching hour," says Mrs. M.

Clarissa looks sharply at the woman. Perhaps sensing an infelicity on the part of his wife, Mr. MacGilvary says, "Might I venture to inquire, Lady Esther, how long Miss Corcoran has harboured her . . ."

"Delusions," says his wife.

"Aye, delusions," he pronounces the word as though to restore to it its rightful delicacy.

"Since first she came to live with my brother and me," says Clarissa. "Her people are from Boston. She remains lucid on that point. But on several others she . . . cannot be persuaded of her misapprehensions."

"Och, 'tis no use persuading," says Mr. MacGilvary regretfully.

"No use whatever," says Mrs. MacGilvary, adding starch.

Clarissa crosses the Rubicon. "Miss Mary Corcoran is my cousin by marriage and, with the death of her last relation, became my de facto ward. She has fallen into an *idée fixe* regarding my brother, believing him to be Lord Henry Bell of the DC de Fayne, whom she met once at my home."

"DC de . . . Who?" asks Mrs. M.

"Fayne." Miffed in spite of herself, Clarissa reflects she ought to be relieved—unless she herself has been infected by the modern mania for renown. "And she believes herself to be my brother's wife."

Mr. M's eyebrows stir like antennae. "And . . . has your brother, Lord—"

"Lord Alfred."

"Has His Lordship a wife?"

"He had. She died in childbed. Recently."

"Ah."

Clarissa continues, "Furthermore. Miss Corcoran believes she herself bore him a son."

"Oh dear. Lord . . . Feen, was it?"

"Lord Alfred, whom she takes to be Lord Henry. Of the DC de Fayne."

"Got it," says Mrs. MacGilvary.

Clarissa concludes, "She labours under the belief that she killed the child in seeking to do away with both it and herself."

Silence. Mrs. MacGilvary looks at her husband. He nods sympathetically . . . quizzically. "And . . . has Lord Henry—Alfred, that is, your brother—has he a son in fact?"

"He had. The child died of fever. There remains a newborn daughter."

"Ah," says Mr. MacGilvary, rubbing his hands together, nodding. "Well then." And poses no further questions. No more does Mrs. MacGilvary.

Clarissa asks, "How many other luna—guests have you?"

"There be three at present. Quiet cases."

"I should like to see them."

"As to that, Lady Esther, I'm afraid we adhere to a strict rule regarding residents' privacy such that none but their relations, physicians or registered friends may visit them."

"Or look upon them," adds Mrs. M.

The couple having passed this final test, Clarissa asks again, "What are your terms?"

The following morning, Henry stands at his study window, watching as the butler carries his sedated wife out and down the stone steps to the waiting carriage. He watches as his sister follows and embarks. Watches as the carriage pulls away, around the gravelled drive, through the iron gates betwixt the privet hedges, and out of sight.

It is accomplished.

To Henry, Lord Bell, Baron of the DC de Fayne, and Lady Marie, a daughter, the Honourable Charlotte Henrietta Geraldine Victoria. June 2, 1875.
The Scotsman

80

THAT VERY EVENING, Mrs. Knox imparts her heart to her old charge. "I wonder not but what I must return to Paisley, Miss Clarissa."

"What? Why?"

"'Tis my home."

"I confess myself mystified."

"I come from Paisley, Your Ladyship."

It is a new idea: that Knox comes from anywhere. It is as disconcerting as if a cornice of Fayne House were to detach and declare itself part of another building. "I see." She does not see.

"There be kinfolk as wilna turn me awa."

"Wait. Knox. Why?"

"Why, miss, I . . ." And Knox unburdens her heart.

Clarissa reports the contents of said heart to her brother.

"She swears she cannot continue with the family if she is constrained to keep to the lie."

Her brother stands before her. She knows he is eager to be gone. To his study. And then, in the morning, to Fayne. Where his child waits—languishes—untreated. That is another matter. Best proceed step by step.

"Which . . . ?" Henry rifles his brain, where various lies are scattered about like bits of bone and beak. "You mean to say the lie regarding Marie having been returned to Morecombe Downs?"

"No, brother. That is what we have told her, and what she believes."

"Then . . ."

"Knox swears she cannot be a party to Marie believing her child to be deceased. Nor to the child believing the same of its mother."

He heaves a great breath. "Does she intend to betray our confidence?"

"Of course not. But she cannot, by her own admission, remain in our employ."

"'Employ'? She is a member of—"

"Nor may we ask it of her." Here, Clarissa's voice catches. She clears her throat, and says, "She'll have to be let go." The veins at her temples contract, her head commences to throb. Not for her the solace of a feeling of unreality, eyes cast upward to a corner of the ceiling, not for her any head-cradling—"Do it, Henry," she barks. Then, calmly, "It is the only way." Moreover Clarissa has denied herself a single daytime drop for nigh on the past seventy-two hours. Pain sharpens the mind. Until it dulls it.

Tears are coursing down her brother's cheeks. Press on, Clarissa, you have "killed" his wife, now banish his beloved nurse—*She was my nurse too!* Cease your whumpering, gel, stand firm. *Yes, Father.*

"And who is to care for my child?" he plaints.

A pause. During which Clarissa lengthens her neck. Looks fate in the eye. Bids farewell to what she had been used to call the rind of a life but which appears in retrospect an orchard, and says, "I shall do my duty by you. I shall remove to Fayne, and help rear your child."

Henry is as still as a crow counting gunshots. Finally he says, "You are too good to me, sister."

Now it is Clarissa who listens for the shot that must kill her. The *Thank you.*

But her brother says, "I'd not for the world see old Mrs. Knox banished to Paisley, whatever claim she may have on the strangers there she calls family. There is another way . . ."

Clarissa listens as her brother explains his idea . . . Until, near giddy with the sense of reprieve, she pulls the bell rope. A glass of water is what she needs. "Havers, sherry."

Byrn has met their coach in the village with the dog cart. Henry is seated next to Knox, who has wept quietly at intervals since they left Bell Gardens. As the cart crests the fell and the house comes into view, Henry breathes a great sigh. He is home.

As to his child: even his sister has seen the wisdom of delaying the surgical procedure until a suitable interval has followed the announcement of Marie's death. They are, after all, supposed still to be abroad. Privately, however, Henry has opted to delay the procedure until his daughter should be old enough to receive anaesthetic. A year or so should do it. All in good time . . .

Knox agreed to see His Lordship safely re-ensconced at Fayne, "Afore I take my leave." It is now five days following their arrival, and she has packed her few belongings. Byrn is standing by with the cart to carry her to the village where she will meet the coach at the Inn at the Kenspeckle Hen, thence "home". . . It has occurred to Knox that she might stop in at Morecombe Downs, just to lay eyes on Her Ladyship one last time. Are they feeding her properly? Does she get a decent airing? Might Knox herself apply for a position there? A flutter in her old heart . . . She takes a last look round her room in the nursery. Then she stoops to the false-bottom bed and retrieves the letters from Her Ladyship's girlhood friend—all those that have arrived since that terrible day at the doctor's surgery—along with the sheet of parchment she retrieved, crumpled, from His Lordship's wastebasket following that fateful night only days ago. Her Ladyship never read the letters—nor has Knox, 'twas no her place, her place was to burn them along with anything else belonging to Her Ladyship that could be reduced to ashes—nor will Her Ladyship ever make use of the sheet of parchment, *Entitling the Bearer to One Trans-Atlantic Passage* . . . But Knox could not bring herself to destroy these few final precious mementoes. And though she knows it is stealing, she tucks the lot into the pocket of her apron. And presses her apron to her old eyes.

She will not bid wee Charlotte goodbye—the bairn is too young to understand, and what need has she to be knowingly wrenched from her nurse, having been already unknowingly wrenched from her mother? What's more, Knox does not trust herself not to fright the child with weeping. *Foolish old woman, you know there be nannies and governesses far better qualified to rear a young lady.* Indeed, better she depart with her burden of truth like a creel of ungutted fish, dripping and stinking.

She leaves the nursery and pulls the door quietly to. Her master has summoned her to his study. She is about to knock at his door, but falters—how can she bear the sight of him, her wee bairn of old? And now she is deserting his own wee bairn. There is no help for it. She is not made of the right stuff to house such a lie in her bosom. It would tear itself free like a bird of prey from within.

For the last time, she knocks and enters His Lordship's study—och, she'd fain be gone in the cart next to the Old Man, but His Lordship has insisted she depart with a goodly sum in lieu of pension, and now the time has come. But His Lordship neither bids her goodbye nor hands her a pouch of sovereigns, instead he bids her be seated. She obeys.

"I'm afraid there is news, Knox. I have received in this morning's post a letter from my sister. You are aware, I think, that Lady Marie has been housed in the locked wing at Morecombe Downs."

"Aye, Your Lordship." Knox colours, for has he read her thoughts? "But I wouldna dream of stopping by to visit Her Ladyship." She blinks away tears.

"You could not do so in any event, Knox—"

"I know she's to be thought—och, I cannae say it." *Dead.* Tears.

"Knox, my sister received word yesterday from the Chief Alienist, Dr. Finch."

Here Henry appears to falter. He breathes in sharply through his nose. Reaches for Clarissa's note upon his desk. "I . . . Forgive me. I bid you . . . read it for yourself." He pushes the notepaper toward her.

Mrs. Knox reaches into her apron for the spectacles which were Lady Marie's gift to her only months ago. And reads.

June 16, 1875

Dear Brother,

I write with grave tidings.

I received word yesterday evening from Dr. Finch, Chief Alienist at Morecombe Downs, that your dear wife, Lady Marie, has died.

In the early hours of June 15, Lady Marie was found to be absent from her room on the locked ward. A male attendant has since been questioned and dismissed for dereliction. It is known that from him she obtained a key to her room, and that he did not detain her when she, clad only in her nightgown, departed the house. I shall not here dilate as to what desperate bargain was struck by your wife with this depraved male.

A search was undertaken of the grounds and environs. It turned up only her nightgown, clinging to a rock on a hazardous stretch of coastline. She is, I grieve to tell you, presumed drowned.

I draw no comfort from the fact that, in walking into the sea, Marie fulfilled her own wishes; but I am eternally grateful that Charlotte is safe at Fayne. And I pray dear Marie find, in death, the peace which was, in life, denied her.

I remain your affectionate sister,

Clarissa

Up in her nursery room once more, Knox sits doubled over, weeping. She did not give way in Lord Henry's presence. She carried her grief, heavy and sloshing, up the several flights and even now, in the privacy of her quarters, she reproaches herself, for her grief can be as nothing to His Lordship's.

No good cursing the lass's keepers. Knox is only too keenly aware that she herself owns a share in the crime; for she too allowed Lady Marie to believe she had killed her own child. And what else but that belief could have goaded her into the clutches of an evil man, thence into the cold cold sea?

When finally Mrs. Knox stops crying, her features have been moulded anew with grief—a grief which converts, as at the wave of a wand, into love for the bairn. Wee Miss Charlotte, who never did anyone any harm. And to think Knox had been set to abandon the bairn. Out of weakness. Out of her inability to shoulder a flimsy lie which has, like a miracle of water into wine, turned into a timber of truth. She picks it up. Shoulders it. Nevermore to set it down, so long as she shall live.

She takes the packet of letters from her pocket and returns it to the drawer of the false-bottom bed. She hesitates before returning the certificate of passage—for all it was precious to Her Ladyship, the fact that she left it behind is testament to her mortal intentions, for she fled that night with no plan to venture farther than the bog. Before Knox can think better of it, she thrusts it deep amid the quilts and blankets. Then she herself returns to her duty, which lies among the living.

Henry has just dispatched Cruikshank with a cable for Boston and one for *The Scotsman*, when he is called by Mr. Mungo to the front entrance where a large lading cart has pulled up. He does not recollect having ordered any new furnishings . . .

He watches as Mungo oversees the unloading, the carrying in, the uncrating . . . and the hanging, of the portrait of his "late wife and son."

He has sealed himself in his study by the time Knox enters the house with Charlotte in tow. The child is carrying a basket of eggs. She sees the great portrait hanging on the landing and cries out in joy, "Momma!"

"That's right, child, 'tis your Mam."

The child drops the basket of eggs and scampers up to the landing where she jumps up and down in an effort to reach the frame, crying excitedly, "Me!!"

Knox comes up, breathless, behind her. "No, child, that be your brother. That be Charles."

Death notice. BELL. Lady Marie, wife to Henry, Lord Bell, 17th Baron DC de Fayne. In childbed, abroad. June 2, 1875. "In the midst of life we are in death." *The Scotsman, June 21, 1875*

———

If the Chief Alienist at Morecombe Downs was given pause by the announcement of the birth of a daughter to Lord and Lady Bell, what with Her Ladyship not having been pregnant mere weeks before, his discretion in not voicing as much was in keeping with the unwritten prospectus whereas the private lives of the aristocratic clientele remain private. The Bell family would not be the first to adopt a "foundling" and claim it as their own. When, however, scarcely a week later, Lady Bell's death notice appears, Dr. Finch allows himself the grim satisfaction of assuring Dr. Hitchcock that—insofar as the death is not unlikely to have been a suicide, given the patient's history—such an unfortunate outcome would not have been the case on his watch; even whilst inwardly register-ing relief that he was not tested on that score.

Miss Gourley writes a note of condolence to Lord Henry. Thank God for rules of etiquette. They hold us up when the language collapses under the weight of calamity. She looks in on Clarissa who is . . . the same. Rosamund is grateful to find herself in company with Lady Nora and Mrs. Heatherington. Murmured condolences, snippets of conversation. Lord Henry, "heartbroken," planning to return from Continent with infant daughter who is "delicate."

Rosamund departs, walks alone, Josey having been banned. For the second time in as many months, a niggle at the back of her mind asserts itself as something akin to . . . is "suspicion" too strong a word? On that frightful night in March, when Lady Marie came to her distraught, with poor wee Charles, Rosamund did not register any sign that Lady Marie was pregnant.

Rosamund finds herself at North Bridge. The sun comes out on what is shaping up to be rather a fine day. And "suspicion" is too strong a word. After all, Lady Marie was cloaked, and clutching her son. Indeed, it was all Rosamund could do to calm her and send for her husband . . .

At Fayne, among the many kind notes of condolence:

Boston, Mass.
June 23, 1875

Dear Lord Henry,
I write to offer you my deepest sympathy for the loss of your beloved
wife, Lady Marie. I beg you may accept from my hand the very deepest
sympathy from my wife, Timothea Blanchard, who is at present overcome, but from whom you may expect to receive a letter at the soonest.

My wife bids me convey to Your Lordship that you may also expect
that the friendship which flourished between her and your wife, will
extend to you and to your infant daughter. I make bold to add here the
offer of my own friendship to Your Lordship and family.

I remain, Your Servant,
Carter J. Blanchard III

81

OVER THE YEARS, the MacGilvarys have proven themselves exemplars
of that undersung but superior virtue, consistency. Clarissa has never
glimpsed any of the other "guests." She has, on occasion, heard them.
There is one who twitters a snatch of song repeatedly. Another holds
forth in a deep drone; Clarissa imagines a dotty old professor reciting—
she catches the cadence in spite of herself—Lucretius? Thus the sounds
too are consistent until, perhaps five years in, the twittering dwindles
then falls silent. The droning continues but is friable now, interrupted by
lapses. A sort of cooing made its debut some two years ago. None of the
sounds would one term positively "insane." *Quiet cases only*. Most consistent of all is the complete absence of sound from the resident of the back
bedroom at the top of the house.

Once a month, Clarissa is escorted up the stairs by Mrs. MacGilvary,
who unlocks the door, hands the key to "Lady Esther" and discreetly
withdraws.

As usual, Clarissa closes the door and relocks it from inside according
to house protocols. She remains standing in the single room. Bright but

spare. Looking at the figure that sits, clad in a snowy nightgown, staring out the barred window—whence a salt breeze, a whiff of fish and fuel.

"Marie?"

Nothing.

Clarissa established, at the outset, the practice of writing to her brother once a month; never venturing a single detail that might not bear scrutiny by a third party.

July 1, 1875

My dear Brother,

I trust this letter finds you and your daughter in good health. I continue tolerably well, bouts of indisposition notwithstanding. I received a call yesterday from Lady Nora. She is the latest among our friends to renew her solicitous inquiry as to your well-being, as well as regards the prospect of your returning to Edinburgh in the near future. I assured her that I would renew my entreaty to you to grace Bell Gardens with your presence.

Apart from the above, there is no news.

I remain, your devoted sister,
Clarissa Bell

At Fayne, Henry opens the monthly letters with trepidation at first. Their bland assurances are like a sheet laid over a body, the outlines of which are unmistakable. Eventually, however, as the sheets accumulate layer upon layer, the outlines are obliterated. And it is as if the body had never been there. *There is no news.*

Added to this reassuring accretion is the fact that Knox believes Marie to be dead—so does the rest of the household along with, of course, his child and indeed the world. But Mrs. Knox is the closest Henry has to a confidante, and she reinforces by word and deed his supposedly widowed condition. It was a stroke of luck, Knox's inability to bear the lie. Henry is the only one at Fayne who knows the truth; but, buffered by the ignorance of those about him, he is spared its searing effects—as with the clash of battle heard from a distance. Thus, Henry grows accustomed to living the life of a retiring widower. And in time, comes to think of himself as just that.

Except that he is sane, and knows himself still to be married. He acquiesced to Clarissa's plan but stopped short of bigamy. Thus far and no farther. Should his wife outlive him, so be it. His daughter will be a wealthy woman regardless, and it is her future which signifies. Henry is not insensible to the enormity of his abdication—the spectre of the unborn Barons Bell rising before him as though in an endless looking glass. The reproach of the dead Barons Bell who line the walls of the portrait gallery. But while Henry has chosen to live a lie for the sake of his child, he will not live in dishonour. Even for the sake of Fayne.

Twelve years on, and Marie has never once turned at Clarissa's entry into the room. Nor has she spoken. But she has grown. Steadily. For along with indicated doses of chloral hydrate, the MacGilvarys have indeed hewed to the "gospel of fatness." Thus, Marie's back is broader, much, than it was when Clarissa brought her here. And her head is shorn. This latter on account of "Miss Corcoran" having sought to hang herself from the window bars with her own hair. "I'm afraid she's never left off wanting to do away with herself, Lady Esther." But there is no danger of that. The MacGilvarys are virtue and vigilance. There is no dropped key. No depravity. No opportunity for Marie to flee. *No news.*

At this rate, Clarissa's sister-in-law will outlive them all; drooling and battening whilst Fayne crumbles and the Bell family line pools in the cul-de-sac of a blighted female. Extinction, thy name is Charlotte Bell.

Clarissa only ever lingers long enough to satisfy herself that her sister-in-law is alive and physically hale. And to say, after a silent interval of ten minutes, "You killed your child."

Before unlocking the door, letting herself out, locking it once more from outside, descending two flights, and handing over the key along with payment for a month's care and board.

Followed by a letter to her brother. Containing the usual entreaty that he favour her with a visit; the cursory report of a friend—a grand-child for the Farquhars—and *Apart from the above, there is no news.*

Only once has Clarissa altered the routine she laid down for her monthly visits to "Miss Corcoran." And it gave rise to an incident. Perhaps seven years ago. She entered the room and locked the door behind her. "Hello Marie." The hulking back. The shorn head. After ten minutes, Clarissa spoke the usual words, "You killed your child." Then she followed them with four singular words: "Your father is dead."

The still, silent form was suddenly neither.

Clarissa made haste to unlock the door, slip out and lock it behind her. Though shaken, she knew herself to have been in no real danger—nor was Marie capable of killing herself or even making much of a pulp of her scalp against the bars, subdued as she was by chloral hydrate. Mrs. MacGilvary mounted the stairs with surprising speed, for "Miss Corcoran" had begun loudly to keen. As could only distress the other guests. *Quiet cases.*

At Fayne, Henry donned a black armband in observance of the death of his father-in-law and acknowledged, in a letter, the kind condolence sent him by Mrs. Blanchard, who continued to wish the best for him and "little Charlotte," and to cherish the hope he might one day voyage to Boston with his daughter.

But Henry has no wish to stray from the safety of Fayne with its baffling and battlements, even to go to Edinburgh. Especially Edinburgh. For that is where his dead wife lives.

Clarissa has stayed the course. But each passing year has leached her of the expectation that her brother, having had the stomach to announce Marie's "death," would have the mettle to remarry. As why else did they go to these lengths? But he has not remarried. Clarissa has implored him to visit—once she has him at No. One Bell Gardens, she might place in his way an eligible young lady or two and soften his resistance. The lass need not be wealthy this time. Indeed, better she be penniless. But Henry will not budge from Fayne. And he will not hear of courting "at present . . ." Why had she ever imagined it might be otherwise? This, after all, is the man who has denied a simple yet crucial medical procedure to his supposedly beloved daughter. Clarissa's blood runs cold at the realization she can no longer put off the truth: her brother has no intention of remarrying while his wife lives. What can't be cured must be endured.

Two drops, hourly during the day. Five drops at bedtime.

Clarissa grows lean. She requires more laudanum to less effect. She understands that she has developed a dependency upon the drug, along with a regrettably ever-increasing tolerance of it. She keeps to a bare minimum dosage, which permits the same degree of pain she was wont to endure before she ever tasted her first drop. This is how she knows that, beneath the thin coverlet of the drug, her disease waits like a bed of burning stone.

Nigh on twelve and a half years pass. And one fine day in late summer, Clarissa receives word from her brother that her niece has achieved the menarche—though he puts it in such obscure terms, Clarissa has to write and ascertain as much from Knox—and that he intends once more to consult Dr. Chambers. He is coming at last! She seizes her chance. Makes inquiries. A Miss Llewellyn is spoken of highly. A connection of the Colonel's. Clarissa invites her to pay a call. And finds she will do nicely. She waits for word of her brother's visit.

Henry receives word from Clarissa that Dr. Chambers is indeed still to be found in Ainsley Place. Though he dreads the appointment, Henry reflects that he is blessed in his sister. He takes a fresh sheet of notepaper and writes:

September 13, 1887

Dear Dr. Chambers,
You will recall I had occasion upwards of some twelve years ago to consult you in company with my (late) wife and our child of twenty-two months. At that time you recommended a course of treatment for her. I write today to inquire whether you might see fit to receive me and my daughter, the Honourable Charlotte Bell, once more, with a view to determining whether treatment is still advisable.

Cordially,
Henry, Lord Bell, Baron DC de Fayne

He folds the letter, inserts it into an envelope, addresses it and sets his seal upon it. The afternoon post will have already gone out. It can wait until morning. He looks about for a free space on his desk, then props the envelope against the legs of the fanciful "chimera."

———

Clarissa waits. Summer turns to autumn and Henry has yet to affirm plans to visit Edinburgh with his daughter. But Clarissa has seen an opportunity.

There may not be another.

She alters her routine once more, arriving at the private establishment in Leith for the second time that month. This does not go unnoticed by the MacGilvarys but it goes unremarked—it is to be expected that a relative might pay a surprise visit in order to ascertain high-quality care of their loved one. "Come in, Lady Esther."

Once in the room, Clarissa adheres to routine. "Hello, Marie."

The obese back, the shaved head. No one would now recognize Lady Marie even if she were to turn up on the doorstep of No. One Bell Gardens itself. Nor would anyone credit the ravings of a madwoman, should she be apprehended by the Edinburgh Constabulary having somehow managed to flee the house at Leith. And if, as is more likely, her body were to wash onto the shore, who could possibly put a name to the bloated form? The wretched creature had wished to die and was saved against her will. Who is Clarissa Bell, or even Henry, to stand in her way? Is it not enough they condemned her to live with an horrific lie? "You killed your child," she says.

Clarissa turns, unlocks the door and lets herself out, pausing as usual to lock it once more behind her. Today, however, prior to descending and returning the key to Mrs. MacGilvary, Clarissa takes from her reticule a lump of wax. And presses the key into it.

What can't be cured must be endured. And what can't be mended must be ended.

82

THE FOLLOWING WEEK, Cruikshank returns from the village with the afternoon post and hands a letter to His Lordship direct from her fingerless gloves.

No. One Bell Gardens
November 17, 1887

My dear brother,
There is news. I beseech you, come at once.

Your devoted sister,
Clarissa Bell

Henry departs immediately for Edinburgh.

He stands in the parlour. Clarissa has placed a glass of whisky in his hand and insisted he be seated.

She lowers herself onto her chair. "Henry, the news regards your wife. I was informed the day before yesterday that she has died."

There are states of distraction which mimic bemusement. "What?" he says, rather affably.

"Marie has gone missing from the private establishment at Leith and is presumed drowned." *Wait*, he thinks, *wait, wait*. But she does not wait. "The proprietor of the establishment found her nightgown washed up at the end of the jetty."

He thinks he has asked, "How could this have happened?" but he has not spoken.

Clarissa, however, answers the question, "The wife of the proprietor carried up Marie's breakfast tray as usual, to find the door unlocked. And the room empty."

". . . How?" His voice dry as chalk. Rhymes with shock. "What's that you . . . ?"

"I said, it is not known by what cunning means she obtained a key to the room."

"We must have the law on them," says Henry, his voice strange in his own ears.

"Brother. Despite the interval of years, I am sensible that this news does not find you indifferent."

"Ha-ha."

"However—" She steels her voice, he sounds hysterical, she won't have it. "It is my hope that it might afford you a measure of relief. And while it is a commonplace that the dead return in memory as they were when in their prime, allow me to console you with the intelligence that your wife was much changed with the years. If I have spared you pain by witnessing, in your stead, that change, it has been no more than my duty. As it is no less now to remind you that, in stealing from her chamber and drowning herself in the sea—thereby denying her faithful husband the solace even of committing her remains to the earth—your wife evinced unwavering determination to put herself to death, the which proves the wisdom of your having, in the first place, put her away."

He is leaning forward with his head between his knees. He feels a spidery touch on his scalp—makes to brush it away and encounters his sister's hand. She withdraws it. He sits up once more. Drinks.

Henry has obliged his sister by agreeing to stay for a few days—it is the least he can do in view of her sacrifices of the past many years—on condition that he be required to see no one. On the third morning he rises in time for tea as usual and Clarissa surprises him by requesting his company on a ride out in the carriage.

"Are you quite sure, sister? I thought . . . That is, will you be quite comfortable?"

"I dare say the air will do me good."

As the carriage bounces over the cobbles of Princes Street, Clarissa digs her nails into her palms, wishing herself rid of her gloves, and fights to keep her voice light as she says, "Why look, there's Fuzzy and his great-niece."

He glances from the window and picks out, down amid the passing parade, Colonel MacOmber, on his arm a young lady. "Mm. Didn't know he had one."

To his consternation, Clarissa waves, "Colonel MacOmber. Fuzzy! Up here!"

Henry watches as the old colonel directs the attention of his young companion upward at the carriage. She turns. Henry does not immediately look away. Nor does he shrink from view when it becomes clear the old gentleman is going to huff and puff his way up the path to greet them—he's always had a soft spot for Clarissa, as Henry knows.

It is the least Henry can do, to descend from the carriage, hand down his sister, and greet the old gentleman properly. And make the acquaintance of—"My great-niece, Miss Llewellyn."

The young lady smiles demurely and offers her hand. Henry takes it and bows over it in the accepted manner. Neither he nor Miss Llewellyn witnesses the look of complicity which passes between Colonel MacOmber and the Honourable Clarissa Bell.

The Colonel blusters, "Now you've had me clamber all this way, least you can do, Clarrie, is give me my tea—oh, and my niece may as well tag along. That is if Lord Henry's not too busy with his birds."

"Not at all, Colonel. Miss Llewellyn, allow me." And Henry hands her up into the carriage.

Henry obliges Clarissa by partaking of tea with Colonel MacOmber and his charming great-niece. The least he can do.

He returns to Fayne a few days later, wearing a black armband.

Knox explains to Charlotte that an old friend has died, "One of your aunt's causes."

And that night, Charlotte hears him through the door of his study, weeping.

The moon lit a path on the water to the black horizon.

Where would it take her, the current? Home? Colder now.

Her Soul strained up from her Body toward the Moon, and grasped a beam. Hanging on for dear Life, to an apron string of the Queen of Tides.

Part Six

When you are face to face with a difficulty,
you are up against a discovery.

LORD KELVIN

83

I AWOKE AS THOUGH FROM ETHER to see my bare feet splashing along bricks—I looked up at the lamps with their rain-lashed halos. I was on North Bridge. I stopped. Behind me was the New Town—a rank of orderly lights. Before me, the Old Town, a jagged line of looming. Below me, the gorge . . . scored by railway tracks. I must return to Bell Gardens, lest morning dawn on my absence and deal Father another blow!

Father—I reached to steady myself at the railing. What right had I even to inhabit the same world as Henry Bell? I had fouled that world. False son. Deformed daughter. Fit for neither the life to which I had so foolishly aspired nor the one for which he so selflessly sought to render me fit; delaying even his own marriage for my sake; nurturing me within the confines of Fayne, safe from contumely, the while I inveighed pettishly against every obstacle to my delusory ambitions. I, the destroyer of his happiness; of his wife. Whose body yet lay in the bog . . . There on the bridge, I withered with shame—like a dry stalk, despite the steady rain.

I was bowed by the image of Father slumped over the soiled certificate of passage, his grief rekindled and rendered the more bitter by the knowledge that his wife had merely sought to flee, her demise all the more tragic in having been accidental—poisonous knowledge that would have stayed safely buried along with her body but for my discovery of the cursed cloak. Even Father's dismissal of my tutor was revealed now as a kindness—one wasted upon me. Prideful misbegotten wretch that I was, no matter they had cut away my blighted flesh, what of my blighted mind? How dare I ever again afflict Father with the sight of me? How live beneath his roof, eat his bread, knowing he was now denied even the balm of my ignorance? This, then, was that vaunted highest good: Truth. But it had not set me free. It had condemned me to knowledge of my own exile. *Monster.*

I buried my face in my arms on the railing and felt the icy rain trickling in at the collar of my nightgown and down my back. In my hand was the crumpled parchment of the certificate. Aunt was right, I ought to have died along with my mother. It was not too late. Indeed, the Truth might yet set me free . . . I lifted my head and looked down upon the tracks.

Shivering with cold, I made to hoist myself onto the railing when suddenly the bricks seemed to shift beneath my feet and I was forced to steady myself. All at once a clamouring arose—a maelstrom of messages of which I was suddenly aware—a tale told by a multitude of voices as filamenty as threads in a spiderweb, a tale of myriad histories and innumerable accidents, of adventures and marvellous transformations. I make sense of it now as best I can: the clay that formed the bricks had travelled epochs, undergone countless convolutions to arrive beneath my feet, and now they were singing of it—had always been singing of it, but in that moment I was able to hear them; they sang of clay composed of matter as old as Earth itself, bits of countless lives, one of which might have witnessed the fern that fell to ground those millions of years ago to become the fossil in Mr. Margalo's hand. And in that moment, I smelled it. The moor.

I "woke" a second time to see once more my feet, slick with mud, my nightgown hemmed in filth as I staggered across the Downs south of the Old Town. It was as though each blink of my eye lasted not half a second but half an hour and more, such that with every blink my eyes opened on quite a different scene, minutes—even hours—removed from the previous. Thus, I walked. And woke. Walked. Woke. Until, far behind me, the glim of the Old and glitter of the New Town were but a smear in the low-lying distance.

Like the peat that waits, cool and heavy beneath the bog 'til it is dug up and ignited, I knew I carried memory. And like a migratory bird, I was drawn by some powerful invisible magnet. South. To Fayne.

84

CLARISSA IS AT THE BREAKFAST TABLE, spine erect. She has forced herself to rise, dress and descend. Normal is as normal does. This might very well be a normal morning but for Henry. Haggard. Haranguing her. "Sit, Henry, sit. Drink your tea." She rings for Maid.

"I incarcerated my wife for twelve and a half years on the basis of a lie."

"She herself told that lie. You acted for the best in light of the intelligence you had. Intelligence she provided. You could not have known she intended to flee rather than . . ."

He has not been to bed. Eyes bloodshot, evening clothes dishevelled. "She died alone, believing she killed her child. It is an enormity, a . . . a horror . . ." Maid enters. "A crime—"

Clarissa cuts him off. "How is Miss Charlotte this morning?"

"I cannae say, Madam."

"Why not? Have you not taken up her breakfast?"

"Aye, Madam, but she's no abed."

"Well where is she?"

Maid looks blank as a billiard ball. "I don't know, Madam."

"Simpleton, find her! Stay. Where is Mrs. Knox?"

Maid hesitates.

"Well?"

"Mrs. Knox is . . . abed." With the latter word, Maid manages to convey an opinion as to the general irregularity of this morning. Such a determination is, however, the sole province of Clarissa. "Go before I turn you out without a character."

Maid bobs and vanishes.

Henry is sagging at the sideboard, his voice a ragged whisper. "Charlotte knows the truth."

Clarissa does not hesitate, for the die has already been cast. "She discovered it for herself. Last night. In my parlour."

He looks at her, stricken.

"She rifled my work basket, goodness know why, and found the photograph."

"What . . . photograph?"

"The one used by the painter. Of the portrait."

"How . . . ?"

"It was addressed to Marie. I opened it. She was past doing so herself."

He shakes his head as though waking into a nightmare. "This is your fault."

"I take no responsibility for my niece having intruded upon my—"

"The photograph was not your property! It was mine!"

"It was your wife's—"

"And therefore mine!" He has roared it.

Clarissa presses her lips together. He looks on the point of striking her. Let him. She looks down. Hears him ask, more calmly, "Why preserve such a thing?"

"Because . . ." Constriction. She scowls back tears. There is marmalade on her cuff. Her voice creaks. "'Tis all I've got left of him . . ."

Henry sighs. "Oh Clarissa. He is not dead. I wish you could see that, sister, and then you might—"

"He is! Gone, and never was, never will be!" She sobs. Clamps hold of herself.

Henry shakes his head. "And now she knows all. God help her. My poor child."

Clarissa concentrates on lifting her cup to her lips. She succeeds. "Will you call on Miss Llewellyn today?"

"Confound Miss Llewellyn!"

"If you had acted thirteen years ago, Henry, none of this would be happening."

"If I had followed my heart eighteen years ago instead of heeding your advice, none of this would be happening! But that would be to wish away my beloved daughter, and that, I shall never do."

"If you love her, you will marry."

A rustling in the doorway. He turns, wild-eyed—"Charlotte?"

Knox is there. "She's gone, Your Lordship."

85

THERE IS THE MINERALLY SMELL of rain, wintry earth and trees. The musk of mushrooms, nests and burrows. The landscape changes, woods give way to rolling pasture stitched with hedgerows, hemmed with drystone walls. Pasture swells, rises to become denuded hills that, at this raw hour, shed darkness like meltwater. And, seen now from high above, emerging from one such pool is a slender figure. Its pace unflagging, it hews as though to the line of a compass. South.

In dormant meadowland, it climbs over stiles without pausing to sit, wades though frigid streams without bending to drink, shades not its eyes from the glare of midday, nor hastens its pace when heavy rain comes, seeks no shelter against the hail. It eats not, neither does it sleep. Night. Day. Night. Day. This is no human endurance.

I could not have said when she joined me, only that soon after the lights of the city sank from view behind me and darkness engulfed me, when I hadn't so much as a star to guide me through unseen clouds, she was there. I felt the great warm shape of her, felt the breath from her great head. I held on to her left horn and leaned into her, yielding to her rumbly walk such that my feet seemed hardly to bear my own weight. When the land rose she pulled me up, and when it fell, she steadied me. Sometimes I fell asleep whilst walking and dreamt I sat rocking along on her broad back; then I would awaken, rested even though I knew it had been a dream and that in reality I had been walking all the while next to Gossamer. Dream and waking, however, had in common that I knew I was safe, and that Gossamer knew the way. At some point on the second night—about midway of our journey—I dreamed I lay sleeping on her back. Then I dreamt I awoke at the sound of her milking song as though sung by a faery choir, and opened my eyes onto a beautiful summer's day amid a field of blue wildflowers. I slid from her back onto a bed of moss. Hardly had I to touch her teats before they gave and, open-mouthed, I caught their nourishment. Sweet and thick, her milk. Restored, I saw nearby a patch of glistening bilberries. Scarcely had I to reach out before they fell into my hands and I ate the delicious black fruit. I gathered forget-me-nots and wove a midsummer crown for Gossy. From this dream too I woke refreshed to find myself walking along as before, one arm slung up over her neck, my hand holding on to her horn, the mosses soft and spongy beneath my feet as though laid out before me in an endless carpet. Whenever I fell—for Reader, more than once exhaustion threatened to rend enchantment and cause me to find myself alone and lost and starving in the wilderness—Gossamer's great tongue scored my cheek and roused me. I struggled once more to my feet, the storm receded, the sun came out, and I walked on.

The slender figure now staggers over cobblestones. She has arrived at a village. Parched and starving she must be, cold and squalid she assuredly is, for she is hatless, hair plastered down her back, clad in a filthy rag, her feet mud-shod and raw. Yet she persists—one foot adamantly after the other, as though drawing chthonic energy from the dark places below . . .

Past a sign in a shuttered window, WE SAY NO TRAIN IN FAYNE. Past the slumbering Inn at the Kenspeckle Hen, past the yews and slabs of the nevermore churchyard; past the vicarage through whose lead-paned parlour window may be glimpsed a nodding silhouette— Mrs. Haas, wake up. Might you help the child as you sought to help the mother? Weary bog-wanderers both.

Out of the high street and onto the bridge over the Water of Feyn the figure glides. Up the steep incline to the crest of the North Fell where the standing stone splits the raging wind—*Child! Stop, do not venture farther!* In vain would a wayfarer cry out to our figure, for who could be heard above the tempest? And besides, our walker is not lost. In the distance is the house, looming grey against an oilskin sky, hollow-eyed, sorrow-struck. And before her is her home—the vast and windswept moor.

Gossamer grew ornery at the crest of the North Fell, nudging me with her blunt horns in her determination to keep me to the track. "Leave off, Gossy. And mind you don't lose your crown of flowers with your nudging." Sensible as I was of her kindness in having conducted me thus far, I was nonetheless determined she should take herself home, for the moor could not be trusted to bear her weight. Thus I dealt her hindquarters a smack and shouted, "Go home!" at which she clomped off, lowing her displeasure. I left the track and, with a dream-like ease akin to floating, descended effortlessly onto the moor.

I awake once more, but this time into a nightmare of icy rain fierce and stinging where my skin is exposed. I struggle to look up but, obscured by gale-torn clouds, there is no telling whether the faint light in the sky be sun or moon. I am drenched and all but naked, bent like a bow by a wind strong enough to keep me down if I should fall, but shy of force to hold me upright. Next instant, the wind drops and I seem to hear Mr. Margalo's voice. "You, Miss Bell, are grass in another form. We are all of us carbon and water." I smell again the silken mud, see with wonder the crystal droplets winking in his palm.

I rise and behold the moor, retreating in swells before me like a sea stilled by the wave of a wand. It smells different at night; opens like a moonflower, releasing its spirit-body of scent to wander like a soul. As I watch, dawn breaks in one swift motion, full-breasted with arms uplifted to embrace the sky. And below, all is emerald. It salves the eye and I seem to see at will each blade, blossom, insect leg of the multitudinous moor; I seem to see the whole of its vastness; I need not see her secret dips and dells to know they are there and stirring. Now the Sun is going swiftly down beneath the weight of Night, who has returned the pressure of her embrace, and off to the east there hovers into view a rogue patch of mist. That is when I hear them.

Chattering, laughing, running before me, and I am running after them. It seems they both beckon and elude me, babbling words just beyond meaning, silvery voices braided in song in an underground spring. What, oh what are they saying?

It is not possible to run across a moor, especially when it turns to bog and reaches up to eat your feet, but I am running. Turf springs back with every footfall, I bound along like Byrn as the merry air draws me onward, effortlessly onward until . . . Silence. Stop.

It clears. Night-time. A gibbous Moon. And there he is. Looking up at me. Rather, at someone just behind me. *Charles.* I dare not move. I wish away the fey child, willing him into the ground, into the myst that plays about his feet like a winding sheet, anything but that he shift his pleading gaze to me, as he does now and, as he has in dreams, commences piteously to cry. This infant fetch of myself . . . I know what he wants. *He?* '*Tis I!* Severed remnant of myself—*my face,* tear-stained, *my eyes,* pleading . . . I will fall insensible in a moment . . . Just then, a voice, neither female nor male, but Present and Everywhere, says,

Look behind you. See what I see, what I have always seen, and re-member me. Please.

I turn.

I see.

A tall figure. Darker against the darkness. Towering over me. In a cloak. Arms outstretched. Its hood is a coal-black halo about the face which is lost in shadow. A word issues thence, in a voice as soft and powerful as the turf. The word reaches me, pierces me—*Charles*. I move toward her. *Momma*, I say—I feel a tug of ineffable pleasure as the word leaves my body and I follow it toward her. But her form wobbles suddenly, as though at a tremor underfoot, and she says, *No*. I do not like that word, I will not heed it. I am drawn by an agony of happiness to be near her, to be in her arms, her embrace, her softness, her smell, my lips are wet. *Charlotte*, says the cloak. I stop. That is a daytime word. I want the magyk word back, the one you said before that drew me like honey and bliss and only you, oh please say it again so I can come to you, for I am stuck now and cannot move, and . . . am I . . . growing taller? No. Momma is sinking.

Slowly, into the centre of her cloak . . . which pleats about her until . . . Her head in its hood lingers a moment above the surface . . . before it too disappears, and she is swallowed. Now the cloak turns in on itself and follows her into the earth with a sucking sound.

I dive in after her. Into darkness and murk, viscid, thicker than blood, tasting of iron and memory, it rushes to fill the vacuum of my nostrils, mouth, *Momma, I am coming to find you.*

86

THE HOUSEHOLD HAS BEEN DISPATCHED to search for her.

The men have scoured the Old Town, every wynd and way and close, every human mouse-hole from Holyrood to Castle Rock.

The women have searched the New Town, including a call to Miss Gourley and Miss Mellor's School for Girls where Miss Charlotte's friend is known to board. Miss Gwendolyn Haas herself has been questioned by Mrs. Knox. To no avail.

Henry himself has walked the bridges, scanning the tracks and ditches below.

He has returned to West Princes Street Gardens and sought out the holly oak, squelching up the rise to part its low-hanging boughs . . . in vain.

And he has passed through a stone arcade in Teviot Place and into a new quadrangle. It is empty. She is not at the Edinburgh School of Medical Arts.

In her nightgown.

In January.

That evening, over the objections of his sister, Henry sends Havers to alert the Edinburgh Constabulary.

Then, without a word to anyone, he returns to the Old Town—on foot this time . . .

At the Refuge, Moira finds the chief in the big main room near the stove with a book in her lap and a weather eye on Brigid, who is huddled in the corner outside the circle of light, shelling beans—Moira is still apt to give this one a bit of a wide berth, there being no telling what might set her off.

"Miss Gourley, there's a gentleman to see you as won't take no, I think it be that same—" The gentleman has entered hot on Moira's heels, the toffey cheek of him.

"Lord Henry," says Miss Gourley.

"Miss Gourley. Good evening."

"What brings you—?"

"My daughter. Charlotte. Is she here?"

It is a wild question. Miss Gourley replies calmly, "She is not, Lord Henry—"

"Oh my God," his arm comes up to cover his face.

"Lord Henry, sit. Now tell me what has happened."

Moira is already pouring from a large all-day teapot on the stove.

His attempt at recovering himself only underlines his desperation. "Forgive me, I call upon you somewhat precipitously for that this morning, I awoke to find my daughter . . . my . . . my Charlotte . . . gone!" He weeps.

"Henry," she says softly. His hand shoots out. Finds hers. She returns the pressure. "Do you mean to say Charlotte has been . . . taken? Or that she has left of her own accord?"

"... I believe the latter."

A scrawny toothless woman is pressing upon him a steaming mug. He sips. Scalds his tongue. Sniffs. "She had ... She is ... As you know ..."

"She was delicate. Is she ill?"

"No. That is. Her condition admitted of cure. Required only ... a minor surgical procedure, the which took place mere days ago. She was healing well, and then ... this morning—" He strangles a sob.

A clattering from the far side of the stove. Miss Gourley turns but Moira is already hustling over to the corner.

"Here now Brigid, you've no tipped the bowl? Jesus, Pete and the Apostles, so you have." In the darkness, Moira sets to picking up. No help from Brigid—ah well, she's not got the full shilling. "Now Brigid," Moira says not unkindly, "Don't you be crying over spilt beans," and rasps a laugh.

"Lord Henry," says Miss Gourley. "Is Charlotte in danger of sepsis or any complications following on from—"

"No, no, she is strong and well. It is only ..." He sips. "She ... harbours hopes—illusions, regarding university, you see but ... I was assured, the physician assured me, such would pass away following the ... the cure."

Rosamund gently withdraws her hand from his. "We shall do everything in our power to find her, Lord Henry—"

"Hush, now, Brigid," says Moira.

"I'll look after her, Moira," says Miss Gourley, rising. "Fetch Miss Elliot. Take any and all who are up to it and search each and every den and doss house—hush, hush now Brigid, please—the whole circuit of the Radical Road, up Arthur's Seat and the Craigs, round the lochs, don't forget the chapel ruins and St. Margaret's Well—wait, Moira! Henry—Lord Henry, describe your daughter. Please."

"She is pretty. And tall for her age. Grey eyes. Long waving Titian locks—"

"How old?" pipes Moira.

"Why ... twelve," he says huskily, and clears his throat.

"Twelve, big for her age, curly ginger, right then, that's me away."

"Hold!" commands Miss Gourley. "Lord Henry, what is Charlotte wearing?"

"... Her nightgown. White."

"What else?"

He shakes his head.

"No cloak? Shoes?"

His face crumples.

Moira says, "We'd best find her soon then, in this weather," and trots off.

Henry watches as Rosamund makes for the corner whence muffled cries. He stops her with a whisper, "Rosamund." His very voice gaunt. He waits for her to turn. It is not possible she can be happy here. Amid the dregs of society.

"What is it, Henry?"

"I have wondered. Always. In light of your absence of . . . some many months. Following our last excursion to Arthur's Seat . . ."

He waits but she does not reply. "Please, Rosamund, can you not guess my question?" His voice breaks on this last like a dry twig.

From the cloakroom comes the kerfuffle of the search party gathering.

Her tone is not unkind but, unlike many who claim never to mince words, Rosamund Gourley does in fact deliver them whole. "You wish to know if our union resulted in a child." He looks away, shocked. "It did not, Henry. But it did bear fruit."

He looks back at her. "On the wall of my private quarters hangs a diploma which designates me Bachelor of Arts."

All these years, he thought it was a private dread: that Rosamund had borne him a child out of wedlock. Now the dread is revealed to have been all along a hope . . . He looks beseechingly at her.

She returns a level gaze. "When you find her, what will you do?"

"Oh. Why, I shall rejoice of course."

"Lord Henry. An educated daughter is not the end of the world. Indeed it might be the beginning."

He falters. Bows and hastens to join the search party in the cloakroom.

Miss Gourley enters the darkness behind the stove. "Now then, Brigid, are you cold?" She does not wait for an answer before retrieving the woman's shawl from the floor and tucking it round the plump shoulders that tremble despite the warmth. Nor does Miss Gourley expect an answer when she looks into the impossibly familiar green eyes and asks, "Who are you?" For Brigid is mute.

87

I AM BREATHING. Under water. No more mud, I have passed through it. Clear and silvery, the water is swift yet calming . . . Have you ever fallen asleep amid the buzz of bees? Aye, like that . . . The water becomes still. I am in a pool of winking crystal blue. And they are all around me, the merry ones, scintillating, felt but unseen. Pure mirth. Light sparkles in the water and . . . She is there. Smiling. At me. Her green hair fans about her lovely face, her hands caress the water as She hovers. She is beautiful! Her dress shimmers, iridescent. She looks as though She has swum through a rainbow! Oh, I want to laugh! Will I drown if I do so? I will ask her. Her Name is upon my lips—then it is gone before I can speak it. What is her Name? I know it, yet know it not . . . She is amused. And I am soothed by her knowing me. She knows everything. I reach out, for I mean to swim to her—and I see my hands. Small, plump, with dimpled knuckles. They are batting away bubbles that cluster about me like pebbles, for I am laughing. And paddling joyously with my feet. My feet: small like my hands, and dimpled too, and there . . . buoyed between my rolly thighs, the wee frond of flesh. I look up once more because the lovely Green Lady has something to tell me. She tells me, and no sooner am I filled with the telling than She and her ravishing smile waver and vanish. I cry like the baby I am—even though I see, by my hands outstretched before me now, that I am once more a well-grown girl of . . . fourteen. My skin . . . is turning blue, like a Pictish warrior . . . my fingers and toes are webbing, like a . . .

Brute, blunt. I am gored in the armpits, hooked and hauled backward and up through muck with wracking force, it will break my neck, pull the tendons from my bones—*Up, up* I am torn from the earth—choking on air, O how can a body be expected to breathe up here, I shall drown in a moment on dry land, let me go back, let me—antlers have me under the arms, I am turned roughly onto my side. I flail, I gag—the bog rips from my lungs, spews up and out, and the naked air, stripped of magyk, takes its place.

———

I wake to find I am warm. Dry. Supine. There is the smell of peat smoke. I open my eyes. The Old Man is there. Face not two feet from my own. Skin the colour of bone on the moor, swept by scavengers and weather. Nose like a blade, pale eyes that never look quite into mine. Head, hairless—a lumpy stone. He physicks me with a dropper—the same one he uses on the sheep, its tip is slimed with green, it is past my lips like a conjuring trick—*foul!* And the reek of it, Byrn's balm.

I was on a cot in Byrn's bothy. It smelled of the old man, all turf and musk and hide. I was covered in a pelt of some kind. Faded brown fur . . .

Byrn muttered, "Evening."

He rose, and turned to his pots on the window sill where the truth of his salutation was borne out by the frosty light of morning. His linen tunic buckled with the motion of his shoulder blades as, one by one, he droppered his seedlings. Yes, those arms of his might feel like antlers . . . I moaned, for it was upon me now, "Why did you bring me back?"

Hot sorrow tore from my chest with the same violence that had pulled me protesting from the ground for I remembered now, but what is memory and what is dreaming? And is not some madness merely memory gauded up in wrong costumes and thrawn words?

"Aye," nodded the old fool—I would be with her now if not for him—I raised my head, only to be sledge-hammered by a waiting memory: my mother, sinking—*Momma!* A warm tongue lapped at my tears— Nolan was cleaning me as she would one of her pups. The Old Man had begun singing to his seedlings. And soon I was singing along with him. Word for word in the Old Tongue. It came to me with the force of simplicity that I had merely forgotten—not the words themselves, but the fact that I knew them. As I sang, my thoughts organized themselves logically, methodically, just as though I were seated at the great scarred library table over in the house, rather than lying beneath a bear skin on old Byrn's cot. My mother had sought to save me from her fate in calling me by the name she knew would stop me in my tracks: the name that exiled Charles to a living death. Condemned to haunt Charlotte. I was Charles. And I was Charlotte. I was dead. And I was alive. These things could not be borne by brain alone. Only spirit, with spirit's language of song, could render these things comprehensible. Thus, I sang along with the Old Man in his "nonsense" words all that day and into the night until he bid me "Good morning" and lay down on the floor beside my cot, curved around Nolan to sleep.

Moments later, it seemed, he bid me "Good evening" and, adroit as a conjurer, slipped the dropper between my lips—*phaugh!* I slept and woke and listened and sang, and whilst I slept the song continued like so many skeins of yarn knitting me back up.

Smell of peat smoke. Nolan's meaty breath. The old man's face. Dropper of—"Byrn." My throat was rough, as though these were the first words I had spoken since he had pulled me from the bog, and yet . . . had I not been singing? For two days. "We must get her body up." I contracted suddenly at a thrust of pain—sewing needle be dashed, it was a rapier between my legs.

"She's no there," said a wispy voice. Cruikshank. My mouth fell open. Filled of a sudden with porridge. She was sitting on the edge of the cot with bowl and spoon. I chewed, swallowed, suddenly as ravenous in body as I was in mind, twin hungers vying for command of my organ of speech—what evolutionary quirk had fitted the mouth for that dual purpose? I bolted the food. I swallowed and caught my breath.

Cruikshank said, "She were alive when he drug her out."

Pierced once again—the pain quite took my breath away. Sharp and remorseless, it drove into the blank crux of me. Just as suddenly, it dropped me—like a cat tiring of a mouse. I felt a cold cloth on my forehead. The rough swaddling of the fur pelt. I neither slept nor woke but before my fevered gaze a phantasmagoria played out upon the walls of the bothy. The stones sweated, pulsed and breathed—spoke too, in the voices of stone—until they were overrun by bright blue salamanders darting every which way. And I saw, sitting before the peat fire, a velvet-antlered buck, Nolan's chin resting in its lap. The buck turned to me and said, "You are mermaid." The bear skin embraced me more closely and, with a low, lulling growl, begged of me a boon which I promised to fulfill, whilst on the windowsill the tender seedlings set to trilling in their earthen pots, and I slept.

———

I woke. Soaked but no longer feverish, beneath the bear skin. Refreshed.

"Evening." Byrn was eating his mash. Cruikshank sat dozing, her head drooping on its stalk. "Cruikshank. You can speak." She looked startled. "I won't tell anyone." She put a bowl to my lips. Water.

They had cared for me. Cleansed me of the bog. Attended to my bodily functions. Had they also sent word to Father? *Father.*

I sat up. I fell back. "I must go. Where are my—? Give me my night-gown."

Cruikshank bent and retrieved a mud-encrusted rag from the floor—a rag with a pocket. I reached carefully in and drew out the certificate of passage, now resembling more a mud-ball than a crumpled parchment. I opened it amid a shower of silt. It was legible. Just.

"What became of my mother?"

Cruikshank answered, "The Old Man drove them to village. To coach."

"Does she yet live?" I whispered.

She shrugged. I turned to the Old Man, who did likewise.

Had Aunt lied to me? As why not, there had been so many lies. Was my mother alive and . . . put away? In a madhouse? *It sounds a very nice one . . .* Or was she dead by some other means? I lay back once more in a bid to stave off fainting. I fought to puzzle it out as I might a prob-lem in logic: Was I prepared to press Father on a subject which already had come near to destroying him? Was I prepared to return to a regi-men designed to render me *marriageable*? Aunt had suggested "a spell at Morecombe Downs." Was I prepared to become a patient of a thera-peutic establishment wherein Mother was perhaps an inmate? I had risked my life to seek my mother's body. Would I risk my freedom? All for the sake of finding out the Truth?

I would.

"Help me up."

Cruikshank did. And caught me before I could fall over. Then, sup-ported by her slight but strong shoulder, wobbling on legs depleted by exertion and weakened by disuse, I made my way toward the door where I paused, suddenly remembering. "Byrn. You were in my dream. You told me I was a mermaid. Of all things."

"Nay."

"I ought to know, it was my dream after all, and you were a—"

"Moor-made."

". . . Oh."

Cruikshank opened the door and we stepped out. O Reader, how sweet the morning air. How crisp the wintry sky. I saw my breath before me. "Leave me be now, Cruiky." With one hand clutching the bear skin beneath my chin and the other arm outstretched, I proceeded, like a tightrope walker, down the path. Before me the barnyard twinkled with frost, a hoof-poached confection. I felt it crunch and melt exquisitely beneath my bare feet as I walked past the byre—I heard Gossamer low softly. I almost wished myself back with her on sunlit meadows but I continued, resolutely picking my way toward the house where I would seek out pen and paper in Father's study to tell him where I was. I stepped onto the cindered forecourt, about to turn in the direction of the portico when I saw, a way off where the cart track crests the Fell, a shape. Approaching.

It dawned on me that I stood now in the same spot where I had stood less than a year ago, next to Father, on the day of my birthday. My *fourteenth* birthday. But now I was naked under the pelt of an extinct bear to whom I had dreamt a promise. Was I dead? Overcome by bog fumes, had I drowned? And was this—all of it—but a curious dying vision? The cinders pricked my soles as though to recall me to my senses as, in the distance, the approaching shape assumed an outline very much of this world, and I recognized the dimensions and cadence of the magnificent Reggie. Mr. Mungo's shire horse. Father's estate manager was coming to seek me. And I was ready to be found. No longer in need of pen and paper, I now required clothing, or at least a bedsheet, in which to meet Mr. Mungo and—yes, a second shape seated behind him on Reggie's great back. Murdoch.

88

AS SWIFTLY AS I DARED, I crossed the forecourt to the portico, mounted the wide stone steps, pushed open the doors, and entered my ancestral home.

Cool as a catacomb. Above my head, the trophies were inert; antlers were drained of animation, flying colours were stilled, crossed swords and cudgels were merely decorative—it was as though all the ghosts had deserted the place. My home? Charlotte's home. That truncated girl of "twelve." Indulged with books and fed on fairy tales of her future. The gullible girl with the tail between her legs, trussed up like the lady they'd soon have her *cut out* to be. These were bitter thoughts, unfair to Father who had only ever strived for my good.

Across the great hall, to one side of the marble staircase, his study door stood closed. Within that room had I spent the sweetest, most formative hours of my life. With the person most beloved of me. Nay, beyond beloved, he was my own "first cause." Initiator of my existence, and proof of God's. Father. I doubled over, as at a blow—Oh, who would have thought the empty spot to have so much pain in it?! I fell, gasping, to the stone floor. Huddled in the bear skin, I forced myself to crawl to the staircase and to climb it on all fours. I reached the landing where, assailed by a fresh spike of pain, I curled into a ball. All at once I understood that the errant bit of flesh, though snipped and gone to be dispersed as carbon in earth or on the air, would give me no more peace than had the "ghost" of "my brother."

Sagged over my knees, drenched in sweat, I plumbed my depths for the will to press on—not to my bedchamber in search of a garment, but to the top of the house and out onto the roof where the currents eddied about the chimneys. I would indeed return to Edinburgh. A corpse. If only it could be Knox to find me, smashed on the forecourt, she who had groomed me with lies to fit me for a life of falsehood and pain. I made to rise. But though the pain had abated for now, I was unspeakably weary. My limbs were like sandbags, my head a boulder.

Summoning all my strength I raised my chin; and found myself looking up into the face I had taught myself to hate. *My* face. *My* halo of curls. *My* gaze both grave and merry. *I* it was who Mother nestled to her breast. *I* whose fingers interlaced the fringes of her silken shawl. *I* upon whom she gazed. Just as it had been I who laughed when pinched . . . I who rolled about on the grass with—*You're in it.* At that, Reader, a force thrust me to my feet and threatened to topple me backward down the stairs. I stood my ground as within me there was brought to bear a tremendous pressure—like two land masses colliding and merging with metamorphic power.

It left me breathless.

But upright.

There followed a series of rumbling aftershocks.

When they abated I felt stronger. Lighter. And taller—as though I stood upon a plinth of two additional years. I looked once more upon the portrait.

My mother was lovely. I had been a bonny bairn. The grass in the portrait was the same as that upon which I had rolled in company with a playfellow who had pinched me and made me laugh; the same grass that only months ago had flattened, frost-bound beneath our two backs as we cloud-gazed, I and that same friend. I spoke aloud, her name, "Gwendolyn Haas." She alone had seen the truth of me and had not wished to alter it. *Don't let them take your extra bit off you, Charlotte.*

But I had . . . *I had let them.* All very well to blame Father, to assert my powerlessness in my own defence, to plead that I had sleep-walked into the abattoir under the mesmeric influence of lies. The fact remained, I had failed to flee. Like a caged bird who fails to recognize freedom when its door is opened, I had remained on my gilded perch. Not only had I *let* them, I had aided and abetted them. 'Twas *I* who had climbed willingly onto the table; *I* who lay down and opened obligingly my legs, *I* who sucked greedily the ether . . . All so that a part of my body, a part of my*self!* could be severed and treated as refuse. Even Father's bird bits met a kinder fate . . . Reader, despite protestations of inexperience, when it came to weeping I proved an able practitioner. I cupped my face and bent my head, the better to harness gravity in drawing the stuff of oceans from my eyes.

Was it loss of mere pleasure? If we were to lose the sun, would we decry the loss of "mere warmth"? Or if the rain, "mere moisture"? "Pleasure" was a flimsy word for an exuberant energy that was greater than the sum of its fleshly parts.

I knew what it was to suffer and that knowledge must henceforth guide my steps.

I looked again at the portrait. And I suddenly understood what the sprites of the swallet had been saying as they laughed and beckoned me on: my name. Both of them.

A gust of cold air, a ruckus below. I darted up and behind the balustrade as light broke in on the great hall and I saw Mr. Mungo entering with Murdoch on his heels. "Miss Charlotte?!" he called.

My late intention of self-slaughter came back to me like the recollection of a nightmare. They had amputated my flesh, but they could not shear my story from me. They had severed the physical link 'twixt Charles and Charlotte. But nevermore would we be put asunder.

"Search the gallery and the upper floors," he ordered Murdoch.

I fled soundlessly up the stairs. Streaked along the gallery between my forebears—all glowering except for the blank of the Blighted Heir—flew up the narrow service stairs to the servants' quarters and stole along the dark passage to Knox's room. I slipped in, pulling the door softly to behind me and, in the dim light of the shuttered windows, raced over to the false-bottom bed.

I knelt and fumbled for the spring mechanism even as boot-heels rang in the passage. It shot open and in a trice I was in the drawer, hauling it closed by means of the bed slats inches from my nose. The next instant I heard the door burst open and boots clomp in and about the room . . . pausing here and there. I heard the *whumpf* of the toy chest being opened and closed, the creak of a cupboard and, drawing nearer, the metal rings of Knox's clothes-curtain being torn aside. The boots resumed their slow-march only to stop inches from my thundering heart. A hefty blow to the wooden drawer-face at the level of my shoulder caused me almost to yelp as Murdoch, whether from petulance or in seeking to test the solidity of the bedstead, heaved a second great kick. It did not, of course, ring hollow because it was stuffed with me! *Stupid Murdoch*—Down, hubris! Help me, Humility, lest Pride foil me and I be dragged naked before my captor. I heard him leave. My heart raced like a stone skipping on the surface of a loch, until long after his footsteps receded.

I waited until, at last, all was silent. Was it near-asphyxiation which imparted the sense of peace? I felt entirely safe. I knew not if, in truth, Bonny Prince Charlie had lain here, but Gwendolyn Haas had. And suddenly I knew what I must do.

I sprang the lock and the drawer shot forth—the air was so chill, I was tempted to remain in my snug sarcophagus. But I clambered out and scooped up the bear skin along with an armload of contents, dropping all on the floor, the better to rummage out my clothing in the half-light. As though bobbing at the surface was the packet of letters in its silken shawl—I plucked it from the heap and tossed it to one side, then quickly rummaged out my cambric shirt and doeskin leggings, exposing as I did so, the tip of a scroll of paper—no doubt a stray letter come loose from the packet. I snatched it up—and paused—not notepaper. Parchment. I opened it and lay it flat upon the floor and made out the words . . . *Entitling the Bearer to One Trans-Atlantic Passage, Saloon Class, Liverpool to Boston.*

It was the pristine twin of the stained and crumpled parchment I had carried in my pocket all the way back to Fayne. I dropped it next to the packet of letters, then reached back into the pile to find my scarlet tunic emblazoned with the blue *Salamander Rampant*. Shivering, I seized my leggings, rose to my feet and, bending forward to step into them, saw, fully restored and nestled pink and plump between my legs, Prickle.

89

THE LAMPS HAVE LONG BEEN LIT and it is well past the hour when one might expect a caller, when Havers opens the door of No. One Bell Gardens to a messenger boy.

Moments later, in the parlour, Henry opens a letter and reads. Clarissa waits, her work idle in her lap. On tenterhooks. There is news.

Henry looks up and says blandly, "Mungo wishes to know if he ought to dredge the bog."

Clarissa lets out her breath. Resumes her work. "Good thinking. It must, after all, be put under the plough at some point. Bearing in mind, of course, the preservation of sufficient moorland to ensure sport." Her fingers fly, agile with the promise of an extra drop tonight. "You may not go in for shooting, Henry, but there is nothing to say your son mightn't. Not to mention the prospect of coal. Why not have Mungo order a survey?"

"He wishes," says Henry acidly, "to know whether I would have him look for Charlotte's body—" His voice disintegrates with the latter word and he hiccoughs. Removes his spectacles. No good attempting to stave off grief. *Howl, howl . . . ! She's dead as earth. Gone for ever!*

"Henry. Henry, I say."

He looks up, face slick and trembling. She speaks firmly. "Mungo is merely being practical. There is nothing to say she has . . . met with misadventure. Either on the bog or anywhere else. Indeed, the notion she might have made her way to Fayne is itself fanciful. She is bound to be hiding somewhere. I would not put it past Rosamund Gourley to be harbouring her even now. She will return when she is satisfied we have been punished sufficiently."

Henry hands her the note.

Fayne
January 26, 1888
Aberfoyle-on-Feyn

Dear Lord Bell,
I attended today your estate in company with my son. Together, in accordance with your instructions, we searched the house and outbuildings, grounds, etcetera. The only intelligence regarding whether Miss Charlotte had been or was still on the premises was provided by Byrn who, under close questioning, gave me to understand he had seen her "on fen." Cruikshank corroborated this by nodding in the usual manner. Cook claimed to have seen no one. It is my duty to inquire whether Your Lordship would have me undertake to dredge the boggy areas of the moor.

Your servant,
R. Mungo

Clarissa folds the note. Hands it back to Henry. Ignoring her, he rings for Havers. "Write to Mr. Mungo and tell him to do nothing. Pack my trunk. I return to Fayne tomorrow. Tell Sanders."

"Very good, Your Lordship."

"Henry if, God forbid, Charlotte has come to grief on the bog, would you not sooner know—"

"If my daughter lies buried at Fayne—" His voice breaks like a dry twig. It costs Henry more than he knows to remain upright and speaking, for the better part of him is on the ground weeping. "If she is to be found, Byrn will find her. Not Mungo and his minions."

"Henry—"

"And Havers. Hang the crape on the door."

"Brother—"

He quits the parlour.

Early next morning I sat on Byrn's stool before his smouldering peat fire and watched as he took from their hook his blade shears. It was all I could do to remain still—it tickled!—as he set about shearing me like a lamb.

I was overcome with joy. The porridge tasted like ambrosia. Never had there dawned such a splendid winter's morning on the moor, all was aglitter with new snow. I was happy to bursting—indeed my chest and shoulders strained against my tunic for I had grown in the intervening months and Cruikshank was obliged to open vents at the armpits and to loosen the waistband of my leggings. They, along with my sleeves, were too short by several inches but there was no time to remedy that and I tucked them into the tops of my hobnail boots. I had slept gloriously in my own bed which Cruikshank had made up for me, and Cook had outdone herself the night before with a hotpot followed by roly-poly pudding. As for my restored anatomy, all was in working order. (Cocoa.) I wondered at my body's capacity for regeneration. To what did I owe it? Certainly Dr. Chambers had not foreseen this. What's more, did it logically follow that, were I to cut off my little finger, it too would grow back? Like the tail of a salamander? Curious though I was, I was unwilling to test the theory.

I ran my hand over my freshly shorn head, soft as the bristles of a newborn piglet. I wrapped my mother's shawl round my bare neck and stepped out from the bothy, relishing the unaccustomed feeling of the cool air upon my scalp. I crunched across to the byre and entered the steamy warmth of hay and manure and hide. There was someone I needed to see before I set out.

She turned her great white head at my approach and cast her brown eye upon me. "Gossy." I put my arms round her neck and hugged her. I thanked her. I breathed in her smell of milk and earth, deep and soft. A snuffling behind me. Maisie. She lifted her snout in insolent greeting. I longed to mount her and feel the fury of the dear old sow. "I'll have you," I told her. She snorted.

In the stable yard, Byrn had Achilles hitched to the cart. Cruikshank brought me my waxed jacket and tweed bunnet from the gun room. "Thank you, Cruiky."

I folded both Certificates of Passage into one pocket, and the packet of Taffy's letters in the other—these latter I somehow saw as a vestige of my mother in need of disinterment along with her shawl.

Cook handed me my specimen case, stuffed with victuals. "Thank you, Cook."

Both servants bobbed. I said to Cook, "What is your name?"

"Adamson, miss."

"Thank you, Adamson."

Byrn mounted the cart and I slung my specimen case up into it. "I'll be right back," said I, and trotted to the house.

I entered my father's study. Various frowsty specimens perched here and there. Overhead a faded sparrowhawk "flew" suspended by a wire in the half light. In a heap on his desk, feathers and beloved broken bits. Atop the bank of pigeon holes stood the creature with the gull's beak, its rainbow plumage the only splash of colour amidst the drab of death. It was laughing—I smiled back. And pulled to the door.

I ran across the cindered forecourt to the cart. The Old Man would accompany me as far as the village but there could be no question of his taking me beyond; Mr. Mungo—to say nothing of Father—must not return to find him gone from Fayne. I might be penniless, but having walked from Edinburgh without food or proper clothing, I was equal to walking back, provisioned as I now was with both. I mounted the cart and took my place next to Byrn.

"Let's away," said I, unwilling to tarry another moment, each of which brought nearer the Mungos who, having failed to find my person in the house, might return to seek my body in the bog.

The Old Man did tarry, however, reaching into the pocket of his smock. He held out his hand to me—narrow and scored and strong as a spade was his palm. In it was a gold coin engraved with the profile of Julius Caesar—he who had been turned back by the Picts and sought but failed to grind the Celts underfoot.

I looked into Byrn's sandstone face and was visited by a fierce clutch in the region of my heart. I became aware of, as it were, a new element in the periodic table, vital and pervasive as oxygen: Love. I loved the Old Man. I loved Fayne, and all its works—the hollow-eyed house, the byre, stables, shed and moat, the moor! The bony fell, the wind. I loved Cruikshank. Welling up, my throat thick with emotion, I said, "Byrn, how did you know I was in peril on the moor the other night?"

"Cow told me."

". . . Gossy? But that was a dream."

"Belike."

"Thank you."

I took the coin. He clicked his tongue and Achilles walked on, following the track, and we ascended steadily the North Fell toward the white stone of lost meaning, sentinel at a forgotten border.

I was dead. And I was alive. I was Charles. And I was Charlotte. Robbed of my past, shorn of my future, I was yet more curious than frightened. I turned to look my last upon those beloved windswept vasts beneath whose drab and wintry dun there slumbered springtime lavender to come.

Then, as the cart crested the brow and descended toward the village, nor did I fear I might be recognized, even by the Reverend and Mrs. Haas, for I was disguised as myself.

90

SOME TWO AND A HALF months before, at the dawn of a crisp November morning, in a district hard by Leith, a comely young woman sits on an overturned crate at the foot of New Lane in full view of the beach, mending a net in company with her mother and mother-in-law, and her sisters and sisters-in-law.

The women are clad in stiff white Dutch-style caps that frame their faces. Some wear brightly coloured jackets. Others are bare-armed. Several wear about their necks broad handkerchiefs of spotted cotton. All sport woollen petticoats striped red-and-white that, kilted one atop the other, fall well above the ankle. They bend to their work and straighten too, paying out ropes, untangling lines—indications that none of them has ever known a corset. Their uniformity of dress is not owing to their shared family ties, but to their shared occupation. They are fishwives of Newhaven.

The comely young woman can see her husband's boat a way out past the pier along with several others, tall brown sails bobbing on the Firth of Forth, some already beyond the lighthouse whose beam has grown faint with sunrise. About to turn back to her length of hemp, her eye is caught by something up by the pier. White and beached. Thinking porpoise, she sets down her portion of net and walks along the shore.

Washed up at the base of a tarred wooden footing, clad only in strands of seaweed, is a body.

A woman.

Not dead.

"Nel, what is it?"

It takes three of them.

Not long afterwards, Miss Gourley is ladling porridge into earthenware bowls and Miss Elliot is leading the morning prayer when there comes a hammering at the door of the Refuge.

Moira slides open the hatch to see, in the sooty light of morning, a sturdy young fishwife, her dress as unmistakable as her odour of brine. Moira shuts the hatch and opens the door.

The young woman stands, feet planted apart, and explains her errand in an accent which is, even to Moira's gnarled ear, all but impenetrable. Her meaning, however, is clear, for next to her is a bicycle, to the rear of which is hitched a wicker cart; and in this clever creel-on-wheels is a person, covered by a canvas tarpaulin.

Miss Elliot arrives in the doorway. "What is it, Moira?"

Moira turns and answers, "Tell the chief, we got another Brigid."

Between the two of them and the fishwife, they carry the woman, still draped in the tarpaulin, into the Refuge. She is hugely fat. "Jesus, Mary and Joseph," gasps Moira—although she is a wiry person whose strength well exceeds her appearance, there are limits.

A knot of children and women crowds round. "Have done with gawking, and go eat your breakfast," snaps Miss Elliot. Miss Gourley hurries over to help and the four of them lay the woman on a pallet near the big woodstove.

Miss Elliot, Moira and the briny young woman stand so as to screen her from view as Miss Gourley lifts the corner of the tarpaulin. The woman is unconscious but breathing regularly. Amid lashings of seaweed and streaks of grime, her massive body is white to the point of appearing bleached. The salt water has been kind to the several abrasions but they will require bandaging and the bruises will require time. Her steel-grey hair is shorn almost to the scalp.

As though in perverse response to the warmth of the stove, the woman begins to shiver. Miss Elliot and Moira snap into action: warm blanket, turn the patient onto her side, rub the limbs vigorously through the rough wool. Wait and watch lest she vomit. When the eyes open, raise the head and, carefully, administer a spoonful of beef tea. Miss Gourley crouches close. "Madam, you are safe. Can you speak?"

The eyes close. Green eyes.

Miss Gourley rises and turns to the lass from Newhaven who has waited patiently—and aromatically. Her cheeks are ruddy with warmth and good health. "However did you manage?"

The young woman replies in a forthright manner, and Miss Gourley is able to glean that, having carried a hundredweight and more of herring and oysters on her back, it was no great feat to cycle with her cargo into Edinburgh—excepting the many stairs were "a bugger."

"You've lost a morning's work," says Miss Gourley. "I'll not see you out of pocket for your good deed."

The lass scoffs good-naturedly at the proffered coins, but cocks her head meaningly at the steaming kettle and fresh loaves stacked on the trestle table. Miss Gourley nods—'tis all very well to do one's Christian duty, but there's a fisherman will need a decent meal when he comes in with his catch at noon. So will the young woman, for when her husband's work day ends, hers begins in earnest, crying *"Caller herring, caller ou!"* door to door through town.

To the pail of porridge, pound of butter and two loaves worth their weight in winter wheat, Miss Gourley adds six rashers of bacon—"Nonsense, you're to take it." The young woman cycles off happily, her cart bouncing on the cobbles behind her.

Miss Gourley joins Miss Elliot standing watch over the sleeping woman. They have not attempted to carry her up to the infirmary on the second storey, but they have brought down a screen and stood it about her.

"Pregnant, I shouldn't wonder," says Miss Elliot.

"Hm."

Pregnancy—not infrequently coupled with a suicide attempt—is among the many reasons a woman finds herself at the Refuge.

It is, however, impossible to tell with this woman, given her corpulence, whether she be pregnant. Indeed she may simply have fallen overboard from a ship. As they watch, the steady respiration is punctuated by shuddering inhalations. Shudders give way to convulsive trembling.

"Moira," calls Miss Gourley over her shoulder. "Send for Mr. Moore."

Miss Gourley and Miss Elliot roll the woman onto her side to prevent her choking then Miss Gourley crouches and grasps the woman in a firm embrace about the shoulders as Moira sits on the woman's legs and they ride out the bucking seizures, while, at no little risk to her fingers, Miss Elliot holds a clothes peg between the woman's teeth to save her biting her own tongue—noting, as she does, the full set of teeth. Clean.

Mr. Moore is all but mobbed upon entry into the Refuge. It is no more than he is accustomed to, and he takes it in good-natured stride, removing his waxy old hat, making his way unhurriedly down the room as a clutch of worried mothers dog his steps—"You'll have a look in his gob, will you—" "The ringworm's crawled over t'other side of her wrist—" "He can't open his eye for pus." Assuring them all of a look-see, he slips round the screen to find the patient seizing in the protective grip of three highly capable women.

The elderly doctor sets down his medical bag and—not without difficulty—kneels at the patient's side. He opens the bag and withdraws a leather-bound case. He lifts its small metal clasps and opens, like a book, his hypodermic kit. Behind him a child screams, a mother scolds, "Good enough for you for peeking, silly goose."

He selects a needle and screws it into the glass-and-metal syringe. A *kerflump* behind him—someone has fainted. Reaching back into his bag, he withdraws a vial. Holding it upside down, he raises it to the light, pierces the seal with the tip of the needle, pulls slowly back on the plunger to draw a clear viscous fluid into the glass tube. Close by his ear, Miss Elliot shouts, "A perimeter of ten feet on pain of exile from the premises!" The woman's arm is thrashing in Miss Gourley's hold. Miss Elliot, without needing to be asked, takes firm hold of it below the elbow, applying pressure that a vein might show itself. Presently, Mr. Moore pierces the needle into the crook of the elbow and injects the contents of the hypodermic syringe. Within seconds, the seizures subside to trembling, and the women are able to loose their hold, rise and wipe the perspiration from their faces.

Moira and Miss Elliot withdraw in order to get things back on track. Miss Elliot can be heard barking orders all the way up to the second floor—Miss Gourley remains while Mr. Moore examines the patient.

The pulse is elevated, which is expected, but the heartbeat is strong and steady, and the lungs sound clear. Reflexes normal, including the pupils as well as the facial muscles, which respond when stimulated, diminishing the possibility of stroke. There is no indication of blockage or mass upon palpation of the abdomen. "Might I trouble you for a lamp, Miss Gourley?"

By the augmented light Mr. Moore is able to ascertain there are no sores in the patient's mouth. Nor are there any on her body, the superficial injuries associated with her immersion in the Firth such as contact with rocks, shingle, debris and the pier footings notwithstanding. Nor are there marks of disease, violence, restraint or, finally, rape. Hypothermia certainly, but well in hand now. That leaves the seizures.

Mr. Moore rises—again not without effort—and covers the patient back up with the blanket. Turning to Miss Gourley, he says, "Florence Nightingale could use you on the battlefield."

"This is a battlefield, Mr. Moore."

"It is that." He nods. "She was unconscious when brought in?"

"Yes. What do you reckon? Pennyroyal gone wrong?"

"Possibly. Though I would expect to see signs of miscarriage by now, considering the seizures. One would almost say a sedative dependency."

"Really?" This would be unusual at the Refuge, such drugs being costly and more or less confined to the "better classes."

Mr. Moore says, "I see no intravenous marks . . ." He bends once more and, taking one of the woman's hands, gently opens it to display the soft, uncalloused hand. The hand of a lady.

"Not to mention the teeth are perfect," says Miss Gourley.

"But her hair, shorn like this . . ."

"I wonder. She may be a nun."

"She may well be."

"Is it possible she is pregnant?"

"I think not. But she does appear to be parous."

"Mm, wouldn't be the first time a nun gave birth, whether before or after becoming a Bride of Christ."

"Psychiatric inmates are sometimes shorn of their hair."

"Against lice?"

"And to stop them pulling it out, or strangling themselves."

Miss Gourley blows out a long breath. The woman lies quiet but for intermittent trembling. "You think she may have escaped from the Asylum at Morningside?"

"There's her girth too, you see," he says, reaching into his bag. "The superintendent there is known for his 'gospel of fatness.' I may just write to him." He hands Miss Gourley a clear bottle along with a dropper. "Here is your culprit, I'm guessing. And your cure."

She reads the printed label: "CHLORAL HYDRATE IN SOLUTION."

Mr. Moore instructs Miss Gourley in the protocols of weaning the patient from the contents of the clear bottle. She must not receive too much. And, as importantly, she must not receive too little.

"I've cleared you a place, Mr. Moore," says Moira. He thanks her and takes a seat at the long refectory table between a boy whose cheeks look to have been scrubbed raw and his mother, who hides her smile with a hand. Around him the room fills up for the noonday meal.

Afterwards, Mr. Moore pushes back his chair and sees to a variety of ailments, swabbing sores, lancing boils, dispensing "oinkments" and advice—"Leave off scratching, if you can." Reassurance—"it'll get better on its own." And, in one case, a promise of surgery to repair a fistula in a young woman named Shelagh who started out as a Brigid until she could be sure Miss Gourley would not send for her father. "An angel, so Miss Gourley is," she says to Mr. Moore.

Meanwhile, Moira and Miss Gourley sponge the new Brigid, dress her in a fresh nightgown and diaper, all with an efficiency worthy of a field hospital. Next order of care is to get the poor woman out of the din of the main-room-cum-refectory and up into the peace and quiet of the infirmary.

91

LESS THAN A WEEK LATER, there is a cot in the corner of the main room behind the screen near the stove, and there Brigid lies.

This arrangement follows an arduous—even hazardous—ascent and subsequent descent, to and from the second-floor infirmary, with the unconscious patient on a stretcher borne by as many able bodies as could fit round it.

Up in the infirmary, Moira, together with a permanently disgruntled woman called Peg who is nevertheless a dog for work, did round-the-clock duty including adhering to the regimen of weaning from the clear bottle—

"Pee-yoo, can't imagine wanting to swaller this, can you?"

"Time was, I thought the same of rum," says Peg.

There were the greater-than-usual exertions required to shift the bedpan in and out from under the patient who, though not quite conscious, had got back the knack of not fouling her diaper. There were the Herculean labours of getting her fed with beef tea and turned and washed—not only to keep her clean but to ward off bedsores. All of this was merely extra effort and might have been borne but for the—well you couldn't call it crying, there wasn't no tears, 'twas more a bellowing this Brigid got up to whenever the room fell silent—there is a limit, even for a Gorbals lass and a Dublin flower-seller when it comes to the basic human need of a wink of sleep. The poor thing sounded like a cow that's down and can't get up to birth.

After three days, a haggard Moira assured Miss Gourley that the new Brigid would die of loneliness if Moira didn't strangle her first unless Peg beat her to it. The patient was precariously returned to the ruckus of the ground floor. Thus, for the past week and a half, Brigid has lain quietly, apparently soothed by the din and the company. At night, Moira, Peg, Miss Gourley and Miss Elliot take turns sitting with her, singing or reading aloud or murmuring softly any old nonsense, the slightest lapse of which triggers the hollerations.

By week's end, there has yet to appear a notice in any newspaper of a missing woman, whether from the Asylum or otherwise—nor even of a shipwreck—and Miss Elliot wonders aloud if it mightn't be time to seek out whatever religious order is shy of a nun, but Miss Gourley hesitates. Given the likelihood the woman did not end up in the Firth by accident, whether by her own hand or that of another, is it not prudent to wait? "Wait for what?"

"Until she wakes and can tell us who she is."

At the end of the first week, amid the cacophony—clattering of objects, a wash of voices, female mostly, some Irish, squabbling, soothing, babies crying, children screeching, laughing—one voice separates out like a thread from a snarl, and Mae recognizes it.

Opens her eyes a slit. What is the woman's name? Hate her. Loves Henry. Horse-face. *Pain.* Need more than what they give her. Shaking. Sweating. Gone. To sleep, or somewhere like it. Wake, or something like it. Through slits. Sees. Narrow back, knotted bun. There are two of them. Women who can't get husbands. Where is Henry? *Pain.* There has been a mistake. *Medicine. Not enough.* A raspy voice, "You're at the Refuge for the Poor Irish Among Us." That's plain funny. *Feel sick.* What a funny dream this is.

"Miss Gourley," calls Moira. And when the chief joins her—"Well she's gone quiet again but she were just now laughing."

Over the next few days, they all hear Brigid's laughter. Sometimes in the dead of night. It is eerie when hollow. Frightening when girlish.

"Any joy from Morningside?" Miss Gourley knows how busy he is, and is almost loath to ask.

"They regret to report, no."

In fact, Mr. Moore received a terse assurance from the asylum's Assistant Alienist: *No such breach of the security of the person has occurred.*

There are private establishments, of course. But, being private, they are under no obligation to disclose the fate of their inmates to any but the persons who put them there in the first place.

They are in the scullery. Miss Gourley is taking inventory among sacks and barrels. Moira is up to the elbows in pink suds, washing the blood from a "jelly rag." "One thing's for certain, Chief, Brigid's no pregnant," says Moira.

"Well that's one question answered," replies Miss Gourley, adding briskly, "You'll need to order three sacks of potatoes, Moira."

By the second week, Mr. Moore is satisfied the patient is out of danger. He replenishes the clear bottle with an ever-diminishing amount of chloral hydrate.

Mae.

When she woke all those years ago on the floor of the great hall at Fayne to find her child dead and gone, the shock undid her. As it must. Shock strikes time still. Paralyzes the body temporarily, as though to give mind, heart and soul a chance to reorganize prior to facing an altered reality; after which, Time can begin again, ushering in the sequence of horror, sorrow and all the terrible etceteras to which we are heir, and without which we can never find our way back into life. But when her husband said, *You drowned her*, the shock that ought to have given way to grief was suspended, as though cast in amber. A suspension which has been maintained for twelve and a half years with the help of drugs and hopelessness. But she is waking up. And her grief is waking with her.

Over the next many days, they all hear Brigid's whimpering. In the night, when it is pathetic. And in the day, when it is bleak.

By the third week, Mr. Moore's concern shifts, for though fully weaned from the drug, the patient seems never fully awake. Her eyes stream tears, but as yet, no one has seen her open them since that first morning.

A blood-freezing cry. Followed by a ragged agony, is it even human? "Miss!"

It is the sound of fresh sorrow, the sound that sirens are modelled on to obliterate thought in favour of fear. In the pre-dawn, Moira grabs hold, and now Peg is here, "Christ on the Cross!"

"Help me, for feck!"

Mae is caught in the current that drags the stricken from stagnant shock to turbulent grief. Because it has just happened! Fresh, oh as fresh today in the stale air of the Refuge as that night in the great hall at Fayne, the mud still wet and caking her body, filling her mouth, stinging her eyes—*She's dead. You drowned her*—it has just happened, just now, just this moment, "Charles!" the name is ripped raw from her throat.

Peg grunts, "I'll hit her back in a minute so I will."

Miss Gourley is there, "Onto her side."

"On three," says Miss Elliot and counts off.

They get her turned, the sobs gush from her like water from a storm pipe. Moira is reaching in her pocket for a clothes peg, Miss Gourley stops her. "It's all right. She's crying. In earnest now." Miss Elliot rocks back on her heels with a sigh. Miss Gourley places a hand on the hectic brow. "It's all right, Brigid."

Moira doesn't need to be asked to put the kettle on. Peg doesn't need to be asked to hold her tongue.

Great gouts of sorrow, no longer a dumb-beast bellow but keening grief, the kind with knowledge in it. O, Grief. Sombre friend, without whom—but why must your ways be so hard?

Come, Grief. Come, Life.

In the fourth week, Mae refuses food and water.

"Brigid. Brigid, can you hear me, my dear?"

His voice is so kind. True, he abandoned her. Like everyone else. Still. There is his smell—it must be raining out, for his coat is releasing the must of innumerable rains, reminding her of . . . *Your father is dead.* She hears the old doctor say, "It feels like the end, my dear, but 'tis not."

She feels the warmth of his dry hand on her brow; feels her eyes open. They fill with the sight of the weathered face, the kind old eyes. She watches as the face takes on an expression of such deep concern that she closes her eyes once more lest they drown in the overflow of her heart. Hears him say, quietly, "Lady Marie?"

She opens her eyes.

He says, "Don't be afraid, I will tell no one. But whatever has happened, dear, you are safe here."

In her first voluntary act since stepping from the pier into the sea, Mae takes his hand.

92

SHE CRIES ONLY in her sleep now. But she sleeps for a full day. And through the next.

"She's like to die," says Moira.

"Let her get on with it, then." Peg.

Miss Gourley is waiting patiently when Brigid wakes and opens her eyes. Beautiful, deep-green eyes—they turn away. "It's all right, Brigid. You have lovely eyes, and I am glad to have finally seen them. I wonder, can you tell me your name?"

No reply.

"Do you remember it?"

Nothing.

"I'll tell no one of your whereabouts without your leave. But it might help me to help you were I to know who you are."

It may be a case of dementia or—oh, there are any number of names and diagnoses, the important thing is, a permanent home must eventually be found for the woman, but why has she not been missed? This preys on Miss Gourley. The woman is a mother. By all indications, a lady. An inconvenient lady . . . ? Gentlemen have, before now, put away wives who went mad. Or sour.

Mae knows she mustn't speak lest she give herself away. They'll send her back. Whatever God wants of her, He wants her alive. And awake. To suffer. But for how long? How long, O Lord?

What year is this? Through how many years did she not grieve? Maybe that is what God wants of her. To grieve for as many years as she was in limbo. Before He'll let her come Home. *To Momma*. Don't say it out loud. Don't say anything. Your baby died. Because you could not keep him safe. But you tried, dear girl. You tried your hardest.

———

"How long we going to keep her?" Peg doesn't bother to whisper.

"I'm sure you'd rather we called you by your own name," coaxes Miss Gourley. She presents pen and paper. "Perhaps you'd rather write it down." The woman's stare is as blank as the page.

Miss Gourley looks for a sign in the woman's eyes. The lovely . . . strangely familiar . . . green eyes.

In the fifth week, Miss Gourley makes a point of accompanying Mr. Moore to the vestibule. He is satisfied Brigid is well weaned of the drug, and can find no physical reason why she mayn't speak, or stand and walk. Miss Gourley says, "We can't keep her indefinitely. 'Tis unfair to those whose need is more pressing, but . . ."

"Time," says Mr. Moore.

"Heals all wounds, aye. Leastways, scabs 'em over."

He chuckles.

"She looks familiar." She has blurted it.

The old doctor cocks his head. "Does she?"

"Foolish, I know, only . . . Mr. Moore, do you not see a resemblance?"

"To . . . ?"

"Lord Henry's late wife, Lady Marie." He waits. She adds, "I said 'twas foolish."

"Not at all, Miss Gourley, stranger things have happened."

"But do you see it? The resemblance?"

He replies, "I can't say as I do, my dear. Which is not to say 'tis no there."

"Of course it isn't there. Lady Marie was your patient through all her . . . travails. If there were a resemblance, you'd be sure to see it."

"Aye, you're right there." He dons his hat, smiles and departs.

A lesser woman might exclaim, but Miss Elliot merely says, "She's lactating."

Dark wet patches on the nightgown. Miss Elliot draws the screen and Miss Gourley unbuttons the nightgown. Says briskly, "Cabbage leaves, Edna."

Miss Gourley waits in silence. Whatever baby suckled at those breasts is long gone, whether grown or dead; and whether the woman is mad, guilty or merely unfortunate, she is bereaved. *I do not know all their histories, nor do I ask.*

Mae.

Breasts weeping along with her eyes.

Miss Elliot returns with several broad pale leaves. Miss Gourley cups the leaves about the woman's breasts. And without turning, says rather tersely, "I'll watch, you nap, Edna."

Edna knows not to argue. It's gone midnight and Rosamund looks all-in, but her terse tone is an indication she is in danger of weeping, and Edna would sooner bathe a cat than get 'twixt Rosie and her private sorrow.

Alone now, Miss Gourley bends closer to Brigid and asks, "What happened?" Her throat constricts, tears stand in her eyes, she stems them. Then, again rather tersely, "Whatever it is, God loves you."

The woman is calmer now. The green eyes look back at Miss Gourley, they focus and . . . their familiarity is disorienting. Perhaps it is this blend of familiarity and anonymity which prompts Miss Gourley to say, "I had a baby too, Brigid."

The green eyes never waver. And Miss Gourley endeavours to keep her voice equally steady as she quietly tells Brigid of the freckled young man with his lost penny whistle and injured ankle. Of the book over which their two heads bent and touched that day. Of Mr. Moore's kindness in finding a loving home for the child. "A baby girl."

Today, Brigid stood up. With the help of Moira, Peg, Miss Elliot and Miss Gourley, before sinking back to her cot.

"Meek as a lamb, God bless her," says Moira on one side of the bedpan.

"And big as a whale," says Peg, on the other.

Today, Brigid rose unaided to her feet and walked, leaning on Moira, to the stove and back. "Well done, Brigid!" Applause from several of the women along with wee Sean Padraig Archibald who looks even younger than his eight years and has been ordered by his mother, Peg, to stop growing lest he be turfed out for being too nearly a man.

Brigid has taken to a chair behind the stove. Her occasional perambulations are now less an occasion of applause than grumbling, for she stands like a rock in a stream and when she does move, seems not to have a grain of sense—"Jesus H, she walked through my dirt pile again afore I could sweep it into the dustpan!"

Listless and staring, while people work and chatter about her, as though she were deaf as well as mute.

"Lost her babby," says Moira on one side of the commode.

"Lost mine too. Down the well," says Peg, on the other.

"You never."

"'Twas drown or starve."

"You're going to hell."

"I've been to hell."

Today, Brigid rose and visited the privy all on her own out back of the scullery.

Applause. "Good on you, Brigid!"

Knocked over a bucket of dirty water on her way back—"Oh, for the love of feck!"

They give her jobs, but she's useless. Either she's forgotten how to shell a bean or she never knew. Moira shows her the way of it but she's all thumbs. Nor does she know her way round a spurtle, can't so much as stir the porridge. Just sits. Following the children with her eyes.

In the fifth week, the Refuge is decked with pine boughs and cut-out paper stars and snowflakes. Following evening prayers, amid the bustle of bedtime while refectory transforms to makeshift dormitory—this time of year always sees an influx—Miss Gourley and Miss Elliot confer in low tones before the screen.

"No one's come to claim her."

"She isn't a lost handbag, Edna."

"No, but she has reached a sort of . . . plateau. She can't do a lick of work, and the care we give her is care taken from others more needy."

"I'll admit, I've been a mite . . ."

"Sentimental."

"Bloody hell, Edna."

"You know I'm right, Rosie."

"We can hardly turn her into the street."

"No, but we can post notice—"

"No."

"Then we'll take her to the Royal Asylum—"

"She'll never be seen again."

"She'll be safe."

"Will she?"

"Safer than in the sea. Safer than wherever she came from."

Miss Gourley sighs, "I suppose we've done our duty."

"I'm sorry, old thing."

"Don't be daft."

"Gives me the willies," says Peg. "Staring all the livelong day, like she wants to eat them up."

Now Peg's said it, 'tis plain to see, Brigid has eyes only for the bairns. Moira scoops up a squalling wee one from young Jenny. "I'll give her back, don't worry."

"I'm worried you will."

Moira places the babby, flailing and wailing, in Brigid's generous lap. Brigid immediately embraces it. It ceases fussing and quiets.

"Abracadabra!" cackles Moira. The women laugh.

Brigid is put to work, holding babies.

Earns her keep.

The food at the Refuge is wholesome and plentiful but does not follow the gospel of fatness. Thus, by the new year, Brigid's bulk has dwindled to plumpness. Her hair has grown too, a thick silver carpet, and defining lines appear in her face. Miss Gourley says, "Why, Brigid. I believe you are quite pretty."

Brigid laughs. Silently.

Then, one night in late January, Henry comes in search of "my daughter, Charlotte."

The goose-flesh streaks in patches the length and breadth of Mae's body.

"Chief, she's got chills."

Shivering.

"She doesn't feel feverish."

Joy.

Too much.

Then: *HE LIED!*

"Quick, hand me a clothes peg."

Mae, stop. Push it away, far, far, keep it at a distance, farther still. Until it is a dot.

On her horizon.

Then, every day she allows it to draw a little closer.

Until a few days later she can see its outline. Like a picture in her mind's eye. The title of which is, *He Lied*.

And by week's end, she can think it—*Henry lied to me. I didn't kill my baby*—without its catching fire and burning her to dust. Most importantly, she can think, *Charles is alive*. My baby boy. My big strong boy. He has run away from his father—good boy! . . . *A minor surgical procedure*—Don't think of it.

You made your peace with it once before.

Men came home from the war terribly injured in just that way.

Charles!

She has screamed it in her head this time.

She will wait until the others are asleep tonight, then slip through the streets and meadows, calling, "Charles! Charles, it's Momma. I've come to find you, my darling!"

93

I EMERGED FROM the thronging platform at Waverley Station into the night. The elegant lanterns on their tapered stands had been lit all along the length of the bridge. The sky was a study in charcoal strokes as, leaving behind the sour scent of trains shunting below, I followed my own distended shadow from pool to pool of lamplight toward the street. In West Princes Street Gardens, leafless trees stood stark, their limbs uplifted as though in supplication, and I touched the brim of my hat to the Scott Monument as though greeting an old friend. My steps seemed to ring out the more keenly in the cold as I strode on, my specimen case jingling against my side and weighed down as though with pirate treasure. The coachman that morning had kindly agreed to accept my gold coin and, in returning to me "the change," obligingly counted out for me the train fare I would need at Berwick-on-Tweed. To this sum he added a fortune in coinage, thus I had more than enough to be getting on with, as Gwen might say.

I knew I must hurry if I was to arrive before the conclusion of evensong. I pulled my tweed cap down more firmly, as much to warm my newly naked head as to obscure my face. If my manner of dress drew looks, my sex attracted none. The coachman had called me "sir" as had the porter in the train. Now as I walked along, freedom enlivened my sinews and sharpened my senses. The selfsame freedom I had only ever enjoyed on the moors at Fayne. Was this all it took? A trick of haberdashery and an overzealous barber? It occurred to me to wonder whether there were, even now, other females comporting themselves in men's attire and with cropped locks. For that matter, might there be men who donned women's clothes? But why a man might choose to exchange his freedom for the fetters of female-dom was as yet still a mystery to me.

My breath puffed out before me as I hurried past the stone columns of the General Post Office. Up ahead was the imperial dome of General Register House. I seemed to see both these monuments to symmetry fairly vibrating with the cacophony of human life within. It struck me that we poor creatures require august edifices to conduct and codify our chaos—that with every moment, every scrap of paper within was returning to dust along with the buildings themselves. And somewhere beneath the Roman dome of Register House, even now dispersing carbon was the record of my birth—Charles's birth. I wondered suddenly whether his—my—death was likewise recorded within. And what of Charlotte's birth?

I kept clear of George Street, though no one from Bell Gardens was likely to be out on a cold "Scotch Sunday" evening, and sprinted up South St. Andrew Street, as though to outrun thoughts of the past. At Queen Street, I made for the low iron fence, vaulting it in a single bound and, like an uncaged animal, pelted the length of its Gardens, heedless of curving pathways and slumbering beds, through thickets and branches, hurdling fences between streets until I came to India Street. My chest chugged like an engine as I forced myself to walk at a seemly pace past the house where James Clerk Maxwell had been born, toward Stockbridge and the gentle curve of Circus Lane.

It was lined both sides with two-storey houses and shops all adjoined and nestled against a backdrop of trees. The smell of wood fires embraced me, and in more than one glowing window there passed unhurried silhouettes. I felt upon my lips the kiss of a snowflake. I looked up to see downy flakes falling lazily from the darkness.

Up ahead, beyond the bend and soaring above the treetops, was the stone bell tower of St. Stephen's Church. The great minute hand was approaching the hour and I hastened along the pavement, softening with snow underfoot, past snug dwellings and purveyors of eyeglasses, lamp oil, finest teas until I came to a house on my left where a sign hung from a standard above an arched oak door. The sign bore a crest: a lamp casting light on an open book, encircled by Latin script, *Libertas per Doctrinam*. And below it, MISS GOURLEY AND MISS MELLOR'S SCHOOL FOR GIRLS. Above the door itself, painted over but faintly discernible: "J. D. Mellor Tobacconist and Snuff Manufacture." Just then the bell of St. Stephen's commenced to toll the hour. I ran toward it. Coming out from Circus Lane, I stopped short before St. Vincent's Episcopal Chapel. It hunkered, Gothic, and altogether Romish to my eye, directly across from tall, pale St. Stephen's. Just then, the timbered chapel door opened, disgorging an ecclesiastical glow. Quickly, I stole up the broad, now slippery, steps of St. Stephen's and into the shadow of its doorway whence I watched as, along with the light, there emerged a generously proportioned lady of erect carriage—Miss Mellor!—followed by two lines of young ladies, identically cloaked and bonneted. I saw her immediately, and it was all I could do not to cry aloud, "Gwendolyn!"

I waited until they had filed into Circus Lane then I slipped across the street and in through the shrubbery. I crept along in back of the houses until I calculated I was behind the school. I looked up. Snow was falling more thickly now. Presently a light appeared, then another and another. I waited until, in a dormer window on the second storey, framed by the branches of a wisteria vine, a lamp appeared. And behind it, a girl. And behind her, Gwen.

Jumping, I grabbed hold of the stone ledge and hoisted myself up and over the garden wall, dropping not quite soundlessly into a barrow of coal clinkers. I paused. Then I crossed to the base of the magnificent vine, its gnarled strength unveiled by winter, and climbed.

I reached the window, and so relieved was I to see Gwen moving about with another girl as they divested themselves of ties, collars and cuffs, that I tapped at the window and smiled. They froze. The girl approached the window and, in a friendly gesture, I doffed my hat. She screamed, Gwen hurried over. I waved and she pushed opened the window, very nearly dislodging me from my perch. Seeing me, she turned and hissed, "Maeve, shutup."

I climbed through the window and it was all I could do not to weep with joy at the sight of that freckled face. But Gwen's look to me was as stern as it was incredulous. "What are you doing here?" And, with a note of concern, "What's happened to you?"

I took heart. "Gwendolyn, I am sorry for the abominable manner in which I treated you when last we met."

"So this is your 'secret admirer,'" said the other girl with a sly look to Gwen.

"Bollocks, 'tis—" She caught herself with a look to me.

I bowed, "Charles . . . Snowe, miss."

The girl giggled. Gwen said, impatiently, "This is Maeve. Miss Beaton, rather."

"Miss Beaton, I am pleased to make your acquaintance." And I inclined my head as I had seen Father do. One could not help but note she was uncommonly pretty. "I have heard good report of you from our mutual friend Gwendolyn."

"I've heard nowt of you, Mr. Snowe." She giggled again. And blushed.

"Maeve, wait in the passage and keep watch."

Miss Beaton made a show of reluctance, but obeyed.

I found I was elated. My cheeks felt warm, the scene before me fairly shone—the snug room was of a simple charm wholly new to me, and of a scent reminiscent of pencil shavings, apples and . . . yes, tobacco. The walls were of white-washed plaster. On the polished plank floor lay a colourful oval carpet of woven rags. Two tidy narrow beds hugged each corner on either side of a door above which hung a framed Bible quote about the Wise and Foolish Virgins, its script as though illuminated by a lamp—the same lamp that figured in the school crest. Flanking the window, a pair of desks held each an actual lamp amid pencils, "scribblers" and text-books. A washstand and plain wardrobe completed the furnishings.

"I say, Gwennie, your room is cracking."

"Charlotte, what's going on?"

"Do you remember when you said I was in the portrait?"

"What of it?"

"You were right."

"Of course I was, your mother was pregnant with you at the time."

I shook my head. I whispered, "I am Charles."

". . . What do you mean?"

"When I was born, they thought I was a boy. Because of . . . the extra bit."

I watched as the import of my words dawned on her. Presently, she drew a long breath and let it out through her lips. "You. Were Charles."

I nodded.

"Then . . . Oh, Charlotte," she breathed. "We've been friends for life." She held out her hands. I took them. "It was you and I on the grass," she said, and her eyes filled with tears.

I nodded.

"'Twas you I pinched."

"'Twas I who laughed."

She hugged me. I wrapped my arms about her, taut and supple as a bow she was, and Reader, so dear.

The door opened a crack. "All right, Gwendo?"

"I'm fine, Maevey, leave us."

"Lights out in twenty, ye wee hussy." The door closed once more.

"Gwen, you were the only one who told me the truth."

"Charlotte," she whispered. "What have they done to you?"

"You told me not to let them."

"And . . ."

"I did let them."

She cupped her hands over her mouth. "Oh Charlotte, dear one, did it hurt?"

"Not at first. Then it did. Terribly. The doctor told me I would never feel anything. In that region. Again."

She covered her face.

"Gwennie, all is well, I—"

The door opened and Maeve slipped in, "Quick, she's coming."

I kicked my jangling specimen case under the bed and dove after it.

A scuffling of feet, a scraping of chairs and a flapping of pages as the girls hastened to their desks a moment before footsteps sounded in the passage and the door opened. I heard a lady's voice. "Fifteen minutes to lights out, gels."

And their reply in unison, "Yes Miss Mellor."

I was of a sudden seized with hilarity. I pinched my nose the way Gwendolyn had taught me those many months ago, and I was still shaking when she hauled me out by the ankles. Maeve too was doubled over and "fit to be tied." Gwen chided us, "Enough. Maeve, out, Charlotte, Charles, whatever your name is, sit."

We obeyed.

Alone once more with Gwen, I made to continue my tale but she broke in, "'Twas you in your mother's belly when she ate of the fen."

My jaw fell open. "'Moor-made.'"

"What's that?"

"Something Byrn said to me. In my dream. If it was a dream . . ."

Scarcely pausing for breath, I related to my friend all that had befallen me; from the fateful moment when I entered Aunt's parlour in search of sweeties, through my flight from Edinburgh; my harrowing vision on the bog, and my wondrous vision within it; my rescue by Byrn, and my recovery at his hands and Cruikshank's; the latter's revelation that my mother had not died in the bog, that indeed neither servant knew what had become of her. Of the physical restoration of my "extra bit" three days following my immersion in the bog. In short, the whole of my recent history with all its shocks and perils and marvels up until the moment I had appeared at her window.

Gwen looked grave. "Your father must know what became of your mother."

"I dare not go back and ask him."

"Aye, but—"

Maeve whispered through the crack of the door—"Five minutes." A stripe of her face was visible, along with one bright green eye, and it was clear to me she had heard at least some of my strange tale, for the look she cast upon me with that one eye was full of wonder. I returned her gaze and, though I could not have said what possessed me, I winked. The door closed.

Gwen brought me back. "You might write him a letter."

"He thinks me dead."

She flinched.

"Gwennie, Father loves me too much to be anything but my jailer and my—" I stopped short, shocked by the word I had left unsaid. "I am to be rendered marriageable, Gwen. You were right. It was the plan from the start." The unsaid word hung in the air: *butcher*.

"Charlotte, I am truly sorry for my part in—"

"Gwendolyn Haas, dancing with you with a book on my head was among the happiest moments of my life."

"It's as though I'd been helping to fatten you for slaughter."

"Then you see why 'tis prudent I be thought dead. And kinder to Father; better a dead daughter than a live monster."

"I take umbrage!" She shot to her feet. "No one, not even you, is permitted to speak so of my friend."

Chills coursed up my sides. I rose likewise. "Gwendolyn, I came here tonight to ask you—"

"Charlotte, you can't stay here, you'll be found out, but I've got an idea—"

"Wait, Gwennie, listen. I have something to ask you."

"What?"

Sensible of the solemnity of the moment, in doubt as to whether I ought to drop to one knee, I clasped my hands behind my back. "As my friend. Will you follow me into exile?"

She appeared nonplussed.

From the inside pocket of my waxed jacket I produced the twin certificates; one good as new, the other smudged, wrinkled and frayed. "We can exchange them. We'll go to Paris. We'll take a loft, you can paint whilst I toil as a tutor. Or artist's model! We'll see Foucault's pendulum! And the *Mona Lisa* of course."

Maeve came in. "Time's up, lovebirds."

"And I've money," I said, ignoring her. "A fortune." With that I overturned my specimen case onto the rug.

"A fortune in farthings," said Maeve. Adding more kindly, "It'll buy ever so many sweets."

"Come quickly, Gwennie, we must fly." I set to scooping the coppers back into my case, aided by Maeve who drew close enough to me that her hair brushed my cheek and I experienced a curiously familiar sensation—

"I can't," said Gwendolyn.

"Whyever not?"

I started at a light touch upon my scalp—Reader, Maeve was *patting* me. "It's lovely and soft, feel it, Gwendo, it's like stroking a hedgehog."

"Charlotte—"

Footsteps along the passage. We froze. Sound of a door opening in a neighbouring room.

"Hide or bugger off," said Maeve, pulling her nightgown on over her clothes and jumping into bed with her boots on.

"Come with me," said Gwen, already opening the window. Maeve shot out from under the covers, dashed to the wardrobe, tore it open and flung at me a cloak for our friend, before leaping back to her bed.

In a deft move which bespoke practice, Gwen put a leg over the sill, turned, and dropped from sight. I climbed out to find her clinging to the vine several feet below me. A last look into the room showed Maeve with the quilt pulled up to her chin. She kissed her palm, then blew on it in my direction. I saw the latch move and, before the door could open, I ducked and flattened myself as far as possible against the vine with its sharp woody scent. From within came the voice of Miss Mellor. "Where's Gwendolyn, Maeve?"

"She's popped out to the jacks, miss, I mean the lavatory."

"In that case, I'll leave it to you girls to douse your own lamps."

"Certainly, miss. Goodnight, miss."

It seemed Miss Mellor would retreat, and we were about to make good our descent when suddenly her voice was directly above me. "I'll close your window, though, shall I? We can't have you catching a chill." As I watched, an ample arm reached forth and drew closed the windowpane.

Hearts pounding, we climbed down to the ground and dashed across to the wall. I boosted her over and together we trudged amid the trees and slipped along the cobbles of Circus Lane, before turning south along Howe Street.

"Where are you taking me?"

"Exile," she said.

94

WE TURNED QUICKLY into Northumberland Street. "Of note on your left is the house where Mary Somerville lived with her—"

"Come on," she exhorted me. "We've got to leg it."

Leg it we did, across Princes Street and onto the Mound. Past the Athenian splendour of the Royal Institution and the serene stone eye of Her Majesty Queen Victoria; past Egyptian sphinxes atop the National Gallery, we two wayward girls fled as though from the wrath of the old gods, running from the Past into the Future—located, ironically enough, in the Old Town.

Once across the Mound, she tripped along ahead of me and I followed the sound of her footfalls up slippery stone steps. We came out into the sloping High Street, past St. Giles', its crown steeple lost in darkness, and the pillar where the unicorn sat as though taking in the view, apparently unbothered by the chain that tethered it.

"Gwennie, is it not strange that Scotland's national animal is a fictional beast?" "Not at all. You can't defeat a beast that doesn't exist." With this Delphic pronouncement she slipped into a close, which came out under George IV Bridge. Here chimney smoke had settled into a ground fog thick as moor mist and as dangerous. I covered my nose and mouth with my cape and pressed on.

She led me through an inky—aye, and stinky—labyrinth with nary a pause—even when we traversed a sinister lane whose name engrimed in the corner bricks proclaimed it Horse Wynd. If it had smelled only of horse it would have been tolerable . . . Past Greyfriars Kirkyard, toward the Royal Infirmary where we slowed to a walk into Teviot Place. I paused, reverentially. "Come on," she urged.

We passed through a stone arcade into a quadrangle, all new in the lamplight with none of the grime of centuries. Looking up, I saw a clock embedded high in the wall, beneath which, inscribed in the stone:

ARS LONGA VITA BREVIS. I trembled with joy. Even as I wondered why Gwendolyn had taken me to the medical school of the University of Edinburgh in the dead of night. Before I could ask, she had slipped between wrought-iron bars into an alleyway. I followed her to the end of what appeared to be a cul-de-sac, and heard the sound of a rusty latch. "This way," she said, and opened a low door in the wall.

We were in a cramped and dingy courtyard, cluttered with barrels and an ash heap. Gwen stooped to pick up a bit of broken masonry and, drawing back her arm, pitched it aloft. It struck a third-storey window. I held my breath, staring up alongside her at the high casement where presently a leaded pane stuttered open. And emitted the head and shoulders of Mr. Margalo.

I sat on the one chair at a rough table on which my old tutor had made space amid books and papers, warming my hands round a mug of tea he had brewed on his penny hob. Gwendolyn sat on his low cot, while Mr. Margalo stood, hands clasped behind his back. We were in his student digs. O Reader, how glad was I once more to behold that pale angular countenance, the high clear brow, those steady brown eyes; to hear the rich reasonable timbre of his voice. He had admitted us via the tradesmen's entrance and spirited us up the back stairs.

I had clasped his hand in both my own and apologized for having believed ill of him. I thanked him for his steadfastness, and delivered, assisted by Gwendolyn, a *précis* of my recent history, concluding with a question. "Mr. Margalo, am I correct in supposing your given name to be Isadore?"

He flushed in the manner wholly familiar to me. He looked at Gwen who was likewise blushing. She said, quietly, "We are engaged."

I stood a moment speechless. Then felt a great smile break over my face, and joy suffused my whole being—my two greatest friends in the world were to be united. "There can be, therefore, no impediment to your accompanying us to Paris, Mr. Margalo." There in his garret, I felt akin to how I'd felt in the mist that day when I learned he was a foundling; that day when I confided to the palm of his hand the word I had heard sobbed on the moor, *Momma* . . . Now there were three of us as though together in a mist. And from within its embrace, I said, "I love you. Both."

They brought me into their confidence. They planned to elope when Gwendolyn turned sixteen years of age. Reverend Haas had vetoed the match, but Mrs. Haas had bestowed her blessing along with her own nest egg, on her daughter. "Enough to see us to Canada." They were bound for the city of Montreal where Mr. Margalo would take up a post in the nascent Department of Botany and Vegetal Physiology at the University of McGill College. As for Gwen, "Montreal isn't Paris, but 'tis *français, quand-même*." Adding, "And you must come with us. Mustn't she, Isadore."

"Yes, you must," said Mr. Margalo, warming to his subject. "You can study medicine, become a licensed physician. And not the first licensed female either, Canada boasts one already in the city of Toronto." His eyes shone, Gwen was beaming, "Say yes, Charlotte."

"Yes," I said. She laughed. They both did. I stretched forth my hands and we all three clasped one another's. "Exile is sweet with such friends."

Gwen sobered. "We must make you safe somehow in the meantime."

There and then, they formulated a plan with an ease that boded well for their married future. Outside the wind had risen, the glass rattled in the window and icy fingers breached the sash. Mr. Margalo said, "'Tis nigh on ten o'clock." No guests were permitted past ten, on pain of expulsion, "And no females at all ever," added Gwen, pulling her cloak snugly about her. We three slipped into the passage, and down the service stairs.

In the street once more, we bent our heads to the blowing snow, leaving behind first the gleaming university buildings, then rows of dignified dwellings where one by one lights were being peaceably extinguished. We passed beneath a span of South Bridge, delving ever deeper into a darkness scored by cries, whether of joy or terror I could not tell, until we were in the Cowgate.

I no longer expected to see women literally fallen onto the cobbles, but one now reeled from an archway to inquire in rough tones and vulgar terms whether I was desirous of intimate assistance. A clutch of ruffians heckled us and I shrank as they lurched into our path as though blown by the squall, but Mr. Margalo did not slacken his pace, thus did I take heart just as I had when following him across the bog, lengthening my own strides, reaching out to tuck Gwendolyn's free arm beneath my own, gallantly flanking her.

Much as the menace of these derelict adults had perturbed me, nothing could have prepared me for the shock of seeing, through the blizzard, three children huddled in a doorway. They were shoeless, with scarcely a shawl between them. I stopped. "What are you playing at?" I shouted over the storm, "Go home!"

They drew further back.

"Where are your parents?"

One of them laughed. Another set to crying.

The biggest one said, "Fuck off."

Gwen said, "Come with us."

The children squabbled, I heard one cry out, "She'll put us in pies."

"You'll be warm, leastways," said Gwen.

They followed, a clutch of shadow at our heels, and I wondered at the extremity of want that could drive children to commit themselves into the hands of strangers despite the prospect of being eaten by an ogre—the which I understood to mean they had reason to fear the appetites of adults.

On we plodded, drenched and near-sightless against the blast until: "Here we are," said Gwen.

The wind had dropped but the snow had turned to bitter rain. Above a recessed door I made out a painted sign. One of its letters, a G, had been overscrawled with the letter S, such that REFUGE had become REFUSE.

Gwen rapped smartly at the door.

"You'll be safe here," said Mr. Margalo, whether to me or the children I could not tell.

A sound like the report of a gun caused me to jump as a hatch shot open at eye level. It was followed by the sound of a bolt sliding, the door opened and a tall woman appeared, her lamp raised. "Have you need of refuge?" she asked in a voice at once calm and commanding.

Gwen stepped into the light. "Yes, Miss Gourley."

Thus did I meet the Angel of Cowgate.

95

WE WERE IN A VESTIBULE where unseen hooks were already over-laden with mean garments. A wiry woman with several teeth missing appeared and took the children in hand—the middle one by the ear—shooing them up a set of stairs, rasping, "This is all we need, we're full up!" By the light of her candle I saw their bare feet stumping up the steps, streaks of angry red showing through soot.

Abandoning our sodden outer-wear on the floor, we entered a cavernous room. Miss Gourley had betrayed no surprise, merely bidding us enter. Guided now by her lamp we walked toward the light at the far end.

Rising from a chair near the stove was a second lady, sharper-featured and, if possible, even more ramrod-straight than Miss Gourley. With scarcely a glance at us, she lifted a steaming kettle.

The circle of light served to deepen the surrounding shadows. The lady handed round mugs of "hot negus" and dragged a bench toward the stove. Mr. Margalo made to assist her but she ordered him "Sit." He obeyed, we all did, grateful for the warmth that was now almost painful in hands and feet. We sipped in silence the fortified beverage as steam rose from our skin and clothing—and from my mother's silk shawl which lay wilted about my neck.

Only now did I perceive, ranged on pallets in rows the length of the room and receding from the island of firelight, dozens of supine human shapes. Women, judging by shawls and wrappings . . . and children tucked marsupial-like in their mothers' garments. A baby whimpered. A woman's voice responded with a snatch of lullaby. Then the only sound was the hissing of the fire in the stove. The sharp-featured lady—"This is Miss Elliot"—had pulled up a chair opposite Miss Gourley and commenced to fill a pipe. Miss Gourley spoke quietly, "Mr. Margalo. Gwendolyn. What brings the two of you and your companion here on such a night and at such an hour?" Not a word did she say regarding Gwendolyn's obvious and serious breach of school rules. Nor did she remark upon the fact that Gwen and Mr. Margalo were confederates in this nocturnal enterprise.

Mr. Margalo replied haltingly, "Miss Gourley, allow me to introduce to you my young friend, Mr. Snowe." He cleared his throat and I held still as Miss Gourley regarded me with an equanimity both reassuring and nerve-racking. Something stirred beyond the stove and I took the occasion to avert my gaze from hers, expecting a cat might slip from the shadows. Miss Gourley returned her attention to Mr. Margalo; as did I, to see him swallow and fall dumb. Gwendolyn, sitting as straight-backed as Miss Gourley herself, piped up and I was soon so rapt with her tale, I quite forgot it was meant to be my own: she had me as a "Heriot's boy," originally a foundling, who was now threatened with "transportation."

Here the second lady interrupted, "Do you mean to say Headmaster Lowe has threatened one of his students with transportation?"

"No indeed, Miss Elliot," said Gwen, eyes wide. "The guardian of one of the other boys has threatened to transport Mr. Snowe."

"I am certain Mr. Lowe knows nothing of it," said Mr. Margalo, with a look to Gwendolyn.

"Then why not tell him?"

Gwen rushed in, "We'd not for the world put the headmaster in difficulties that he's in no position to remedy, the guardian of the other boy being very rich and vengeful. Mr. Snowe needs sanctuary 'til such time as he can emigrate. To Canada. Where he has friends."

More rustling. No cat.

I watched the blush creep from Mr. Margalo's collar to his brow. The round, woodsy aroma of Miss Elliot's pipe was in contrast to the wordless tension. It appeared Gwen had spent her last false coin, and I could see it cost Mr. Margalo dearly to lie, especially to Miss Gourley, who had herself engaged him to teach at Gwen's school.

At length she spoke. "What is the nature of the crime for which Mr. Snowe faces transportation?"

Gwen replied coolly, "A crime against nature, Miss Gourley."

Miss Gourley betrayed no surprise. Notwithstanding I knew myself to be considered a "mistake of Nature," I had no idea of what a "crime against Nature" might consist. Miss Gourley turned to me. I took a sip of the fortified brew. "What say you, Mr. Snowe?"

A drop went down the wrong way causing my eyes to water and I heard myself say, "I humbly beg shelter, Miss Gourley" in a high-pitched voice. Miss Elliot's brow rose. Miss Gourley's furrowed.

Gwendolyn shot a look to Mr. Margalo—who appeared somewhat at sea—then blurted their elopement plan, concluding with, "We have my mother's blessing, Miss Gourley, but I . . ." Gwen's face grew pink amid her freckles as, chin high, she fought back tears, saying, "I want yours too. You've always—You've always believed in me. I'd like to know you still will. Afterwards."

Mr. Margalo rose. "I wish to assure you, Miss Gourley, my conduct toward Gwendolyn has been honourable, as are my intentions. I will love and cherish her always."

"Mr. Margalo, is your benefactor aware of your plans?"

"He is, Miss Gourley."

She turned to Gwen once more. "You've a good mother, Gwendolyn. It is my honour to add my blessing to hers."

Gwen blew her nose and Mr. Margalo resumed his seat by her side, though somewhat nearer now. Miss Gourley appeared about to say more when from behind the stove came, no longer a rustling but . . . a chuckling? Miss Elliot rose and went toward the sound. "Did we wake you, Brigid?"

Miss Gourley's tone was suddenly crisp. "Now then, I do not doubt you both have the best of intentions. But I am sure your young friend would not wish to run you afoul of the law by accompanying you to Canada."

Gwen looked wary but said nothing.

Miss Gourley turned to me and, with a note of regret, "You do not, I presume, wish harm to your friends. Do you, Miss Bell?"

I froze. My tongue fused to the roof of my mouth.

She spoke quietly. "Gwendolyn, Mr. Margalo, it is best you take your leave now and we shall say no more about it." Turning to her colleague, "Miss Elliot, please send for Lord Henry."

I opened my lips to cry, *No!* but not a sound issued thence.

"Rosamund, oughtn't we to hear her out?"

"We've no right to harbour her, Edna, much as I might—we have no right, and we've much to lose." She cast her eye into the darkness and the dozens of sleeping forms.

"Miss Gourley," said Gwen. "Please let Charlotte come with us, please, don't send her back, she's in terrible danger—!"

"Indeed she may be, Gwendolyn, having only just undergone a surgical procedure—"

"Miss Gourley," said Mr. Margalo, "I will take responsibility for Miss Bell as her protector and provider, with the promise to see to her university education."

I could not move. Like a deer who, about to be eaten by a lion, lies with eyes wide, perfectly still; like a patient under anaesthesia; I was immobilized as, all about me, events moved inexorably toward my demise. Gwen was protesting through tears, a baby had begun to cry, Mr. Margalo was studying me with a look of concern, Miss Gourley was shaking her head with half-closed eyes, Miss Elliot had risen to send word to Bell Gardens, when—"Charles," came a thick voice from behind the stove. And, as though giving birth to a shadow, the darkness bulged and a shape emerged.

A beggarwoman, by the bundled look of her, shuffled forth. A woollen shawl draped about her head and shoulders obscured her face.

I heard Miss Elliot say, "Why Brigid, I am very glad to know you can speak."

The woman ignored her, standing as though transfixed.

"What is it, Brigid?" asked Miss Gourley.

As I watched, the woman's arms opened. Her shawl slipped back to reveal a head of cropped silvery hair not much longer than my own. Her face now exposed, it was plain to see she was staring. At me.

In blithe tones now, strangely at odds with her appearance, the woman said, "Charles." Her voice—her accent—worked on me as a sort of spell. Woozy of a sudden, I grasped the edge of the bench. Time itself seemed to shift along with the floor.

"Hush now, you'll wake others," chides Miss Elliot. "'Tis no your baby, Brigid, 'tis a young lass—"

Brigid bares her teeth at them. Inhuman, the snarl. All too human, the sobs as she bends over the girl, clasps and rocks her—grieving the long-lost child she claims to have found, weeping, "My baby, my baby, my baby . . ."

Babies awaken as though at a summons, and the darkness is jagged with their crying. Some mothers seek to soothe with singing, others swear.

Miss Gourley is silent. Staring at the pietà at her feet.

Miss Elliot says firmly, "Brigid, let her go."

Miss Gourley says quietly, "Lady Marie?"

Brigid looks up. The face is smeared with grief, but the eyes are clear—wide with fear—and unmistakable.

"It's all right," says Miss Gourley, holding the desperate gaze. "I'll not tell a soul. You are safe here. And so is your child."

There is no loosing her arms from about the lass, but Lady Marie suffers Miss Gourley to put water to her child's lips.

I coughed and opened my eyes. To find I was looking into those of the portrait. Deep, dazzling green. Alive. Gazing back at me. Though dimly aware of noise all round me, I had ears only for Her voice. It seemed to issue not only from her lips but from deep within me . . . Her embrace, I recognized it: soft. Her scent, *home*. I lifted my hand—to see, tangled amid my fingers, the fringe of her silken shawl. My lips parted. "Momma," I whispered.

"Charles," she crooned.

My tears flowed even as I shook my head and sought to rise.

"Lady Marie," said Miss Gourley carefully, "Charles died long ago, this is—"

"Charles!" she cried, as though scrawling with her heart in blood on the darkness.

"Mother."

"My sweet darling boy," she cooed, "does it hurt very much?"

"Not anymore, Mother."

"He can't hurt you ever again, Charles. Momma won't let him."

Tears coursed down her face; so piteous was her sorrow as she cradled my head, so pathetic her misapprehension of so much, that I said, "Mother, he failed. He tried, but . . . I fled. I am . . . I am as I was born."

She clutched me to her heart and I felt its thunder and wondered whether, in assuaging this grief, I had predisposed her to a greater, for I knew I was not, and never would be, her son.

"Mother, please let me go."

She loosed her hold with a smile. I rose to my feet. Legs trembling, heart pounding, I turned to the Angel of Cowgate. "Miss Gourley. I was born the Honourable Charles Bell, June first, eighteen seventy-three. I did not die. But I was buried. Inside the Honourable Charlotte Bell. We stand before you now."

The room had hushed. Apart from a stray whimper, the babies were quiet, and their mothers too, though whether the latter slept or listened, I could not tell.

"Oh Charles, that's a story your father made up," said my mother. "He and that horrible doctor."

"Lady Marie," said Gwen. ". . . Hello."

"Little Gwendolyn." My mother smiled. "You're all grown up and pretty as a picture. And he seems nice, your fiancé."

Mr. Margalo rose, bowed. "Lady Marie, my name is Isadore Margalo, and I am honoured to make your acquaintance."

Suddenly we were as though in a drawing room. I felt giddy.

"How's your dear sweet mother?" she asked Gwen.

"She is well, Lady Marie, thank you."

I interrupted this bizarre display of dross—"We must tell Father. He is broken-hearted, thinking you dead." Whereupon, a strange sound bubbled up, as from a cauldron: my mother's hollow laughter.

"She's hysterical," murmured Miss Elliot.

"Edna," rebuked Miss Gourley. "Fetch the whisky." But Miss Elliot was already halfway toward the darker end of the room. I heard a door swing open.

My mother was doubled over now, clutching her sides—laughter is contagious and not always agreeably so. It took an effort of will to suppress my own rising hilarity. "Mother. How comes it you are alive?" With the question came a fresh wave of faintness—I felt Gwen's grip, strong and lean as hickory, guiding me back onto the bench, only to look up and find it was Miss Gourley.

My mother's laughter ceased like a drop in wind and her features fell. She shook her head slowly as though the very air had thickened, and through fluttering half-closed lids could be seen the whites of her eyes. Miss Elliot was there with a bottle of amber liquid. She tipped it over a soup spoon and raised it to my mother's lips. My mother took it, sputtered, coughed, and fanned her chest with her hand in a gesture disconcertingly—almost grotesquely—coquettish. In a hoarse voice, she said, "He put me away."

In the silence which followed I looked to Gwen to find her eyes already upon me, and I said, "In Morecombe Downs."

High girlish laughter made an unsettling contrast with her appearance. When she spoke again, it was in the sparkling tones of a hostess drawing out her guests, contradicting none, uniting all. "Quite right, Morecombe Downs came first, darling. Then came a horrible house in

Leith." The façade crumbled along with the voice, "For over twelve years."

"Why?" My voice, a strand of cobweb.

Brightly once more, "He thought I had tried to kill myself and you. Silly me, I left a naughty note."

"But. Afterwards. When Byrn pulled you out. Why didn't you tell Father you'd been running away? How could you let him live with the sorrow all these years? How could you allow yourself be imprisoned?"

Her tone now curiously flat, she replied, "He told me you were dead."

"Who did?" I asked.

"Your father!" She shrieked it.

96

THE ROOM SWAM. She went on shrieking. A wailing and lamenting fit to fell the walls of Troy. I scrabbled for purchase on the floorboards as though in an attempt to scale those walls. Then I was sitting up, my head between my knees, a rug draped across my shoulders. The room had erupted again, nearly drowning out my mother. Shapes were moving in the darkness, women pacing with their babies, skirting the periphery of light cast by the stove and Miss Gourley's lamp—I heard Miss Elliot and Moira moving among them, exhorting and reassuring by turns.

Mr. Margalo and Gwen were crouched either side of me. Mother quieted and sank to her knees. Miss Gourley wrapped her own shawl about Mother's shoulders. Spittle had formed at Mother's lips and she said in a quaverous whisper, "His sister came. Every month for over twelve years. To pay my keepers. And each time, she visited me in my room. And at each visit she said to me"—her voice dropped to a shudder—"'You killed your child.'"

Miss Elliot knelt and held my mother in a firm embrace from behind as she shook and continued through chattering teeth, "And then, on her last visit. She left me a key. On the windowsill. And that night, I took it. And unlocked my door, and left the house. And went into the water." Her eyes streamed, but her face was calm.

I was cold, Reader. So cold. As cold as wee Charles outside my window in the dead of night . . .

Miss Gourley was saying, "Miss Bell. Charlotte. Can you hear me?" I looked up and nodded. "Your mother was brought to us, having been pulled from the Firth and near death, some upwards of two months ago. Your father must now believe her dead, whatever he believed before."

My mother stood. "Charles," she said forthrightly and reached down a hand to me. I grasped it in both my own. "Mother," I said, my own eyes streaming. "I am Charlotte."

Her smile was full of love. And she said, "It's all right, Charles. You don't have to pretend anymore. Come, let's go."

She made to pull me up by the hand but I let hers go. She looked bewildered.

I rose of my own accord, reached into my pocket and withdrew the soiled certificate of passage. My mother's eyes widened at the sight of it. I explained how it came to be in my possession, courtesy of Mr. Margalo. "Father knows now that you were fleeing that night. He knows his mistake, Mother, and grieves it sorely."

She scoffed, but took from me the certificate as though it were a precious relic. I produced its perfect twin, and likewise handed it to her. "These are your property. You may return to Boston, as was your original intent."

She shook her head sadly. "Taffy deserted me too."

I reached back into my pocket, and gave her the packet of letters.

Gwen reached out and squeezed my hand.

Mother sank to the bench and we watched as she perused the letters for the first time. I feared another explosion what with her learning the truth of how her friend too had been deceived—instead, a bittersweet smile played upon her features in which I discerned, for the first time, the lineaments of a young woman. She looked up and wiped tears from her cheeks.

I said, "You must write to her."

She shook her head.

"Mother, whyever not?"

She clamped shut her lips as though holding back a flood.

"She will be so very glad to know you are alive," I persisted.

"Even if Taffy is. Alive . . ." She was unable to continue.

"Mother, she is. Father and I received Yuletide greetings from her only last month, she is like nothing so much as clockwork when it comes to—"

I felt Miss Gourley's hand on my arm. "Your mother is still, in the eyes of the law, your father's property. He would be within his rights to pursue her."

Mother looked up at me. "What happened to your lovely curls?"

"Father is about to be married. He believes you dead, you must employ the fact to your advantage and be gone."

"I don't care what happens to me now. I can die. I can scrub floors."

"You can't, we've seen you try," said Miss Elliot.

"Then I'll stand on the street corner and sing 'til they put me away again, the only thing that matters is I've found you, Charles—"

"Mother, my name is—"

"You are your father's rightful heir—"

I spoke over her, "I am not, I am the Honourable—"

"You're the next Baron of the DC de Fayne—"

"I am no such—"

Miss Gourley broke in, "Lady Marie, have you any money of your own?"

"Not a red cent."

"No account in your own name at a bank? Here or in America?"

"Nope."

"Nothing whereby a proof of life might release funds?"

"I haven't got a thing except my Bonny Prince Charlie." And she gazed adoringly at me.

I shrank.

Miss Elliot tapped her pipe. "I'll give Lord Henry this: many men in his position would have long ago procured a quiet divorce."

My mother began to titter, the which grew quickly into an all-out belly laugh. I feared lest she become hysterical once more, but she sighed and fanned herself with the certificate of passage saying, "Henry would never divorce me. Daddy made sure of that. A little thing called a codi-cil." And with a saucy elevation of the eyebrows, and a faux-demure look to Mr. Margalo, "Sounds a little naughty, I know."

She explained that my grandfather, the late Gerald Corcoran, "Bean Baron of Boston," had obtained my father's signature on a marriage contract stipulating that in the event of divorce or annulment, my mother's dowry would revert to her. "Then you must threaten to tell the world of how he has treated you," I exhorted her. She tilted her head and smiled indulgently at me.

In the time it took for Miss Elliot to fill a fresh pipe, I saw through new eyes—the eyes of "the world": What was my mother's tale of torment compared with my father's plight? A gentleman—a nobleman at that—might be forgiven for having put about a falsehood regarding the death of his insane wife, especially if he had done so for the sake of his daughter whose marriage prospects, dimmed already by delicate health, would be dashed quite by a public disclosure of maternal madness—and especially if he had in the meantime remained honourably unmarried. Moreover, if a gentleman's wife were to survive "a second suicide attempt," he would be within his rights to commit her to an asylum; one better equipped to humanely secure her person until such time as she might be seen to "die" all over again—this time, perhaps, in fact. One's heart quite goes out to the gentleman: saddled with a sick daughter and a mad wife, and he too honourable to cast aside the latter in divorce.

"So that's that," said Lady Marie Bell.

We were silent for a moment.

My thoughts began quietly to gather and put themselves in order. "You say she left you a key."

"Who? Oh, yes, that's how I—Yes."

"Either my aunt was in league with your keepers, or she obtained it by some other means."

"Oh Charlie, what does it matter?"

By way of answer, I dilated to the assembled party the plan which was even then formulating itself within my brain. It was logical. It was bold. And by no means fool-proof. When I had done, silence reigned—even in the huddled darkness. My mother was first to speak. "It's worth a try."

Miss Elliot said, "You'll need legal assistance regardless."

"Where can you find a lawyer in this town who won't run straight to Henry?" said my mother.

Miss Gourley turned to Mr. Margalo. "I shall write to your benefactor." She rose. "But for now I think we could all do with some rest." In the amber light her features showed drawn with the strain of the preceding hour. Before she allowed Gwen and Mr. Margalo to depart, however, she took pen and notebook from her pocket and dashed off a note which she handed to Gwen. "Slip this under Miss Mellor's door when you return."

"Thank you, Miss Gourley."

The Angel of Cowgate paused and looked sternly at Gwendolyn. Then, stepped forward and embraced her.

When at length she released Gwen, I saw my mother's hand slip forth and squeeze Miss Gourley's own.

97

MY LIMBS LEADEN with fatigue, I followed Miss Gourley up to the top of the house and her private quarters: a garret chamber, where she bade me take my rest upon her own bed. I demurred, "I'll not deprive you of your—"

"Do as I say."

Half in a dream already, I mumbled the question I had meant to ask Gwen before she'd left—"What is a 'crime against nature'?"

"It refers to sexual relations between two individuals of the same sex."

I surfaced. "You mean . . . congress?"

"Yes."

"And is it? A crime?"

"According to the laws of Man, yes. According to those of Nature? Not a bit of it."

She pressed me firmly back against the pillow. "Sleep. You are safe now."

Miss Gourley watches as the young person instantly complies, their breath shifting to the regularity of sleep; and wonders what might have transpired had she herself, thirteen years ago and in this very room, spoken the latter words to the mother.

She crosses the hall and beds down in Edna's room, the latter having slipped away to spend the remainder of the night with John.

I woke to see, inches from my nose, the slope of a ceiling. Was I in Paris? Had Gwen and I fled after all? A clatter of hooves and wheels from below reached me through the porthole window whence a watery light. I raised myself to my knees and looked down.

Several storeys below, vendors streamed past with barrows and carts, a boy led two dray horses by their bridles, and more followed behind him, a river of horses flowing up the Cowgate to the Grassmarket. Across the street, a clutch of shoeless children was shooed from a doorway by a man with a crop—surely not the same children? No . . . they were smaller still, and numbered five. I became aware that the bed I was in, and the floor upon which it stood, jutted into midair, and it seemed I might almost reach out and touch the washing hanging from the scutcheon of the house opposite.

I sat up. The room was sparsely furnished. No larger than Mr. Margalo's student digs but better, if modestly, appointed. I threw back the comforter and arose. An odour of mothballs assaulted my nostrils and drew my eye to where a suit of clothing was laid out over a wooden chair. A tailed frock coat of a dubious black now fading to green. A plaid waistcoat. Shirt and celluloid collar. Checked trousers with braces. And a fresh set of linen smalls. At the foot of the chair, my boots. I rose.

The collar on the frock coat was high, like that of a banker's from a previous era. The waistcoat was threadbare about the pocket, as though the original owner had oft dipped his fingers in search of watch or snuff box. The garments were straightforward enough, however, no experience of monkey-puzzling required, and I donned them quickly, shivering against the cold.

Though I was nearly long enough for them, I was insufficiently wide, thus with the clothes fairly hanging off of me, I ventured down to the third floor where I paused at the sight of a remarkable arrangement; the entire floor had been rendered one single chamber with white-washed walls and green-painted floors where some two dozen narrow iron beds were ranged. Each was tidily, if spartanly, made up and furnished with a foot-locker. The small high windows of this dormitory were thrown open. A scrawny flame-haired woman of indeterminate years—and intermittent teeth—was sweeping energetically. She addressed me in a rasping voice and I recognized her as the woman who had ushered the children upstairs the previous night. "What became of them? The children?" I asked.

She did not answer but trotted down one storey. I followed, and she stepped aside with a nod in the direction of an open door. Seated at rows of scarred wooden desks were upwards of two dozen ragged-looking youngsters—three of whose feet were shod only in soot. Their faces, however, were clean and they sat like the others with hands folded on the desk before them, looking up at Miss Gourley. Behind her was an immense "blackboard." Written there in chalk were several phonetic combinations along with a column of three-letter words. This, then, was a schoolroom, however rude. Tacked up on one side was a map of the world; on the other side a chart depicted, by means of a series of illustrated panels, "The Elements of Hygiene" beginning with a pair of hands afoam in soap suds; proceeding through the cleansing of ears and nose; culminating with a mouth aiming bolts of lightning into a handkerchief. On a third wall, rough-hewn shelves were sway-backed with books. And stuck higgledy-piggledy on every available patch of wall were drawings and paintings—many rudimentary, some arresting. Miss Gourley nodded to me, and carried on: "C, A, T, sound it out, Aoife." I withdrew.

On the other side of the passage stood a closed door with "INFIRMARY" hand-painted in block letters. Here an odour of carbolic, like that which had pervaded Dr. Chambers's surgery, insinuated itself through the crack beneath the door and I came near to swoon in dread—an ill omen considering my medical aspirations.

Thence to the ground floor and the great room—where chaos reigned amid a horde of scrawny children, squalling babies and women of all ages who seemed to be ransacking the place. Soon enough my eyes adjusted and I discerned patterns amid the ruckus; a work party of girls and boys dragged several long tables to the centre of the room while others carried chairs like trophies from where they were stacked in avalanches along the walls; younger children tended to those still smaller whose shrieks and random wobbly-legged movements fairly dizzied me. I was more than once obliged to step aside lest I be knocked over, so little regard had they for their betters. I picked out lines of supply—stacks of kindling carried from what must be the scullery at the far end, beyond the claw-foot stove where last night the world had shifted on its axis—and oases of industry: here a woman mopped the floor, there another toted slops, a third sat soothing a brace of babies— my mother.

An urchin bumped past me without a by-your-leave, an empty clay bowl cupped in his hands—"Watch yourself, Sean Padraig Archibald," carked a woman whose features looked etched in bitterness, and without missing a stroke in her sweeping she dealt him a clip on the ear—his recoil afforded me a glimpse of his left eye crusted closed with a sticky-looking substance.

He was followed by numerous others of similarly grimy and thread-bare appearance—between the lot of them there was insufficient meat on their bones to make a meal for Maisie. From behind an immense pot set on a trestle table at the foot of the room, flame-haired Moira—she was everywhere—commenced ladling porridge into the bowls they held up like famished chicks. They set the bowls on the long tables but rather than falling to, they fetched more empty bowls and returned to the caul-dron until before each empty chair there sat a steaming bowl.

A fresh din was borne on a gust of frigid air and I turned to see a line of wretches more abject still, women and children, filing in from the street—among them, yes, the five barefoot ragamuffins from across the street. "What is happening?" I asked stupidly of no one, of everyone.

In a Gorbals (as I would learn) accent, a taut-faced chapped-nosed lass replied—so far as I could make out—"'Tis Saturday, blockhead," and brushed past me with her bowls which she set before two more of the less fortunate who now filled the places at the table.

Suddenly silence, and I saw Miss Elliot at the head of the room, ramrod-straight and ringing out, "Bless this food and those who eat it. Amen!" A prayer whose brevity was the soul of mercy—the women and children fell to with a clatter. No sooner had the meal begun than it was over and the whole process was flung into reverse, as those with full bel-lies filed out and the scrappy resident children cleared the crockery and set to replacing it with full bowls and clean spoons. I retreated toward the stove where my mother was cradling an additional two infants, all of whom slept to the raucous lullaby of the Refuge, safe in her ample embrace. I made to bid her "good morning" but she looked up and said—absurdly—"Shush."

I set to helping with the clearing of the crockery, at some risk to my coat—and to the crockery—as a second rank of eaters took the places vacated by the first; followed by a third, and a fourth—numerous men this time of whom several neglected to remove their caps as they hunched over their bowls. *Ruffians.*

Following a billow of steam toward the back, I entered the scullery where I doffed my frock coat, rolled up the sleeves of my shirt and planted myself next to the chap-nosed lass who was elbow-deep in a basin of sudsy water. Her strength and competence as she seized a ewer of scalding water and replenished the basin were in inverse proportion to her slight frame and tender age, for I surmised she could not be more than ten years old.

"What's a dandy like you doing in a place like this?" she asked. I comprehended the question only after she obliged me by thrice repeating it. Before I could answer, she posed another query, pronounced slowly and loudly, "Do you speak English?!"

I replied, "I should like to be assistance if I may."

She rolled her eyes and elbowed me—painfully—out of the way as she lifted a bowl from the basin and set it on the draining board. I stood, arms limp at my sides.

She said something quite unintelligible, then thrust a clean rag at me. Which I understood perfectly.

Thus I endeavoured to fall into step with the rhythm of the place, finding myself refreshingly inexpert and slow to learn in the domestic sphere with its overlay of chaos and its underpinning of repetitive chores. It struck me that my backwardness was comparable to that of so many when confronted with a problem in calculus or a page from Tacitus. Indeed Fiona—she of the sharp elbows—persisted in treating me as though I were a half-wit, curtly declining my offer to teach her sums, for after all, "fat lot of good it's done you, Mr. Charles."

The Saturday performance was reprised on Sunday, Monday, Tuesday and Wednesday, with two out of three meals per day in rotation, breakfast, luncheon—"What's that?" demanded Fiona, after which I learned to call the midday meal "dinner," which in turn I learned to call "supper." By the second Monday I was elbow-deep in the basin and wielding hot ewers. The Lord's Day saw a longer prayer before the meal, and a thinning of the ranks owing to the many who left long enough to attend services— whether in thanks to or fear of a God who could count the hairs on their heads but seemed incapable of putting food reliably in their mouths.

By Thursday, my hands were cracked and raw and I was reassigned to slops. Behind the scullery the wash house was little more than a steam-choked cubby through which one passed with the slops to access the courtyard—surprisingly large. Unsurprisingly grim. Its cindery surface was pockmarked here and there with crabgrass. Who knows but what it concealed an ossuary from the last plague or witch-burning. Here, children played, sometimes under the supervision of Miss Elliot who, with hiked skirts, joined them in kicking about an inflated pig's bladder, the while a large white hog named Robert the Bruce glowered from his pen into which I tipped the slops.

There were few enough slops, for there was little waste at the Refuge, thus Robert the Bruce's diet was supplemented daily with perfectly good porridge. Were they fattening him for slaughter? No. He was a pampered pet. Wherefore, in the midst of want, a make-shifting community kept a pig for a pet was beyond me. But the children regularly kicked the bladder toward his pen and he frequently returned it via his snout. I feared him, for he tried to bite me the first time I brought him his victuals, ungrateful brute. But with the passage of days, I discerned in his supercilious countenance a hint of Maisie; might not he be one of her many descendants? I decided to do him the honour of mounting and riding him.

The bone of my wrist healed more swiftly than Miss Gourley and the surgeon anticipated—"Remarkable," pronounced Mr. Moore—and within forty-eight hours I was back washing crockery next to Fiona whom I now understood hailed from "Garbles, is it?" I asked, thinking it apt, considering her manner of speech. "Gorbals!" she bawled back, "Eediot!" I did not repeat my experiment with Robert the Bruce.

Mr. Moore was a kindly old surgeon and "man-midwife." Seeing I was captivated by his trade, he schooled me in the basics of human physicking such that I became something of a fixture in the Infirmary, having first got over my dread at the smell of anti-septic—and perhaps it was as well I should know this dread, for it engendered in me fellow-feeling for my "patients." Strange to say, as repulsive as a reeking, leaking baby was to me, in no wise was I repelled by the weeping sores, suppurating wounds and parasitical blooms that tormented so many of the Refugees. Thus I swabbed the crusty eye of the bumptious Sean Padraig Archibald (his name was longer than he was), trading him a currant for each subsequent treatment until his pink-eye cleared up. I then did likewise with his ringworm—along with the various rashes and infestations of the dozen or so women and children who took to queuing up behind him.

Mother continued to be known as Brigid and so too did I address her, except in those rare moments when we might not be overheard. I was irked not so much by her insistence upon calling me "Charles"—for everyone now called me "Master Charles," the which I found not disagreeable. It was, rather, her refusal to call me "Charlotte" that rankled. Even in those private moments when I begged her, "Please, Mother, 'tis my name as much as the other," her face closed, she turned away and became as implacable as stone.

The dormitory upstairs being reserved for mothers with children, I slept on a pallet in the scullery next to Peg of the bitter tongue, who never ceased to frighten me in the night with her mighty snoring, and by day with her habit of pinching my buttocks.

My education proceeded apace: I picked up a small child. Its nose streamed, its mouth screamed. I carried it—arms straight out in front of me so as not to sully my waistcoat with effluvia—to its mother, a girl of fifteen called Jenny. I got so that I was able to tuck one in the crook of my arm whilst holding a milk-sopped crust for it to gum. All this engendered in me no desire to sprout bairns of my own, but it did go some way to moderating my aversion to those of others.

Sean Padraig Archibald took to dogging my steps, causing me more than once to trip. When I suggested to him he might make a tasty morsel for Robert the Bruce, he laughed. Soon enough he was pointing over my shoulder at words and pictures in outdated issues of *The Scotsman* that I salvaged in my few moments of leisure. Having personally deloused and disinfected the lad I deemed it not incautious to suffer him to sit next me. "Next" became "quite near" which evolved into a positive burrowing beneath my arm until the boy was ensconced in my lap— evidently his destination all along—together with a pestilential rag tied on a stick, the which rudimentary effigy he addressed affectionately as "Bun." When I asked Sean Padraig Archibald why he himself had three names, he answered, "The first ones died."

I soon learned that fearsome Peg was mother to Fiona and Sean Padraig Archie. And to seven older ones who had emigrated or otherwise dispersed. Along with five who had not survived childhood, the youngest of whom "fell into the well," Fiona told me with a sidelong look, arch beyond her years.

I was clearing the tables of Sunday lunch—dinner, rather—tallying as I did what I owed the Refuge in broken crockery, when I saw a gentleman enter from the vestibule, carrying a large leather hold-all. I dropped what I was doing, adding to my debt—in my defence the crockery was less than sturdy—and hastened to join Miss Elliot in greeting him. This must be the gentleman who would furnish us with legal advice and to whom we would entrust our plan. The *frisson* I experienced in striding toward him, however, was not owing to his being our solicitor as much as it was to his being Mr. Margalo's benefactor: he who had found my future tutor in a basket and delivered him safely to Heriot's Hospital School. To my surprise, I was overtaken by my mother—for all her bulk, she was light on her feet. As she swept past me I heard her say, "Josey, oh, I'm so happy to see you!"

98

I HUNG BACK as the gentleman removed his somewhat shabby silk hat and bowed to my mother. She extended her hand gracefully as though she were in the drawing room of her own home, and he took it. Neither spoke for a moment. Then the gentleman murmured, "Lady Marie. I was so pleased to learn you are alive and well." A slight hesitance of speech only added to an overall impression of graciousness—and if he was shocked by my mother's appearance, he gave no sign.

"I don't know about 'well' but I'm alive."

Miss Elliot interjected, "Thank you for coming, Mr. Baxter. Allow me to introduce the Honourable Charlotte Bell."

"Charles is my son," said Mother, looking daggers at Miss Elliot.

Turning to me, he bowed.

He was pale, with a somewhat unkempt mane of salt-and-pepper hair, grizzled side-whiskers, a high lined forehead and dark eyes in which there mingled intelligence and kindness. I warmed to him immediately.

Scarcely had I time to wonder how it came to pass that my mother was not only acquainted with my tutor's benefactor, but was on terms sufficiently familiar to admit of her having hailed him by his first name, when Miss Elliot said, "Rosamund's waiting for you, Josey, go straight on up."

As we mounted the stairs, Mother played the hostess, chattering as though for the benefit of her guests, "Mr. Baxter was your father's great friend, in fact the three of them—Henry, Josey and Miss Gourley—were great friends. A bird-watching trio, isn't that right, Josey? 'The ornithological musketeers,' ha-ha! Miss Gourley saved your father's life. If not for her he'd have fallen from the Salisbury Craigs and I'd never have met him. And you'd never have been born. And I'd do it all over again, every last nightmarish bit of it, for the sake of having my beautiful boy."

Soon my mother, Mr. Baxter, Miss Gourley and I were seated about the latter's deal table under the sloping timbers of her garret quarters, and now Moira popped in with a tray and set before us mugs of tea and slices of shortbread. Miss Gourley said rather sharply, "And who is helping Miss Elliot while you're up here spoiling us?"

"John's here, miss," rasped Moira.

"Oh, that's all right then," said Miss Gourley.

From his bulging brief-bag Mr. Baxter produced an envelope. Opening it, he withdrew and unfolded a document. "This you may recognize as your nuptial contract, Lady Marie, signed by your father, Gerald Corcoran Esquire, and by Lord Henry Bell."

My mother did indeed recognize the contract. Taking it, she flipped to the last page and stabbed it with her index finger, "The codicil! God bless you, Daddy." Whereupon she crossed herself like the Irish Papist she was.

"Have you any property in hand, Lady Marie?" asked Mr. Baxter.

"Only these." And she produced the two certificates of passage. Indicating the soiled one she said, "This is the one I took with me that night. Thanks to dear Maggie Sheehan . . ." Her eyes misted over and I feared lest we lose her to a flight of reminiscence, but she narrowed them and looked at me. "It's how come I was able to run away in the first place." Then she sat back and folded her hands over her girth, resembling more a portly codger than a plump chatelaine. "Well now. As Gerry Corcoran might say, let's talk turkey."

Miss Gourley took a triangle of shortbread and dipped it into her tea as Mr. Baxter explained the various legal avenues he judged worth pursuing and proposed a date some two weeks hence "when matters might be brought to a head in the presence of all parties." He then reviewed with me the plan I had formulated on the night of my arrival at the Refuge. "It may not come to that," he concluded. "Lord Henry may sign the writ without further inducement."

"I should think he may, Father is a gentleman."

Neither my mother nor Miss Gourley remarked on this.

Mr. Baxter drew forth a second document. Its heading: "Writ of Divorce." He went through it, page by page, with my mother, then handed her a pen and, pointing to a dotted line below which appeared her name in print, bid her "Sign here." With a steady hand, Lady Marie Bell signed her name to the writ which, if finalized, would strip her of that name forever. Mr. Baxter said, "As witnessed by . . ." And passed both pen and page to Miss Gourley who likewise signed. No look or word passed between the two women, but I sensed a fleeting vibration that, were it visible, I might have called an electrical current. As the ink dried on the writ of divorce, I saw opposite my mother's signature another dotted line, as yet empty, below which appeared, in print, "Henry Lord Bell, Baron DC de Fayne."

I felt my heart pounding. But could not understand why. After all, none of this came as a shock, I knew full well the point of the entire exercise was that my parents should be divorced. My mother, as though from far away, was urging me to eat some shortbread, "After all, you're a growing boy."

Mr. Baxter had my mother and Miss Gourley sign three more copies of the writ. He allowed them to dry before replacing them in the envelope, which he stuffed back into his brief-bag. Mother and Miss Gourley rose as one. Mr. Baxter hastened to his feet and Mother said, once more the charming hostess, "Dear Josey, you're still so handsome."

"And you, Lady Marie, are the picture of loveliness."

These two middle-aged people, each clearly the worse for wear, swore the other was a vision of youth and beauty. I wondered . . . in years to come when Gwendolyn should be a papery old lady, would I yet see the sprightly girl?

Mother and I rejoined Moira and Miss Elliot and the usual rabble of children in the refectory where preparations were already underway for supper. Crossing the room and carrying three stacked chairs was a new woman in high collar, narrow tie, tweed coat and matching skirt, her hair scraped flat against her scalp into a knot at the base of her neck. Miss Elliot said, "John, this is Brigid and Mister Charles."

John nodded, "How do," and carried on pitching in. My mother whispered to me balefully, "My land, Charles, did you ever see such mannish women?"

99

OVER THE ENSUING TWO WEEKS, Time both flew and deepened. I determined to earn my keep at the Refuge by redoubling my efforts in every domain during the remainder of my sojourn there. Thus I plunged in.

I attended the successful birth of a healthy, welcomed baby. Having nothing to do but observe, I fainted.

I witnessed Miss Gourley turn from the door a woman coughing blood and pleading for shelter. "One must not succour the few at the expense of the many," she said as she shot the bolt. I could not decide whether her spine was steelier or her heart more tender. I learned a new word: *triage*.

I assisted Moira in the delousing of the inhabitants and, as I plied the comb and squished nits between my nails, my ear became attuned to every accent from County Cork to the Gorbals. On one such occasion, Moira asked me to fetch the vinegar and lard, "There's a good lass."

Returning with the vat, I whispered, "How did you know?"

"I'm a witch." She saw my consternation and laughed. "Och, you're no the first lass to pass herself off as a laddy. Nor vicey-versy, come to that, there's many a lad does the same."

"Really? Why on earth would they wish to?"

She threw back her head and cackled.

Miss Elliot's friend John, a taciturn librarian, was a frequent visitor, and from time to time, Miss Elliot rode off with her, the two of them bouncing along on bicycles—marvellous machines! I prevailed upon John to instruct me in their operation. I healed swiftly.

One morning, Mr. Moore watched as I stitched the elbow of a tiny wee lad who'd been rescued from a chimney flue. The child sat, preternaturally patient, while I worked and when I finished he asked for a "glass of stout," the which Miss Elliot gave him. I accompanied Mr. Moore to the vestibule and, on impulse, out into street. Hatless and coatless I walked with him and, as he threaded his way west and south from the Cowgate, confided in him. "I am not Charles Snowe. That is, I am not only he. I am also Charlotte Snowe," said I, and told him my tale, without revealing that the Brigid whose embrace worked like magic on colicky babies was also my mother. I told him of my parents' horror at my "defect," of its surgical removal and subsequent regeneration. "Mr. Moore, have I not now all the more cause to be called a mistake of Nature? I know myself to be female, but I know myself to be as well, Charles." The old gentleman paused. We were outside Greyfriars Kirkyard. He said, "Nature doesnae deal in mistakes so much as differences. We can never know when one of them might wind up saving our skin. It saved yours." He smiled. Then added gravely, "Take care whom you tell, at least 'til you're of age. There be those who'd sooner study you than listen to you, Miss Bell." Seeing my disconcertion, he reassured me. "Your mother told me. Though she calls you Charles."

"You know . . . my mother?"

"Lady Marie was my patient afore you were born."

"And you've kept mum."

"Such is my patient's wish."

"I wish to be a physician like you."

"I'm only an old man-midwife and surgeon."

"Then that's what I'll be. Will you teach me?"

"You've more to learn than I can teach, you're the future, lass."

"How'm I to get there through a present that blocks me at every turn?"

"How do the grasses grow up and through the paving stones of Holyrood?"

"You'd wish me so hard a life?"

"The grasses do not dash themselves against the stones. They persist. They exert a pressure that splits the stones as surely as Samson broke his bonds."

". . . I haven't that much time."

"How do you know?"

The crown of his broad old hat was dilapidated with innumerable Edinburgh rains, a sheen to the brim where it was doffed and donned. He touched it now with a nod, before turning to amble off toward his next patient. I lingered before the gates to the kirkyard. I saluted, in silence, the remains of James Hutton that I knew lay within—not rest-ing, but multiplying backwards into all the constituent parts of matter wherein *we find no vestige of a beginning, no prospect of an end* . . .

I was in the scullery, peeling potatoes—and not infrequently my epidermis—pausing to watch with interest as the nicks in my hands closed up on their own, swiftly and without a trace. My mother startled me and, absurdly, I made to hide my hands. "There you are, naughty boy, where've you been?" On her hip she dandled a baby who drooled and gnawed on her knuckle.

"I was out walking with Mr. Moore. He told me you were his patient long ago."

She smiled. "I was, the dear man, and it's thanks to him my second baby was buried in the kirkyard instead of . . . Well, you know, *poof.*"

". . . How many did you have before me?"

"Three. Two miscarriages and a still-birth but that's all women's troubles, Charles, you don't need to bother about that, and don't be going out for walks, even if you do look so manly your own father wouldn't recognize you."

"Mother . . ." My heart commenced pounding the way it had a few days before when I watched her and Miss Gourley sign the writ.

"What is it, handsome?"

"Only . . ." A dangerous lump in my throat. I stammered, "Might you . . . ? If Father—" I swallowed hard. "What if he were to apologize? And beg you to return? Would you . . . ? What would you do?"

"I'd cut out his heart and feed it to his sister."

I set down the paring knife.

She went on, "It's bad enough what he did to me, Charles, but think what he tried to do to you, look what he did do, making you live all those years as a—"

"Mother, can you not see I am as much Charlotte as I am Charles? As much your daughter as your—"

"You are your father's son and heir and one day you'll be the Baron."

"I hate you."

Shocked to have said it aloud, I braced myself for havoc. I stole a look up. She was smiling through tears. "Momma loves you no matter what, Charles." The baby in her arms gurgled.

I steeled myself. I would not batten as Charles only to starve as Charlotte. Gathering within me now like a thunder-cloud was anger. Anger at my father who must maim where he loved. Anger at my mother who must do likewise, if with words rather than knives. Rage that anyone should presume to name what was mine alone, namely my very Self!

On she yammered, "When all this is sorted out, we'll get on a great big ship and sail home to Boston just like I tried to do with you all those years ago. Taffy's going to love you, and you'll meet your little cousin, Tess—not so little anymore! I can't wait to write and tell Taffy we're fine and we're coming home!"

I did not bother to contradict her. I was done with her. I said through gritted teeth, "This 'Tess' is not, in fact, my cousin."

"How do you know that?"

"She wrote to me."

My mother clapped and squealed, the baby did likewise. "Did she?! Oh darling, you've been pen-friends this whole time?"

"If by that you mean we kept up a lively correspondence, no. Following the initial inanities, I allowed it to lapse."

For a moment I thought she might reproach me—but she turned on me her adoring gaze. "Well isn't that just like a boy your age."

Miss Gourley counselled patience. I had sought her out in her garret quarters where she had been writing a letter which she set aside beneath a sheet of blotting paper.

"She is willfully blind," said I.

"She is your mother and she loves you."

"'Tis Charles she loves, she hates Charlotte!" I pummelled my head with my fists—Miss Gourley seized my wrists and held them. "You are permitted to harm no one beneath this roof, including yourself. Do you understand?"

I nodded. She released me. I kicked over the deal table, sending paper, pen and divers books flying, I seized the chair she had lately vacated and hurled it against the door where it splintered, I jumped and slammed my feet to the floor in hopes of plummeting the entire room into the street five storeys below.

Presently, Miss Gourley said, "Give her time."

"She's had years!"

"Years in which she was incarcerated, drugged and driven to suicide. It is a wonder she is alive at all."

"I wish you were my mother."

"You're like her."

"I'm not!"

"Throw anything you like except for that crock on the shelf, it contains honey."

"How am I like her?" I asked in a small voice, bracing myself for the answer.

"You're both made of strong stuff."

I could find nothing to refute in that statement.

She bent to right her table. I hastened to help, and picked up her chair—now more of a stool. She collected her papers, I found her pen between the wall and baseboard. Nib intact.

"Remember that when it comes to next week," she said. "And whatever happens, Charles Charlotte Bell, you have a friend in me. Now go fetch a rag and set about mopping up that ink while I write to your father."

On Sunday, Gwen arrived in company with Mr. Margalo. Miss Gourley conducted him up to the schoolroom, while Mother commandeered Gwen, insisting she enter into plans for a "real wedding when the time comes," detaining her further with the plea that she help in choosing between two dresses Mother had found in the donations cupboard. "Flowers or stripes?" When at last I was able to pry her away, commending her display of feigned interest, Gwen assured me that on the contrary she had enjoyed herself immensely and that my mother was "loads of fun."

We repaired to the privacy of the courtyard in back of the scullery where, shivering with cold, she said, "I've something to tell you about Isadore."

I felt my stomach drop.

Overhead a kerfuffle as a third-storey window was thrown open and the excited voices of children reached us. Gwen hastened to add, "It's nothing bad. At least nothing that reflects badly on him."

Just then, two objects whizzed past us, hitting the ground at the same time—a potato and a lump of coal. "Sorry!" came Mr. Margalo's voice.

He was at the window, where smaller faces bobbed either side of him. He turned back and we caught snatches of his instructions, ". . . make certain there be no one below . . ."

Gwen continued, "His benefactor, Mr. Baxter, has told him something of his parentage."

"I say, have his parents found him at last?"

"Em. I don't know they've been looking for him, but any road, Mr. Baxter says his mother was an Irish maid who emigrated ages ago and may be living in Boston."

"Maggie Sheehan."

"How did you know?"

"She was my mother's lady's maid. 'Twas she sent Mother the certificate of passage."

"Then she was a good soul in the end, Mr. Baxter said as much to Izzy, a clever, comely lass—"

"So that's where he got his peculiar name."

"'Tisn't peculiar, Isadore means 'gift of—'"

"I mean his last name. Mr. Baxter named him for his mother, you see? 'Maggie' is a form of 'Margaret,' and so is 'Margalo.'" This I deemed logical, like identifying the link between two members of a single genus, but Gwen's eyes filled with tears. "How lovely," she said.

"Did Mr. Baxter say who his father is?"

"He wouldn't. I know what you're thinking, I thought the same but 'tisn't Mr. Baxter. It was a nobleman."

"Look out below!" came a child's cry. We stepped handily from the path of a bulging sack and the makeshift football—which bounced into Robert the Bruce's pen and woke him.

"Gwennie . . ." It dawned on me with the force of a magic wish, "What if he is my brother?"

Her eyebrows rose, followed by the corners of her mouth. "That would make loads of sense, now wouldn't it, considering you two peas-in-a-pod."

"He must seek out Maggie Sheehan, and ask her."

"Izzy claims not to care, says Mr. Baxter is all the father and mother he's ever needed."

A cry of distress from above. Sean Padraig Archie's beloved rag-and-stick effigy was being dangled from the window by a bigger boy who was laughing, "Let's see if he can fly!" Sean Padraig Archie looked fair to fall from the window himself in reaching vainly for "Bun!" when he was pulled back by his sister Fiona. Mr. Margalo appeared the next instant but too late to stop the older boy dropping it. Sean Padraig Archie cried out in anguish as the wretched thing tumbled earthward, rag-head first, its "hair" flying crazily. I stepped forth and caught the odious "Bun."

As for for the pig's-bladder football, however, Robert the Bruce had eaten it.

Henry does not look up as Cruikshank's fingerless-gloved hand sets his post on the desk before him. The letter has been forwarded from No. One Bell Gardens. He recognizes immediately the hand. Reflexive joy is quashed by dread. Why has Rosamund written to him? He can hardly bear to open it. On the other hand, what if it should contain news of his daughter? Has she been found? Impossible. She lies here, some-where beneath the mosses of Fayne. He sits, his will paralyzed. Presently he sees his hands, as though taking orders from some dim chamber in his brain, take up the envelope and open it.

The Refuge
The Cowgate
February 16, 1888

Dear Lord Henry,
I write to ask leave to pay you and your sister a call at No. One Bell Gardens this Sunday at an hour convenient to you. I have news that is best conveyed in person.

Knowing how you suffer at the disappearance of Charlotte, and to spare you further pangs, I hereby assure you she is alive and well, and presently residing at an undisclosed location. She has told me her history. I appeal to your honour that you not seek to discover by force your daughter, who will herself appear willingly on Sunday.

Cordially,
Rosamund Gourley

He rings for Knox.

At the sight of his tear-stained face she fears the worst. Then he tells her.

If there were a bell tower at Fayne it would be ringing out now. *Charlotte is coming home!*

During her time at the Refuge, what my mother had lost in physical size, she appeared to have gained in outward manner. As that final week dawned, she laughed more loudly. She exhorted me more frequently, "Oh Charles, have some fun!" She squeezed my cheeks, planted kisses on them; grasped my shoulders, saying, "You'll fill out in no time." She joked and sang and gossiped with the other women. She broke into the stores of sugar, worth its weight in sterling, and indulged the children, who ran about shrieking all the more wildly. She was "Brigid," pulled from the sea and larger than life—and prettier too with each passing day as though with the waning of an evil spell, to the point where the other women speculated she was a mermaid cast out from the deeps for being too fond of humanity. *Moor-made*, I thought but did not say. She doted on me, was amused by me and, yes, amused me, for Reader I had determined to heed Miss Gourley's counsel and give her time. Thus by degrees I shed my shyness with her and unstoppered my own reservoirs of mirth—such as when I allowed myself to be cajoled into Irish dancing with the children, my lack of skill conducing to much levity. But her blandishments and merriment, her maternal pride and caresses were meant for Charles alone.

Thus, as the intervals of fun expanded, so did pain contract my heart; for the more I loved her, the more I hated the woman who, like the false mother in the story of Solomon's chalk circle, would willingly see the child she claimed as her own, cut in two—like Edinburgh itself.

When her brother arrives unannounced on Saturday evening, Clarissa permits herself a measure of optimism. Even if he has returned only to renew the bootless search for his daughter, he has nonetheless thought better of his self-imposed exile. He is lonely. That is to the good.

As if in vindication of her hopes were his words upon retiring this evening, "I expect to have good news for you before long, Clarissa."

Her brother is too honourable to have summarily broken his engagement with Miss Llewellyn. Rather, he had retreated to Fayne with a promise to release the young lady should she think better of yoking herself to a man whose life was all mourning. And though it appeared that in the short term Clarissa's niece had once again—with her death as with her birth—scuttled Henry's prospects, and those of Fayne, in the long term it was no bad thing to have the girl out of the way once and for all. Like her mother.

Five drops only, this evening.

On Saturday night, with the tables pushed back and the pallets not yet spread on the floor of the big main room, Moira pulled up a stool and, with a barrel lid in one hand and a smooth bone in the other, commenced striking the wood with both ends of the bone by means of her rapidly flicking wrist. Accelerating and slowing by turns, she altered as well the pitch, higher near the rim of the lid, deeper toward the centre where the wood sang low and rich. Soon it seemed all the residents had gathered in a circle, several bringing lamps, some sitting on the floor, others on chairs or benches, children scooting this way and that or sitting cross-legged, rapt. I pulled up a chair of my own, making room for Sean Padraig Archie who squeezed next to me, hugging to his chest his beloved bacterial Bun.

As Moira drummed, a humming arose, a repetitive almost-melody. I could not tell at first where it came from or whether it was one voice or many, but in fact it was only hers. Presently, her lips parted on a sinewy *"humm an ahumm ana humma nana humm an a hum an a hummananna hummanna."* It became tuneful within a narrow band of pitch that grew slowly wider. By now, several women, some nursing their babies, others mending clothes, were beating time with their feet. They added their voices—singly, then in twos and threes and I seemed to see the voices as lengths of yarn that wove and thickened the tune itself, venturing higher and lower, faster and slower, but always looping back to the pattern, as if the whole song were shunting back and forth on a loom.

Moira's drumstick of bone never faltered, and now the sonic weave was shot through with a bright thread of—were they words or mere sounds that Moira started singing?—each one a variation, so far as I could tell, on *deedle-dydle-dyddle-dydle-deedle-dydle-dum* in a lilting rhythm that seemed to owe something of its precision to the gaps in her lower teeth. Now wee Fiona got up, skipped to the centre of the circle and, arms held straight to her sides, began to dance, her feet moving with a grace and agility that matched Moira's wrist. Women and children rose and joined in with greater or lesser degrees of intricacy, all with faces impassive, their feet, as it were, expressing all. Then all at once, as though on cue, they ceased.

And fierce Peg commenced to sing in a voice as taut as twine. And in words that ran up my spine like newts—for they were the nearest I'd ever heard to Byrn's when he was chanting in the Old Tongue. I listened, transfixed, every hair of my body standing on end.

This song too did not end so much as stop. And when it did, a whoop of appreciation and clapping rose up. My mother said, in a voice that sounded heavy as though with sleep, "What language is that?"

"Och, 'tis all nonsense words," scoffed Peg.

At which Moira remonstrated, "Just because we don't understand 'em anymore, don't mean they're nonsense." And turning back to my mother, "Peg's got the way of it, whether she likes or no."

My mother stood up, and started dancing.

Moira resumed her drumming and I hoped the sound might rein my mother in, for she had begun to stomp and, with arms held straight against her sides, to whirl in a sort of step-dance-cum-tarantella, skirt flying, head thrown back. I opened my lips to beg her to stop but . . . a different sound issued from my mouth.

The words sang themselves out of me as Moira drummed and Mother danced.

A whoop brought me back to the room with the women and children and the close smell of bodies and breath and the sounds of . . . clapping. For me. Presently there came another sound—wheezy and reedy, a grace-noted melancholy air. The girl Jenny was playing a small instrument like a bellows, squeezing it between her hands. Miss Gourley stood holding Jenny's baby. By the stove, Miss Elliot was puffing on her pipe with one hand and holding John's with the other.

Jenny played, Moira drummed, and many a ballad in Irish, Scots, Gaelic and English was sung, verse after verse—some, I suspected, made up on the spot. Tales of love, woe, work and wonder.

My mother showed no more signs of flagging than did the others, so I crept to her cot behind the stove and drifted off to the chatter and snatches of song, all a balm to my brain, as refreshing as a stream in springtime chuckling through my mind. I seemed suspended in a bower held up by Wee Folk whose song soothed my sleep . . .

Od y tayse en drow ny hawse,
Od y mayse en trow ny mawse,
Bryg en braw,
Bryg en yd,
Bryg en braw,
Na Caylyx yd

100

SUNDAY MORNING DAWNED mild and therefore grey. I was unable to touch a bite, managing only a swallow of tea. In the vestibule, Miss Gourley straightened my tie, then stood for a moment, scrutinizing me. "Are you very frightened, Charlotte?"

"Of course not," I sputtered.

"Then how do you propose to be brave?"

"I am terrified, Miss Gourley."

"Good show, there's your first step. Remember, all must feel fear. The important thing is not to be ruled by it." She took up her hold-all and stepped out into the quiet street. I followed her.

She decreed we should walk. It had the effect of steadying my nerves—the which, no doubt, had been her intention.

I was perspiring beneath my heavy overcoat by the time we passed between the gates in the privet hedge, and mounted the broad stone steps to the handsome front door of No. One Bell Gardens.

I stood to one side as Miss Gourley pulled the bit of crape on the door-bell.

Fiona had brushed my morning coat and trousers, laundered my shirt, wiped clean my collar and cuffs, and John had lent me an emerald-green velvet waistcoat. A Homburg hat, being a half-size too big, sat low on my forehead and shadowed my face. I saw a twitch at the parlour curtain and presently the door opened.

Havers said, "Miss Gourley."

"Hello, Mr. Havers. Lord Henry is expecting me."

The butler swept me up and down with a look but stepped aside and I followed Miss Gourley into the airy foyer that had so cheered me when first I beheld it a scant two months—and a lifetime—ago. "First" beheld it? Reader, such is the slippage of memory against memory like two land masses across a fault line, for of course I had, in infancy, known this foyer and every inch of the house, including its fearsome female occupant—then so tender toward me. *Cwissa.*

"Rosamund!" came Aunt's cheery cry. I knew not whether to be more surprised by her tone or her use of Miss Gourley's first name. "Come in! Havers, don't leave her lurking in the foyer."

Miss Gourley handed her hat to the butler and asked as though by way of afterthought, "I'm having the locks re-keyed at the Refuge, Mr. Havers. Miss Bell mentioned to me a locksmith she had occasion to use, oh sometime in the fall I think it was, only the name escaped her."

"McGrievy's it was, miss," he replied blandly, "in Princes Street."

"Thank you, Mr. Havers."

Miss Gourley exited the foyer and Havers extended a hand for my hat but I kept it on my head and ducked past him, stationing myself to one side of the parlour door. I heard Miss Gourley say, "Hello Clarissa," and was again taken aback. No mere acquaintances, these two ladies were on intimate terms. The rustling of silk told me Aunt was rising from her chair. "To what do I owe the pleasure?"

I felt my palms grow moist. I stepped into the parlour doorway. She looked thinner. I swiftly bowed my head.

"Are you canvassing for subscriptions, and with one of your beneficiaries in tow? 'Deserving,' is he?" She cast a glance in my direction.

Miss Gourley answered, "I believe so."

"Wanting work, is he? In that case, he may report to Sanders—"

"My young friend has escorted me here for a different purpose, Clarissa."

"Well then," Aunt resumed her armless chair, "Sit you down, Rosie, and tell me all about it." Miss Gourley obeyed.

"In fact, Lord Henry is expecting me."

"Is he. Henry arrived last night, and in good spirits too, though I shouldn't have thought he'd be at home to anyone at all 'til tomorrow."

My amazement at the evident friendship between Aunt and Miss Gourley had obscured what I now registered as a strange dissonance:

Aunt, far from being in mourning for the presumed death of her niece, seemed in rather a holiday mood.

"Clarissa, I . . . confess I would not have anticipated so hearty a welcome."

"The return of the prodigal friend," said Aunt, adding rather grandly, "All is forgiven."

Miss Gourley cleared her throat. "Now is perhaps not the time to inquire what it is for which I've been forgiven."

"I come in for a share of the blame, Rosamund, having neglected you sorely, but we'll soon put that to rights. How fares the Refuge? I trust the stream of poor Irish flows unabated. I should like to subscribe, I know Henry does and, after all, your work provides a sanitary buffer between the wretched and their betters."

"That is generous of you, Clarissa, but—"

"Nonsense," said Aunt with a severity that betrayed tender feeling. "Tea," she pronounced, reaching for the bell cord.

"No thank you. "

"Sherry, then," she countered, a mite roguishly.

"Clarissa, Henry took me into his confidence regarding the disappearance of your niece." *Henry.*

Silence. I glanced up to see Aunt's cheek had gone from chalky to patchy.

Miss Gourley went on, "He asked that I alert him if I came by news of her."

"And have you? 'News'?" I heard a chilling note in her last word—it seemed to hint at a coiled hope now lifting its fanged head.

Miss Gourley turned to me; Aunt followed her look and barked, "Remove your hat, boy."

I obeyed.

Behind me I heard, "Rosamund."

"Lord Henry."

I turned my face to my father.

He was blinking, squinting at the light. His hair was awry, newly thin. His cheek, never florid, was hollow. In place of a morning coat he wore a dressing gown and he was shod in the carpet slippers I had embroidered for him at Yuletide. It smote my heart.

Recognition did not so much dawn on his features as melt them. "Charlotte," he said with fathomless love. And opened his arms.

I felt my own features distort with emotion, heard my strangled cry, "Father," as I went to him and he gathered me in his embrace.

Presently he drew back and, looking at me as though merely puzzled, inquired, "Where have you been, my treasure?"

"Home." I wept. Like a willow, lately a girl, now inconsolably a tree.

"At Fayne? But I looked for you there."

"I . . . did not wish to be found, Father. I am sorry!"

"Rosamund," faltered Aunt. "We are in your debt, but . . . Might we be given to know how it comes to pass my niece is here in company with you?" Here her gaze fell heavily upon me. "And with so strange an appearance?"

"Some four weeks ago, she sought refuge with us in Cowgate—"

"Four weeks?!"

"During which time—"

"How dare you?" Aunt breathed, and it seemed to me a trace of smoke issued from between her lips.

"Aunt, Miss Gourley is here to speak with Father."

"Go upstairs at once and put on decent clothes."

"No."

"Dear heart," said Father to me. "You are, I see, prudently disguised for your own protection." He smiled. "Thank God and thank you, Miss Gourley." Here he turned upon that lady a look of untrammelled . . . tenderness.

Miss Gourley cast down her eyes momentarily. Only then did I realize her efforts on my behalf and that of my mother came at some personal cost. "Lord Henry, I am here today with your child in order—"

"Father, I know the truth, and I would rather die than grieve you, but I believe all might yet be well—"

Aunt broke in, "You've come near to killing him with your recklessness, we were on the point of submitting your obituary for publication."

"Nor would it be the first time," I shot back.

She regarded me warily—and seemed to sniff the air.

"Which brings us to the matter at hand."

Miss Gourley's admonishment was meant for me, but Aunt's eyes narrowed like those of a shrew at bay as she said in a dangerously level tone,

"Miss Gourley, you have harboured a runaway and abetted my niece's flouting of the laws governing proper attire, therefore count yourself fortunate if I do not this instant summon the Constabulary."

Father said, "Now Clarissa, let us turn the page. My daughter 'who was dead is alive.'" He smiled on me, his lashes glistening with tears, and opened his arms once more. I hung back.

"Your son too," I said.

"What's that, my dear?" he inquired genially.

"Charles too is alive."

"Oh as to that, my darling, you may put it from your mind, there never was a Charles."

"There is, Father. He stands before you."

Father's smile grew vague and he allowed his gaze to drift upward. To a corner of the ceiling.

"I did not kill my mother," I said dully. "Nor was she dead through all the years of my childhood."

"That's a lie," seethed Aunt.

Stung back to life, I addressed her, cold with anger, "I have learned that, only months ago, my mother escaped from a house in Leith and entered the waters of the Firth of Forth—"

Aunt rounded on Miss Gourley, "This is your doing. When did he tell you, eh? And this is how you repay his confidence, always had your hooks in him, hadn't you, well you can't have him, not then, not now—!"

A moan escaped Father.

"Henry!" cried Aunt and Miss Gourley in unison, the latter springing to his side as he swayed on his feet. Aunt pulled the bell cord. Father leaned on Miss Gourley's forearm, allowing himself to be guided onto the chair she had just vacated.

From the doorway arose a keening. Knox was there—her face a mask of grief.

I beheld the old liar. Procuress of pain, evil witch—

Aunt cried out in agony, "Knox! Knoxy! It was for your good! For the good of the child, for the good of us all—!" She struggled painfully to rise but Knox turned and left. Suddenly dizzy with rage, 'twas all I could do not to follow the old hag, to thrash her with invective, to poison whatever grief she now tasted—

Maid was there with salts, but my aunt swatted her away. From the foyer there reached us the sound of the front door closing. Aunt's face was in her hands. The old nurse was gone.

Havers arrived with a glass of water for Father who drank it and allowed himself to recline for an instant against the chair-back until, at the sight of Miss Gourley standing, he rose to his feet. "Henry, please—that is, Lord Henry. Be seated, I implore you."

"Charlotte," said Father—pausing to steady himself. He clasped his hands behind his back and proceeded with the grace befitting a gentleman under duress. "All I have done, I have done for your good. And you have my word that, were I vouchsafed the opportunity, I would do all as before. With one exception. I would have obtained for you a cure while you were still an infant." His voice shook. "For that, I am sorry. For that, I beg you may find it in your heart to forgive me. And I pray that God might do likewise."

Miss Gourley sat down, freeing my father to do likewise—with a sigh—and from her hold-all produced a document stamped with the seal of the General Register Office for Scotland. She handed it to Father. He squinted, eyelashes aflutter, and fumbled in the pocket of his dressing gown for his spectacles. Donning them, he perused the document, passed it absently to Clarissa, then tilted his head and regarded Miss Gourley quizzically.

A short laugh from Aunt, "A writ of divorce? What an absurdity, Lady Marie is dead." She took the writ disdainfully between thumb and forefinger and, seeming on the point of dropping it into the fire, contented herself with depositing it on the occasional table.

Trembling, I crossed the parlour to the window and, coming within inches of my aunt, drew aside the curtain and raised a hand, by way of signal, to the hansom cab that now waited in the drive. I watched as its door opened and Mr. Baxter alighted. Behind me, craning her narrow neck, Aunt exclaimed, "Josey!"

"Surely you do not mean to say Baxter is here," said Father reproachfully. "I wonder you invite the man, Clarissa, knowing I forbade him the house."

"He is not here at my bidding, Henry." Aunt's voice wavered with contrition. She sounded oddly young. She turned back to the window, unable to hide her eagerness. "Who is that with him . . . ?" Her voice died and she merely stared. I returned to Miss Gourley's side.

There was the sound of the front door opening and presently Havers entered and announced, "Mr. Baxter and . . ." Here he was seen to hesitate. He raised a loosely closed hand to his lips and emitted a slight cough, before continuing, "A lady who declines to give her name but claims long acquaintance with the family." Whereupon he melted away. And Mr. Baxter entered with my mother upon his arm.

She was dressed in a simple floral-print silk gown, out of step with the season but perfectly matched with her hopes. Her short silver-streaked hair was combed behind her ears. Her figure was matronly, her face was lined, but her carriage was erect. And the eyes were the eyes of the portrait.

Father fell back in his chair and stared up at her, one hand shading his eyes.

What blood there was, drained from Aunt's cheeks.

"Mae," gasped Father.

I did not take my eyes from him, fearful lest he be overcome quite. He slowly lowered his hand and gazed upon my mother.

My mother returned his look and, far from savaging his breast in quest of his heart, said simply, "Hello Henry."

He cupped a hand over his mouth and I could not make out if he were on the point of choking or rejoicing.

My mother continued. "You haven't seen me as recently as Clarissa has, so I know it must come as a bit of a shock. I'm not the girl you put away nearly thirteen years ago."

He was ashen. But he rose to his feet. In the presence of a lady.

Miss Gourley spoke with signal calm, "Lady Marie was rescued from the Firth of Forth and brought to the Refuge—"

Aunt snarled, "I'll see you in chains, Rosamund Gourley, and your 'Refuge' razed to the ground—"

"I see I have further cause to thank you, Miss Gourley," said Father, suddenly the unflappable gentleman.

I fought a sense of unreality.

Miss Gourley went on, and there was about her a quality I had grown up believing the preserve of gentlemen and myself: honour. "Lord Henry, we did not recognize Lady Marie, and it was some time before she disclosed to us her true—"

Mother interrupted, "It wasn't until my son turned up that I spilled the beans."

"Your son?" said Father.

"Charles," said Mother.

"Josey," pleaded Aunt. "Help, can't you?" Her voice had softened. I turned to her in surprise to see that so too had her eyes—and with an emotion I recognized from long ago: love.

"I'm sorry, Clarissa," said Mr. Baxter.

Clarissa.

How much had passed already among the adults in this room? How much of friendship? Of trust? Of love? And heartbreak. How much of life had been shared by these, my elders, to render the present moment pregnant with the past?

As though breaking a spell, Miss Gourley returned us to the here and now. "Mr. Baxter has come in his capacity as solicitor to witness your signature on the writ, Lord Henry."

Clarissa snapped, "Don't be ridiculous. My sister-in-law is mad, she may count herself lucky my brother did not abandon her years ago."

Miss Gourley countered, "I don't know that luck comes into it, Clarissa. Lady Marie is entitled by law to the return of her dowry upon divorce from Lord Henry."

With a horrid smile, my aunt tugged at the bell sash. Havers returned instantly. In a voice terrifying for its treacle and poison, Aunt said, "Havers, send for Dr. Chambers."

"Very good—"

"No!" cried my mother, suddenly wild-eyed. The butler paused in the doorway. Mr. Baxter placed a hand on Mother's arm but addressed my father, saying gently, "Henry, it would be best to sign."

Henry.

"How dare you set foot in my house, Baxter?" said Father with a curl of his lip.

A plaintive note in Aunt's voice, "Henry, please—"

Mr. Baxter said, "Clarissa, I don't mind, really, and won't stay longer than—"

"You're just mean, Henry," said my mother.

My father looked at her and his sneer faded. Somehow I could see past his care-worn features to a younger man. "Marie. I do not deserve your forgiveness. But perhaps . . . with time . . . I might earn it."

I looked at my mother. Past the lines in her face I saw, as though through the fine cracks in an old painting, a young woman. Cheeks and eyes aglow. Holding her beloved child; posing with him for a photograph.

"Marie," said Father. "This is your home."

I looked from one to the other. I saw a handsome couple. And, for the first time since I'd been a two-year-old boy, I saw my parents. Together. For a moment I thought that if no one said a word, it would seal up again—the chasm in my family. And those whom I had put asunder, I would reunite.

"Henry," warned Aunt, "She is a danger to herself and—"

I whirled on her, "You viper—!"

"Sweetheart—" said Mother.

"Mother!" I was near breathless. "Father is sorry, you can see that, all might yet be well, we can be as we might have been if not for . . ." Shaking with rage, I beheld my aunt—a withered stick in black silk, wracked in body, thrawn in soul. "This was all her doing!"

"Sweetheart," repeated my mother, waiting until my eyes met hers before continuing, "She's not the Baron. He is."

I looked at my father.

He squared his shoulders and, with an urbane note of regret, "Quite right, Marie, and I'm afraid I shan't sign your writ."

"Havers," said I in a tone which amazed me with its airiness, so like Father's.

"Yes, Miss Charlotte."

"Tell Sanders to fetch Mr. McGrievy from his locksmith shop in Princes Street."

Clarissa looked up as though at distant thunder.

"Very good, miss—"

"Stay," said Aunt.

The butler obeyed, apparently unperturbed. "Is it still your wish, Madam, that I send for Dr. Chambers?"

"Forget the locksmith," said my mother, "Havers can tell us himself how he got the key copied last fall." I marvelled at her *sang froid* as she took from me the baton, as it were, and advanced the plan I had conceived.

Father said, "What 'key'?"

"Do you really not know, Henry?"

"Well, Havers?" said Father.

"Not a word, Havers," said Aunt.

The hesitation was but a hair's breadth before Havers turned to the Baron and, as smoothly as ever, said, "I know not whether it was the key in question, Your Lordship, but a wax impression of a key was given me by Miss Clarissa some months ago with the instruction that I should order a new key to be made from it, which I did, whereupon I gave the newly cut key to Miss Clarissa."

"Well, what of it?" said Father, with a hint of pique as though at matters domestic.

"Mother used a key to escape from her room at the house in Leith—"

"No," quavered Aunt.

To my surprise, I took no pleasure from the next words to pass my lips—indeed they tasted sour to me: "Aunt Clarissa gave her the key, knowing Mother would likely do away with herself." I felt fouled, and I understood for the first time why much of what ought to be said remains so oft unsaid: the saying sullies the speaker. I felt unwell.

Father was stock-still. Presently he said, "I cannot believe it of my sister."

"Clarissa visited once a month, Henry." My mother's accent cut through, flat and matter-of-fact. "And each time she said, 'You killed your child.' I guess she was afraid I might forget. What with the drugs and all."

Father's lips parted. He drew a breath and began very slightly to tilt backwards, catching himself with a look to Aunt, as though grappling onto her gaze. He shook his head a little spasmodically—it was an expression of dismay and dawning horror such as I had never seen and hoped never to see again.

I turned to my aunt. "Shall I summon the Constabulary?"

There ensued an incendiary silence. Broken only by the purring of the fire.

Presently, Father took the writ from the table, along with a pen from Mr. Baxter and, with nib hovering above the signature line, inquired in the tones of a gentleman whose amiable manner admits of no alteration, "On what grounds?"

Mr. Baxter said, "Desertion."

A drop of ink splashed to the page. Father bent forward and signed. In quadruplicate.

Mr. Baxter then signed in witness and held the signature pages before the hearth that the ink might dry quickly. He returned one copy to my father, and two to his brief-bag. He placed the remaining copy in an envelope which he handed to my mother.

"Thank you, Josey." She rose. My father did likewise. "You know, Henry, I told Charles that I'd like to cut out your heart. But I take it back. I don't think you have one." Turning to leave, she said, "I'll see myself out, Havers."

Mr. Baxter bowed, then turned and followed her. Miss Gourley rose and looked at me, but I shook my head. She hesitated, then exited, Havers dutifully on her heels.

Clarissa sat motionless, hands folded in her lap. She appeared diminished—near mummified. I poured out a glass of water and offered it to her. She waved it away. My father lowered himself back onto the chair. He looked as friable as one of his specimens. I would stay. He would concede I was meant for a life of the mind which did not admit of matrimony. I would attend school. He would marry and carry on the Bell line. I would remain with him for the rest of his days, a devoted spinster-daughter and physician, the better to minister to him in his advancing years. I opened my lips to say all this, but said simply, "Father." And wept.

"Charlotte, my darling. Don't cry."

"Father. Might you not. Even once. Call me Charles?"

He looked bewildered, the ghost of a smile playing about his lips. "You are, and always will be, my precious Charlotte."

A sob escaped me. "Please, Father, say it, and I shall never ask it of you again." But he was mum. I cried like a child.

He reached into the pocket of his dressing gown and, with a look of infinite tenderness, proffered a snow-white hanky. I took it. I held it to my face and breathed in his scent. Of wool and sealing wax and tobacco and soap. I felt his hand pat my head. Heard him say in cherishing tones, "Charlotte."

I doubled over slowly, the handkerchief pressed to my face as though to prevent the latter from falling off and onto the floor. He went on. Gently but firmly. "The doctor said you might experience confusion. But you mustn't fret, you are cured. These torments soon will pass."

"Please, Father, please. Please. Please." I heard rising notes of panic and calamity in my voice. Hardly trusting myself to behold once again those guileless blue eyes and yet craving only that, I looked full upon him. But he was looking at a corner of the ceiling.

My heart froze.

And I might have turned to stone, but that Aunt, her voice vibrating with hatred, said, "Go put on decent clothing and cease to scandalize your father."

I mopped my face. Blew my nose. "Goodbye, Aunt."

She stared at me murderously. "Foolish girl, your father will not allow you to stray a second time from under this roof."

"No more will my mother allow me to be mutilated a second time."

She regarded me warily. "What can you mean?"

"My severed flesh has grown back."

Her features contracted in disgust.

Father closed his eyes.

He was the Baron.

I turned, and left the house.

At the sound of the front door closing, Clarissa sighs—even a sigh is painful, tearing as it seems to do at the lining of her chest. "Henry, I know you think me wicked."

He rises, waving her off mildly, and makes unhurriedly for the door, shuffling somewhat in his slippers.

"But I have only ever acted in your interests. Henry?" Did he chuckle just now? "Brother, you are finally well and truly free, you may marry—not Miss Llewellyn of course, she is penniless, but a young lady of means . . ."

He turns in the doorway. "My dear sister. It is accomplished."

". . . What is?"

He smiles. "Oh Clarissa. If only you had inherited."

101

I WISHED TO WALK.

And to be alone with my thoughts. In hopes of disentangling them from my feelings.

"Charles," trilled my mother from the window of the hansom cab. She had been waiting outside the gate and now she paralleled my progress along George Street. Would no one rid me of this troublesome mother?

The temperature had dropped and the sun had come out. The air was crystalline. As I walked I felt the bands of a spell snap from about my rib cage. No spell has power over love, and Reader, I loved my father as much as ever I had. What broke was not love but illusion. Illusion is a comfortable garment thrown over an uncomfortable truth which, left too long covered, must rot. I had been magyked, in thrall to Father's fragility. But he was the Baron. And now I was free. I was cold. So cold.

"Charles, wait!"

I wished to be colder.

"Good luck, Mother," I called back without looking, and turned up a side street. The cab turned likewise and I quickened my steps, ducking into a mews, sliding on stone—for ice had formed in the shadows—squeezing through a narrow passage between two houses and out into a street that gave onto a small private park.

The gate swung open at my touch for it had been left unlocked. Drawn perhaps by the cooing of pigeons, and longing to throw open the windows and hatches of my fevered brain to set free all trapped thoughts, I entered. The path branched in three directions. At its confluence stood a bench. Seated there was an old woman. She was surrounded by pigeons. They strutted and lofted about her feet and jostled one another to perch on the back of the bench. She was feeding them from a paper sack. She looked up. "Hello, pet."

I was cold. So cold.

In the winter sun, her face showed finely etched, the tracery about her eyes, the lacework of her cheeks—it was a face sculpted by time and work. And love. And lies.

"I'm sorry."

"That does not signify." I felt nothing.

"'Twas ne'er meant to harm you—"

"I am harmed!" It flew from my mouth like a bird from a house—"You lied!" A house in flames—"You were my jailer! You groomed me, lulled me, helped undress me; laid me out, stood by as they photographed my . . . *me*!"—foaming with rage, faint with naming—"whilst he drugged me, thrust his instruments up into me, then you left me alone with that woman and him and his burning knife!"

"Child . . ."

All the anger I could not muster toward my father, in excess even of that which I had heaped upon my aunt, surged now, but even as I lashed out I understood I had never, for one moment, been burdened by the need to protect my old nurse from my wrath—any more than I'd had to protect the gnarled spectre of Aunt. "I hate you!"

I ran blindly away, slipping on fallen leaves candied in ice, back to the gate. Parked before it, a hansom cab. At the window, my mother's face, pink with the brisk air, smiling. Shining with tears. O Reader, I had had enough of tears. Tears that professed love for me, tears calculated to shield from guilt the one who shed them, tears meant to claim injury on the part of the injuring party—enough! "You got your divorce, what more do you want of me?"

The cab door opened. She stepped down and walked toward me—then past me. To Knox. The old woman rose, clutching her paper sack of seeds, her breath visible in puffs. I watched as my mother went to her and the two women embraced. I lingered as though enchanted, even as I ordered myself to turn my back and begone; even as I inwardly scoffed that the length of time they held one another sufficed for the preparation of a soft-cooked egg. I hated them. I hated women. I hated men.

"Charles."

Enough.

"I need to talk to you, Charles."

But I had finished with her, finished with human speech. I was leaving, to join earth, trees, sky. It seemed effortlessly within reach now, the intricate transformation; as though accessible all along had been that promiscuity beyond time and space. I heard it—a mathematical tinkling, it scintillated my brain, was intensely pleasurable. All was distinct, and

yet at one with all else—the air, the bench, the women, the trees, the sky,
I. Nothing that is not beautiful, nothing that is not connected, nothing
that does not dissolve in bliss . . .

"Charlotte."

I seemed to awaken.

It was my mother's voice.

"I've lost enough babies, Charlotte," she added. "Please come with me."

A kerfuffle about my feet. I looked down to see the pigeons strutting
and chookering. I took the paper sack from Knox's hand and with a
wave of my arm, spilt an arc of golden seed and flapping wings.

I heard Mother laughing. It sounded like the waters of the swallet
that had drawn me with its merry, riddling words.

I turned to my old nurse. "Knoxy? Look after Father."

"Aye, pet."

And I stepped up into the cab with my mother.

In her garret quarters atop the Refuge, Rosamund Gourley fills her pen
and bends to an empty sheet of paper.

The Refuge
The Cowgate, Edinburgh
February 26, 1888

Dear Mrs. Haas,

I write to you, not in my capacity as Co-Foundress of your daughter's
school, but as a woman who wishes humbly to express to you her
gratitude. And to take the liberty of informing you of a fact which,
until recently, I deemed best kept hidden. I ask as well that you might
forgive my intrusion onto your privacy.

Some nearly sixteen years ago, you took, from Mr. Moore, loving
receipt of a female infant to whom I had given birth.

It has, as you know, been my privilege to count your daughter,
Gwendolyn, among my pupils, and to see first-hand the fine young
woman she has grown to be, owing to the loving care of her parents,
not least you, her mother.

I have not imparted this information to Gwendolyn. I leave the
determination of whether and/or when to do so, in your hands.

I am forever grateful.

Please know that your family has a friend in me.

Cordially,
R. Gourley

102

FROM THE STERN of the *Scythia*, my mother and I watched the coast-line of Great Britain shrink to a smear on the horizon. The wind set to flapping the flower-pot hat she held in one hand, and rippled the leg-of-mutton sleeves of her peacock-blue dress with its mandarin lozenges; it lifted my dashing new burgundy cape and set to flying like a pennant my silk bowtie of Mother's own choosing. To Mother as well I owed my velvet waistcoat with its clever wooden toggles, and the matching trousers with the grenadier-style stripe along the outside leg.

She turned and, leaning back against the rail, cropped hair fluttering about her face, looked up at the tilted smoke-stacks and twin masts of the ship. She brought her hand to her mouth and bit into a succulent pear. Wiping her chin with her wrist, she said, "Well, Charlotte, it sure beats a plague ship."

Overhead, a wheel of gulls seemed to laugh, and she threw back her head and laughed with them.

At No. One Bell Gardens, a transformation is taking place. Framed poetically as a journey to that "bourn" from which "no traveller returns" it is in fact a process that conjures every magyk known and unknown in achieving the awesome alchemy of death. Few have slipped the bonds of time and space long enough to know their true nature and returned to tell the tale. Of those who have made the round trip, few find it tellable. As for the rest of us, we must die into knowledge, and once only.

Clarissa is not one to whinge. Thus, while there is still time, an inventory:

It feels, daily, as though her flesh were becoming bark—fascia hardening, tendons stiffening, all in a gathering grip from within. Every morning, agony. Every evening, dread. There is a moment in the afternoon of comparative ease. She is not bedridden, bed is to be avoided. Stone bed. Rather, she is chair-ridden. Bone-ridden, her skeleton the rack upon which her tissues are stretched, the screw turning, tighter each day.

She is quite thin now. But in a malevolent reversal, the lighter her body becomes, the heavier it feels to her, each limb weighed down by pain.

Beside her, the blue bottle sits stoppered and untouched. After a week, Maid goes to the chemist for its successor.

And its successor.

Until a third bottle sits stoppered and untouched.

Maid risks wondering aloud at Madam's staunch refusal to avail herself of a drop of relief and is threatened with dismissal (invalids are testy). Madam is a rare one for pain.

Today, having helped her on and off the commode, Maid half-carries her to the—"not the bed, eediot!"—down the stairs to the parlour. Madam is so light, it is like carrying kindling (kindling that whimpers in pain with every movement). Settling her gingerly onto the armless nursing chair by the window, arranging the cushion just so—earning a slap—lighting the fire in the hearth, "Is there anything else I can—"

"Go."

Maid goes.

Clarissa sits, hands idle in her lap. There is no longer any question of taking up her work basket.

The fire pops purses and coffins.

She is not a tree. But imagine, Reader, if you will, that a tree is innervated such as to be a network of pain; and that the tree is able now to direct the movement of one thin leafless limb.

Clarissa watches her arm, starkly outlined by the sleeve of her nightgown, as she wills it to elevate—weight of lumber; wills it to reach—lightning-strike of pain—wills it to lever rightward. Wills twig-fingers to close about the first blue bottle. Wills the twigs of the other hand to close about the tiny cork and remove it. Both sets of twigs cluster about the bottle now, and both pain-heavy branches raise it to lips that are turning to bark.

Relief.

Repeat.

Bliss.

Repeat.

Oblivion.

He is bent over the wing of an Arctic tern. A tap at his study door. It opens.

"Penny," says Knox.

He looks up . . .

Death notice. BELL. The Honourable Clarissa Catherine Beatrice, sister to Henry, Lord Bell, Baron DC de Fayne. At No. One Bell Gardens, Edinburgh. Aged fifty-six.

Henry's first thought: "Now Rosamund and I may marry." And he weeps.

～❧

Part Seven

I'm no longer fighting. I'm inviting.
POLLY HIGGINS

Arrival

THE *SCYTHIA* SAILED serenely into Boston Harbor on a glorious June morning. Mother leaned over the forward rail like an ample bowsprit and spread her arms as though to embrace the fishing boats dotting the waters of the port side, and the islands to starboard—she pointed to one. "That's where your Granny and Grandpappy were held half-starved, Charlotte, and don't you ever forget it."

"Why, what had they done?"

"They had the nerve to be Irish."

We emerged into the South Channel and were greeted by an unobstructed view of the coastline with the city laid out upon it. On a rise near its centre there glinted a spear of morning light, and my mother gasped, "The State House."

"What is the State House?"

"It's the place where your Grandpappy showed them what an Irishman can do when he sets his mind to it. Your Grandpappy also sold me for a title and a heap of mud and don't you forget that either."

A towboat guided us into harbour and we nosed into a berth amid a wilderness of masts and smoke-stacks, and as the gangplank was lowered onto the great wharf, I offered my arm to my mother.

Thus, Reader, did I set foot in the "New World." New to whom? I would come to that question in time—the latter of which I would have aplenty.

Our cab drew up before a house with a bright-red door in Chestnut Street, in the heart of a pleasant purlieu remarkable for its resemblance to Edinburgh's New Town, but for its red bricks and wooden window frames.

"I'm shaking," said Mother, grasping my hand. I gave hers a reassuring squeeze. "Don't worry, Mother, Mrs. Blanchard will recognize you despite the passage of years and the acquisition of flesh."

She smacked my hand, and the next instant seized me in an embrace before straightening my bowtie and dusting my collar.

We alighted. She with her handbag and I with my specimen case, we walked up the brick path to the red door. I heard her catch her breath. "All right?" To which she replied, "The porch swing." Once again, Mother's answer to a simple question was more intriguing than informative. I reached out to take hold of a brass horse-shoe knocker but the door opened suddenly and a young woman stopped short with a smile—"Oh, hello."

"Taffy," said Mother, smiling through tears.

The girl glanced at me with a sort of polite panic in her eyes. Brown eyes. The next instant, an older woman in cap and apron appeared in the doorway, "Here now, what's the ruckle, Miss Tessy, thought you'd left, who's this?" County Cork. Same as Peg. Softened but unmistakable.

"Annie!" cried Mother.

"Annie? What is it?" came yet another female voice—calm, melodious. And the population of the doorway increased by one. The lady stopped when she saw my mother. And stared. My mother did the same. Then, in an infinitely gentle gesture, the lady reached out a hand, cupped my mother's cheek, and said, "Mae."

They embraced. Patiently. As though they had known for a very long time—considerably longer than the month or so since Mother's letter—that it was coming. They wept.

I stole a look at the girl to find her eyes upon me. She looked away, then back again. We exchanged a smile as though equally at a loss and both of us looked away once more.

When at length they drew apart, Taffy said, "Dearest Mae, this is my daughter, Tessy."

My mother turned to the girl whom she had mistaken for her mother and with a look full of love said, "Of course she is." She turned on me a look no less loving but darkened with something deeper, something mortal. Earth. "And this, dear Taffy, is my son, Charlotte Bell."

I saw their politely suppressed surprise. Mindful of my obligation as a gentleman to set others at ease, I bowed. "How do you do,

Mrs. Blanchard, Miss Blanchard. I am Miss Corcoran's daughter, Charles."

We were shown to our rooms, but Mother refused to take a quiet supper there in the interests of "recovering from your long voyage."

"Are you talking about the sea-crossing, Taffy, or my whole life since I left for Rome eighteen years ago?"

"Dearest Mae, both I should think, forgive me, you'll want to rest."

"I've had enough 'rest' to last me a lifetime."

The house was comfortable, if a touch overheated. "Isn't it wonderful?" sighed Mother.

Mrs. Blanchard was a person of such innate modesty and moderate temperament, I wondered at her having claimed Mother for a bosom friend—but I supposed anyone might have thought the same of me and Gwendolyn Haas.

As for Miss Theresa Blanchard, she regarded me with a polite wariness, and I made a mental note to refrain from any unseasonable display of mnemonics. She was uncommonly pretty. An observable fact.

Nor was I in want of lofty pursuits. Over the next several weeks there were lectures and concerts and walks and dinner guests of a kind wholly new to me. At the Blanchards' table I met an attorney-at-law named Mr. Tubbs, who had been born a slave—the very word a stinging lash such that I hesitate to commit it here in ink lest it ignite the page.

At the Blanchards' table too I met ladies from the Women's Education Association, and on one eminently memorable evening, listened, amazed, to a lively discussion of industrial chemistry, mineralogy and biology among students of the Women's Laboratory at the Massachusetts Institute of Technology. O brave new world that hath such women in it! Among them—each and every one worthy to be ranked with Rosamund Gourley—were several pairs who cohabited in what my mother titteringly referred to as "a Boston marriage."

Mother herself was less high-minded in her pursuits, whether "brazening it out" with one Katie Buxton, or producing her chequebook at the dining table and making out a large sum to a suffragist who had established a "settlement house" for women and children "regardless of creed or colour."

"You remind me of a friend of mine back in Auld Reekie," said Mother, signing with a flourish.

We visited the grave of Miss Blanchard's uncle who had been killed in "the war between the states"—a war to which I heard Miss Blanchard's father refer, in a low voice, as "far from over."

And we visited my grandfather's grave. Mother lingered, hands folded, eyes fixed on his granite stone, looking for all the world as though she were about to say something . . . before stepping aside, and kneeling before that of her mother. She closed her eyes, I saw her lips moving, and assumed she was praying.

After dinner one evening, Mrs. Blanchard said, "Come with me Mae, I've got something for you." I found Mother in her bedroom, weeping and laughing. She looked up from a packet of papers on her lap. "My letters."

I was mercifully left to my own devices when it came to matters sartorial. Owing perhaps to his never having grown old enough to be breeched, I felt most Charles when wearing a frock, and most Charlotte when in trousers—provided they itched not overmuch. I could not abide stiff collars, nor ties arranged like nooses about one's neck. Likewise, when frocked, I eschewed "foundation garments," opting for simple flowing dresses which, in Mother's opinion, lent me an air of having "just wrapped yourself in a tablecloth."

I had written to tell Father of our safe arrival. He had replied, and the sight of his handwriting—as familiar to me as his dear face—contrasted starkly with the impersonal tenor of the words themselves. Thus I both dreaded and craved the hour of the post, for Gwen and I kept up a lively correspondence. I devoured her news of school, of merry Maeve, of Miss Mellor, Miss Gourley, Miss Elliot and John, of her parents (her father had "come round" to her engagement) and especially of Mr. Margalo. The margins of her letters were lined with sketches often bearing humorous captions like something out of *Punch* but beautiful.

About a month into our sojourn on Chestnut Street, there arrived from Gwendolyn a letter with the most remarkable news, which she had only lately received from her mother and which she assured me was "as strangely unsurprising as it is shocking and, of all things, it's brought me and Mam closer. Dearest Charlotte, I'm really rather proud of all my parents." Having her permission to do so, I conveyed, still reeling, my friend's news to my mother—to whom it came as no surprise. "Mrs. Haas wrote and told me that Miss Gourley wrote and told her, and of course I'm not going to tell Mrs. Haas that I guessed as much and that it was me who advised Miss Gourley to write to her in the first place."

A month or so later, I was inspecting the mechanics of the "porch swing," a contraption not dissimilar to Foucault's pendulum but that suspended from its frame was a bench of a size to accommodate two adults. I wondered if, with the ever-keen assistance of Miss Blanchard's younger brother and sister, I might fit it with a motor. "Hop on, it won't bite," said Miss Blanchard. And she sat and patted the spot next to her. Before I could join her, the wee terrier set to yapping. (The dog did no work and lived in the house. It slept on a cushion. On a sofa. In the drawing room.) A postman trundled up the walk.

"Mailman," she corrected me.

"Male man?"

"Mailman."

"Oh. Quite."

He handed her the "mail."

She shuffled through. "This one's for your mom."

It was from Miss Gourley. I braced myself for news of Father.

"Are you okay?"

"I am."

"Sit."

I obeyed. I felt the world shift beneath me.

"It's just the swing," she said.

"Quite."

"What's the matter, Miss Charles?"

I shook my head. I could not speak the words. I dreaded he might be dead. And I could not imagine the world could continue afterward.

She left with the letter and returned shortly with my mother. Forcing myself to rise, I searched her face for a sign—perhaps, after all, it was only news of his remarriage. Not to Miss Llewellyn of course, but to a young lady of means. To be followed soon after by news of an heir, all of which was devoutly to be wished for the sake of Fayne and my beloved moor, scene of my fast-receding childhood—both of them.

Mother showed me the letter. It contained a clipping from *The Scotsman*, wherein the death of the Honourable Clarissa Bell was announced. She sighed, folded it away, and said, "Poor Henry."

Then she breezed back into the house.

Miss Blanchard bid me once more be seated. I did so, immediately setting the machine in motion, falling into an agreeable rhythm with my companion.

"Who's Clarissa Bell?" she asked.

"She was my father's sister. She went to great lengths to ensure the continuance of the title."

"I'm sorry for your loss."

I replied airily, "No need, Miss Blanchard. I say, does this thing go any faster?"

I felt nothing at the news of Aunt's death. By dinner I had quite forgotten it. A delicious "Irish stew." Followed by pudding—which they called "dessert," as though one had earned it—a distinctly Puritan outlook—consisting of "pumpkin pie." A peculiarly Yankee notion: the turning of animal fodder into a "treat."

That night, however, under cover of darkness, I wept hot tears. Because, for all she had hated Charlotte, she had loved Charles. And much as Charlotte had hated Aunt, Charles loved her. It was no good pummelling my head, smacking my wet cheeks. I would weep for *Cwissa* . . .

Our mothers primped and fussed over Miss Blanchard as though she were a doll and she good-naturedly endured it. Unless it was possible she enjoyed it? I inquired. She replied, "It's fun." This propensity for fun she shared with Gwendolyn Haas. Indeed, she shared much that I loved in my friend. Miss Blanchard, however, radiated something new in my experience. Calm. An amused calm. She was a pattern young lady who seemed never to misbehave or even wish to—but with none of the appertaining priss so often associated with the breed. She knew her own mind, and if life had prepared her to expect ease, plenty and gentle treatment, this expectation had not muffled her in a cotton-wool of ignorance; on the contrary, it seemed to have girded her with a strength that even then she was turning outward.

We were on the porch swing.

"I wish you could meet my friend Gwendolyn. I think the two of you might 'hit it off.'" I hesitated, then added, "I've told her about you—your family, that is. And Boston as a whole." I had no wish to lend the impression that my letters were full of Miss Blanchard this, Miss Blanchard that—the which they were.

"Tell me about her."

"She is an artist. She is engaged to my tutor and oldest friend, Isadore Margalo. She is devoted to things French."

"Tell me more."

I did.

At length she said, "Gwendolyn's my friend too now, and you can tell her that in your next letter."

We swung in silence for a time. Presently, I asked, "Have you artistic leanings, Miss Blanchard?"

"Please call me Tessa."

"Tessa." The word seemed to release a capsule of warmth. Like a spiced brew.

She was saying, "Well as for 'leanings,' I suppose I have all sorts, Miss Charles."

"Do call me Charles. Or Charlotte. As you like."

"What would you like me to call you?"

"What would you like to call me?"

"Sweetheart."

She blushed but did not cease to smile. As did I—blush, that is. I longed to look away, I longed never to look away.

She said, "I'm going to be a teacher."

Her statement might have been a *non sequitur*—or at the very least, abrupt—if it had not seemed between us that time was of the essence. It was as though we knew that the threads connecting one thought to another would keep, along with all the narrative skeins of our lives to date; as though we knew we would one day sit together on either side of a hearth, weaving those threads like a tapestry; but that for now, the urge to mate and migrate was paramount. And if the hearth were to be attained, we must prepare to fly.

She settled upon "Charlie."

———

We were boating in the Back Bay Fens. Summer haze, like a visible hum, lay on the marsh; all was veiled in lazy shimmer as we meandered the narrow waterway, gliding through carpets of lily-pads that parted before our prow, leaving bubbles in our gentle wake. Our mothers were a distance ahead, having the advantage over us of being each a skilled oarswoman, whereas in our boat, there was but one—I had yet to gain the knack of proceeding in anything but a circle. Tessa, however, was tireless. In her loose dress of pale iris she rivalled me for the latest in table-linen couture. Blue damsel-flies zigged about, came together on her sleeves, and whizzed away again. We rounded a bend into a corridor of stately elms. She stowed the oars and allowed our craft to drift. I gazed into the water at our reflection amid the trees towering in the depths. I saw her fingers trailing in the water. I looked up. She leaned forward and kissed me. Time did not stop. It expanded.

How had I lived until now?

We pledged our troth, but did not declare ourselves to our families, who indulged our "girlish" attachment as a tender prelude to the womanly fulfillment of marriage. Had I been a thoroughgoing young man, heir to title and fortune, we would have been all but thrown together—and therefore wrenched apart, there being in that case no question of spending hours unchaperoned. Thus, our summer idyll.

But as summer turned to fall, Tess became more and more the object of male attention, and the drawing room in Chestnut Street was host to numerous suitors.

"Don't be silly, Charlie, they're old friends."

This did not assuage my misgivings. That they were honourable was not in question. That their fawning gaze was, at times, directed to me in my table-linened guise, struck me as incomprehensible. "Miss Bell, may I have the pleasure of your company punting on the Charles River?" inquired a jug-eared youth, one Gordon Peabody Junior. (Great ones for "Juniors" and I's, II's, III's were these Americans. As though they had never quite got over kicking out the monarchy.) "You may not."

Tess would marry in two or three years, she must.

"Says who?"

"Says your family, says the world."

"I want to marry you."

"I have no rejoinder."

She laughed. She loved me. I cannot explain it. Love is a miracle. Nothing to do with "dessert."

There came a day when, on one of our aquatic excursions, we pulled our rowboat up to where a willow swept the bank and parted to welcome us into a green world. In the dappled light, amid the scent of earth and moss soft enough for Faery, we lay down in one another's arms. Reader, I would not court bathos in detailing what followed. But as a scientist, it behooves me to report: bliss.

She asked me one day, as we lay in one another's arms, to tell her about Fayne.

I did so.

Much as I had meant to keep it closed like the covers of an enchanted book, I opened for her the prospect of my beloved wild moorlands. The standing stone. My trout stream. The house. The ancient Dispute. I regaled her with the "tail" of the Blighted Heir. And more soberly, the tale of my own "blighted" birth . . . To my surprise, the telling felt more balm than bane. And it occurred to me that memory is shaped not merely by events and their retention, but also by the telling, and by the listening. Thereby, too, is shaped the future.

She rose on one elbow. "So you have, what do you call it, a 'case.'"

"A claim."

"Yes."

"No."

"But you can inherit as a woman in Scotland."

"But not in England."

"Can't that just count as another dispute?"

"No, it is a difference, only, in law between one side of the border and the other."

"But if the border is in dispute in Fayne, then—"

"Were I to inherit according to Scottish law, the Dispute would be settled."

"Good."

"No."

"Why?"

"To acknowledge the primacy of one law or the other is to trigger the dissolution of the estate, the absorption of its lands by the winning side, and the extinction of the title."

"Golly."

"Quite."

"Still, it's your birthright."

This gave me pause. As Charlotte I had grown up with no expectation of inheritance. But what of Charles?

I wrote to Mr. Baxter.

He replied that in his opinion my claim was "not without merit" and offered to assist me in his "capacity as solicitor and friend." I thanked him. And put it from my mind. I was in no hurry to part from Tess.

I might have forgotten Fayne altogether, but that as summer turned to fall, a series of odd occurrences snagged my notice like mental burdocks. One evening at dinner, the surface of the water in my glass wrinkled as though at a seismic wave. I turned to the young twins, Amy and Ethan, about to explain the "earthquake" in their water glasses, when I saw that the surface in theirs was smooth. As was that of every other glass on the table as well as the water pitcher. Suddenly prey to an uncanny fear, I drained my glass to expunge the sight—for it must be a hallucination—half-afraid as I did so, that I swallowed a spell of sorts.

It occurred again the following evening.

Then, whilst drifting along the Muddy (it wasn't) River, I glanced over the side to see reflected in the water a face not my own. Reader, it was not the phantasm of my own infant face such as had surprised me on the bog that long ago day with Mr. Margalo—but it was a face I knew as well as my own: *Byrn*. Staring up at me with his blue pebble eyes, his time-planed face like bleached bone. He appeared both older and younger, resembling more strongly now the playful Celtic-style drawing Gwen had made of him as a faun. He was summoning me. Not over the side of the boat, but *home*.

"What's the matter? asked Tessa.

"I just saw an old friend," I whispered. "In the water."

"Who?"

And I told her.

I felt better for having talked to Tess. I put all the watery phenomena behind me, I was having too glorious a time. I had everything I'd never dreamed of, what's more, I had accustomed myself to Boston society so far as to surmise that, rather than evidence of madness, my hallucinations might be viewed as a psychic ability much prized in its salons of those days—had I stayed, I might have made quite a splash as a "spirit rapper" in a Boston marriage with Miss Tessa Blanchard. Reader, it would have been a wonderful life.

One night, not long afterwards, I woke to the sound of rushing water. My first thought was that the Charles had flooded. I threw off the covers. Tessa said groggily, "What's the matter?"

I flew to the window and looked out through the spreading branches of the chestnut tree, expecting to see the waters rising about the house. Instead, there was the garden slumbering beneath the blue light of the moon. The rushing in my ears became a trickling . . .

"Charlie?"

. . . and the trickling become the chatter of the underground spring. The swallet had surfaced in my brain and was singing my names, along with a third word—one so familiar, yet just beneath comprehension. A word compressed as though it had lain buried. A word preserved, like something pulled from the bog. Alive.

I turned to Tess. "You did not hear it?"

She shook her head. "It was only a dream."

I left.

With a promise.

Return

I TRAVELLED AS young Mr. Charles Corcoran, a bookish lad of solitary inclination and, in an itchy tweed suit, unexceptional appearance. Apart from having more than once to rebuff the unwanted attentions of the purser on shipboard, whom I at first feared had guessed my secret, my journey was uneventful, and scarcely more than weeks later, I accompanied Mr. Baxter to the eastern end of Princes Street and the General Register Office for Scotland in New Register House.

Here I would see first-hand the document Mr. Baxter had already copied, notarized and caused to be witnessed. And I would not-see first-hand those documents which were absent because they were non-existent.

With the dome soaring a hundred feet above our heads, our footsteps echoed as we sought out an archivist clerk—a constricted-looking man, reed-thin but with the purplish complexion of a corpulent one—to assist us with the red volumes on the first tier: *Births*.

Followed by the black volumes on the second: *Deaths*.

I had been "summoned" to Fayne by Byrn, but Reader, it was Father who preyed on my mind. Cherishing no hopes that he might ratify my claim, I was keen only to assure myself as to his well-being, and feared to find him fallen on hard times following the withdrawal of Mother's fortune.

Mr. Baxter accompanied me by train to Berwick-on-Tweed, during which trip I had leisure to observe that his degree of genteel unkemptness never altered. His collar was never more nor less crumpled than previously; the salt-and-pepper hair lapping at his collar, never longer nor shorter. His whiskers, likewise. He smelled of tobacco and beer, paper and ink and faintly of Macassar. The scent of a gentleman and a bachelor.

There is, in such a shared journey—provided both passengers be facing in the same direction—the possibility of shared confidences; not unlike that which inheres in a sudden mist. Such was the case with Mr. Baxter. For my part, there remained little to confide in this solicitor and old family friend—save for the fact of my beloved Tessa. But there was a question I longed to ask him. One which I thought might be best snuck up on, like a grouse in the heather. To that end, I broached the subject of Mr. Margalo and his impending union with my bosom friend, Gwendolyn Haas. Thus it transpired that I learned it was in fact Mr. Baxter to whom I was indebted for the treasure of Mr. Margalo's tutelage; for not only had Mr. Baxter acted as benefactor and parent to the latter, he had made a timely intervention which would prove critical in determining the course of events, to wit, when Mr. Margalo announced his intention to apply for the post of tutor to the child of Henry, Lord Bell, Seventeenth Baron of the DC de Fayne, Mr. Baxter counselled his ward to remove from among his glowing character references Mr. Baxter's own.

"Why?"

"I had by then become *persona non grata* in the eyes of Lord Henry," he replied quietly.

"Again, why?"

He turned to me and said, "Do you know what a Uranian is?"

"An inhabitant of the eponymous planet?"

"No. A Uranian is a man who loves, in the fullest sense, another man. And in doing so, commits a crime in law."

I ventured to ask, "Mr. Baxter. Were you too 'misapprehended in your sex'?"

He smiled. Shook his head.

"Father cast you out, solely for that you love another man as other men might love a woman?"

"Yes."

"Are there female Uranians?"

"They are called Sapphists. Generally speaking."

It struck me of a sudden that my personal plight was part of a wider injustice. How were those such as Mr. Baxter and I—especially as regarded my anatomical trespass across what was widely viewed as a divide between two sexes—to live in accordance with our nature when that nature was deemed criminal in the eyes of the law? In adhering to that highest Stoic virtue of Truth, we harmed neither the person nor property of any man or woman—except insofar as woman was deemed the property of man, and therefore had no legal right even to claim harm on her own behalf. I felt outraged, yet exhilarated. I peered round at my fellow passengers and out the window as a farm rattled past, then a village. The very existence of a law whereby Mr. Baxter risked jail was enough to persuade me that, if he and I escaped notice, it was not because we were few but because we were in hiding. I studied his profile. I wished to learn to recognize our ranks. I longed to sound the "all clear" and see us come out from where we hid in plain sight. "I say, Mr. Baxter, there must be a goodly number of us."

He smiled, almost sadly.

Staring straight forward, I plunged in. "Mr. Baxter. Is Mr. Margalo my brother?"

"He is as much your brother as he is my son," he said gently. "That is to say, yes, though not by blood." He hesitated, then added, "By something perhaps stronger."

There rose a lump in my throat that put me in mind of the one I had first seen bobbing above Mr. Margalo's stiff collar. I was grateful we were facing forward.

Thence by coach to Aberfoyle-on-Feyn and the Inn at the Kenspeckle Hen, where we shouldered our way through a midday throng and onto a bench at a rough-hewn table amid ostlers and miller's hands and a trio of mud-spattered labourers. We were conspicuous by our city clothes and complexions but not by any outward sign that I was a citizen of that debatable land between the sexes—certainly no one saw me as female. In the lull before battle, we tucked into large servings of cottage pie. Mr. Baxter drank a glass of stout and I took a dram of whisky, an experience which I imagined akin to having the epithelial cells of my throat stripped by turpentine. I was pondering an antidotal treacle pudding when, out of the masculine rumble there flew, like a flint from the plough, the word "Fayne" and I pricked up my ears like Nolan. Thus Mr. Baxter and I learned that allotments would soon be offered for purchase by Mr. Mungo, "estate manager as was to Lord Bell over to Fayne, selling up is His Lordship."

"Aye, all but the old manor house where he looks fair to die."

"A ready-made mausoleum, into the bargain!" Laughter.

At my suggestion we walked from the village so as to attract as little notice as possible—merely two gentlemen out for a ramble on the moor. We crossed the bridge, the track rose sharply and the standing stone pierced the brow of the North Fell. We crested it and met the wall of wind. Before us were spread the bleak and swelling vasts of Fayne, and the sight, more than the wind, took my breath away.

The November sky was immense and grey as pewter. A brace of hawks wheeled high overhead, while lower down, skimming the faded heather, flew a trio of red grouse. The smell of the bog arose as though in greeting. In the distance stood the house.

We set off out down the long sloping track, sleeves luffing and coat tails flying.

Presently, I discerned a carriage standing on the forecourt. I assumed it was Father's and that he had either just arrived or was set to depart. I was about to remark on the good luck of our timing when I was shocked by the report of a gun. We looked up and saw, plummeting to earth, a grouse. As we watched, a second and a third bird flew straight up from the heather, their wings whirring, only to be felled, one after another, shot for shot.

"Hai, you there, put up your gun!" I ran ahead of Mr. Baxter toward the figure blending in with the fall rusts and greens of the moor.

It was a gentleman, and if his tweed hunting jacket and knicker-bockers had not alerted me to his class, his haughty tones would have as he said, without turning, "I say, Ebby, hand me the flask." He had spoken to a glum-looking youth, similarly attired. The gentleman now turned to me, his gun broken across his arm, and drawled, "One can hardly call it sport when the silly things are so willing to be shot." I was about to see him off when Mr. Baxter caught up, breathless, alongside me. "Hawley?"

"I say, Josey! I'll be deuced, you look like a piss-pot, old man, grab a gun, it's on me. Oh, this is my son, Ebeneezer. Ebby, this is my old school chum Mr. Josiah Baxter." Turning to me, he added, "Who's this? Your son? Or just 'yours'?" he asked, with an insinuating elevation of brow.

"I am Charles Bell."

I had the satisfaction of seeing the smug face fall. Hawley recovered himself with a giggle, "Jolly good, who are you, really?"

"I am heir to Fayne and you, sir, are trespassing."

"That's where you're wrong, dear boy, I bought the shooting rights." Languid once more, he went on, "Not to mention poor old Henny-Penny hasn't got an heir." He shouldered his gun once more. A retriever bounded up and dropped a grouse at my feet.

"Even your dog knows who's master here," I said.

Another shot rang out, and the youth Ebeneezer—as pretty as his name was sombre—cast me a baleful, even pleading look before I turned on my heel and stalked off.

I was furious. "The idea Father would invite anyone to kill his birds!"

Mr. Baxter said nothing. "You don't think it can be true, do you, Mr. Baxter?"

"Hawley is worse than a prat. But he's no liar. Among equals at least."

I would have broken into a run toward the house but that Mr. Baxter showed no inclination to sprint.

We were overtaken by the trio of mud-spattered labourers from the inn, shovels on their shoulders. They passed us in silence and I caught the familiar reek of loam and peat. A short distance ahead they abruptly left the track and marched east toward the bog. "You there! What are you doing on His Lordship's land?"

One of the three turned back without stopping and answered, "Draining it."

I broke into a run.

It was not Father's carriage. On its side in ostentatious gold were entwined the letters R and H. Nor was it Sanders who slumped, dozing and liveried, on the box above a pair of chestnut geldings that stood likewise dormant. Nothing stirred. There was not a bark. Even the wind had dropped. The crunch of cinders beneath our feet was the only sound. An eerie calm blanketed the premises like an enchantment.

A still-deeper silence greeted us when I pushed open the great doors. There was no sign of Knox. Nor Cruikshank either. I walked on the balls of my feet as though loath to wake some mythic beast, to the door of Father's study where I tapped and paused. Silence. I turned the knob and peered through the crack.

Dust motes hung in the weak light that seeped through the curtains. Specimens now crowded every surface and, suspended from the ceiling, birds that had never in life flocked together flew forever united in death. I heard Mr. Baxter's intake of breath behind me. There was not space to open fully the door and scarcely enough to step into the avian crypt. Everywhere were bits and faded heaps. I gasped as at my feet a wing fluttered as though about to take flight—I turned it over with the toe of my boot to reveal a cluster of writhing larvae. On its perch atop the pigeon holes stood the chimera. Its plumage was bright as ever but its laughing gull-beak was now more a rictus of despair.

"Mr. Charlotte," said Mr. Baxter. "'Tis well you prepare yourself. It may be your father is much changed."

We withdrew. And followed the sound of muffled voices to the door of the library—my erstwhile schoolroom. I pushed it open.

Father was there. Seated at the end of the great mahogany table that had once been a tree in Africa. He was bent over a document, a pen hovering in one hand. The ink in the pen had once been iron and oak gall. And would be again. Beside him stood Mr. Mungo.

"Father."

He looked up. Removed his spectacles, squinted and smiled. Reader, he had grown old. He said, so pleasantly it hurt my heart, "Why, Charlotte." And, placing both hands flat upon the table, rose like the gentleman he was.

"Father. What is happening?"

He looked in my direction while seeming not quite to focus upon me. I drew nearer and spoke more clearly. "I've brought Mr. Baxter."

Mr. Baxter stepped forward. "Lord Henry, I am here in my professional capacity as—"

"Come in, come in, old friend." Father reached out his hands in welcome. Much changed indeed. Mr. Baxter remained at my side.

Mr. Mungo murmured something to my father who resumed his seat and took up his pen once more.

I went to him and knelt at his side. "Father, there is a man out on the moor, killing the grouse."

"Oh," he smiled in mild regret, "Can't be helped, Charlotte, you see, it's all up."

"What do you mean?"

"My dear, I shall retire to Edinburgh and the estate shall . . . Well I've sold it, you see, so there is no estate. There is no Fayne. No baron. No bother." He continued smiling, his voice gentle, and I feared for his brain.

"Father, no."

He took my hand. "My darling. Come with me to Edinburgh, we shall live there very well indeed and—dash it all, you must pursue your medical studies, as for the life of me I cannot recall a single impediment thereto."

"Except that I am female."

"Ah. So were the ladies pelted with sheep, and they survived."

Before him sat the document, its heading plainly visible: "Deed of Conveyance."

"Father. What have you done?"

"I've . . . oh, bother the details, explain it to my daughter, would you, Mungo?"

Father sat back with his hands folded across his chest as though listening to an old tale as Mr. Mungo explained that Father had agreed to sell the shooting rights to Lord Richard Hawley, and the land to Mungo who even now was preparing to "cure the bog." The peat would be harvested, the soil drained and treated with lime to dry it up, preparatory to putting twelve thousand previously worthless acres under the plough.

A voice behind me added, "Don't forget mineral rights, Father."

I turned. "Murdoch."

". . . Miss Charlotte?" A sneer in his voice.

I rose. "You will address me as Mister Bell, for so I am."

He snorted, incredulous.

"Father, I am your heir male of the body, I have proof, you need not sell, you must not!"

"You sound like my dear late sister, heh."

"Father. It is my birthright you have placed upon the block."

Murdoch did not bother to conceal his amusement. "*Miss* Bell, there is coal beneath the moor."

"That will do, Murdoch," said Mr. Mungo, and turning to me with wonted severity but no incivility, "I have agreed to pay a generous percentage of the proceeds in perpetuity to Lord Henry."

"Tut-tut, there shall no longer be a Lord Henry," said Father mildly. He took my hand between both his own. "Charlotte, my treasure. Fayne is an albatross. It ends here. With me." And he took up his pen once more.

I stayed his hand. "Father, I beg you. Hear me out before you sign."

Mr. Baxter stepped forward, and from his leather hold-all withdrew a red-bound document. I laid it atop the Deed of Conveyance. Father donned his spectacles once more and, his nose nearly touching the paper, read what was written below the stamp of the General Registrar of Scotland duly registering: *The birth of Charles Henry Gerald Victor Bell, son of Henry, Lord Bell, Baron DC de Fayne, on the first day of June in the year of our Lord Eighteen Seventy-Three.*

I watched, trembling. When he looked up, I spoke. "There is no registration of Charles's death because Charles did not die. There is no registration of Charlotte's birth because Charlotte was never born. 'Tis I, Father, your lawful son and heir."

He did not speak.

I added, "I shall be rich too, for I am likewise heir to my mother's fortune, thus you have nothing to fear regarding maintenance of the estate."

He looked upon me with some of the old delight—as though I had just recited a passage from Bewick's *History of British Birds*. And for a moment I felt we were on our old footing—Father was not changed, but restored!

"My dearest child . . . It was churlish of me to deny your request these many months ago when you begged me to call you by your old given name. Had I obliged you then, perhaps we would be already living together quite happily . . ."

I held my breath. An impish thought leapt in: *If Father had acceded to your wish then, you might never have crossed the ocean and met Tessa.* He went on, "I find it costs me nothing now to oblige you, for what does it matter? What does anything?" He chuckled and patted my head, saying, "Charles."

I could not speak for happiness. Neither could I move or cry out when I saw him take up his pen and sign the Deed of Conveyance.

I stumbled from the room. Past Murdoch who smirked, past Mr. Baxter who looked sadder than ever. And out. Onto to the forecourt.

I beheld the moor. Sprawled on her back and laid out for the taking. The air thinned about me. Beneath my feet the earth loosed its hold. I felt off-kilter. There came the crack of a gun. Then all was sterile silence once more. In the east I spied the trio of shapes, bent over their shovels.

I was seized by fear—*Where was Byrn?!* It struck me that his absence was at the core of this unnatural silence.

I ran toward the byre—whence not a sound. Had they been put, every one, to the axe? I dared not look in. At the top of the path was the bothy and the welcome sight of smoke issuing from its chimney.

I pushed at the silvered planks of the door with its widening cracks and furred edges. Knox looked up from her stool next to the cot; Cruikshank from tending the kettle on the hob. Neither said a word. On the cot, beneath a thin blanket that showed plainly the diminished outlines of his body lay the Auld One, curled on his side, his head resting upon the folded bear skin. I saw the base of his skull, the tender nape of neck so like a child's now. On either side of his hairless scalp, more prominent with the thinning of skin, were the nubs of his misshapen crown. Like all of us, Byrn had been born into life. And now, it seemed, he was being born into death.

My eyes filled and overflowed.

My tears consisted of the same water as that which rained and fed the seas and flowed through my veins, the same water that sluiced the century and all its filthy works, yet was endlessly cleansed, somehow, by Earth. And returned to us. The same water as the swallet which had, those weeks ago in Boston, whispered to me a word. A word submerged below hearing. Compressed, as though it had lain beneath the peat, one of its syllables lost to the pulverizing weight, one of its vowels squashed 'til it sprouted a tail . . . A word preserved by the bog, hauled up to breathe and expand, restored to its full meaning. I drew near the cot, stood over Byrn's shrinking shape, and spoke the Word: "Baron."

He turned his head on its delicate stem and looked up at me with the blue pebble eyes. With one arm, long and bowed like a scythe, he put off the coverlet from his body and rose to his feet.

Terribly fragile he looked. And yet he was all bone, and what is stronger? His skin was nearly blanched as bone too, and rather than hanging from his frame in loose folds and spent sinews, it was taut; beneath the arc of his ribs was a concavity so gaunt it seemed it must meet with his spine in back. His organs of generation were screened not by hair, but by a dull white pelt, and his penis was evidenced insofar as a furred sheath, tufted at its end, depended from his loins.

There was a hush. I looked to Knox and Cruikshank—their eyes were upon me, their breath held. I understood they had already witnessed the Auld One's nakedness and waited now to see what I would make of it.

I bent to the cot and took up the bear-skin robe. I draped it round his spare shoulders and, in doing so, saw his tail. Short. Bushy. The tail of a deer.

"Can you walk?" I asked him.

He nodded. We turned to leave and I saw Mr. Baxter standing in the doorway, amazed.

Together, we five exited the bothy and processed, strangely regal, across the muck and toward the manor house.

Father and Mr. Mungo were both seated, drinking a dram to seal their transaction. Murdoch lounged behind his father's chair.

Father looked up, vaguely amused at the sight of our pageant. Mr. Mungo did not rise at my entry, saying only, "What's this then, take him away, he stinks of the bog."

"Your contract with my father, sir, is null and void."

Murdoch gave a short laugh for which he received an admonishing glance from his father, who now rose. "Miss Bell, your father's signature and seal are upon the transaction."

"My father has no right to sell Fayne."

Father cradled his forehead.

Murdoch could not contain himself. "Och, you're nowt but a lass in mannie's clothing—"

Mr. Mungo ignored him. "Miss Bell, your claim to inheritance is not at issue, and perhaps with the connivance of a slick Edinburgh solicitor you might even prevail. But there is no law of entail or otherwise to prevent the current baron exercising his right to sell the land."

"The baron may have that right, but my father is not the baron."

Father sighed. "You are so like your mother at times."

"You are not the baron!" I proclaimed. "Nor was your father, nor his before him, nor—"

"My dear, I really must ask you to help dear old Byrn from the room, the smell does begin to impinge."

I composed myself. I drew nearer Father and gestured to the Auld Man to join me. He did so and I removed from him the bear-skin robe.

A moment of silence. Then, a gasp from Father. Mr. Mungo stared. Murdoch gaped.

"I give you the Thirteenth Baron of the DC de Fayne," said I. "'The Blighted Heir.'"

Silence.

Followed by a crescendo of sputtering from among the men. I turned my back and, together with Cruikshank, helped Byrn, Lord Bell, from the room. I looked over my shoulder to see Father tear in two the contract.

Mr. Mungo, however, would experience no such Damascene moment. He was waiting for me when I emerged from the bothy, where I had helped to settle the frail old Baron back onto his cot. I brushed past him.

Red-faced with anger and dogged by Murdoch, he followed me, shouting, "The contract was witnessed and signed, no mere ripping up of it changes the fact this land is mine!"

Reaching the cinder forecourt, I turned on him smartly. "In the name of the Thirteenth Baron of the—"

"I know not what you're playing at, missy, but no monster, whether true nor feigned, has a claim to my property."

"I command you, cease your digging and be gone—"

"We've our own monster!" cried Murdoch, breathless with excitement as he looked out toward the North Fell.

I became aware of a rumbling. Away off at the break of slope, a bizarre silhouette was advancing along the track.

"I'll give you 'digging,'" he sneered.

The thing grew closer. Larger. Louder. Clanking, snorting, rocking side to side. It was an iron box fitted with a smoke-stack and perched on great metal wheels.

"What in God's name is that?" asked Mr. Baxter.

"It is a marvel," I replied, for it was not this exemplar of mechanical innovation to which I objected, but the purpose to which it was to be put. Like a dumb beast, it knew not what it came to do. "It is a steam-driven plough."

Murdoch had already turned away and was striding up to meet the machine. He waved his arms and it came to a shuddering halt with a belch of smoke. With a grinding sound, the machine swivelled and, wobbling, came to a stop facing the boglands to the east. With a groaning exertion of its engine it lurched forward and I had a view of its wheels; girded with segments of steel track, they revolved inexorably onward, throwing up divots of earth in their wake as the plough bore down and onto the open moor. Murdoch followed, quite skipping.

"Miss Bell," said Mr. Mungo, his courtesy restored with his confidence, "The bog will be ditched and drained and cured in a matter of weeks. This time next year, Fayne will yield food and profit in exchange for honest labour. I advise you take your winnings, your butterfly collections, your blue blood, your fairy tales and freaks of nature, and hie you home to Edinburgh."

I commenced to sing. The words flew from my lips on a twist of melody such that the song sung itself. I was aware of Mr. Mungo's expression of disgust. He shook his head.

Mist gathered. Thickened. Enveloped all until I could not see my hand before my face.

From off, I heard the machine sputter to a halt, then fall silent.

"What the devil?"—I heard fear in his voice, and knew I courted danger.

Murdoch cried out from the mist, "Father!"

"Stay where you are, Murdoch!" roared Mr. Mungo. He was enough of this land to know its perils.

I made a bold gambit. "I will not take off the mist until you agree to drop your claim." Reader, I was no less shocked than Mr. Mungo at the atmospheric phenomenon. But whether magyk, miracle or happenstance, it was a gift.

"I'll have you for witchcraft," he snarled, and I heard him backing away.

Mr. Baxter's voice cut through the fog. "In my capacity as solicitor to Henry Bell, formerly known as Lord Bell, I advise you, Mr. Mungo, that the Deed of Conveyance is null and void, it not having been registered in the local Register of Sasines. Accordingly, and whereas by these presents 'Fayne' shall mean the lands appertaining to the estate of the DC de Fayne, exclusive of the manor house notwithstanding its contiguity therewith to be severed, Fayne remains without prejudice the property of the Baron of the DC de Fayne."

The mist lifted.

Lord Richard Hawley was happy to relinquish his shooting rights. "Rum weather in any case."

Young Ebeneezer leaned out the window of his father's coach and addressed me shyly, "I think you splendid whoever you are." Not only a pretty youth, he was something familiar—perhaps it was the high planes of his forehead, the slight perturbation of brow. And an earnest look in his eyes which, though blue, put me in mind of the first pair of brown ones I had ever seen . . . As the carriage pulled away, I waved to him and he remained at the window, curls flying for as far as I could see.

It took a team of shire horses to pull the poor metal beast from off the moor.

Father detained Mr. Baxter in the library prior to dinner. "Josey, a word."

———

Over the course of three cycles of the moon we nursed Lord Byrn as he
wasted away. I spoke with him in the Auld Tongue—it came back to me;
rather, Byrn watered the tiny shoots within my mind and they matured
such that I soon surpassed my two-year-old self in fluency.

He taught me to listen to Brigid. He taught me the filling of the buckets with her bounty. I went yoked onto the moor according to the Auld
Ways, and returned night after night until he was satisfied. He taught
me to read Fenn by sight, smell and feel. And taste. Thus, my tutor:
bedridden, illiterate and innumerate.

I asked him where he had learned his craft and he replied, "The
Women."

What women?

"The Auld Ones."

When?

"Long ago."

Who were they? What were their names?

"Janet."

He sang the songs, those I knew and some new to me.

I kept vigil in the bothy. Cruikshank kept us fed. Together we kept him
clean and comfortable as he failed. Knox looked in from time to time but
her duty lay in the house, with Father.

Byrn's flesh sank about his bones, and the two lumps on either side of
his crown increased in prominence such that I feared lest his thinning
skin give way.

At the solstice he made to rise. I made to stop him. He brushed aside
my hand with a weakness of body but a firmness of intent such that
I helped him to stand.

I helped him into the bear-skin robe. With one of his longbow arms
draped about my shoulders, and one of mine about his reed-thin waist,
we walked out onto the moor under a low sun that was somehow dark as
though gestating the shadow of winter.

We walked until the bog quaked beneath our feet and I wondered if it
was his intention to commit himself there and then to Brigid. Instead, he
showed me how to find the swallet.

———

He died next day. Cruikshank wept. Knox prayed for the repose of his soul. We washed his body. We wrapped him in the bear-skin robe. On his scalp the bumps had broken through—just as the hair and fingernails of a corpse continue to grow after death, the bony nubs had pierced the skin in the hours following his death. They looked to be covered in delicate grey fur. I touched one: velvet.

I had determined to see him entombed with the barons—three of them false, for they were usurpers—in the chapel floor. I sought out the trio of men from the village who had been digging at the Mungos' behest, and bade them come up to the manor house and open the crypt; the which they did, and I stepped back from the dark exhalation of imprisoned time.

I paid the men twice what they would have earned in draining the bog, and returned to the bothy to fetch the body of Lord Byrn, Thirteenth Baron of the DC de Fayne. "The Blighted Heir."

Knox and Cruikshank were present when I bent to his frail corpse, slipped my arms beneath his shoulders and knees, lifted him, and he fell to dust.

I wrapped the fur about his remains and carried the bundle out into the flinty December day, across the moor and up to the North Fell, where the standing stone marked the windiest point. I opened it and loosed his dust. It flew, a sheet of ash on the wind, whirled, reversed, and dispersed.

I returned to the house, to tell Father that he was now Fourteenth Baron of the DC de Fayne. He received me affably, in his study.

The room was a haze of motes, and the only creatures which flew amid the suspended flock were moths.

He did not acknowledge my announcement, rather he asked me very kindly if I might help him find, amid the heaps on the floor and the piles on the desk, the spinal disc of the capercaillie.

I repeated my news.

He responded, "Heh."

I set to hunting for his missing bit.

"Here it is, Father."

"Good show, Charlotte."

I realized he had been blind for some time.

———

Knox and I kept him fed and watered. And loved.

I found him, shortly after Hogmanay, in his study, his head resting on his folded arms. He was as still as his beloved birds.

Before him, on the desk, was his seal ring. He had removed it. I stroked his head, and kissed him. Father.

I took the ring, and found it fit my middle finger. Over the years, it has migrated among fingers and thumbs, and now that I am all twig and vine, as it were, I wear it on a chain about my ropy old neck.

The work of the men from the village was not in vain. We laid Father in the tomb of the barons.

Mr. Baxter produced my father's last Will and Testament, which he had revised according to Father's instructions on the day of the mist.

I made myself known under the seal of the Salamander to Her Majesty's Herald, as Charles Bell, Fifteenth Baron of the DC de Fayne.

I wrote to Tess.

Reader, she came to me.

Brigid's Children

MR. BAXTER WROTE a letter to Mr. Margalo. In due course, I received one from Gwen telling me that while Isadore was chagrined to learn that his natural father was an ignoble nobleman, he was not averse to meeting his half-brother, Ebeneezer. And he had been positively cheered to discover, courtesy of my mother, that his own mother resided in Boston, a mere day's journey from Montreal. She had become a well-known businesswoman, operating a thriving chophouse known all along the waterfront as "Sheehan's Shaheen." He wrote to her in the most delicate terms, and she replied immediately, exhorting him to visit and bring his wife, *and heers the ferst class fayr.*

Gwennie added, *I am B with C! Well, not particularly Big yet, I grant you, but I am definitely with Child. If it is a girl, I shall call her Charlotte, and if it is a boy, I shall call him Charlotte. And if there is any question as to sex, I shall call them Charlotte.*

Mr. Margalo and I would keep up a lively decades-long correspondence. He specialized in the hydra. If I had it to do over again, I would devote my life to slime.

Tess and I took up residence at No. One Bell Gardens. Thanks to the courage of the "Edinburgh Seven" nearly twenty years before, there was no riot, and no abuse—certainly no sheep—was hurled when I entered the Medical Arts Building; but an impudent sergeant-at-arms made to debar my entrance to Anatomy Hall, even whilst grubby young gentlemen—and some less than gentle—brushed past me in a cloud of pomade and perspiration.

"My good man," said I. "I am here to audit lectures on Anatomy Especially as Pertains to Matters Gynecological."

"No females are permitted, miss."

"I am Lord Charlotte Bell, Fifteenth Baron of the DC de Fayne, and I bid you step aside if you value your post."

It would take another few years before female students would be admitted to the university and permitted to earn a degree in any course of study, but I was certainly not the only woman enrolled; I was, however, the only one to be enrolled as such and to be openly attired in other than feminine garb (I had by then reverted entirely to capes, tunics and leggings in repertory with flowing shirts, loose trousers and waistcoats). I suspected there was at least one other woman in my anatomy class who was "mansquerading" (*per* my jest) but I did not query her lest she, not possessing the protection of rank, be hounded, threatened and prosecuted. I supplemented my university training with clinical classes at Leith Hospital given by the heroic Sophia Jex-Blake herself: leader of the original "Seven" in the face of male invective, threats and, yes, sheep.

As Charlotte and Tess we were known as "the ladies of Bell Gardens." As Charles and Tess we married by mutual consent and declaration before our witnesses, Miss Gourley and Mr. Baxter, in the foyer of No. One. Tessa became Theresa, Lady Bell, Fifteenth Baroness of the DC de

Fayne. And my lawfully wedded wife. Mr. Baxter himself saw the record of our marriage filed on the top shelf of the dome at New Register House among the green volumes: *Marriages*.

Our respective mothers and her father made their peace with our union. In time.

Once I became a licensed physician, we found ourselves more at Fayne and less in Edinburgh. I made a living bequest of No. One Bell Gardens to Miss Gourley, who established a "settlement house" devoted to advancing the Rights of Woman and placed Moira in charge as Head Administrator. In appreciation of the gift, Miss Elliot presented me with a handsome meerschaum pipe carved with the head of Julius Caesar— I find it draws particularly well when I am facing north, in the direction of the undefeated Picts. Tessa resigned her teaching post at Miss Gourley and Miss Mellor's School for Girls and set about founding a school in Aberfoyle-on-Feyn.

Cruiky, Knox and Cook—Mrs. Adamson—stayed on at Fayne. Fiona and Sean Padraig Archibald came for lunch and moved into the guest wing. Tess trained up Fiona as a teacher and I took over tutoring Sean Padraig Archie.

I revived the vegetable garden, hauling buckets from those places and at those times according to Byrn's teaching. I physicked the villagers and farmers of the county, who came to accept me as "Lord Charlotte" and paid me in meat and produce. Reader, I was a trained physician and surgeon, but Byrn it was who had made of me a healer versed in the uses of mosses and balms, and it was Knox who made of me a "man-midwife." I became known simply as "the doctor" and as time went on, there was not a family in the county to whom I had not ministered, and the children grew and multiplied whom I had helped into the light of day. I tended my patients in their homes and in my surgery at Fayne House in the former conservatory. I performed minor and not-so-minor surgical procedures and administered vaccinations against smallpox and a growing list of pathogens in the ensuing years. Sean Padraig Archie was particularly helpful, performing hand-puppet shows to distract children and adults alike from "the jab" and, following a period of medical apprenticeship, he assumed formal duties as my assisting nurse.

I took on the three labourers as all-round estate helpers. Good diligent hands they were and together they did the work of one Auld Man.

Two were brothers, both called Farleigh. The third was called Malcolm. He had a green thumb.

Tess and I made plans more than once to voyage to the Sahara. To the Amazon. To the Galapagos, Antarctica, Patagonia. And to Montreal and Boston, of course. But always something delayed our plans. Life was full.

Reader, I come now to Time.
    They began to die.
    Gossamer.
    Maisie.
    Achilles and Hector.
    Cruikshank.

All those about me acquired Time's traces. So did I, but far more slowly, as though within me there ticked a different clock. Tess knew. As did a handful of others—my friends, including Ebby and of course Gwen and Isadore—and some among the many who came and went at Fayne, drawn by rumours of "old-ways" agriculture, free thought and "free love"—so they called it before the Great War, when so many chose to eschew the bonds of marriage (Tessa and I remained quite happy with our own bond) along with the conventions of sex *vis-à-vis* there being but two.

Knoxy died. Uncertain of her own age, which she put in the neighbourhood of ninety-five.

And still they came, some for a weekend, some for a lifetime. They pitched tents and caravans (and—eventually—Volkswagen vans). I regularly retrieved visitors from off the bog, rescuing them from drowning and a leathery future as a museum exhibit. I tended the garden. It gave several times a year, thus my guests were fed, even if I never learned all their names or causes. As a physician I was, like it or no, privy to all manner of complaints and confidences, and a steady trickle of babies were born at Fayne. I remembered what the Green Lady had told me.

———

Tessa's mother, dear Taffy, died of the influenza in 1919.

All were welcome to come and work and tend the sheep and mend the house and outbuildings; or spend days simply loafing on the moor, or arguing in the schoolroom about various systems of government and schools of thought. Some of them painted. Some wrote. Too many believed themselves to be musicians.

My mother, dear Mae, died of stroke in 1931.

I will tell you that Fayne House became a military hospital during the Great War of 1914 to 1918. Tessa and I tended to wounds both seen and unseen. Several soldiers and nurses stayed on.

And I will tell you that Fayne became a home for evacuated children some twenty years later, during the Second World War. Even some of the older children even took to calling Tess "Mummy." One day we saw a bomb fall into the bog. I got on the tractor and pulled it out. That was a grand day for the children. Several of them would stay on, grow up, work, play. Die of old age.

There were the unspeakable events which came to light toward the end of the Second World War.

And so many others.

Another time, perhaps.

Gwennie and Isadore died within a year of one another in 1959 and '60.

The Green Lady had told me my children would be legion. It took me a long while to understand, for I knew I was not for birthing. Nor did Tess seek to increase the number of children she nurtured and educated by bearing one herself. Not but what I sometimes wish it had been otherwise.

Tessa died in 1963.

———

I grow tired. A walk up to the standing stone has left me quite winded, if you will pardon the pun. I am undecided with regard to a proposal for a turbine to be erected at this spot. It is a subject of spirited debate among my guests but it is my decision to make. Decisions used to energize me. They weary me now. Another sign.

After Tess died, I began to wonder at my continued existence, which seemed of small utility to me. Without her. Then it occurred to me that my failure to die might be in connection with my lack of an heir. For how could I die and leave Fayne without a custodian? Fayne. Fascinating to naturalists, maddening to energy companies (whether fossil or green), seductive to pharmaceuticals. Annoying to governmental agencies tasked with draining British swamps and rendering them fit for agriculture, or at the very least tree farms. Fayne. My albatross . . . Why not let it go?

But I failed to die.

Along with her correspondence, Mother left the bulk of her fortune to me, the which she had exponentially increased in size. This was due less to her financial acumen than to a well-timed call upon a lady medium in Lime Street who, in the second week of October 1929, told my mother that she had a message from her late father, Gerald Corcoran: "Sell up and stuff the mattress, Mary." Whereupon Mother immediately converted to gold.

Fayne thrives, having escaped all attempts to cure it. Visitors are still welcome. (Please deposit this Guide on the console table in the great entry hall, beneath the drawing of Byrn by Gwendolyn Haas-Margalo, for the use of future visitors.) If arriving by car, they exit the dual carriageway, bypass the city of Aberfoyle-on-Feyn, cross the Water of Feyn by means of a concrete bridge, park in the car park and walk up the hill. The white standing stone rises into view, and when they reach the brow of the North Fell they step into the wind. Some lose their hats.

I am seen as an eccentric. My longevity is doubted.

———

As I ply my pen to put the finishing touches on this revised Visitor's Guide, I sit at Father's desk. His moth-eaten specimens are long gone for I burned them shortly after we interred his body in the floor of the chapel—all but one: our chimeric creature of many species. It continues to stand tall on the desk in its rainbow plumage, alert and vibrant despite the years, as though it were about to break into laughter.

At the turn of the millennium, I paid a late-registration fine and registered the birth of the Honourable Charlotte Henrietta Geraldine Victoria Bell, born June 2, 1875. It was a small matter to have it notarized and warranted, there being none left living to dispute my word. I journeyed for the last time to Edinburgh and myself saw it entered into the digitized records of the General Register Office.

I followed this up by giving notice to Buckingham Palace and to the Court of Scottish Registrars, under the seal of the Salamander, that henceforth I was to be known in England as Lord Charlotte Bell, Fifteenth Baron of the DC de Fayne, and in Scotland as Lady Charles Bell, First Baroness of the DC de Fayne. Some eleven years later I received the provisional decision of the Court of Scottish Registrars in favour of "deferring the matter in the Disputed Baron-*cum*-Baroness of the DC of Fayne." I await a reply from the Palace.

These days, along with the strays, the estate is host to two or three foundations and a "think tank," and there is more than one NGO about the place. Someone hung a disco ball in the chapel. I have allsorts here. Veterans and neophytes of every good fight from the four corners of the Earth flow through the place. When argument turns to bickering, when the acronyms grow longer than can be supported by a cantilever of good intentions, when hyphens proliferate to the point where they are no longer bridges but darts, I gradually reduce the central heating.

And what have I done over the years with Fayne? Nothing. I have left it to its own devices. No need to "rewild" it for it has never been "de-wilded." I fill the buckets at certain times. I have my ways. Auld Ways they are.

———

In 2014 I kept my promise to the bear who long ago inhabited the hide in which Byrn wrapped me and in which he died. I contributed a large sum anonymously to a here-unnamed community body in the north which acquired, under Scotland's Community Right to Buy, a vast estate which they proceeded to enclose, and into which brown bears have been quietly released.

Scientists are among those who have come to Fayne. Over the years they have drawn samples of mud and water, and I donate material from my buckets—though I have never so much as mentioned the swallet. Reader, in wetlands such as Fayne there is much to discover and observe, from medicines to the mechanisms of species diversification among plants and animals and fungi and all those in between and at the margins where Nature burgeons most. I might trace my own genital variation, the which I am content to describe as an intersex trait, to my mother's ingestion of mud whilst in her twelfth week of pregnancy, for moor mud has been found to contain hormone-like substances which influence sexual morphology. I might even trace my unusual capacity for tissue regeneration, and therefore longevity, to the soup of species in that same swallet-fed mud, and speculate that certain exogenous genes caught a ride into my own genome on the backs of those myriad bacteria without which human life is impossible. After all, what is this thing called "I"? I am legion, and so are we all, Reader. Old Byrn and I bore Nature's marks at a macroscopic level, but before Van Leeuwenhoek peered through his lens, a person could be burnt as a witch for suggesting there might be life teeming in a drop of rainwater. Medicine. Magyk. Science. Faith. Fact: Fayne absorbs about one thousand tons of carbon from the air per year and stores about eight million tons overall. This used to be interesting. It is now life-and-death. In addition to all its known and unknown marvels and mundanities, Fayne is one vast held breath. I have lately determined that my legacy should include a mighty amount of unexhaled carbon dioxide. It is the least I can do—rather, it is the least I can not do.

I would have thought the Holocene was good for another few millennia. I never dreamed I might live to inhabit the Anthropocene. There used to be a lot of places like Fayne. There are fewer every day. Byrn had me to take up his mantle as custodian. But to whom could I bequeath guardianship in turn? Upon my death, the Dispute would dissolve, and Fayne would be placed on the block; a border would be drawn, a line straight and true with no blurred and burgeoning edges—edges where diversity thrives and life makes love to itself. Fayne would become a "resource." And it would, at last, exhale . . .

Thus did I undertake a quest to achieve the conditions under which I would be capable of dying.

Soon.

I feel myself, even now . . . rewilding. Here you may imagine I wink, *id est* ;-). And what of my mortal remains? I have made clear that any form of disposal or dispersal is preferable to being laid in the floor of the chapel—disco ball notwithstanding.

There are so many beautiful young people, from all parts of Earth, back and forth through the great doors of the manor house and at times camped out on the moor, surely one of them . . . Gwen and Izzy's great-grandchildren still visit with their grandchildren, perhaps one of them . . . Or indeed, Fayne.org, which is an entire movement. But a movement is not a person, no matter how many good people sign on. A movement, like a corporation, cannot be personally accountable. Therefore it cannot be wholly moral. And I require morals. And morals require love in order not to run roughshod. And love requires agency . . .

In 2017, I circulated a petition in Greater Aberfoyle-upon-Feyn to have Fayne declared a person. Many signed. I submitted the petition to the local Scottish council and proposed a bill to that effect. The council voted against it. I submitted the petition and proposed the bill to the local English district authority. It passed. This was in consequence of the English councillors' determination not to cede, to Scotland, territorial authority over Fayne, lest Scotland claim the land in the event it should separate from the United Kingdom. Thus it is now a matter of Dispute whether Fayne is a person, and therefore whether Fayne may be owned by anyone at all. The Department of National Heritage (gov.uk) is involved, as is another community body, this one composed of retired geologists from the Northwest Highlands who seek to purchase the land and "leave it the fuck alone." I have accordingly, in my will, bequeathed my money to Fayne and named as trustees the local Scottish and English council and district governments, all of which remain reliably at odds. I have named Brigid's Children as co-executors and stewards in perpetuity. (There is no need for you to join, Reader, you are already a member.) It is my fervent hope that lawyers have yet to be born who will earn their livelihood in perpetuation of the Dispute.

A patch of mist is on the east moor. I hear the swallet. It is calling me . . .

. . . to a quiet place . . .

of dry bracken. If you are very still, and can wait, they will come out to look at you. Eyes. Nature has so many of them. Eyes are one way of seeing. Nature has so many ways. Up on their hinds-of-many-legs they stand, insects in their fine-stitched suits. Antennae inclined. Nature looking back at you. A rabbit. A fox. A bird alights. Looking . . . Flight and pursuit are set aside. Even the dry grass is bending attentively with the ascent of a beetle; nearby stirs a fringe of dwarf birch and willow, loosely woven as though Nature were hinting how to make a basket. Nature is full of hints. And warnings. Be so quiet they cannot mistake you for anything but attention. And they will come. They bring tidings of the dark pool that rises and sustains us all; now the trees are bowing their crowns, they know. If you wish to see the face of God, be still and God will come to look at you. Will you see that face if you rip off its mask? No, it will turn away. Will you see it if you pluck slowly at it, thread by loosed thread? No, it will unravel. If you wish to see God, let yourself be seen.

The dark pool winks now into view in a bolster of mist.

Eye of Creation.

Oh Reader, why not let it go?! Consume and incinerate. All of it, the Earth. Each of us will die, even I shall die, I know this now; why ought we to persist in inflicting life on innocent generations who, over and over, must open their eyes to the horror of their own mortality—and our species' capacity for destruction?

God so loved the World, She created Herself that She might create It.

God so loved the World, He creatured and planted It that He might see It.

Let us cherish the mud, and cultivate compassion for the stars. Feel the gnarled embrace of roots, and not begrudge the final feast of our body to our fellow creatures. Celebrate the transubstantiation of food into energy to thought to love. We live in perpetual transformation amid the alchemy of every moment, death into life, filth into food, every creature a cosmos of many creatures, every consciousness a miracle, all from a speck, a swerve, a word.

Merely to be.

To say, *I am here*.

I am possible.

I am more things than are dreamt of in our philosophy. Look into me and see our shared infinity.

God so loved the World, They did not wish to miss a single moment of It.

The last thing in my line of vision is the Creature of many species, with its rainbow plumage and herring gull's beak. It is laughing. So am I.

Fin

ACKNOWLEDGMENTS

I time-travelled gloriously in the course of writing this novel. I journeyed through so many books and articles and places, so much beautiful and harrowing science, history, and art, so many objects, implements, traces and adornments, from our own time and far before. So I will limit my written thanks here to those with who helped me in person and in "real time". Thank you!

In Scotland: Eva Faber, Janet Fulton, Pete Harrison (and the rest of the geologists in the van), Mandy Haggith, Faye Hammil, Doug Macdougall, Joan Michael, John Penman, David Robinson, Moira Telfer, John Urquhart (Iain Urchardan), Louise Welsh, Ruth Wishart.

In Canada and the US: Chris Lyons and the Osler Library of the History of Medicine at McGill University, Lauren Williams, Rare Books and Special Collections, Dr Victoria Dickenson; professors, Paul H. Glaser, Tim Moore, Nigel Roulet, Helen Tai, Bernie Zebarth; Judith Bowden, Miles DaSilva, Susan Doherty, Edward W. Gordon, Margaret Ann Fitzpatrick-Hanly, Hal Hannaford, Reid Hannaford, Honora Johannesen, Isobel McDonald, Duncan McDonald, Sarah Howard, John-Hugh MacDonald, Heather Macdougall, Alanna Palmer, Fiona Robinson, Lillian Szpak, Sue Warrrington.

The Wylie Agency, especially Andrew for your love of *Fayne* in all phases, and especially Tracy for your wise and ongoing guidance.

Doctors, David Baker, Willi Broeren, Alison Doucet, George Ecker, Michael Stein, Gwyneth de Vries. You got me through it.

A special note of thanks to the academics, film-makers and activists who continue to live, lead, study, and tell of the struggle for equal rights and protections under the law for people who are born with Intersex traits. You fight for us all.

Thank you to my extraordinary publishing team at Knopf Canada, including Ashley Dunn, Lynn Henry, Kelly Hill, Ann Jansen, Melanie Little, Emma Lockhart, Rick Meier, Owen Torrey, Gillian Watts, and truly extraordinary sales team, including Mary Giuliano, Sara James and Matthew Sibiga. Thank you, Marion Garner for guiding all my books into the welcoming open waters of Vintage Canada. Thank you, Sharon Klein, for being in my corner everywhere and always; thank you Kelly Hill, for making the book look the way we dreamt it; thank you Susan Burns, without whom no books exist. Thank you Kristin Cochrane and Anne Collins for your vision, wisdom and steadfast support. And to the incomparably kind, brilliant, intuitive and laser-focussed Martha Kanya-Forstner—yes, Martha, it's all out of the basket now, that's the whole scarf.

Thank you, Alisa Palmer, my loving wife, colleague, and best friend. Thank you Isabel MacDonald-Palmer and Lora MacDonald-Palmer, my daughters and great loves. Everything is better because of you three. Thank you Chester, gentleman canine and companion of the endless and otherwise solitary days and nights.

Thank you, Reader. It is all, and always, for you.

Herewith a note on dialect by way of apology to citizens of Edinburgh and those from the Scottish Borders and Northern England, should some words and phrases fall oddly on the ear: in certain cases I have deliberately mingled modes of speech (in the spirit of "the dispute") while in others I have simplified things for readers who haven't the privilege of knowing first-hand the beautiful and culturally rich area where *Fayne* is set.

ANN-MARIE MACDONALD IS an award-winning novelist, playwright, actor, and broadcast host. Her writing for the stage includes the plays *Goodnight Desdemona (Good Morning Juliet)*, *Belle Moral: A Natural History*, and *Hamlet-911*, along with the libretto for the chamber opera *Nigredo Hotel*, and book and lyrics for the musical *Anything That Moves*. She is the author of the bestselling novels *Fall on Your Knees*, *The Way the Crow Flies*, and *Adult Onset*. Ann-Marie is a graduate of the Acting Program of The National Theatre School of Canada. In 2019 she was made an Officer of the Order of Canada in recognition of her contribution to the arts and her LGBTQ2SI+ activism. She is married to theatre director Alisa Palmer, with whom she has two children.